BENEATH THE TWISTED TREES

BRADLEY P. BEAULIEU

BENEATH THE TWISTED TREES

Book Four of
The Song of the Shattered Sands

DAW BOOKS, INC.

DONALD A. WOLLHEIM, FOUNDER

1745 Broadway, New York, NY 10019

ELIZABETH R. WOLLHEIM

SHEILA E. GILBERT

PUBLISHERS

www.dawbooks.com

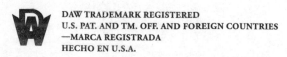

For Rick.
Rest in peace, friend.
You left us too soon.
Thanks for all the laughs, the good times,
and above all, the donuts and grape soda.

The Story So Far

The Song of the Shattered Sands is a vast and complex tale. I consider that a good thing, and if you're reading this, you likely do too, but it can present a problem. It's easy to forget what happened in the earlier volumes. I do my best to catch readers up with little reminders along the way, but even so, I recognize the need for a refresher.

It is with this in mind that I provide the following synopses.

As always, thank you for joining me in this grand tale. I hope you enjoy your return to the Great Shangazi.

—Bradley P. Beaulieu

* * *

The Song of the Shattered Sands

The Song of the Shattered Sands is an epic fantasy series in the vein of *One Thousand and One Nights*. The story centers on Çeda, a young woman who lives in the slums of the great desert city of Sharakhai and fights in the pits for money. In the eyes of the city's wealthy, she is nothing. She is one step above slavery, a fate that constantly nips at her heels. Through clues in a book left to her by her mother, Çeda realizes she is also one of the thirteenth tribe, a legendary group of nomads who were nearly eradicated by the Twelve Kings of Sharakhai four hundred years before.

In the decades that followed those dark days, Sharakhai became the single, unquestioned power in the desert, but in recent years the iron grip of the city has weakened. The asirim, strange and powerful creatures of the desert, have always protected Sharakhai, but they have become fewer, their power more feeble. Sensing weakness, the kingdoms bordering the Great Shangazi close in like jackals, hoping to snatch this jewel they've so long coveted, but it may be the wandering people of the desert, insulted by the very presence of Sharakhai, who in the end destroy the city so that no one—especially outsiders—can control it.

Though Çeda doesn't know it, her heritage and the book her mother left her put her in a unique position. The asirim were once people of the thirteenth tribe. After a grand bargain with the gods of the desert, they were betrayed by the Twelve Kings of Sharakhai and transformed into the wicked creatures they are now. Fearing retribution, the Kings sent the asirim to hunt their kinsmen, to kill every man, woman, and child who had blood of the thirteenth tribe running through their veins. The asirim wept, but they had no choice. They were bound as surely as the sun shines on the desert. Çeda's book is one of the last remaining clues to that secret history.

Of Sand and Malice Made

Çeda is the youngest pit fighter in the history of Sharakhai. She's made her name in the arena as the fearsome White Wolf. None but her closest friends and allies know her true identity, but that changes when she crosses the path of Hidi and Makuo, twin demigods who were summoned by a vengeful woman named Kesaea.

Kesaea wishes to bring about the downfall of her own sister, who has taken her place as the favored plaything of Rümayesh, an ehrekh, a sadistic creature forged aeons ago by Goezhen, the god of chaos. The ehrekh are desert dwellers, often hiding from the view of man, but this one lurks in the dark corners of Sharakhai, toying with and preying on humans. For centuries, Rümayesh has combed the populace of Sharakhai, looking for baubles among them, bright jewels that might interest her for a time. She chooses some few to stand by her side until she tires of them. Others she abducts to examine more closely, leaving them ruined, worn-out husks.

At Kesaea's bidding, the twins manipulate Çeda into meeting Rümayesh in hopes that the ehrekh would become entranced with her and toss Ashwandi aside. To Çeda's horror, it works.

Çeda tries to hide, but Rümayesh is not so easily deterred; the chase makes her covet the vibrant young pit fighter all the more. She uses her many resources to discover Çeda's secret identity. She learns who Çeda holds dearest. And the more restless she grows, the more violent she becomes. But the danger grows infinitely worse when Rümayesh turns her attention to Çeda's friends. Çeda is horrified that the people she loves have been placed in harm's way. She's seen firsthand the blood and suffering left in Rümayesh's wake as she hunts for those she craves.

Çeda is captured but manages to escape, and in so doing delivers Rümayesh into the hands of Hidi and Makuo, who torture her endlessly. But the ehrekh is still able to reach out to Çeda, forcing her to relive the torture as well. Knowing that she can never be free unless she liberates Rümayesh from the godling twins, Çeda recruits the help of a gifted young thief named Brama. With Brama's help, Çeda steals into Rümayesh's hidden desert fortress in hopes of freeing her through the use of a sacred ritual.

Çeda succeeds, but at the cost of Brama becoming enslaved instead of her. Knowing she can't leave Brama to the cruelties of an ehrekh, Çeda searches for and finds a different, more ancient ritual that prepares a magical gemstone, a sapphire, to capture Rümayesh. In a climactic battle, Çeda manages to trap Rümayesh within the stone and free Brama. In the end, Çeda knows that Brama is perhaps the one person who would be most careful with the sapphire, and so leaves it with him.

Twelve Kings in Sharakhai

Çeda uncovers secret poems hidden in a book left to her by her mother. Through clues in the poems, she learns more about Beht Ihman, the fateful night when the people of the thirteenth tribe were enslaved and turned into the asirim. She also learns that she is herself a descendant of the thirteenth tribe, which gives her some clue as to what her mother was doing in Sharakhai. She later discovers, to her shock and revulsion, that she may be the daughter of one of the Kings, and that this too was part of her mother's plan.

Refusing to let the mystery go unresolved, Çeda goes into the desert to the blooming fields, where the adichara trees shelter the asirim. The Kings are immune to the adichara's poison, and their children are resistant. To all others the poison is deadly. To prove to herself once and for all that she is the daughter of one of the Kings, Çeda poisons herself, and later is brought to the house of the Blade Maidens, the place where the warrior-daughters of the Kings live and train. There, with the help of an ally to the thirteenth tribe, Çeda survives and is allowed entry into the House of Maidens.

As she recuperates and trains with the Blade Maidens, Çeda investigates the clues left in her mother's book, her one treasured possession. Her mother died trying to unlock the secrets of a fabled poem that promises to unlock the secrets of the past and show Çeda the keys to the Kings' power and the way in which they can be defeated.

Meanwhile, the Moonless Host, a resistance group that hopes to end the reign of the Kings of Sharakhai, hatches a plan to break into the palace of King Külaşan, the Wandering King. Hidden in its depths is his son Hamzakiir, a blood mage and a man the Moonless Host hopes to use for their own purposes. It won't be so simple, however. The Kings stand ready to stop them, and their resources are vast.

There is also Ramahd Amansir, a lord from the neighboring kingdom of Qaimir, and

Princess Meryam, who travels with him. They have plans for Hamzakiir as well. Ramahd came to Sharakhai in hopes of gaining revenge for the loss of his wife and child at the hands of Macide, the leader of the Moonless Host. He stumbles across Çeda in the fighting pits, and the two of them come to know one another.

They might even have become involved romantically, but Çeda has more to worry about than love, and Meryam has other plans for Ramahd. Meryam knows that allowing Hamzakiir to fall into the hands of the Moonless Host would be terrible for her cause, so she makes plans to steal Hamzakiir from under their very noses.

At the end of the book, Çeda manages to unlock the first of the poem's riddles. Along with her best friend, Emre, who against Çeda's wishes has joined the ranks of the Moonless Host, she infiltrates King Külaşan's desert palace and kills him. Emre and the Moonless Host, meanwhile, manage to raise Hamzakiir from his near-dead state and steal him away from the palace. Before they can reach safety, however, Meryam and Ramahd intercept them and take Hamzakiir.

With Blood Upon the Sand

Çeda has become a Blade Maiden, an elite warrior in service to the Kings of Sharakhai. She's learning their secrets even as they send her on covert missions to further their rule. She's already uncovered the dark history of the asirim, but it's only when she bonds with them, chaining them to her will, that she feels their pain as her own. They hunger for release, they demand it, but their chains were forged by the gods themselves and are proving unbreakable.

Çeda could become the champion the enslaved asirim have been waiting for, but the need to tread carefully has never been greater. The Kings, hungry for blood, scour the city in a ruthless quest for revenge. Emre and his new allies in the Moonless Host, meanwhile, lay plans to take advantage of the unrest in Sharakhai. They hope to strike a major blow against the Kings and their god-given powers.

Hamzakiir has escaped the attentions of Queen Meryam and Ramahd, and has insinuated himself into the ranks of the Moonless Host. Through manipulation and sometimes force, he is slowly taking the reins of power from Macide and his father, Ishaq. His plan for Sharakhai is bold. The many scarabs of the Moonless Host, who itch for more progress, buy into Hamzakiir's plans.

Those plans are nearly upended when Davud, a young collegia scholar, is captured along with many others from his graduating class. Hamzakiir's spells trigger Davud's awakening as a blood mage. It is that very awakening that gives Davud power, nearly stopping Hamzakiir and his dark agenda. Davud fails, however, and burns his fellow classmate, Anila, in a cold fire, almost killing her.

The Moonless Host fractures in two, many following Hamzakiir, others following Macide, who is revealed to be Çeda's uncle. In a devastating betrayal, Hamzakiir kills many of the old guard in the Moonless Host, giving him near-complete control of the group. With them at his beck and call, he attacks Sharakhai, planning to take for his own the fabled elixirs that grant the Kings long life.

Emre and Macide, however, want the elixirs destroyed so that neither Hamzakiir nor the Kings can have them. Meryam is sympathetic, and commands Ramahd to help Emre.

An attack on Sharakhai unfolds, where the abducted collegia students, now grotesque monsters, are used to clear the way to King's Harbor. As the battle rages, both Hamzakiir and his faction, and Macide and his, infiltrate the palaces in search of the caches where the fabled elixirs are stored. Two of the three primary caches are destroyed. The third falls into Hamzakiir's hands.

Çeda, meanwhile, caught up in the battle in the harbor, tries to kill Cahil the Confessor King and King Mesut. The Kings are not so easily destroyed, however. They discover Çeda's purpose and turn the tables, nearly killing her. Sehid-Alaz, the King of the Thirteenth Tribe, is so fearful of Çeda's death that he manages to throw off the shackles of his curse and protect Çeda long enough for her to release the wights, the trapped souls of the asirim, from King Mesut's legendary bracelet. Thus freed, the wights come for their revenge and kill King Mesut.

Having been revealed, Çeda flees into the desert.

A Veil of Spears

The Night of Endless Swords was a bloody battle that nearly saw Sharakhai's destruction. The Kings know they won a narrow victory that night, and since then, their elite Blade Maidens and the soldiers of the Silver Spears have been pressing relentlessly on the Moonless Host. Hundreds have been murdered or given to Cahil the Confessor King for questioning. Knowing their movement is nearing the point of collapse, the scarabs of the Moonless Host flee the city.

Çeda, who has already fled the city, is captured by Onur, the King of Sloth. Onur has returned to the desert and is raising an army of his own to challenge the other Kings' right to rule. After escaping Onur, Çeda finds the scattered remains of the Moonless Host, who are now calling themselves the thirteenth tribe. Her people are reforming, but the nascent tribe is quickly being caught in a struggle between Onur's growing influence and the considerable might of the Kings who, with Sharakhai now firmly back under their rule, are turning their attention to the desert once more.

In Sharakhai, meanwhile, a deadly game is being played. Davud and Anila are being kept by Sukru the Reaping King. They're being groomed for their powers, Davud as a budding blood mage, Anila as a rare necromancer. A mysterious mage known as the Sparrow, however, is trying to lure Davud away from King Sukru for his own dark purposes. As Davud and Anila both grow in power, they fight for their very lives against the machinations of the Sparrow.

In the desert, Emre comes into his own as a prominent member of the thirteenth tribe. More are looking to him as a leader, including Macide. Emre helps to navigate the tribe toward safety, but the threat of King Onur grows by the day. Even with Emre's help in securing allies among the other tribes, it may not be enough. Things grow worse when the Kings of Sharakhai sail to the desert to confront Onur. They hatch a deal with Onur: crush the thirteenth tribe first, and they can deal with one another later.

Çeda knows that the thirteenth tribe will be destroyed unless she can free the powerful asirim from their bondage. She vows to lift the curse the gods placed on them, and soon returns to Sharakhai and its deadly blooming fields to do just that.

The Kings have not been idle, however. Nor are they fools. They know the asirim are the key to maintaining power. Making matters worse, their greatest tactician, the Kings of Swords himself, has made it his personal mission to bring Çeda to justice for her many crimes. Queen Meryam has also decided to throw in her lot with them. She's even managed to steal away the sapphire that contains the soul of the ehrekh, Rümayesh.

The night before the final confrontation, Çeda manages to liberate the wights still trapped inside Mesut's bracelet. The tribes and the Kings clash. As the battle unfolds, Ramahd, Emre, and the young thief, Brama, stage an ingenious attack on Queen Meryam's ship. There, they free Rümayesh, adding a powerful ally to their fight.

Near the end of the battle, it is revealed that Queen Meryam has long been dominating the mind of the blood mage, Hamzakiir. She has designs on more than just Macide or the Moonless Host. She wants the city for herself. In order to secure it, she forces Hamzakiir to take on the guise of Kiral the King of Kings. Kiral himself, meanwhile, is sent into the battle and is killed.

In the battle's closing moments, Çeda is nearly killed by the fearsome ehrekh, Guhldrathen. Guhldrathen, however, is swept up by Rümayesh and destroyed. This frees the path for Çeda to kill King Onur, which she does in single combat.

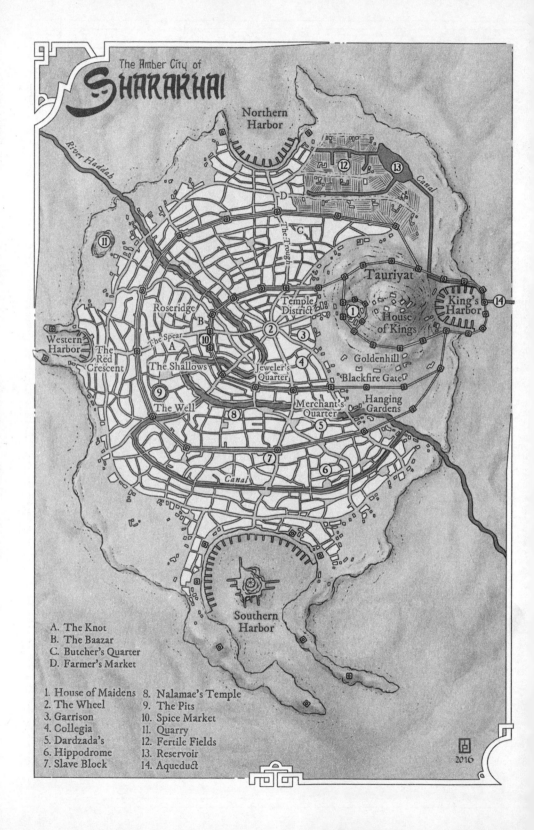

The Amber City of

Sharakhai

Northern Harbor

River Haddah

The Trough

Tauriyat

King's Harbor

Roseridge

Temple District

House of Kings

Western Harbor

The Spear

Goldenhill

The Red Crescent

The Shallows

Jeweler's Quarter

Blackfire Gate

Hanging Gardens

The Well

Merchant's Quarter

Canal

Southern Harbor

A. The Knot
B. The Baazar
C. Butcher's Quarter
D. Farmer's Market

1. House of Maidens
2. The Wheel
3. Garrison
4. Collegia
5. Dardzada's
6. Hippodrome
7. Slave Block
8. Nalamae's Temple
9. The Pits
10. Spice Market
11. Quarry
12. Fertile Fields
13. Reservoir
14. Aqueduct

2016

Chapter 1

UNDER COVER OF DARKNESS, leagues east of Sharakhai, three women navigated the endless dunes of the Great Shangazi. Çeda led the way on her zilij, a skimwood board that hissed as she rode it. Like the runners of sandships, the board had been painstakingly treated with a special wax which, coupled with the qualities of the wood itself, allowed it to glide slick as a lemon seed over the desert's surface. Melis and Sümeya, wearing their old uniforms, their Maiden's black, rode just behind her on zilijs of their own, and while they might not be as deft as Çeda, they were passable and they made good time toward their destination: the blooming fields.

Golden Rhia and silver Tulathan hung high overhead, pendants in a star-swept sky shedding light on the spindrift that lifted from the dunes like smoke on the wind. Both moons were full. Beht Zha'ir had returned to the desert, which partly explained why, despite the night's heat, all three women wore battle dresses. Melis and Sümeya's were well worn and made from black cloth, while Çeda's was newly sewn and dyed in rich amber hues, colors more typical of the desert tribes. Hanging easily from Çeda's belt were her mother's knife and her shamshir, River's Daughter: the ebon steel blade that had once felt so foreign, a sign of the Kings' oppression, but was now her truest, most trusted friend.

The weapons gave comfort against the boneyard chill trying to seep its way into her heart, but did nothing to prevent the whispers of doubt. *Turn back*, the whispers said. *There's no hope in this. The Kings will sense you.* They were echoes from the asirim, those pitiable souls who lived beneath the twisted trees. The words were meant to discourage, but served only to harden Çeda's resolve. What she was about to do was *necessary*—for the good of the asirim, for the good of her tribe, for the good of the desert—and it was long past due.

After following the crest of a dune, Çeda leaned into the downward slope, built speed toward and through the trough, then kicked along the incline with full-body strokes of her leg. Melis and Sümeya followed suit, and when they reached the peak, all three of them stomped the end of their zilijs, flipping them over to prevent them from sliding away.

"Breath of the desert," Sümeya said, "it feels like years since we were here."

"Like another life," Çeda replied.

So much had happened since then: their flight into the desert, their meeting with the thirteenth tribe, the battle against King Onur and his tribe built through conquest, then the larger battle where the other Sharakhani Kings and the royal navy joined in. It had all begun here, when Çeda, hoping to reveal the truth to Sümeya and Melis, had chosen a family of asirim to speak with. They'd told their story, but King Husamettín had dominated them immediately after and forced them to do his will. Only with the help of Dardzada, the old apothecary, had they managed to escape Husamettín and his Blade Maidens, and even then it had been a near thing.

The sand was soft beneath Çeda's callused hands as she crouched and studied the blooming fields. *Today might be a different day*, she thought, *but it's every bit as dangerous.* From their distant vantage, the long line of trees looked harmless, a line of ink spilled across a rolling piece of parchment. To the careful observer, however, more was revealed. The branches of the adichara trees swayed, their night blooms open, each a pale, blue-white flame, brighter than the reflected light of the moons could account for. *Like a river of souls*, Çeda mused, *searching for the farther fields*.

She studied the shadows beneath the trees and the gaps between the groves for any telltale signs of soldiers. She spread her awareness outward, wary of spikes of emotion from the asirim that might indicate the presence of one of the Kings.

She had once needed an adichara petal to do such things. Not so now, especially this close to the blooming fields. It was a miracle of sorts, a power that flowed from the old wound in the meat of her right thumb, a wound she'd given herself to prove once and for all that she was a daughter of a Sharakhani King. Through the poison that still resided there she could feel the trees and the asirim. The tattoo around it, given to her by the Matron Zaïde, had saved her life. It helped to hem the pain in, but it could only do so much. This close to the blooming fields the wound was a fount of anger and vengeance.

She'd learned that she could draw upon that anger so long as she didn't let it overwhelm her. She did so now, squeezing her hand until the pain sharpened. Her sense of the blooming fields sharpened with it.

"Well?" Melis said gruffly.

Çeda ignored the note of impatience in her voice, completing her inspection with care. "There's nothing," she replied when she was done. "We're safe for now."

Melis stood and stomped on her zilij to flip it back over. "Then let's get bloody moving." With one hard kick, she slid into motion.

Çeda and Sümeya shared a look. Melis had been acting like this more often of late, but now was hardly the time to discuss it. They followed and had just reached the peak of the next dune when a lonely wail swept like cold rain over the desert. Çeda shivered from it. The sorrow in that call stemmed from the asir's pain, its helplessness to stand against the voices of the gods that whispered in their minds: *Go to Sharakhai. Take tribute. Kill for us.*

Çeda had once viewed the asirim as ruthless monsters. Now she saw them for what they truly were. Slaves. Slaves to the gods' decree. Slaves to the will of the Kings. On this holy night, they would go to Sharakhai and kill the ones King Sukru had marked, then return to the blooming fields with their tributes, where the bodies would be tossed into the arms of the adichara to be torn limb from limb, their blood feeding the roots of the twisted trees.

It was all still so daunting, her mission to destroy the Kings, but she couldn't forget how far she'd come. Six Kings lay dead or powerless. Azad had been felled by Çeda's mother, Ahya. Külaşan, Mesut, and Onur were dead by Çeda's hand. Yusam's death was still a mystery, though Çeda wouldn't be surprised to learn that one of his brother Kings, Ihsan being the most likely, had done it. And then there was Zeheb, the Whisper King, driven mad by his own power.

As she reached the edge of the grove, more and more of the blooming fields were opened to her. More of the asirim were as well. She felt so much pure *need* in them it was nearly overwhelming, but she suppressed those gnawing feelings as best she could, concentrating solely on the grove that lay before her. As she, Sümeya, and Melis entered it along a tunnel-like path, the adichara branches moved snakelike, rubbing against one another, the sound of it like twigs breaking underfoot. Beneath the light of the blue-white blooms, an arsenal of thorns stood out starkly along the branches.

They made their way to a clearing where they'd first met the asir named Mavra, a matriarch who had somehow managed to keep her family together over four terrible centuries of enslavement. As had been true the last time she'd come, Çeda felt not only Mavra, but her kin as well: the children, grandchildren, and great-grandchildren. Most were asleep, caught in the spell that kept them in place until called upon by Sukru and his infernal whip, or pressed into service by one of the other Kings.

"Rise, Mavra," Çeda said aloud. "Rise and wake your children."

Like moonlight rippling over a pond, Mavra's will spread amongst the others. They roused, and their anger flared. Emaciated hands broke the sandy surface beneath the trees. Their ceaseless hunger gnawed at them as they crawled like termites from rotted wood. A dozen cadaverous shapes lifted from the ground, their blackened skin shriveled, tight against their bones. More followed, and more still, until they all stood trembling, mouths agape as their eyes swallowed the light of the adichara blooms.

Only Mavra remained in her grave.

Come grandmother. Leave the roots behind.

A few paces from where Çeda stood, an ungainly form broke the surface and pulled herself tall. Mavra was large, with broad shoulders and pendulous breasts. Lank hair hung before her face in dust-ridden strands. Her whole body quivered, making her look fragile, as if she were standing through sheer will alone. Only in her flinty stare could Çeda see some glimmer of her former, awesome strength.

"*Threeee of mine died when last you came,*" she said in a reedy whisper.

"What happened was a tragedy," Çeda said. "But the Kings caused it. Surely you see this."

"*Haaaaddd you not coooome*"—her voice had grown stronger, her sorrow palpable—"*they would still be aliiive.*"

Her brood were becoming more animated. Sedef, the most overprotective of her sons, crept closer on all fours. His limbs were long and lanky, his thoughts dark, echoing the murderous look in his eyes. The others parted as he came.

"You're right to be angry," Çeda said, keeping one eye on Sedef, "but direct that anger against King Husamettín, who has hidden the truth for four hundred years. Direct it against King Sukru, who summons you to Sharakhai. Direct it against King Kiral, who rules them all. Not against me, nor my sisters, who have come to see you freed."

Çeda could feel Mavra's heart skip at the word *freed*. She might hate Çeda for what had happened, but she recognized the truth in Çeda's words. Sedef, however, was not so patient. He growled and groaned until the others backed away and cowered from him, even Mavra.

It was in the following moments, as Sedef charged and Mavra did nothing to stop him, that Çeda understood: Sedef had supplanted Mavra as the leader of their family.

With long strides he stormed toward the clearing.

"Control your son, Mavra!" Çeda called.

Melis, breathing rapidly, drew her shamshir. Çeda immediately whistled, *Stand down!* Melis knew better—Çeda had told her not to touch a weapon—but her fear of the asirim was overriding it. Still, she complied with Çeda's order, though by then Sedef was nearly on top of her.

Now! Çeda whistled.

As one, Çeda, Melis, and Sümeya tackled Sedef. Çeda felt his long claws rake her dress across the thighs. The armor held, but the next moment he was reaching for her neck.

Like all the asirim, Sedef was inhumanly strong, but Melis and Sümeya had both taken petals, and Çeda had the power of the adichara running through her as well. Together, they held him at bay. But Sedef was no newcomer to battle. He rolled. He clawed. He bit. Sümeya, Melis, and Çeda all took cuts from his nails, or were struck by his elbows, his knees, his feet.

"Mavra!"

Sedef head-butted Çeda. Stars mixed with the brightness of the adichara blooms. Sedef threw her back and sent a kick into Melis's gut, and then, in a blink, had his arms around Sümeya's waist. He lifted her high, ready to throw her into the poisonous adichara thorns.

"No!" Çeda cried, coming shakily to her feet, too far away, too woozy to help.

With a roar, a dark form tackled Sedef from behind. It was Mavra. She was using her weight to force Sedef to the ground while Sümeya fell against two winding adichara boughs.

"Sümeya!" Çeda reached her a moment later and helped her to her feet.

"It's all right," Sümeya said. "The thorns didn't pierce."

Çeda's relief was short-lived. Sedef's strength was terrible, and Mavra seemed unable to stop him. When Mavra spoke to him, however, everything changed.

"Throw away your chance for freedom if you will, but don't do it for us all. Think of Amile and how he's suffered. Think of all the others, your brothers and sisters, your nieces and nephews and countless cousins."

Sedef still fought her, but Mavra was displaying the sort of power she surely possessed when she was young. The mood in the clearing shifted. Mavra's children had felt lost without her. Her return, though it came at the cost of Sedef's defeat and shame, gave them hope. They *wanted* Mavra to win. And so, Çeda suspected, did Sedef. How else to explain his slowed movements or his faint sense of hope as Mavra drove him down and pressed a forearm against his throat? When his body finally went lax, she lifted herself up and pointed to the darkest part of the nearby trees. There, the adichara parted, creating a path. Like a scolded child, Sedef rose and followed it, shoulders bowed, and the trees converged behind him.

Mavra's broad frame heaved with every ragged breath she took. She turned to Çeda. *"Tell me now,"* she said, her words little more than a long wheeze. *"Tell me how we can be freed."*

All eyes shifted to Çeda.

"I must know something first," Çeda replied, and waved to the adicharas as their branches clicked and clacked. "Would you leave this grove? Would you leave the only home you've known for the past four hundred years?"

It was not a simple question. Mavra's old life was like a dream to her, distant and discomfiting even compared to the embrace of the adichara's roots. No matter that they were a symbol of her enslavement, these twisted trees had long ago become her home.

Mavra considered, her childlike worry plain on her face. *"Yeessss,"* she said. *"I would leave."*

"Would you strike against the Kings?"

"Gleefully." She spat the word.

"Lastly, Mavra, would you follow *me*?"

All around the grove, the tortured voices of the asirim rose. It made the hair on Çeda's arms and the back of her neck stand up. Some, heedless of the thorns, grabbed the nearby trunks and shook the trees, making the light from the blooms above flicker wildly. Mavra, however, was a guiding star. The asirim settled themselves, deferent, waiting for Mavra to decide.

"Will you free all of us?"

"I will."

"Our King as well?"

She meant Sehid-Alaz, who as far as Çeda knew was still trapped in King Husamettín's palace.

"That is my hope," Çeda said.

Mavra considered, her jaundiced eyes searching. *"I want more,"* she finally rasped. *"I want more than to simply be free."*

"What more do you want?"

Çeda thought she knew the answer, but she wanted Mavra to say it out loud. Mavra leaned aggressively toward Çeda. Her heavy cheeks shook. Her eyes opened wide in a yellow leer that spoke of hunger and rage and little else. As much as she wanted to say the words, she couldn't. She was forbidden to speak of such things, so Çeda spoke them for her.

"You want revenge. You want to taste the blood of Kings."

Mavra couldn't so much as nod, but Çeda felt the desire within her, boiling like a witch's cauldron.

"Follow me, Mavra, and we will go to Tauriyat. Follow me and together we will free our king from his imprisonment."

Mavra's hope lit like a beacon. *"Husamettín's will is strong, and he knows the asirim best now that Mesut lies dead. He will not let Sehid-Alaz go easily."*

"No," Çeda replied, "which is why we'll kill him first."

Chapter 2

A MAN NAMED BRAMA trekked north along the peak of a knife-edge dune. A hot wind blew, scouring the dune's windward side, sending spindrift to swirling. It tickled the fingers of his left hand, collected in the furrows between his scars. More than the heat, more than the give of the sand beneath his sandals, he felt a thing that couldn't be seen. It came when the wind picked up, as it had for many days, and in this way was predictable, but it was defined more by its ephemeral nature. Each time it came, Brama would concentrate on the feeling, but he'd no sooner begun to sense its inner workings than it would dissipate.

He wanted to learn its nature—something deep inside him *needed* to learn it—but he'd failed so many times by trying to impose his will upon it, so instead he relaxed. He let his senses go. *Come to me if you wish*, he mused. *I'll chase you no longer.*

Like a meager wind toying with the canvas of a sandship, a new sensation filled his chest and cradled his heart. *Not unlike love*, Brama thought. He took in the desert anew. All about him lay the golden dunes of the Great Shangazi, breathtaking in their simplistic beauty. He'd seen much in his time since the great battle between the Sharakhani Kings and the thirteenth tribe, and had come to love the desert like nothing else.

Nothing? he mused.

Not so long ago, his only love had been for Rümayesh, the ehrekh, the ancient desert creature he'd been bound to for years. But Rümayesh was off exploring the desert. When she would return Brama had no idea. He couldn't even remember when she'd left. Days ago? Weeks? Since then, he'd been free to see the desert for what it truly was: a treasure.

The curious feeling spread. It tingled along his arms and he became increasingly aware of a line of low rocks, too far for the eye to see. He felt the oases beyond, and the life that thrived in and around them. He'd never had much fondness for the desert when he was young. The few times he'd left the city for the sand had felt interminable. Now he felt like a blind man who'd been granted the ability to see for the first time. The strange new world that had been opened to him was chaotic, even garish, but no less wondrous for it.

It felt as if he was coming to know the desert as a *part* of it. The notion caused his newfound senses to falter and he immediately halted, closed his eyes, and lost himself in the sigh of the wind as it tugged at his curly hair. He felt the sun's relentless heat along his left side. While he listened to the breathy sigh of sand along the dunes, he found peace once more, and the strange sensation returned.

He opened his eyes to see the sand swirling before him in lazy patterns. The patterns held meaning, he knew, but they felt unknowable. They may as well have been the writings of an elder god. And yet he knew enough to know they *had* meaning, which was a miracle in itself. It was Rümayesh's influence, a thing he ought to be more concerned about, but he'd given up trying to escape her. He'd agreed to walk with her for a time, so why not learn more of the desert while he did?

The moment became so powerful he realized he could feel Rümayesh somewhere far, far away. He felt as if, were he to take one step toward her, he would turn to sand and be borne upon the wind until he was lain at her feet, whole once more. She would kiss the crown of his head and the two of them would become as one. They would explore the desert together, as she'd promised, and she would shelter him from all danger. Through ages they would walk, side by side, the lord of all things coming to take his hand only when she'd tired of his company.

He was nearly ready to do it. The urge was intoxicating, almost overwhelming. But he was jarred by a bitter scent on the wind. Something new had come to this part of the desert, which might be friend or foe. He turned and breathed deeply, knowing, without knowing *how* he knew, that he would find it in that direction. In the moment he'd made up his mind to learn more, the swirling wind vanished and the sand fell about him like rain.

After shaking it from his hair, he considered the horizon. Whatever he'd sensed, it was something old, something deeper than the desert. He felt heady from it. For days and nights he followed that scent, and one morning spotted an amber haze lifting along the horizon. His first thought was a caravan, but this was something much, much larger.

Rümayesh had said before she'd left, "War has come to the desert."

"Are you certain, then, that we should part?"

Sensing his true meaning, she'd smiled and caressed his cheek. "You have nothing to fear. And you need time to learn the desert on your own."

He hadn't known what she'd meant then, but in the days that followed, his new senses had been born—his ability to see the magic that made up the world—and he'd come to know the desert in ways he could never have before. He knew he should hate Rümayesh for all she'd done to him, but for this he was glad.

As high sun arrived he reached the edges of Aldiir, the largest caravanserai along the desert's northerly passage, roughly halfway between Sharakhai and the southern border of Mirea. To the right of the cluster of mudbrick buildings were daubs of blue-green, pools of water choked with all manner of greenery, from tall grasses to spearsheaf bushes to the occasional date tree.

Beyond the serai, a great fleet of ships was arrayed in a protective ring. Brama had heard of them. Dunebreakers, they were called, four-masted affairs with double-decked forecastles and aftcastles. And they were tall, taller than he thought sandships could be. They had strange, huge wheels affixed to the sides of the hulls at the ships' centers, apparently to help dig them out of trouble, though if that was the case why wouldn't they just make the damned ships smaller to begin with? They were so cumbersome it hardly seemed they could navigate the desert, much less bear an army toward Sharakhai.

A horn blew, and three riders left the ring of ships and came riding toward him. The lead rider sat atop a dappled brown mare. He wore light leather armor and a conical reed hat. More curious was his cream-colored skin and his hair, which was paler than bleached bones. The other two riders wore lacquered armor, their faces hidden by the grinning demon masks of their helms. They rode qirin, powerful mounts with the body of a horse but the neck and head of a dragon, with huge coiled horns atop their heads. And while their coats along their midsection and haunches were chestnut roan, the scales along their forelegs, neck, and head were a powdery blue that shone red under the light of the hot desert sun.

The lead rider urged his horse ahead of the qirin knights. His icy eyes pierced Brama as he reined to a stop. Though they made no move to raise them, the knights behind him each held a bow with an arrow nocked. In the glaring sun, the arrowheads glinted like diamonds. It took Brama a moment to realize why. They *were* diamonds. The thief in him wondered how many more were in their quivers. He wondered at their quality. But those were old instincts from a different life, and he set the thoughts aside as useless.

Their albino leader took in the weave of scars covering Brama's face, neck, and hands. "State your name," he said in perfect Sharakhan.

"I am Brama Junayd'ava. And you?" A memory tickled at the back of Brama's mind. He'd seen the man before, but couldn't place where.

He peered at Brama's scar-riddled face. "You're the Tattered Prince, the one who used to heal addicts in the Knot."

Brama gave him a theatrical bow. "We are one and the same."

The man scanned the horizon beyond Brama as if he expected someone else to be there. "Your business here?"

It was that word, *business*, that unlocked the memory. Brama had gone to the fighting pits often when he was young, and he'd seen this Mirean man there, quite a few times actually, usually as a guest in Osman's personal seats. "You're Juvaal . . . No, Juvaan. The Mirean ambassador."

Juvaan's eyes remained cold. "I asked you your business."

Brama smiled. "I need give no answers to an interloper in the desert."

The qirin warriors, one to either side of him, lifted their bows and drew their diamond-tipped arrows back, but at a wave from Juvaan, they lowered them again. Juvaan slipped down from his saddle and walked across the grasping sand, stopping several paces from Brama. He was wary—more than Brama would have expected on finding a lone man walking in the desert—but there was no fear in his eyes. "I must know what brought you here."

"Is curiosity not a good enough answer?" Brama waved toward the towering ships. "It's not every day one sees an army invading the Great Shangazi."

Juvaan seemed disappointed. He retrieved something from a small bag at his belt: a glazed, plum-sized pot with holes in it. When he lifted the lid, an emerald green dragonfly with pink wings flew out. It glittered as it flew, the color of its wings shifting from pink to blue to green and back again. It hovered before Brama, buzzed past his ear, only to return a moment later as if waiting for something.

Brama crooked a finger toward it, and there it landed, fanning its wings like the dragonflies along the Haddah in spring. Of a sudden it began beating its wings in such a way that it created a drone. It was louder than Brama would have given it credit for. He felt it in his chest. Goezhen's sweet kiss, it made his *mouth* itch. Juvaan, as though he'd been expecting this, gave nothing away. He set the lid of the pot against the clay rim and began circling it slowly. It produced another sort of sound, a crystalline ring. The dragonfly, clearly summoned by the sound, launched itself, arced through the air, landed on the pot, and crawled inside.

Juvaan quickly replaced the lid and secreted the pot inside his bag. "Would you care for some tea?"

"*Tea?*" Brama waited for further explanation, but Juvaan only smiled and waved to the encampment. "What did that bloody thing just do?"

"All will be explained." Juvaan waved again, this time bowing his head. "Please. My queen would be honored if you would join her."

Brama laughed. "Well then, by all means, let's have tea with the queen!"

At a quiet word from Juvaan the two qirin warriors rode away, taking Juvaan's horse with them. Juvaan then led Brama on foot beyond the caravanserai and toward the ring of ships. As they passed between two of the tall dunebreakers, more knights in lacquered armor and demon masks watched them pass from atop the decks, bows at the ready. Workmen called. Soldiers moved to and fro. From somewhere beyond the circle of dunebreakers, a strange call sounded—a cross between an elephant's trumpet and a sand drake's hiss. Brama looked to his escort, but none of them seemed put off by it.

In the center of the camp was a pavilion of white silk that shimmered as the wind made its roof roll in easy waves. Around it, in a circular pattern within the ring of ships, stood similar but smaller tents. Some few soldiers stood sentry here, but by and large servants seemed to dominate the space.

Why are they camped here anyway? Brama thought. *If their purpose is conquest, shouldn't they be sailing hard for Sharakhai?*

Juvaan led them inside the central pavilion, where the sand was covered by a host of fine Mirean carpets, a variety of low tables, and piles of pillows meant for sitting. All around the pavilion, standing inside the wooden poles, were more warriors like the first two, each wearing a demon mask, each with a diamond-tipped arrow nocked across their bow.

Across the tent from Brama was a dais, upon which rested an ornate wooden chair. Sitting cross-legged upon it was a woman of perhaps fifty summers wearing a fine silk robe with long, flowing sleeves. The black silk was embellished with thousands of tiny pearls in the shapes of lotuses and marsh grasses. A wide crimson belt wrapped her waist. Her lustrous black hair was done up a in perfect bun, which was held in place by an ornamental headdress and a pair of gleaming steel pins, each as long as her forearm.

Juvaan bowed and spoke quickly in Mirean, then bowed again and said in Sharakhan, "My Queen Alansal, I bring you Brama Junayd'ava."

The queen smiled as Juvaan backed away and left them in peace. Her smile was pleasant enough, but her eyes were hungry. "I'm pleased you found us." Her Sharakhan was noticeably slower than Juvaan's, and had a thick Mirean accent. Holding one sleeve, she used her opposite hand to wave to the pile of pillows before her. "Sit if you would."

Brama did, more curious than anything else. He had no idea why they were treating him this way, but he was willing to play this game if they were.

They brought him rice wine that tasted of grapes and fennel and fresh cut grass. They served him dumplings filled with minced pork, onion, and water chestnuts that were both savory and sweet, with a texture that was at first chewy but then melted in his mouth. These were followed by disks of steamed, jasmine rice with bull's-eye centers made from a fragrant radish and pickled carrots. More platters came, all bearing bite-sized food with flavors the likes of which Brama had never tasted. The last had crunchy black seeds that made his lips and tongue tingle.

When he was sure he would burst if he had another bite, he lounged against his pillows and sipped from his glass of sweet plum wine. "What is it you need?"

The abruptness of the question didn't seem to faze Queen Alansal. "As you may have guessed," she said, "my fleet has come to the desert to topple the twelve Kings, now somewhat fewer in number, from power."

"That's hardly a surprise."

The queen smiled, fine lines showing at the corners of her eyes and mouth. "No, no surprise, but I wonder. Would it bother you?"

"If the Kings no longer sat atop Tauriyat?"

Holding her long sleeve with care, the queen smiled and took a sip of wine. "Yes."

"No, I don't suppose it would."

"And would you care to help?"

The game, such as it was, was becoming more elaborate by the moment. "How?"

"The Kings will meet us here soon enough, and we will defeat them. No matter that the Mad King of Malasan has sent a fleet to take the Amber Jewel. No matter that Kundhun supports the failing, flailing Kings. No matter that the Qaimiri Queen thinks to swoop in when the Kings are at their weakest. We will still win, and I wish to avoid as much bloodshed as possible. Help us convince the Kings of this inevitability now. Help us crush their fleet and leave them defenseless as we advance on the city. Our fleet is mighty, and with you at our side we could do just that."

Through the alcohol haze, Brama thought he was beginning to understand. The queen thought he was an ehrekh. Rümayesh's taint on him had caused the dragonfly to land on him and buzz in that strange manner. And it was the promise of an ehrekh's power that had led to the queen of Mirea making an offer to a man who otherwise looked like what he truly was: a one-time thief who'd somehow, improbably, befriended one of the most ancient and powerful creatures in the Great Shangazi.

Brama wasn't about to give up the game just yet, though. "I see how *your* aims might be furthered, but there is nothing free in the desert."

This drew a smile that made the queen seem ancient. It was a knowing smile, the smile of a woman who knew the hearts of men at but a word. "Nor beyond the mountains," she said softly. "There are many things Mirea might offer you. You have but to name your price."

Brama might be young, but he was no stranger to bargaining. "You put a scent on the wind that I might be drawn near. You did so because you already have something to offer, something you're sure will be of interest."

At this Alansal paused. She set down her glass of plum wine and stared more deeply into Brama's eyes than she had before. "It is said that Goezhen bestowed upon you his own thirst. It is said that you hunger for the touch of the lost gods. It is said that you would pay dearly for but a glimpse of who they once were. Is it not so, *Brama Junayd'ava?*"

She spoke his name in singsong, as though the two of them were conspirators and she knew that some other name, his true name, hid behind it, waiting to be spoken. He might even have felt a compulsion to tell her what it was. But he resisted that call, thinking more on what she was implying. He'd felt Rümayesh's cravings. Most often it was to taste mortal women and men, to experience life as they did, but that desire was driven by something deeper, something as much a part of her as her midnight skin and curving horns. She'd never said it, but Brama had felt her thoughts. She wanted the touch of the old gods. She needed it. It was why she occasionally gave in and tortured some of her victims, so that she might taste the blood of mortals, and through them, the blood of the old gods, who had given of themselves that mortal man might live and follow them to the farther fields once they'd died.

Now here was the queen of a distant land, claiming to offer him the same: a touch of the lost gods. Something greater than the blood of mortals, which an ehrekh could have at any time she wished.

"What do you have?" Brama asked.

From around her neck Queen Alansal unclasped a necklace, the pendant a glass vial with a cork stopper. Brama couldn't quite make out what was inside it. It was dark, whatever it was, and scintillant. It reminded him of raw iron ore.

"The first gods left these shores long ago," the queen said. "Half an age passed before mortals even learned of it. The young gods searched for them and, upon learning of their departure, wept. Some went to the places the elder gods often visited, to remind themselves of happier days. Others collected and hoarded artifacts made by their elders. Others searched for their bodily remains, then hoarded them away. Not all were found, however, and when mortals learned of this, they searched as well. Wars were fought over pieces as small as a fingernail. The young gods sometimes entered the fray, such was their desire for these remnants." She peered into the vial. "Such was the power of the elders who made our world."

She let the words settle between them like a hand offered in friendship. Brama couldn't claim to understand it all, but he understood enough to know what was inside the vial. He nodded to it as casually as he could. "That's what you're offering me, a taste of the old gods?"

"No." She handed the vial to a servant, who delivered it to Brama. "I have an entire finger bone of Raamajit the Exalted. This is but a scraping from that very bone, which I offer to you freely that you might know what I say is true."

As Brama stared at the vial in wonder, the queen motioned for him to continue. With great care, he held the vial to his nose, pulled the cork, and breathed in the scent.

His head tipped backward from the feeling of power that stormed through him. His fingers tingled. His bones ached. He tried in vain to keep it all in, but the urge to laugh came bubbling up from inside him. He laughed long and hard, a child before an unexpected thousand-layer sweet.

When he and Rümayesh had joined hands after the Battle of Blackspear, the great battle King Onur had waged against the thirteenth tribe, it had freed Brama's mind of all the pain and doubt burdening him like hundredweights. But that same transaction, whether Rümayesh had intended it or not, had transferred some small amount of her power to him. It had been a rush the likes of which he'd never experienced before. This was similar, but deeper, wider. However connected to the Shangazi he'd felt before, now he was the desert's master. It was incomprehensible that the mere scent of a thing could possess such power.

"What say you, Rümayesh?" Queen Alansal said. "Will you enter into this bargain with us?"

Brama might have been surprised to hear Rümayesh's name had the bone's power not been running through him, but much of what had been hidden moments ago was now revealed, as if the shutters had been opened in an ill-used room, revealing motes of dust in the air, a layer of dirt on the floor. The diamond-tipped arrowheads of the nearby warriors seemed to glow. There was a palpable sheen to Queen Alansal's skin. And there was a thread that ran from him to another. Rümayesh. Her presence had been veiled but was now clear as day, the connection gaining substance until it felt like a tendril of wool, easy to grip, easier to cut.

Brama swallowed hard, hoping Rümayesh hadn't sensed his sudden nervousness or that, if she had, she attributed it to his standing before the queen of Mirea, not from the thought of what he might do with so much power.

Tell her yes, Rümayesh spoke from her hiding place somewhere west of the Mirean camp.

She was near, he realized. Very near. And suddenly he understood why. *You thought this was a trap,* Brama said. *You caught the same scent, weeks before I did. That's why you left me.*

She paused. *They would never have harmed you.*

If you believed that why wouldn't you have come yourself?

It had to be this way. The queen knew you were but an emissary within moments of speaking to you. And I didn't lie to you. There were things that needed tending to. He was about to reply, but she spoke over him. *Look at her, Brama.*

Despite the feelings of betrayal, he obeyed. The sheen on Alansal's skin had intensified, while the look in her eyes had darkened; they looked like two black pits in a field of stardust.

Queen Alansal has spent her days collecting things like the bones of the old gods. Few could harm an ehrekh, or trap us like Çedamihn did with the sapphire, but there are some that might. How foolish would I have been to have gone to her without knowing more?

It felt strange to be so closely watched by a queen whose powers he could only guess at while another sort of creature stared at him from within. In that moment, he would do anything to make it stop.

"How large is the bone?" Brama asked Queen Alansal.

"It is a piece the size of a chestnut."

"If we help you, all of it goes to my lady."

For the span of a breath, the queen considered, then nodded. "Very well."

"Very well," Brama echoed. "Rümayesh agrees to join you."

He felt Rümayesh's relief, which was strange in and of itself. He hadn't realized how desperate the ehrekh would be to gain such a thing. But he was glad for it as well, because it hid his own secret: that for the first time since being caught up with Rümayesh, he had a chance to be rid of her once and for all.

Chapter 3

Within the adichara grove, Çeda drew her kenshar and balled her right hand. The pain was already high, but she forced it higher by pumping her fist, then pressed the tip of her kenshar into her palm. Blood welled, dark and glistening in the pale light of the wavering blooms. When enough blood had gathered, she held her open palm to Mavra.

Mavra hesitated, but not for long. She knew this was her path to freedom. With a hand that felt impossibly warm, she reached out and gripped Çeda's wrist, then ran her too-dry tongue up Çeda's palm, accepting the offered blood. Çeda felt a terrible thrill run through her, a quickening of sorts, while her link to Mavra, so weak and tentative a moment ago, crystallized into a bond that was every bit as strong as the one she'd shared with Kerim, the asir who'd accompanied her into the desert after the Night of Endless Swords.

"Good," Çeda said, ignoring the ache in her hand and wrist.

Behind Mavra, the adichara were pulling back, allowing Sedef to return. It was Mavra's doing. She knew, as Çeda did, that Sedef's consent was crucial. Perhaps Sedef did too. It would explain why he seemed so wary, why he walked in a hunched, distrustful manner until he reached them. Only then did he pull himself up to his full, towering height. He smelled like a charnel and looked as if he were on the verge of savaging her.

If it was meant to intimidate her, it didn't work. Çeda refused to be cowed. She held her bloodied palm out to him.

Sedef stared down at it, and Çeda saw the flash of an image: Sedef's tongue being cut from him over a century earlier by King Cahil after Sedef had hesitated to obey an order. Unable to speak aloud, his words rang in her mind. *We trade one form of slavery for another.*

And suddenly his show of strength made sense. He was scared. Not for himself, but for his kin. Çeda refused to lie to him, to any of them. They would all know the truth before they joined her.

"Make no mistake," she said, "you will be bound to me. It can be no other way until the curse is lifted. But you will be as free as I can make you."

Sedef's eyes, those jaundiced eyes, looked as if he were about to break down and cry. Çeda could feel his thirst for revenge. It was greater than even Mavra's. But he also knew that if this failed, they would all be hunted down by the Kings.

"Please, Sedef." She shook her hand. "Join me."

After a moment's pause, he took her hand. With much of his tongue gone, he could only kiss her palm, then suck on his blood-glistened lips. But he managed it, and Çeda felt the bond with him grow. In some ways it ran *through* Mavra. She was their undisputed leader once more.

As the ache in Çeda's right hand deepened, a frail female form stepped forward, one of Mavra's daughters. Then a waif of a boy, shriveled and blackened like the rest. Each licked her palm, forming a bond with Çeda, and the ache in her hand grew. She bore it with a smile, because the thought of freeing *some* of them, even imperfectly, made her heart soar.

On and on they came, some two dozen in all, each pushing Çeda's agony farther. She could hardly flex her hand for how terribly it hurt. The skin was angry and swollen, as if it were infected. The small red scar at the center of her thumb, the old puncture wound where the adichara thorn had pierced her skin, looked as if it were about to burst and release blood or poison or pus. For as long as Çeda could remember, she'd been able to sense the blooming fields, but never had her awareness felt so complete as it did now. She felt the blooms, the branches, the roots, even the strange cavern below Sharakhai where the roots all joined.

"Çeda?"

She also felt, for perhaps the first time, an enmity for the trees themselves. Perhaps it was a reflection of the asirim's hatred. Or perhaps it was her own growing awareness of the part the trees had played in the enslavement of her people.

"Çeda!"

She turned to find Sümeya staring at her.

"The night is wasting. The Kings may still come."

Çeda spoke in a distant tone, "We're nearly done."

But when all of Mavra's children had completed the ritual, Çeda remained where she was, simply *feeling* the trees. She took a sudden breath, her mind beginning to clear. Husamettín had likely felt what they had done, and what they were *about* to do would alert all of the Kings—how could it be otherwise? That danger had made her second guess her decision for weeks, but the chance that it might sever the asirim's ties to the blooming fields, or at least allay their burden, was one she couldn't pass up.

"Unearth the trees," Çeda said to the asirim. "Tear them up by the roots."

"No!" Melis said, stepping in front of Çeda.

The asirim hesitated.

"The trees must go," Çeda said.

She hadn't expected any objections, but now she could see she'd misjudged the situation. Melis had always been the calm one, but now she was incensed.

"The adichara are sacred!" Melis shouted.

Çeda spoke calmly. "The trees are not sacred. They are a tool created by the gods to imprison my people."

Melis motioned to the gathered asirim. "We have what we've come for. It worked. I can *feel* it."

"Mavra and the rest have called these trees home since the days of Beht Ihman. They're bound to them, Melis. The trees are part of what enslaves them." When Melis made to speak again, Çeda pointed to the darkest part of the grove and talked over her. "You were taught that these groves were called the killing fields, were you not? They said it was because of the way the asirim, the *holy warriors* of Sharakhai, chased down her enemies, enemies whose bodies were thrown to the trees that they might drink of their blood. They have a different meaning to us. Death reigns here each month, Melis, when more tributes are collected. But for the asirim it is their *own* deaths, denied to them these many centuries, which the killing fields and these trees represent. How can you defend the very symbol of what is most reviled?"

Melis stared at the clearing as if she couldn't understand how she'd wound up there.

"Let them take the trees," Sümeya said.

Melis glared at her as if it were the worst sort of betrayal. Her hand on the pommel of her ebon blade, she stalked away.

"You should've told us," Sümeya said once she was out of earshot. "You should've trusted us."

Çeda stood there, feeling foolish. "You're right. It seemed so obvious to me, but I should have realized."

Sümeya looked as though she'd been expecting a different response. She waved to the asirim, who seemed agitated, on edge. "Best get on with it."

Çeda nodded. "Go," she said to Mavra and the rest. "Tear the trees down, all of them that housed you."

They set to immediately, tearing at the trees, ripping up the smallest among them that they might reach the larger ones. Were these normal men and women, they would have no hope of tearing up these trees with their gnarled trunks, not without tools. But these were the asirim, and their strength was breathtaking.

One tree broke with a great crack near its base. They threw the trunk aside and began digging up its roots. Nearby, Sedef and several others tore up another, larger than the first. Behind Çeda two more were falling to the strength of the asirim.

It was loud, all around her, but Çeda was numb to it. She was coughing, bent over, left hand on her knee to keep herself from falling to the sand while her right hand covered her heart. It was beating so strangely, its rhythm like tripping down a set of stairs. And it *hurt*, as though each beat were causing irreversible damage.

She tried to reach out to the asirim, but couldn't. Her mind was running wild. She felt a presence, watching with keen interest. It reminded her of the visions in Nalamae's tree, a hundred perspectives shown in the hanging crystals, except in this case *she* was the one being observed. It felt divine in nature, but she was certain it wasn't Nalamae. It was another of the gods. Which, she wondered in growing fear, Yerinde? Tulathan? Rhia?

She found no answer, and the vision faded, but her panic refused to ease. "Make them stop," she said. But it came out too softly.

Sümeya was suddenly at her side, one hand on her back. "What's happened?"

Çeda felt so weak. Her heart had begun to skip. "Make them stop!"

Sümeya was not bonded to the asirim, but she had taken a petal. Çeda felt Sümeya *press* upon the asirim as she screamed for them to stop. It felt distant and muffled, but Çeda could hear the panic in her voice. It was that, more than anything, that brought Çeda back from the edge. She dropped to her knees, clutched her chest, and focused solely on her breathing, her heartbeat, willing both to fall into their proper rhythms.

The asirim, meanwhile, listened. They felt Çeda's pain and worry. It echoed within them. Mavra, Amile, Natise, and the rest. Even Sedef. They didn't love her, but they at least saw her as an ally, and a woman whose blood ran thick with their own blood, and that meant much in the desert.

The tearing, cracking sounds ceased. The clicking and clacking of the adichara resumed while the asirim closed in around her. Their worry cradled her like down. For a moment, she simply basked in it, realizing that the pain in her right arm had eased.

"Are you well?" Sümeya asked, kneeling by her side.

When Çeda didn't respond, Sümeya felt the pulse on Çeda's neck. She lay the backs of her fingers along Çeda's forehead. It felt good, to be cared for. Beyond her, the twin moons had lowered in the west. She knew it shouldn't, but the night felt strangely serene.

That was when Çeda felt a new heartbeat. One she was sure hadn't been there a moment ago.

"Someone has come," Çeda said, but it came out in a whisper. "Sümeya, someone has come!"

Sümeya heard her this time. She stood, drawing her shamshir in a blinding flourish, and turned to the precise location where Çeda had sensed the new heartbeat. In a burst of movement, she dove right and whistled, *Enemy! Beware!*

Something dark streaked through the air where Sümeya had been standing. The black shaft of an arrow sunk deep into the chest of an asir who wailed as she was spun to the ground.

Mavra lifted her arm and pointed beyond the trees. *Beşir!* she called. *King Beşir has come!*

Sedef was suddenly by Çeda's side, pulling her to her feet.

Sümeya sprinted along the pathway toward the open desert. *Attack!* she whistled to Melis. *Protect our flank!*

Çeda saw movement to her left. The trees were parting. A tunnel of sorts opened directly ahead of her, giving a narrow view of the desert. On the sand stood a dark shape, bow drawn, sighting along the shaft of another arrow.

The bowman released, the arrow flying straight for Çeda's head. She'd begun to move, but already knew it was too late.

Sedef charged into the arrow's path and took it deep in the chest. He reeled from it, then grabbed the shaft and yanked it free. Bits of flesh and dark blood flew. He turned and loped with the others along the paths through the grove, following Sümeya.

Çeda felt lightheaded. Her ability to feel those around her wavered. She felt King Beşir's presence, but then he was simply gone. With a meaty thump, an arrow struck Mavra's side where she was lumbering behind Çeda. Mavra screamed, a pitiful, high-pitched sound that turned into a growl. Sedef reached her side, placed a hand around the shaft, and drew the arrow from her ribs. He caught another of the black-fletched arrows in his thigh for the trouble.

They fled from the blooming field and into open desert.

Melis stood ready with her short bow, the string already pulled to her cheek. Sümeya had just strung hers and was drawing an arrow from the quiver along her back.

"If we don't do something," Sümeya said, "he'll kill us all."

From within the blooming fields, more arrows streaked through the night. Melis and Sümeya let fly with arrows of their own, but their shots never found their target. Beşir's angle of attack was always carefully chosen and their arrows were often caught in the branches. Whenever their aim came too close, Beşir simply moved to a new location where the branches would part for him, opening up a new pathway for his deadly fire. He was concentrating on the asirim, sending them into a panic, but Çeda waited with River's Daughter drawn, her mind open and aware, knowing that sooner or later Beşir would return his attention to the three of them.

She felt a shift, and Beşir's dark silhouette appeared inside the blooming fields twenty paces away. His bow was already drawn and aimed toward Sümeya. Çeda slid right and lunged with her buckler as the arrow was released. It struck her shield hard and ricocheted with an ear-piercing *ting*.

Beşir loosed two more in rapid succession, one for Çeda, another for Melis. Çeda dodged the one meant for her and blocked the other, though this time the arrow struck the face of her buckler with so much force her entire arm went numb. Her joints were just starting to tingle, the feeling returning, when she felt a tug along her lower back, then a burning along her skin, evidence of a grazing arrow that bit into the nearby dune with a sound like crunching gravel.

It took Melis and Sümeya only the beat of a heart to aim and loose their arrows, but by then Beşir was already gone. The tunnel he'd created in the trees slowly shrank back into place.

Çeda suddenly felt him near. Very near. Just behind Melis, where Çeda couldn't easily use her sword to meet him. Melis felt him as well. She turned, holding her bow like a staff, but Beşir, clothed in a black khalat and turban, was already swinging his own bow across her guard.

He struck Melis on the side of the head. Even before she collapsed in a heap, he was on Sümeya, using her position and his own quick footwork to prevent Çeda from reaching him. Sümeya blocked the swing of his tall bow with her shorter one once, twice, but when she tried a third time Beşir dissolved like a shadow and reappeared behind her, his bow across her neck.

"Well, well," Beşir said, his voice sonorous and expressive, not unlike Ibrahim the storyteller, "if it isn't the black sheep who began it all."

Sümeya struggled, but Beşir had her at an extreme disadvantage. He held her steady, the bow slowly cutting off her air supply. Her movements were coming slower, her resistance weakening as she blacked out. Çeda was ready when Sümeya slumped to the ground. She charged and attacked, but Beşir parried her blows, batting them away with sharp twists of his bow.

Several asirim were galloping toward them on all fours, including Sedef, who favored his wounded side. Beşir seemed unconcerned. "Husamettín thought you would reappear in Sharakhai before you dared the blooming fields." He blocked another of her blows. "But I bargained you would come here, to do exactly this."

Çeda felt for Beşir's heart. She tried to reach for it, to *press* on him, but it was as though his heart were able to disappear and reappear, just like the man himself.

"Some of the other Kings might be impressed by what you've managed to do. But I'm not. It ends here, Çedamihn Ahyanesh'ala. It ends tonight."

She knew he was going to use his god-granted power on her, just as he had with Sümeya. It was only a question of when.

From her right, Çeda felt the lifting of the sand. Mavra was kneeling, one of her great hands pressed to the ground, and the sand was blowing in a gale before her. At this point it was no more than a stiff wind, but Çeda could tell she was readying for something. Sedef was nearing, and he was dragging a bulky object behind him.

Çeda and Beşir traded several more blows as Sedef's heavy footsteps brought him closer. Then Beşir retreated. By all appearances he was a man who'd seen fifty summers, but he moved like a gazelle. He drew an arrow from the quiver at his hip as he did so. She'd just begun to charge as he nocked the arrow.

And then she felt it.

The strange *tug* inside her that she now recognized as Beşir's intent to shift among the shadows.

She felt desperately for where he intended to go, but it was simply too brief. In a blink he was standing to her left, several paces away. She'd just begun to shift toward him when a scouring of sand lifted from the dune. It gusted, blowing around her as it reached for Beşir.

Beşir loosed his arrow. Çeda was too late in bringing her buckler around, but Mavra's wind was strong enough to blow the arrow off target just enough that it only pierced the boiled strips of leather over her ribs.

Beşir already had another arrow nocked. The air was so thick with sand

Çeda could barely see him. She saw enough, though. He was drawing his bow back when she heard an almighty grunt from somewhere behind her. To her left something long and ungainly flew through the air.

The bough of an adichara, Çeda realized. End over end it flew, the thickest part striking Beşir across the head just as he loosed his arrow.

Çeda twisted her body to one side while bringing River's Daughter up and around in a tight arc. She felt the arrow's path. Felt her blade slice it neatly in two. Saw the two ends spin up and into the night.

Then she sprinted for King Beşir.

He was on the ground, prone. Head lolling as he stared toward the sky, a great bleeding gash along the left side of his face from his forehead, across one eye, and down his cheek. Çeda brought her sword up as he blinked, mouth yawning wide. He caught her eye as the sword swung down toward his neck.

And she felt it.

His *shift*.

"No!" Çeda cried as River's Daughter came down against the sand.

She stared at the spot, feeling desperately for where he might have reappeared. But she felt nothing.

Beşir was gone.

Chapter 4

EVENTIDE'S GRAND HALL was bedecked for a wedding. A thousand had come to witness the marriage of King Kiral, the King of Kings, to Queen Maryam of Qaimir. Waterfalls of flowers clung to the pillars, lacing the air with scents of rose and lilac and blooming desert sage. High above, the palace bells tolled, while the long purple carpet leading from the entrance to the foot of the dais divided the hall perfectly in two. To either side of the carpet were padded benches, now nearly full with lords and ladies and their children, their chatter filling the lulls between the bright peals of the palace bells.

As the last were led to their benches, King Ihsan sat himself in the gallery with the other Kings. It was a senselessly grand affair, a puppet show meant to appease the highborn in Sharakhai. *Things can't be so bad,* the ostentatiousness said, *if the Kings would take time for a wedding such as this!*

Despite the expense, Ihsan couldn't deny that the sleight of hand was necessary—the highborn *did* need appeasing—but it galled him that Queen Meryam had somehow inveigled her way into Kiral's life, and that Kiral was too blind to see he was being played. Appeasement or not, they hardly needed another mouth sitting at the high table, asking to be fed.

"Perhaps you should be grateful," Nayyan had whispered to him last night in bed.

Ihsan had gaped at her. "Grateful? To that cadaver? That ghul in queen's raiment?"

"She isn't so bad."

"No? Have you not heard the rumors, that it was no ehrekh that consumed her father, but Meryam herself? They say she dined on his heart over an open fire before returning to Sharakhai to cry her story to anyone who would listen."

Nayyan had made a face. "You believe that?"

He'd shrugged. "I wouldn't put it past her."

"I don't know if you've heard, my good King, but there are two fleets sailing for our city. Sharakhai is in dire need of allies, and Meryam has offered us much."

He'd looked at her warily, playfully. "She's got to you too, hasn't she?"

Nayyan slapped his shoulder. "Let Meryam play at being King. It's a long way to the end of this war. If she makes it to the other side, she'll prove no more difficult to be rid of than the other Kings."

"No more difficult . . ." Ihsan pulled her against him and spoke to the ceiling. "Just you wait and see. Nothing good will come of this union, and Meryam will be difficult as ringworm to get rid of."

Of those gathered in Eventide's hall, the royalty of Tauriyat and Golden-hill and Blackfire Gate were the most numerous. Several hundred haled from Qaimir. And with Kundhun receiving more and more favor from Sharakhai, their numbers had swelled; their imposing figures and colorful clothing mixed with the more staid garb of Qaimir.

King Beşir, sitting to Ihsan's left, adjusted his seat and said, "Bloody gods, the desert will crumble before this comes to an end."

Beşir had said it more to himself than anyone else, but Ihsan leaned in and spoke to the dour King anyway. "Best to watch your tongue these days."

Beşir turned his long face toward Ihsan, but not before glancing at the other four Kings, who sat to Ihsan's right. "This is *my* bloody city. If anyone needs to watch their tongues"—he waved angrily to the crowd, especially toward the back, where most of the lesser guests from Qaimir and Kundhun were sitting—"it's *them*."

Ihsan smiled. "It was but a jest, my good King."

Beşir stared at King Azad, who was watching their exchange with mild amusement. "Has no one told you?" Beşir turned his sober look on Ihsan, then weighed him as carefully as he might the gold in the city's coffers. "The time for foolery has passed."

"What unfortunate news," Ihsan said back. "You'll be sure to let me know when smiles no longer lead to the gallows."

King Azad, who was Nayyan in the guise of her father, snickered. She liked Beşir as much as Ihsan did, which was to say not at all. Beşir, meanwhile, scoffed dismissively, then turned his attention back to the crowd, pretending Ihsan didn't exist. Beşir had been in a foul mood since losing Çedamihn out in the desert two days before. It wasn't merely that he'd failed, but that he'd been forced go in the first place. He'd long since lost himself in pursuits of his own design and was becoming increasingly vexed that the weight of a King's mantle had been laid across his shoulders once more.

Ihsan realized King Husamettín was staring at him. Ruggedly handsome and dressed impeccably, he towered over Sukru and Cahil at the end of the gallery seats. As the pealing of the bells came to a sudden end, Ihsan nodded to him. Husamettín nodded back.

The event was finally on them. King Kiral and Queen Meryam stepped through an archway built into one side of the hall. Kiral was bedecked in raiment of gold and rust with accents of ivory. Queen Meryam wore a dress that poured like a river of rubies down her undernourished frame. She wore no veil, as many in Qaimir might, but walked with her face unmasked, as was the custom in the desert.

They heard words from Yerinde's high priest, a small rabbit of a man who, it was said, had the ear of the goddess herself. The King and queen spoke vows to their right hands which, instead of sand, gripped handfuls of shells delivered from the Austral Sea. As they released their grips, the shells pattered against the rich purple carpet with a sound like distant drums. A child near the front dove and grabbed some before she was snatched up and pressed back into her seat by her red-faced mother. The crowd laughed.

The mixing of customs continued with songs from both countries, desert cymbals that Kiral and Meryam crashed together, the tying of their wrists to one another, not with a cord of leather but with an old, beaten necklace, a thing Meryam had had since she was a child, apparently. When it was done, the couple and their guests adjourned to a nearby hall.

Many of the guests, ready to enjoy the relatively cool day, took drinks on the adjoining patio which overlooked the eastern desert and King's Harbor. It was a strange choice, Ihsan thought. Kiral curated his imagery carefully—projecting strength, always—and yet the vast majority of the royal navy had sailed north to meet the threat of the Mirean fleet, leaving King's Harbor practically empty. The city looked defenseless.

No one seemed to mind, though. They ate. They drank. Ihsan spoke to several Qaimiri nobleman, needling them for information about Meryam. They refused to share anything of import, and Ihsan let it go. He'd gained much in recent months, particularly with King Zeheb, the King of Whispers—now called the Burbling King, the Mad Bull of Sharakhai, or even the Lord of Muttered Ravings—and he wouldn't see it all undone because he'd allowed his impatience to get the better of him by using his powers where others, Meryam in particular, might sense it.

Ihsan returned to the hall to find the high priest throwing rose petals into the air, showering Meryam and Kiral. As he watched, a shiver ran through the crowd. Smiles and laughs turned to deep frowns and worry. It swept through the rest of the room like a wave. Ihsan felt it too, a shift in his gut not unlike the feeling one gets when a loved one is in immediate danger. The guests were looking at one another as if they might have an explanation for their strange and sudden discomfort. Somewhere, a child cried, and a susurrus of conversation rose.

When a shout of surprise came from the opposite end of the hall, all eyes turned. Spilling forth from an archway leading to a verdant garden was a host of dark, fluttering shapes, a cloud of moths with black, iridescent wings that reminded Ihsan of a moonless, star-filled sky.

The moths billowed outward, causing fright as they neared the crowd of Sharakhani lords and ladies. People shied from them. Some ran. Darkening the portico beyond the arch was a tall figure, taller than any man or woman inside the building, including the towering Kundhuni, including Kings Kiral and Husamettín. It was the goddess, Yerinde, beautiful and fearsome in the same breath. She was naked save for the black moths, which covered her thighs, her sex, her stomach, her breasts. With each step the goddess took, some of the moths lifted, exposing her, but Yerinde seemed not to care. She strode across the room, not toward Kiral and Meryam, as might be expected, but toward the tables set aside for Ihsan and the other Kings.

Unlike the last times Ihsan had seen her, Yerinde's black hair was unbound. It fell across her shoulders and down her back and chest in lazy curls, making her look like a wild woman, a goddess newly fashioned by the hand of the elder gods.

Husamettín led the way across the gold-veined floor. Ihsan, and Beşir followed, with Sukru, Cahil, and Azad coming last. Kiral joined them as they neared the goddess. Meryam wisely stayed back, but she watched this exchange with dark, glittering eyes. *Always hungry for more, Queen Meryam of Qaimir.*

As one, the Kings genuflected. The crowd of onlookers did the same. A command slipped into Ihsan's mind like sunlight through gauze:

Rise, Yerinde said.

The Kings rose, while all others, including Meryam, remained on bended knee. Yerinde turned her gaze to Kiral. She stared at him as if he'd offended her and was trying to determine what, after the proper weighing of his offense, should be done with him. Kiral stared back much as he always did, with a supreme confidence that would rankle even the most gracious man or woman.

Going against that very nature, Kiral opened his mouth to speak, then closed it again. The pockmarked landscape of his cheeks rolled as the muscles of his jaw worked. He swallowed once. Twice. His mouth opened again, but no words came out.

Ihsan couldn't decide whether it was Kiral's own uncertainty that stayed him or some command from Yerinde. Whatever the case, Yerinde turned away from Kiral—away from the King of Kings!—and laid her eyes upon Husamettín instead. Ihsan could not imagine a greater insult for the man who thought himself above all others, yet here he was, overlooked by a creature infinitely more powerful than he, as if she likened him to the black moths fluttering about her frame.

Weeks have passed since we spoke below this mountain, Yerinde said to Husamettín. Her lips were pressed tightly, unmoving as she spoke. *Words were exchanged. Vows were made.*

"The goddess speaks the truth," Husamettín replied in a loud, clear voice. *Name thy promise.*

For the first time, the emotionless edifice of Husamettín's face cracked. He glanced back at the lords and ladies huddling like a herd of oryx. Finally he said, "To bring you the head of Nalamae, the one who has wronged us."

Just so, replied Yerinde. Around her, the moths turned darker, their wings becoming black as an endless void, like the eyes of the lord of all things. For a moment they seemed to draw all color from the room. *But now I wonder, where is my prize? What have the Kings of Sharakhai, so graced these many years, so showered with favor, done to deserve it?*

Husamettín bowed his head, though while doing so shifted his right hand to the hilt of his god-given weapon, Night's Kiss. It was an unconscious act, surely, but one that courted ruin.

"We have searched the desert far and wide," he said. "We have sent ships to gather word. We have worked with our soothsayers. Our seer, King Yusam, is dead, but we have scoured his journals for any signs that might lead to her. We have searched for the home of the desert witch, Saliah, whom we believe was her last incarnation before she realized her true heritage. We have yet to find it, but in the meanwhile we've searched for those who visited her there, and questioned some, but none knew her whereabouts, or how we might lure her from hiding. We have searched a thousand paths and more, but none have so far delivered news of her whereabouts."

At this, Yerinde stared down, her face a mask of dispassion. As Husamettín spoke, the moths had flown up and about, leaving her utterly naked. They spread outward, fluttering, flying, flitting to and fro, expanding like a flower in bloom until they'd surrounded the Kings and Yerinde, cutting them off from the rest of the crowd, cutting them off from Meryam as well.

The frightened sounds of the crowd abated as if they'd all been turned to statues. Kiral seemed confused. He blinked as if he'd suddenly found himself in an entirely new place.

Yerinde pulled herself to her full height. Her black hair lifted, flowing on an unseen wind. *Tribute was demanded of the Kings of Sharakhai. You will set Nalamae's head before me.*

Husamettín bowed low and spoke in a firm yet reasonable tone. "We will, though surely the goddess will admit that Nalamae is gifted at remaining hidden."

Ihsan had known none of this—not of Yerinde's prior visit, nor her strange request, nor the efforts of the other Kings to fulfill it. Based on the reactions of several other Kings, however, he saw that they'd been privy to it and had decided, for whatever reason, not to share it with him. Husamettín had known, of course. So had Cahil and Sukru. Perhaps Kiral as well, though the man was acting so strangely it was difficult to say for certain.

This was a strange thing to be faced with. The gods had asked for so very little over the years, after all. It was common knowledge amongst the Kings that Nalamae had deigned not to join her siblings on the night of Beht Ihman. It was also common knowledge that Nalamae had been hunted and killed many times by her brothers and sisters. *Why then does Yerinde need us to perform this service? And why now?*

He had few enough answers, but one thing was certain: this was not an opportunity to be passed up. "If we might ask a small boon of the goddess," he said, "a way for us to gain her scent. Had we but that, we could easily do the rest."

Yerinde blinked languidly and turned her violet eyes to Ihsan. As in the past, his insides melted. His mouth began to water. It was a feeling akin to love, but so much more dangerous. She seemed to be weighing him. He felt it in his bones. Felt it in the pit of his stomach. Felt it in the way his cock suddenly swelled, feelings of passion and fright and simple confusion over what he *ought* to be feeling warring inside him.

She was quicker to assess him than Kiral, and seemed to come to a more favorable resolution, for as she stared at him, she smiled. At first he thought it might be for his benefit, an act, but he could see some few of the moths turning blue, an effect that looked like the flames of an arcane bonfire lifting toward a midnight sky.

What wouldst thou request of me?

"Forgive me," Ihsan said, "but it seems to me that if one wants to draw the hare from hiding, one doesn't go blundering about its warren. One *lures* it. Only then can it be shot through with an arrow."

A lure . . .

Ihsan nodded.

Yerinde's eyes flared. For a moment his feelings became markedly stronger. His cock strained against his trousers. Pleasure mixed with pain mixed with worry. He wasn't even sure Yerinde was aware of the effect she was having on him. Whatever the case, he refused to flinch from it.

A moment later, the feelings subsided. *A lure I might grant thee*, Yerinde said, *but how to measure thine earnestness. Wouldst thou slay the goddess were she standing before thee now?*

Ihsan wasn't sure what to say—this was a strange request, one that could shake the foundations of the desert. Before he could say anything, though, Beşir raised his low, sonorous voice.

"Of course we would."

Yerinde turned to him, stared into his piercing eyes. *Wouldst thou?*

The few blue moths shifted black, and Beşir cowered but then seemed embarrassed to have done so. The look on his face hardened.

"Of course," he said again, practically spitting the words.

Kill one thou lovest?

"I have little love for the goddess."

It wouldst be different, I promise, were she standing before thee now. She was the last, the one closest to thy mortal hearts. The love long buried within thee, Beşir Adem'ava al Okan, wouldst spring forth. Of this thou must have no doubt.

"My aim would not flinch, goddess. Have no fear of that."

And yet I do!

The cloud of moths churned around them, their movements wild, almost angry. The goddess waved toward the crowd standing beyond the wall of black moths. An archway was made, and a lone moth flew out. Nearly everyone cowered from it, but there was one, a young woman who'd seen no more than twenty summers, who stood transfixed. Beşir's daughter, Kara, one of the very few children he'd sired in recent generations. He doted on her, in his own, overly protective way, preparing her, most said, for the role of vizira when she grew older. The moth's wings changed as it flew toward her; they were now a perfect match to Yerinde's violet eyes. When it reached her, the moth landed lightly upon her forehead. Its wings flapped lazily, and the woman's eyes blinked in time, as if the two were now one.

Kara strode forward, a woman walking to her grave, and the moths swept in behind her. Her movements were slow and languorous, but it was plain to see she was terrified. Her eyes pleaded with Kiral, with Husamettín, but most of all with Beşir, begging them to free her from this spell.

Yerinde's voice boomed, shaking the Kings. *If Nalamae stood before thee, if love filled thy heart, thou wouldst honor thy vow and end her life?*

At this, something happened that Ihsan could not ever recall seeing before, not at any time in his more than four centuries walking the earth. Beşir, one the most self-absorbed men Ihsan had ever known, *blanched.* Yerinde had found one of very few things—not merely the death of his own daughter, but the lifting of his own hand to do it—that would give the man pause.

Beşir licked his full, bloodless lips. "Of course I would, but she is not the goddess."

Yerinde stared down at him with a mixture of amusement and no small amount of self-awareness. The shift of her violet eyes toward Beşir's daughter spoke volumes. *No longer do we speak of the river goddess.*

Of course not, Ihsan thought. *This is now about loyalty. It is about the Kings and our debt to the desert gods.* It was a message from Yerinde to each of them—should they fail, those they loved most would be forfeit.

Beşir's eyes moved to Kara. Then to Kiral, who was taking it all in as if he'd had an epiphany. Whatever truth he'd seen had apparently shaken him to his core. Beşir's look pleaded with Husamettín, who had stepped into the void of leadership left by Kiral's inaction. Husamettín, however, had always been a calculating man, one who faced life's tough realities unflinchingly. His stern look, his very stance, stiff-backed and aloof, told Beşir all he needed to know.

Beşir curled in on himself. For a moment he looked more like Sukru than the touchy, reticent man Ihsan had known for centuries. But then, pulling his knife, he took two long strides, grabbed his daughter's hair, and used the blade to open her throat. Blood spilled. Over Beşir especially, but also across the shoes and khalats of all the nearby Kings—all, miraculously, save Ihsan.

They stared. At the blood as it spread. At Kara as she fell. At Yerinde as she smiled, transfixed by the expanding pool of red and the rapidly dulling eyes of Beşir's daughter. When the river of crimson touched her bare feet, a shiver ran up her towering frame and the black moths went wild. They turned red, a cavalcade of crimson storming around them all. With it came a frisson of fear and pain and, strangest of all, pleasure; an insistent thing that felt real and true and, for that very reason, decidedly *wrong* in this context. Beyond the sphere of moths, things were markedly different. The guests of this once-joyous occasion had their hands to their ears. Pain distorted their faces as they screamed, the sounds of their agony dulled by the magic of the moths.

Yerinde fixed her gaze on Ihsan. *Thy request was for a way to lure the goddess.*

Ihsan replied as easily as he could manage. "It was."

And so I grant it.

She put out her hand. Upon her outstretched finger landed small blue bird: a sickletail, with long, curving feathers that trailed behind it like a wedding train. As Yerinde smoothed her fingers over its back, it changed shape. Its wings widened and lengthened. Its body grew. Its beak curved like a falcon's, and its talons turned sharp and cruel. It became huge, as big as the buzzards that plagued the northern desert.

Give it some remnant of the White Wolf and it shall lead thee to her. Such is Nalamae's care for her child that, if threatened, she will come.

"We have no such thing to give it," Ihsan said.

Do you not?

"None that I would rely upon."

Is there no one in thy possession who might find such a thing? The absent smile Yerinde gave as she ran the backs of her fingers over the blue bird's wings left a hollow in Ihsan's heart. Without another word being spoken, the bird hopped down and began to lap obscenely at the blood near Kara's feet. The goddess, meanwhile, turned and left, her moths following her like a pack of well-trained hounds.

Chapter 5

RAMAHD AMANSIR LIES on ground as hard as glass. The sun rests along the horizon, half swallowed and glowing like a forge fire. Striding toward him is a woman, a huntress wearing a bright red dress that flares wildly in the evening wind. It is Meryam, his queen. Her eyes are bright with anger. Her mouth is set in a line, grim as an unsheathed sword. And her face . . . By the grace of the one true god, she has been restored, fully fleshed, as if the years of abusing her body in favor of the red ways have all been swept away. She is the Meryam of old, and she is beautiful beyond words.

In her right hand she bears an iron, the sort cattlemen use in Qaimir to mark their steers. The sign upon it, however, is nothing like a brand. It is a sigil, a thing meant to cast a spell on him, one that will remain with him forever should she catch him and sear it into his skin. Ramahd is no blood mage, but he recognizes the symbols that combine on the brand's glowing end. One is *forget*. Laid over it is the sign for *eternity*. Meryam isn't merely trying to kill him; she hopes to erase him from the world for what she views as his betrayals: the disobeying of her orders, standing against her as she fought beside the Kings of Sharakhai, attempting to expose to the world the fact that she murdered her own father.

A nest of black tendrils snake from her opposite hand. They twist, ever-reaching, hypnotic movements bending not only to Meryam's will but to their own infernal workings. Ramahd uses his power and cuts one as it nears. In that severing, some small amount of the magic Meryam is using to feed the spell is severed as well. The black tendril dries and crumbles in the wind, dissipating like ash.

He cuts a second and a third but, Mighty Alu, there are so many. Meryam has become frighteningly powerful, as has her thirst for blood. His blood. Night after night she comes for him, granting few reprieves. Her gaze is baleful, her eyes golden and misshapen like a bull's, not unlike those of Guhldrathen, the ancient ehrekh she once bargained with. And her hair! *Oh Meryam, what have you done?* Sprouting from among the cleverly woven braids are two small horns, rounded nubs no larger than a kid's.

"I loved you, you know," Meryam tells him. Her face, a study in anger and disgust and rank dissatisfaction, belies those words.

"How could you have done it, Meryam?" Ramahd asks as he cuts another dark tendril, this one just inches from his neck. "How could you have killed your own father?"

She steps forward, wind whipping her hair, her bright red dress billowing, curling like a demon manifesting in the night. "What he did to Yasmine's memory was unforgivable."

"What do you mean?"

"You're trying to distract me, Ramahd. My father will have his reckoning when I see him again in the farther fields."

"And when you're there, will you look upon him with anything but shame?"

Blood streaks from her eyes to paint her rounded cheeks. "I'm not the one who should be ashamed. He abandoned our cause. He abandoned the memory of his own daughter. He was prepared to let her killer walk when the hill became too difficult for him to climb. He was ready to abandon her memory for *gold!*"

"So you killed him for it?"

She pauses as if she's said too much. "You'll see. Things are different there. He'll admit that he was wrong, and if I deliver to Qaimir all that I've promised, he will take me in his arms and tell me how proud he is of his daughter."

"That's what you think?" A tendril wraps his ankle and squeezes, burns where it touches his skin. Worse, it stalls his retreat. "That you can do whatever you wish, and it will all be forgiven in the next life if you deliver glory to our kingdom?"

When another tendril slips around his opposite ankle, it stops him completely. Meryam smiles and drops onto his chest, then raises the brand high in both hands. "Do you doubt it?"

"What you've done, what you're doing"—he struggles to break free, but more black ropes are circling his wrists—"it carries no glory at all, Meryam."

She laughs while her golden eyes flash. Scalding blood pours from them to patter against his neck. "Such a simple fool. Haven't you learned by now, Ramahd?" Down comes the brand, searing deep into his skin. "Conquest carries all the glory in the world."

Ramahd woke to someone shaking him hard enough to rattle the cot he slept on.

"Wake up, Ramahd!" It was Vrago, a man who had been handsome once but now looked terrible. His eyes were heavy and listless. His face was haggard. "She's back. You have to cut her off!"

Ramahd blinked, taking in the crumbling, mudbrick room where he, Tiron, and Vrago were lying. He sat up, eyes wide, heart pounding. The image of Meryam's inhuman eyes haunted him. He touched his chest, his skin itching where the brand had struck.

Vrago shook Ramahd harder. "Ramahd, cut Meryam off!"

Ramahd blinked, remembering the endless nights spent in the Shallows, the slums of Sharakhai's west end. The hovels in which he and his men had been hiding blurred before his eyes, one like the next and the next, but at last his memories returned, along with his vow to stop Meryam's attempts at finding him, which were coming almost every night.

He felt for her presence and found it, faint though it was. She was growing ever more subtle in her search. She knew he'd returned to Sharakhai— the squadron of Silver Spears she'd sent to the buildings where they'd first hidden was proof enough of that—but she had yet to locate him precisely.

While awake, Ramahd had become adept at sensing her. Whenever he did, he cut her off, which had forced Meryam to change strategies. She began searching for him in the small hours of the morning. Twice they'd nearly been caught. But the very fact that she was using his own blood to track him—she still had several vials of blood she'd collected before she ordered Basilio to have him taken to the desert and killed—had the effect of rousing him from deep sleep, at least enough so that one of his men, either Cicio, Vrago, or Tiron, could notice and wake him.

Their war escalated. Ramahd adjusted his sleep patterns to foil her new approach. Meryam responded by searching for him at random intervals of day or night. Since then, the only way he'd thought to counter her was to sleep less. It couldn't last, though. The weariness was weighing on him, dragging him down. One day soon Meryam would catch him too deep in slumber, and then she'd have them all.

Meryam's spell felt like a starving bone crusher approaching in the dark of the desert night. Ramahd didn't cut it off completely, but instead made it seem as though her sense of him was fading, as if he were moving farther and farther away. Meryam, after all, was no longer the only danger. With the might of Tauriyat at her beck and call, she often had the Kings' forces ready as she closed in, and she would send them rushing forward when she felt Ramahd beginning to cut the fabric of her spells.

But then he remembered. By the breath of the one true god, his dream. The tendrils. The brand. She'd *already* found him.

Shouts came from the stairwell just outside their room. Someone cried out in pain, then a ship's bell began to ring. The bell was picked up somewhere on the floors above, then more came in from neighboring buildings. It was a signal, and the pattern—two short, two long—was an indicator that it wasn't merely the Silver Spears who'd arrived, but Blade Maidens.

Ramahd tried to keep his heart in check. He'd never had to face a Blade Maiden one on one. Alu willing, he wouldn't have to tonight.

Vrago took Ramahd by the nape of the neck. He smiled, and for a moment, the young, handsome man that had come to Sharakhai with Ramahd returned. "You're awake?"

"I'm awake."

He slapped Ramahd's neck lightly several times. "Good," he said, then broke away. "I'm going to scout the way ahead. Tiron stays with you. He knows the path." He flashed one last smile and was gone.

Ramahd was still blinking away sleep as he gathered his things, including a heavy sack that contained the head of King Kiral—the *real* King Kiral, the one Meryam had sent to his death at the hands of the ehrekh, Guhldrathen. Ramahd had been hoping since his return to Sharakhai to use it, to put his plan into action, but it wasn't time yet. The allies he needed were still weeks away from the city.

When Ramahd made to grab his bag of clothes, Tiron forestalled him. "Too dangerous." He motioned to the sack. "Bad enough we're still lugging that thing around."

Now wasn't the time to discuss the head, so Ramahd simply nodded and Tiron led him from their tiny room. Like thieves they slipped along the narrow corridors of the tenement. When they reached a darkened stairwell, he took them up to the fifth story landing, where Cicio was waiting. Cicio, who cut a compact shape, pointed to the open window nearby, then slipped through it with liquid ease onto the roof of another tenement building. Tiron followed moments before the sound of splintering wood came from behind them.

As pots and pans began clanging all through the building, Ramahd, Tiron, and Cicio rushed across the roof. By the light of the twin moons, Tulathan a narrow silver scythe, golden Rhia a near-perfect disc, Ramahd crouched at the roof's edge and spotted several men rushing away from the building. Some were met by a tall black shape.

A Blade Maiden, Ramahd knew. He immediately began looking for more, as they often worked in groups of five known as hands. He didn't see any, but sweet Alu, he swore the one below was looking directly where he was peering over the edge of the roof.

A sharp, piercing whistle rose above the sounds of clanging.

It was echoed moments later by another, then another, in buildings on either side of the alley. They'd spotted him and were trading information so that they could close in.

"Bloody gods," Cicio said under his breath as the alarm continued to spread.

They sprinted across the rooftop. Tiron, in the lead, leapt across the gap between this roof and the next and landed with a roll. Cicio followed. Ra-mahd came next, but as he flew through the air he felt something snap around his ankle with a sound like a thunderclap. He was pulled up short just as the bright pain of the whip strike was registering. He twisted awk-wardly, the easy leap becoming a fight to simply reach the other building.

His body fell across the roof's mudbrick lip, and the sack slipped from his grasp and onto the roof. Glancing behind, in the direction the whip was pulling him, he saw a black shape at the top of a set of stairs attached to the building he'd just leapt from. Like one of Meryam's tendrils, a dark line ran from the Blade Maiden's hands to Ramahd's ankle. He adjusted his grip on the roof as the Maiden pulled in the slack. Fearing a fall at any moment, he drew his kenshar and in one wild motion swiped it across the outside of his ankle.

The knife's keen edge cut through the braided end of the whip, and he was freed. He lost sight of the Maiden as Cicio began hauling him over the edge of the roof.

The whip cracked again and Cicio screamed. "Bitch!" he cried. "Son of bitch!" Inexplicably switching to Sharakhan.

The whip struck again, this time against Ramahd's left thigh. It felt like a bloody stab of steel. He grunted hard against the pain while scrabbling over the edge. He'd just rolled over the lip when a resounding clap came behind him, loud as breaking lumber, the whip narrowly missing.

Then he was up and running, and Tiron was shoving the sack back into his hands. "*You* carry the blasted thing."

Ramahd bore its awkward weight as they made for the far side of the roof. Behind them came a thud and a scraping sound, as of someone rolling along the gravel-strewn roof. A Blade Maiden, ebon blade drawn, was sprint-ing toward them, swift as a gods-damned cheetah.

Ahead, Cicio leapt from the edge of the building into darkness. Tiron followed. Ramahd had no choice but to leapt blindly. Mimicking Tiron's speed and direction, he flew across a narrow alley and through a massive hole, one story down, in the crumbling building that faced it. He slipped on the rubble scattered across the floor. Knowing the Maiden would be just behind him, he didn't bother trying to get up. He rolled quickly away, mak-ing room for the others to fight.

He could just make out Tiron and Cicio nearby, plus a shadowy form in the open doorway. The crunch of the Maiden's landing was followed by the twang of a crossbow. The shape was Vrago, and he'd just released a bolt at the Blade Maiden, who was crouched only a few paces away. But the Maiden . . . Breath of the desert, the way she moved. Vrago had a marksman's aim, but the Maiden had anticipated it and dodged.

As the crossbow bolt crunched into the mudbrick wall of the opposite building, Tiron rushed the Maiden. Her shamshir was up and ready. Tiron's bright steel flashed, met by her ebon blade. The Maiden spun and sent Tiron reeling with a kick to the gut. She dropped, continuing her spin, and sent Cicio tumbling to the floor. Tossing the sack aside, Ramahd drew his own sword. The Maiden met two of his blows with bone-rattling blocks.

Then another twang sounded. It was the second of the dual crossbow's bolts being released.

The bolt punched into the Maiden's chest, just over her heart, sending her staggering back. One hand gripping the bolt, she blocked several more of Ramahd's blows, each block weaker than the last, but then she snapped a sharp, powerful kick into Ramahd's chest with a sharp *kiai*. He was sent reeling, but it was a desperate move and the Maiden stumbled as well.

By then Vrago had charged, his crossbow clattering to the floor as he drew his fighting knife.

"Leave her!" Ramahd called, knowing it was only a matter of time before she fell.

But Vrago didn't listen. He managed a vicious swipe across her forearm. Another across her thigh while ducking the swing of her sword.

"Retreat!" Ramahd shouted.

But the order came too late. With another *kiai*, she delivered a crosscut to his ribs, and when Vrago punched her across the jaw and curled toward the wound with a groan, she recovered and brought her ebon blade up and across his throat.

Vrago stumbled, both hands clasping his neck. It was a wound he couldn't recover from, though. Ramahd could already hear the stream of blood spattering against the floor.

The Maiden stumbled backward. Her heel caught on the rough opening, and she tipped through it silently. A moment later, there came the sound of her battle dress's skirt fluttering in the warm desert air. The sound faded until a meaty thump rose up from the courtyard below.

Cicio knelt by Vrago's side. Ramahd joined him. Vrago stared into their eyes, one then the other, then up to Tiron where he stood looming in the darkness. He looked scared and confused, a little boy waiting for death to take him. But then he blinked and steeled himself and looked straight into Ramahd's eyes. "Go," he managed to say in a toneless rasp.

Ramahd, blinking tears away, nodded and stood, then pulled Cicio to a stand as well. The sounds of pursuit—whistles among the other Blade Maidens—were coming closer. After retrieving the sack, Ramahd, Cicio, and Tiron fled, taking the winding path they'd scouted earlier in the day.

The darkness made it a harrowing escape, but of the Maidens, Mighty Alu be blessed, they saw no further signs.

Their next safe house was a root cellar that smelled of garlic and turnips and piss. Cicio, wordless after the loss of Vrago, left to scout the area and begin the work of planning their escape routes. The old woman they'd contacted days earlier, and paid a deposit to set the room up if need be, watched them warily, but took the extra coin they laid in her palm and left them in peace.

Tiron, sitting on the cot across from Ramahd, gave the door a stony look and waited for her footsteps to recede. "That one will cut us up and put us in her soup, we're not careful," he said in Qaimiran.

"We'd make shit soup, you and I." They'd both lost weight after the ceaseless running.

Tiron, stony in the best of times, turned dour. He hated it when he thought he wasn't being taken seriously.

"We won't stay long," Ramahd said.

It was a constant problem. He didn't like their temporary landlord any better than Tiron did, but they'd been forced to scramble for contacts they thought safe from Meryam. Nearly all of those Ramahd had cultivated over the years were known to Meryam and her advisor, Basilio, and those who weren't might be found at any time.

"We should leave when the city wakes," Tiron ventured.

Ramahd nodded. Much as he'd like the day to rest, it would be wiser to find a host less likely to try to make a few sylval by selling their whereabouts to the Silver Spears.

Tiron's gaze drifted down to the sack beneath Ramahd's cot. "We can't go on like this, my lord."

"I know," Ramahd said. "Mateo will arrive soon."

Before Ramahd and the others had sailed back to Sharakhai, they'd stopped in the caravanserai of Mazandir. Their immediate purpose was to trade the *Blue Heron* for a smaller, cheaper ship. It gave them the money they needed to operate in Sharakhai but also ensured their ship wouldn't be recognized. Ramahd had also arranged for the desert tribe he'd traded with to intercept the inbound Qaimiri fleet with a message for its admiral, Duke Hektor, King Aldouan's brother and next in line to the throne. When a woman from the tribe had arrived in Sharakhai a week ago, she'd confirmed that the message had been delivered and that Hektor had agree to send Vice Admiral Mateo Abrantes ahead of the fleet to meet him.

"My lord, we don't know what Mateo will say, and even if he arrived today it wouldn't change the fact that Meryam has your blood, and that sooner or later she will have you. We've been here for three weeks searching for the Enclave. You know how they operate. If they wanted us to find them, we would have by now."

"I'm not certain of that. War has arrived. They'll be busy readying themselves."

"And if we don't find them soon, Vrago's fate will be ours."

The Enclave were a group of blood magi who lived in the cracks of society in Sharakhai. Ramahd needed them. It was a gamble, what he was doing. The Enclave might very well side with Meryam in this. But he knew things they didn't. Meryam had dominated Hamzakiir, a fellow blood mage, a thing strictly forbidden by the Enclave, even among magi who weren't part of the Enclave. Ramahd was sure if he revealed the truth about Meryam and Hamzakiir, who she'd disguised as King Kiral, they would aid him, keep Meryam off his trail until Ramahd could speak to Duke Hektor face to face.

But the Enclave were highly secretive, so much so that Ramahd had no idea how to reach them. Very few did. Meryam knew, of course, but there'd be no getting the information out of her.

Her recent ascension to queen of Sharakhai had left him an opening, however. After Ramahd's departure, she would have needed a new go-between to the Enclave. He was certain that person was Basilio. Ramahd had paid a goodly sum to a washerwoman to learn that Basilio had been missing from the embassy house since shortly after Meryam left for the Battle of Blackspear. Ramahd then paid the woman even more to try to find him. That very night, not coincidentally, Meryam made her first appearance. She'd nearly caught him at the small perfumery where they were to meet the washerwoman—a dozen Qaimiri soldiers had tried to take them and they made a narrow escape. Meryam was perhaps unprepared for Ramahd to have become so adept at nullifying her spells.

The washerwoman had been killed, an unfortunate tragedy that also served to cut off one avenue of gaining information. They continued the search for Basilio, offering handsome sums for information that would lead them to either Basilio or the Enclave. But few accepted their offer, worried about retaliation from the House of Kings, and those who did accept offered leads worth less than rubbish.

"Let's *go*," Tiron pleaded. "Let's go to the embassy house and find your blood. You said yourself she'd likely not bring it to Eventide."

Ramahd had been struggling with this very thing since their arrival. Destroy the vials of his blood Meryam still had and she'd lose her power over him. But there was no guarantee they'd find any in the embassy house, nor that they'd find anything that would point them toward Basilio. It would be a mission conducted at great risk to his men, and he'd already put them through much. Bad enough that security around the embassy house would be fortified. The House of Kings, which sheltered all the major embassy houses within its walls, was closely watched at all hours.

"A day or two more, Tiron. That's all I'm asking."

Tiron was a hard man, one who didn't back down easily, but after a moment's consideration he nodded grimly and fell onto his cot.

Despite Vrago's death, or perhaps because of it, relief at escaping the Blade Maidens was finally hitting home. Even as it did, though, he remembered Vrago's handsome smile and felt terrible. "The saving of one's country," Ramahd mused. "They said it would be easier."

"They . . ." Tiron smiled a miserable smile. "Those fuckers are always lying."

Ramahd laughed. It felt good to laugh. "It's enough to drive a man to drink."

"Or have a dance with the dark mistress," Tiron replied.

The dark mistress was slang for black lotus, a drug Tiron had been heavily addicted to for a time. Ramahd had flirted with it as well. As he considered Tiron's somber words, visions of an old estate along the banks of the Haddah swam before him. Then another, of an ancient woman in a black dress, a bottle of fine Qaimiri brandy on the table between them as she and Ramahd spoke of Tiron. A jolt ran through Ramahd's body. He sat bolt upright and swung his legs over the side of the cot.

"What is it?" Tiron asked.

"There may be another way," Ramahd said, "only . . ." Breath of the desert . . . Tiron was ever strong, ever stout, always willing to do what it took, but Ramahd wasn't sure he could bring himself to ask this of him.

Tiron's face had turned hard again. "You need but say it, my lord."

"There's another way we might find Basilio. But it would require just that, Tiron, a dance with the dark mistress." Tiron knew immediately what he was talking about—Ramahd could see it in his eyes—but he stated it baldly anyway. He needed Tiron to know what he was getting into. "I need you to return to one the Widow's drug dens, Tiron. I need you to lay a story at the feet of those who work there, a story strong enough that it will be brought back to the Widow herself."

Tiron considered, but not for long. "Very well."

Ramahd searched his eyes. *Fresh winds of the sea, how I wish I could see into the hearts of men.* "Tell me you can handle it, Tiron."

"I can handle it."

"Then why do you seem so bloody eager?"

He took in the earthen walls of the cellar. "A chance to get away from this, even for a night?" He laughed. "I'll take it, my lord. I'll take it gladly."

Tiron was filled with bluster. Ramahd didn't think he was lying, but he'd known Tiron since they were children. There was little that scared him, but just then, as his gaze slid beyond the walls of the dank cellar, he looked a child lost on a storm-wracked sea.

If they left him there too long, Ramahd was certain the dark mistress would have him, but they needed this. They needed to find Basilio. "It would only be for a night," Ramahd said. "Two or three at most."

"I know," Tiron said. "I'll do it."

Alu help me, Ramahd thought. But then he said the words. "Very well."

Chapter 6

EMRE STOOD AT THE CREST of a dune with Aríz, the young shaikh of Tribe Kadri. Aríz had inherited the mantle from his father, Mihir, after he'd been killed by King Onur in the desert. He was wise enough for his age in the arts of diplomacy, but he was in sore need of training in the art of war, which was why Emre had an unstrung bow slung across his shoulders. Aríz had a bow as well, but his was strung and ready, an arrow already nocked. Not far away, along the top of another dune, Frail Lemi, Emre's towering, muscle-bound friend, was practicing spearcraft in his typically impressive form, slashing, advancing, blocking, riposting. The sound of his movements, his percussive grunts, even the whirring of his greatspear, filled the hot, parched air.

"Dayan has seen thirty-nine summers," Aríz was telling Emre, "and by all accounts has ruled Tribe Halarijan with an even hand."

"It's been tumultuous, though, no?" Emre said easily. "I heard one of his cousins tried to take his seat." Without warning, Emre swept his bow like a staff at Aríz's shins.

Aríz leapt over the swing, rolled to a stand, and fired the arrow at the woolen target set into the slope of the opposite dune. The arrow fell short in a burst of amber sand.

"No!" came Frail Lemi's bellowing shout.

Lemi was practicing with Umber, King Onur's massive black spear they'd retrieved after the great battle between the tribes and the Kings. No one but Lemi could wield the heavy weapon easily, so they'd given it to him.

One night over a campfire, Hamid—a childhood friend of Çeda and Emre—had asked Frail Lemi, "Why call it Umber?"

Lemi had shrugged. "That was his sign, wasn't it? Silver on umber."

"Yes, but the spear was the silver part. Why not call it Silver? Or Black? He wasn't called the Black Spear for nothing, you know."

"I know," Frail Lemi said with a dispassionate air, and would not be dissuaded. Umber it was, and soon everyone else was calling it that too.

Aríz glanced Frail Lemi's way, clearly annoyed, and shouted, "Aren't you bloody tired yet?"

Lemi only laughed. The sun glistened off his dark skin as he spun and brought Umber across his body in a vicious arc. He'd been at his forms for nearly an hour and seemed as full of energy as he had when he'd begun.

Aríz grit his jaw as he picked up another arrow. "Yes, Dayan has had challenges to his rule, but he's skilled at sniffing such things out." He nocked the arrow and watched for Emre's next move. "Each time it's happened he's cut the head from the snake before it managed to lay eggs."

When Emre swung his bow high, Aríz ducked beneath it, drew, and let fly. Though not far off, the arrow struck to the right of the target.

With no break in his movements, Frail Lemi shouted in a long, barely discernible growl, "Not good enough!"

Aríz threw his bow to the sand. "It's too hard! I'll never be able to fight like this."

Frail Lemi stopped his forms and leaned against his spear, laughing. "Aw, baby boy miss his target?"

Color rose along the dark skin of Aríz's cheeks as he glanced Lemi's way, and Lemi laughed even harder. Emre was about to reason with Aríz when a voice called out behind him.

"I tell you again it's improper."

It was Ali-Budrek, Aríz's vizir, walking side by side with Hamid. They were coming from the camp: a grouping of Tribe Kadri's ships that had been arrayed in a circle beside a small oasis. Among them was the *Amaranth*, the ship assigned by Macide to represent the thirteenth tribe on this diplomatic journey—as was *Calamity's Reign*, the ship owned and captained by Haddad, a fiery woman and caravan owner who was acting as an emissary of sorts to the Malasani King.

Ali-Budrek and Hamid came to a stop nearby. Hamid seemed strangely sanguine. Ali-Budrek, however, was anything but. His scowl was dark as the shadow his rotund figure cast against the sand. "If Shaikh Aríz is going to be trained"—Ali-Budrek's crossed his arms over his barrel chest in a pose that defined him more than any other—"Can you at least tell that walking grain tower to stop barking at the shaikh like a bloody jackal?"

"We're doing this for a reason," Emre said.

"And what reason is that?"

"To ready him for battle."

"No. You're filling his head with so much nonsense it will confuse him to the point that he'll *fail* when battle comes!"

"He's doing better than I did at this stage."

"He's not lying!" Frail Lemi shouted from the opposite dune. "Emre was terrible! Couldn't hit the desert surrounded by fucking sand!"

"Show him, then," Hamid cut in. He wore that smug expression of his, the one that revealed how jealous he was, how eager to see Emre knocked down a peg or two.

Hamid had been annoyed when Emre was assigned to represent the thirteenth tribe at this meeting and not him. Since then, he'd been pushing Emre in small ways, every chance he got.

"My skills aren't the ones that need sharpening," Emre replied.

"You're the one teaching him," Hamid shot back. "Don't you want to give young Aríz something to aspire to?"

"He has a point," Ali-Budrek said.

Aríz watched all this in silence.

"Show them, Emre!" Frail Lemi bellowed.

Emre knew he shouldn't give in to Hamid, but the smug look on his face was more than he could bear. He strung his bow and told Aríz to give his to Hamid. Hamid caught it with a smile and moved between Emre and the target. Emre, meanwhile, took five arrows, pinched four between the fingers of his right hand, and nocked the fifth.

Hamid gave him no time to prepare. He came at Emre, swinging the bow like a staff, first high, then low. But Emre was ready. He ducked, then leapt and released his first arrow. It struck the target as Emre rolled back to evade another swing. Two more thumped into the target when Hamid overcompensated. The fourth flew just past Hamid's hip as he charged, angry and red-faced.

Hamid was hoping to embarrass Emre, but he'd always had more bluster than true skill with sword or spear. When Hamid overcommitted, Emre poked him in the chest and sent him tumbling backward. He looked like an overturned crab, limbs flailing, as Emre let his last arrow fly with a release that approached perfection. It sunk into the center of the target, surrounded by the other four arrows.

Aríz tried and failed to hide his amusement while Emre, stifling a grin of his own, offered his hand to Hamid. Surprisingly, Hamid showed some composure for once, even as Frail Lemi's laughter became pure, almost childlike. "Hey, Hamid! You want I should carry you to bed? Ickle Hami need a nap after his spanking?"

Hamid pretended to ignore them all as he took in the spread of Emre's arrows. "Not bad."

Ali-Budrek frowned. "Even so, allowing the shaikh to train in silence could only help his concentration." He waved to Frail Lemi, who had dropped to one knee and was laughing uncontrollably. "This is humiliating."

"He stays," Aríz cut in. Emre wasn't surprised. Aríz had grown closer to Frail Lemi than anyone would have guessed. And for his part, Lemi had come to look upon Aríz like a little brother—though in truth, Aríz was more like the big brother in their relationship. Frail Lemi's mind had become simple after breaking a fall from a granary tower with his head when he was young, while Aríz was intelligent and sharp, and often seemed much wiser than his fifteen summers would imply. He might be half Lemi's age, and size, but he had twice the wisdom.

Aríz, eager to prove himself, took up his bow with the sort of vibrance Emre loved to see. "Let's go."

"It won't come in a single afternoon," Emre said.

Aríz nodded, clearly shrugging off the warning, and waited for Emre to begin. Ali-Budrek, meanwhile, eyed Emre with that stubborn badger stare of his. Thankfully he left a moment later, leaving Hamid their only spectator.

Aríz picked up from their earlier conversation. "Shaikh Dayan will come to our council with an open mind if not an open heart. He doesn't trust easily, but he recognizes the truth when he sees it, and his tribe has been as hurt as any other by the Kings."

"It isn't Dayan we need to worry about," Hamid interjected. "It's Neylana."

Neylana was the shaikh of Tribe Kenan, but Emre had no reason to think she'd be any trouble. "What do you mean?" he asked.

Hamid glanced pointedly to Aríz. "Later."

Aríz caught his look. "If there's something I should know then, for the good of the alliance, say it."

"Forgive me." Hamid bowed stiffly and waved toward Emre. "I wouldn't presume to share something Tribe Khiyanat's emissary hadn't had a chance to consider."

He would say no more, and Emre refused to play his game. He continued drilling Aríz, stopping only when Aríz had scored a hit just beside Emre's best. As Aríz went to work on his spearcraft with Frail Lemi, Emre walked with Hamid toward the ships.

"Care to tell me what that was all about?" Emre asked.

Hamid took his time, sauntering like a fat caravan owner surveying his fleet. "Early yesterday morning, I spied a skiff sailing hard from the southeast." Hamid had been assigned to a scout ship. He'd returned in the middle of the night. "It had the look of a Malasani craft."

"And?"

"I think it was the *Calamity's*."

Emre wanted to laugh. "I've never known you to beat around the bush so much, Hamid."

"I've never known you to be so thick."

"You're suggesting Haddad sent it."

Hamid's mouth fell open and his eyes went round with feigned shock. "Well, will the wonders of the desert never cease?"

Emre sneered. "Why would she have sent a skiff?"

"To speak to the bloody tribes we're about to take council with!" Hamid threw a hand out toward *Calamity's Reign*, Haddad's dhow, resting on the far edge of the circle of ships. "She's here at her king's behest. She speaks for Malasan in this camp and perhaps beyond. Or have you conveniently forgotten that?"

Emre felt awkward. He'd grown close to Haddad after the Battle of Blackspear, while Hamid, likely *because* of that, had come to distrust her more and more. "I don't know why you're so worried about Haddad," Emre said. "Both tribes said they were open to negotiations."

"That's a far cry from joining the alliance, Emre. And remember, Shaikh Neylana was one of those who began funneling money to Hamzakiir when he tried to take the Moonless Host from Macide's father, Ishaq."

There was no denying it. Neylana had been one of the most brazen about it. But she'd made amends. She'd already sent a small ship with gold and supplies to aid them, the thirteenth tribe. It was part of the reason why Macide was certain she would agree to join the alliance, the growing coalition of tribes banding with one another for mutual protection against not only the Sharakhani Kings, but the desert's invaders as well: Malasan, Mirea, and Qaimir. And then there was Neylana's letter, which had accompanied the ship and the gold. She'd given no hard promises, but it was clear she was open to discussions as long as mutual benefit could be found. Shaikh Dayan had sent a similar letter. Assuming Emre didn't make some terrible mistake, both tribes seemed ready to join the alliance. More tricky by far would be the journey to the Malasani encampment. It was there that Emre, along with Haddad's help, would broach the subject of peace between Malasan and the tribes.

"Why do we even allow her presence here?" Hamid asked. "She's a bloody foreigner."

"We have no argument with the Malasani."

Hamid looked at him, aghast. "No *argument*? Goezhen's pendulous balls, Emre, can you even hear yourself? Have you forgotten Rafa?"

"Of course I haven't!" Rafa was Emre's brother, who'd been killed by a murderous lout of a man, a Malasani, after a trick Emre, Hamid, Tariq, and Çeda had pulled on him. "But that debt has been paid. Saadet is dead."

"Yes," he said, practically spitting the words, "by *Çeda's* hand."

"Saadet is dead and we have a tribe to protect."

"How is that different from running the streets for the Moonless Host in Sharakhai?"

Emre stopped and faced him. The sun beat down on them both. "That's your problem, Hamid. You're still acting like it's just a few of us, like if we make a mistake others won't pay for it. But we're all together now. We could lose *everyone*. I don't like seeing the Malasani invade the desert any more than you do, but if we make a mistake now, the entire tribe suffers."

"Allowing the Malasani to sail the desert without a fight goes against everything we joined the Host for."

"Yes, but things change, Hamid. We're fighting a different war now."

Hamid's eyes went emotionless, a sign his anger was threatening to boil over. "It's weakness."

"No, Macide has the right of it. Inciting the Malasani to become our enemies before we see how things play out in Sharakhai is pure foolishness. We need to bide our time, gain allies, learn what the Malasani plan to do once the war is settled."

"Is that why you're sleeping with Haddad? So you can learn of Malasan's plans?"

Emre went red in the face. He hadn't been hiding the relationship, exactly, but he hadn't been advertising it either. "That has nothing to do with it."

"If you're so sure then why don't you ask her about it?"

"Why don't you stick to your own business, and let me worry about Haddad?"

Hamid took him in with a look of disgust. "Bakhi's bright hammer, I knew *Çeda* had you wrapped around her little finger. I had no idea it was *all* women." He began walking away, back toward their ships.

"Not everything is a conspiracy, Hamid!"

Hamid didn't reply.

Late that evening Emre lay with Haddad in her cabin on *Calamity's Reign*. Scout ships had reported that both the Rushing Waters of Tribe Kenan and the White Trees of Tribe Halarijan were near and would arrive at the oasis the following day.

As the sun went down, Emre and Haddad made love. After, while Haddad's cheeks and chest were still flushed, she opened the cabin window that faced the setting sun and prayed to the androgynous god, Tamtamiin, one of the Malasani triumvirate. Much of the cabin lay in ochre shadows, but the sun's golden light struck her face just so. She looked beautiful like that. The sunlight made it seem as though Tamtamiin were staring directly at her, granting her the peace the god was known for.

When she was done, she left the shutters open and lay beside him. The dusk breeze licked the sweat from their naked bodies, providing relief from the relentless summer heat. Emre lay on his stomach, taking her in, while his chin rested on his folded arms. Haddad lay beside him, one arm running over his back.

"A sad day is coming," Haddad said.

"Oh? What day is that?"

"Your sister tribes are nearly here. Then we'll be headed to meet the Malasani army. And after that"—she lifted her arm and slapped his bare ass—"you'll abandon me to go and meet your shaikh."

Emre smiled, enjoying both the sting and the simple fact that she'd done it. It felt like she'd claimed him. "You could join me."

She laughed, which stung a lot more than the slap had. "*Join* you? I'll need to report to my king at some point, won't I?"

"Yes, but what then?"

"Exactly. What then?" She shifted closer, pressed kisses along his arm. Her fingers trailed through his long, unbound hair, raking his scalp. "I don't know, Emre." She spoke softly now, her dark eyes and intent look sending a thrill running through him. "There's so much happening. I don't know what he'll want me to do."

"You won't take up your caravan trade again?"

"I'll do as my king and Ranrika tell me"—she kissed his elbow with languid ease and lay back down—"but yes, likely I will. It's in my bones. But who knows when? If the Sharakhani Kings win, there's no telling how far they'll go to punish Malasan, nor who they'll implicate in the war. It could be years before Malasani caravans can safely brave the sands. And even then, I would likely still be a target."

There was truth in her words. "I've never visited Malasan, you know."

Haddad laughed louder than before, then tempered it when she saw his reaction. "You'd really come to Malasan for me?"

"I'd come to visit its wonders." He kissed the round of her belly. "There must be one or two."

She looked affronted as she twisted in the bed and slapped his ass again, and when he tried to kiss her breast, kept him at bay with a hand to his forehead. "Malasan *is* filled with wonders."

"No doubt," he said, slipping one hand under her leg and between her thighs.

She spread her legs as he played with her, her smile increasingly satisfied. She lay her head back and stared at the ceiling, her hips starting to move in slow circles.

"A skiff was spotted by the scouts." He felt a right bastard for bringing it up now, but they'd be asleep soon, and tomorrow would be busy for them both. "They thought it looked like yours."

She pulled him up until she could kiss his lips. "Yes. I sent one out."

"Why?"

"To speak with the shaikhs."

Emre leaned away from her next kiss. "Both of them?"

"Well, of course!"

"Haddad, why?"

"To do exactly what we just talked about. To secure trade."

"While war rages in the desert?"

She shrugged. "War is the best time for certain things."

"Like what?"

She gave him a shove so that he was lying on his back, then straddled him. "Whatever they're most desperate to get rid of. Whatever I think I can turn over somewhere else for a profit. In the case of Halarijan, its bows and arrows and spears fashioned from their fabled trees. In the case of Kenan, it's the healing paste they gather from the Haddah in late spring." She leaned down and kissed him deeply, her breasts just touching his chest while her hips began to grind.

He broke away. "But your ships are gone. You've nothing to trade."

"If you think they'd turn their nose up at good Malasani gold then you're a bigger fool than I thought."

Her explanation made sense. She *was* always looking for trade, whether it was jewelry, black laugher hides, intricate pottery. Her hold was full of it: treasures from the desert she would one day bring back to Malasan or trade along the way if she found a better deal. She'd even managed to get a pair of bottles of Tulogal from Macide, a legendary liquor rarely seen beyond the desert.

"But . . . why not do that when they're here?"

She looked at him as if he were daft. "I wasn't delivered from my mother's womb yesterday, Emre Aykan'ava. If I wait, Kadri might have secured a deal before I can. Or the two tribes might have traded with one another. I needed those deals *before* the meeting."

It was a crafty move, the sort Haddad was famed for. Emre was embarrassed and angry with himself for believing in Hamid's paranoia. "You got what you wanted, then?"

She winked. "I always get what I want."

He took in her body, which was beginning to writhe deliciously against his stiffening cock. "Is that so?"

"Yes." She kissed him again, biting his lip this time. "I do. Now are you going to fuck me or not?"

He returned her kiss with interest while moving his hips against hers. "Depends on whether you really want it."

She didn't answer, merely smiled that smile of hers, reached down between his legs, and began stroking him.

"Oh all right, I'm going to fuck you."

"That's what I thought."

Their laughter filled the small cabin.

Chapter 7

AVUD WATCHED FROM THE EDGE of the bazaar. He felt strange, wearing a turban and veil. He'd grown up here, in the bazaar and the spice market and the neighborhoods that surrounded them. His sister, Tehla, the baker, was only a short walk away through the bazaar's choked aisles. He'd watched her working for a time but had refused to go near her. No one could know where he was, least of all his family—they were in enough danger already.

As it always did near the noonday meal, the sounds of the bazaar and the distant spice market became an unyielding roar. It was so loud it would drown out some of the lesser storytellers, but not old Ibrahim, who had a booming voice that never failed to cut through the din. Just then he was making a dramatic face at a young, raven-haired girl while many in the crowd looked on with smiles. The girl stared wide-eyed as she listened to one of the many fanciful tales of Bahri Al'sir, the patron saint of tail spinners all across the desert.

In this tale, Bahri had just run afoul of the shaikh of Tribe Halarijan, a vengeful man who was angry that Bahri had stolen a kiss from his daughter. *Strange,* Davud thought, *how a man from the desert can seem so foreign, so exotic*. But with the city's origin as a humble caravanserai faded by time, it was the simple truth: the people of the desert *were* foreign to those in the city, and vice versa.

Bahri Al'sir, hoping to make amends, had gone to the southern mountains to steal an egg from the great rocs that nested there. He would present the egg to the shaikh in apology and ask for his daughter's hand in marriage. He was about to make his escape when the roc returned.

Ibrahim had gathered his long beard into a fist and was using it to describe how Bahri Al'sir escaped the angry roc with not just one egg in his pack, but all three. He was using the girl as a prop, making her reactions as much a part of the show as his story, and the crowd loved it. They poked at others to look as the girl clapped her hands at the series of clever antics that saved Bahri time and again.

That was when Ibrahim's eyes passed over Davud. Davud's face was covered, and it had been years since they'd seen one another, and yet a moment later, as Ibrahim described how one of the roc eggs had hatched a young but fully fledged roc, which had rescued Bahri Al'sir as he was falling down the mountain to a sure death, he winked at Davud.

As he closed the story, coins flew and constellations of copper and silver formed on Ibrahim's midnight blue carpet. With practiced ease, he gathered every last coin and six-piece into a pile, then swept them into the beaten leather bag between his feet. As he rolled his carpet up, hoisted it over his shoulder, and began walking down the street, Davud fell into step beside him.

"I thought you lost to the House of Kings for good," Ibrahim said without even glancing his way.

"For a time, so did I." Davud glanced at a passerby. "Ibrahim, I need to speak to you. Can I walk you home?"

"I'm not going home. But you can walk with me."

Ibrahim led them down a narrow street. As the raucous din of the bazaar faded, replaced by the drone of the city, Davud removed his veil. It felt good to speak face to face for once.

"You always used to go home," he said, "to Eva."

Ibrahim looked as if he were about to say something biting, but then his expression softened. "Eva passed a few months back. I haven't the heart to go home for lunch any longer."

"Oh, Ibrahim." Davud laid one hand on Ibrahim's bony shoulder. "My tears for your loss. Truly, hers was a flame so bright we'll surely see her walking in the farther fields."

Ibrahim glanced up as if he thought he might see her in the sky, then he reached over and patted Davud's hand. "I'll tell her you said so when I see her again. She'll like that."

"What happened?"

"I woke one morning, and she was gone. Passed in her sleep." He looked to Davud and smiled through his pain. "Do you know the last words she said to me?"

"What?"

"'Would you like some cardamom cookies for tomorrow?'"

Davud had to laugh. They were his favorite, and Eva's were the best in the neighborhood, better than Tehla's even. More than once, Davud had stolen a few as they were cooling on her kitchen windowsill. He'd thought her foolish to leave them there. It was years before he learned she put them there on purpose, knowing some would get pinched.

"My mouth is watering just thinking about them."

Ibrahim blinked, and his tears fell like sun-brightened crystals. "I used to tell her how sick of them I was, just to tease her, but she would only smile and make more, or whatever else she pleased."

They came to a tea house with several tables and chairs outside in the street. A few were occupied. Ibrahim set his carpet against the wall and took the table farthest away from the other patrons, then motioned for Davud to join him. When they'd both been left alone with their steaming cups of tea, Ibrahim picked up his cup, took a sip, and spoke in a low voice.

"The Spears have been asking after you."

"I know."

"They said the Kings themselves wish to speak to you."

"One King in particular, I expect."

Ibrahim raised his hand. "This is a story I don't want to know, Davud."

Davud sipped his tea, an infusion of lemongrass and ginger. It reminded him of a girl he'd liked at the collegia. A poet. "I haven't come about that."

"Then what *have* you come about?"

"I'm looking for someone. A woman named Dilara."

"Dilara . . . ?"

Ibrahim's gaze dropped to the ring Davud wore on his right index finger. A blooding ring. Along one side was a thorn of sharpened steel, a thing he could twist toward his palm to draw blood, from himself; from another, when needed. Months ago, Davud would have been embarrassed. He would have hidden the ring. His face would have flushed. But he was no longer running from his nature. He was a blood mage. He may not like it, but he'd come to accept it. Holding Ibrahim's eye, he wrapped his fingers around his teacup, the ring clinking against the ceramic as he did.

"Dilara," he replied, taking a long sip.

Ibrahim's eyes slid to the table sweep, a young boy who placed the empty cups and saucers onto a tray. When he'd walked back inside the tea house, Ibrahim said, "Would you like to know the most important lesson I've learned since Eva passed?"

"Please."

"Be satisfied with what you have. Give thanks for it, because one day, perhaps sooner than you'd like, it will all be gone. Whatever happened while you were being held by King Sukru, you're free of him now. Leave the Kings be, Davud. Find a nice, quiet place in the city. Or leave for a caravanserai, at least for a year or two."

"I can't do that."

"Why not?" He sat back and flicked his long fingers eastward, toward Malasan. "I promise you, after the war, the Kings will have forgotten all about you."

"Ibrahim, I need to find her."

"Need to find *them*, you mean."

Ibrahim knew. He was referring to the Enclave, a group of wizards who hid among the populace of Sharakhai, who'd long ago banded together for mutual protection against the Kings' aggressions. They were precisely who Davud needed to find. Still, he left Ibrahim's comment unacknowledged.

"You're still with the woman you escaped with? Anael?"

"Anila. And no. She died three weeks ago."

Whatever words of advice Ibrahim had been about to impart died on his lips. "I'm sorry to hear we share in our sorrows. What happened?"

Anila wasn't dead, but he couldn't have Ibrahim, or anyone else for that matter, knowing so. The more who thought she'd succumbed to her nature as a necromancer, the better.

"She was wounded badly in Ishmantep. It was her desire for revenge that had kept her alive in the House of Kings, but when we escaped . . ." Davud shrugged. "Well, it wasn't enough."

Ibrahim nodded as if he understood. "Your time in Ishmantep was terrible, I'm certain. As was your time in the palaces." He leaned in as his gaze swept over the other patrons and the street beyond. "But now you're *free*. There's no need to go meddling with people who would just as soon swallow you whole."

"It isn't so much that I want to," Davud said evenly. "I need to. If I don't, they'll find *me*, and I can't have that. I won't."

The sound of clopping hooves rose up on a nearby street. Dozens of horses were galloping through the city, likely a squad of Silver Spears or several hands of Blade Maidens. Davud sat up straighter, ready to run if need be, but thankfully the sounds began to recede.

Ibrahim set down his cup. "Would you like to know what I think?"

"I would."

"I may have heard rumor of a man speaking to the storytellers of this city. If the rumors are true, he's spoken to at least seven, and each time he's asked after the Enclave. Sometimes using the name Dilara. Other times Esmeray. Or Esrin. Those three magi are said to live in or near the Shallows." Ibrahim's gaze circled the sky for a moment. "Near this very tea house, in fact. But it's curious . . ."

"What's curious?"

"The likelihood of the storytellers having direct contact with any of those people is slim, wouldn't you agree?"

"Oh, I don't know," Davud replied easily. "Storytellers know quite a few people."

"They also *tell tales*."

"And?"

"I think you're using them. I think you're trying to spread the word, so that the Enclave comes to *you*."

Davud smiled. "As I said, I need to find them."

Ibrahim leaned so far back in his chair Davud thought he might tip over, then linked his fingers over his stomach. "The Enclave demand loyalty from those who join their ranks. They enforce it through blood. They're hardly better than the gangs of thieves who run the Shallows."

Hardly better than the Kings, either, Davud thought, *but what am I to do?* "Are you telling me you have no way of reaching Dilara?"

"None."

"Could you ask around?"

"I could, Davud, but I won't. I didn't live to see my wife led to the farther fields in her old age by taking risks like that."

The other storytellers had been reticent as well, but a few of them, Davud was certain, would ask around, perhaps even spin his tale in the oud parlors over a glass of araq. Ibrahim was an exception, though. He knew Davud. Knew his family as well. He was trying to be protective, but if he knew how much trouble Davud was already in, he'd see that the Enclave was by far the lesser of the two dangers. *It's certain King Sukru hasn't given up,* Davud thought. *He's still chasing me, and if I'm not careful, I'll land myself back in his clutches.* He refused to share it with Ibrahim, though. The chances of the Kings somehow learning of it and coming for *Ibrahim* were simply too high. They still had their Kings of Whispers, after all.

Davud stood, leaving more than enough coins to pay for their tea. "I'm sorry about Eva. I really did love her cookies."

"Me too," Ibrahim replied with a sad, kind smile. "I'm sorry about Anila."

Davud left and wandered the city for a time. There was something about staying in one place that made him worry King Sukru would use his blood and come for him. He could still feel the prick of the needle as Sukru himself extracted it from his arm. How foolish he'd been to give it up, though he'd really had no choice.

As he paced along the streets of Roseridge, he felt for the ward he'd placed around himself that morning using his blood and a combination of the sigils for *search*, *magic*, and *warn*. It was imperfect, he knew, but was designed to sense anyone near him who could use magic. He felt as if he were fishing, only for three very dangerous fish.

He wandered until near nightfall and couldn't decide if he was disappointed another day had passed without contact. Ready to head back to his room at last, he stood in line to head through the gates of the city's outer wall, a thing that was becoming more difficult by the day as, if reports were true, the Malasani fleet crept closer to the city. There were still fifty people ahead of him when he felt a peculiar tingling at the base of his throat, like a bee had gotten trapped halfway to his stomach. The likelihood of a sting felt ever greater as the line slowed to a crawl. Some merchant woman who looked more Mirean than she did Sharakhani had been stopped while her hand-drawn cart was searched.

Davud swiveled his blooding ring toward his palm and squeezed. He felt its bite, felt his own blood tickle along the folds of his skin. With one finger he traced a master sigil from the more basic signs for *obfuscate* and *mortal man*. As he felt the warmth of the spell taking effect, he stepped out of line and walked serenely forward.

A bright-eyed baby girl looked up from the arms of her father and stared straight at him. An expression of discomfort passed over her face, then she began to cry. Her father shushed her, oblivious to the fact that the baby had somehow seen through Davud's spell. Everyone else in the line was watching the merchant woman shout and point beyond the wall. "You see? There's nothing there! I have to get home! My babies are sick!"

Davud kept a steady pace. It wasn't that the people in line couldn't see him, it was that he'd fallen beneath their notice. *The less power used, the better.* But the tingling in his throat was growing stronger.

As he neared the guards and the choke point beneath the gates, the woman's cart was just being rolled away by a Silver Spear. A second soldier was leading her away by the arm. All eyes were on her, save for the guard who'd come to relieve the others and begin questioning the next in line. He stared straight at Davud, and Davud thought he'd managed to pierce the spell as well.

But when Davud continued to walk with a steady pace beneath and beyond the looming gate, the Spear's eyes moved back to the pair of men at the head of the line as if Davud were a captain of the guard and had every right to go where he wished. Davud breathed a sigh of relief and released the power of the spell.

Forcing himself not to run, he entered the Red Crescent, the neighborhood surrounding the western harbor. Sunset was nearing as he reached a stone archway, the entrance to an old boneyard. He headed toward the back, where a fresh grave stood out from the others. The gravestone read: *Here lies Fezek Fatim'ala: Poet, Playwright, Father, Friend.* The tickle in Davud's throat was now so strong he was forced to release the spell of detection lest it distract him. No sooner had he done so than the world tilted and spun around him.

He tried to keep his balance. His arms windmilled like an inattentive child tripped by an unseen foot. But it was no use. He fell face first onto the fresh dirt. The vertigo didn't abate. It was all he could do to roll over without throwing up. His breathing came heavy as a harvest ox.

When a lone figure came into view beneath the archway—a woman, Davud thought, though he couldn't be sure—his fear soared to new levels. He pierced the palm of his right hand with his blooding ring. Felt the prick on his skin. Felt hot blood flow. It was more than enough to cast a spell, but by the gods who breathe, the world was turning so quickly he couldn't gather his thoughts.

The feminine figure strode confidently forward and crouched beside Davud. The world began to slow, and he saw her clearly for the first time. A woman who'd seen twenty-five summers, perhaps, she had dark skin and wore a turban that gathered her many, many braids into two thick hunks that rolled down her back. On her cheeks and between her eyebrows were red tattoos, their designs like bittersweets, the bright, four-petaled flowers favored in many rites of spring. Davud didn't need any of that to tell him who this was, though. The wild look in her eyes was enough. She was the crazed one. The zealot.

"Esmeray," he said, "I only wish to speak."

"A collegia scholar, awakened by Hamzakiir, taken by Sukru and since escaped the attention of the Kings."

"I only wish to speak."

"And little wonder, but I tell you"—she leaned forward, a blooding ring of her own on her thumb, and used the needle-sharp tip to press against Davud's eyelid—"you aren't *welcome* in the Enclave. Do you hear?"

Davud cringed, sure she was about to put his eye out.

Just then a dark figure wearing a hooded robe appeared in the arch of the boneyard's entrance. It was Anila. Stepping beside her into the boneyard was a lanky man with arms long enough to encompass Davud's entire family.

Esmeray noticed. "Begone. This is no business of yours."

The lanky man lumbered ahead of Anila. Davud's world, meanwhile, spun, righted itself, and spun again, making the man seem to lurch in queer and unexpected ways. He felt good and truly drunk.

A tendril of darkness stretched between in Esmeray's palms. "I told you to go." With a low thrum the spell thickened. The tendril became a strand, the strand a thread, the thread a rope. Ever twisting, it seemed eager to be free of her control.

"I'm terribly sorry," the lurching man replied while picking up speed, "but I'm afraid I don't have much of a choice in the matter."

The spell hummed as it flew through the air like a wriggling snake. It struck the man in the gut, and a sizzling sound filled the cramped space of the boneyard. Clothes and skin were blasted away, yet the man hardly lost a step. Esmeray's eyes went wide as he loomed ever nearer. She clapped her palms and spread them while backing away, but tripped over a low grave marker. The lash of darkness she was forming flew harmlessly into a salmon-colored sky.

The lumbering man was on her a moment later, gripping her wrist in one hand, her neck in the other. His hood fell back and his lank hair swayed as he thumped Esmeray's head against the ground and she kicked and screamed. She clawed at his face with her free hand, but it was a losing battle. On the third strike, she went limp.

Footsteps approached, lighter than the lumbering man's. Davud lifted his head, still fighting the world as it lurched, to see Anila walking toward him wearing a dress of sapphire blue. The midnight skin of her face was largely hidden by her headdress and veil. A blanket was folded over one arm. She reached out to Davud with her free hand and pulled him to his feet. The vertigo was so strong that for long moments all he could do was take short breaths while pressing one hand to his stomach.

"Time to get some answers?" Anila asked when he'd straightened up.

She looked dead tired, but worse, seemed to be in pain. She was staving off the urges that had consumed her over the weeks since escaping Sukru's palace. As always, he wished he could help, but this was well beyond his power. *Reach the Enclave,* he told himself for the hundredth time. *Tell them our story, and they'll help us.*

He nodded to her. "Time to get some answers."

Anila opened her mouth to speak, then closed it. Her pain seemed to grow worse. Her lips and chin quivered badly. Tears collected in her blood-shot eyes. Ever since they'd learned of Hamzakiir's death in the desert at the hands of the ehrekh, Guhldrathen, these episodes had grown worse. Her purpose, which had saved her from sure death in Ishmantep, had been her burning desire to see Hamzakiir dead. Robbed of her anger, her fight against the call of the farther fields was like a slow slide toward the edge of a cliff. Death was inevitable. It happened to all necromancers sooner or later.

Unless I do something about it. Davud took her hand and squeezed. "Just a bit longer."

Anila nodded, then jutted her chin to Esmeray's unconscious form. "Best we move quickly."

Davud couldn't agree more. He knelt by Esmeray's side, pierced the skin of her wrist with his blooding ring, and brought the wound to his lips. He felt a rush of power as he fed on her blood.

The ghul was named Fezek, and he was beholden to Anila. She'd raised him in this very boneyard, his grave only a few paces away. His robe was burned, his skin as well, but his face held no look of pain. He studied everything Davud was doing with a look of naked wonder, then spoke in feathery tones. "Do you suppose, having drank her blood, her family will recognize you as one of their own in the farther fields?"

"Be quiet," Anila said.

"He's stealing a part of her soul, after all." His voice sounded tattered and threadbare.

"I said be quiet."

"Yes, who am I but the man you robbed of his afterlife? Why ever would you grant me the answer to one of life's greatest riddles?"

"That's hardly one of life's greatest riddles."

Fezek's cloudy eyes were brimming with shock, the sort a stage performer might put on for the cheap seats in the back. "Surely you jest! With the answer to that one question, the riddle of our very nature might be unlocked!"

"Be quiet," Davud said. "Both of you."

Having swallowed enough of Esmeray's blood, not only for what he needed to do now, but for the meeting that would soon take place, he dabbed a finger to the wound, collecting some of the blood.

Fezek, meanwhile, muttered under his breath, something about wounds deeper than those that kill. The man was worse than a braying mule, but Davud forgave him for it. Whenever he annoyed Anila, she seemed to forget about her pain for a while. Besides, Anila was so weak, were they to lose Fezek, she might not have enough power to summon another ghul. Putting up with his millstone of a mouth was worth the protection he afforded them.

Working quickly, Davud painted a sigil onto Esmeray's forehead, combining *guise* with *search*. He negated them both by adding more precise arcs over it, the sigil for *annul*. It would be sufficient, he hoped, to hide Esmeray from those who would soon be searching for her. He drew another that would keep her in a state of sleep until he wished otherwise, then ran his thumb along her wrist. The wound closed with a sound like a skewer of goat being thrown on a smoking hot grill.

Anila tossed the blanket she carried to Fezek, who caught it clumsily and wrapped Esmeray in its folds. Once he'd hoisted her over his shoulder, the three of them left the boneyard and lost themselves in the shade-filled streets.

Chapter 8

ÇEDA'S LEGS WERE ON FIRE. Her throat burned. Her chest heaved like an oryx that had just slipped a pack of black laughers. She refused to slow down, though. Sümeya, still unconscious and badly wounded, lay on the makeshift litter Çeda was hauling. She hadn't so much as groaned since Çeda strapped the zilijs together, laid Sümeya on it, and set out for Leorah's yacht. With the moons set and true night fallen, Sümeya looked like one of the dead, and more and more Çeda felt like an undertaker delivering her to her grave.

Beside her, the towering frame of Mavra's son Sedef plodded along. They were a study in contrasts: Çeda's pace uneven, Sedef's rock steady; Çeda glancing back to Sümeya constantly, Sedef with eyes fixed forward but taking childlike care to ensure that Melis, cradled in his long arms, was as comfortable as he could make her.

The rest of the asirim, including Mavra, followed a quarter-league back. They were wary of the open desert, and shaken by their confrontations, first with Çeda and then King Beşir. Better they remain back. The other women, those of the thirteenth tribe who'd agreed to accompany Çeda, had been told what to expect from the asirim, but meeting them face to face was another thing entirely. Better for them to meet Sedef first, to ease their transition. Çeda would introduce Mavra and the rest of her kin later.

Little time had passed since Beşir's attack. Çeda supposed she should count herself lucky—they might all have been killed and the asirim returned to their graves beneath the adichara—yet still she was angry Beşir had slipped through her grasp. Sedef's mighty throw of the adichara branch had nearly rid Sharakhai of another King. And just after, she'd missed taking his head from his neck by a whisper. While tending to Sümeya and Melis, she had reached out, trying to sense his presence again, the whole time fearing the return of his rain of black arrows, but there'd been nothing. Wherever he'd gone, he was too far away to sense.

She was frustrated at how wrong she'd been. She'd chosen the night of Beht Zha'ir for this raid primarily because the asirim were more awake, and she thought it might give them more ability to oppose the Kings' will. But she'd also chosen it because Rhia would be full. Beşir's bloody verse had been one of those hidden in moon letters in her mother's book of poems.

Sharp of eye,
And quick of wit,
The King of Amberlark;
With wave of hand,
On cooling sand,
Slips he into the dark.

King will shift,
'Twixt light and dark,
The gift of onyx sky;
Shadows play,
In dark of day,
Yet not 'neath Rhia's eye.

Not 'neath Rhia's eye. It seemed to indicate he would be weakened by Rhia's golden glow, or that his power would be stripped of him while Rhia stared down from the heavens. Of all the Kings, she'd thought them safe from Beşir.

Please, Çeda whispered to Nalamae, *let him be taken by his wounds.* Or if not his wounds then the adichara poison—she'd seen a scattering of small punctures all over his face from the thorns.

Sedef, picking up on her thoughts, glanced her way. *You gaze upon a mirage. The Kings' blood is proof against the adichara's poison.*

He was right, of course. And there was little hope of Beşir dying from the sheer trauma of his wounds. Assuming he'd reached safety—and surely he had—the King would merely consume one of the healing draughts. The Kings had few after the Night of Endless Swords, a night that had seen their three main caches of elixirs destroyed or taken, but surely all the Kings still had some squirreled away. At least she'd forced him to consume one, maybe several, thereby shrinking what must be an already-meager supply.

Her makeshift litter sighed as she ran down along a dune to the trough. As she reached the far crest, she spotted it at last: Leorah's ship, a small, two-masted yacht known as *Wadi's Gait*, barely visible under the dim light of the stars.

She pushed herself hard and reached it as a small lantern was lit on the deck, casting a golden glow against the rigging, the sails, and the ancient woman standing on deck, waiting. To all who saw her, she looked like Çeda's great-grandmother, Leorah, but in truth she was Leorah's sister, Devorah. The amethyst on her right hand, a purple stone that glittered like a shooting star in the lamplight, was one of Iri's four sacred stones—the Tears of Tulathan—which could, and did, store the soul of a woman or man. Leorah and her sister Devorah had been using it for decades to share Leorah's body. When the sun set, Leorah diminished and Devorah's soul woke. She would live out her hours, enjoying the moon and the stars and the cool desert air. When the sun rose, Devorah relinquished her hold, and Leorah's will became dominant once more.

A half-dozen women wearing battle dresses similar to Çeda's stood beside Devorah. They were but some of the warriors who'd agreed, with Macide's blessing, to join Çeda in her quest to free the asirim. "Shieldwives," they'd dubbed themselves. *We protect the tribe,* Jenise, the boldest among them, had said to Çeda, *and we protect you. We are a shield for our people.*

The six women dropped down to the sand and met Çeda and Sedef. The first three lifted Sümeya from the litter and carried her up the gangplank and into the ship's hold. The other three, despite Çeda's attempts to prepare them, stopped well short of Sedef's towering shape with looks of naked fear on their faces. They refused to go near him. Sedef, after the battle with Beşir, was on edge as well, so Çeda took Melis from his arms and bid him return to the others until they set sail.

Where will we go? he asked. There was a defensive tone to his words, bordering on fear.

To the desert, Çeda replied.

He stared at her, his face unyielding as granite. *You said we would free Sehid-Alaz.*

She knew then that he'd guessed her intentions. She'd thought he might the moment they saw the women warriors standing on the deck. Çeda had been working tirelessly to mask her thoughts, but she'd clearly failed.

There was nothing to do about it now, though. *We go to the desert,* she said to him, *so that you and the others can bond with these women.*

Distaste flooded his mind even as revulsion and fear grew on the faces of the women at the mere sight of him.

Bond . . .

Yes, Çeda replied, *bond . . . I'm not strong enough to hold all of you forever. I need others, my tribe—our tribe—to help me.*

Sedef stared at each of the Shieldwives in turn with a look not unlike the one he'd given Çeda before charging her in the blooming fields. Çeda tried to read his thoughts, but felt only raw emotion. Hatred. Anger. And no small amount of confusion. She was about to say something, to try to convince him that this was the right path to take, when he turned and trudged away. As he headed toward the other asirim he left a coldness in his wake that, while not unexpected, was certainly disheartening.

Change and grief are bitter siblings, Çeda's mother used to say, *one chained to the other. We fight for the world we want, Çeda, but know that the world will fight back. Be ready for the tears. Shed them even as you return to battle.*

Çeda brought Melis to the deck and gave her over to Jenise, a woman with striking green-and-gold eyes who Çeda had already come to trust. Like the other Shieldwives, she was not wholly comfortable in the presence of the Blade Maidens, but for Çeda's sake she accepted them.

"What?" Çeda said.

Jenise forced a smile. "Nothing."

With the help of the others, Jenise carried Melis belowdecks. Çeda wished they had more time to rest, but dawn would soon be on them, and they had to be well away from the blooming fields by then, so they set sail soon after. As the yacht gained speed, the asirim fell in behind. Their dark forms clustering in the yacht's wake, they looked like a pack of hungry jackals.

Çeda left the care of Melis and Sümeya to the others, choosing instead to sit with Devorah amidships in chairs that were fastened to the deck.

"Well?" Devorah asked.

Çeda told her everything, from the asirim's reaction to Beşir's attack.

"It's curious about Beşir's bloody verse," Devorah said, "but we knew the Kings would respond in some way." The lamp swinging from a hook on the boom made the crags in her face seem to sway. "More worrisome are the asirim, how they'll take to the others."

Far behind the ship, one of the asirim yipped. Others picked up the call, howling or barking as they ran.

Çeda felt a deep sorrow for all they'd been through. "They'll need time to adjust."

Devorah waved a hand, indicating not the ship, but the women crewing it. "We have little enough to grant them. We must begin the bonding soon."

"I know." Çeda flexed her right hand. The pain was bad but manageable. Their growing distance from the blooming fields helped, but Çeda knew it was going to grow worse in the days ahead. Left unchecked, it would eventually overwhelm her. The only question was whether they could forge the bonds between the asirim and the Shieldwives before that happened. "We'll start as soon as we join up with the other two ships."

"I tell you again," a voice came from the hatchway, "you cannot risk more than a week."

Çeda and Devorah turned to see Sümeya making her way unsteadily toward them. In place of her turban, a bandage now wrapped her head. She reached a chair and lowered herself gingerly into it, wincing as she went.

"How do you feel?" Çeda asked.

One eye pinched more than the other as a wave of pain swept over Sümeya's face. "Like a pair of desert titans are taking turns hammering my skull." She rolled her tongue inside her cheek, repositioning the pinch of black lotus she'd been given to stave off the worst of her pain.

"Why only seven days?" Devorah asked.

"The Kings may decide to retreat," Sümeya said, "to further fortify the city. If that happens, Malasan and Mirea will make for Sharakhai like falcons. And we don't know what Qaimir has planned. If the rumors of marriage between Kiral and Meryam are true, that means reinforcements from Qaimir are on their way." The ship rolled over a dune, shifting them all in their seats. "If we're to rescue your King, Sehid-Alaz, it must be soon."

They'd had this argument several times. And Çeda didn't disagree, but to leave for Sharakhai when these women were unprepared would doom their mission from the start. "We'll move as fast as we can."

Sümeya held her eye. "One week, Çeda."

"We'll move as fast as we can."

They sailed through the following day and near nightfall reached a small oasis where two more yachts, *Red Bride* and *The Piteous Wagtail*, were moored. On them were eleven more Shieldwives.

With night approaching, Çeda thought it unwise to try bonding now. She wanted to make their attempt in the light of the day, free of the moons' influence. And she wanted to give everyone—the Shieldwives *and* the asirim—more time to acclimate to one another.

As they ate a simple meal of flatbread and hummus and pickled onions, however, Çeda started having second thoughts. She worried that waiting would do them no good. Her right arm ached terribly. Worse, she felt echoes of emotion from the asirim, who huddled closely in the desert. Many were worried they'd made the wrong decision. They yearned for sleep beneath the adichara, not the miserable vistas of the open desert. Some nearly broke away, to try to go off on their own. Each time it happened, the urge was quickly put down, but not without the occasional scuffle during the night. Çeda heard them—as did the rest of the camp—growling and scrapping, then yowling in pain as Mavra or Sedef returned their family to order.

A meal that had begun by sharing tales over a fire fell into to an uncomfortable silence. Çeda tried to lighten the mood by telling them a tale of her days running the streets. Emre had come up with the scheme of selling skunkweed as a rare aphrodisiac to anyone who looked remotely new to the spice market. The story ended with Yahya, the man who sold red lotus powder, the most expensive aphrodisiac to be found in Sharakhai, giving chase and Emre trying to leap over a manure cart only to trip and fall headfirst into the steaming pile. Yahya had ended up laughing so hard he'd forgiven Emre, and even given him a vial of red lotus.

"You're going to need it," Yahya told him. "When word gets out that you use skunkweed, no woman is going to want to sleep with you."

"It doesn't have to get out," Emre had pleaded.

"Oh, yes it does," Yahya had replied with a smile. "I'll make sure of it."

It was a story that never failed to raise a laugh, but with Çeda's arm increasingly hot and painful, and everyone so conscious of the asirim, it went over like a marriage proposal at a funeral.

That night Çeda lay awake while Sümeya lay in the bunk across from her. They stared at one another, both worried. For a long while, Sümeya looked as if she was about to say something, but she turned to face the hull instead. Çeda knew what she was going to say: Çeda had overextended herself by taking Mavra's entire family. The bond she'd formed with them was already weakening, and the desire to break it was like an infection that was only going to spread.

In the morning, Çeda called the Shieldwives together. They gathered on the sand away from the ships. Leorah was having trouble with the heat and remained on *Wadi's Gait*. Melis said she'd remain as well, claiming Leorah needed looking after. Even when Leorah told her to go, she remained, saying her presence was the last thing the ritual needed.

"The Shieldwives may not accept you yet," Çeda had said to her in a low voice, "but they need to. And they will, if only you'll reach out to them."

Melis frowned. "I'm not here to make friends, Çeda."

"Then why *are* you here?"

"I've been asking myself that very same thing."

Çeda paused, wondering how to broach the subject. *Attack it head on*, she thought to herself. *At least then we'll both know where the other stands.* "The other night, at the blooming fields, you drew your weapon after explicit instructions not to."

"What of it?"

"I don't claim to have as much experience as you or Sümeya. Far from it. Except when it comes to the asirim."

"As you say."

"If you're going to remain . . ." Çeda fumbled for the right words. She'd always looked up to Melis. She was a rock, and here Çeda was, trying to order her around. "You have to accept my orders, Melis. Do you understand? It can't be any other way."

It looked as if Melis were trying out a thousand responses before replying in a simple, calm voice, "Very well."

Çeda waited for more, but Melis seemed unwilling to take it any further. "Very well," she said in reply.

Çeda left Melis there and joined the Shieldwives on the sand. Sümeya stood by her side. The rest formed a line, all of them wearing the same sand-colored battle dresses and turbans as Çeda. Their shamshirs hung easily at their sides as they faced the asirim, who huddled in the distance like a herd of frightened oryx.

Çeda motioned to Ramela, a woman twice Çeda's age and calm as a pillar of stone. She was a broad woman with a wide face who had a penchant for biting the insides of her cheeks, especially when she was nervous. She did so now while staring at the asirim in the distance.

"As we said," Çeda prompted. "Raise your hand. Feel for them."

Ramela stepped forward and swallowed hard, her gaze fixed on the asirim as if, were she to look anywhere else, she would lose heart.

Sümeya snorted and spoke loud enough for everyone to hear. "Every single Blade Maiden goes through this ritual. Are the Shieldwives lesser women than they?"

It was transparent manipulation, but it worked. Ramela's look hardened as she took Sümeya in from head to toe. When she turned her gaze back to the asirim, it was with a stiff back and a wooden stare.

"Good," Çeda said. "Now raise your hand."

Ramela complied, lifting her right hand so that her palm faced outward. In the center of her hand was a puckered wound, the reminder of the ritual she and all the rest had performed two weeks ago with Çeda guiding them. Like Çeda's wound, it was the kiss of an adichara thorn. The Shieldwives had been twenty-five in number at the time, but eight of them had succumbed to the poison. The rest had been tattooed by Leorah, who had worked tirelessly to copy Zaïde's techniques and hem the poison in. It gave each woman a connection to the adichara that would serve as a conduit to the asirim. It was this that Ramela needed to draw upon now, only she'd never done it before and was clearly having trouble.

Her wide brow furrowed. Her nostrils flared.

"One of them will stand out to you," Çeda said to her. "Call that one near."

Ramela's eyes flicked to Sümeya. The two women were of an age, but in that moment, Ramela looked like a girl not yet passed into womanhood. With a show of will, she focused her attention on the asirim. Soon one of them was breaking from the others, crawling on all fours, then standing and walking with a strange gait—sideways, as if he couldn't bear to look upon the gathered women directly. He had the bearing of a man bent with age, but his resolve was undeniably powerful.

Your name, Çeda called to him.

An echo of the name he'd once used came to her. *Amile.*

His fury at all that had happened was bright as molten steel. Everything in his heartbreaking past fueled it: Beht Ihman, the endless torture he'd endured, the murders he'd been forced to commit in the name of the Kings, the very presence of two Blade Maidens, whom all the asirim despised. Most of all, he hated that he and his family had just been freed only to be enslaved once more. He knew that those before him were his kin. He just didn't care.

"Choose another," Çeda said, trying to keep her growing concern from leeching into her voice, "not Amile."

"You said to choose the one that stands out," Ramela replied. "Amile's anger is a reflection of my own." Ramela had lost five brothers and two sisters to the Kings, four of them in an ambush near Sharakhai's western harbor after trading raw gemstones in the city.

"You cannot fathom the anger of the asirim," Çeda said. "You cannot know how deeply it runs."

"He is the one I choose."

Ramela was a proud woman and spoke with conviction. Çeda looked to Sümeya, who shrugged and nodded. Çeda wasn't wholly comfortable with it, but in the end agreed with her. If anyone could bond with Amile, Ramela could.

Çeda watched as Amile approached using that crooked gait of his. He wore only a tattered loincloth. He was bald. His beard was filthy with dirt and sand. As he neared the line of women, he crouched low and moved like a crab, his thin arms akimbo. His eyes flicked between Ramela and Çeda and the rest with a restrained rage, a small glimpse into the well of fury confined within him. When he came within a few paces of Ramela he crouched low, folded his knees, and placed his hands wide upon the sand. He would only look sidelong at Ramela, never in the eyes.

A thing from a nightmare, Çeda thought.

Amile glanced at her, smiled a wicked smile, then returned his attention to Ramela. A muffled sort of conversation was happening between them. Just what it was, Çeda couldn't say, but the longer it happened, the more concerned she became.

"Draw him near," Çeda said. She couldn't tell if Ramela had heard. "Draw him near, Ramela. Join hands, and I'll release my hold on him."

Ramela was beginning to tremble. Her hand with the puckered scar and the intricate tattoos was lowering. An image flashed through Çeda's mind of Amile leaping aboard a ship. Ramela had a strong and immediate reaction to it: a memory of her own, of the fears she'd had for her family when she'd learned how a lone asirim had torn through the crew of her family's ship, killing all before a single Blade Maiden or Silver Spear could step foot on deck. Amile's memory was not of the same attack on Ramela's family, but it was similar, one of many mass murders he'd been forced to commit.

In the vision, Amile had reached the rigging. He tore at it, as was the will of the Blade Maiden he was bonded to. As the tops of the canvas sails began to float free, Amile dropped and landed heavily on the deck. A tribesman came at him with a sword, but Amile was too fast. He dodged and surged forward. His nails sunk deep into the man's chest, clutching him, preventing him from retreating. Amile had broken his bones, pulled his flesh free, and now he was forcing Ramela to live that pain too, as if *she* were the man he was attacking.

"Amile, stop it," Çeda said.

But the vision was unyielding. Amile moved on to the next tribesman, an ancient, gray-haired man with widely spaced eyes and scars all over the left side of his face. In quivering hands he held a spear, which he used to catch Amile across the ribs with a sharp thrust, but then Amile was on him, pressing him down to the deck with one hand while the other reached across his throat. With one wrench, blood flew high, all across the deck. It pattered against Amile's skin, almost hot to the touch. How satisfying it was to feel it, even as, deep down, it tore at the remains of the man he'd once been.

Ramela's breath came in terrified gasps. Her hands were at her throat. She couldn't take her eyes from Amile, who stared up at her with a smile on his shriveled, blackened face.

Amile! Çeda cried. *Stop this now!*

She tried to force her will on him. It was something she was loath to do, but Amile was leaving her no choice.

Except it wasn't working. The vision dimmed. The sounds dulled. Somehow that only seemed to make Ramela's terror increase.

In the vision, Amile flew across the deck, launching himself off the hatch to fall on a cluster of women firing arrows and launching fire pots at the Kings' galleon. One of the women, a crone with a shock of gray, wiry hair, tried to stab him with a knife, but Amile snatched her wrist and forced her down to the deck. Before she could cry out, his jagged teeth tore out her throat. Her lifeblood flowed, sending a sickening thrill through Amile. His emotions warred within him: glee at fulfilling the mission given him by his bonded Blade Maiden, fury at the Kings of Sharakhai, and an unending loathing for himself and his fate, a thing that spanned centuries.

It was then that Çeda realized that Ramela, just like the old woman in the vision, had drawn her kenshar. She'd been so wrapped up in the memory that she'd reacted as if *she* were being attacked.

"Ramela, watch out!" Çeda ran toward her—but Amile did too, and he was faster.

Amile, I beg you, don't do this!

Her pleading seemed to amuse him. As in the vision, he grabbed Ramela's wrist and bulled her down to the sand. Before Çeda could reach him, he ducked his head and tore out her throat.

Çeda drove one shoulder hard into Amile's side, and he was thrown off her. But the damage had been done. Ramela twitched, grasping ineffectually at her neck.

The Shieldwives drew their shamshirs as Amile sprinted away. With only the loosest bond remaining to tie him to Çeda, he didn't run toward open sand, but toward the other asirim. They parted for him, then closed ranks with Amile at their center, as if they expected Çeda and the Shieldwives to attack.

Çeda dropped by Ramela's side. Sümeya as well. The others closed in around them. Ramela blinked, took in Çeda and the others as her throat convulsed and a terrible, pained confusion played out over her features. Breath of the desert, she looked ashamed, as if she'd failed Çeda.

Tears streamed down Çeda's face as she gripped Ramela's right hand. She tried to find the right words—a wish to send her off to the farther fields—but felt completely inadequate to the moment. As she knelt there, mute, Ramela's eyes went glassy and her body fell slack.

Chapter 9

SEVEN KINGS SAT within the council room of the Sun Palace. Kiral and Husamettín, as they had for centuries, took the two central seats. To Husamettín's left sat the youthful Cahil, the bent form of Sukru, and the resigned Beşir, who was still lost in grief over having been forced by Yerinde to take the life of his own daughter only a few hours earlier in Eventide. Along the far end of the table were Azad and Ihsan, who had been carefully measuring the mood of the room since this hastily arranged council had begun.

In their centuries spent in council in this room, kings and queens had stood before them. Emperors and empresses had delivered impassioned pleas of kinship. Such visitors were welcomed, so long as they bent the knee. But others were met with distrust or even outright belligerence if they had not yet learned that the will of the Kings would not be denied. Never in all that time had one joined them as an equal. Until today.

Occupying the seat to Kiral's right, the seat formerly filled by King Mesut, was frail Queen Meryam. She held the same level of authority as the Kings of Sharakhai, or so Kiral would have them believe. None of them truly believed it, Ihsan wagered, not even Kiral himself. Ihsan certainly didn't. But they were all aware how much they needed Qaimir and her resources. War was breathing down their neck, and Sharakhai, as they said in the city's west end, was in dire need of cousins with sharp knives.

They'd spent much of their time so far discussing Yerinde and what her sudden appearance meant for their collective plans. Meryam had held her tongue for much of the discussion, asking a question only when the plans for Qaimir's inbound fleet might be affected. But at a pause in the heated conversation, she turned suddenly to Ihsan and said, "Why did you speak to her?"

Kiral's muddled reactions had vanished shortly after Yerinde's departure, and his typically imperious manner had returned. He seemed piqued at Meryam's words, but said nothing against her, choosing instead to sit tall in his seat and address Ihsan as if the question had been his. "A fair question."

"The better question," countered King Azad, "is why you didn't tell us about your promises to the goddess. A god of the desert comes to you in the bowels of the House of Kings and you bind us all in a *promise* to her, and you never thought it worth telling us?"

Ihsan and Azad had agreed to play certain roles in this conversation. Azad would be affronted. Ihsan would be the voice of reason, at least until the other Kings gave him cause to change course.

Kiral, in a rare show of discomfort, scratched the stubble along his neck. "The battle in the desert with King Onur was already brewing. Malasan and Mirea were preparing their assault. There was much to attend to."

"And after the battle was won?" Azad pressed.

"Things were already set in motion. You would be told when the Kestrels we'd sent to the desert returned."

The Kestrels were the Blade Maidens' elite. Nine in total, they were master spies and assassins, gifted linguists, masters of subterfuge, trained in tactics and strategy like no other. They had taken orders from King Zeheb, before his bout with madness had forced them to choose another commander. Now they reported to Husamettín.

"The Kestrels have returned, have they not?" Ihsan asked.

Husamettín nodded and replied in that majestic manner of his that Ihsan found so annoying. "The last returned only a few days ago."

"A few *weeks* ago," Ihsan countered.

Husamettín shrugged, his annoyance showing in the way he shifted the goblet of watered wine sitting before him. "What of it?"

Azad stood and stabbed a finger across the table's curving expanse. "You dare ask such a question? Our right to know such things will not be denied!"

"And if it is?" Cahil added blithely. "What will you do then?"

The relationship between Husamettín and Cahil had been chilly of late, so it was strange to see Cahil come to Husamettín's defense, but Cahil and Azad had ever been at odds. From the moment they'd brought up the idea, Cahil had been against Nayyan wearing her father's skin, and Nayyan had never forgiven him for it.

"It shall not happen again," Azad said, "and you will reveal anything else you've hidden. The plans you've set into motion for Nalamae and for the thirteenth tribe. All of it."

"My good Kings," Ihsan said with a raised hand. Cahil was working himself up to say something stupid and brash. Better to calm the argument now before things got out of hand. "What's done is done." He made a show of looking around the table. "We are but seven now, and Kiral has the right of it. There is much for us to do and—"

"Eight," Cahil cut across him.

"What?" Ihsan said.

"We are eight."

At first Ihsan thought he meant with Queen Meryam. But no. Cahil was alluding to Zeheb, and by his exclusion Ihsan had revealed just how little he thought of the Mad Bull of Sharakhai. Cahil had never loved Zeheb, but Ihsan could tell he harbored suspicions over the way Zeheb had first been implicated, and later turned up mad as a spring hare in Sukru's dungeons. Now, however, Zeheb was in Eventide, under Kiral's control.

"Whatever our number"—Ihsan gave Meryam a polite tilt of his head—"we'll accomplish none of our goals if we continue to bicker. Now more than ever, it's important we combine our efforts lest we perish apart."

Kiral tilted his head, tacit agreement and the only apology Ihsan was likely to get for being left out in the cold. "You've thought about Çedamihn? About finding something of hers to give Yerinde's bird?"

"I have, but I need time to explore the possibility, and to talk with the Whisper King . . ."

Kiral sniffed, considering the request. From time to time Ihsan had been granted leave to speak to him, to attempt to suss out secrets if he could, but each request had fallen under more scrutiny than the last. Kiral didn't suspect that Ihsan had orchestrated Zeheb's fall, but he'd begun treating the King of Whispers like their supply of elixirs: as a rare and exhaustible resource that needed careful supervision.

"You may speak to Zeheb," Kiral said at last, then moved on to their efforts to slow down the Mirean and Malasani fleets.

Ihsan listened with only one ear until the subject of a particular alchemyst was raised. "Alu-Waled reports that his serum has now been tested on the asirim," Meryam was saying, "and is ready for dispersal."

Alu-Waled was a gifted alchemyst who had long been in King Sukru's employ. He'd been tasked, at Meryam's urging and with Kiral's blessing, with developing a plague that could devastate the incoming Mirean fleet. And now it appeared he'd succeeded.

"I still think it too risky," Ihsan said, "to unleash such a thing."

"Yes, well," Cahil jumped in before Meryam could speak, "you've always had a tender stomach when it comes to war."

"It isn't weakness that drives me, but simple prudence. This serum may well decimate the entire Mirean fleet, and perhaps they deserve it for waging war against the Amber City—"

An incredulous bark of a laugh escaped Cahil. *"Perhaps?"*

"Whether it does or doesn't," Ihsan continued, all but ignoring Cahil and the smile on his babylike face, "isn't the point. We cannot predict what will happen when it reaches the city, and I'll bet my palace that it will."

Meryam, who'd been rubbing the red beads of her necklace, the same tatty one she'd used in the wedding ceremony, let it fall and turned all her attention on Kiral. "Must we have this discussion again?"

"It's a discussion worth having," Ihsan cut in.

"It will all go as planned," Meryam replied.

"No. There's too much riding on this to take your word for it."

"What would you have me do, go to the warfront myself?" Meryam had a penchant for turning cross when it suited her. This time, however, it didn't seem premeditated.

"If you insist on this course of action," Ihsan replied easily, "I would have you do precisely that."

Kiral raised his hands. "Let's not be hasty," he said to Ihsan. "With

Malasan on our doorstep, the place for our queen is right here in the city."
Ihsan tried to break in, but Kiral talked over him. "Your reservations have
been duly noted, Ihsan, but we've all decided it's worth the risk."

Duly noted, Ihsan mused. *Duly tossed in a fucking midden heap, more like.*
Meryam had been winning far too many of these battles of late. Not surprising, he supposed, but galling all the same.

Husamettín gave them an update on their progress to the north, where
their fleet was moving to intercept Mirea, and an update on the state of the
city's defenses, which were being readied for the assault from Malasan. Soon
their meeting was complete, each with their assigned tasks, none as important to their survival as Ihsan's. Yerinde must be appeased, after all.

After a ride up to Eventide, and a writ from Kiral to allow him in, Ihsan
was led to a room deep in the bowels of the palace where two Silver Spears
stood at attention. The room was a small affair with multiple layers of carpets
on the floor and padding on the walls. They'd been installed not only to
muffle Zeheb's incessant screams but also to prevent further injury, a constant danger with the way he sometimes threw himself at the walls or writhed
on the floor.

As the door clicked shut, Ihsan sat cross-legged next to Zeheb, who was
curled in a corner like a child frightened of a sandstorm. The irony of the scene
wasn't lost on Ihsan. It was a near complete reversal of the moment in Zeheb's
palace where a Kestrel had shoved Ihsan's face into the carpet while Zeheb
knelt calmly nearby. Ihsan wagered he was about as smug now as Zeheb had
been then. Whether Zeheb was as scared as Ihsan had been, who could tell?
The man's eyes darted to and fro. The nonsense spewing from his mouth was
ceaseless. The only reason he was still alive was that he was being force fed
twice a day. Still, he'd lost half his bulk. His skin *hung* from his frame.

"There was a very interesting meeting earlier today," Ihsan began. Zeheb
gave no indication that he'd heard. When Ihsan spoke again, he allowed
some of his power to leach into his words. "With the goddess, Yerinde."

From Zeheb's parted lips came a rustle of sounds, *"Goddess, modest,
oddest . . ."*

"She wants Nalamae's head. Did you know? Did the whispers tell you?"

"The Goddess." The words were stronger now. *"Yerinde. Nalamae. Tulathan. Rhia . . ."*

"Yes, Yerinde told us to follow young Çedamihn, told us that if we did, Nalamae would come to save her. We have a gift that will allow us to do it, a bird, but it needs her scent. Çeda's scent."

"Scents, sends, rends . . . Goezhen may come."

"He may. But we must play this game out. The pieces are before us, and it's our turn to make a move."

Zeheb's entire body convulsed. *"Move, prove, reprove . . . So many voices, Ihsan . . . There are so many . . ."*

"I know," Ihsan replied. "Tell me. You spent months listening to Çeda. Listening to those who spoke to her. Who they spoke to in turn. Who might have something of hers, a thing that defines her?"

"Asking, tasking, masking . . ."

"Concentrate, Zeheb."

"Masking, asking, tasking . . ."

As willing as Ihsan was to set the other Kings up for a fall, he couldn't do so here. The chance that Yerinde would do something rash were they to fail was simply too high. With a wave of her hand, the goddess could undo generations of Ihsan's careful preparations.

He wondered again why she would be gone for so long, only to return centuries later and demand the Kings kill her sister goddess. He yearned to read Yusam's lost journals, the ones that resided in Eventide, this very palace. Kiral had taken them, hoarding yet more for himself. Did the riddle's answer lay there? There must be *some* hint of it, something that might help head off the worst of Yusam's visions: a Sharakhai laid to waste.

"Come, Zeheb. I need something of Çedamihn's."

"Tasking, masking, fighting, striking . . ."

"Zeheb!" Ihsan was loath to allow too much power into his voice. He could already feel the effect of his power weakening. It happened when he used it too often on the same person, and he had on Zeheb. He wondered how long it would be before he'd need to arrange for Zeheb's suicide. He prodded Zeheb's ribs with the sharp toe of one boot. "Zeheb, lead me to Çedamihn!"

Zeheb cowered, but only kept mumbling to himself. *"Masking, unmasking . . . The master. The master of the mask."*

Ihsan was ready to kick Zeheb in the gut if only to loosen his tongue, but then it struck him. *What a bloody fool you are, Ihsan.* Zeheb *was* giving him something; it was just that he was speaking in riddles again.

"Who? Who is the master of the mask?"

"The master of the mask . . . The master now taken, whispering in a cell of his own . . ." As Ihsan tried to puzzle out his meaning, Zeheb giggled. *"A cell for a spell . . . Oh, how he fell . . ."*

Zeheb fell silent soon after, and would say no more.

I'll have to try another day, Ihsan decided, and left the room, wondering what in the great wide desert he was going to do about Yerinde. Behind him, the cell door closed. The lock clanked, the key ring jingled, and a memory sprang to him. In a burst of insight, he realized what the Whisper King had been trying to tell him. He felt foolish for not having thought of it himself, but then again, how often had he ever visited Sharakhai's fighting pits?

"Here, my Lord King!"

As Ihsan strode along the pier toward a two-masted ketch named *Yerinde's Needle—the gods are not without their humor,* Ihsan mused—the warden of his assigned hand of Blade Maidens waved to him from the hatch leading down into the ship.

On the ship's deck stood a woman name Djaga Okoyo. She was hemmed in by two Blade Maidens, who stood at the ready, hands on the hilts of their shamshirs. Djaga's closely shorn hair, her angry look, even her stance, made her look like her one-time moniker from the pits, the Lion of Kundhun. Ihsan was tempted to have the Maidens wipe that defiant look from her face, or take it out on the surprisingly delicate Mirean woman she kept, but decided to question her a moment first.

"Have you seen Çeda in recent months?" Ihsan asked her.

Djaga couldn't help but glance at the Mirean woman by her side. She wasn't scared for herself, but for her lover. "No," she eventually replied, in the sort of short bark that many Kundhuni used when they were angry.

"Have you seen her?" he said again, this time letting power into his voice.

For a time, Djaga said nothing. She swallowed hard. She blinked. But then gave in, as all those under his spell eventually did. "No."

Ihsan wondered for a moment whether it was simple defiance or her love for Çeda that made her unwilling to tell him. Likely it was both. Djaga hadn't reached the pinnacle of pit fighting by backing down from anyone.

Ignoring her impudence for now, he stepped past her and took the ladder down into the ship. He'd just come from the internment camp where hundreds of the Moonless Host were being kept, along with Mirean and Malasani dissidents. There, huddled alone, in the corner of a tight mudbrick structure, was a once-great man, at least as far as such things went in the west end of Sharakhai. His name was Osman, and he was a hollow-cheeked ghost of the gladiator he once was—Zeheb's master of the masks, the one who decided who would fight in which helms and gladiatorial armor. Çeda had been one of his gladiators once and had worn a mask of her own.

By the time he departed, Ihsan was impressed with Osman. In his many years, he'd found only a handful who could resist his commands. Osman had managed it for many long, shaking breaths. In the end, however, his lips had quivered, the tortured look on his face had broken, and he'd given Ihsan that which he sought.

Ihsan reached the captain's cabin, where the warden of the Blade Maidens was holding back the hinged lid of a wooden bench. Within, nestled among blankets and bric-a-brac, was a helm fashioned into the likeness of Nalamae. Atop it was a wolf pelt, the empty pits of its eyes humorless and hungry. And beneath, a faded set of leather armor—gladiator's breastplate, battle skirt, bracers and greaves—all dyed white.

Ihsan picked up the helm and ran his fingers over Nalamae's primitive features. "Well, well, well, perhaps we'll find you after all." He wondered again if he should abandon this search—he had no idea where it might lead and what might come of it—but in the end he came to the same conclusion as every other time he'd considered it. It was simply too dangerous to defy the goddess after opening his fool mouth and begging for her help.

Taking up the helm and armor, he left the ship and made for Eventide.

Chapter 10

BRAMA RODE TOWARD THE SUMMIT of a hill on a lively chestnut mare. The small, mountain-bred horse, Kweilo, was a gift from Queen Alansal of Mirea, and her name meant *little bird* in Mirean, because of how she liked to skip and prance when unsaddled or when given free rein.

Near the base of the hill to Brama's left, where dry, rocky ground met waves of amber sand, stood dozens of standing stones in two rough lines, like the ribs of some half-buried titan.

Rümayesh sat atop one of the misshapen pillars. She surveyed the desert's expanse, crouching like a condor on the lookout for prey. If this day went like any of the others they'd spent scouting, she would remain atop that stone until nightfall. With her so preoccupied, Brama retrieved the vial of powder the queen had given him—a scraping from the finger bone of Raamajit the Exalted, one of the old gods. He cracked the cork open and inhaled the wondrous scent. There was little enough powder inside, but its very odor sent a rush of power coursing through him, power he used to shore up the mental walls he'd erected against Rümayesh.

When Kweilo's lazy pace delivered him to the summit at last, Brama replaced the stopper, hid the vial away, and dropped down from the saddle with a heavy thump against the stone. Kweilo immediately began nibbling on the nearby ironweed. Rümayesh, meanwhile, swiveled her great horned head toward him. Amusement rolled off her in waves, but she said nothing, and neither did he. As her attention returned to the sand, Brama lifted his spyglass and studied the horizon, looking for the telltale signs of ships.

They were a day's ride from the Mirean encampment, where Queen Alansal had a small fleet of cutters ranging far ahead along the caravan trail and elsewhere to spy for the Kings' fleet. But she'd ordered a dozen more teams to search nearer to the caravanserai: a second line of defense should the Kings capture the Mirean scout ships. The queen had overwhelming numbers. If the estimations of her generals were correct, the Kings' galleons might outnumber the queen's dunebreakers slightly, but the Mirean ships easily housed twice the number of soldiers.

But all knew the size of their forces was but half the story, and perhaps the lesser half at that. The Kings had had centuries to gather their strength for just such an attack. They had the favor of the gods. They had the asirim. They had their Blade Maidens and Silver Spears. If that weren't enough, they'd scoured the desert for its magical artifacts, hoarding all they could find. The Kings might have been loath to use such artifacts in the past lest knowledge of them escape, but Alansal was certain they would use them now that their rule was in jeopardy.

As the sun began to set, Brama rode down the slope. To the northeast, he spotted movement. A pair of qirin drove across the desert, kicking up sand, the sun shining red off the sapphire-blue scales of their maned necks while their long, burnished tails trailed like pennants in the wind. Their riders were Mae and Shu-fen, twin sisters and the very same warriors who had accompanied Juvaan when Brama had first arrived at their camp.

They were two of the Damned, warriors who'd sworn their lives to the queen. Like all the Damned, they wore brightly painted armor and helms with demon masks that covered their faces. Brama had assumed they'd been assigned their mounts or that they'd hunted them in the wilds of the Mirean highlands, but Juvaan told him that the *qirin* had chosen the twins. Both Mae and Shu-fen had been sentenced to life working in the queen's mines for premeditated murder. Legend had it the beasts could look into a mortal's soul and see a path toward redemption. If they did, the prisoners were freed.

So it had been with Mae and Shu-fen—the two qirin had, in no uncertain terms, saved the lives of the warriors who rode them. It was a sacred honor, but more than this, it was an unbreakable bond between the saved and the savior.

As Mae and Shu-fen neared, Brama hailed them. They didn't return the greeting, however. They were too busy trying to calm their mounts. The qirins' coats twitched. Their tails flicked. They fought their reins. Mae let it go on for some time, watching what they would do, but then she issued a trilling whistle and the qirin calmed.

"What is it?" Brama asked.

"They feeling something," she said in halting Sharakhan. "How you say? Dangers?"

"Something dangerous," Brama replied.

"Something dangerous," Mae said imperfectly. She smiled a quick, proud smile and then spoke in rapid Mirean to Shu-fen.

Over the past few weeks, Brama had often lost the sense of the desert that had come so easily to him when he'd been alone. But just then it returned in a rush. He had a sense that something wasn't quite right, that the world around him was different somehow, in the midst of a change. His gut churned from it.

He drew his shamshir and stared across the dunes, trying to locate the source. He knew it was out there somewhere, but the desert ahead of him was completely empty, devoid of all save a rise of dark stone in the distance and the occasional cough of spindrift. Kweilo, against her nature, was eerily calm. Her ears were pinned back and her tail was low. The qirin began to prance. They tugged hard at their reins as Shu-fen and Mae fought to keep them still. Waves of heat and steam trailed from their nostrils. These were beasts trained for war, and qirin met fear with aggression.

Rümayesh still sat atop her column of stone, staring down like a lynx that heard a scorpion shifting beneath the sand.

What is it? Brama asked her.

Receiving no answer, he pulled his gaze back to the landscape ahead. He swore something had just *shifted*. Most likely it was just the heat rising off the dunes, but it hadn't felt that way.

There. He saw it again.

At the top of the next dune, a strange phenomenon presented itself. The horizon seemed to tilt, then tumble, then right itself before tilting again. It looked as though the air itself had been given life, an elemental of some sort, or a demon.

From the corner of his eye he saw Rümayesh leap down from her perch and charge across the sand. To his left, Shu-fen let out a "Hiyah!" and spurred her qirin forward. Mae mirrored her, the two of them charging toward some other perceived threat.

Brama, however, couldn't take his eyes from the strange vision ahead. A dozen paces away, sand was kicking up with soft but quickly intensifying crunching sounds. Footsteps, Brama realized, charging straight for him. He lifted his sword and managed one hard swing before he felt something barrel into his chest.

He was thrown violently to the sand. Kweilo skipped away, and the sky seemed to melt, revealing a shriveled, blackened face. An asir, he saw, a girl once, now a wisp of a thing with the features of a starving gutter wren: emaciated ribs, cadaverous face, sticklike limbs.

Searing lines of pain lit along Brama's chest as her long claws tore at him. A great bellow of pain escaped him, half caused by fear as the asir opened her jaws impossibly wide, a rabid bone crusher going in for the kill. The asir fought to reach his neck around the shamshir Brama had managed to wedge between her jaws. The terrible swipes of her clawed hands continued to tear at the flesh along his ribs. He couldn't keep taking this kind of damage but, Bakhi's swift hammer, he dare not take his attention from girl's mouth. He rocked the sword back and forth, cutting deeply. Black blood oozed. Fell hot against Brama's face, dripped in his mouth. The asir hardly seemed to care about the mess Brama's sword was making of her cheeks, teeth, and jaws. She fought with a mad, singular intent: to end his life.

Only when Brama had pulled the sword free and managed to lever it against her neck did she have any sense of self-preservation. She rolled away and came up quick, swiping viciously at his shamshir. So inhuman was her strength that the blow sent the sword spinning from his grip. But Brama was already reaching for his belt. He managed to pull his kenshar free and was bringing it up hard as the asir darted in again. He drove the knife beneath her jaw. Gripping the top of her head, he sent it further, levering it back and forth like a thief's blade working the lid off a chest.

The asir's entire body fell into a paroxysm. The terrible scream she released was a thing that felt separate and alive. The sound *crawled* across his skin, but he kept sawing, until finally the asir fell silent and slumped over him. He threw the frail body aside, wondering at how little she weighed and the terrible strength she'd just exhibited.

Ignoring the foundry of pain in his gut, Brama made it to his feet. He looked wildly around, expecting more asirim to come rushing at him, but there were none. To his left, Mae and her qirin fought an asir with long, gangly limbs. The asir's whole left side was burning in blue flames, but it hardly seemed to notice. As Brama limped forward, the asir charged. Mae's demon mask grinned as she pulled at the reins and her qirin reared. Its hooves pounded the asir's upraised arms, and then it twisted with sinuous grace to avoid the asir's lunge. Its mouth stretched wide and it doused the asir in fresh turquoise flames.

The asir staggered and fell to its knees. In that moment, Mae rode past, swept her tassled dao sword across the thing's neck, and it fell back to the sand. Its head, nearly severed from its neck, twitched a moment and then lay still as the flames licking its body sent dark smoke billowing into a cobalt sky.

Near the standing stones, Rümayesh had come upright from a dark shape lying prone on the sand. Another asir. Rümayesh leapt, and suddenly there was a taller, gangly asir caught in her grip. She bore her weight down on it, pinning it to the sand while all three of her tails pierced its chest over and over. When she bit into the asir's neck, it lost its struggle, and Rümayesh yanked her tails free. Black blood flew in three grand arcs.

Shu-fen was riding hard up the windward side of the dune to join Mae. She slowed her mount when she saw the asir lying there unmoving, its body aflame. The two of them reined their qirin over, wary of more asirim, but no more materialized. Mae's armor had been scored in several places. Shu-fen, however, was favoring her right side, one gauntleted hand pressed tightly against her thigh. Brama knew serious wounds when he saw them; the flow of blood was enough that he wondered if she'd make it.

"Can I help?" he asked.

Shu-fen lifted her head. A moment later, she used the tip of her sword to point at Brama's chest. Her face was hidden behind the mask of her helm, but Brama could feel her stare.

Brama looked down. He was so accustomed to pain and his body's ability to heal itself that he hadn't realized how bad his own wounds were. Pain was pain. Give it attention and it would soar to the heavens, but let it be and it would eventually dwindle. Still, as he took in the mess the asir had made of his flesh, he felt some of the same terrible twinges he'd had when he'd been a prisoner to Rümayesh and she'd tortured him daily.

For just a moment, he lamented the life he might once have led, the loves he might have had had his body not been ruined by her attentions. He thought again of returning to Sharakhai. Of returning to Jax, the woman he'd come to love and who'd somehow come to love him. But he couldn't. Do that and Rümayesh would use her against him.

I would never use her against you, not after all you've done for me.

Brama cursed himself. He'd grown more adept at keeping Rümayesh out of his mind, but the pain had caused his concentration to slip. He began the process of replacing his barriers and said to her, *Are there more of them?*

He felt the warbling sensation near his heart—Rümayesh's laughter as felt through their shared bond. *I don't know why you won't believe me, Brama. Your wish is my command! Tell me to leave your Jax alone and it shall be so. Tell me you wish to return to her and it will happen.*

With the pain it was difficult, but Brama felt the walls slip securely into place at last.

As you will, Rümayesh said, and crouched over the asir she'd slain as if she were about to dissect it.

As Shu-fen took a bag of medicinals from her saddle bag and began to dress her own wounds, Brama wondered why the Kings would send only a handful of asir. He had no answers, and soon Mae was dismounting to tend to *his* wounds. The bandages she wrapped around his waist were quickly soaked with blood. With her demon helm off, Brama could see her face clearly at last. She had fair features and eyes of bright, jade green, a sign of good fortune in Mirea. She kept glancing at Brama with worry, but he merely shook his head and tried to reassure her. "All will be well." Mae's pinched lips and pallid cheeks made it clear how unconvinced she was.

Soon he, Mae, and Shu-fen were headed back toward camp, while Rü-mayesh remained to look for more asirim. They arrived near nightfall, and Brama and Shu-fen were led straight to the hospital ship. The physic, a man who looked too young to be going to war, and far too young to know anything about medicine, tended to Brama first. As he unwrapped the blood-soaked bandages, Mae's eyes went wide. The deep gashes hurt terribly, but they had already started to mend. Many had closed. By morning the bleeding would have stopped entirely. By the following evening, all the wounds would be closed and scar tissue starting to form.

Mae and the physic engaged in hushed conversation, excluding Brama. When they'd gone on for some time, Brama broke in. "I'd like to speak to the queen." When neither responded, he said, slower this time, "Queen Alansal."

They refused him. When he became insistent, they made hand signs for him to remain for a short while. He was just about to leave the hospital, their concerns over his well-being be damned, when Juvaan Xin-Lei, the tall Mirean with ivory skin and snow-white hair, came striding in.

"Say anything you wish to say to the queen to me," he said when Brama repeated his demand.

Brama considered pressing him, but what would be the point? Juvaan pulled up a chair to his bedside, and Brama told him all of it: the attack, the strange asirim, how crazed they were.

At this, Juvaan sniffed. "The asirim have always been crazed."

"So the stories say," Brama replied, "but have you ever heard of them being masked as they were, almost impossible to see?"

"No, but we are fighting not only the Kings of Sharakhai, but a Queen of Qaimir as well: a known blood mage."

"Even so, why would the Kings send the asirim against you in that way? Why be content to attack a few forward scouts?"

"An excellent question," Juvaan said, standing, "one my queen and I will consider carefully." He bowed from the waist. "Thank you, Brama Junayd'ava. There's no telling what might have happened had you and Rümayesh not been there. We are in your debt."

Brama gave a nod in return, and Juvaan left.

Late that night, Brama felt something stir. He'd become well attuned to

Rümayesh and the impression she made on his senses. She was distant, still in the desert. But there was another scent very much like hers. And it was near. Very near.

Night had fallen, but by the light of the small lamp near the infirmary's entrance, he could see that the other patients were sleeping. He crept toward the door, slipping easily into the gait that had served him so well in his days slinking over Sharakhai's rooftops.

When he heard footsteps and a hushed conversation approaching the top of the stairs leading up to deck, he tested several of the cabin doors across the passageway, finding the third one unlocked. He waited for the voices to pass by, then slipped quiet as a shadow up to deck, over the ship's side, and down to the sand. He was careful of his wounds, but it still wasn't enough. Eyes screwed tight, one hand clawing the sand involuntarily, he waited for the pain to pass.

Rhia was a crescent in the sky, leaving much of the camp in darkness. A scattering of pockets were lit by hanging lanterns. Brama avoided them all, sliding from shadow to shadow, heading steadily toward the queen's pavilion.

The pavilion's canvas walls were in place to keep away the night's chill, and there were a dozen guards posted outside, making it all but impossible for Brama to get anywhere near it. He didn't need to, though, for just then the pavilion's flaps were pulled wide, and out stepped a creature that, despite all Brama's experience with Rümayesh, made his knees go weak.

It was tall, with skin that glistened in the moonlight. Twin horns curved like scimitars up and away from its bald head. A tail moved, snakelike, behind it. When it had taken several steps from the tent, its four arms moved rhythmically, seeming to draw in the night. It was gathering power, Brama realized. He could feel it. But then its arms stopped, and its head swiveled toward his hiding place in the darkness. Eyes that seemed too small for its head shone like pearls. Brama couldn't be sure, but it seemed to smile. Then burst into a cloud of locusts. A droning sound made Brama flinch, made his wounds itch. The cloud flew up and away in an undulating mass and in moments was gone, leaving behind a chill that prickled Brama's skin.

Chapter 11

R AMAHD WAS CROUCHED, as he had been for the last hour, along the edge of a roof overlooking the dry, cracked bed of the River Haddah. Even for Sharakhai the day was scorching. The wind was listless, the very air hot as a foundry. It was near high sun, a time when most would be indoors, taking meals with their families and having a nap before returning to work, yet the streets were busy. It was a sign of the looming war. Many were nervous that the Malasani fleet, which had been spotted to the southeast, would arrive any day.

The spyglass Ramahd held to his eye was trained across the riverbed on an old mansion, the finest along a stretch of homes that might once have been grand but now reflected, at best, a middling affluence. The windows of the central room, and the double doors open on its far side, offered a limited view of the mansion's central patio. On that patio, sitting and talking easily with one another, with a bottle of what looked to be fine Qaimiri brandy between them, was a bent old woman dressed in funereal black and the portly frame of Basilio Baijani.

They'd been speaking for some time and things appeared to be wrapping up. The woman, a figure known to most in Sharakhai as the Widow, was pointing east, perhaps toward the House of Kings, while Basilio, arms crossed over his ample chest, seemed to take in everything she was saying, then nodded and stood. He made a few placating gestures before kissing the Widow's offered hand.

As Basilio was led from the room by a servant boy, Ramahd moved to the edge of the building and slipped down a rope to ground level. He strode along the near side of the river while, on the far side, Cicio fell into step twenty paces behind Basilio, who was flanked by two guards, a man and a woman Ramahd knew quite well. All three were dressed in ordinary Sharakhani garb.

Ramahd was pleased that their gamble with the Widow had paid off, but he was still uncomfortable with having sent Tiron off to a drug den to lay the trap. Cicio had been incensed, especially considering they'd just lost Vrago, Cicio's closest friend. "We can still go to the embassy, my lord," Cicio had said in Qaimiran, pleading with Ramahd. "We'll find your blood so Meryam can no longer track you. We'll see you safe. Just don't send Tiron into those fucking dens again."

It was the same argument he'd had with Tiron. "We'd never make it," Ramahd said, "and if somehow we did, we'd never make it out again."

Cicio knew better than most how tight security around the House of Kings had become. He'd scouted them on their return to Sharakhai and told Ramahd it would be no good trying to sneak over the walls, not until the war was over.

"Let *me* go," Cicio pleaded. "*I'll* take the lotus."

Tiron had agreed to smoke a bit of black lotus while he was there. It was necessary for his story to be believed.

"No," Ramahd said. "Tiron's been there before. They'd suspect something if it was you."

In the end Tiron had decided to go to the same drug den he'd used in the past. While there, after breathing in the smoke that loosened so many tongues, he spun a tale within hearing of those who ran the den: that Lord Ramahd Amansir of Qaimir had found a way to the Enclave and, fearing they would only shelter one person from Queen Meryam's anger, had abandoned Tiron to his own fate. It was bait, pure and simple, designed to lure Basilio out of hiding. The story would reach the Widow, and the Widow,

Ramahd had gambled, would have a way to contact the queen. As it was Enclave business, Meryam would send Basilio to investigate.

And so she had. Now it was simply a matter of convincing Basilio it was in his best interests to share.

Ahead, Basilio and his escort wove around a mule cart and turned a corner. Cicio, instead of following, hopped an ironwork fence and ran quick and low toward the rear of the mansion's small estate, planning on catching the group from another angle while Ramahd chased them from behind.

Ramahd picked up his pace, weaving through the crowd and turning the corner. The street ahead eased to the left. Dozens walked along it: men with clothes baskets on their heads, gutter wrens squatting in the shade near a tea house, a clutch of collegia students in flaxen robes listening to a portly priest of Bakhi. Of Basilio, however, Ramahd saw no sign. Nor did he see his guards.

His heart beginning to pound, Ramahd loped to where the street met the cart path that ran along the rear of the estate where he thought he'd find Cicio, but Cicio had vanished too. Ramahd continued down the street, craning his neck to look farther along the curve. In the distance he thought he saw Cicio's cocksure stride taking him through the arched mouth of a narrow alley, but that didn't make sense—Cicio hadn't had the time to run that far.

Ramahd sprinted after him. The crowd stared, but Ramahd was well past the point of caring. He reached the alley, where the buildings were four stories high and crowded shoulder to shoulder. It left the alley in deep shade. It was also perfectly, completely empty. No Cicio. No Basilio. No one at all.

There was something off about this. Like a home that had witnessed some recent, violent death.

"Cicio?" he rasped as he ran down the alley, looking through the doorways, through the slats in the windows. By the time he reached the next intersection, he was out of breath and drenched in sweat despite the parched desert air.

"Cicio!"

He continued straight, his stomach twisted in knots. Far ahead, he caught the flare of an embroidered silk skirt passing beneath an archway that led to an abandoned building. Ramahd sprinted toward it and found an empty floor covered in dirt and stones, filled with the detritus of forgotten industry. Other doorways led deeper into shadow. Rats scattered as he headed for the one opposite the arch.

In the room beyond, he caught sight of a window and halted in his tracks. The window, little more than a gaping hole in the mudbrick, gave a view of the desert. Ramahd blinked at it. Spit gathered in his mouth quickly, painfully. He was supposed to be in the center of the city. He *was* in the city's center. And yet the view was of the open land to the northwest of Sharakhai. It was rocks and sand dunes as far as the eye could see. Looking back the way he'd come, he saw a square arch, and a stairwell leading down. The hum of the city had been replaced with a faint sound of whistling wind.

Years ago Ramahd had traveled to his uncle's estate along the edge of the Austral Sea. He and his cousin had hiked through an ancient forest to the shore and watched the sun set. They'd laughed at the stories their parents used to tell them: stories of a forest alive, that harbored ill intent, stories of snatchers who lived in the trees, dead men and women who were drawn to those who lingered. When the sun went down, however, it took their courage with it. The forest that had seemed meek only hours ago now seemed indomitable. Malign. Hungry beyond all measure. They who'd felt like conquerors now felt meaningless, and each step felt as if it were summoning the very snatchers they'd earlier scoffed at. The hopelessness Ramahd felt as he wandered the abandoned building felt the same. He was trapped in a place he could never hope to understand, much less gain sway over.

He was no longer some impressionable young man, though. The twisting feeling in his gut had swelled since he turned down the street after Basilio— and passed through the outer edge of the spell that now held him in its sway. He was no stranger to the inner workings of magic, but this particular weaving was so refined, so intricate, he could discern neither its edges nor the pattern of its fabric.

When he heard the sound of scraping from below, he took a set of stairs down and began to expand his awareness. He stood there, wrapped in wonder, as the spell and its sheer scope became known to him at last. Dozens of threads reached out, supporting it like a grand spiderweb, connecting this place not only to others in Sharakhai, but to more in the desert as well. He considered dismantling it but had no idea where to begin. It was easy to undermine a spell as it was being formed, but quite another to unravel one that had already been cast. This one felt complex as clockwork, as if many had lent a hand to its making, and in so doing had concealed the method of its creation, and therefore of its destruction.

He followed the hall at the bottom of the stairs to a courtyard. Of the four people standing there, Ramahd recognized three as members of the Enclave's inner circle. There was Prayna, their de facto leader: a woman Ramahd's age with a serious face and soulful eyes. Undosu: an old Kundhuni man with wrinkled black skin and a leather cap with a pattern of shells sewn into it. Nebahat: a man with dark skin, a smile as bright as sunshine, and a painted yellow forehead with a bright red stripe running down its center. The last was a young Mirean woman of perhaps fifteen summers whose light skin appeared untouched by the harshness of the desert sun. Ramahd had heard of her: Meiying, a prodigy who'd risen quickly through the Enclave's ranks and seized the inner circle's final seat, not merely by means of the power she commanded but the clarity of her insights.

Calm Prayna, evenhanded Prayna, stepped forward. The sun cut in through a hole above and shone on her pale green head scarf and its golden chains. "Out of respect for our past dealings we offer this one meeting."

"Where's Cicio?"

Prayna glanced to one corner of the room. As a cloud passed over the sun, Ramahd saw him, Cicio, lying on the dirty floor, unconscious but breathing. When the sun returned, he was gone.

"What do you want?" Prayna asked.

"I want us both to prosper," Ramahd replied.

Prayna's humoring smile made the purple scrollwork tattoos over her eyebrows curl. "You want to be saved from your new queen's vengeance."

"The last I checked, she was your queen too. Besides, wouldn't saving myself be considered prospering?"

Nebahat's smile grew wider. "What does that have to do with the Enclave?"

Ramahd felt as if he were walking a tightrope—one misstep and all would be over. "When Meryam first came to Sharakhai, she accepted your offer to meet but refused to join your ranks." Ramahd took them in one by one. "She claimed, as I recall, that it wasn't necessary, that it would be imprudent given her position as the daughter to King Aldouan and heir to the throne."

The pipe Undosu had to his lips had no tabbaq in its bowl, but he puffed on it just the same. After considering Ramahd with a wary stare, he removed the pipe from his mouth, pointed the end at Ramahd, and spoke in a thick Kundhuni accent, "No mage is *forced* into the Enclave. You know this as well as we do."

"And yet you must have wondered, despite her claims, if there were other reasons behind her refusal."

Prayna, ever the pragmatist, frowned. "Say what you mean to say."

"Meryam declined because it would give you too much power over her. It freed her to use your charity against you. She made a study of you and your ways, your capabilities, your politics. She's gained more power through her marriage to Kiral, and now she'll use that knowledge against you as she moves on to another conquest: mastery of the Enclave itself."

Uncomfortable glances passed between the magi. "Do you have proof?" Prayna asked.

"In Qaimir, she broke Hamzakiir's mind. She's been dominating him since, using him as her slave."

Ramahd thought they might argue with him, claiming, as many would, that Hamzakiir had been killed by the ehrekh, Guhldrathen, during the Battle of Blackspear. It hadn't been common knowledge at first, but the returning soldiers had told their tales, and the story had spread like wildfire through Sharakhai. Instead, Prayna turned and motioned to a sack on the floor, the sack that contained Kiral's head, the one he'd secreted away in the back rooms of an armorer he'd come to trust.

Behind Prayna, one of the windows had come to life. Instead of shadows and an abandoned room beyond, it showed the back room of that very armory. Silver Spears were tearing it apart, looking for something. A Blade Maiden stood among them, guiding their search.

"It's fortunate for you," Prayna said, picking up the sack and holding it out for Ramahd to take, "that we are not thieves."

The vision through the window faded as Ramahd accepted it and looked inside. There, as he'd left it, was the head of Kiral, King of Kings, the man whose face and body had been altered by Meryam to look like Hamzakiir.

"You know the truth, then," Ramahd said. "She's already enslaved one mage. What makes you think she won't enslave *you*?"

Nebahat—for some reason his orange turban had become bright and almost painful to look at—seemed surprised. "You speak of crimes against the Enclave." He waved to the sack. "Hamzakiir has much to answer for in this regard."

"Which may become part of the problem. Even if Meryam's designs on Sharakhai were entirely innocent—and I assure you they are not— Hamzakiir's will would eventually affect her. He trusts no one. Meryam is the same. They will not suffer the Enclave's existence once they take the reins in Sharakhai."

"What do you want from us?" Prayna asked.

All around him the windows, the doorways, and the broken section of wall changed. They revealed different places, none of them like the next. Some rooms were shaded, others bright as the sun-scorched desert, others lit by candles or hearths. Men, women, even children stood within them, silent, expectant, as if awaiting Ramahd's answer. This was a full meeting of the Enclave, then. They had all come to hear his plea. And when he was done, they would render their verdict.

"I want Meryam to answer for her crimes," Ramahd said, turning to take them all in. "I want the rightful heir to the Qaimiri throne, Duke Hektor, to take her place. But in order to do that I need help. I need protection. I need to be shielded from Meryam's attempts to find me until I can reach the House of Kings and expose her."

It was a straightforward request, and Ramahd felt hopeful. Some of the magi opened their arms, palms facing him, a gesture of acceptance in the desert. But more and more, the gathered magi gripped their hands into fists and crossed them over their chests. By the time the circle was done, crossed arms outnumbered open palms three to one. Ramahd thought the inner circle might vote as well—and perhaps they would have had it not gone so heavily against him—but what did it matter in the end? They could count as well as Ramahd.

Nebahat's bright smile faded. As did Undosu's curious, piercing stare. Meiying had a troubled expression that made Ramahd think she wasn't altogether comfortable with the decision just made by the circle. Still, she remained silent, watching and waiting. Prayna merely smiled, a pleasant enough thing, Ramahd supposed, though clearly at odds with her pitiless gaze. "I'm afraid your request must be denied"—she motioned to the sack gripped in his right hand—"but you must do as you see fit for you and your nation. We won't interfere in your quest."

"She's got to you," Ramahd said, staring into Prayna's depthless eyes. "She's already made an arrangement with the Enclave, hasn't she?"

The circle remained silent. Many in the windows began to fade.

The disappointment Ramahd had felt at the vote was already turning to fear. "You'll come to regret this." Gods how he hated the pleading sound of his voice. It was just that he'd pinned so many hopes on this meeting. "You cannot cede so much power to Meryam and expect it to go unpunished."

More magi faded. One, a woman with a scowl on her face who'd voted for Ramahd, stared hard at Prayna before turning and fading like the others. Soon Ramahd was alone with the four members of the inner circle. Prayna was the first to leave, then Nebahat with a sad smile. Undosu puffed on his unlit pipe and turned away as if Ramahd didn't exist. As they left through different doorways, Ramahd felt them being whisked away to other parts of the city, each departure undoing a part of the spell that had constructed this strange meeting place.

The doorways and windows, instead of revealing homes all across the city, now opened onto the dirty floors and broken walls of the abandoned building. All save one. Only Meiying remained.

"Please," Ramahd said to her. "Don't do this."

"It's already done," she said, her tone polite but firm as new-forged steel.

She waved to the final doorway, which showed a dark, smoke-filled room. Men and women lay sprawled over the floor, eyes fluttering, their minds taken in what Ramahd recognized as the pall of black lotus. Among them Ramahd saw Tiron, curled on the floor like a child, his eyes closed, fluttering madly as if gripped in nightmare.

"You should hurry," Meiying said as she headed toward the doorway.

The view changed as she stepped through—into a comfortable looking room filled with shelves and scrolls and carvings of ivory and jade. Then it too faded, and Ramahd was left alone with Cicio, who was lying in the corner as before.

"Come," Ramahd said, rousing him. "Tiron's in trouble."

When they reached the drug den, Tiron was curled up as Ramahd had seen through the vision. His eyes were no longer moving, however. Cicio dropped to his knees and shook Tiron, but Ramahd didn't bother. Tiron was dead.

Cicio stood and stared at the young tough, Pony, who ran the den. "You let him die, ah?" Cicio pulled his knife and pointed the tip at Pony's chest. "You let him die?"

Pony raised his hands, his long hair unbound and falling around his shoulders. "He paid for what he wanted!" He backed up as Cicio advanced. "He paid! What was I supposed to do?"

Before he'd even finished, Cicio barreled into him and drove him down against the filthy floor. Pony screamed and twisted as Cicio stabbed him through the ribs. Over and over Cicio drove the knife home while, Mighty Alu shield his eyes, Ramahd stood and watched. It felt like sweet justice, a righting of this terrible wrong. Of course, it was anything but. This wasn't Pony's fault. It was Ramahd's. Ramahd had sent him here knowing full well how sweet the lotus's call would be to Tiron.

By the time Ramahd pulled Cicio off, Pony's kaftan was soaked red with blood from a dozen wounds. Cicio spat on him, kicked him as he writhed on the floor and stared wide-eyed at the ceiling.

"Tiron," Ramahd said to Cicio. "Help me with Tiron."

The look Cicio gave him was crazed, as if he had half a mind to attack Ramahd as he had Pony, but then he put his knife away and moved to Tiron's side.

That night, they buried their friend in the desert.

Chapter 12

As the Shieldwives carried Ramela's body away, the color drained from Çeda's world, leaving everything a washed-out haze. Shame over Ramela's death filled her like a fetid stream. She wished she could wash the taint of it from her, but how could she? It was all her fault.

She should have waited. She should have forced Ramela to choose a different asir, any but Amile. She should have had another Shieldwife attempt this first bonding ritual. Now it was ruined. The other asirim had seen what Amile had done. They'd *felt* it. Would they follow his lead? Would they allow their pent-up anger and frustration, sentiments that had been building for four centuries, to outweigh their desire for revenge against the Kings?

And who among the Shieldwives would even be willing to try? One or two might be brave or stupid enough, but even if they did, their fear might cause them to falter at the worst time. Çeda couldn't allow any of them to risk it until she knew how to forge their bonds safely.

She suddenly realized she was alone with Leorah. The others had all left, and Çeda couldn't rightly recall if they'd spoken words in parting and, if they had, whether she'd responded.

"They've lost so much," Leorah was saying. "It's been eroded, generation after generation, so that now, in some of them, there's practically nothing left."

The memory of Amile attacking the ship played out in Çeda's mind. He'd *wanted* Ramela to attack him, and had used her fear of the asirim to make her do so. And when Ramela had succumbed to that desire and drawn her sword, it had allowed Amile to sidestep his bond with Çeda and sever the one that Ramela had been trying to create with him.

"His will is so strong," Çeda breathed.

"No," Leorah said. "You have it precisely wrong. Amile acted as he did not because he wanted to, but because he has so little will left. In his moment of weakness, the compulsion laid down by the desert gods to protect the Kings of Sharakhai drove him."

"But I bonded with Kerim. It lasted for months."

"Kerim, I fear, was a very special case. Mavra and Sedef may be forged of the same stuff as Kerim, perhaps one or two others, but how many more? And how to tell them apart? We may not know until their will breaks and they attack."

Çeda's arm was burning so badly she sucked her breath through clenched teeth while shaking away a bit of the pain. Leorah studied her, the concern plain on her face. "It's not too late to send them back to the adichara. Try again another day."

"If we do that, the Kings will kill them all."

In the distance, several asirim wailed.

Leorah glanced their way, then turned quickly as the wind threw sand and dust against her. "Of that there can be no doubt," she said, blinking the dust from her eyes, "but you must see that if you don't find a solution soon, the bonds you now share with them will break. You'll be risking not only their lives, but your own and the lives of your Shieldwives as well."

It was true. Çeda felt her links to the asirim weighing on her. The wailing in the distance ceased, though a moment later one of them began to sob pitifully.

Just past nightfall, as the sun lit the western clouds a terrible, burning orange, Çeda went into the desert and beckoned to Mavra. With plodding steps she came, stopping some distance away. Amile remained sheltered by the others, his mood murderous, while Mavra's worry for him shone like a beacon. She feared the same might happen to her, or to any of her children. She feared Çeda's response if it did.

Before Çeda could say a word, Mavra spoke in a thin rasp. *"I heard you. Speaking with your great-grandmother."* She waited, perhaps hoping Çeda would answer her unspoken question. When Çeda didn't, she went on, *"Will you do it? Will you send us away?"*

Çeda was uncertain about many things, but not about this. "I would die first."

There were tears in Mavra's eyes. She could feel the honesty in Çeda's words, and was grateful for it. *"Your friend,"* she began. *"My heart fills with salt at her loss. Amile was once so gentle."*

"I remember," Çeda said, recalling many of her sweetest memories of him.

"It wasn't him."

"I know," Çeda replied easily. "I know it wasn't Amile's fault. But we can't proceed until we're sure it won't happen again."

Çeda could feel Mavra's desperation, her worry that she would, just as Leorah had said, lose everyone because she'd agreed to leave the blooming fields. In a display of perfect helplessness, she spread her hands wide. *"I don't know how to help."*

"I know."

"Then why have you summoned me?"

Çeda stepped forward but stopped when Mavra took a step back. She tried again, and this time Mavra remained. Çeda embraced her. "To let you know, all of you, that we will find a way through this. I won't rest until it's done. Do you hear me?"

Mavra didn't respond, but Çeda felt her fear diminish. There, where the fear once was, a hope was born. It was small and tentative, but after so much worry among the asirim, it was infectious—Mavra waddled toward her children with a lighter heart, and Çeda felt the rest of them begin to hope too, even Amile.

Sedef stood apart from the crowd, tall, unyielding. *It won't last.*

Çeda faced him. "For now, that isn't what matters. Sleep. Rest. We'll find a way."

——— ● —→

Two days after Ramela was buried, while the evening meal was being prepared, Çeda was sitting with Sümeya on the deck of Leorah's yacht. Sümeya hummed an old Sharakhani folk song while inking a new tattoo across Çeda's left arm. It was a welcome respite from the rhythms of the last few days. The tapping of the needle, the constant pinpricks into her skin, were helping to distract her from the pain in her right arm. The ache had grown over the course of the last few days, but focusing on the sharp pain from the new tattoo—indeed, focusing on the various tattoos she now had over her body— helped to take her mind off the slowly growing knowledge that she couldn't keep Mavra and the others bonded to her like this forever.

Sümeya switched to another bowl of ink, one of six she had sitting around the deck, and pointed to the inside of Çeda's bicep. "Here." When Sümeya had shifted her stool into better position, Çeda twisted her arm so that it rested on Sümeya's thighs. "Now hold still."

"I always hold still."

"No, you don't." She was staring at Çeda's right leg, which was bouncing up and down again. Çeda stilled it, and Sümeya laughed. "You're like a little girl with a whole tray of baklava."

Çeda glanced over the side of the yacht, where several Shieldwives were preparing food.

Sümeya paused, following Çeda's gaze. "Sometimes you're like an open book, Çedamihn. Why don't you just spit it out?"

"It's nothing."

Sümeya rolled her eyes and went back to work.

"It's just," Çeda said under her breath, "I don't know what to do."

Sümeya continued to concentrate on Çeda's arm as if she hadn't sensed Çeda's desperation. "I've told you my feelings on the subject."

"Just let them go?"

"Or choose a pairing yourself." She jutted her chin toward the sand, where Jenise was drilling ten others in spearcraft. "Jenise is strong. So is Sedef. Take them. Or another two. There must be some combination that would work. But do it soon. Waiting is only going to make it worse."

Çeda watched them, Jenise shouting the sequence, the women spinning or thrusting their spears to the proper position. They were drills Sümeya had taught them only a week earlier, and for the most part they'd taken to it well. They were far from perfect, however, and Çeda wondered how far they could advance given how engrained their bad habits were. But they were eager to learn and rarely grumbled when asked to correct their mistakes.

Çeda had said as much to Sümeya last night, and Sümeya had laughed long and hard. "Çedamihn Ahyanesh'ala . . . I never thought I'd see the day."

"What?" Çeda asked.

"There may be a bit of Sayabim in you after all."

Sayabim had been Çeda's instructor in bladecraft in the House of Maidens. She'd been an exacting mistress, always complaining that Çeda was too old to learn properly. Çeda started to laugh too—she supposed she *had* learned more from Sayabim than she'd thought—but the sounds of their laughter had only seemed to sour Melis's mood, who was trying to read in her bunk.

As Sümeya tapped away, Çeda considered her counsel and remembered Kerim, the asir who had bonded with her before the Battle in King's Harbor. "We might find a pair who could bond as Kerim and I did, but how many more?"

"You may not *need* more. Sometimes all it takes to loosen a jam in the streets is to get that first cart to move. Find two who can bond and the rest may follow."

"Yes, but if we choose wrongly again, that may be the end of it."

Sümeya shrugged, as if to say *who can tell?*

"We have to be certain," Çeda said, her words half question, half declaration.

"The future is *never* certain."

"I can't gamble with others' lives."

"You already have, and will again." Sümeya lifted her head and stared at Çeda, the gaze of the First Warden returning. "We're entering a proper war now, Çeda, and whether you recognize it or not, war is a study in attrition." She returned to her inking. "You have time yet, but don't lose the opening battle because you refused to make a move."

Çeda knew Sümeya was right; there was a path through this forest. Çeda just had to find it.

As Sümeya continued to expand the image along her bicep, Çeda concentrated on her right hand, where Zaïde's tattoo hemmed in the poison from her adichara wound. Staring at it always brought her back to her roots. It gave her perspective to think about the dizzying sequence of events that had led to Dardzada depositing her on a cart and leaving her in front of the House of Maidens in a last ditch attempt at saving her life. Her acceptance into the Blade Maidens had followed as a result, and set her on this long, strange, and winding course. Zaïde's tattoo made a sort of fingerless glove around her hand, words and traceries and sigils combining to tell the tale of Çeda's life as a young woman, with hints at her heritage. *The lost are now found*, it said in one place, and nearby, *Bane of the unrighteous*. Zaïde had always meant for her to be a knife, bent toward the heart of the Kings. Çeda's true nature, her purpose, had been there in plain sight for all to see, though most read it differently and assumed it was meant in honor of her service to the Kings.

Her time in the Blade Maidens had led to another tattoo, the one on her left hand. Sümeya had designed and inked it after Çeda had killed Külaşan the Wandering King. A peacock wrapped around her wrist, head low as if bowing. On the back of her hand, surrounded by verdant leaves and lapping water, were the words *Savior of Sharakhai* in beautiful calligraphy. Sümeya, thinking Çeda had been trying to save Külaşan, had thought Çeda a hero. They hadn't spoken of that day since Sümeya had inked the tattoo, but whatever Sümeya's thoughts, Çeda was proud of the images and all they represented. Külaşan had thought of his death as a release, and for Çeda's part, she had never regretted killing her first King.

On her back was the first tattoo Çeda had ever received, this one from Dardzada, the apothecary who'd taken Çeda in after her mother died. Çeda hadn't asked for the tattoo; he'd forced it on her in a drunken rage over what he viewed as intolerable disobedience. *Funnily enough, over my first visit to the blooming fields.* It was an ancient sigil, writ large along the skin between her shoulder blades. For a long while she'd thought it had meant *bastard*, but she'd found out years later from King Husamettín himself that it more properly meant both *one of many* and *many in one*.

Around that tattoo, subsuming it, Leorah had inked another design that spread across the whole of her upper back. It recounted Çeda's involvement in the Night of Endless Swords, the great battle in King's Harbor. Mount Tauriyat, as viewed from the harbor, now hovered over Dardzada's sigil. Around it was wrapped a lyrical retelling of everything that had led up to the battle and what had happened after, including Mesut's death at Çeda's hands. The way Leorah had inked it made the entire design look like a spread-winged falcon, the tips of the wings wrapping around Çeda's shoulders and the rounded muscles of her upper arms.

Only a few weeks ago, Sümeya and Leorah had begun combining their efforts to create sleeves of imagery and words along Çeda's arms. The new additions recounted everything that had led to the Battle of Blackspear. Leorah had continued from Zaïde's design on Çeda's sword hand, connecting it to the falcon wings near her shoulder. Hers told Çeda's tale from the point of view of the tribes, how Çeda had come to the desert, how she'd breathed her spirit into the gathered forces when times were their most bleak, how later she'd fought and then killed Onur with her own knife. The mighty wyrm wrapped her arm, its head resting along her forearm. Onur's great spear, the one given him by the desert gods on Beht Ihman, was pointed toward the gaping maw of the wyrm—one of the great dragons of legend.

Sümeya's design continued from the one she'd inked on Çeda's left hand, telling Çeda's tale from the point of view of a Blade Maiden. How she'd bonded with the asir, Kerim, how she'd brought Mesut's magical golden band to the desert, how she'd used it to create the seventeen: the Forsaken, the asirim who, once liberated from Mesut's bracelet, had vanquished the wyrm in the final battle and helped to turn the tide. Sadly, all of the Forsaken had died shortly after the Battle of Blackspear. Days after the battle had ended, without warning or preamble, those who'd survived had simply fallen to the sand, never to rise again.

Leorah had finished her tattoo on Çeda's right arm two days ago. Sümeya was nearly finished with the one on her left, but there were several important elements remaining. Sümeya was using bright white ink to render Salsanna, the brave woman who'd found the way to free the asirim from Mesut's bracelet. She'd later sacrificed herself to allow one of the Forsaken to take her form. Çeda's pride in her swelled as her likeness took shape.

As Sümeya's clever fingers adjusted Çeda's arm, her thoughts drifted to their time in the desert before they'd reached Ishmantep. They'd shared something then, the two of them losing themselves to passion. For Çeda it had been mixed with a desire to learn more of the Kings' secrets. Even so, her feelings for Sümeya had been real. She'd long wanted to bring it up, to see if Sümeya still felt the same way. But she was worried that Sümeya would be angry, or that she'd tell Çeda it had only been her loneliness and her desire for Nayyan coming through.

And yet the way Sümeya had responded in the blooming fields when she thought Çeda was in danger—terror had filled Sümeya's voice, the sort one saves for those closest to them—made her think that maybe she *should* bring it up. Right then.

She was just about to say something, anything, when Sümeya lifted her hand and stretched. The sun was just touching the horizon. "We'll have to finish tomorrow."

"Sümeya . . ." Çeda began, but just then Melis climbed up from below-decks. Çeda hid her disappointment as Sümeya prepared the salve and bandages she would wrap around the newly inked areas. Melis saw the two of them there and seemed unsure of what to do, what to say.

Çeda twisted her arm, showing her what Sümeya had done. "What do you think?"

"Lovely," she said, and moved past them to sit heavily in one of the four chairs fixed to the deck.

"Don't mind her," Sümeya said to Çeda while applying the salve. "Her moon day has yet to pass."

"*My* moon day?" Melis stood.

Sümeya ignored her.

"*My* moon day?" Melis's face had turned red. "A bit of blood would do you good! At least then you might care about what's *happened*, Sümeya Husamettín'ava." She practically spat the name of the King, Sümeya's father. "You stand here with these women, training them, acting as if the betrayal of all you've come to know and love is nothing! Acting as if what you do will somehow erase the shame you've brought upon yourself. Çeda can't *fix* what the Kings have done. Don't you see that?"

Sümeya finished applying the salve and turned to face Melis. "If you believe that, then why do you stay?"

Melis stared at her own hands, which were shivering with rage or impotence, or both. "I cannot *return* to Sharakhai!"

"That's why you remain, Melis Yusam'ava? Because you fear you'll be killed when you return?"

"I will be! So will you!"

Sümeya spat over the side of the ship. "The Melis I know would never use that as an excuse."

Melis stabbed a finger at Sümeya. "Everything I love is gone!"

"No," Sümeya countered. "You have always loved truth. You have always loved justice. We are finding those things now." She waved to Çeda. "Make no mistake. Just because we now walk the same path as Çeda doesn't mean we believe in all the same things. We have common cause. That's all. Let us walk the path a little farther, see where it takes us. There are more truths to uncover, and I would find them. Then, together, you and I will see where justice truly lies."

Melis looked out into the desert, where the asirim still huddled. They'd hardly moved in the last few days, and their hunger was gnawing at Çeda. It was gnawing at them all.

"They . . ." Melis began.

"They what?" Çeda said.

Melis turned her broad, freckled face toward Çeda, and then she seemed to lose heart. She said no more and left the ship, heading in the opposite direction from the asirim.

Late that night Çeda lay in her bunk, alone in the cabin she shared with Sümeya and Melis. She listened to the songs being sung by the campfire. A dozen voices were raised, and with them, Çeda's mood was lifted as well. Ramela had not been forgotten, but her death was not the heavy cloud it had been two days earlier.

And yet I'm no closer to solving this riddle.

The song came to a rowdy end, accentuated by a reverberant belch from Jenise and a round of drunken laughter from the others. When someone farted loudly, and a new round of giggles ensued, someone started up an ancient camp song about a mare and a stallion. It was Devorah, Leorah having given way to her as the sun had set. The song was bawdy, and Devorah sang it lustily, a fact made all the more amusing for how serious she typically was. As the women began to neigh the notes of the chorus, Çeda heard footsteps reach the deck and climb down into the ship.

Melis came into the cabin, silent and brooding. Instead of going to her bunk at the far end of the cabin, she stopped near Çeda and sat on the edge of Sümeya's bunk. By the light filtering in through the porthole, Çeda could see she was holding something. A small pot. She held it out for Çeda to take.

Çeda sat up and accepted it. "What's this?"

"White ink, to use on the likeness of Salsanna." When Çeda stared at it, confused, Melis went on. "For the tattoo, on your arm."

"I know what it's for"—Çeda opened the lid and smelled the floral scent—"but Sümeya already has ink."

"Not like that she doesn't."

Then Çeda realized. The floral smell . . . "You made this from adichara petals."

"In part, yes."

"The petals are dear to us now."

Melis paused, her hands on her knees, for all the world a lord readying to mete out judgment. "We have enough. I'd rather see that tattoo made in the old way, as Zaïde would have done."

Çeda lifted her right hand. "Zaïde?"

"Yes. She would have mixed petals into the ink for your tattoo, not just soot from the branches." She flicked her hands toward the pot. "Salsanna deserves it."

It was a precious gift, not just the ink but the knowledge of what Zaïde had done. They'd prepared ink for all the women's tattoos, but as Melis had said, they'd used burned branches after removing the thorns. "Thank you," Çeda said.

"It's nothing." Melis slipped into her nightdress and lay down in her bunk, facing away from Çeda.

"Melis, will you tell me what's been eating away at you?"

"Not tonight."

Çeda felt like pressing her, but thought it best to leave it at that. "Very well. Sweet dreams."

For the first time in all their time together away from Sharakhai, Melis responded. "Sweet dreams."

Çeda smiled as she lay her head back down.

The following morning, she woke with a jolt.

Sümeya, sensing it, awoke too. "What?" she asked blearily.

But Çeda ignored her, turning instead to Melis, who was twisting in her bunk, her expression half annoyance, half confusion. "The ink," Çeda said.

"Yes?"

"We use it to tell our tales."

"Yes, but—"

"The asirim can't." Çeda got up, changed into her battle dress. "They have *no one* to tell their tales."

"Of course, but—"

"Meet me outside, both of you." She took to the stairs, and called over her shoulder. "And bring Leorah. Quickly!"

Chapter 13

EMRE ACCOMPANIED YOUNG Shaikh Aríz to greet the two tribes as they arrived at the oasis. The Rushing Waters of Tribe Kenan had arrived early, their fleet like a herd of akhalas surging over the dunes. By the time the White Trees of Tribe Halarijan joined them near sunset, a feast was already underway. They ate a stew of roasted lamb, tomatoes, and sweet onions, then charred flatbread with smoked eggplant, crumbled cheese and fire-roasted peppers laid over it, and finished with a rice pudding that was so creamy, so perfectly spiced with cinnamon and clove, it put a smile on everyone's face.

There wasn't as much to go around as everyone would have liked—they were all aware of the need to preserve supplies, especially as they headed into late summer—but everything had been prepared with love, and the night was filled with so much dancing, music, stories, and drink that no one gave much heed to the fact that their bellies weren't completely full.

There were even a few games of skill and strength and riding. The one most watched was the test of strength. Any could enter, but it soon became clear that the only two worthy of the title were Frail Lemi and a White Tree, an ox of a man named Gall. The man was just as large as they said, and very strong, but when they came to the stone toss, and Frail Lemi threw his the length of a ship, Gall had simply dropped his own onto the sand and started laughing. Frail Lemi had laughed with him, childlike, and no one was quite sure whether Frail Lemi knew *why* Gall had found his throw so funny.

When their laughs had faded, Gall held out his hand to Frail Lemi. "The gods gave you too much."

To this, Frail Lemi, in one of his rare moments of pure clarity, had sobered and pointed to his shaved head and the scar there, evidence of the fall that had robbed him of his wits. "What they gave in some places they took in others." Frail Lemi broke into a wide grin.

Gall seemed unsure whether to laugh or not, but then he did, harder than before, and clapped Frail Lemi on the shoulder. "Come," he said. "In drink at least, I'm certain to win."

Day shifted to night, and carpets were laid around campfires. One campfire was so sought after that many stood just to get a glimpse of the three shaikhs talking around it. Shaikh Aríz of Tribe Kadri, Shaikh Neylana of Tribe Kenan, and Shaikh Dayan of Tribe Halarijan sat on piles of pillows, raised glasses of araq, shared news and jokes, and listened as storytellers told tales of prior meetings between their tribes. They were often joyous tales of marriage, or of mystic adventures in the desert.

The topics of war and battle were assiduously avoided—no one had a wish to enflame old grievances—though since they'd come to speak of the thirteenth tribe and a potential alliance, it was almost impossible to avoid mention of the days leading up to Beht Ihman, when all the tribes had banded together. It made for a bit of discomfort for Emre and the others from the thirteenth tribe, for theirs was a tale of betrayal and of being forgotten for centuries. Their tribe had been sacrificed by the Kings and transformed into the asirim, or else killed in the massacre that followed when the asirim were sent to hunt and murder their own kin. Mere handfuls had escaped, either by hiding in Sharakhai or by living amongst the other tribes, forsaking their names, their blood, their past.

Later, while wandering the camp, Emre would meet a dozen men and women who confessed they had blood of the thirteenth tribe, nine of whom stated they wished to join him when he returned to Macide. It was a sign of healing. A small one, to be sure, but it did Emre's heart good to witness it.

Logs were added to the fire, sending great plumes of embers high into the night. At Shaikh Dayan's bidding, Emre recounted the days leading up to the Battle of Blackspear, and the harrowing battle itself. It felt a bit surreal, telling it from the distance these past few months had added. In years past, Emre might have embellished his own role in it, maybe winked at a girl who'd caught his eye, but to embellish here would feel ridiculous. The tale was so fantastic as it was he wondered if anyone would believe it.

He found himself wishing not for some pretty woman to sit near him at the fire, nor even for Haddad to come from her ship, where she'd sequestered herself—*this night is for the tribes alone*, she'd said when he'd come to invite her. No, he wished Çeda were here. How he missed her. Her quirky smile. Her simple, stark beauty. Her wit. For what felt like the thousandth time since she'd sailed away with Leorah and the Shieldwives, he told himself the fates were determined to keep the two of them apart. *Very well*, he thought, knowing that to rail against them would only make things worse, *but could you at least give me a sign that we'll be together again one day?*

Aríz added more to the tale of the Battle of Blackspear from his own perspective. By then the campfire was choked with people, some standing on tiptoes to hear. They were impressed, Shaikh Dayan especially, who seemed to wear his heart on his sleeve. Neylana was more reticent, but even she nodded as Emre and Aríz came to the high points: Mihir's one-on-one battle with Onur, the flight from the dragon, the spying of tribe Khiyanat and the jubilation that followed, and finally the lengthy battle that saw the arrival of the Sharakhani Kings, the queen of Qaimir, a pair of ancient ehrekh locked in battle, and the death of Onur at Çeda's hands.

"You ordered the *Autumn Rose* to charge Onur's ship?" Shaikh Neylana asked. She was a woman of fifty summers with a face that seemed unaccustomed to smiles. The running joke was that Neylana was too busy feasting on the blood of her enemies for humor. And now Emre could see why. The fire's ruddy glow softened many of the faces sitting around it, but against Neylana's skin it somehow gave her the look of a crag owl, hungry and wary as it waited in the night.

Emre waved to Aríz. "I made the suggestion, Shaikh Aríz approved it."

"And you led the attack on the King of King's ship?"

"I joined in, with two others."

"And after all that, the Silver Spears just let you go?"

"Yes, and they were thoughtful enough to give me gifts before our parting." He pointed to the right side of his head, where a scar could be seen before being lost in his dark hair. "This." He pointed to another on his neck and pulled his thawb away to reveal one more on his shoulder. "And these, before I was so kindly escorted from their ship."

Neylana smiled. "Even so," she said, "an entire ship against three men."

"Three men and one ehrekh."

She nodded, brows raised, as if the explanation were perfectly reasonable, but Emre could tell she found his story anything but. She pressed no more, and the feast continued, but Emre began to worry. He'd thought this council was going to be more ceremony than a true negotiation. It was clear, however, that he would have to keep his wits about him; Shaikh Neylana, and possibly Shaikh Dayan as well, were not as committed as he'd thought.

The following morning saw the start of the formal council between the tribes. In a large pavilion, Aríz, Dayan, and Neylana sat with their viziers. Aríz wore traditional garb, a thawb with ornamental bracers wrapping his forearms and his turban set at a jaunty angle, as many of the younger men in Tribe Kadri were beginning to do. Shaikh Dayan wore a brilliant yellow khalat and a turban with a malachite brooch shaped like the delicate flower after which he'd been named. His raiment was the richest in the pavilion, a thing he was famed for, and noticeably more impressive than Shaikh Neylana's, who wore a plain black abaya, a headdress of pale green beads, and a sky-blue hijab that hung loosely over her head and shoulders. Haddad's long, unbound hair and bright bodice and skirt set her apart as a foreigner, but you wouldn't know it by the way she sat, looking as if she belonged in the circle every bit as much as the shaikhs. Lastly, there were Emre and Hamid, who sat as equals, representing the thirteenth tribe.

Aríz did much of the talking early on, laying out the proposed terms of the alliance that he, Macide, and the other shaikhs had nominally agreed to. It offered mutual protection and mutual trade, free of the dictates of the Sharakhani Kings who often pitted one tribe against the other for their own benefit. No mention of war against Sharakhai was made, but all knew that the larger the alliance grew, the more likely such a thing became.

Dayan was the first to touch on one of the more difficult subjects. He nodded to Aríz and spoke softly. "It seems generous of the eastern tribes to cede ground to Khiyanat, the thirteenth, but you seem to be implying that we should cede ground as well."

Aríz, showing more aplomb than his years might indicate, motioned easily to Emre and Hamid. "We welcome our brothers and sisters and rejoice that they no longer need to hide from the Kings. All we hope to do is restore the old territories."

"The old territories?"

While the pavilion's roof above them snapped in the morning wind, Aríz unfolded a map. "The lands of Tribes Kadri, Salmük, and Masal would shift like so. While your borders"—he circumscribed the new territories for Tribe Kenan, then Halarijan—"would move here." When Dayan's pleasant smile turned humoring, Aríz seemed to lose confidence. Suddenly he looked less the statesman and more the wide-eyed young man of fifteen summers he truly was. "It's hardly land you would miss."

"And how would you know what Kenan would miss and what it wouldn't?"

Aríz pointed again to the map, specifically the desert tract and the portion of the mountain ranges Kenan would be giving up. "There are few enough resources to be found there. And because of the agreements reached between your father and my grandfather, neither of us have sailed there in any case."

"But now you *would* sail there." He leaned back from inspecting the map. "It's a good bit of land to give up."

"Made less so by the amount Halarijan would cede in turn, and Narazid to them, and so on."

"Assuming that all the tribes agree."

Aríz nodded, ceding the point. "Which we are hopeful will happen."

"Presumptuous of you," Dayan said, though not in a way that provoked, Emre thought. He was merely being realistic.

"Nothing will change right away," Emre said. "It will take time. Years, in fact. Macide merely hopes to secure your agreement now that we might find our place in the desert."

Dayan picked up a stuffed grape leaf and took a bite. "So not only are you asking for land, you're asking for food, medicine, armor, weapons, and ships."

Emre tipped his head. "We cannot sustain ourselves without help."

"And the coffers of the Moonless Host that we contributed to over the years?"

"Spent, the last of it lost in the flight from Sharakhai."

Dayan took another bite with a calm, unconcerned air. "You would have us believe there's nothing left?"

"Please understand. There are hundreds upon hundreds who lived in Sharakhai but who now face life in the desert. After generations of living in the shadows of the tribes who protected us"—Emre bowed his head to both Dayan and Neylana—"some have come to us to help, but most are new to your way of life. Skills you take for granted must be learned anew. Trade agreements that were established by your tribes generations ago must be forged from scratch. And meanwhile, we do not have the jobs we once had in Sharakhai to support us. That helped to sustain us and our families, and many had well-paid work that allowed contributions to the needs of the Host. That's all gone now, ripped from us in our flight from the Kings."

"Life in the desert is harsh. Better, perhaps, if you had remained in hiding."

Hamid's face turned red. "You might have forgotten what it was like before the Moonless Host was born, but the scarabs do not. It was the *Host* who turned the eyes of the Kings from the desert to the city. It was the *Host* who spilled blood to take down the Kings, who weakened them, sparing you from the skirmishes and killings that once kept you in line."

Dayan sniffed, his lips becoming a meandering line filled with skepticism. "The Kings continued to do those things."

"Yes, but they were considerably worse before us. Where would you be now had we not fought your fight for you?"

Emre put a hand on his arm, and thankfully Hamid quieted. "I might not have put it so bluntly, but what Hamid says is true. The tribes helped the Host, and the Host helped the tribes in return. On the back of the long campaign we waged in the city, you profited for years, generations."

"Oh?" Dayan said. "How so?"

"If I recall, Kenan had no trade agreements with Sharakhai, and no right to trade in the caravanserais, before the birth of the Moonless Host. But when the Kings began to ask your great-grandmother for help to root us out, she exacted concessions from them: the trade agreements that survive to this day." Emre turned to Neylana. "The same is true of Halarijan. And more than once, when some of your tribe were wanted for piracy, we fed you information to avoid the Kings' navy. There's more besides, but I don't wish to dwell in the past. The truth is that the thirteenth tribe, Tribe Khiyanat, *deserves* a place in the desert. We're asking you to respect that right, to make way for us, and to profit with us once we've found our legs. With your help, that will happen sooner than later."

Dayan, usually careful not to tip his hand, seemed impressed. Neylana seemed anything but. "Does Macide hope to make himself a King in the desert?" she asked abruptly.

"No," Emre said. He'd discussed this very topic with Macide at length. The thirteenth tribe's existence was tenuous, but it was also colored by their history. They arose largely from the Moonless Host, and the Host had long wanted to see the Kings fall. They'd never come close enough for anyone to wonder what would happen if they succeeded, but the question now arose: as Macide gained more influence, would he use it go beyond mere survival?

"And yet," Neylana said, "he sent you here to gather others beneath his banner—"

"Not beneath it," Emre corrected, "*beside* it."

"You," Neylana went on, "a man who risked the life of Mihir, Shaikh of Tribe Kadri, in the vain attempt of stopping King Onur."

Aríz, seeming affronted, sat straight. "We *did* stop him."

"No. As we heard from Emre's own mouth, the ehrekh stopped him. Çedamihn Ahyanesh'ala stopped him. Why wasn't *she* sent to treat with us?"

Emre felt his face flush. Çeda's shadow had been growing longer and longer. He'd no idea it extended this far, though. "I'm here—" Emre began, but Neylana cut him short.

"You're here to beg, as you've already admitted. You're here to ask us to cede ground that has been ours since the desert's dawning. You're here to ask us to weaken ourselves that you, who were drummed out of Sharakhai by the might of the Kings you sought to bring down, can profit. And now you are trying to convince us that you have been *owed* it all along." With an abrupt flourish of one hand, she tipped her glass of araq over, spilling it onto the sand. "Well I won't have it. What's ours is ours, and we won't give it up for you"—she stood and cast her gaze pointedly at Aríz and Dayan—"or for anyone else."

With that she paced from the tent as if she were queen of the desert.

Dayan looked shocked. Emre could practically feel him reworking his previous calculations. If Tribe Halarijan was unwilling to shift the boundaries of their territory, what did that mean for his own tribe?

As Emre feared, the negotiations that followed went horribly. Dayan would only assist with food and supplies. They gave up a single ship, an old schooner, under the proviso that it would be returned in a year's time, or a better one given to Tribe Kenan. And they promised to aid the alliance if they were outright attacked by the Kings or by the invading Malasani fleet. But he would go no farther than that.

Throughout the entire conversation, Haddad had remained silent. And when Emre confronted her about it after, she looked at him with a bemused expression. "It wasn't my job to convince them, Emre. It was yours."

"Well I hope you're bloody proud of her," Hamid said that night as the sun was going down. He was staring at Haddad's dhow, where she was leaning on the gunwales with her rangy cuss of a first mate.

"What do you mean?"

For once, Hamid's look of calm arrogance faded, in favor of a look of profound disappointment. "I have no idea what Macide saw in you, to send you here."

"I spoke to her. She said she made a few trade arrangements. Where's the harm in that?"

"I swear to all the gods of the desert, Emre, in you their quest to forge a pure, unadulterated idiot was fulfilled. It may have looked like we failed today"—without looking, he stabbed a finger toward Haddad—"but it was already set up to fail. Trade agreements or not, she asked them to keep away from us."

"Why would she do that?"

"For her king! For Malasan!"

"That makes no sense."

"It makes perfect sense if you're King Emir. Would *you* want a fucking alliance forming at your back while you're preparing to attack the greatest city in all the Five Kingdoms?"

"Well, even if she did"—Emre was confused more than anything—"what do you want me to do about it now?"

"In Sharakhai, we had easy solutions for such things."

Those solutions all amounted to the same thing: the long sleep for the one giving the Moonless Host trouble. "We're not in Sharakhai anymore. And killing Haddad may have no effect at all. It may push them *toward* Malasan, not farther away."

Hamid regarded Emre with that flat, hangman's stare of his. "Fix this, Emre, before I'm forced to fix it for you."

With that he stalked away, leaving Emre's failure feeling even more complete than it had moments ago. He looked to Haddad, who spotted him and waved. After a moment's discomfort, Emre waved back, feeling a perfect fool for doing so.

Chapter 14

Taking up the ink Melis had given her and Sümeya's bag of tattoo-ing needles and inks, Çeda rushed from the ship before either Sümeya or Melis could say anything more to her. She was too excited to re-main, too excited to even speak of it until she was out under the sun with the asirim near to hand. She was worried the idea would start to fade like a dream. But it didn't. Not as she left the ship. Not as she went to those sleep-ing around the now-cooled fire. Not as she found Jenise lying beside her lover and sister Shieldwife, Auvrey, their arms entwined.

"Come," Çeda said to Jenise after rousing her.

Jenise's sun-bleached hair was unbound. She blinked the sleep from her eyes then looked about in alarm. As she took Çeda in, however, her worry faded. With care, she unwound herself from Auvrey's embrace, then wrapped her wheat-colored turban around her head with practiced ease. The two of them walked side by side, away from the ships and toward the asirim, far enough that they could speak without waking the whole camp. By then, Melis was walking by Leorah's side, supporting her as Leorah thumped Nalamae's tall staff into the sand. Sümeya came just behind, and soon Çeda was facing the four of them.

Çeda held out her right hand, then motioned to the hands of the others, who all had tattoos in roughly the same place, even Leorah, though hers was the lone tattoo not designed around the prick of an adichara thorn. "The tattoos," Çeda began. "We all have our tales to tell. And we've done so, not just with our words but in the stories we've inked into our skin." She waved to the asirim, who huddled in the distance. "But the asirim have been bound for centuries. They *cannot* tell their own tales. They're bound by the gods, forbidden from speaking it, and few enough will tell their tale for them. Were we to give them a way to do so, however, I think it would free a part of them."

They all stared at her.

She lifted Melis's pot of tattoo ink, the one made from the branches and blooms of the adichara, and focused her attention on Jenise. "*You* will become the canvas for their tales. You and all the others. You will forge your bonds through *story*."

"And if you're wrong?" Sümeya asked.

The idea felt so right that Çeda nearly denied her out of hand—she *needed* this to be true—but she knew that was her younger, more callow self speaking. Gone were the days when she could let her impulses rule her; she was responsible for so much more now. "If I'm wrong, I may lead another to the farther fields. I would let them try it on me, but that would prove little. I'm already bonded to them. And having them try it on either Sümeya or Melis is out of the question. Their anger would be too hot."

Jenise was no fool. She knew very well why Çeda had brought her here. "I'll do it," she said.

Leorah groaned and grumbled, her tongue searching for something inside her cheek. "Sharakhai was not built in a day. Let us take some time to think on it."

"No," Jenise replied, her voice soft and distant. "I can feel the hope in Çeda's heart, and I can feel it spreading among the asirim." She stared intently at the huddled group, lit purple in the pale morning sun. "Some will deny it, though—Imir, Natise, even Sedef—and that is a blight that will only grow."

She took the pot of ink from Çeda, then opened the case and took out an inkwell, needle, and striking stick. Çeda hardly knew what to say. She wanted to yelp with joy. With the sun rising, and Jenise taking up the torch Çeda had lit, it felt like they'd all been saved. But she worried as well. The images of Amile's teeth tearing into Ramela's soft throat were playing over and over again.

The others had been roused, and were joining them, watching with a strange fascination. Auvrey was at their head. "What are you doing?" she asked Jenise.

"I'm doing what we came here to do." Jenise walked to the top of the next dune. Auvrey made to go with her, as did Çeda, but Jenise stopped them both with a raised hand. "I go alone. They must see that I'm unafraid."

"But"—Auvrey, her hands gripped over her heart, looked perfectly impotent—"why now?"

"Because waiting will bring ruin." Jenise's eyes lifted to the sunrise. "Because now is the perfect time."

"It's all right," Çeda said, trying to calm Auvrey, trying to calm her own nerves as well. "We know the signs. We'll be ready to protect her."

Auvrey held her tongue, her eyes full of fear. Jenise, meanwhile, moved to the next dune and sat cross-legged. After placing the ink, needle, striking stick, and basin on the sand next to her, she stared over the distance between her and the asirim and reached out to them. Unlike Ramela, she wasn't waiting for one of them to respond to her. She was calling to them, summoning one in particular.

In the distance, a figure stood, towering over the rest of the huddled asirim. He broke away, back hunched, his body turned sideways as if he couldn't bear to look at Jenise as he approached.

"No!" Auvrey cried. "Not Amile, Jenise. Not Amile! Please!"

When Jenise didn't respond, Auvrey sprinted forward but slowed when Melis intercepted her. Auvrey was so upset she tried to bull past, but Melis caught her and sent her reeling backward with a powerful shove. In a blink, Auvrey had a knife in one hand. Melis didn't wait for her to advance. In a whirlwind of lithe movement, she slipped past Auvrey's initial swing, snatched her wrist, and twisted her hard to the ground.

After disarming her, Melis stood and used the tip of Auvrey's knife to point at two of Auvrey's friends, who were rushing forward to protect her. "Jenise has chosen to sit on that dune so that none of *you* would have to be the first. Don't think to dishonor her by taking that choice from her."

Auvrey, more than a little shocked, stood and backed away. Her expression was no less worried, but she let the ritual continue. Jenise sat calmly, waiting, for all the world an ascetic in commune with the Great Mother. Amile approached, his thoughts every bit as black as they'd been before he'd tricked Ramela into attacking him. It wasn't all darkness, though. There was curiosity as well, as if he'd found a strange fruit lying in the desert and didn't yet know what to make of it.

He lurched down the slope of one dune, climbed the next. Soon he was approaching Jenise, walking low to the ground, defensive, as if he expected Jenise to attack *him*. Jenise said something, her words lost in the bluster of the morning wind. Amile replied in a stream of sibilance that barely rose above the hiss of spindrift. Çeda felt his mixture of confusion and anger, both so near to his bottomless well of rage that she nearly ran forward to stop him before it could go any further—if they lost another of their number, there would be no convincing the women *or* the asirim that this process of bonding was worth pursuing—but it was in this moment that Jenise turned away from Amile, undid the ties of her dress, and slipped free of the bodice and sleeves, baring her chest and back down to her waist. Gathering the sleeves into her lap, she leaned forward, exposing her back to Amile in a display of trust that was so complete it elicited gasps from many of the women, Auvrey and Çeda included.

All the women stared, rapt, as Amile crawled forward like an insect, wary, his thoughts dark as a winter storm. Auvrey whispered prayers to the gods as Amile reached Jenise's back. He sniffed her hair, her exposed neck. A flare of anger rose in him. It was so strong and frightening that Çeda nearly called out a warning. Leorah, however, sensed Çeda's mood and grabbed her wrist before she could utter a word. It gave Çeda the patience she needed to wait a moment more.

With studious care, as if he daren't disturb a thread on her dress, nor allow his blackened limbs to brush her copper skin, Amile sat on the sand behind Jenise, cross-legged, just as she was. He stared at her back and for a long while simply shook his head. Çeda had seen a boy in the bazaar like this, the son of a carpetmonger who'd been kicked in the head by a mule when he was young. He could perform simple tasks—fetch water, carry carpets, brush the very mule that had kicked him—but most often he would sit on the carpets and shake his head just as Amile was doing now, as if each intermittent thought caused him some small amount of surprise or pain or worry.

With trembling hands, Amile took the small pot of ink, lifted the lid and smelled the contents. His head arched back, and Çeda heard a groan the likes of which she'd never heard from the asirim before. There was pleasure in that sound, but also yearning, like a man who'd once had the perfect bottle of araq and, on smelling some component—new leather, a whiff of jasmine, a copper bracelet on his skin—longed once more to taste it.

Amile poured some of the ink into the empty well. He looked like an aging painter who knew his palsy was incurable, but who'd also found his life's inspiration, and refused to give in until his masterwork was complete. Setting the pot aside, he took up the needle and striking stick, dipped needle into ink, and began tapping it into Jenise's skin.

For a long while, no one spoke, but then Sümeya broke the silence. "You feel it?" she asked, to no one in particular.

By this time there were tears streaming down Çeda's cheeks. She had no idea when they'd started to fall. She nodded while wiping them away. "I do."

The feeling was slight, but unmistakable: Çeda's bond to Amile was weakening, while a new bond was forming between Amile and Jenise.

Chapter 15

DAVUD AND ANILA walked into an empty stone amphitheater. Behind them came the ghul, Fezek, carrying the unconscious form of Esmeray the blood mage. High above, a stippled bank of clouds was lit by the lowering sun, making them look like dahlias, fire-filled and fallen on a field of cobalt blue. The rows of seats arced around a shaded, semicircular stage. Other than a layer of dust and a bit of graffiti here and there, it was a clean space, as if the owners had left on a short holiday and would be back at any moment.

A holiday perhaps, Davud thought, *but it isn't likely to be a short one.*

The amphitheater had long been the home of a legendary show. The owners, a Kundhuni couple and their three children, had trained condors and falcons and other birds to perform tricks. Through entertaining lectures interspersed with displays of the birds themselves, they spoke of the birds' lifestyles, their habitats, even their feeding habits, including displays of how they would dive on prey from on high. Davud had been to it several times. It was a treasure. But when rumors of war struck, the couple had taken it as a sign and, unable to find anyone to buy the show or even the land, had packed up their family and sailed for the hills of Kundhun.

No squatters had yet claimed it, and the walls of the stadium itself were high enough that it provided a place for Davud and Anila to meet the Enclave with little chance of being observed. It was a convenient place for the coming confrontation.

Anila motioned Fezek to the stage. The tall, lanky ghul lurched to the place she'd indicated and set Esmeray down. Fezek pulled the hood of his robe back and placed himself near her head, ready, at Anila's command, to lift his foot and crush her skull should the need arise.

The Enclave would already be looking for Esmeray. Of that Davud was certain. The only thing preventing them from finding her was the sigil of masking he'd painted onto her forehead. They were an extremely secretive lot, the Enclave, and given their long history of betrayals from within, were wary of new members. It sometimes took months, even years, for them to approach new magi and offer them a place among their ranks. Davud didn't have that much time. They'd managed to avoid Sukru so far, but they couldn't keep it up forever.

After exchanging sharp nods with Anila, Davud took Esmeray's wrist and blooded her again. This time, however, he took off the ring and collected her blood in the small reservoir worked into the underside of the claw. After closing the wound with a swipe of his thumb, he moved around Esmeray in a circle, allowing the blood to drip onto the dry earth. When it was complete, he touched his finger to the last of it and drew a sigil upon Esmeray's neck that combined *sense* with *magic*, then *trigger* and *shear*. He infused the blood with intent as he did so, giving the symbols the life they needed to trigger the spell without his interference. He finished with a line across her neck, then stood and regarded his handiwork.

The spell would, if it sensed magic crossing the boundaries of the circle of blood, cut Esmeray's neck like a knife through butter. It was one of the most complicated sigils he'd yet created. Any small mistake would ruin it, leaving both him and Anila exposed, or worse, having it trigger under the wrong conditions and kill Esmeray when he didn't mean for it to. But he was satisfied that all looked proper.

"It would make for a fine playhouse," Fezek said, staring up at the seats.

Davud licked his thumb and began wiping away the blood on Esmeray's forehead, thereby lifting the spell of hiding he'd placed on her.

Anila, meanwhile, sighed. "This isn't the time, Fezek."

"Of course not, but perhaps we might revisit it? It does seem like a waste to show off a bunch of *birds* and hardly speak a verse!"

"Fezek."

"Of course, of course," he said absently, though none of the wonder had left his cloudy eyes. "I'll give you time to think about it."

The sigil that had masked Esmeray's presence was gone, leaving only the one that kept her asleep. Davud suspected it would work for hours, perhaps even days, on anyone else, but he could already feel her stirring. Even so, he decided not to reapply it. One way or another, this wasn't going to take long.

Indeed, a few scant breaths later, movement in the clouds caught his attention.

"There," he said, and Anila nodded.

It was little more than a smudge at first, as if the clouds were daubs of paint being smeared by the finger of an overexcited child. It twisted and turned, wending its way toward the amphitheater. Then it rushed downward to a place on the third row of seats. There, suddenly, stood a handsome, dark-skinned man whose face bore more than a few similarities to Esmeray's. He wore a tan turban, cocked to one side, a matching thawb, and a rope of a necklace with grape-sized beads that ran halfway down his chest.

He held a kenshar with sigils engraved into the blade in one hand. He pointed this at Davud and Anila. "Step away from my sister."

"I warn you, Esrin, to come no nearer." Davud pointed to the blood on the dirt. "None of us wants Esmeray to be harmed, but she will be should you or a spell or even that blade of yours cross this line."

Esrin stepped forward, stopping short of the circle of blood. "I told you to step away from my sister."

"I'm afraid we can't do that. Not until we've come to an accord."

A voice called from behind them, "An accord?"

Davud turned to find a woman standing near the wooden stage. She wore a flowing red jalabiya with a headdress of lapis and silver. Blue tattoos marked her chin and cheeks and ran above her eyebrows in arcs. Like Esrin, she had a striking resemblance to Esmeray. She was Dilara, their sister.

"You think you can come to an accord with *us*?"

Davud had hoped they would face only one of them, need to convince only one that he meant no harm, but there was nothing for it now. "Not an accord with you," he said, "with the Enclave. We're here to request sanctuary."

Esrin adjusted the aim of his kenshar, pointing to Esmeray's wrist. "You *blooded* her." He stepped down along the seats, then dropped to the amphitheater floor with a clomp of his leather boots. "You'll die for what you've done."

"Esmeray would tell you herself that *she* attacked *us*," Anila replied easily.

Dilara approached the line of blood and stared at it warily. In the dim light it looked like ink spilled over a mottled piece of parchment. "That doesn't sound like my sister."

A blatant lie. The tales told of Esmeray all spoke of a woman who lost her temper more often than a sick mule. "She tried to gouge my eyes out with her ring!"

Dilara had yet to take her eyes off the circle of blood. She was looking for a weakness and thankfully couldn't seem to find one. "Well, if that's the case, this doesn't have to end in bloodshed. Dismantle your spell, and we'll let you walk away."

"I can't do that. We're being chased by the Kings. They're hoping to use us, or see us dead. Wasn't the Enclave formed to protect magi against precisely that?"

At this Dilara looked up, her indignation masked by a calm face and a sweet smile. "The members of the Enclave protect one another," she said. "You think any of us could trust you after this?"

"Not you," Davud explained again. "The inner circle. One meeting is all we're asking for, to tell our tale and to let *them* decide."

Dilara smiled, her white teeth shining in the heavy shadows of the stadium. "Right now, we *are* the inner circle."

Davud caught movement on his left. Esrin, staring at the circle with an expression of pure concentration, lifted one hand toward it.

"Davud!" Anila called, mere moments before the stone beneath the circle of blood began to shatter in an expanding line. The spell on Esmeray's neck should have triggered, but the exact opposite was happening. The spell was being dismantled before their eyes, and the release of its energy was pulverizing the stone beneath the blood.

Something bright and blue crossed the gap between Dilara and Davud. Pain was just beginning to register when he saw the glowing tendril running from Dilara's hands to his ankles. Smiling, Dilara yanked on it hard, and Davud toppled to the stone, banging a knee and one elbow in the process. Worse was the pain now running through him. It tightened his muscles. Rattled his bones.

"Please!" he called over the pain. "We only wish to speak!"

Anila, however, wasted no effort on words. Her hands were spread toward Esrin, who stood several paces away. His eyes were wide, haunted, as if he were witnessing his own death. He stumbled to his knees, and his hand went to his heart.

"No!" Dilara shouted, and sent another glowing rope lashing toward Anila's neck.

Fezek intercepted it with a blinding swipe of his right hand. "You'll forgive me," he said, "but I can't allow you to do that." The spell had caught his wrist, but didn't seem to affect him as it had Davud. With a perfectly calm expression, he began to draw Dilara nearer, pulling the bright lash hand over hand, forcing her to release the spell with a ripsaw buzz.

The other spell was still very much alive, however, and the pain was growing worse by the moment. Davud could try to cast a counterspell to stop her, but with his body bucking like an unbroken stallion it was impossible. There was only one thing he could think to do.

As a guttural moan escaped his throat, he threw himself over Esmeray's legs. Immediately, Esmeray's body began to spasm as well.

Seeing it, Dilara released her spell.

Feeling like he'd fallen from the heights of Tauriyat and struck every stone on the way down, Davud managed to gain his feet. By then a roiling ball of green flame was gathering between Dilara's hands. Davud was just trying to summon a shield, a thing he was nearly certain to fail at, when a gravelly voice called, "Enough!"

The resonance in that voice, its deep command, caused Dilara, Anila, and Esrin to turn. Fezek, however, was staring at Esmeray as if he regretted what he was about to do.

As he lifted one foot, Davud cried, "No!" and tackled him across the waist. Fezek, however, was stout-bodied, and wouldn't go down easily, not with someone as thin as Davud trying to tackle him. At least Davud fouled his aim. Fezek struck only a glancing blow with his foot, doing little more than dislodging Esmeray's turban. Desperate, Davud used a maneuver he'd seen Çeda use once: he hooked Fezek around one ankle and pushed hard until they both fell tumbling to the ground.

Fezek was suddenly fighting Davud. His big hands pummeling him, sending Davud reeling. And then Fezek was on top of him. Gone was his kind look. Gone was the innocence in his eyes. He'd turned into someone else. Some*thing* else. He had both hands clasped, lifted high, ready to deliver a killing blow.

Before it could land, however, Anila raised a hand. Thin tendrils of fog traveled between her palm and Fezek, and he went still as stone, staring into the middle distance, bewildered. Davud, meanwhile, crawled quickly away and regained his feet. After a moment, to make sure Fezek was under control once more, he turned toward the entrance tunnel, where a bowlegged Kundhunese man was walking into the theater proper.

He had dark, wrinkled skin and a short wiry beard. His roughspun clothes spoke of a simple life, a simple man. So did his tassled leather cap with a beaten coin on the front and strings of seashells sewn into the top and sides. Most arresting was his gaze, which was deep, as if his experience went beyond this world.

"You're Undosu," Davud said as he reached the stage.

"My reputation spreads so far?" His Kundhunese accent might be heavy, but his tone was as light as his smile. Then his reddened eyes fell upon Dilara and Esrin, and that all changed. "It's true then?" His smile disappeared, and his tone became that of a disappointed grandfather. "You discovered their nature and thought to leave me in the dark?"

It looked like Esrin wanted to speak but was having trouble breathing. Dilara stepped into the silence. "He was asking around the city for us, but he comes from Sukru's palace."

"No," Anila interjected, "we *escaped* Sukru's palace. We were his prisoners."

Dilara gave Anila an icy glare, then returned her attention to Undosu.

"It's a trap. How many of us must suffer at the hands of the Reaping King before we learn?"

Undosu closed his eyes as if he'd heard this argument too many times before. "The Kings have not broken the pact."

Dilara looked as if she was biting her tongue. "You think that won't change?" She gestured toward Tauriyat and the House of Kings. "You think Sukru won't do whatever he needs to win the coming war?"

Undosu waggled his head from side to side. "And how would killing *us* serve that purpose?"

"He worries that we'll be used by the enemy! Or that we'll decide on our own to aid them."

"The Enclave would do neither."

"I know that, but the Kings don't. And if you can't see that then you're a fool!"

"Well," Undosu said, "perhaps I *am* a fool, but you know very well that only the inner circle alone has the power to decide who enters our ranks. Not you. Not your brother. Certainly not your fool-headed sister." Without waiting for a response, he spun toward Davud. "We'll take you to the inner circle to present your story, and then we will decide whether sanctuary will be granted."

"That's all I ask."

Behind them, Esmeray was waking. Undosu went to her and helped her to her feet, though Davud had the impression it was as much for Davud and Anila's sake as it was for Esmeray's. It took Esmeray a moment, but she seemed slowly to recall the events that had delivered her here. Then her eyes met Davud's and a burning fury was kindled. She lifted her hands, but Undosu grabbed them both and pushed her back. "No, no, no, fool girl! They've been granted sanctuary."

"I don't care what you or anyone else has granted them!"

"You will or you'll end up like your brother, and this time Dilara and Esrin will follow."

At this, the fire in Esmeray cooled, making it clear how much she cared for her siblings. And it hinted at the fate of the fourth—Davud didn't understand what had happened to their brother, exactly, but it was clear his fate was final.

After one last deadly look at Anila and Fezek, Esmeray allowed Undosu to lead her from the amphitheater in that strange, waddling gait of his. Esrin followed, leaving Davud and Anila alone with Dilara.

She stabbed one finger toward the exit. "Well, get on, then!"

Davud did, with Anila by his side. Fezek, his confusion gone, his cheery expression returned, lumbered in their wake.

Chapter 16

BRAMA WAS SHAKEN by the sudden arrival of the second ehrekh in the Mirean war camp. His skin still itched from the buzzing as it had vanished in a cloud of locusts. He wasn't ready to return to the hospital ship—he'd only feel confined there, trapped—so he wandered the desert instead, wondering why the ehrekh had come.

Had it been drawn here by the same scent as Rümayesh and Brama? It was the likeliest explanation. Queen Alansal hadn't mentioned any other ehrekh—the notion of trying to keep two of them under control without destroying her own fleet made Brama's head spin—but he wouldn't put it past her. Alansal was nothing if not bold. Except she'd already promised the bone of Raamajit to Rümayesh. What did that leave for the other ehrekh?

Or maybe he had it all wrong. Maybe the queen had made a pact with the other ehrekh *before* Brama had arrived at their camp. But if so, why wouldn't Alansal have mentioned it?

Did you know anything about it? he called to Rümayesh.

She didn't reply. In fact, he realized she'd completely closed herself off to him. At least when he'd arrived at the Mirean camp he'd had a vague awareness of her presence. Now he couldn't sense her at all.

He headed back to camp as the sun began to burn along the eastern horizon. Near the hospital ship, a pair of soldiers were carrying a woman on a stretcher. They took to the gangplank as she moaned and coughed, twisting where she lay. Brama couldn't understand her words—they came in breathy gasps, as if she were in a fever dream.

He picked up his pace and realized it was Shu-fen.

He lost sight of them as they reached the deck high above. A knot of worry began to form in his gut. He made his way back to the infirmary, the long room with all the cots. An old woman wearing the simple robes of a physic and the young man who'd tended to Brama the day before were at Shu-fen's bedside along with the two foot soldiers who had carried her in. Brama's steps were heavy as he made his way toward them.

They'd removed the bandages around Shu-fen's right thigh. The wound had been stitched, and there was a poultice that glistened over her skin. The flesh around the wound, however, wasn't right. It was dark. Black. Less than a day had passed since the asirim's attack. The asir's claws had clearly infected her flesh, but it was spreading faster than anything Brama had ever seen and, if the grim expressions on the faces of the two physics was any indication, he was not alone.

Just then a terrible coughing fit overtook Shu-fen, and she looked up at Brama with a surprised expression, as if she'd just realized he was there. It was in that moment, with their eyes locked, that Brama realized a terrible, horrifying truth. He could somehow feel the effect the infection was having on her, like some dark demon clawing toward a pit and dragging Shu-fen with it.

And Brama *liked* it. His sense of its hungry growth sent thrills running through him. He was horrified Shu-fen might die, and yet the disease itself was like an old, favored meal that had been laced with spices he'd never tasted before. It completely changed the dish, made it new again.

This is how Rümayesh feels. This is how she experiences us, whether it be joy, love, pain, or anguish. They are all but flavors to be savored.

He wanted to give Shu-fen hope, but how could he do that when he couldn't even hold her eye?

"Are you well?" the young physic asked him in Sharakhan.

Brama blinked, realizing the man must have been staring at him for some time. He was saved from replying when Shu-Fen's twin sister, Mae, burst through the doorway, out of breath, as if she'd sprinted the whole way here. She wore not the lacquered armor of the Damned but simple blue silk shirt and trousers. Shu-fen's look immediately softened. She stared at Mae with a mixture of confusion and helplessness, then seemed to notice Brama again. Her expression turned serious, and she spoke to the healers quickly while pointing to Brama's midsection.

The young physic motioned to Brama's bandages. "May we see?"

Glad for the distraction, he removed his shirt, tossed it on a nearby cot, and unwound the bandages wrapped around his chest. When his skin was revealed, both Shu-fen and Mae gasped. What had been a furrowed landscape of fresh wounds yesterday was now a collection of angry but mostly healed flesh. Only a few spots still wept clear fluid, and there was no trace of darkened flesh.

"Did your mistress heal you?" the physic asked.

Brama shrugged. "In a manner of speaking, yes."

The physic nodded as if that were a perfectly reasonable answer to give. "Can she also do this for Shu-fen?"

"I can ask her upon her return."

"And when will that be?"

"I don't know."

He seemed disconcerted at that, but smiled anyway. "You'll let us know?"

"I will."

He bowed from the waist. "Thank you."

Don't thank me yet, Brama thought. *I've no idea what she might demand in return.*

Over the day that followed, Shu-fen's condition worsened. She lay in her cot, either awake and coughing or asleep and thrashing. And the infection in her wounds continued to spread. They came to Brama several times to ask about Rümayesh, but he told them the same thing each time.

"She's gone, and I don't know when she'll return."

By the end of the following day, they couldn't wait any longer, and decided to amputate her right leg. Despite the milky serum they'd administered, her screams filled the entirety of the hospital ship.

Brama asked to speak with the queen again, planning to broach the subject of the ehrekh. He thought it too much of a coincidence that the very night Rümayesh had chosen to leave the Mirean camp had been the same night the other ehrckh had spoken with Queen Alansal. In reply, he was told that the queen would be happy to speak to Rümayesh. When he told them Rümayesh went where she would and could not be summoned, they said they understood and would he please inform them if he somehow found a way.

In the eyes of the queen, I'm nothing more than a lackey.

The following morning, guards were assigned to him. They didn't prevent him from leaving the ship, nor walking in the desert if he so chose, but they accompanied him everywhere and insisted he remain away from the pavilion.

That night, Shu-fen died.

Surely it was as much to do with the strange infection as it was the loss of blood and amputation of her leg. As was the way of the Damned, Shu-fen's qirin died as well. Apparently, it had simply lain down beside the pool where the qirin were being kept, closed its eyes, and never got up again. The two were buried together in a deep desert grave.

The following day, Mae came to Brama and asked if he would return to scouting with her and a squad of the Damned who'd been assigned to her.

He waved to the two guardsmen standing nearby. "How can I? I'm being watched."

"I request for you to join us. My queen grant it." She bowed her head to him, a gesture that was both sincere and filled with hope. "Please. I don't wish for more asirim to come, to reach camp."

Brama had little else to do, and in all sincerity didn't wish for the asirim to reach the camp either. So he nodded and left that morning with Mae and a dozen other qirin warriors. Their mood was understandably heavy; they had all trained with Shu-fen for years. But they were stoic warriors, and seemed filled with purpose, eager to deliver vengeance for their fallen comrade against the asirim, or the Sharakhani fleet, should they arrive.

Juvaan Xin-Lei decided to join them too. He rode a plain-looking stallion with a patchwork coat. His ivory armor was beyond its prime but still more than serviceable. And he seemed at ease with it, and with the well-worn sword, a red-tassled dao, at his belt. Warring with the rest of his garb was the conical reed farmer's hat he wore instead of a helm. It was old and weather-stained, the sort of hat that would be changed over every few seasons; this one had withstood the test of time, however. The full effect made Juvaan look like one of the famed warrior poets who, after tiring of a life of war, wandered the mountains of Mirea in search of enlightenment.

Juvaan's gaze occasionally drifted toward Brama's mare, Kweilo—or more accurately, Brama soon discovered, to the way he sat the saddle. "If you don't mind my saying, Lord Brama, you don't look very comfortable with reins in your hands."

"No, never have been." Brama patted Kweilo's neck, sorry that she'd been paired with such a poor rider.

A sly grin overcame Juvaan. "Is that why we found you walking in the desert?"

Brama laughed. "Sadly, yes. Rümayesh gifted me with the finest akhala the desert has ever seen, but I rode the poor beast into the sand."

"A pity," Juvaan said.

"A pity, indeed. And you? Do you enjoy them?"

He looked down at his mount. "Let's just say there's a reason I remained in Sharakhai for so long."

"Your hatred of horses?"

Juvaan shifted in his saddle and grimaced. "My love of a life free of saddle sores."

They laughed and rode in silence for a time, but as they headed up the incline of a knobby hill, Juvaan asked, "Have we done something to offend your lady?"

"Not that I'm aware."

Juvaan nodded in a friendly manner. "Do you know where lady Rümayesh has gone?"

Brama steered Kweilo onto a less rocky path. "As I've said, she didn't tell me."

"Of course, though I will admit to some confusion. Why do you suppose she would have left without telling her most trusted servant?"

Precisely what I'd like to know, Brama thought. "I've learned that it's wisest to let Rümayesh come and go as she pleases with no questions asked, although I rather think it has something to do with the ehrekh that visited the queen in her pavilion the other night."

Brama was good at reading people, but he had to admit Juvaan masked his emotions well. He exhibited no embarrassment over his queen being caught speaking to another ehrekh, nor anger at being surprised and challenged by a foreigner. But his protracted silence proved he hadn't known Brama was aware of it. "Behlosh's arrival was unexpected, though not unwelcome."

"Behlosh has agreed to help the queen as well?"

Juvaan shrugged. "He has yet to make his decision known."

"And his reward?"

Juvaan turned and stared with those icy eyes of his. "I thought Sharakhani were more direct."

"Fine. Your queen promised Rümayesh a reliquary with the bone of the old god."

"My queen promised her *a* bone of the old god."

Brama blinked several times. "Your queen found more than one."

Juvaan said nothing as they came to the hill's summit and dismounted. They stared south across a desert overcast with the sort of clouds that teased rain but would likely boil off by afternoon. As Brama stared over the endless dunes he wondered if the wavering curtain along the horizon would soon part for the Kings' fleet. The attack by the obscured asirim still confused him. Only a handful had been sent. Were they meant to be assassins? Somehow Brama doubted it, but he had no better explanation.

"You'll forgive me for saying it, I hope, but treating with two ehrekh is madness. Using the bones of the old ones in payment makes it doubly so." Those bones were the sort of thing the ehrekh would stop at nothing to obtain. Even the gods of the desert coveted them.

"I leave such things to my queen. What we need from you are assurances that Rümayesh will return and finish what she's started."

"She'll return when she returns," Brama said. "As for the rest . . ." Brama lapsed into silence, feeling every bit as impotent as Juvaan.

"Might she have been summoned by her lord?" Juvaan ventured.

By her lord? What on earth was Juvaan talking about? "Rümayesh has no lord." But then Brama understood, and his fingers, so often numb from the abuse they'd taken, started to tingle. There was only one being that might hold the title of lord over a creature like Rümayesh. Goezhen, god of chaos, god of demons, god of shadows and covetous urges.

As the implications began to roll over him, another thought occurred to Brama. "Did Behlosh come as a herald of Goezhen?"

Something most strange happened then. Color came to Juvaan's cheeks. He was *embarrassed*, Brama realized. He'd been a diplomat once, a good one from what Brama had heard of him, and he'd just given Brama clues as to Behlosh's nature while receiving nothing in return for it.

"Is he, Juvaan?"

But Juvaan would be pushed no further on the subject. Brama didn't need his confirmation, though. His silence spoke volumes. What worried him more was the inevitable conclusion: the god of chaos had come to play in the desert.

Brama and Juvaan saw no signs of the asirim that day. Nor did Mae and her squad of the Damned. They spotted no ships along the horizon, either. The day's excitement came only when they returned to camp. There was a commotion near the hospital ship. On the sand near the ship's gangplank, several of Queen Alansal's generals were speaking with three of the servants who tended to the patients. Juvaan rode forward at a brisk pace and joined them.

Mae, riding her qirin alongside Brama, glanced at him warily, as if she suspected him of wrongdoing, then she kicked her mount into a faster pace, following Juvaan as the rest of the Damned rode their qirin toward the far end of the encampment.

When Brama arrived, the generals were heading up the gangplank. Juvaan followed, waving for Brama to accompany him. A hollow of dread had formed in Brama's gut on seeing the generals and the anxious looks on their faces, and each step he took in Juvaan's wake chiseled it out just a little bit more, so that by the time they reached the infirmary, he was queasy with it. In the center of the long room lay a young man, the physic with the kindly smile, the one who'd helped Brama when he'd first arrived. Next to him, lying in another cot, was the old woman, the physic who tended to the Damned. They were both awake and resting, but dread filled their eyes. The eyes of the old woman turned angry when she saw Brama. The young man, however, still looked at him in a kindly way. A small amount of hope seemed to mingled with his fears. He began to cough a moment later.

Both had sallow skin. There were notes of a gray, ashy color around their eyes and lips and nostrils. One of the physic's nurses, normally a reserved woman, was speaking to the generals in a strained, high-pitched tone. She pulled back the young physic's lower lip to reveal gums the color of rotted fruit.

A pall fell over the gathering. Many took a step back; Brama doubted they even realized they were doing it. These men and women were accustomed to war, but there was little that robbed one of courage like seeing death at the hands of disease.

Juvaan looked like the desert had just been turned upside down. "What do you know of this?"

Brama shook his head. "What would I know of such things?"

Juvaan translated, after which a rush of conversation followed, with some of the generals pointing to Brama. "You were cut as deeply as Shu-fen, yet you escaped the infection." He waved a hand to Brama's midsection. "They're now wondering why."

"How would *I* bloody know?" Brama didn't like where this was headed. He didn't like it at all.

Juvaan chose not to translate Brama's response. "They'll want a better explanation than that."

"They're aware that I heal quickly. It's likely proof against the infection."

"They also know that your mistress granted you power. And that your mistress is now gone."

"The *asirim* dealt those wounds to Shu-fen!" Brama said.

"And Rümayesh was close at hand."

"If you think Rümayesh somehow caused this, then you're a bloody fool." Brama looked to the generals. "You're all bloody fools."

Juvaan bowed his head, a gesture Brama found somehow infuriating. "Please. The generals are only asking prudent questions, questions you would want asked were you in their shoes."

"The asirim dealt those wounds," Brama said again, "and the *Kings* sent the asirim." He waved toward the stricken physics. "They *wanted* this to happen." Brama never thought he would defend a creature like Rümayesh, but in this he felt confident. He'd felt no workings of magic from her at the time. She had nothing to do with this.

But if that was so, a little voice inside him said, *why did she leave? Why hasn't she returned?*

Juvaan's wintry eyes stared into Brama's. He looked like a man on the cusp of a difficult decision. Anyone else, anyone not protected by Rümayesh, would likely have been thrown into the brig of one of their dunebreakers, or tortured until they told the truth. But the likelihood of vengeance upon Rümayesh's return was simply too great.

Juvaan worked his jaw, then nodded crisply. "Go," he said, "but remain in camp." Then he turned to the generals, all but ignoring Brama. A conversation that began in calm tones quickly became heated as Brama left.

Over the following day, another five were discovered with similar symptoms to Shu-fen, including two of the generals. The day after that, over a dozen more were delivered to the hospital ship. "The scourge," they were calling it, and already there were whispers that the gods of the desert had come to destroy the invading fleet.

Chapter 17

ÇEDA WATCHED IN WONDER as Amile expanded his tattoo on Jenise's back. He worked for the entire day, the Shieldwives erecting a sun-shade to shelter them. Only twice were they interrupted, both times to bring Jenise food, to give her a chance to relieve herself beyond the oasis. But then she returned and sat while Amile continued. When the sun set, Amile returned to the huddle of asirim while Jenise returned to the fire where she'd lain the previous night with Auvrey. She spoke little and ate sparingly. She was acting like one does when they see death for the first time, though Çeda knew good and well Jenise had sent dozens to their graves and seen many more die. When Jenise finally laid herself down to sleep, it was with Auvrey at a noticeable distance, the two of them holding hands as she fell asleep.

Amile continued his tattoo throughout the next day. Again Jenise showed extreme patience, sitting still for long hours with few breaks while Amile added more to his design. Finally, just past high sun on the third day of the work, Amile stopped. With furrows of clouds raking their way across the sky, he set the needle and striking stick aside, wiped the excess ink from Jenise's skin, and sat with his knees pulled to his chest, simply staring at what he'd done.

When Çeda approached, Sümeya, Melis, and Auvrey followed. Amile shifted uncomfortably on the sand and pushed himself away from Jenise like a boy caught stealing bread. His eyes shifted between the tattoo and the approaching women, as if he couldn't decide whether he wanted to be there when they saw it or not. In the end, he stood and bounded over the dunes on all fours, sand kicking up behind him as he went. He wailed, a long, warbling bray, and headed not for the other asirim, but toward open sand. Soon he was but a dark speck in the distance.

In a way, Çeda was glad to see him go. He needed time to adjust. Time to grieve over all the memories he'd been forced to dredge up. Time to consider his new future with Jenise. He was a complete cypher to Çeda now. Her bond with him had been severed, replaced by one with Jenise that was every bit as strong as Çeda's had been with Kerim—stronger, even. Amile recognized how close he'd been to losing himself entirely, and how crucial Jenise's offer had been to returning his sanity.

Jenise waited as they came, allowing them all to see Amile's story. It was nothing like Sümeya's work, or Leorah's, or Zaïde's. It was done by an inexpert hand. It was sloppy. Some of the images Çeda could hardly recognize. And there were few words. But the sheer power in it . . . The central image was of a man holding a child up to the sun. Beneath that image, around it, were thorns. Blood. Darkness. They hemmed the man and child in. Trapped them. The most common image in the dark border was people. Sometimes faces. Sometimes figures in the night. Sometimes only eyes or mouths or hands or feet.

They were his victims, Çeda realized. The men and women, sometimes children, that Amile had been forced to murder and deliver to the blooming fields to feed the twisted trees.

Auvrey knelt by Jenise's side, describing what she saw. Jenise hadn't seen it, of course—she'd been the canvas—but when Jenise dropped her head into her hands and began to cry, Çeda realized she'd known. She'd felt those images as Amile had pressed them into her skin. Not once had she broken down during Amile's hours of effort, but now she was wracked, inconsolable with grief.

Auvrey, with the care and devotion of a mother for her child, applied salve to Jenise's back, wrapped bandages around her chest, then guided Jenise's arms back into the sleeves of her dress. Leorah led Jenise away, the two of them retiring alone to *Wadi's Gait*.

"And now?" asked Auvrey.

The Shieldwives huddled close. They'd all known the purpose of Jenise's tattoos, and now, clearly, it was their turn.

"You begin in the morning," Çeda said. "All of you."

Auvrey glanced at the others, then bowed her head in reverence. "If it's all the same to you, Çedamihn, we'd like to begin now."

Çeda was taken aback. She'd thought they might still have reservations. "You've all spoken?"

Auvrey bowed her head again. "All of us. Jenise included."

Çeda couldn't help but think of Sümeya's counsel: *We cannot risk more than a week,* she'd said, and she was very likely right. "We'll begin tonight, but not everyone. It's too much emotion all at once." Çeda cast her gaze over the Shieldwives. With Ramela gone and Jenise bonded, there were fifteen left. "Six can begin today. If all goes well, the others can start in the morning."

Soon enough the six had been chosen and were standing in a line. One by one they called to the asirim, as Jenise had, and the asirim came. They were in awe as much as the women were. Their rage still burned, but a hope had been kindled beside it. They were so eager to tell their tales that many yowled or yipped like hyena pups. Some even rolled on the sand.

That Natise came first was no surprise. He'd been an innocent in life and was perhaps the most human left among them. To Çeda's complete surprise, Sedef was next. He seemed as eager as the rest—perhaps *more* eager after having lost his tongue—to see his story written, even in so ephemeral a form as a tattoo. Three more followed, and the last were Huuri and Imwe, twin boys, Mavra's grandchildren. They made their way shyly to a single Shield-wife: Sirendra, a lithe gazelle of a woman. Each of them took one of her hands. There were others like the twins, two or sometimes three who were especially close and didn't want to be parted, who joined to a single Shieldwife.

In fits and starts, the asirim began to craft their tattoos. Some, like Jenise's, were placed on the Shieldwife's back. Others already had tattoos there and offered their legs instead, or their chest and stomach, or their arms or neck. The asir sometimes merged their designs with the older tattoos, or confined them to a single space. The twins started theirs on the tops of Sirendra's feet, and did so cruelly at times, striking the needle harder than they needed to, each glancing at Sirendra as if they enjoyed every ounce of pain they were giving. Sirendra took it all stoically, hugging her legs and giving the boys the freedom they needed. Eventually the boys slowed their movements, then stared numbly at Sirendra as tears streamed down her cheeks. They moved with care after that, tapping their needles only as hard as was necessary, giving Sirendra time to rest between sessions.

Some were skilled in the art, but most, as had been true of Amile, possessed little skill and less precision, making the images blurry and broken. But it wasn't the final rendering that mattered; it was how deeply they sung the song of their life while forming their tattoo, and how closely the Shield-wife listened to it. The images were powerful and painful, but also purifying. And the Shieldwives lived their pain, making their bonds that much stronger.

"Goezhen's sweet kiss," Sümeya said near sunset, "the horrors they've seen."

Çeda was left speechless. It wasn't just the sheer volume of pain that made her feel sick to her stomach, but the creativity the asirim had shown in inflicting it.

Çeda surveyed the field of women and asirim around her. "Where's Melis?" she asked. "She should see this."

Sümeya shook her head. "I've asked her. She won't come."

Çeda fumed, but decided against ordering Melis to come. This day was for the asirim, and she refused to taint it.

As it happened, only Mavra was left without a bond, and so, later that day, Çeda took up a cloth bundle filled with inks and tattoo needles and walked into the desert toward the huddled asirim. Mavra waddled forward to meet her. She stood before Çeda, chin up, perhaps sensing Çeda's purpose.

"We are bonded, grandmother, and will remain so"—Çeda lifted the bundle—"but I would have you tell your tale." She paused, suddenly unsure of herself. "If you would."

Mavra's shoulders, so tight a moment ago, relaxed. She glanced at the bundle in a way that revealed how touched she was. It was the sort of look that might have stolen over her centuries ago when a grandchild offered her a perfectly imperfect statue: a thing made of clay and love and childish moldings, held up in tiny, hopeful hands. To Çeda's offer, however, she shook her head. She motioned to the asirim behind her, then to those who were tattooing their stories on the Shieldwives.

"My story is already being told, Çedamihn Ahyanesh'ala al Malakhed." Her voice was high and thin, like stone scraping stone. She'd used the old name for the thirteenth tribe, Malakhed, the name she would have learned as a child. It was a sign of acceptance, of welcoming Çeda to her family. It made Çeda's heart swell with pride. *"And you have your own to tell,"* Mavra went on, *"one that will eclipse mine. One that must eclipse mine."*

Çeda felt foolish standing there, her offer denied. "You're certain?"

Shaking her head with a smile, Mavra looked in that moment like any number of proud grandmothers Çeda had seen in Sharakhai, a woman who, upon reaching the sunset of her life, had looked upon her life's work and found herself content with all she'd accomplished. *"Go,"* she said. *"Tend to your flock, while I tend to mine."*

Three days passed and sunset was nearing as the last of the tattoos were completed. Çeda's bonds with the asirim were gone, all but Mavra's, which had grown incrementally stronger as each of her children was passed off to one of the Shieldwives.

Through Mavra, Çeda felt the other bonds. They were different from the old. They were pure and dark and strong as ebon steel, but also complex. The asirim battled between their centuries-old struggle for freedom and the siren call of submission, between a wish to find peace and the desire for revenge, between their instinct to shield the weakest among them and the repressed hope that they might lay aside their anger and simply heal for a time. It was all in constant flux as the Shieldwives and asirim improbably, beautifully, learned to live with one another.

Like a tribe, Çeda thought. Tears formed at the very notion.

The pain in Çeda's right hand had eased; not fully, but it was a manageable pain now, and a great relief. She wasn't sure if she could have gone much longer without beginning to fray.

Near sundown on their sixth day at the oasis, the camp began to tear down. Tomorrow, they would sail for Sharakhai, to liberate Sehid-Alaz.

No, Çeda thought. *Not liberate. Not really.*

She'd become convinced that in order for the rest of the asirim to be free, Sehid-Alaz had to die. It saddened her terribly, so much so that she'd hidden it from everyone, even Leorah.

Not everyone, child, Mavra called to her. *I've known since we left the blooming fields. But I pray that you'll free him first. Let him taste the desert air once more before we take that step.*

Çeda was embarrassed over her slip, but felt relieved all the same. *Thank you, grandmother.*

Mavra's cold indifference felt like a shrug. *We all die, Çedamihn. Sehid-Alaz has known the truth of it for centuries. Likely he'll welcome it.*

She'd thought Mavra would fight her, but she seemed as prepared as Çeda to do what was needed. And so they would. They would free Sehid-Alaz and see what might be done for him, but Çeda was increasingly certain that for the rest of the asirim to be free, Sehid-Alaz needed to die. *We'll do it our way. We'll honor him as he steps toward the farther fields. He will go with his head held high.*

When morning's light broke along the horizon, they made the ships ready and were about to pack the last of their provisions and set sail when a blood curdling scream came from the *Red Bride*. Cries of fright and alarm followed. The Shieldwives aboard the *Bride* were pointing up through the rigging. Above the yacht, something dark streaked through the charcoal sky. Çeda drew River's Daughter and squinted. She saw a hint of flapping wings, but little more.

Jenise and Auvrey, swords at the ready, came running toward Leorah's ship. "Imadra's badly hurt," Jenise said. "A gash across her neck."

Çeda could hardly take her eyes off the sky. "From *what?*"

Jenise shook her head. "I saw only a flash of wings. It flew like a demon—"

A piercing shriek like a salt flat eagle cut through her words. It went on and on, and the longer it did, the more Çeda's skin prickled, the more her guts turned to jelly.

All eyes turned to the western sky, where a dark form swooped closer. Its beak was made for rending. Its talons were wickedly curved. Broad wings batted the air, pinions spread like a display of freshly forged shamshirs. And billowing in its wake, a train of slate blue plumes. *A sickletail*, Çeda thought, *but grown to grotesque proportions.*

Arrows flew but the sickletail avoided them with lazy twists of its wings, flying ever closer to two Shieldwives who were pulling furiously on a rope, drawing up the *Red Bride*'s anchor.

Melis, who'd just gained the deck, sprinted forward, her ebon blade drawn, calling, "Lai, lai, lai!" in a high ululation as she imposed herself between the bird and the women hauling on the anchor rope. Her sword was poised, ready to strike, but at the last moment the bird swerved around the mainmast's starboard shroud and fell upon the rearmost Shieldwife. Talons raked. Wings drummed, and then it launched itself into the crisp morning air with a leap and a sweep of its broad wings.

The Shieldwife's hands shot to her neck. She staggered backward as blood spewed from the wound left by the bird's talons. She collapsed to the deck a moment later, eyes wide, staring at the sky as if she couldn't quite believe what had just happened.

Leorah sat nearby in one of the chairs affixed to the deck. The amethyst on her right hand glimmered, its glow only partially attributable to the rays of the rising sun. She looked tired, weary as the world. She hardly seemed able to keep her head up. Lifting a quivering hand, she pointed over the gunwales and mumbled something too softly for Çeda to hear.

"Ships!" a Shieldwife shouted from atop the mainmast. She was stabbing one arm northwest, the same direction Leorah had just pointed. "Four clippers! The royal navy!"

Sensing danger, the Shieldwife switched her grip on the mast and spun, mere moments before the sickletail swooped up behind her. She tried to fend it off, but the bird had fearsome speed and reflexes. It sunk one of its talons into her forearm, the other into her turban. As its wings pummeled the air, its curving beak darted down again and again, knifing into the flesh of the Shieldwife's face. She reeled, then slipped, but before she plummeted she managed to grasp the bird's leg, clearly hoping to take it down with her. The bird, however, would not be so easily defeated. With mighty beats of its wings it gathered the dry desert air to its chest. It lifted her above the rigging, above the sails. Only when it had borne her twice the height of the ship did it start pecking and clawing.

In moments the Shieldwife's hands were a ruin of flesh and sinew. She fell, and like a tumbling stone twisted end over end until she met the deck with a resounding thud. As she lay there, unmoving, the sickletail flew away, lost in the gloaming once more.

Several rushed to the Shieldwife's aid, but the sinking feeling in Çeda's stomach told her it was already too late. She focused on the approaching ships instead. There were four of them: sleek and dark, their sails full and golden in the morning light. Their prows were capped in dark iron.

"Bakhi's bright hammer," Çeda swore, then bellowed to the other yachts. "Sail! Sail! All ships set sail!"

Chapter 18

"CALL YOUR ASIRIM TO PUSH THE SHIPS!" Çeda cried. "Keep your swords loose and your bows close to hand. Sharp eyes, now! And sail smartly! Our lives depend on it!"

In a rush of activity, they all began to prepare the sails, ready buckets of blue dousing agent, and pull the anchors. Çeda, meanwhile, asked for aid from Mavra. The asirim were nervous. They moved to obey, but not quickly enough. They were terrified, and suddenly Çeda realized why. The Kings. The Kings were aboard the approaching clippers.

Come, children, Mavra said. *They have no hold on us now!*

They moved faster, their courage building. They gathered around the struts just as the sails of their three yachts were beginning to billow. Such was the strength of the asirim that the ships lurched into motion, knocking Çeda off balance for a moment.

"Beware!" Sümeya called. "We're attacked from the south!"

Çeda turned and spotted the sickletail flying low over the dunes. Its wings brushed the crests, creating strange, almost mystical patterns in its wake.

Gripping River's Daughter with both hands, Çeda stepped in front of

Leorah to protect her. Sümeya, Auvrey, and Jenise, meanwhile, lined up beside her. Çeda tried to feel for the sickletail's heartbeat, as she could with mortal man. She hoped she might press upon it, slow it down, enough that one of the others might slice it from the sky. The moment she spread her awareness, however, she felt something open up inside her. It started in her heart, delicate as a newfound worry, but quickly expanded into a dread that threatened to consume her.

Her head tipped back. Her eyes went wide. She stood on a precipice with a terrible expanse before her: a wide, dark, scintillant void. She felt another presence, something *beyond* the sickletail. The bird was a window to another world, Çeda on one side staring in, and on the other . . .

"Breath of the desert . . ." A name came to her numbed lips. "Yerinde . . ."

The goddess was beautiful and powerful and fearsome. So different from Nalamae. Nalamae felt grounded, a part of the mortal world, where Yerinde seemed of the heavens—a reluctant observer of mortal man—and yet Çeda was certain that Yerinde had fashioned this strange creature and given it to the Kings, an act of encumbrance that bound the goddess to the Kings and the desert at large. It was the reason, Çeda suspected, that she could sense the goddess at all.

The sickletail swept over the bow, a gale of wings and wind, but instead of attacking the women, it sliced clean through the mainsheet, the rope that held the mainsail's boom in position.

"Gods, no!" Çeda breathed.

Çeda ran for the rope's severed end—the one still attached to the boom—but the boom was already swinging sharply into the wind, going wide of the ship until the sail was heading to the fore. Çeda cringed as the boom cracked near the mast.

It took several long moments for the import of that sound to hit home. They weren't lost. They could repair the mainsheet, and the ship was still moving. The jib was full, and the asirim were pushing hard against the struts below. The enemy, though, was at full speed and closing quickly.

Çeda looked at the *Red Bride* and *The Piteous Wagtail*. They were beginning to move with more speed. If need be, one of them could steer alongside *Wadi's Gait*—they could abandon the wounded ship and still escape. But they had no hope at all if they couldn't do stop the sickletail. The bird arced into the sky like the swing of a sword. Having wounded *Wadi's Gait*, it seemed intent on doing the same to the other ships. As its path curled toward them, Çeda cupped her hands and bellowed, "Aim true, Shieldwives! Protect the rigging!"

They tried. They truly did. A dozen arrows inked sharp lines in the magenta sky. Some even clipped the bird's tail feathers—their severed tips fluttered down as the bird's powerful wings beat ever onward. But the bird dove and swooped, bending its course with deadly ease.

Still feeling the presence beyond the bird, Çeda gathered herself and reached toward it. This time she felt Yerinde's eyes falling not on the ships but on *her*. Çeda felt amusement. Anticipation. At the same time, a change was overcoming Çeda. Not since she'd climbed Nalamae's tree and looked into the hanging shards of glass so long ago had she felt so connected to the desert. She had no idea what it might mean. Perhaps it was her experience with Nalamae echoing in another of the desert gods. Whatever the case, she ignored her feelings of awe and *pressed* on the bird, *pressed* on Yerinde.

Çeda felt a tug in return. She felt like a child trying to yank on the lead of an ox, and the ox had decided to pull back. But it worked. The bird's wings faltered, and in that moment, Jenise released an arrow. The shot blurred, a stroke of black, piercing the bird through the chest. Down it went, wings aflutter, twisting, tailing, wheeling toward the desert floor to land with a thud and a spray of sand.

As one, the Shieldwives raised their hands and shouted with joy, while Çeda pressed one hand to her chest. She was bent over and coughing, the experience having caused her heart to start beating like a top sent tumbling down a set of stairs.

Sümeya was by her side, bent and talking low. "Are you well?"

"Well enough." With Sümeya's help, she tried to stand tall. She felt another coughing fit coming on and managed to get out, "Guide them, Sümeya," before it overtook her.

For a heartbeat, Sümeya stared, her concern plain on her face, then the old Sümeya suddenly returned and began calling orders crisply. She ordered the *Red Bride* and *The Piteous Wagtail* to abandon their attempt at rescuing those on *Wadi's Gait* and to sail southeast. As they moved to comply, she ordered *Wadi's Gait* steered windward. With the wind helping, they swung the mainmast aftward and lashed the wounded boom in place. It would make for dangerous sailing, but it would allow them to capture the wind and save the vessel.

The Kings' ships had closed within a league. By the time they'd brought all three ships up to speed, they'd cut the distance in half and were still gaining. They were royal clippers, sails full and powering over the sand like a pack of black laughers who'd sensed their next kill. There were dozens of Blade Maidens aboard, and the crews would have grapnels ready, fire pots prepared.

Worse, they had asirim of their own.

Çeda saw them bounding over the sand beside the ships. They were released moments later. They came on, baying, barking, braying as their speed ate the distance between the tall royal ships and Çeda's feeble fleet of three.

"We can still outrun them," Çeda said.

Sümeya's expression was grave. "No, Çeda. This is now a choice between fighting to the death and surrender."

Seeing how quickly the asirim were moving, Çeda realized she was right. They couldn't outrun the Kings' ships. Not any longer. Not with the wind so strong and the direction so favorable for the clippers. She looked to Jenise and Auvrey, looked to the other ships, where all eyes were locked on the clippers and the galloping herd of asirim. Their fear was plain—swords lowered, shoulders slumped. She *felt it* through the bonds they'd all made with the asirim.

Mavra and her children wailed, not because they might die, but because they were about to do battle against their own—more misery to be piled on the ziggurat they'd already built.

Sümeya took a step closer and spoke so that only Çeda could hear. "You can still surrender, Çeda."

She waved a hand toward the clippers. "You think they'll let any of us *live*?"

"There's at least a chance," Sümeya replied.

"To live what sort of life? Most of us would be slaughtered. Some few would be kept as bargaining chips, or worse, bait, to use against the thirteenth tribe." She held Sümeya's striking brown eyes. "I can't give them up. I won't."

"We cannot win. Even you must see this."

"We all die, Sümeya," Çeda said, suddenly awash in a fey mood. "What we do today may open the door for another."

Sümeya seemed to weigh her words, then nodded. Çeda couldn't be sure, but Sümeya seemed pleased, if such a thing were possible on a day like today. "What would you have us do?"

Çeda used River's Daughter to point to the oncoming ships. "There are Kings aboard those ships. Let's make them pay for what they've done."

As the Kings' asirim came ever closer, Çeda moved to the foredeck and studied the terrain ahead. There were some few rocks. Not many and not very tall, but it would give them a slight advantage. She called out her plan, such as it was, and it was relayed to the other ships. If they could make it to those rocks and pull the ships into a circle, they could fight and take as many of the Kings and their soldiers with them as they could.

Her Shieldwives pulled their veils into place. Sümeya followed suit a moment later. Çeda did as well, then turned to the trailing clippers. They were close enough now to make out individuals: King Sukru standing on the foredeck of one ship, his whip already in his hand; King Cahil on another in golden armor, a shield and war hammer at the ready; King Beşir on a third, his tall black bow to hand.

And on the fourth, standing at the gunwales, King Husamettín. Tall and dark in his black armor, he had one boot propped up on the railing as if he were preparing to leap for Çeda's ship. His two-handed shamshir, Night's Kiss, was unsheathed, held loosely by his side. Even at this distance Çeda could see how it devoured light. A terrible thrill ran through her at the sight of him—her father, if Ihsan were to be believed. The Honey-tongued King had told her so after the Battle of Blackspear. It might be a lie, but Çeda didn't think so. It felt true, and had from the moment the words had left Ihsan's mouth.

She meant what she'd said to Mavra in the blooming fields. She would kill Husamettín if given the chance. But she wished to know certain truths before she did: how her mother, Ahya, had come to him, how she'd got into his good graces, what Husamettín had done on the night she died. Now, though, Çeda doubted she'd ever get the chance.

"So be it," she said to the blustering wind.

Soon the Kings' asirim were so near Çeda had no choice but to send their own. *Go!* she called to Mavra. *Go, and fight for us as we will soon fight for you!*

Mavra and Sedef, Amile and Natise, Mehmet and Gevind and Lela, all broke away from the yachts and bounded to meet the oncoming wave of asirim. The sand swirled ahead of them, driving against those chained to the Kings. This was Mavra's doing. A moment later, however, Çeda saw another asir in the opposing line who had such gifts. Several did, in fact. In mere moments, an entire swath of desert was caught up in a fog of sand and stone. It swallowed the yachts, drove hard against their sails. The cracked boom groaned under the added strain but, thank the gods, it held.

The air became so thick the four clippers faded like memories, but it wasn't long before they became visible once more, resolving from the golden fog. Cat's claws were released. Twin balls of black iron twisted through a haze-filled air, a writhing chain strung between them. A half-dozen fell short of *The Piteous Wagtail*, but they were only ranging shots. Then one struck the *Wagtail*'s stern. It may have fallen harmlessly off the hull and thudded against the sand, the second one as well, but it was only a matter of time before . . .

The third streaked in like a pair of fighting crows and wrapped around the rear strut of the starboard ski. The ship immediately started to slow as the claws raked the sand.

"Oh, gods," Çeda breathed. One of the Kings's ships, Cahil's, was turning. Çeda knew what it was going to do, and ran toward the stern, yelling, "Free it! Free it!"

One of the Shieldwives slipped down to the skimwood runner ski along a rope. She navigated the ski, balancing with one hand still on the rope, until she'd made it to the strut where the cat's claws' chain was wrapped. She knelt and tried to pull the device free, but the iron balls at the ends had a dozen long hooks worked into them. They were designed to dig into the sand and slow a ship down. Freeing one while a ship was at speed was nearly impossible.

The Shieldwife pulled desperately at the chain, but didn't have the strength to free it. Another Shieldwife joined her, ready to help. All the while, Cahil's clipper sailed on, turning easily toward the *Wagtail*, not slowing in the least.

Jenise had reached Çeda's side. Her face was veiled, but Çeda could hear the horror in her words. "They're going to ram it."

Çeda had known it from the moment the clipper had peeled away from the others. The Shieldwives on the ski were straining against the cat's claw, but it was too late. They'd just managed to pull it free when the clipper came barreling in amidships.

The *Wagtail*'s portside struts buckled as the ship was driven by the massive clipper. The hull crashed against the sand and the iron caps along the clipper's prow crushed the yacht's hull like kindling. On its momentum bore it, driving both ships forward, splitting the *Wagtail* neatly in half. Before the interlocked ships had even come to a rest, the Blade Maidens were storming over the forecastle gunwales, leaping down to the deck or hull, both of which were tilted at an angle.

While the three other clippers sailed on, Çeda struggled with whether to turn back, to try to save the women on the wounded yacht. Sümeya caught her mood. She shook her head and, when Çeda still looked to the fallen ship, reached out and gripped her wrist hard. "Your responsibility is to save the rest."

She was right. She was right, but gods, to leave them there . . .

The rocks, Çeda decided. *We have to reach them, and draw as many of the clippers with us as we can.*

It was soon clear, however, that her hopes were in vain. The clippers were close. Cat's claws were flying in and a fire pot struck aft, orange flames spreading across the deck and over the side just behind the pilot's wheel.

Grapnels arced high, launched from the nearest of the ships, Husamettín's. It landed across the angled forestay, slipped down until it met the deck and was pulled tight. And then Husamettín himself was leaping for the rope. With a gauntleted hand he gripped it and slid toward *Wadi's Gait*.

Çeda was already on the move, rushing across the deck, ready to slice the rope with River's Daughter, but Husamettín had anticipated her. As the nose of his clipper drifted away, it pulled the rope tight as a bowstring. He used it to launch himself toward the yacht. He fell short of the deck and landed on the starboard ski.

Çeda leaned over and swiped with River's Daughter. Ebon steel rang as he blocked with Night's Kiss, which emitted a buzzing sound as it moved.

After another block, he sprinted along the ski, grabbed the gunwales, and swung himself up to deck ahead of the pilot's wheel. Leorah was there, Nalamae's staff in her quivering hands, but Husamettín sent her sprawling with a backhanded blow across her head.

Sümeya met him, her blade a spinning, a charcoal blur. Çeda arrived a moment later, swinging River's Daughter aggressively but holding herself in check. Take chances with Husamettín, and she was as likely to lose her head as score a glancing blow. Across the central deck they fought, Çeda and Sümeya slipping into their old habits, their spacing, their timing, complementing one another.

Husamettín was lithe and powerful, his blows deadly accurate. Auvrey, who'd been throwing dousing sand onto the fire, rose and charged Husamettín from behind. But the King was ready. He ducked her blow and brought his sword up in a devastating uppercut. Night's Kiss gave a violent rattle, cutting through armor, skin, and bone like wet paper, opening her from hip to shoulder.

Auvrey staggered, eyes wide and disbelieving, her innards just beginning to spill as she tripped over side of the ship. Jenise's scream came a moment later. Her grieved cry was echoed by Yildi, the asir Auvrey had bonded with, from somewhere inside the battle the asirim were waging. Jenise came storming over the deck, her shamshir in hand.

Çeda blocked her path. "Jenise, no!"

But Jenise refused to listen, and Husamettín used her emotions against her. After containing her initial fury of blows, he brought Night's Kiss down with so much force that it cut clean through her shamshir. Its shattered pieces flew end over end, glinting from the sunlight filtering down through the dust. Blood welled in Jenise's turban, a wound that would have been much worse had the strike been anything but the follow-through.

As she crumpled to the deck, dazed, Çeda and Sümeya engaged, one to either side of him. Çeda rarely saw Sümeya overcommit herself, but Husamettín's fearsome display was forcing her hand. When she went for a more forceful swing, Husamettín launched himself off the hatch into a high, backward leap. He arced over Sümeya's head, blocking her riposte as he went. When he landed, he spun, ducked beneath yet another overreach by Sümeya, and snapped his leg out to catch her knee. Her leg buckled and she fell, her head striking the deck hard. Her ebon blade slipped from her lax fingers and went sliding across the deck.

With her eyes glazed, blinking slowly, King Husamettín laid Night's Kiss across her neck. "Drop your sword, Çedamihn."

As the desert wind blew, Çeda gripped River's Daughter tightly. The deck bucked. The clippers behind her loomed. Despite her words to Sümeya earlier, that she would fight to the death, Çeda realized she couldn't. Not after all Sümeya had done. Not after she'd become such a beacon of hope. If the First Warden could believe, then who else might?

Çeda was just about to lay down her sword when a figure rose up behind Husamettín. The King sensed it and turned to find Leorah, standing wobbly, using Nalamae's staff to hold herself steady on the shifting deck. Her right hand was raised high, her fingers splayed wide. And her amethyst ring . . . By the gods who breathe, it was bright as the dawn.

Husamettín tried to evade her touch, but Leorah was too close. Her palm fell across his face, and the King's entire body went rigid. He groaned like a sick child and his head arched back. And his eyes . . . They were visible through Leorah's outstretched fingers. They'd gone impossibly wide, as if he were witnessing his own death. Leorah followed him to the deck, keeping her hand on him the entire way down. He went limp as his head thumped against the deck boards.

Leorah was trembling as she stared at the approaching ships. "He is only one." Her breath came hard. Sweat gathered on her upper lip and her bloodless cheeks. "There are more to come."

Leorah was not easily cowed. She'd told Çeda many times how prepared she and Devorah were to die, that they knew they'd both received well more than their allotted time. *When the lord of all things comes for me, I will take his hand gladly and walk with him to the farther fields.* But now she was fragile and frightened, a woman about to see her life's work undone before her very eyes.

Çeda helped to rouse Sümeya and Jenise, who were woozy but conscious. Jenise returned to the wheel, while Sümeya recovered her sword. They all watched the approaching ships.

Husamettín's clipper sailed only a dozen paces off the starboard quarter. Another, King Sukru's, was a mere twenty off the port. Jenise had managed to cut the boarding lines, but the ships were launching more, several of which fell across the rigging. Another fire pot crashed against the deck and the sealed companionway, spraying fire so high the foot of the mainsail caught fire. A dozen Blade Maidens were lined up along the bow of both ships, preparing to leap. Sukru himself stood at the prow, above the lion figurehead, his whip uncoiled and his small eyes hungry. Off the starboard quarter, Beşir's clipper hounded the *Red Bride*, with two grapnels already secured and more flying toward it. Melis was flying over the deck, pointing and ordering the Shieldwives to defend their ship.

At the wheel, Jenise's face was a mask of awe and confusion. She lifted one hand and pointed off the port bow.

Çeda turned.

Ahead, standing among the rocks she'd spotted earlier, was the figure of a woman. She was tall and regal. Her hair plaited and hanging down her chest. "Nalamae," Çeda whispered. "Breath of the desert, leave the wheel!" she shouted to Jenise. "Cut the boarding lines! We must reach her!"

Çeda and Sümeya ran aftward, cutting the grapnel lines thrown from the Kings' ships. Jenise tied the wheel in place and joined them. But more grapnels were already flying in. One was so high up it caught against the mainmast, and there was no hope of reaching it quickly.

Sukru, smiling, cracked his whip over the gunwales, catching Jenise across the shoulder in a bright burst of blood. But just then a disturbance arose behind the Reaping King. An asir, Sedef, crashed into the Blade Maidens and tore into the King. In a blink Sukru was lifted and thrown over the side of his own ship. Down he tumbled, cawing like a crow in his surprise. Before he struck the sand, he twisted and lashed a shroud line aboard the clipper with a miraculous flick of his whip.

As he swung aftward to safety, Sedef, bound onto the gunwales and leapt high through the air toward *Wadi's Gait*. He reached the last grapnel line as the Maidens' arrows harried him. Several struck deep into his back and thighs as he grabbed hold of the line and pulled, his thin muscles going taut.

The rope snapped like thread, and Sedef fell down toward the deck as *Wadi's Gait* sailed on, the boom creaking, the rocks coming ever closer. Leorah's staff thumped over the deck as she made her way to the starboard bow. Nalamae stood just ahead, her hands high, palms facing the oncoming ships. As the ship bumped over a patch of rocky ground, Leorah reached the gunwales and flung the staff over the side.

Nalamae caught it in both hands. As the yacht sped past her, she brought the butt down against the stone.

A sound like the breaking of the earth rent the hot summer air. The yacht lurched, the aft end lifting off the sand, throwing everyone to the deck. Çeda spun about, staring in wonder as the ship sailed on and Nalamae's tall form dwindled into the distance.

The rock shelf around Nalamae exploded outward as if Iri himself had brought down his fist. The effect was terrible in its power, and much more pronounced in the direction of the Kings' ships. The earth lifted in an almighty burst of sand and stone that sent both clippers reeling, heeling, masts tilting, the desert itself driving against their hulls. As a cloud of amber towered in the sky, the port ski of Sukru's clipper gave way. It capsized, dark-clothed bodies flew from the ship like an overturned fig cart. Husamettín's ship righted itself, then came crashing down hard and turned sharply starboard, heeling away from the yacht's line of sail.

Wadi's Gait and the *Red Bride* were hardly touched, but the wave struck Beşir's clipper hard. Sails were ripped away, split along their seams or snapping the rigging and leaving them flapping in the wind. Buffeted by the wind, the ship slid over the sand, then slowed precipitously, its skis sinking deep like wagon wheels in mud.

A dozen asirim, including Mavra, Amile, and others from her clan, came bounding out of the cloud, chasing *Wadi's Gait*. Arrows rained toward Nalamae from the Blade Maidens aboard Husamettín's clipper, but Nalamae, holding her staff tight against the ochre stone beneath her, was beginning to crack and splinter, bits of her crumbling and falling away as if she were terracotta, not flesh and blood.

Near Çeda, sand began to swirl over the deck. It tightened into a spinning column, then flaked away in clumps, leaving Nalamae standing there, whole once more. Her eyes were closed, one ear pressed to her staff as if she were listening closely to the mood of the desert. In that moment, Çeda felt something atop the sealed companionway. She knew before she turned who it was—she'd felt him use his power in the blooming fields.

There, bow drawn, stood Beşir, half-shadowed by the drape of the foresail.

"No!" Çeda cried, lifting River's Daughter as the arrow was released.

She felt her blade nick the arrow, but it wasn't enough. The shaft sunk deep into the center of Nalamae's chest. Çeda charged Beşir as she lifted River's Daughter high. Beşir's eyes went wide. He started to retreat, but Çeda was already there, bringing her shamshir across his body.

It sliced deep, and he fell backward. The speed of his withdrawal carried him over the gunwales at the rear. Çeda sprinted aft, ready to leap down and kill him where he fell, but as she stared at the sand along the wake of *Wadi's Gait*, he was nowhere to be found.

Chapter 19

THE DAY AFTER the failed council with Shaikh Neylana and Shaikh Dayan, Emre went to the circle of Halarijan ships and asked to speak with Dayan alone. He was allowed, and soon found himself with the shaikh in the captain's cabin of his ship.

"Please," Dayan said, motioning to the opulent chair opposite him. Emre sat and arranged himself. Before sitting, Dayan poured two stiff helpings of araq from a bottle with a distinctive oval shape. It was from tribe Tulogal, and was a liquor most would use only for the most special of occasions. Emre took it, raised the citrine liquor in a gesture of good health, and took a healthy swallow. Dayan followed suit, though he savored the liquor much more than Emre had. "Now, tell me how I can help before you go to meet with the King of Malasan."

"I won't waste your time stomping around the rabbit's den. I'm here because I think you're making a mistake."

"Is that what you told Neylana when you met with her this morning?"

"Yes," Emre replied.

"And what was her response?"

"Somewhat less favorable than I'm hoping yours will be."

Dayan laughed, an honest sound that spread throughout the cabin. "I'm guessing she wasn't so generous with her liquor either."

"She was not." Emre liked this man, with his bright clothes and brighter smiles, but he did have the annoying habit of rubbing one's nose in his generosity. "I'm not going to meet with the King of Malasan for my own sake, but for my tribe's. And you must see that I won't be representing Khiyanat only, but the whole of the desert people."

"It's brazen, don't you think, to claim to wield so much influence?"

"It's the truth," Emre shot back. "Whatever the king and I discuss will set the tone for his dealings with other tribes." Emre stared into the liquor, savoring the scents of anise and sweetgrass and slightly burnt naan. "There was a time when I would have died before speaking to a Malasani as an equal."

"Your brother, Rafa, yes?"

Emre shouldn't have been surprised Dayan knew of his brother. He was a careful man, and would have made inquiries. "Rafa was murdered by a man named Saadet ibn Sim over something *I* did. A stolen purse, nicked from Saadet's belt on the night of Beht Revahl. He took my brother's life over a handful coins, and made me watch as he did it. That night I swore I would see the desert rid of the Malasani's taint."

"A tall order."

Emre shrugged. "There were rather more of them than I'd realized."

Dayan chuckled, nodding in a way that made it clear he shared in Emre's pain. "And then there was Haddad."

"Yes," Emre admitted, "crossing paths with Haddad was an unexpected surprise. She's enchanting, dangerously so, but she isn't the reason my hatred for the Malasani has cooled."

"I've a feeling we've reached the point of our discussion."

Emre sipped his araq while, outside the ship, there came the rhythmic clanking of a windlass being wound, a reminder of how close Dayan's fleet was to setting sail. "Before I fled the city with Macide, I'd hardly been out of Sharakhai for more than a day at a time. I knew—still know—little of the ways of the desert. But what I saw in the forming of the thirteenth tribe changed me. I sat by fires and traded stories. I stood beneath an open sky, unconfined by city streets. I listened to the rattle of sand as the ceaseless winds drove it."

"What happened to you"—with his glass, Dayan waved to the ship's hull, a nod to the desert beyond—"we call it the Great Mother's kiss."

Emre tipped his head. "The perfect phrase. The Shangazi infused me and made me realize how precious life is in the desert. Not just the tribes, but Sharakhai as well. If we take one wrong step, we could be gone."

"You see our reality, then. Some small part of it, in any case. You are but a child to the desert by your own admission, but now you see how carefully each of us must tread, each tribe, lest we be caught in the storm, a thing not of our making but which might kill us all the same."

"This is my point. Just as I cannot understand how life has been here in the desert, you cannot see what life has been like in Sharakhai. Together, however, we might find a way to navigate the dunes."

"You're about to tell me that the Kings are ready to fall."

"They are, but that isn't my point. The cruel Sharakhani Kings, the Mad King of Malasan, the ageless Queen of Mirea, the blood mage who inherited the throne of Qaimir from her father." It was Emre's turn to point beyond the walls of the ship. "Do you see the game they play? Do you see how little they care whose territory they sail through, be it Kadri, Salmük, Kenan, or Halarijan?"

For the first time, Dayan seemed put upon. "Their ships number in the hundreds. Their soldiers in the tens of thousands."

"Yes, but what would the combined ships of the desert tribes number? How many spears might be rallied to *our* side?"

Dayan snorted. "A question whose answer has no value. It will never happen."

"But it can."

"Neylana has already denied you."

"All it takes is one. Then another and another. We have four already. Macide is speaking to Ebros, Ulmahir, and Tulogal. We are at the tipping point." Emre lifted his glass. "Join us, Shaikh Dayan. Join us, and the western desert will follow. Join us, and Neylana will be forced to join as well. She will not be left out, not when all the other tribes have entered the alliance."

Dayan stared into his glass. His smile had long since faded, but he was staring at the araq as if he now found it distasteful. He lowered the glass, then set it down with a clack against the desk before him. His look was so unlike the Dayan Emre had come to know over these past few days that Emre was certain he'd lost him, that Dayan was offended in some way. But then Dayan's expression turned resolute.

"I want first salvage rights once the Malasani fleet has been defeated. Twenty ships of our choice."

A white flame of joy lit inside Emre—he could hardly believe his ears—but he quickly tempered his enthusiasm. Dayan had not yet agreed, after all. "We don't yet know how many ships there will be, but surely we can promise ten."

"Give us twelve, plus all their plunder."

Emre made a show of considering, then stood and held out his hand. "Done."

"Very well, Emre Aykan'ava"—Dayan stood and gripped Emre's forearm with a bejeweled hand—"Kenan will join the alliance."

Emre smiled as they shook arms. "The desert united."

Dayan considered the phrase, and seemed pleased by it. "The desert united."

In the end, Dayan agreed to give them five ships, each outfitted with warriors who would be at Emre's beck and call until the full alliance had had a chance to meet and discuss their plans. They were given a host of supplies as well, including crates of their famed healing unguent that would serve the alliance well.

By the time Emre and Dayan were done talking, the camp was abuzz with the news. But Emre's conversation with Hamid was still bothering him. His mind kept wandering to the replies they'd received from Dayan and Neylana before the meeting, their abrupt turn away during the council.

And there was Hamid as well. He hadn't let things rest since their last conversation. Twice Emre had seen him on deck, glaring at Haddad's dhow, *Calamity's Reign,* like he wanted to march over to it and do what Emre wouldn't. Both times he'd turned to Emre as if he knew full well he was being watched, then gone on about his business as if Emre didn't exist. As Emre returned to the *Amaranth,* the bright glow he had from getting

Dayan to agree to join the alliance dimmed after a chilling exchange with Frail Lemi.

The big man was standing on deck, cracking his knuckles, the muscles along his arms and shoulder rippling in the sun. "Time to take care of things, Emre?" It was the sort of thing he used to say in Sharakhai before leaving to get an unruly scarab, a soldier of the Moonless Host, to step back in line, or to send an unmistakable message to the Host's enemies.

In this case, however, Emre had no idea what he was talking about, not at first. "Take care of what, Lem?"

He jutted his chin at *Calamity's Reign*, staring at it much as Hamid had. "Hamid said we'd be going soon."

Suddenly the reason for Frail Lemi's excitement was crystal clear. But Emre kept the confused look on his face. He couldn't have Lemi getting himself worked up, and the best way to do that was not to order him to stand down but to pretend to be confused. Like the spreading of an infectious yawn, it always seemed to scatter Lemi's darker thoughts.

"I've no idea what you mean. Going to do what?"

He shrugged as if he couldn't understand why Emre didn't know what he was talking about, but didn't want to admit it for fear of embarrassing himself. "To take *care* of things."

Emre felt bad. He could see Frail Lemi trying to work out where he'd gotten things wrong, but better that than him heading off to *Calamity's Reign* on his own with a spear in his hand. "Let me go talk to Hamid, okay? I'll get this all straightened out."

Without waiting for a reply, he went belowdecks. He found Hamid sitting on his own bunk, sharpening a straight razor on a whetstone. In Sharakhai, the razor had been Hamid's weapon of choice when dealing with the Moonless Host's looser ends.

"Didn't I tell you to tend to your own business?"

"I have been. The question is whether you've been tending to yours."

"Put the fucking razor away, Hamid."

Without taking his eyes off Emre, Hamid folded the razor, dropped it and the whetstone into the chest at the foot of his bed, and gave the lid a gentle shove. It set home with a hollow thud.

"Leave Haddad alone," Emre said.

"Certainly."

Hamid stood and tried to walk past, but Emre took the front of his thawb in both fists and shoved him backward until he thumped against the cabin wall. Staring straight into Hamid's cold-blooded eyes, he said, "Leave Haddad alone, and *stop* putting things into Lemi's head."

"I would dream of nothing else."

His amused look nearly made Emre punch him across the jaw. Gods help him, he thought about waiting until they were asleep and taking that razor to *Hamid's* throat. But what would that solve in the end? Violence was a cancer.

He shoved Hamid against the wall one last time, then left the hold and headed across the deck toward his own cabin. He slammed the door and sat, fuming for a long while, rocking back in his chair. Across from him, in a series of shelves, were a half-dozen bottles of araq, all of different shapes, all from different tribes. No Tulogal, though.

The taste of it was still on his tongue. It was a rare thing, Tulogal, especially in this part of the desert. It was conceivable Dayan had traded for the bottle he'd shared with Emre long before their council. But Macide had had several bottles, which he'd made a point of spiriting away from the city before the Moonless Host had been driven into the desert. Haddad had traded for two of them. One each for Dayan and Neylana? A way to soften them as her negotiations with them began?

He went and poured his own drink, an araq with a strong bite and a clean copper finish.

He knew his anger with Hamid was as much about embarrassment over his own inaction as it was fear for Haddad's safety. He'd been putting off speaking to her precisely *because* Hamid had made a stink about it. As mad and bloodthirsty as Hamid was, Emre had to admit he had a nose for rooting out trouble—even when they were kids. It was a sixth sense that had kept him and others alive time and time again. He might be sick to death of Hamid's constant pushing, but he couldn't jeopardize the tribe just because he didn't want to listen to Hamid's advice. He had to know the truth.

Before he knew it his steps were leading him down the gangplank and over the sand toward *Calamity's Reign*. When he arrived, however, Haddad was gone.

"Where is she?" he asked her lanky first mate.

The crewman made a sour face. Acid scars covered much of his neck and face, evidence of the battle with the great wyrm during the Battle of Blackspear. It was his sneer, though, that made Emre want to punch him. "You think you're entitled to special treatment aboard this ship, but you're not, scarab."

Emre took a step forward. "I asked you where Haddad was."

"Off fucking your lamb of a father, I suppose."

When Emre made for Haddad's cabin at the rear of the ship, the mate intercepted, drawing his slim knife as he did so. "Wouldn't do that if I were you."

"I'm going to speak to her," Emre said.

The mate didn't budge.

"I'm going to speak to Haddad"—Emre put a hand on his own knife—"now get that ugly, dungheap of a face from my sight before I—"

"What do you want, Emre?"

He and the mate both turned to find Haddad stalking up the gangplank. She reached the deck and made straight for her cabin, but Emre met her near the mainmast. "We need to talk."

She stopped, taking a deep breath before looking him in the eyes. "I'm rather busy at the moment." Her Sharakhani accent was thick, the way it got when her blood was up.

"Make the time."

She looked ready to say something rash, and Emre could feel her first mate looming behind him. Emre was ready for him to make a move, but just then Haddad deflated with a sharp huff and waved her mate away.

She made for her cabin, but Emre immediately said, "In the hold, Haddad."

She spun, a look of terrible anger darkening her features. *Not embarrassment,* he realized, *nor worry, but pure anger.* He walked to the hatch, where the first mate was standing. He had a leg on it, preventing it from being slid aside so that Emre could enter.

"Open it," Haddad said.

The mate remained where he was, eyeing Haddad with a stony stare.

"Open it." This time it was a sharp command spoken in Malasani.

The mate did, and Emre and Haddad descended.

"You're a bit upset," Emre said when they were alone.

"You're bloody well right I'm upset! You would be too if I'd just upended all of your negotiations with Dayan!"

"And how did I do that?"

"By forcing him to shift his plans!"

"You got what you wanted ahead of the council. You said so yourself. You practically rubbed my nose in it!"

She waved to the stacks and stacks of roped-off crates around them. "Do you know *anything* about business, Emre? I made an arrangement with Dayan to buy a few crates of unguent, yes. But do you think for a second that was the end of it? I've worked for years to secure a handful of lucrative contracts, but that's all turned to shit because of King Onur and his aggressions against the eastern tribes, and now the war. I might make a few deals here and there, but if I want to *survive*, if I want to feed my crew and their families back home, not to mention my own, then I need sustained trade. Sustained, Emre. *That's* the bread that feeds. Not the crumbs that come from a few crates of healing mud."

"Did you give them bottles of Tulogal?"

She stared at him as if he were mad. "Yes!"

"Why?"

"To wax the skis, Emre!"

"Hamid thinks the money wasn't for trade, but to buy them off. That you paid them to look the other way as the war plays itself out, and to get trade routes ready for when Malasan takes Sharakhai."

"That's what *Hamid* thinks or what *you* think?"

"Did you?"

Her look turned cold. She looked hurt, but Emre genuinely couldn't tell if she was faking it or not.

"Open the crates, Haddad."

She raised her eyebrows. "You really want to do this?"

"I have to know."

"Do this, Emre, and it will be the end of us."

He wished it hadn't come to this, but for the tribe, for the desert, he needed to be sure.

"Very well," she said, and stalked over to a set of crates marked with the rusty red sign of Kenan. She pulled at the ropes securing them to the hull, took up a pry bar hanging from a nail, and levered the lid open. Inside, cradled in straw, were piles of clay ointment jars. She opened one and slapped it into Emre's palm. As the pungent smell wafted into the stuffy air of the hold, she moved on to another crate, similarly filled, and another and another. She took out longer crates and opened those as well. They contained trays of unstrung bows made from the wood of the fabled ivory ash trees found only in Halarijan territory. When she'd opened them all, she swung the pry bar back and forth as if in that moment she wanted nothing more than to bring it crashing against Emre's head.

"Satisfied?"

Emre stared down at the gray unguent streaked with purple. He closed the lid and tossed it into the crate it had come from. "I had to know."

"I don't blame you," she said, though her look belied her words. "Now get the fuck off my ship."

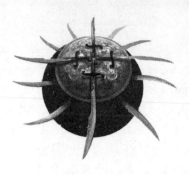

Chapter 20

I AM KIRAL, KING OF KINGS, Lord of Sharakhai. I am Kiral, King of Kings, Lord of the Amber Jewel.

It was a refrain that played often in his mind, especially when his new bride, Queen Meryam shan Aldouan of Qaimir, was near. He walked by her side now, the two of them on their way to hear the counsel of King Beşir, who a day ago—or perhaps it was several days, he couldn't recall—had raised the alarm regarding the city's finances.

Over the next hour, Beşir tried his best to detail how dire things truly were, but several times he lost track of where he was. It was unlike him. Kiral was almost certain of it.

Meryam paused their conversation with a lift of a hand from her teacup. "We could speak of this another time."

Beşir's disarray was because of his daughter, the one he'd recently been forced to kill to prove his allegiance to Yerinde. Kiral knew he should offer condolences, or thank Beşir for his sacrifice, or at the very least echo Meryam's offer of a postponement of these proceedings until he'd had time to recover himself. But the truth was he could think of nothing but how he felt trapped within his own body.

I am Kiral, King of Kings. I am Kiral, King of Kings.

"No," Beşir said, sharing a rare and all-too-brief look of gratitude with Meryam. "This needs to be done now. I leave as soon as this is over to join the others in the desert."

Husamettín, Sukru, and Cahil had left days ago with the sickletail. The hunt for Çeda was on, all in hope of flushing Nalamae from hiding. Beşir, remaining behind to take care of several important points of business, would depart soon to join them. He continued the rundown of his assessment, making it clear how expensive their swelled ranks of soldiers were to recruit, outfit, and train. *I am Kiral, King of Kings.* It was necessary to defend themselves, of course, but Kiral wondered aloud whether there might be another way in the coming weeks—when the fighting would be at its worst—to call upon the loyalty of the Sharakhani people to rally to the city's defenses.

Beşir sighed, combing his beard with his fingers. "As I just mentioned, the overture has been made, but few have taken up the call, and the ranks they fill suffer a high attrition rate. Many abandon their posts after too long, seeing how the Spears are being paid while they receive only promises."

"Then it's time," Kiral said. "We'll begin conscription, as we discussed."

He might have uttered those words, but they weren't his. He glanced to his left, at Queen Meryam, who pointedly did not look his way. *What thoughts lay behind those dark, calculating eyes? What have you done to me?* As much as he wanted to know the answer to those questions, his attention was drawn back to Beşir as if Meryam had laid a finger across his chin and compelled him to do so.

It was then that he felt a glimmer of the man behind the mask. He had gone by another name once. What was it? By the gods, he couldn't remember. And now that it came to it, he remembered thinking this same thing many, many times before. Now, as then, the answers were just out of reach. He recalled glimpses of waking in the catacombs beneath his father's hidden palace. Of being taken to Qaimir by Meryam and her man. Of being assaulted day after day by Meryam in that dank room in Viaroza.

"Hamzakiir . . ."

The word came to him from beyond the fog of his thoughts. Someone had spoken it. Beşir? Or his stocky vizir who'd just entered the room? He knew not. Like an alchemycal reaction, however, his memories coalesced around it, and the truth crystalized. Beneath the mask Meryam had placed on him, he was another man. A powerful man. Hamzakiir. Hamzakiir Külaşan'ava, rightful heir to the Wandering King's throne.

I am Hamzakiir Külaşan'ava. I am Hamzakiir, son of the Wandering King. I am Hamzakiir . . . He held the thought close, like a talisman, yet try as he might his memories slipped through his grasp like so much sand.

"I . . ."

Beşir and Meryam turned to him. He wanted desperately to say it—*I am Hamzakiir, son of the Wandering King*—but the words wouldn't come.

Beşir, who'd been speaking, seemed annoyed. "Yes?"

Soon he'd shaken his head. "Nothing," he muttered. When Beşir looked at him strangely, he waved impatiently for him to continue. "Go on."

He felt himself falling into the darkness, an oubliette of Meryam's making. *I am Hamzakiir*, he said once. *I am* . . . And then he was lost completely, the King of Kings once more.

Weeks later, Kiral wasn't sure how many, he sat within the Sun Palace at the base of Tauriyat, Meryam by his side. A council of the Kings had been called. Sukru and Cahil, returned from their failed mission in the desert, sat on his right, while Beşir, Ihsan, and Azad were on his left. With Husamettín taken in the desert by the traitor Çedamihn, and Zeheb lost to madness, they were a poor group indeed. And King Azad wasn't even truly one of them!

And what about you?

Gods, how muddied his mind was. What had he just been thinking about? *Azad. His daughter's true identity masked.* But as happened so often lately, the thought was lost like a stone swallowed by the sand.

"The other Kings have grown impatient," Azad was telling them.

"Impatient," Sukru spat. "We have more important things to worry about than pretenders to the thrones."

"Not pretenders," Azad said forcefully. "The rightful heirs."

"Well," Sukru replied with a sneer, "we all know where *your* loyalties lie."

"They lie here, with us," Azad said. "I'm merely advising caution when it comes to the inheritors of the thrones left vacant by recent events. They are not a problem now, but they will become one if we continue to ignore them. The war keeps them in check, but when it's over, they'll come to us with demands."

"What demands?" Meryam asked.

King Sukru stiffened at this. He still hadn't fully accepted Meryam's presence at council. Nor had most of the others. But they suffered it for Kiral and for the power she was bringing to Sharakhai's defense.

"They'll each want their full twelfth of proceeds from taxes, as their forebears had. They'll want full representation in our councils."

Cahil laughed. "Why should we pretend to care what they want? They'll get what we offer and be glad for it, or we'll find another to take their place. There's no shortage in any of the lesser Kings' houses."

The term *lesser Kings* had been coined to describe those who had inherited the thrones of the dead Sharakhani Kings. They were the rightful Kings, but hadn't been blessed by the desert gods, and thus were referred to as *lesser*, while those who had lived since the time of Beht Ihman were often referred to as the *greater Kings*.

"It isn't wise to use that term," Kiral said.

"What?" Sukru spat, incredulous. "They *are* lesser Kings."

"Perhaps, but the illusion that they aren't is a useful one. And we mustn't discount them so easily." Kiral's mouth might have uttered those words, but he knew very well it was Meryam who'd spoken them. He had some few thoughts of his own, and was allowed to voice them from time to time, but she always seemed to know when their minds differed, and stepped in with an ease that was frightening. He also felt how important this was to her—to smooth things over with the lesser Kings—and it made him wonder why. Before he had a chance to develop a theory, he was waving to the empty seats around the curving table. "Whether we like it or not, they hold some power in Sharakhai. Perhaps more than any of us would like to admit. Dozens of influential families and businesses sit beneath the shade of their trees." Sukru had opened his mouth to speak, but Kiral raised his hand. "We would do well to consider how to bring them to the table without giving them a seat, as it were."

Sukru, as always, seemed displeased, but pressed no further. "I have something more urgent to bring to the council in any case. The matter of Davud Mahzun'ava and Anila Khabir'ava."

"Who?" Cahil asked.

"The two magi," Sukru said.

Cahil sneered. "Why didn't you just say *the magi who killed my brother and escaped my palace?*"

Sukru dragged his sour look to Kiral and, surprisingly, Meryam, who he normally ignored. "I request permission to speak to the Enclave, and demand they be delivered to us."

"You know that isn't part of the covenant," Meryam countered.

Sukru pounded the table. "Then they will know that we make formal claim on them! They will refuse them sanctuary, and any other form of help they might request."

What followed was lost on Kiral. Davud's name had been like a stone thrown into a thicket, causing more and more memories to lift like a flock of frightened pheasants, each taking him somewhere else. To a ship sailing toward Ishmantep. To encountering a young man on its deck, a budding mage with great potential. To speaking to him from the top of a pit, asking him to consider his future carefully. He'd been undergoing the change, the first step in becoming a blood mage, and he, Hamzakiir, had been trying to help him survive it.

In the end, Davud had relented, and aiding him had cost Hamzakiir. He'd used his skills and the power derived from Anila's blood to douse the flames Hamzakiir had unleashed on several of the ships docked at the caravanserai.

The conversation in the council room drifted in and out of consciousness. Meryam was pressing Sukru about his past encounters with Davud and Anila.

As Sukru spoke of training them, Kiral was reminded of the collegia students. How he'd changed them in dark ways. How he'd delivered them to Sharakhai and unleashed them on the aqueduct and the great gate of King's Harbor. He remembered returning to the House of Kings to find the cache of elixirs he'd so long pursued, and his own pleasure at having gained them for Meryam.

He remembered the trip to the desert with Meryam and Ramahd and King Aldouan. Summoning Guhldrathen, Meryam and Ramahd escaping—and his falling back into her clutches.

The discussion about the Enclave was winding down. All agreed that Davud and Anila were dangerous, and that allowing them to ally with the Enclave would be unwise. Meryam would speak to the Enclave herself and demand they refuse sanctuary to them.

They spoke of the war. Meryam gave her report on the plague's progress. All was going according to plan, she said. Scores were now infected. Soon it would be hundreds, then thousands. In little time, the Mirean fleet would either leave or attempt to throw their strength against the gathered Sharakhani fleet. Either would prove their undoing, and the Sharakhani fleet would be in good shape to return and pit themselves against the forces of Malasan.

"But there's been a wrinkle," Meryam said.

"What wrinkle?" Sukru asked.

"The alchemyst, Alu-Waled, has been taken by an ehrekh. We fear it is Rümayesh, who seems eager to meddle in our affairs."

Cahil spun a knife on the table with one finger, as if none of this mattered to him. "I told you we shouldn't have sent the alchemyst."

"There's more," Meryam said, dismissing Cahil's concern without so much as looking at him. "Our kestrels report having seen a second ehrekh."

Nervous looks passed throughout the room, not only from the vizirs and viziras but the gathered Kings as well. They knew the sort of havoc ehrekh could cause. Several had seen it with their own eyes over the centuries, most recently during the Battle of Blackspear, where Rümayesh and Guhldrathen had fought.

"If the description is accurate," Meryam went on, "the second is Behlosh."

"Forgive me," Ihsan said, "but I'm rather behind on my demonic lore. Who, by the gods who walk this earth, might *Behlosh* be?"

"An elder," Meryam said. "One of the first Goezhen made."

"As is Rümayesh?" Ihsan replied.

Meryam nodded.

Ihsan made a show of taking in everyone at the table, everyone but Meryam. "My Kings, I thought the reason we . . . entertained the idea of having Qaimir take a seat at our table was precisely because we were promised we would get an ehrekh on *our* side, while simultaneously ridding ourselves of another."

"We *did* rid ourselves of another," Meryam said.

"No thanks to you," Ihsan shot back. "You *left* when the one you promised would grant you the power you needed was freed by Brama, a bloody backstreet thief!"

"And how pleased you seem by it!"

"Do you see me smiling? We gambled much on the Battle of Blackspear, largely because we"—he emphasized *we* while staring at Kiral—"believed you could deliver us a victory."

Ihsan was making a play, that much was clear. He wasn't usually so aggressive, but he had argued hard against releasing the scourge on the Mirean fleet. He might even have believed his own words. The turn of events would have annoyed the real Kiral. He, the man hidden behind Kiral's mask, might have been amused had he been free to think his own thoughts. As things stood, however, this disagreement between Meryam and Ihsan felt like an opportunity.

Meryam's lips were pinched. "We *were* victorious."

"Victorious?" Ihsan's face was full of mock amazement. "Did you say *victorious?* Ships lost. Men killed. Our standing in the eyes of our people shrunken to the size of a shriveled up prune. But at least the Moonless Host slipped through our grasp again! And even better, they did so with three other desert tribes backing them and more sure to follow."

Meryam tried to wield the weight of Kiral's word before the council. *What's done is done*, she tried to say. He felt them on the tip of his tongue— *What's done is done! What's done is done!*—but he fought her with every dram of fight left in him. He fought her, and he won! He felt her keen displeasure. She would be wroth when this council was done. She'd make him hurt himself again. But unless she was willing to spend more effort, a thing that, if done in front of the other Kings, might tip her hand, she was unable to tilt the scales.

"What's done is done," Meryam said to the others. "We must look to the shoring of our defenses—"

"So we must!" Ihsan cut in. He was a man afire, quite unlike the circumspect manipulator they were all accustomed to seeing. "In our history, the Kings have all gone to battle in the name of Sharakhai. We've bled to defend our thrones." He waved to her place at the table. "As my good queen now enjoys the same fruits as we do, I would suggest she go to the warfront to ensure Mirea's advance is halted."

"I did go to war," Meryam said.

"And then fled."

"I've spearheaded the effort to unleash the plague on Mirea. A tactic that is paying vast dividends."

"So you say. But what better way to protect that investment than to check on its progress yourself?" Ihsan looked about the table. "What say you, my good Kings?"

An uncomfortable silence followed as all waited for another to speak. Queen Meryam pressed hard on Hamzakiir. *Come, my Kings,* she wanted him to say. *This is foolishness. We need Meryam here.* But he resisted. A trickle of sweat crept its way down his forehead, but he maintained his hold on himself.

Ihsan, meanwhile, seemed to be focusing his attention on Azad, clearly hoping for him to rally to his side. They were lovers, Ihsan and the King-in-disguise, and yet Azad remained silent.

It was Sukru who ventured into the silence first. "We have all fought," he said while swinging his gaze to Meryam. "Our new Queen should as well."

"And given that we're confident in holding off the Malasani threat," Cahil chimed in, "and that we have spent and will spend so many resources to stop Mirea, it does seem prudent to have our queen—who promised us much as her dowry—prove her worth."

Again Meryam tried to have Hamzakiir intervene, and again he resisted.

"My fleet has already set sail!" Meryam's voice echoed harshly off the hard walls and sharp edges of the room. "Thousands are coming to the defense of Sharakhai."

It was Cahil who replied. "And in your absence they'll be positioned as we see fit." He spoke in that infuriatingly easy manner of his. For once Hamzakiir was glad for it. It was pushing Meryam beyond reason.

"I must be here when my fleet arrives."

"Did you not say that your Vice Admiral Mateo would be arriving soon?" Ihsan asked.

She had. There was no denying it now, and the implication was clear. Her orders could be given to him on his arrival, at which point she could depart the city.

Meryam remained silent, and in that silence she pushed Hamzakiir as much as she could. The balance was precarious. Ihsan, Sukru, and Cahil had all effectively voted in favor of Meryam going. Azad and Meryam, who had a vote at council as well, were clearly against the idea. With Beşir fallen into a deeper silence than normal, waiting for other voices to chime in, it fell to Kiral.

Cloaked in silence and a burning will, Meryam tried to break him. With all her might she tried, but she'd been pushing herself hard for weeks. She had little strength in reserve, and she hadn't expected Hamzakiir's sudden awakening. He wanted to tell them who he was. Who he truly was. But that truth was a heavy weight, and he found himself unable to lift it.

To side with Ihsan and the others, though, was simpler. A more bearable task. It was a thing Kiral might do, and the cage around Hamzakiir's mind was built to let such things through. So it was that he found himself with both the will and the words.

"Queen Meryam will go."

The statement struck like a gavel. The silence that followed yawned ever wider, the Kings swiveling their heads to Beşir even though, in effect, the decision had already been made.

"Very well," Beşir said.

Azad was then forced to tip his head in agreement, at which point they moved on to other business.

Meryam burned in silent fury. Hamzakiir had been right. When they returned to Eventide that night, they retired to their bedchambers and she forced him to strip and kneel before her.

She handed him a flagellation whip. "Draw me my blood."

He didn't try to resist. He was well aware he wouldn't be able to, not now that they were alone and he and his pain was her sole concern. However, as he swung the whip across his shoulder, as it struck skin, as blood began to trickle down his back, he smiled from within.

He'd defied Meryam. And that meant he could do it again.

Chapter 21

IN AN OCTAGONAL ROOM OF rich walnut panels and golden candelabra, Davud and Anila sat side-by-side in two lustrous, high-backed chairs. The close air smelled of linseed oil and fragrant kyphi, which burned in brass censers set on pedestals in all four corners of the room. Fezek, who upon reaching the rich manor had tried reciting a new sonnet on the futility of life to anyone who would listen, had been left in the antechamber outside.

He and Anila had been treated with respect, and their words given more weight than he could have hoped for. They sat in a circle with the Enclave's members, including Esrin, Dilara, and Esmeray, whose cold, humorless expression hadn't changed since the circle had convened. More than their manners, Davud was relieved to see their story taken seriously. It gave him hope for the first time since leaving King Sukru's palace that they might find some respite from a life constantly on the run.

The first hour of the circle was spent detailing their time with Sukru, and later with his brother the Sparrow, finishing with their harrowing escape. The nature of the Enclave's questions made him increasingly convinced they would grant them sanctuary, perhaps even allow them into the Enclave formally. Undosu, the old Kundhuni with the beaten leather cap, asked for particulars about Davud's awakening as a mage and about Anila's transformation into a necromancer. Meiying, a Mirean girl who'd surely seen no more than fifteen summers, was curious about the blooming fields and the strange crystal in the cavern below the city, whereas Nebahat, a Malasani man who had a painted golden forehead with a red stripe down the center, seemed most interested in the Kings and their dealings with one another.

As time wore on, however, they began asking more pointed questions, particularly Prayna, a strikingly beautiful Sharakhani woman. She focused on King Sukru, to the exclusion of everything else. How long had each of them been mentored? Who did the mentoring? What sigils and other knowledge had they been supplied with? How had his brother, the Sparrow, become involved, first with Davud and later with Anila? And, perhaps most importantly, what sort of assurances had Sukru demanded before allowing them to remain in his palace?

"Did he take your blood?" Prayna asked.

In that moment she was all cold calculation. Davud hadn't mentioned the taking of their blood and neither had Anila. He thought about lying, but the chance of its being discovered—indeed, of the Enclave already knowing the truth—was too great.

"Yes," he said.

"Both of you?" she pressed.

"Yes," Davud replied.

Prayna nodded with her lips pursed, then looked to the others as if she'd heard all she needed to hear.

The others continued for a time, but the tone had now changed. They had the air of botanists who had to be quick in studying a rare and dying breed of flower. They asked more about the Kings and their capabilities, and delved deeper into the peculiarities of necromancy and Anila's relation to it. But soon it was done and they filed from the room to deliberate. When they returned, the mood, formerly so optimistic, was funereal, so it came as no surprise when Prayna leaned forward in her chair and smiled sadly. "Your request for sanctuary has been denied."

"But why?" Anila demanded angrily. "We are brothers and sisters, are we not?" When no one responded, she stood and glared over the assemblage. "We are being *hunted* by your enemies!"

Prayna stood tall, a regal figure every bit Anila's equal. "The Kings are not our enemies. Nor are you. You came here begging favors, and we've declined. There's no more to it than that."

"Not your enemies?" She spread her arms wide. "The Enclave was only formed because the Kings were hunting you down!"

"That tale began and ended centuries ago," Prayna countered, "and has little to do with our current arrangement with the House of Kings."

"You think any of you wouldn't be hunted down were you to disavow yourselves of the Enclave's protections?"

At this, Esrin and Dilara looked uncomfortable, while their sister, Esmeray, fumed.

"Go," Prayna said, motioning to the door in the corner.

"You think any of you wouldn't be taken and tortured and killed?"

"Go!" Prayna's command echoed in the harshness of the wooden-walled room. "You won't be told a third time."

Anila took them in with a disgusted look. "Cowards."

Before she could say more, Davud raised his hands and stepped between them. "Enough," he said, and took Anila by the arm.

"Don't touch me!" She ripped her arm free and stalked from the room.

When the door closed behind her with a boom, Davud faced the assemblage. "I came here with two hopes. While you've denied the first, I hope you won't deny the second. You know Anila's story. Necromancers need an anchor, a tie to the world of the living. With Hamzakiir's death, that tie is fading, and her connection to the farther fields grows stronger every day. I would save her."

Prayna lifted her hands, palms facing outward, and put on a look as if that one simple gesture had absolved her of all responsibility. "I fear that's beyond us."

"Surely you have some knowledge amongst you. Or texts that might illuminate her condition, perhaps even point to a cure." He looked pointedly to Undosu. "And you in turn, may have more questions for us."

Before Undosu could say a word, Prayna waved toward the door. "Steer clear of the Enclave and its interests, and none of us will do you harm. Beyond that, you're on your own."

The fading of her heartless words took the last of Davud's hope with it.

It wasn't enough that they'd condemned Davud to a life of being hunted; their decision was a death sentence for Anila. "I remind you we've done nothing wrong. King Sukru, if he has his way, will destroy us for killing his brother, the Sparrow, a man who for centuries has preyed upon those who might otherwise have entered your ranks. You are the poorer for that, and you're the poorer for the decision you've made here today."

Davud could see that Undosu, the old Kundhuni, regretted what had happened, but he spoke no word in his defense, nor did anyone else. As they'd been on the way in, Davud and Anila were blindfolded and bespelled before being led away and deposited in the boneyard where they'd fought Esmeray. Fezek was already there, staring at his own gravestone. The Enclave had at least had the decency to find him new clothes and a hooded cloak so that he didn't look like, well, like what he was. A ghul.

"Come," Davud said, and led them away.

With the twin moons bathing the city in a soft silver light, they headed back to the cellar they'd rented in the Shallows. Once inside the dank, light-less space, Fezek sat in the corner and leaned back against the cool mudbrick.

"Would you like me to recite a poem to help you sleep?"

"No, thank you," Davud said. His poems were terrible.

"A sonnet, perhaps."

Before Davud could respond, Anila lay down and stared at the candle by her bedside. "Tell me again about Meiwei."

Fezek was deflated, but thankfully took the hint and fell silent. Davud, meanwhile, crossed his legs on the bed and leaned his back against the wall. Anila, who had seemed so indomitable a short while ago, now looked de-feated, a woman ready to accept whatever the fates had in store for her.

She sensed his reticence, his unwillingness to dredge up the past. "I need it, Davud. Tell me what you remember."

Since learning of Hamzakiir's death, she'd insisted Davud share his memories of their fellow graduates from the collegia. He knew very well it wasn't the memories she was interested in, per se, but the horrors they'd been put through. Their abduction. Their travel by ship to Ishmantep. His and Anila's escape and subsequent return to the caravanserai in hope of freeing the friends they'd spent years studying with, only to find that they'd missed Hamzakiir by minutes, the man who had done this to them all, the one they'd hoped to exact their revenge against. Worst of all for Davud was his personal horror at having used Anila's blood, which left her like this: halfway between life and death.

There were times when he felt like this macabre ritual of reciting tales was hurting Anila more than it was helping—the tales might feed her anger, but they also ate at her soul. Yet he'd found no more effective ways to help her. So, as the candle's light shone golden on the snakelike patterns in Anila's skin, Davud told her all he remembered about Meiwei. How pretty her smile was, how her notes were always a mess but how she very often had the highest marks on their tests. How shy and polite she was, and how she would skip when she was excited to tell you something. He told her everything: the funniest memories, the saddest, the most touching. Through it all, Anila's eyes were closed.

"Now Collum," she said when he was done.

Davud found he could no longer look at her, so he lay down and stared at the wooden beams running across the ceiling. He told her Collum's tale, but instead of giving in to the anger, he recounted memories of affable Collum in a way his fellow graduates would approve of: with grins and laughter, a gleam in his melancholy eyes.

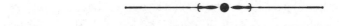

Davud woke to the feeling of being watched. He lifted his head and looked toward the corner. He shivered as he saw Fezek staring back at him. Fezek was sitting in the exact same position as earlier, his unblinking eyes glaring like lanterns at Davud. "Gods, Fezek, what is it?"

"I'm sorry about yesterday."

"What do you mean?"

"The woman. Esmeray. I nearly . . ."

Nearly killed her, he meant. Davud could still see the crazed look in his eyes as he'd raised his foot high, ready to bring it down on top of her skull, and his subsequent rage when Davud tackled him.

"It's all right, Fezek. It's what we told you to do."

"Yes, well, it's not like me. I don't know what's happened."

It's no mystery, Davud wanted to say. *Anila brought you back from the dead, and now you're not all there.* They'd had this conversation before, though. Bringing it up only made Fezek more upset. "It's all right," Davud said soothingly.

Fezek smiled half-heartedly. "Thank you," he said. "You can go back to sleep." But those cloudy eyes of his didn't budge.

"Look, I don't mean to be rude, Fezek, can you please stop staring at me? It's ghastly."

"More ghastly than me being dead?"

"They're both ghastly. Now will you please stare somewhere else?"

With an affronted look, Fezek raised both hands and turned his head away. "Heavens forbid you become *uncomfortable* when the dead poet stares at you. I mean, it's not as if I'm doing it to remember my time amongst the living, a thing that comforts me like a warm blanket in winter. No, why would you think *that*?"

Before Davud could say anything else, there came the sound of scraping from outside the cellar door. It was rhythmic and getting louder. Someone was descending the steps. Fezek's hearing wasn't very good, but his head now swiveled toward the door, and his eyes widened. As Davud swung his feet off the bed and placed them on the cold, packed earth, Fezek rushed to the door, opened it, and lunged into the night.

There came a yelp of fright, then sounds of a struggle. "Let go of me!"

Fezek dragged a woman with dark skin and wild hair into the room. By the gods, it was Esmeray. Fezek had her by the wrists, his grip so tight Esmeray was wincing.

"Enough, Fezek," Davud said. "Let her go."

Fezek complied, his expression wary as he stepped back into his corner. Esmeray seemed as angry as she'd been in the boneyard, but her look softened as she turned her gaze to Anila, who was still lost in her dreams, her eyes moving wildly beneath her lids. Davud thought about waking her, but decided against it. The dreams helped, not because Anila found them restful, but because she'd found a way to dream of exacting her revenge against Hamzakiir.

"What do you want?" Davud asked.

Facing Fezek, Esmeray raised her hands defensively, but Fezek apparently no longer saw her as a threat and squatted down in his corner once more.

Keeping one eye on him, she turned toward Davud and crossed her arms. "If it's true what you said, that King Sukru took your blood, it won't be long before he comes for you."

Davud stared at her open-mouthed. "Which was precisely why I was seeking sanctuary!"

She motioned to Anila and went on as if he hadn't spoken. "And even if he doesn't, she won't last much longer. Isn't that right?"

Davud felt his face growing hot. "If you've only come to rub my nose in it, you can leave."

"Has it ever occurred to you that you have other options?"

"Like what? Attacking Sukru while he sleeps?"

Esmeray's tattooed eyes went unexpectedly wide with pleasure. "*Precisely* that. Let Sukru have his way and he'll take you at his leisure. But take the fight to the *Kings* and you might stand a chance. Or at the very least you'll not be taking it like some old, useless mule waiting for the hammer blow."

It was so strange to see a woman who'd been ready to scratch out his eyes offering him advice that Davud smiled. "Why ever would you care?"

Her look was proud, even flinty, as if she were fighting a host of difficult memories. "I lost someone I loved dearly to the Kings. I wish I'd had the courage then to fight harder for him."

"Couldn't you still?"

Her look turned incredulous. She stabbed a finger at his chest. "Why do you think I'm here?"

"Wait, you're offering to *help* us?"

"Me and one other, a Qaimiri lord who came begging for the Enclave's help, a man who, despite his compelling story, was conspired against by the inner circle. His request, like yours, was denied."

"Why would I care about him?"

Esmeray's bright white smile made her look like a thief who'd stumbled on easy prey. "Because you could help one another. The Kings are after him as well. As is the city's new queen."

"Queen Meryam?"

"Just so."

Davud shook his head. "This man's name?"

"Lord Ramahd Amansir."

Chapter 22

IN THE WEEK FOLLOWING THE ATTACK by the diseased asirim, Brama witnessed a hundred more being brought to the Mirean hospital ship. Knowing how dangerous it was for any to tend to them, he decided to remain on the ship and help where he could.

The two physics, the old woman and the young man, died a week after showing signs of the disease, but before succumbing they offered up a host of ideas for how to fight it. Some of the afflicted had been placed on fasts. Others were put in sweat lodges. Others still were blooded with leeches. All treatments had a minimal effect, some made the symptoms worse. And the medicinals applied to new patients' skin had only seemed to ease the pain of the necrosis, not treat the condition. Queen Alansal had given up a small amount of a fabled liquor called brightwine in hopes that it would help. It gave those who imbibed it hours of bliss, but when it, too, proved ineffective, the queen put an immediate end to the practice.

Brama had hoped that the sickening sense of joy he felt while near the afflicted would vanish, but it didn't. If anything it grew. It was nearly enough to make him stay away from the ships, but he buried the thought the moment it reared its ugly head. Whatever discomfort he might experience, it was nothing compared to the suffering of the afflicted. Still, it had the effect of compounding his growing hatred of Rümayesh and the fact that he was becoming more like her by the day.

Several more times he heard the same strange trumpeting sound he'd heard while walking with Juvaan days ago. It came from beyond the camp this time, well beyond the oasis, and was accompanied by clouds of dust. Brama asked what it was, but the only thing anyone would ever say was *gui shan*. The calls reminded him of the elephants he'd seen brought to Sharakhai years ago, though the sound of these animals was deeper, rougher, more resonant. "May I see them?" he asked several times, intensely curious.

But the answer was always an emphatic no.

Nine days after the attack, Brama was changing the sheets of a fallen soldier when several new patients shuffled into the infirmary. Brama gasped when he recognized one. "Gods, no," he whispered, and made his way toward her.

Like all of the Damned, Mae's hair was closely shorn along the top and sides of her head, with a long braided tail at the back. She stared at him with her vivid green eyes and put on a pleasant face as Brama neared. She was a brave woman, but gods, the fear behind her smile. "I was so certain the gods had shone on me," she said, referring to the way she'd been spared from the disease so far.

Indeed, so had Brama. Mae had been there when it all began and had escaped the first wave of victims, while her twin sister, Shu-Fen, had succumbed to it. But now here she was, her lips turning gray, her eyes turning red. Brama sat on a stool by her bedside and took her hand. "Some have beaten it."

"Only six," she replied.

"And you'll be the seventh. Seven is a lucky number."

Her smiled turned genuine. "Not in Mirea." Then she paused and became pensive. "I more scare for Angfua than I am for me."

Angfua was her qirin. As with Shu-fen's qirin, Angfua would die if Mae succumbed to the disease.

"How did Angfua find you?" Brama asked. It was a terribly personal question, as he well knew. It was taboo to ask the Damned of their crimes or the circumstances around the bonding with their qirin. But he was not

Mirean, and he wondered if the Damned themselves wouldn't like to talk of it from time to time.

At first Mae only picked at the fringe of her blanket, and he thought she would decline to answer, but then she looked at him defiantly. "I kill the man who rape my younger brother." Her jaw worked, as if the memories were working themselves out in ways she couldn't express. "They suspect him of other crimes like this, but he was constable in the village, and town elders stood behind him." She shrugged. "I didn't see how a man such as this should be allowed to live."

"Understandably," Brama said. "Justifiably. Shu-Fen joined you?"

"Shu-Fen try to stop me, but they didn't believe us, and sentenced her to a life in the queen's mines alongside me."

"I'm sorry," Brama said. "That's how you found your qirin? You called for one?"

As Brama understood it, any accused who thought themselves in the right, even when committing a terrible crime, could forego a trial and call for a qirin to judge them instead. If they were chosen, the bond was forged. If not, the qirin would find them unworthy and gore them to death.

Mae shook her head. "Judgment pass already. Angfua and Jin come to village square where Shu-Fen and I would be whipped. They touch their horns to the ropes that bind us, and the knots come undone. We rode them from village and no one stop us."

Brama wondered at the bond created between them, one of love and respect. *So different from the one I have with Rümayesh.* "Is there no way to release Angfua?"

Mae's smile was strained. "I wish it—" She paused. "Possibril?"

"Wish it was possible."

She nodded, embarrassed. "I wish it was possible, but our bond, it made for life."

"And the Damned? I thought the queen selects them herself."

"She do. We wanted no more dishonor on our family, so I travel to the capital to beg the queen to join her service. She is wise, our queen. She agree, and asked Shu-Fen to come as well."

Brama's thoughts were interrupted by a commotion near the entrance.

Brama turned and found Juvaan standing there, beckoning to him. "Queen Alansal summons you."

Brama nodded, then squeezed Mae's hand. "In the desert, there are seven gods. Seven will be your number. Just you wait and see."

With a stony expression, Juvaan led Brama to the queen's pavilion, refusing to say why she wished to speak with him. But when Brama entered and found several of the Damned watching him from behind their grinning masks, their diamond-tipped arrows at the ready, he was fairly certain it wasn't for tea. He wondered, given how closely linked he and Rümayesh were, whether those arrows would affect him the same way they would her, but he tossed the thought aside as useless. The desert, as the old saying went, holds a thousand and one ways to die. What was one more?

In the center of the dais, sitting cross-legged on her wooden chair, was Queen Alansal. She wore a resplendent dress of blue silk with a bright orange sash across her waist. Her hair was intricately coiffed in a headdress with two steel pins holding it in place, but she looked haggard, with dark bags beneath her eyes, and while some of her grim determination remained, she looked small just then, like the fabled fox who'd challenged the hyena and been eaten for his trouble.

"What progress in contacting your mistress?" She sounded weary, but there was a clear note of desperation as well. She would not remain patient much longer, but what could Brama say?

"I've been trying, your Excellence. But I'm afraid she's not responding."

"Where has she gone?"

"I don't know."

Alansal straightened her back. "What would you think was happening, were you in my position?"

"I would think that ehrekh are mysterious, and their purposes cannot always be known to us, and that we should trust her at her word when she says she is here to help us."

"Us?"

Brama hadn't meant to say it, but he supposed it was true. Despite the fact that they were sailing to wage war against the city that birthed him, he felt sympathy for these people. At least, for those who might die at the hands of this dark disease. They didn't deserve long, lingering deaths. If things continued as they had been, the plague might swallow the entire Mirean fleet whole.

"She agreed to help," Brama said, "and she will."

"I wish I shared your confidence." Her chair creaked as she adjusted her position. "Tell me something that will restore a bit of mine."

What could he say? "Why don't you ask Behlosh where she is?"

"Behlosh is not your concern. Not unless you've become *his* mouthpiece as well." She looked him up and down with a piqued expression. "Have you become his mouthpiece?"

"No, Excellence, I have not."

"Then kindly tell me something about your mistress's whereabouts. Tell me what she knew about the asirim before the attack. Tell me what she knows about this disease."

The queen was normally so composed. The anger in her words and in the pinched expression on her face made it clear just how hard the past days had been on her. He hadn't noticed how tense the guards were, how ready for action, but he did now. Queen Alansal was ready to press him to the point of violence if need be.

He tilted his head toward the nearest of the Damned, a tall fellow with a bright red circle painted onto the center of his armor. "This isn't the wisest course of action, your Excellence."

"My people are *dying*!"

"And killing me will do nothing to bring them back."

"Do you wish to know what I think?"

"Please," Brama said, his voice no longer pleasant.

"I think the asirim were sent by the Kings, but that *Rümayesh* put the taint upon their claws so this disease could work its foul magic on my people. And I think she fled and left you behind so that she might have eyes and ears within our camp." Alansal lifted a finger. Bows creaked as a dozen arrows were lifted and aimed at Brama's chest. "So I ask you one final time. Where is Rümayesh?"

Brama felt his chest expand and collapse with each breath. His skin prickled. He could feel each of the arrowheads pointed at him. "You've convinced yourself of lies."

Alansal's head tilted, her brows pinched, and her look of barely controlled anger deepened. "Then convince me of the truth."

"That won't be necessary," a deep, feminine voice spoke.

All eyes turned toward the pavilion's entrance, where a towering black form ducked low. In one long, sinuous movement Rümayesh entered the pavilion, and she didn't come alone. Behind her, she had an old man by the ankle. She dragged him across the sand and onto the pavilion's carpeted floor. The archers, who'd been training their arrows on Brama, shifted to Rümayesh. Rümayesh ignored them all, focusing on the queen. Rümayesh did spare one glance for Brama, and in that moment, he felt a flash of annoyance, a thing clearly echoed in her flinty gaze.

Along her forehead, between the sweep of her horns that sprouted there, was a deep wound, only half healed. There were more signs of struggle along her body. A nick along one of her three lashing tails. A cut along the back of her head, where the long black thorns, her *hair*, had been severed in a crescent-shaped arc. There were two puncture wounds along her abdomen, and dark, almost black bruising to her already-dark skin.

She tossed the man to the foot of the dais.

"What is this?" Queen Alansal spoke the words as if Rümayesh had just presented her with a box of confectioneries. How she managed to stay so calm Brama had no idea. He knew Rümayesh, and had little to fear from her, but she was a mercurial being, and this was strange indeed.

"This," Rümayesh said, "is the alchemyst who created the scourge currently running rampant through your fleet."

The man was balding and had a graying beard that traveled halfway down the chest of his blue khalat. He was filthy and bloodied. Sand fell from his wiry hair as he came to a stand. He took in his surroundings with the look of a man standing in the shadow of his own gibbet.

"Your name?" said Queen Alansal.

"My name is—" He cleared his throat and bowed his head. "My name is Alu-Waled."

Alansal lifted the folds of her skirt and arranged them in a more pleasing pattern. "Is this true, Alu-Waled? Did you infect the asirim? Are you the man who delivered the scourge upon us?"

Alu-Waled seemed to have something caught in his throat. He swallowed and kept swallowing, his eyes darting between the queen, the Damned, and the towering ehrekh standing behind him. He was shivering badly.

"You set it upon the asirim and sent them here," Alansal pressed. "Which of the Kings ordered you to do this?"

He shook his head, and a sifting of sand fell to the carpets. "Not a King."

Alansal feigned surprise. "Was it not?"

"No, your Excellence. It was a queen. Queen Meryam."

Queen Alansal seemed confused for a moment, then her face went blank, as if not only did she accept Alu-Waled's claim, but thought herself foolish for not having thought of it sooner. "However much Sharakhai's new queen might be taking the reins, she didn't do this without permission."

The shivering along Alu-Waled's body grew worse. It made Brama nervous just to look at him. "No, Excellence. King Kiral gave his assent."

A hummingbird smile flitted across Alansal's lips. "We'll return to that. For now, tell me about the scourge. We need the cure."

"As I've—" His face pinched, as if he were reliving some painful memory. "As I've already told the ehrekh, it cannot be undone."

"Surely you jest."

This time, the shaking of Alu-Waled's head dropped enough sand to fill a teacup. He cringed as he spoke. "I'm afraid not. It was what I was told to do!"

"And if you'd been been ordered by Queen Meryam to create a cure?"

He peered into the pavilion's corners as if he might find a miracle hidden there. "If I had my full complement of assistants, the proper equipment and components, then perhaps."

"You may have any assistants you require. Any equipment. Any agents and reagents you might name."

It was a sign of Alansal's desperation that she would even entertain the notion. Recognizing her words as the lifeline they were, the old alchemyst nodded. "I can try."

At this, one of Rümayesh's tails lashed out and struck him across the back. "The truth," came Rümayesh's liquid voice.

With a terrified glance backward, Alu-Waled nodded and said, "It would likely take years, your Excellence. And even then . . ."

"You see no other way?" The anger in Alansal's voice was clear, but so was her worry for her people.

Alu-Waled shrugged, a gesture of perfect impotence. "It is easier to harm than to heal."

"So it is." Alansal motioned to the guards. "But I wonder if one might lead to the other. Take him to my chambers, and we'll find the truth of it."

Alu-Waled hardly struggled as two of the Damned led him away. "I was only doing as I was told." As they approached the entrance, he looked over his shoulder at the queen. "They would have killed me! I have seven children!"

A pall settled over the pavilion. Alansal turned her attention to Rümayesh, who waited patiently, her three tails swishing to and fro. It looked as if Alansal were debating whether to berate Rümayesh for abandoning them without a word, or praise her for delivering the one man who might find them a cure.

"For finding answers to some of the riddles that plague us, I thank you." Holding one sleeve, Alansal motioned to the place where Alu-Waled had just been standing. "A pity you weren't able to find the cure as well."

"A pity. I learned the truth shortly after taking him from the Kings' ships, but thought it best if you heard it yourself."

"And what now?" Alansal asked. "You know what's happening. Is there naught you can do?"

Rümayesh tilted her head. "What would you have me do?"

"I would have you heal them."

"Alu-Waled spoke the truth. There is no cure. And I'm no healer." She waved one arm toward Brama. "Just ask my herald."

"And yet your herald went untouched by the scourge."

"You misunderstand. What Brama has is no gift from me, but from Goezhen himself. *I* was granted such power, and when Brama and I joined hands he was granted some of the same."

For the first time in Brama's presence, Alansal's stony facade cracked. She was out of her element, impotent, fearful for her people, and willing to do anything to save them. "Surely there must be *some* way for you to help."

"My skills are limited."

"If you could but try."

Rümayesh considered, then tipped her head in agreement. "Very well. Bring one to me."

Queen Alansal did as Rümayesh asked. A cot was laid on the sand near the hospital's gangplank and one of the inflicted was carried out—none other than Mae. It only made sense to choose one of the Damned—they were highly trained warriors, and the lives of their qirin were also in the balance—but Brama still found himself breathing a sigh of relief to know that Mae might be saved.

Rümayesh crouched before her while the queen, her court, and many of her generals watched from a safe distance. The physics, several surgeons, and their assistants, who all wore white masks over their faces, stood closer. Their eyes darted constantly to Rümayesh, as though fearful she might attack them at any moment.

Rümayesh squatted and held one hand over Mae's face. Her fingers bent crookedly, swaying like grasses in the Haddah's clear, springtime flow. She tilted her head this way and that, her movements trancelike. Rümayesh's presence spread throughout Mae's body, and her curiosity rose. She wanted to know more about the disease. But then something revolting happened. Like a magpie, Rümayesh collected experiences, even painful ones. So she'd done with Brama. So she'd done with countless others. She was doing so again now, reveling in feelings she'd never felt before, her pleasure increasing the more that Mae's unique blend of pain, fear, and worry became known to her.

Long minutes passed, and Rümayesh became lost in the sensation. With the sun beating down, waves of self-indulgent bliss rolled from her, a euphoric sense of joy distilled not just from Mae's fear, but the intense, almost painful anticipation of those who watched, waiting, hoping Rümayesh would soon lift her head and tell them she'd found a way to cure their young soldier. It sickened Brama. So much so that he was ready to step forward and put a stop to it.

You knew my nature long before you led me to this place, Rümayesh said to him.

And I like it no better than I did then.

You have but to leave if it so offends you.

She knew he couldn't, though. He might walk away, but he would still feel her efforts. And even if he tried to shut her out, he couldn't do so for long. She knew this was too important to him.

Stop, Brama said, *or I'll tell the queen what you're doing.*

Rümayesh's hand paused over Mae's face. *You know, I believe you would.* At last she stood and faced the queen. "The nature of the disease is insidious. I might be able to slow its spread in one or two for a time, but no more."

As the desert wind tugged at the fabric of her ornate silk dress, Queen Alansal cloaked herself in silence and took her time to consider Rümayesh's words. She bowed her head. "You have my thanks for trying."

Rümayesh bowed her great, horned head in the same manner, though not without a soft smile that mocked, as if, despite her words, she considered all of this—the war, the queen, her entire army—beneath her notice. She stalked off beyond the circle of dunebreakers and into the desert, and the queen and the others dispersed.

Brama trailed after Rümayesh and found her near the edge of the caravanserai. She stood at the edge of a rocky overhang, looking out over pools of water with thick strips of grasses and bushes surrounding them. Beyond them were the dozen buildings of the caravanserai, which were dwarfed by the Mirean fleet in the middle distance.

"Why not just refuse her?" Brama asked. "Why go through that charade?" She hadn't tried to heal Mae. Not truly. She'd merely worn the guise of a healer while steeping herself in Mae's pain.

"You know me well enough by now to answer that question."

"She promised you a reliquary, a bone of Raamajit the Exalted. Ask her for it in exchange for lifting the scourge. She'd agree. I'm certain of it."

"Your care for these foreigners astounds me." Her head swiveled, and her yellow eyes shot straight through him. "They're here to wage war on *your* city."

"War was coming no matter what I did, but it's bigger than that now. Queen Alansal is considering ordering her fleet home. If she does, the scourge might reach her homeland. It could decimate their entire population."

She turned her attention back to the verdant pools of water. "What of it?"

Brama stared at her, his mouth open. "You would wallow like a sow in that as well? You would find joy as tens of thousands, perhaps hundreds of thousands, perished?"

She remained silent for a time. It was then that Brama realized. She was *brooding*. "What are human lives to me?"

"They meant something to you once."

"You can look upon your own flesh and speak those words?"

"Is this because of Behlosh?"

"Begone, Brama."

"Is it because of Goezhen?"

Brama had felt rage from Rümayesh before. He'd felt hunger and need, even jealousy, but he'd never felt so much as a twinge of sorrow. He did now, and it made him wonder: Sorrow over what? Sorrow over whom? "I made a vow to keep you safe, Brama Junayd'ava. But I warn you, I will forsake it if you speak of Goezhen again."

He had to wonder why she was so sensitive about it, but he felt the truth in her words. This wasn't the time to press. "Don't leave them to suffer like this." He waved toward the circle of tall dunebreakers. "Don't let the scourge escape the bounds of this encampment."

"It is beyond me," she repeated.

Brama waited for her to say something more. When she didn't, he said, "I've thought many things of you, but I never thought you a coward."

He thought he'd made a terrible mistake. Such was the anger within her. But then she burst into a cloud of beetles and flew away, into the desert. As the cloud dwindled beyond sight, Brama turned and walked back to camp, to help with the sick as he could.

Chapter 23

IT WAS THE MOONLESS PART of the night as Çeda stood in the forward cabin of *Wadi's Gait*. Before her, lit by a lantern hanging from the ceiling beams, the goddess Nalamae lay in the cabin's lone bunk. A blanket covered her, but only from the waist down. Her chest was wrapped tightly in bandages. Her hair was no longer braided but hung about her arms and shoulders like a golden mantle. As tall as she was, her legs dangled beyond the foot of the bed.

Sümeya was slumped in a chair in the corner, snoring softly. With night fallen, Devorah now occupied Leorah's body; she sat crook-backed on a padded stool beside the bunk, unwinding a bloody bandage from around Nalamae's wrist, one of the many smaller injuries the goddess had sustained. It still felt so strange. Gods weren't supposed to lie in sickbeds. They weren't supposed to need help from mortals. Yet here was Nalamae, pallid, shivering, being tended to by an aged woman who seemed every bit as frail.

Nalamae hadn't awoken since the battle, either because of the arrow she'd taken from Beşir's bow or from the power she'd expended to save them. Likely it was both. At least she seemed to have stabilized, thanks to Leorah, Devorah, and Sümeya's tireless work.

Çeda put her hand on Devorah's shoulder. "I'm going to get some fresh air."

Devorah reached up and patted her hand. "Say a prayer to the old gods."

The old gods aren't listening, Çeda thought. *Why do you think we're in this mess?* But Çeda couldn't say that. She was convinced the old gods wouldn't have left their children to do such things without being punished for it.

Çeda lifted Night's Kiss, Husamettín's great, two-handed shamshir, from a shelf and took it up to the deck. The ship swayed as they sailed beneath a scattering of stars. The dunes were shallow in this part of the desert, the sand powdery, making their passage sound like an approaching rainstorm.

The *Red Bride*, commanded by Melis, sailed along their port side. Husamettín was on that ship, bound with ropes in the hold. In addition to Çeda, Leorah, Sümeya, and Melis, ten Shieldwives had survived the terrible battle, along with twelve asirim. The Shieldwives, many of whom were lying on the decks of the two ships, seemed content to wrap themselves in silence. The asirim were of like minds, galloping in silence behind the ships. Mavra was inconsolable with grief, Sedef righteous with anger.

The rest of their beleaguered company, six Shieldwives and twice as many asirim, had been killed outright or lost in the battle. They'd had no chance to do more than sweep by *The Piteous Wagtail* and transfer the survivors to Leorah's yacht. Three Shieldwives had been injured terribly. Before the sun rose, Sirendra would likely die from a chest wound that refused to stop bleeding. The two asirim bonded to her—the twins, Huuri and Imwe— lagged behind the pack, not from injuries of their own, but because they feared the lord of all things would soon come for Sirendra.

While heading to the stern, where Jenise stood at the wheel, Çeda scanned the horizon for the telltale rake of sails or the glimmer of lantern light. "No sign of them?"

"None," Jenise replied stiffly. She'd insisted on piloting them through the night. *I won't be able to sleep,* she'd told Çeda. *Not tonight.*

"Jenise, we've hardly had a chance to speak. Everything happened so quickly. Husamettín was there, and . . ." Çeda swallowed to clear her throat. "Auvrey was gone before I knew it."

"Such a stupid thing to do," Jenise said, "going after the King of Swords on her own."

"It was brave."

"It was the most beetle-brained thing I've ever seen. She was always so headstrong. And overprotective. A terrible combination, really." She stared fixedly ahead, as if she were reliving Auvrey's final moments over and over. She probably had been since the sun went down. As the ship slunk into a wide trough, she glanced Çeda's way. "But yes, she was brave as well."

Çeda gripped her shoulder. "She was a bright light among us."

Jenise patted her hand while staring up at the heavens. "She still is."

While Jenise navigated the way ahead, Çeda gave the horizon behind them a more careful inspection. After the battle the day before, one of the Kings' ships had given chase. Over the course of the morning it had closed the distance, but then Çeda had ordered *Wadi's Gait* and the *Red Bride* to sail for a swath of rocky terrain. They'd reached it just in time, using their maneuverability to put distance between them and the clipper once more.

Çeda wondered what would have happened if the clipper had caught up to them. They knew the goddess was with Çeda and the Shieldwives. Would they risk Nalamae's using her power again? Maybe not. Maybe they were giving chase only to learn where they were headed, information they might use once a larger force had been rallied.

Çeda thought it more likely King Beşir was aboard that ship. Surely he hoped to finish what he'd started. In the closing moments of the battle, Çeda had delivered a devastating blow that would have killed a normal man in moments, but Beşir would have brought healing elixirs with him and a day or two of rest would see him back on his feet. Three days, and he would be well enough to draw his bow again.

Despite their losses, it was hard not to look at the battle's outcome as anything but miraculous. Without Nalamae's intervention, they would all have died or been captured by the Kings.

Mavra wailed. *That's cold comfort, daughter of Ahyanesh.*

Cold comfort indeed, Çeda thought. The battle had been a terrible blow, the Kings proving once again how the gods favored them, how impossible Çeda's task was.

Setting those worries aside, Çeda lifted Husamettín's sword. She'd had no chance to satisfy her curiosity until now, and it was difficult to hide her awe. The entire desert had heard of this blade, even if only in folk tales. Even in the lands beyond the desert, tales were told of the King of Swords and the hunger of his ebon blade. Much like the Blade Maidens themselves, the sword was a symbol of fear, a sign of the Kings' power. And now she held it in her hands.

The blade had a grim beauty about it. Its grip felt unnatural, nothing like River's Daughter, and it was *weighty*, though not so heavy as she would have guessed. If the legends were true, Goezhen himself had forged it. Çeda had few doubts that he had; the most striking part about it, even sheathed as it was, was the power emanating from within. It *hummed*. And when she pulled the blade free of its sheath, it buzzed with a sound like a beetle in flight. The ebon steel swallowed the stars as she swung it overhead, and in the wake of its passage a black void fluttered, a sheet of night that dissipated, foglike, in the blink of an eye. Swinging the blade across her body, she felt the vibration in her bones, first in her hand, then up her wrist and along her arm.

During Çeda's training as a Blade Maiden, Sayabim had always harped on about making one's sword an extension of her body. River's Daughter had always felt like a willing partner in that dance. Night's Kiss, however, refused to be led. It resisted her movements, sometimes feeling more weighty than it had moments ago. Then it would change its mind and lean into her movements. Time and time again it set her off balance and ruined her timing. She felt like a child swinging a real sword for the first time. But it became easier when she focused her will upon it, not only because it made her more mindful of the sword's tendencies, but because the sword seemed somehow pleased.

Most disturbing was the yearning she felt within the darkened steel. She'd been communing with the asirim for years, longer if she included some of her earliest memories of the blooming fields. She'd felt their hunger to kill—an impulse laid upon their shoulders by the gods but no less real for it. This blade had urges that were similar, but it was starkly different in one key way: it fed off her intent. As she responded to the urge to draw blood with memories of her own—the strongest being her deep desire to slay the Kings after her mother's death—the blade responded in kind, and she had to sheathe it lest it overwhelm her. When she did, the blade's murderous urges became muted then faded altogether. She felt its satisfaction, however, as if this first foray with its new master had gone well enough.

Hearing movement, Çeda turned to find Sümeya climbing up the hatch stairs. When she spotted Çeda, she stopped halfway and motioned to the ship's lantern-lit interior. "She's awake, and she's asking for you."

Çeda felt a cold dread as she accompanied Sümeya to the forward cabin. She was convinced the goddess would say that the wound from Beşir would soon take her life. She found Nalamae in her bunk, Devorah by her side, feeding her broth from a steaming bowl.

As Çeda sidled past Devorah to stand near the foot of the bed, Nalamae rolled her head toward Çeda's position. Her eyes weren't fixed in the right place, though. They stared *beyond* the boundaries of the ship. To the heavens? To the Kings' ship still trailing behind them?

"Leave us," Nalamae whispered.

Sümeya hesitated, but Devorah was soon up and ushering her out with brisk waves of her hand. With a smile that Çeda supposed was meant to give her heart, Devorah handed over the spoon and bowl of broth, then left. The door closed with a thump behind her.

Çeda felt small in the silence that followed.

Perhaps sensing it, a smile formed on Nalamae's broad, handsome face. "Here," she said, patting the stool.

Çeda hesitated. She'd been angry with Nalamae for not aiding them sooner, for hiding in the shadows when she could have helped the thirteenth tribe. But she could see now that she'd been acting like an impetuous child, unable to see the consequences of her desires. Now, they were plain as day. The moment Nalamae had left her place of hiding—to save Çeda and her mission, no less—she'd nearly paid for it with her life.

"Come," Nalamae said, "sit by my side. The broth is good, and I would finish it before it grows cold."

The broth's rich scent brought Çeda back to her senses. She leaned Night's Kiss in a corner. The blade had quieted to the point that it seemed almost mundane. An effect of being close to Nalamae?

Çeda sat and fed the goddess, and soon the broth had been consumed. Nalamae seemed comforted, but even in that brief time the bandages across her chest, pristine when Çeda had arrived, had developed a spot of red over her breast.

"Will it heal?" Çeda asked.

Nalamae lifted one arm to test the wound, but she hadn't even touched the skin around it before she paled and her arm fell back. Long moments punctuated by her quick, shallow breathing passed before her color returned.

"It will be no simple thing," the goddess said weakly. "The bow that delivered that arrow was crafted by Yerinde herself. But yes, I think I will recover."

"Yerinde arranged all of this," Çeda said. "We think they want you dead. Permanently dead. Is that so?"

"Of course."

"Would it have worked, had Beşir's arrow been aimed with a sharper eye?"

Nalamae shrugged, cringing from the slight effort. "I cannot say. I won't deny the possibility. But I've had so little control over my rebirths thus far."

Çeda shook her head, terribly confused. "But how can that be?"

"You are under the mistaken impression that I do it consciously, and that therefore I must know what I'm doing. I'm afraid I don't, Çedamihn. So much has been lost to me, including the nature of the spells that save me time and time again." She raised a hand before Çeda could protest. "You must understand. So many of my earliest memories have been lost. When I am reborn, I find myself somewhere in the desert. This time it was as Saliah, witch of the desert. In times past it was as others. Always I am naked and alone. Blind. I know so little."

On the deck above, Sümeya called orders to adjust the ship's course. The rudder turned. The ship heeled for a moment, the hull creaking before giving over to the hiss of the skis once more.

"Slowly but surely, however," Nalamae went on, "I discover tools to remember. When I came to the acacia where we first met, I made the glass chimes you saw. I wove thread from gold and hung them. I saw the countless visions the acacia had gathered into its branches, but never did I see visions about myself. My true nature was hidden from me. Only when some few came to me for help, like Leorah and your mother, or others with blood of the lost tribe, did I begin to see myself in some of the visions.

"It took years, but in time more and more of my past was revealed. I collected those visions like pearls. I stitched them against the fabric of my life to better understand what my brothers and sisters had done to the Kings, what they'd planned from the start. The days leading up to Beht Ihman are still lost to me, but I understand much now, Çedamihn. I know that the day is nearing when they reveal what they've so meticulously planned. This is why they fear me. This is why Yerinde sent the Kings to deal with me once and for all. We have but to unlock the final riddle."

From the purse at her belt, Çeda took out a silver vial. Within was the acacia seed her mother had stolen from the House of Kings. She unscrewed the top and tipped it onto Nalamae's palm. She told Nalamae the story of her mother's finding it and later giving it to Leorah so that it would find its way to Çeda.

Nalamae held the seed for a long while, rolling it between her palms. When she spoke again, her voice was reverent. "To hold it . . ." She pinched the seed between two fingers, brought it to her nose, and inhaled deeply. She looked like a woman awaiting news of a lost child, fearful yet still holding out hope.

"What's happened?" Çeda asked. "Have you seen something?"

Nalamae turned toward Çeda, and her worried look vanished. "One of the visions your mother had was of you visiting Leorah on this very ship." She patted the hull. "I tried to tell her that visions are not certainties, that they're merely one possibility among many, but your mother would hear nothing of it. She was convinced that it would happen."

"Does that mean I was meant to deliver the seed to you? Did she see any of this? Yerinde? The Kings? Your wound?"

"This is the failing of so many mortals. You think the things the fates show you are preordained. They are not. The visions the acacia grants, the visions seen in Yusam's mere, they are places one might land, but only if the right course is followed."

"I didn't know I was following a course."

Nalamae smiled. "Sometimes that's best, Çedamihn, for only in that way can you wash ashore in the right place and at the right time."

Çeda wasn't sure she believed that, but there was no point in arguing. Instead, she asked the question that had been worrying her since she'd found the seed in the box her mother had left her. "Does it mean you will die?" Warm tears filled her eyes, crept down her cheeks. "Will I use this to plant another tree for you?"

Nalamae reached up and wiped the tears away. Their eyes met, and for once she seemed to be looking directly at Çeda. "That I cannot say."

"But you must know something. If you die, it may be years before the tree is large enough to call to you. Decades, perhaps, before you return to us."

"That's true"—she took the vial from Çeda, slipped the seed inside, and pressed it back into Çeda's hands—"so perhaps we should ensure that I don't."

Çeda screwed the cap back on and hid the treasure inside her pouch. "Can you stop the other gods?" she asked abruptly.

"That is the wrong question. We've reached a crossroads. I don't know what my sisters and brothers have planned, but we know that they've seen fit to watch everything from afar. It is as if they set up a pillar of stones on Beht Ihman and that every action taken by the Kings chips away at the foundation. If we do nothing, it will soon come tumbling down. And now Yerinde has entered the fray, which means they've become nervous, perhaps of my presence. Or of yours."

"Mine?" A chill ran down her spine. "No, they want *you*. Ihsan told me so."

Just then a bell rang three times. It was the *Red Bride*. They'd been told to signal *Wadi's Gait* when Husamettín awoke. Nalamae seemed disturbed by the sound. When she spoke again, she sounded weary. "There's no doubt the other gods would like to see me dead, but take note that they threatened *you* in order to force my hand. They know, as I do, that you will play one of the biggest roles in the coming conflict."

"What are you saying?"

As Nalamae closed her eyes, orders were called to bring the two ships near to one another, and Çeda's eyes were drawn to the stain of red on her bandages. Already it was wider than when Devorah had left. The goddess remained silent for so long Çeda thought she'd fallen asleep, but then she stirred and spoke. "When the sun rises, Çedamihn, we must part ways. I will sail with Leorah to Mount Arasal to heal and await your return. You must go to Sharakhai. There is little time, I think, for you to continue as you've planned. So go. Find Sehid-Alaz. Free as many of the asirim as you can, then meet us in the valley below the mountain."

Çeda's right hand was tingling. The old pain was flaring, not as it had in the past with outright pain, but as if she'd finally mastered it. She squeezed her hand into a fist, enjoying the prickle of pain that spread through her palm, fingers, and wrist. "Yerinde herself may move to stop me."

"Yes, but I'll see what I can do to force her hand. I've become particularly gifted at hiding my presence from them. But I will allow them to see some signs of where Leorah and I are headed. Not so much that they know where precisely, but enough to draw their attention from you. It will, I trust, convince them that I am weakened, and that it might be best to kill me while they have the chance."

As the hissing sound of the *Red Bride*'s skis grew louder, Nalamae took Çeda's right hand and forced it to unclench. "Go, speak with the King of Swords."

Çeda lifted Nalamae's hand and kissed her fingers. After calling Devorah to tend to the goddess, she headed up to deck, ready to transfer to the other ship.

Chapter 24

THERE WAS SO MUCH MORE that Çeda wished to speak to Nalamae about. But the morning had brought with it a howling gale. An amber fog obscured the desert, stinging exposed skin. They could see no more than a quarter-league ahead. It was dangerous weather to sail in, to be sure, but it also presented an opportunity: part ways with *Wadi's Gait* now and they could do so without being spotted by the Kings' ships.

They decided to take it. After saying their farewells, Çeda and Sümeya swung over to the other yacht. From the deck of the *Red Bride*, Çeda watched as *Wadi's Gait* was swallowed by the swirling sand, then asked to speak to Husamettín alone. Sümeya seemed ready to argue, but after a sharp nod she left Çeda to it and set about the business of helping Melis to prepare the ship for their journey to Sharakhai.

Çeda took Night's Kiss with her belowdecks and arrived at the small hold in the ship's stern, where Husamettín had been bound with rope and tied to the hull. He looked strangely whole. It wasn't right that they should be so battered and he so unscathed, but Çeda counted her lucky stars that Leorah had somehow been able to knock him unconscious. His armor had been taken from him. He wore woolen stockings, black trousers, and a simple ivory kaftan stained by time and sweat.

Strangest of all, his turban was gone, leaving his pepper-black hair to flow down across his shoulders and chest. She'd never seen him this way: looking mortal, ordinary. It lent their meeting an air of intimacy that served to remind Çeda of her mother's absence. It put her in a right foul mood.

"It's interesting, don't you think, that the gods saw fit to place the fate of my own father into my hands?"

Husamettín held his tongue and seemed warier than he'd been moments ago.

"How did my mother come to you?" Çeda asked. "Who did she pretend to be?"

"What matter is that?"

"What matter is it to withhold it?"

He shifted himself against the hull so that he sat more upright. "She came as a trader in fine antiques."

"Antiques of what sort?"

"Silverwork, mostly. Gold. Some tin."

Absently, Çeda sat on a sack of rice, close enough to touch Husamettín's legs, and thought back to her childhood. There were things her mother had tended to hoard, and they were generally of a certain sort. "Chased pieces," Çeda said. "Embossed. Usually small. Lockets and cases and the like." When Husamettín gave a shallow nod, she pulled her teardrop locket from beneath her dress. "Like this?"

As his eyes fell on the locket they filled with wonder, but only momentarily. They hardened quickly, making her wonder what these pieces meant to him. So he'd been lured, at least in part, by Ahya's bringing him a certain kind of antique. Doing a bit of educated guesswork, she said, "You were collecting pieces of your past, weren't you?"

She didn't need the dark look on his face to know it was true. It made perfect sense. It was likely something he'd hidden from many people and when her mother found out, she'd used it as an opening, a way to insert herself into his life. "What do they mean to you?" She thought further on the works her mother had collected, and remembered how similar they were in style. "Were they from your tribe?" And then she remembered how old Husamettín was, how lonely one's life might be if they lived to see everyone they knew die. "It was someone you knew, wasn't it? A sister, perhaps, or one of your lovers."

Husamettín remained stubbornly silent, but she could tell she'd hit the mark.

"Look at you." All the venom she'd harbored for the Kings returned in a rush. "You pretend to value family, and yet you sacrificed your brothers and sisters. You sacrificed a woman you loved. You would have sacrificed me as well, your own *daughter*."

"You think your mother deserved anything less? You think a spy who'd infiltrated the ranks of the Moonless Host would be met with mercy by Macide Ishaq'ava?"

"I'm no scarab. And whatever my mother did to you, it wasn't enough. None of you deserved the gifts the gods gave you."

Husamettín snorted. "You're blind if you think the thirteenth tribe are so different from the Kings."

"How dare you compare us! The thirteenth tribe fights for its very survival, while you hope to murder us, finishing what you started on Beht Ihman."

"The gods themselves anointed our cause."

"You're speaking to the wrong woman if you think you can wipe the blood from your hands by invoking the gods. They may have made you an offer, but it was *your* consent that led to the slaughter of thousands." She was getting none of the satisfaction she'd hoped for from this confrontation. She'd expected catharsis but found only bitterness and bile. "I've long wondered," she went on, "if I would do to my father as he did to my mother."

"What is it you think I did?"

The image of her mother hanging upside down from the Kings' gallows returned unbidden. Ahya had been bloody, naked, her throat slit wide. Ancient runes had been carved into the skin of her feet, hands, and forehead. "You *tortured* her." Çeda blinked to clear the terrible image. "Cut foul words into her skin so that she'd be marked in the farther fields."

And then Husamettín surprised her. There was a flash of regret in his eyes. "That was Cahil."

"You think that makes it better?" His reaction made her wonder, though. Was he still hurt by what Ahya had done? Hurt by her lies? Had he *loved* her? No. One didn't do that to people they loved. He *coveted* Ahya, and when he found he could no longer have her, that he'd *never* had her, he'd beaten her, given her over to the cruelest of the Kings for questioning, and watched while it happened. The very thought enraged her. Her feelings were echoed by Night's Kiss, making them impossible to ignore. She was forced to suppress them lest the heightened emotions rob her of all reason.

Husamettín glanced down at the sword, still held in her left hand. "Its call is powerful. You might come to regret taking it from me."

"I'll manage." She felt some small acknowledgment from the sword—deference to her as its new master—but she also sensed the undeniable kinship it felt toward Husamettín.

Husamettín shrugged. "When the twin moons return to the desert, we'll know the truth of it."

"And what happens then?"

"Its will becomes stronger."

"Which implies that it wants something."

He looked at her as if it were the most mud-brained thing he'd ever heard. "Well of course it does. It wants blood! It will demand it."

She'd brought Night's Kiss with her to get some of her questions about it answered, but it felt as if the conversation were too much in his control, so she altered her tack. "Was that the cost to seal your pact with Yerinde? Blood?"

To her satisfaction, his brows pinched momentarily in surprise. "The gods have stood behind the Kings of Sharakhai for centuries."

"Azad dead by my mother's hand. Külaşan, Mesut, and Onur by mine. Yusam is gone as well. Zeheb has been driven mad. Is that what you consider the gods standing behind you?"

"Sharakhai is still ours."

"And yet your position grows more tenuous by the day." The wind gusted and the hull creaked as the ship leaned over a dune. Night's Kiss tried to fan her anger, but she stifled it, focusing on her reason for speaking to Husamettín alone. "Have you considered the possibility Yerinde is acting without the consent of the other gods?"

He remained silent.

"What did she promise you? What did she want in return? Was it the thirteenth tribe, or Nalamae?"

Again that pinching at the edges of his eyes, more carefully hidden. "Who told you that?"

"Come now. It should be no surprise that whispers of your hunt for the goddess have drifted to the desert. I'll admit, it seemed preposterous at first." She pointed beyond the hull. "But then I *felt* Yerinde. I felt her hunger for Nalamae. Don't you think it strange that after four hundred years the goddess would suddenly appear in Sharakhai and ask this of you?"

"I presume you have a point?"

"You still have the power to make your own choices. Even you must admit Yerinde's demand is strange. There is a greater purpose behind it. Tell me what you know, and perhaps together we can discover it before it's too late."

He laughed, a rare thing from the stone-hearted King of Swords. "You think I would do anything to help *you*?"

"Not me," Çeda said. "You would be atoning for your sins before you leave these shores. You would be helping Sharakhai."

"Are you a priestess of Bakhi now, to offer me salvation before I die? And what matter is Sharakhai to you?"

Çeda jabbed the hilt of Night's Kiss into his chest. "You may not believe it, but Sharakhai is in my bones. It is *my* city as much as it is yours, and I love it. No matter what you and the other Kings have done, Sharakhai is still a place of wonder, and I will fight to protect it. But now the jackals of Mirea and Malasan are closing in. Worse, the gods themselves are playing us all for fools."

"If you knew me as well as you pretend, you wouldn't waste your breath. I would never share our secrets, nor take counsel with a traitor."

"I may be a traitor to *your* cause, but I am loyal to Sharakhai."

"Loyal to the people of the desert, you mean."

"Them as well, yes."

Husamettín sneered. "You think your tribe wouldn't tear the city apart if given the chance?"

"You don't know them. Not anymore. You've demonized them for so long you think they're just like the tribes who came to Sharakhai four hundred years ago, ready to tear the walls down. But they aren't. They no longer wish to see Sharakhai destroyed."

Husamettín's face turned angry. "You would sit before me and claim that the Moonless Host wishes for *peace*?"

"There are those who would mete out violence. What do you expect after all you've done? But Tribe Khiyanat is not the Moonless Host, nor is it the same tribe you and your brother Kings allowed to be sacrificed. It is a thing made anew, and I tell you, Macide is ready for peace. So are the other shaikhs. Offer them a way to prosper and they will join you. They would help save Sharakhai from her invaders."

"The tribes know how peace can be found."

"By bowing to you, men who think themselves the rightful rulers of the desert?"

The look on his face was one of supreme entitlement. "How else?"

Çeda was so angry she gripped the hilt of Night's Kiss and bared a foot of its ebon steel. It hummed angrily as she spoke. "What power you have, you gained through the lives of my people!"

"All is fair in war, Çedamihn."

She stood and bared the full length of Night's Kiss, tossing the sheath aside. "That was not *war*!" She pointed the sword at his chest. "That was murder. That was betrayal. *You* are the traitor, Husamettín. *You* are the one who broke all confidences. Have you no shame for what you've done?"

His face was grim and undaunted as he stared at the tip of the ebon blade. "You think me cowed by the sight of steel?"

She knew very well that Night's Kiss was heightening the rage within her. She let it. She would let it rise as high as it wished to go. "You should be."

"Why?" His eyes were flinty. He smiled. "What will you do with it?"

The blade pleaded with her to use it against its former master. She drew it back, ready to bring it across his throat.

Do not! came Mavra's reedy voice. *Do not!*

Çeda sensed her running along the sand beside the others, who held similar reservations. Those who might once have pushed her into rageful action were now the voice of reason.

What are you afraid of? Çeda asked them.

Sheath it, Çedamihn. It was Mavra, and her fear was plain.

Sheath it, said Sedef.

Sheath it, called the others.

They were *pained* by the unsheathed sword, she realized. Or by the miasma of dark emotions that emanated from her. She tried to ask them more, but like so many things related to the Kings, their curse forbade them from speaking of it. That realization, and their collective fear, threw cold water on her fury. Her breath coming hot, her right hand burning white with pain, she picked up the sheath and slid Night's Kiss home. It rested there with an angry buzz.

"Why does Yerinde want Nalamae dead? You cannot be so blinded that you don't care about the answer."

Husamettín only stared.

"Give me Sehid-Alaz, then."

"*Give* him to you?"

The smug look on his face was too much. She threw Night's Kiss aside, straddled his waist, and drove her fist into his mouth. "Tell me where he is! Tell me how to lift the chains you've placed on him!"

"Chains?" Husamettín was not a man of humor, but he laughed at this, blood dripping down his chin from his split lip. "You think I've chained him?"

She crashed her fist into his mouth again. "His chains!" She hit him again, and finally he stopped laughing. "Like the asir you treated like a hound." Çeda could still see that sad soul, crawling along beside the gaoler, never leaving his side, his mind hungry to devour. "You did the same to Sehid-Alaz, didn't you?"

Blood stained Husamettín's lips and teeth. His eyes, however, were filled with mirth. "I placed no *chains* on him. I learned how to neuter the asirim long ago. It makes them less useful overall, but they become docile, willing to adhere to my needs. Once done, they come to heel forevermore. Once done, it cannot be *un*done. Sehid-Alaz is now as the one you saw in my dungeons."

Çeda became pure red rage. The sword no longer drove her. Instead, it was the frustration and rage that had been building since before her mother's death. It was the knowledge of all that Husamettín and the other Kings had done. This was for those who'd died on Beht Ihman. For those who'd been hunted like jackals ever since. For those the asirim had been forced to kill in the name of the Kings. This was for all the asirim who yet lived, waiting for their release. And it was for Schid-Alaz, whose people had been taken from him, and now his very identity.

Over and over again her fists powered into Husamettín's face. She realized she was screaming. Someone was in the hold with her, trying to pull her away, but she shoved them back.

Husamettín's face was a wreckage of cut skin and hair and sweat and blood, but still she drove her fists into his flesh.

Sümeya, Çeda realized. Melis had come as well. They were trying to pull her away.

"You'll kill him!" Sümeya was shouting.

Grabbing a fistful of his hair, she pounded his face twice more. And when they grabbed her arms and dragged her away, she sent her boot into his jaw and heard the satisfying crunch of broken bones.

Husamettín's eyes fluttered shut and his head lolled to one side, unconscious. Blood dripped from a dozen wounds along his mouth, cheeks, nose, and the bony ridges around his eyes. But Çeda didn't care. She wanted to kill him, consequences be damned. Another King would be gone. Another blight on the desert removed.

Sümeya was saying something.

Çeda's breath came in great heaves, making it nearly impossible to hear. With a great effort of will, she focused her attention on Sümeya.

"Ships!" she said. "We've spotted ships!"

"What?"

"Swift dhows and ketches. At least a dozen of them flying the colors of Malasan."

Slowly, Çeda's breathing slowed. She saw then what she hadn't noticed before. Husamettín's kaftan had been ripped down to his stomach, revealing a knotted landscape of old scars. Had he been tortured? Maybe. Maybe one of his enemies had taken him centuries ago. It might even have been someone from the Moonless Host, someone from the thirteenth tribe.

The prospect sobered Çeda. Husamettín, the King of Sharakhai, seemed to shrink before her. No longer was he a King, a figure to be feared. He was but a man, a sad, broken man who deserved nothing but death. Part of her longed to give it to him, but there was still work to be done in the desert. Her people needed a home. The surviving Kings had to be dealt with. The gods were playing a game she knew little about. And there was still a chance that Husamettín, this pitiful thing of flesh and blood that many had thought immortal, could help them.

So he would live. He would live until he proved himself no longer useful. Picking up Night's Kiss, she spat on his unconscious form and left the hold.

Chapter 25

IN THE DEPTHS OF SHARAKHAI's trading district, Davud watched from the shaded portico of an old hostelry as an uncovered araba pulled by a pair of dusty brown akhalas turned off the Corona. The air was streaked with amber sand. The storm that had swept in that morning seemed to accompany the news that dozens of ships had been spotted along the southern horizon. The vanguard of the Malasani fleet had arrived.

"That him?" Davud asked.

Esmeray nodded. The veil of her orange turban covered her face.

Anila had remained in their cellar room in the Shallows. She'd wanted to come, but the simple truth was she was too weak. In any case, Davud wanted to gauge Lord Ramahd Amansir and his story before putting Anila at risk, so he was glad for the excuse. And yet, the very fact that Anila had agreed with hardly a fight worried him. The old Anila would have insisted on joining him. And likely would have won the argument.

The coach jingled nearer. The driver wore a patterned white scarf, tied inexpertly around his head. His curly black hair had snuck free in several places and was whipping around his head like a dervish as dust and sand

whorled around him. He pulled to a stop before the portico and stared down
at them as if they were naughty children he'd just caught harassing a cat.

"Who you wait for, ah?" His Qaimiri accent was thick.

"Aman-bloody-sir," Esmeray shot back, and climbed into the back of the
coach. "What happened, your coach with a gods-damned roof break a wheel?"

When Davud joined her, the coachman spun around and eyed him. "She
a funny one. A *jonglari*," he said, giving the Qaimiri word for fool. His eyes
slid to Esmeray. "Why you no help when he come to you?"

He meant Ramahd, when he'd come to the Enclave for help, but Esmeray
was having none of it. "I'll not trade words with Amansir's *servant*."

"My name Cicio." He pointed to the portico. "And you trade or you stay."

When Esmeray looked as if she were about to give him a biting reply—
there was hardly a moment when she didn't seem angry—Davud waded into
the conversation with a raised hand. "We don't represent the Enclave."

"No?" The look he gave Davud was one of disdain and dry amusement.
"Then who you *represent*, ah?"

"Only ourselves."

For a moment the wind turned the scarf so poorly restraining his hair into
a mound of writhing snakes. Cold mirth filled Cicio's eyes as he pulled a long
knife from his belt and held it up for them to see. "Whoever you here for, you
betray Ramahd and I take this to you throat." He ran the tip across his stub-
bly neck with a laugh. "My knife *represent* my anger. You understand?"

Esmeray rolled her eyes and eased back into the bench, calm as summer
sand. Cicio, after a bark of a laugh at Esmeray's reaction, returned the knife
to its sheath, turned forward in his seat, and snapped the reins.

The araba lurched into motion, and Cicio delivered them to a boatyard, a
place along the city's now-dry southern canal that made a bit of extra money
in the rainy season by renting out flat-bottomed boats. The driver led them
away from the wagon and among the dry racks and overturned punts, and
there they found Ramahd Amansir. He was dressed in Sharakhani clothing—
a simple kaftan, sirwal trousers, and leather sandals—but wore no scarf. He
was a handsome man with dark eyes and several days' growth of beard darkening his tanned face. His long hair was tied neatly behind his head. Despite
the wind, not a single strand was loose, giving Davud the impression of a

fastidious man, the sort who rarely let details escape him. Like the wagon driver, he looked haggard, as if he hadn't slept properly in days.

As they came to a halt, an alarming thing happened. The spell Davud had worked in order to mask himself from King Sukru began to unravel. He dispelled and recast it every morning in hope of hiding from the King. When he'd started using it, he had no idea whether it was strong enough to stop Sukru, though given that they hadn't been found so far, Davud suspected it was. And yet as firmly as it had been in place a moment ago, as comforted as Davud felt by its presence, it was undone, leaving him feeling lost and un-armed, a mark in a den of thieves.

"Stop!" Esmeray said, and Davud knew that whatever spells she'd woven before coming here were unraveling as well.

"I'd rather we speak without magic standing between us," Ramahd countered.

The abilities Ramahd was displaying weren't new to Davud—King Sukru's man, Zahndrethus, had had similar powers—but he'd never expected them from a Qaimiri lord. Davud took in Cicio, Ramahd's wild-haired servant, more carefully. He didn't have his hands on his weapons, but he was clearly ready to act, and suddenly the threat he'd made on their way here didn't seem so casual.

Ramahd questioned Davud first. He seemed to know something about Davud's story already, perhaps from Esmeray's message, their offer to speak. Davud thought it odd that he would be so interested, but he began to understand when Ramahd's questions shifted to Çeda. He pressed for more information on her state of mind while being held in Sukru's palace. He asked for the details of Davud's assault on her, a thing Davud was still mortified by. He'd been compelled by Ihsan, the Honey-tongued King, into attacking Çeda with the intent to kill. That Çeda had made it out alive made it no less horrifying.

Ramahd finished by asking whether Davud had seen her since his escape from the House of Kings. *He's smitten with her*, Davud realized.

Then Ramahd asked Esmeray her reasons for arranging this meeting. To this she would only say it was a debt that needed repaying.

"A debt to whom?" Ramahd pressed.

"What is that to you? You came to the Enclave begging for help"—Esmeray made a ridiculously theatrical flourish toward Davud—"and now help has come."

Ramahd hardly seemed impressed. "You're telling me you have the Enclave's backing?"

"I'm telling you beggars can't be choosers."

"Perhaps, but only fools ally themselves with other fools."

"I owe the Kings a blood debt, and I mean to pay it back." In that moment Esmeray was like an ancient desert power, an efrit in the guise of a woman. "If that's not good enough for you, you can tell me so now."

Davud felt the conviction in her words and so, apparently, did Ramahd. He nodded to her, and began telling his own tale, the same one he'd shared with the Enclave a week before. As Ramahd spoke, movement along the Haddah drew Davud's attention. From behind a swath of still-green but fading rushes, a spotted serval cat with teacup ears and hungry eyes had wandered out and onto the cracked riverbed. Their native home was in the grasslands of Kundhun, but the large cats had become favorites of the lords and ladies of Goldenhill. After a brief, inquisitive pause, the serval turned, showing off the white spots behind its ears, and lost itself among the brown rushes.

Ramahd was not yet done with his tale, but Davud was feeling uncomfortable out here in the open. "That you want to bring your queen to justice is understandable," he said. "I would as well. What I don't understand is *how*."

"It won't be easy. Your help will be a start, but it won't be enough. I'll need the backing of several Qaimiri lords."

Davud shook his head, confused. "And you'll arrange that when you're here in Sharakhai how?"

"The first of the men I need is already here. Mateo Abrantes, the vice admiral of Meryam's fleet. If I can convince him, his commander, Duke Hektor, is sure to follow. And if I can secure *Hektor's* help, we'll be halfway to making Meryam pay for her crimes."

Davud shook his head. "What crime would be enough for them to want to overthrow their own queen?"

"Using Hamzakiir to murder her own father would be enough on its own, but there's also the murder of Kiral the King of Kings and disguising

Hamzakiir to rule in his place. The fear of retribution from Sharakhai will force them to—"

"Wait, Hamzakiir is alive?"

"Yes," Ramahd said. Ramahd hadn't finished his tale, but he did now, telling Davud what he'd learned shortly before the Battle of Blackspear: that Hamzakiir and Kiral had exchanged guises, and that it was *Kiral* who'd died in the desert, not Hamzakiir.

Davud stared at Esmeray. "Did you know this?"

She looked confused. "Yes."

"Why didn't you tell me?"

She motioned to Ramahd, vexed. "He's telling you now."

The sound of the wind was suddenly loud in Davud's ears. He felt the push of it against his back. Smelled the desert's warm scent. He turned and stared across the river toward Tauriyat, whose outline could barely be seen through the thick amber haze. If Hamzakiir was still alive, Anila might still find purpose. Hatred and thoughts of revenge were terrible things to center one's life around, but just then Davud didn't care. If it could grant Anila a renewed lease on life, he would take it, and worry about a more permanent healing later.

He was just thinking about returning to Anila when he saw something small and round lift into the air. It had been launched from the opposite bank of the Haddah from behind a stone wall, a short distance from where the serval had wandered onto the riverbed. It was arcing toward them, he realized.

Ramahd had sensed something was wrong, and was following his gaze. With Ramahd distracted, Davud did something that felt foolhardy, but was necessary to gain the power he needed—he launched himself forward and grabbed Ramahd's wrist.

"Ey!" Cicio shouted from behind him.

The crunch of gravel came as Cicio, Davud presumed, darted toward him. The object, meanwhile, a clay pot, plummeted toward them. Using his blooding ring, Davud pierced Ramahd's wrist. Ramahd shouted, tried to push Davud away.

Davud smeared a trail of Ramahd's blood over his palm as Cicio tackled him.

"I'm trying to save us!" Davud said.

Cicio didn't seem to care. "What I tell you, you little pig fucker?" He had his knife out and looked ready to use it, but in that moment Esmeray swept in and grabbed Cicio's wrist. The palm of her other hand was bloody. She pressed it against Cicio's forehead, at which point his mouth went wide and his eyes rolled up in his head.

A dozen paces away, the pot shattered, coughing a billow of black smoke into the air. Another pot was lifting behind it, launched from the same position as the first.

Ramahd recoiled from the wound Davud had delivered, but seemed to understand that Davud meant him no harm; he waited as Davud smeared the blood over his palms. As the black cloud swept toward them, Davud curled his arms in precise motions, rendering a sigil in the air before him. Over *defend* he layered *impurity* and *air*—a simple but effective spell. As the barrier formed around him, he pressed his arms outward, spreading the effect so that it encompassed not only him and Esmeray, but Ramahd and Cicio too.

A moment later, a roil of gray gas swallowed them. The second pot struck closer, its dark, billowing cloud adding to the first. For a moment it was so dark it occluded the sun. Even with the spell he'd woven, the noxious fumes threatened them. Davud's eyes watered, and he began to cough.

As quickly and carefully as he could, he traced another spell. Upon *veil* he added *regard, resonance,* and *redolence.*

It manifested just in time. He heard footsteps approaching, and through the cloud spotted dark shapes. Dark swords drawn, a hand of Blade Maidens prowled through the racks of punts. A second hand of Maidens followed the first. They wore black battle dresses and turbans, but instead of their normal veils, each Maiden wore a muzzle of sorts that covered her nose and mouth.

Whatever had gone into the making of those muzzles was proof against the gas. Davud was tempted to cast a spell to weaken the straps and remove their protections, but it was too dangerous. There were too many, and any one of them might manage to sense where Davud and the others were.

"Move calmly but quickly," Davud said. "And do not speak. Not until I tell you."

His words were muted, and would be all but imperceptible to the Maidens, but the Maidens had powers he could only guess at. Indeed, the nearest

of them, their warden, stopped in her tracks and raised one fist. Those behind her instantly froze while the warden's gaze swept over the six of them
as they slowly backed away.

Davud was ready to unleash a spell should the warden sense them, but
thankfully the more they backed away, the more uncertain the warden
seemed. Eventually she waved her Blade Maidens forward and they swept
deeper into the boatyard. The moment they were lost from sight, Davud and
the others headed into the city streets.

That was when a chilling thought occurred to Davud.

"Oh gods," he said. "Anila."

Understanding dawned on Esmeray. "Let's go."

"What?" Ramahd asked as he helped Cicio to walk.

Davud was already sprinting down the Corona, heading back toward
their room in the cellar, but Esmeray called behind him, "If the Kings
tracked us to the boatyard, they could easily have found Anila as well."

Davud knew what he'd find at their rented cellar room, but it was still a
shock to see. The door lay in ruins. The room was empty. Fezek lay crooked
on the landing outside the door. Gods help him, he was trying to hold in his
guts, which were spilling out as fast as he could rake them back in.

Davud knelt and pushed him back so that he lay flat on the packed earth.
"What happened, Fezek?"

Fezek's jaw worked, but he couldn't seem to say anything. He hardly
seemed to know Davud was there. Davud felt terrible for it, but he shook
Fezek hard, and slowly the ghul's cloudy eyes focused on him.

"Sukru," Fezek said in his hoary voice. "Sukru came and took her."

Chapter 26

As the wind scoured the alley, Ramahd stood at the top of the stairs to the cellar room where, apparently, the young blood mage, Davud, had been hiding with his friend Anila. What remained of the door hung awkwardly on its hinges. The rest was shattered.

The rangy man to whom Davud was speaking seemed nearly as broken. His name was Fezek, and he was a ghul, some unfortunate soul who'd been raised by the necromancer, Anila. Bad enough he'd been ripped from his rewards in the next life; now the poor man was lying with his back to the wall, trying to hold his intestines in against a gaping wound. Ramahd could only guess Sukru had torn him open with a crack of his whip. Davud was crouched by his side, speaking softly, a look of terror slipping through the cracks of his calm facade—not for Fezek's sake, but for Anila's.

Everything Ramahd had learned about Davud had shown him to be a kind, calculating sort, someone who planned his steps carefully before acting and with thought for others before himself. That he cared deeply for Anila was obvious. He felt responsible for her having being stolen away by King Sukru, and perhaps he was. Ramahd vowed to keep an eye on him; such things had a way of forcing one into emotional decisions.

Esmeray seemed furious at the turn of events. Ramahd had the impression she was more angry with herself than King Sukru, though. And she was nervous. He could tell by the way her eyes kept flitting to the rooftops and to the opposite end of the alley, where Cicio stood guard.

She's right to be worried, Ramahd thought. *It isn't wise to linger.* He took the stairs down to the landing, where Davud was using needle and thread to sew Fezek's belly back together. The sound of it, like day-old stew being stirred, turned Ramahd's stomach.

"You hardly need to be so precise," Fezek was saying while craning his neck to stare at Davud's handiwork.

Davud hardly seemed to notice Fezek had spoken. He was too focused on the curving needle, brow knitted as he worked with precise, confident technique.

"Don't be too hard on yourself." Ramahd said to him. "You couldn't have known."

"I knew very well Sukru was coming for us." Davud finished the last of the stitches. "I just thought . . . I thought she'd be safe for a few hours. I thought she'd be safe *here.*"

As Davud packed the needle and thread into a small bag, Fezek stood without a hint of pain and lumbered to the top of the stairs. A moment more for Davud to collect his things, and they were all standing in the alley.

"I have a place we can go," Ramahd said, "but it's inside the walls."

Davud nodded, not quite piecing together the challenge that getting there would present, but Esmeray took his meaning. With the arrival of the Malasani fleet, it was going to be difficult getting so many of them through the city's outermost defenses.

"I can get us there," she said, and headed into the blustering wind.

She'd not taken three steps, however, before a man and woman resolved from the dust-strewn air ahead of them. Ramahd recognized them from his meeting with the Enclave as Esmeray's brother and sister: Esrin and Dilara. Cicio immediately moved to intercept, but came to a halt when Esmeray raised a hand and said, "Leave them be."

"You're being rash," Esrin said calmly. He was a handsome Sharakhani with dark skin like his sisters. He also had a patronizing look on his face, a thing that seemed to spark Esmeray's fury.

"I'm doing what I should have done a year ago."

"Our brother Deniz is dead," Dilara replied, "and nothing you do will bring him back. For once, Esma, think with your head and not your heart." She placed a hand over her chest while touching Esrin's shoulder. "What you're doing puts *us* at risk as well. It puts the *Enclave* at risk."

Dilara's voice and manner were softer than her brother's, but Esmeray seemed no more receptive to them. "The Kings must pay for what they've done."

"They *have* paid. King Sukru's own brother, the Sparrow, lies dead!"

She waved to Davud. "By *his* hand, not by ours. His and that of the woman just taken by Sukru."

"What of it?"

Esmeray's eyes went wide as the moons. "Who do you think gave Deniz to the Sparrow? Who do you think came here and stole away a woman who came *begging* for sanctuary?"

"You know the covenant as well as I do," Dilara said. "They'd been marked by the Kings. The Enclave *couldn't* take them in."

Esmeray spat on the ground. "The covenant has always been a coward's agreement, to the Kings' advantage."

Esrin's handsome face grew hard. "The covenant has kept us alive. We all loved our brother, but he was a stubborn, beetle-brained fool. It wouldn't have been so bad if he didn't have so much bloody ambition to go along with it. That combination got him into trouble with the Kings, got him expelled from the Enclave's ranks, and got him killed. You are as dear to me as anyone, Esma, but you have more of Deniz's leanings than you're willing to admit. It isn't your fault—you got it from our father. But I beg you now to see this for the fool's errand it is. Don't make the same mistakes Deniz did." He waved to Davud and Ramahd. "They aren't worth it."

Esmeray met his gaze with a silent stare, but Dilara stepped into the silence. "The Enclave doesn't interfere in the lives of the Kings."

It was a threat, an indication that, were Esmeray to take this any farther, the Enclave would be forced to act.

In the months since awakening to his abilities, Ramahd had become more and more adept at sensing when power was being gathered. He felt it now in Esmeray, a weight ready to come crashing down. Thankfully she took it no farther. "A debt is owed," she said, "a debt the Enclave should have paid the moment Deniz was found lying in the Haddah. A debt we three should have paid together. You tell me you find your purses empty. So be it. I've enough coin for us all."

Her brother and sister shared a look of regret.

As he had with Esmeray, Ramahd felt another spell gathering, this time from Dilara. No, he realized, Dilara and Esrin were working together, creating a spell stronger than either could weave on their own.

Thin black tendrils reached from the two of them toward Esmeray. Ramahd tried to sap their power. Neither was a match for Meryam, not even close, but together they were strong, making it difficult to interrupt the spell. He gained a foothold as the vinelike tendrils whipped outward, and once he had that, he found the path to the spell's dismantling. The tendrils crumbled to dust and were taken by the wind.

Esrin tried to weave a new spell, and this time Ramahd stopped it before it had even begun. Esmeray, meanwhile, had summoned a shield. It shimmered wildly with faint cerulean light, sand and dust curling around its edges, and grew as Esmeray poured more power into it. It formed a dome that protected her, Davud, Ramahd, and Cicio.

Davud glanced at Ramahd, clearly embarrassed that he'd been caught so flat-footed by Dilara and Esrin's attack. Ramahd was hardly surprised, though. Davud was a collegia scholar, not a foot soldier.

Dilara stared at them as the strong wind tugged at her beautiful headdress. "This is how you want it to be?"

Esmeray said nothing.

"So be it," Dilara said.

After sparing a final, flinty look for Ramahd, Esrin joined her and the two walked away, side by side, until they were swallowed by the storm.

Esmeray led Ramahd and the others in the opposite direction, to a small tenement north of the Red Crescent. She walked right into one of the homes and nodded to an old woman she found sitting in a rocking chair with a cat in her lap. The old woman did no more than glance up, as if intrusions by strangers were something that happened every day. They continued to the cellar where, in a small room filled with root vegetables, was the entrance to a tunnel. When they'd all filed into the darkness, Esmeray flicked her fingers in the air, and a small blue light floated ahead, leading their way through the stone-lined tunnel.

"That could have gone bad quickly," Ramahd said to her softly.

"Yes, but it didn't, did it?"

"Your brother Deniz ran afoul of the Kings?"

"Never mind about my brother."

"If it's likely to happen again"—Ramahd pointed with his thumb back the way they came—"we deserve to know."

Esmeray shot his thumb an annoyed look. The two of them were in the lead. Behind them, Fezek was yammering on about something, the futility of life or some such, loudly enough that it covered Ramahd and Esmeray's conversation. Even so, she waited for a turn in the tunnel before speaking.

"Esrin wasn't wrong. Deniz was always a bit of a fool. For all his gifts in the red ways they never brought him the adoration he craved. He loved akhalas and owned several powerful enough to race but not enough to win. Though it was strictly forbidden to interfere with the interests of the Kings, he got it into his head that a few races won would go unnoticed and would open doors that, having been born in the Shallows, had always been closed to him."

"Let me guess. His efforts didn't go unnoticed."

"Nor unpunished. He ignored the Enclave's warnings to desist and soon became known all about the city as a new force in the racing circuit. For months he was feted in some of the richest halls in Blackfire Gate and Hanging Gardens. Then he was summoned to Goldenhill by the great-grandson of King Sukru, a man who, as it turns out, only wanted to ply Deniz for his secret to training horses. Sukru was there as well and learned of Deniz's sudden blossoming. It took little time for the Reaping King to guess that Deniz had been using hidden talents to tilt the field toward his horses."

"But surely he wouldn't have been expelled from the Enclave for that?"

"Not if he'd stopped then, no, but Deniz had his eye on the greatest race of the year. He was warned that if he raced a single horse, even in the preliminaries, he would have to give up his seat in the Enclave. Stubborn fool that he was, he continued anyway. I begged the Enclave not to abandon him. I begged Deniz to stop, but neither listened." They took a dip in the tunnel, then entered a small cavern. In the distance came the sound of dripping. "Three days later, Deniz disappeared from a pre-race feast in the hippodrome. He left the stadium without saying goodbye to anyone and was never seen again. I looked everywhere for him, using every means available to me, and never found a trace. Months later his body was found along the Haddah, face-down on the stones." Esmeray's voice was amplified in the echoing space of the cavern. "His body had been ravaged, sigils written in blood, some fresh, some dried and flaking, others barely apparent on his dark skin. They told a story of pain and anguish, of cruelly inventive experiments, likely conducted at the hands of King Sukru, or his brother the Sparrow."

"And you?" Ramahd asked. "Why wait all this time to seek revenge?" He regretted putting it so bluntly, but he still wasn't sure he could trust her.

She looked him straight in the eye. The blue light she'd conjured lent her such a haunting aspect she looked as though she'd risen from the dead right alongside Fezek. "Because I was a coward. I let my brother and sister convince me that revenge against the Kings was destined to fail, and that I would be jeopardizing not only the Enclave but them specifically. Members of the Enclave or not, how could the Kings allow a pair of siblings to live when the other two had assaulted them so baldly?"

"Is all of that not still true?"

"Perhaps"—she gave him a reluctant shrug and resumed walking—"but I refuse to live in fear any longer."

"But why now?" he asked, following in her wake. "Davud's sudden appearance wouldn't have been enough to change your mind."

"No?"

"No. There's something deeper at work."

"You're persistent," she called over her shoulder. "I'll give you that."

"It happens when I'm worried."

"Do you believe in the fates?"

"Doesn't everyone?"

"You'd be surprised," she said with a bark of a laugh. "But *I* do. Their signs are everywhere. I thought I could let Deniz's death go. I thought I would heal in time, but each day that passed saw my soul burn a little bit more, until it felt like only charred remains. And then the fates saw fit to deliver Davud to the Enclave, one year to the day after Deniz's death." She paused as if that were explanation enough. "I won't go to the farther fields having done nothing to avenge him."

They met several more tunnels but soon were climbing a set of winding stairs into a shop filled with all manner of metal and glass cages filled with lizards, toads, frogs, snails, and insects. The symphony of calls reminded Ramahd of the wet forests of Qaimir, but here in Sharakhai they seemed wrong, as if a part of his homeland had been stolen and hidden away here in the desert.

An old woman sitting behind a high counter nodded to Esmeray. Esmeray nodded back. Cicio, meanwhile, was craning his neck to look through the nearby window. "Not much time left, no?" he said in Qaimiran.

Ramahd nodded. It was already nearing high sun. He didn't have much time to reach Alu's temple, and today was likely the only day he'd have a chance to speak with Mateo. "Take them to the workshop," he said to Cicio.

Ramahd had arranged the safe house himself. An old friend in the city, a locksmith, had a small room above his workshop. He'd agreed to let Ramahd use it for as long as he liked.

"Take *them*?" Cicio looked at Ramahd as if he were mad. "No, I'm going with you to the temple, then we'll *both* take them."

"Nothing's going to happen with Mateo. Better you see them safe."

Still he refused. When Ramahd took them outside and pointed sternly west, however, Cicio relented. As he led Davud, Esmeray, and Fezek toward the safe house, Ramahd headed east, toward the temple district.

Chapter 27

THE VEIL OF ÇEDA's turban was pulled tight across her face as she peered over the *Red Bride*'s port bow. With the screaming wind, the landscape was little more than an amber haze, but a half-league distant, she could just make out the telltale signs of ships. The dark smudge of hulls, the cut of sails above them. They marked a line that ran roughly parallel to the *Bride*'s line of sail.

"They're all Malasani?" Çeda asked.

"Looks like it," Sümeya replied. She and Melis stood next to Çeda, the wind whipping the heavy fabric of their Maiden's black.

"Adjust course," Çeda called above the wind, "one point starboard."

"Aye," Jenise called from the pilot's wheel, "one point starboard."

The *Bride* creaked as Jenise pulled at the wheel. The enemy ships drifted farther away, fading as they went. Çeda held her breath as they were lost to the sand entirely, but it was only a few moments later, as the *Bride* was leaning into the swell of a dune, that they came back into view.

"Goezhen's pendulous balls," Çeda said under her breath.

"We outrun them," Jenise shouted. "It's the only way."

"No." Melis lifted a hand and pointed to the Malasani line. "Half of those ships could outpace us."

"Then why are they holding back?"

No one had an answer.

Seven Shieldwives, the healthiest of those who'd survived the battle with the Kings, crewed the ship. There was a stiffness about them, and a silence that spoke of their growing nervousness. These were stout women, more than ready for battle, but the numbers against them were daunting.

Behind their yacht came a pack of nine bounding forms—Mavra, Sedef, Amile, and the others who'd remained after *Wadi's Gait* had made for Mount Arasal. There was no fear in them. Quite the opposite, in fact. Their battle lust was building. Çeda could hear it in their thoughts like whispers on the wind: *rend, tear, kill.*

Night's Kiss, hanging from Çeda's belt, echoed their sentiments. The two were starting to work in concert, the sword's and the asirim's dark thoughts intensifying Çeda's emotions. To make matters worse, Çeda's right hand was on fire. The whole length of her arm felt hot and infected, and more than once she found herself flexing her hand near the hilt of Night's Kiss. Each time she'd had to force it back by her side. She had half a mind to take the sword belowdecks and leave it there, or better yet, throw it overboard. Yet whenever she thought overlong on either possibility, the urge dissipated like spindrift in a growing gale.

Just then a whistle came from the stern. *Enemy,* a Shieldwife called. *Behind.*

They all turned and saw the subtle shapes. Three, then five, then eight. More of the Malasani fleet, sailing to hem them in.

"That's why they haven't attacked," Melis said grimly. "While we gawped, they were working to cut off our escape."

Çeda stared at the two lines of ships, wondering how they could have executed their trap so perfectly. "It makes no sense. Their fleet sailed for Sharakhai weeks ago."

"True," Sümeya said, "but we know they were sailing hard for the city, likely so that they could beat Mirea to the prize. They would have left dozens of ships behind to secure the caravanserais. Likely that's done and now they're sending unneeded ships to the city."

The crew was nervous. Çeda could see it in their eyes, in their stiff movements.

"What do we do?" Jenise asked.

Çeda's eyes were fixed on the line of ships off the port bow. "We punch our way through." She squeezed her right hand, letting the pain course up her arm and into her shoulder, but stopped when Sümeya took note of it. "We'll call the asirim to us, have them run ahead and shatter their line."

Break them, Mavra echoed.

Grind them, said Sedef.

Çeda did her best to ignore their collective urges, but it wasn't easy. "When they do, we sail through. The Malasani will think twice about following after that."

Melis and Sümeya shared a look, but then Sümeya nodded. "It's as good a plan as any."

Jenise began calling orders to the other Shieldwives to make ready and to call their asirim closer to the yacht.

Come, Çeda called to Mavra, but she was already bounding ahead of the others, her children fighting to keep up. *Let's show them what it means to invade the Great Mother.*

Just then Sümeya gripped Çeda's right wrist. Her hand felt like a forge fire, her arm a bar of molten steel. She was torn between wanting to strike Sümeya and asking her to grip it harder.

Sümeya spun her around until the two of them were face to face. "I've seen what that sword does to my father. He's had centuries to master it. It, in turn, has had centuries trying to master *him.* That sword *hungers* for blood. Don't let it blind you to what we need to do."

Çeda twisted her wrist from Sümeya's grasp. "We have a battle to prepare for."

But Sümeya didn't budge. "Why not give it to me before we engage?"

"I'll keep the sword."

"You'd have it back once we're safely through."

"I'll keep the sword," she repeated, then walked sternward and bent her attention to the asirim. It was not lost to her how pleased Night's Kiss seemed, nor how Mavra's worry seemed to echo Sümeya's, but Çeda ignored it all.

The asirim bounded ahead as horns sounded—orders being relayed to the other Malasani ships, orders that were crisply obeyed. As both lines began to close in, there were two narrow gaps the *Red Bride* might sail through, but both cinched tight before the *Bride* could take advantage. They were surrounded. Four ships began to break from the rough circle and close in.

Çeda drew Night's Kiss and used it to point over the port bow. "Direct the asirim there! Attack the ketch with the dark sails and the dhow behind it, but don't risk lives. The asirim's blood will be up. They'll want to do more than disable the ships, so be ready to fight them over it."

As her orders were relayed by the Shieldwives, the asirim bounded ahead of the *Bride*, galloping on all fours and separating into two ragged groups. Mavra was like a bear leading her cubs. Sedef, the tallest, powered over the sand beside her. After the battle with the Kings and the loss of several of their number, they were ravenous.

Mavra called the desert to her aid. A great gout of sand and rock lifted before her and buffeted the ketch with the dark sails. It rocked the ship and whipped the rigging mercilessly. The canvas began to rip just as the other group of asirim reached the dhow. They leapt to the deck, scrabbling over the sides while warriors in scale armor ran to defend. The warriors stood little chance, however. The asirim were too fast. Too powerful. They stormed the deck, taking down the pilot, leaping up to the sails and pulling at the rigging.

One by one their swordsmen were felled. Three flew over the side in a tumble of limbs when Amile bulled into them. As they were lost to billowing amber dust, Amile flew up the mainmast toward the vulture's nest, where a crewman was blowing a signal horn.

The pilot, however, had regained the wheel. He was cranking at it madly, guiding their ship toward the *Red Bride*. Jenise was ready for it. She steered the *Bride* expertly away so that the dhow, which had lost a lot of speed, passed narrowly behind them rather than ramming them as intended.

As Jenise adjusted course again, guiding the *Bride* away from the Malasani ships along their starboard side, three bulky shapes dropped from the dark-sailed ship. They were large, and dressed in armor that reminded Çeda of her days in the pits.

Why the Malasani would have dropped three of their soldiers from the back of a ship she had no idea, but she was instantly worried. *Stop them*, she called to Mavra. *Don't let them get near the* Bride.

Mavra, Sedef, and the three others in her group moved to intercept. The first of the bronze warriors met Mavra with a lowered shoulder. For all her bulk, Mavra was thrown aside like a child trying to stop a horse, but not before she swiped one massive hand across the warrior's face. Beneath the force of her blow, massive chunks of cheek and nose were ripped free and went tumbling through the air before landing with a splash against the sand. What remained of the face turned wild and angry.

"A golem," Melis breathed. "They're golems."

Mavra was up again in a moment, chasing after it. Arrows began to streak in. The Shieldwives returned fire. Sümeya, Melis, and Çeda joined them a moment later, but Çeda was transfixed by the golems pounding their way toward the *Red Bride*.

Mavra caught up to the first and took it down from behind, then tore at it mercilessly, but not before the golem struck her across the face in response. The blow would have destroyed a mortal woman, but Mavra seemed only enraged. Looming over the golem, she lifted her massive right hand and brought it down like a sledgehammer onto its chest and pressed.

The golem's body, armor and all, collapsed inward. Its chest was now a misshapen hollow, but the blow hardly seemed to have affected it. As it continued to struggle against Mavra, however, the sand beneath it began to part like water, drawing it down, deeper and deeper. It thrashed wildly and bludgeoned Mavra, connecting against her arms, her chest, but Mavra, the blackened skin of her face locked in an expression of rage and fierce determination, kept her hand firmly pressed until the golem was swallowed by the desert.

When Mavra raised her hand toward the other charging golems, the effect of the sinking sand spread. Çeda's hand tingled from it. She felt her awareness of the desert expand, a thing she'd only ever felt near the blooming fields. It was strange to feel it here, so far away from Sharakhai, but she had no time to wonder over it. As she launched more arrows, and the Malasani ship on their starboard side closed in, its warriors prepared to swing over on boarding lines.

The slipsand caught another golem, allowing Sedef to tackle it from behind. The other asirim closed in like wolves. But the golem was far from defenseless. It hammered several, and then Natise came too close. The golem grabbed her by the throat, then brought its closed fist down against her head in a terrible blow. Bone and ichor exploded. Natise crumpled to the sand, her shriveled, blackened limbs gone slack, while the other asirim howled and tore into the golem with renewed rage.

The third golem had escaped the effects of Mavra's spell and was pounding like a warhorse toward the *Red Bride*. It would reach the ship in moments.

Çeda swung Night's Kiss toward Jenise. "Drop a rope off the transom!"

As Jenise moved to comply, Melis covered her with a shield against the incoming arrows and Çeda sprinted toward the bow.

Sümeya whistled sharply behind her. *Halt!*

But Çeda kept running. Along the bowsprit she flew, Night's Kiss raised high. The fire in her arm had reached her heart. She felt like a herald of Iri, a demigod of sand and stone and scorched desert air.

Reaching the end of the bowsprit, she launched herself toward the golem. In a grand arc she flew, bringing the great, two-handed shamshir across the golem's hastily raised defenses. With a terrible rattle that shook her bones, the sword cleaved through its upraised arms, its head, and halfway into its wine-barrel chest.

Çeda's momentum carried her into the golem. It felt like striking the face of a cliff. She fell to the sand while the golem merely staggered sideways and remained standing. The split halves of its body widened like unfired potter's clay as it turned toward her and raised one leg. She twisted away from one thundering stomp. The golem loomed over her, but she stopped its advance by setting both feet against the golem's chest. With the darkness of the *Red Bride*'s hull looming ever larger, she released an almighty grunt and pressed with both legs.

The yacht swept overhead and the keel connected with a hollow thud, sending the golem sprawling to the sand, arms and legs flailing.

Catching, the rope Jenise had dropped off the back of the ship, Çeda swung herself up and around the back of the ship, landing just inside the transom. Sümeya and Melis had gained the deck of the dhow off their starboard side and were pressing the enemy back. Their aim was not to engage with the Malasani soldiers, however. When they'd gone far enough, Melis sliced the mainsail's halyard while Sümeya did the same with the foresail's. The wind flung the canvas away, leaving the sails to drape over the ship's far side, covering a good many of the crew in the process.

Nearer to Çeda, four Malasani warriors leapt over the gap between the ships. Jenise intercepted the first. The second fell to a swift uppercut from Night's Kiss, the sword buzzing like a ripsaw as it cut deep into his chest. The shamshir emitted a satisfied drone as it sheared through another warrior's buckler and halfway through his forearm. The shock in the man's eyes was plain as he tipped over the gunwales behind him and plummeted toward the sand.

The sheet of darkness that trailed the shamshir's movements was thicker now. The last of the Malasani soldiers watched *it* more than her movements, which proved his undoing. After a blinding but desperate exchange the man had no hope of keeping up with, she sliced his leg, then caught him across the neck when he dropped his guard.

Night's Kiss thrummed in her right hand. It sensed Çeda's revulsion over its thirst for blood, but was smug in its certainty that she would do nothing about it.

I could, she said. *I could throw you overboard.*

And yet the sword remained in her hand. It took all her will to sheath it. As it set home, it emitted a sound like a hyena's barking laugh.

With their sails now flapping in the wind, the dhow beside them was beginning to flag. Melis and Sümeya, after unleashing a flurry of swings, leapt back to the *Red Bride*. The gap between the ships widened ever further, and the Malasani crew did nothing to prevent it. They'd had no idea the sort of warriors they'd find aboard their ship, and seemed relieved they would no longer have to face them.

"Ahead!" Jenise called from the wheel.

Directly ahead of the *Bride*, the same ketch that had dropped the golems lowered a rake into the sand to slow its speed. They hoped to match the *Red Bride*'s pace and board her, but Mavra and the other asirim had resumed the chase. The crew launched fire pot after fire pot, hoping to stave them off, and the sand behind the ship lit in bursts of orange flame and billowing smoke.

Several well placed strikes lit one of the asirim ablaze, but then the rest were up and onto the deck. The crew didn't stand a chance. It was a slaughter that sobered Çeda, dousing the blood lust that Night's Kiss had instilled in her.

She took in the ships around them, which continued to close in. And while the dhow to their port side had been decimated by the other group of asirim, Çeda knew they couldn't continue like this. They had to escape.

"There," Melis said, pointing toward a line of low rocks the enemy were steering to avoid. Their ships skirted inside the rocks, bringing them closer to the *Red Bride*, forcing them to cluster more than was wise.

"Yes," Çeda said, seeing Melis's intent. "Jenise, ready the ship. We'll turn toward those rocks."

Çeda bent Mavra's will toward the yellow-sailed dhow at the head of the largest cluster of ships. The other Shieldwives, sensing Çeda's intensity, urged their bonded asirim to do the same. As the asirim moved to obey, Çeda stepped to the ship's pulpit, spread her arms, and tilted her head back, feeling the desert like never before. Her right arm burned like a beacon fire, a star in a sand-laden sky. She lifted it high, gripped her right hand tight, and called upon the wind, summoning it to her, drawing it up and along the path of their yacht.

And it obeyed. The sails stretched. The hull creaked. And the ship was driven forward, fleet as a falcon.

"Now, Jenise."

Jenise guided them unerringly. They skirted the now-pilotless ketch along their port side and continued toward the tight line of Malasani ships. Moments later, the asirim reached the yellow-sailed dhow and overwhelmed it, howling all the while. The dhow slowed sharply, forcing the trailing ships to avoid it, but hemmed in as they were by the rocks, they couldn't all do so.

Ahead of the dhow, an ever-widening gap was made. It was into this that the *Red Bride* flew. As they reached open sand, the asirim disengaged, another ship fallen to them. Horns blew, and the few Malasani ships that had started to give chase disengaged. The cost of taking the *Red Bride* was simply too great.

Çeda continued to guide the wind. Not until well after the Malasani ships had been swallowed by the storm did she unclench her fist and lower her right arm. The wind calmed, her deep awareness of the desert dimmed, and at last they eased into a less frantic pace over the sand.

Çeda turned to find the Shieldwives staring at her with a reverence that made her supremely uncomfortable. "We've wounds to dress and repairs to make."

"Aye," came their chorus.

As the Shieldwives set to it, Çeda was caught by the looks on Sümeya and Melis's faces. Even with their veils drawn, Çeda could see the awe in Sümeya's stare and the look of utter revulsion in Melis's.

Chapter 28

INSIDE THE LONG, narrow infirmary of the bustling hospital ship, Brama knelt beside Mae's cot and lifted her head. "Please drink."

He couldn't tell if she heard him or not. Her eyelids quivered and her lips trembled, as if she were caught in the midst of a terrible dream.

The disease had progressed at a steady pace. Her lips had turned dark, her skin had blackened around her eyes and nostrils, she had terrible coughing fits, and her piss and shit were both laden with blood. She'd lasted longer than most, but she didn't have much time left—a day or two at the most. Brama tried using a spoon to give her more of the tea, but most of it dribbled from her lips. She held her stomach and moaned, uttering a long, rapid string of Mirean.

The infirmary was overflowing with those afflicted by the scourge. Twice the normal number of cots had been brought in to allow for three hundred in the primary hall of healing. The other decks held more, so that a full five hundred now lay diseased and dying within the ship. Four days earlier, a dunebreaker had been assigned to help. Soon it, too, would be full. The scourge was sweeping through the Mirean encampment like a scythe.

As Brama prepared to move to the next cot, one of the boys tasked with ferrying messages to the main encampment entered and scanned the room. Brama waved to him. The boy, spotting him at last, waved back and began weaving his way through the aisles. The entire room watched him with fleeting hope, as if he'd come with news of a cure, but hope faded when it became clear who he'd come to see.

Like the others tending to the sick, the boy wore no mask, having recovered and thereby developed an immunity. The scourge had left him with a light graying around his eyes, a darkening of his lips. He hadn't even developed a cough. There were now enough survivors like him who were the only ones allowed to tend to the sick. Regular inspections and quarantining efforts had further slowed the disease, but it was still spreading at an alarming rate.

"Juvaan send." The boy's voice quavered as he spoke, a common symptom of survivors. His limbs trembled as well. "He wait."

Brama signaled to the nurses that he was leaving, then followed the boy. Juvaan waited a good distance away on his horse. He held Kweilo's reins, ready for Brama to take. In the distance, the Mirean encampment squatted beside the caravanserai like a pack of bone crushers. The two ships filled with the afflicted had been separated from the rest to avoid the possibility of ill humors being borne on the wind to the healthy ships.

Brama mounted Kweilo, and he and Juvaan rode together toward the main encampment. Juvaan looked haggard. He'd been shouldering the brunt of their efforts to halt the spread of the scourge, and it showed in his eyes, in the dulled way in which he scanned the horizon. "You asked to speak alone," he said in a listless voice.

"Yes. I need to ask you a question. And I need you to answer it as best—"

"Just say it," Juvaan said wearily.

"I need to know what your queen asked of Behlosh when he arrived. And I need to know his answer."

"You're asking me to betray my queen's confidence."

"I am, but for good reason." He waved to the ships behind them. "You're *dying*, Juvaan. Alu-Waled's medicines had no effect, and I'm willing to bet they never will." He did not mention that Rümayesh was barely helping. She'd agreed to ease the pain of some few chosen by Queen Alansal, but like Mae, the rapid progress of their symptoms hadn't been slowed. "If something doesn't change," he went on, "your entire fleet may be lost."

Juvaan rode in silence for a time, his face in deep shadow beneath his conical farmer's hat. "Let me pose a question. Were you in my queen's place, would you not be suspicious?"

"Of course I would."

"Would *you* trust the servant of a creature like Rümayesh?"

"That would depend on his words and deeds."

"My queen is appreciative of all you've done on the ships," Juvaan said, "but we all saw Rümayesh's attempt to heal Mae. The queen thinks she withheld her power. Is she wrong?"

Brama had known the question would come. It felt strange to want to keep Rümayesh's secrets, but he refused to protect her any longer. "No, she isn't."

"Why?" Fire bled into his words at last. "Why would Rümayesh do that?"

"I don't know," Brama answered truthfully, "which is why I need to know more about Behlosh."

Juvaan nodded, as if he'd expected that answer. "What good will it do you?"

"I need to convince Rümayesh to help you. If I can't, your cause is lost. Knowing Behlosh's purpose will help."

Juvaan rode in silence, stiff-backed. Brama thought he'd lost him, but then Juvaan's head swiveled, his attention caught by something to their left. Brama turned as well, and saw buzzards circling lazily over the mass grave.

"My queen was surprised when a second ehrekh arrived," Juvaan said. "She thought her gamble with the bones might lure one at most. She certainly didn't expect Behlosh, another of the Shangazi's eldest, to answer her call. But he did. He arrived in her pavilion and demanded to know why such a scent was on the wind. When my queen answered and presented him with a vial similar to the one you now possess, Behlosh seemed intrigued, even tempted—who can tell with such creatures?—but instead of agreeing or denying the offer, he said he would bring it to his lord."

"To Goezhen."

"Who else?" Juvaan replied.

"That's why you asked about Rümayesh. It's why you thought she might have gone to Goezhen as well."

"It can't be a coincidence that she failed to return from the desert on the very night Behlosh arrived."

Brama acknowledged the point with a nod. "Has Behlosh returned?"

"No."

Brama reined Kweilo to a stop. Juvaan mirrored him.

"I have to meet with the queen," Brama said.

"I know. But I've already presented your request twice and been denied. Alansal won't suffer a third request, not even from me."

As he had for days, Brama considered forcing the issue. He could find a way to steal into Alansal's capital ship and meet with her. But he knew the queen well enough to know that she wouldn't listen. Not like that. *Not everything can be solved by leaning a shoulder into it,* his father used to say. *Sometimes it takes a bit of oil.*

Brama stared into Juvaan's ice-cold eyes. "Your queen *will* suffer another request, because this time you'll impress upon her the importance of it. You'll make it clear I'm offering a way for her to save her people. And you'll ensure that it be just the two of us, none of her generals. I won't have their influence affecting her decision."

To Brama's relief, Juvaan didn't become angry. "You think I have so much influence over my queen?"

"You have more than you're letting on. And more than you've used thus far." Brama clasped his hands before him, a gesture of supplication in the desert. "You cannot let this go on, Juvaan. Fail now, and your survivors will be able to return to Mirea on a single ship."

Juvaan seemed hesitant and weary and inclined to send Brama away with a half-hearted assent to consider his appeal, but just then a skimwood sleigh broke away from the circle of dunebreakers. It was a common sight these days: another group of scourge victims being ferried toward quarantine. For a long time, Juvaan could only stare.

"I'll get you your meeting," he said, then urged his horse into a gallop.

Brama rode Kweilo across the desert. True night reigned, but a cavalcade of stars accompanied him on his journey. The sky was so brilliant, the dunes so dreamlike, it felt as if they were riding not over the desert, but across the firmament itself.

A rope ran from the back of Kweilo's saddle to a sleigh, which carried Mae. She was blanketed against the night, but it was hardly necessary; she'd developed a fever, one of the last stages before death. Brama was doing his best to ignore how captivated he was by Mae's condition, how close she was to crossing over, but it wasn't easy. The best thing he'd found to combat it was to steep himself in the physicality of this place—the sights, the sounds, the smells—and ignore Mae altogether. He felt callous for doing so, even shameful, but it was better than the alternative.

As Kweilo crested a dune, her hooves and the trailing sleigh sent waves of sand hissing down both sides of the peak. From this vantage the line of dark hills Brama had been heading toward stood out like a jagged line of broken pottery. Those hills were where Brama would find Behlosh. Brama could feel him, lying in wait like a ravenous wolf. Whether he, in turn, was aware of Brama's approach, Brama had no idea.

He received his answer a short while later. As Kweilo neared the top of the next dune, a soft rattling sound broke over the desert. The sound became a hum became a thrum. Far ahead, an undulating cloud occluded the stars, flowing eel-like toward him. It descended onto the dune, then shaped itself, forming a solid figure from the dark, writhing mass. As the sound faded, a four-armed beast was revealed, a creature with two great horns like scythes sweeping back from its forehead.

It was Behlosh. Kweilo had stopped, but Brama urged her forward. The skin along her shoulders twitched but, brave horse that she was, she plodded farther along the dune.

As Behlosh's head swiveled to watch them, he lifted to his full height, two of his four arms crossing like some inflexible guard before a shisha den. His restless tail pounded the dune, creating a spray of sand with each blow. "Rümayesh's pet," he said in a voice that threatened like thunder.

After reining Kweilo to a stop, Brama dismounted. The hair along his arms and the back of his neck stood on end. The gulf between their two dunes was wide, but just then it felt insignificant. Brama was reminded of the first time he'd seen Rümayesh—his terror, the power that rolled from her in waves. There was no doubt Rümayesh had always been conniving and cruel, but she at least harbored genuine curiosity about the lives of mortals. The empathy it lent her might be slight and unpredictable, but at least it was there. Not so, with Behlosh. The glint in his eyes, the set of his mouth, the way he began to pace like a caged lion, made him seem malicious, angry, and above all *hungry* to inflict his desires upon Brama.

After taking a deep breath, Brama spoke clearly into the night. "Behlosh the Elder, I come to you in peace, to offer you a bargain."

Behlosh's hungry eyes cut through the night. The sinuous movement of his tail looked purposeful and arcane, a spell being woven. "Thine undying queen hast already laid a bargain at my feet."

Brama blinked, shook his head, cleared his mind of the cobwebs that had suddenly appeared. "A bargain you've neither accepted nor declined. I've come with one of my own."

"Name it."

Brama waved toward the sleigh. "Here lies a single one of the diseased. Heal her, and your part of the bargain is fulfilled."

Behlosh stared at Mae. "But one . . ."

"But one."

The ehrekh came storming down the dune. It took only six long strides for him to reach the summit of Brama's dune. Brama took a half step back but then steeled himself while Behlosh, head twisting, horns sweeping, stared down at Mae. "In her veins flows the blood of thy queen?"

"No."

"Someone favored by her then? A lover?"

"She is favored, but no more than many of the soldiers in her army."

Behlosh stepped around to the back of the sleigh and crouched so low his face was inches from Mae's. Kweilo, ever brave, stood still, though her tail swished constantly. Finally, Behlosh stood to his full, towering height. "Why hast only one been brought?"

"That isn't part of what I'm offering."

"Then what *is* thine offer?"

From around his neck Brama retrieved the necklace given to him by Queen Alansal. On the end of the chain was an amulet, which Brama held out between thumb and forefinger for Behlosh to see. The golden amulet was the size of a fig with a hollow core that was visible through the elegant filigree work in its walls. It reflected the starlight, while the object inside swallowed the night.

"A bone of Raamajit the Exalted," Brama said. "Yours if you heal this woman."

Low laughter rolled from Behlosh. "A lone soldier from a dying army in exchange for the bone of an elder god?"

"You agree, then?"

"A lone soldier for the bone of Raamajit . . . ."

"It would make for a pretty prize for your lord, would it not? Or for you to call your own?"

Behlosh's four hands tightened into fists. His tail swished faster than before, slapped the sand harder. "Dost thou hope to master the second bone? Or mayhaps thy wish is to play on Rümayesh's tenderness." Behlosh waved toward Mae. "Thou thinkest that healing this one might guilt her, sway her to join thy cause. Thou thinkest that if she breaks from our lord Goezhen, thy precious fleet might be saved."

"My reasons are my own." Using the chain, Brama spun the amulet in the air, a thing Queen Alansal had assured him would put the bone's scent on the wind. "What say you, Behlosh? Will you enter into this bargain with me?"

Behlosh stared at the twirling amulet and Brama was sure he'd erred. He was certain Behlosh had taken offense and would leave. Or would take the amulet from him by force, perhaps delivering it to Goezhen. It was what he and Alansal had both feared as they'd discussed this plan. She'd nearly declined, she was so set on keeping the treasures of the bones, but she'd come to see that her gambit had failed, that for some reason Goezhen had interceded to prevent her from sailing as easily as she'd hoped toward Sharakhai. If she hoarded her power and refused to allow Brama to use one of the bones to forge an agreement with Behlosh, she risked the destruction of her entire fleet, or worse, her homeland.

As they'd sat within her private room in her capital ship, Alansal had taken one of the steel pins she always wore through her hair and used it to draw an intricate design in the air before her. On the final stroke, a chromatic line had appeared. The line flowed, gentle as a summer breeze, and Queen Alansal had thrust her hand into it. When she pulled it free, she had the amulet in her hand.

She'd held the priceless artifact out for Brama to take while the scintillant line closed itself with a soft *tick*. All of the self assurance Alansal had shown in their earlier meetings was gone, replaced with a worry that seemed depthless. "Go," she said. "See my people safe."

The small bone inside the amulet was plain to see, but it was the new senses granted by Rümayesh that allowed Brama to feel the power emanating from it. It was a remnant of a distant age, a fragment of the raw potency wielded by the elder gods. How many such things remained in the world? Brama accepted the amulet with reverence, but made no promises to Alansal. They both knew theirs was a desperate hope.

Behlosh stared at the spinning amulet. He was hungry for it. Brama could feel it. "Rümayesh will not turn on her master for thee." He waved dismissively to Mae, a gesture that somehow felt wrong coming from a creature with four arms. "Nor for them."

Brama stilled his hand. The amulet wrapped his forearm, then slowly started to unwind. "Do you accept or not?"

Behlosh leaned over Mae. Two arms supported him while the other two gripped Mae's chest. Behlosh's thumbs pressed into her skin, above her breasts. Black claws pierced her and Mae struggled, but she was too weak to do anything more than writhe beneath Behlosh's terrible strength.

Brama studied Behlosh's every move. He steeped himself in the ritual being performed. The scourge had a tight grip on Mae, but Brama felt its ill humors being burned away like the chill of the night at the desert sun's rising. Brama felt once more that strange sense of satisfaction at her pain.

Please no, Brama pleaded. *Not with Mae.*

But his unspoken wish only seemed to intensify the feeling. What made it worse was disappointment—his *disappointment*—at feeling the scourge fade. The combination was so powerful he reacted to it physically. His mouth watered; his nostrils flared in disgust.

By the gods who breathe, how I hate what I've become.

The last of the scourge was driven from Mae's body. Then, like a brand pressed to a wound to stop the bleeding, Behlosh proofed her body against reinfection. The damage the scourge had done was not pretty—Mae might never be whole again—but the disease was gone.

When Behlosh stood and held out one hand, Brama threw the amulet to him.

Brama said, "Why does Goezhen wish to see so much death inflicted upon the Mirean fleet?"

For a long time, Behlosh was silent. "Tell Rümayesh my thoughts still linger over the taste of her first love." There was a sneer in his words.

He burst into a cloud of buzzing locusts, lifted, and was gone, leaving Brama alone with the softly breathing Mae. He mounted Kweilo. "Come on, girl," he said, snapping the reins. "We've lots to do, and little enough time to do it."

Chapter 29

E MRE SAT IN THE CAPTAIN'S cabin of the *Amaranth,* recording in the log the ship's position and the events of the last few days. Writing was still torturous for him. He'd never learned as a child. Çeda had tried over and over again to teach him, but he'd been a terrible, ungrateful student, and now he was paying the price. Pens were cursed artifacts that turned his hands to stone.

He sat back to look over his handiwork. "Iri's black teeth, a strutting hen could do better."

"Ships ho! Ships ho!" called a voice.

Grateful for the distraction, Emre put the book and pen away and rushed from the cabin. Off their starboard bow, sailing easily over a smooth plain of sand, was *Calamity's Reign.* No other ships accompanied them. Young Shaikh Aríz and his vizir had both said, and Emre agreed, that only a single ship from the tribes, the *Amaranth* itself, should be sent to treat with the Malasani king. Aríz had, however, agreed to hide his tribe in a range of low, rocky hills a half-day's sail from Sharakhai. Should Emre have need, he had but to send a skiff to warn them.

Hamid and Frail Lemi joined him at the bow as a swath of masts and sails and dark hulls came into view along the horizon. The Malasani fleet was quite a sight. Hundreds of ships arrayed in a vast line, their masts so numerous they looked like the bristles of an untidy brush.

Beyond the Malasani fleet loomed the blooming fields, an ominous stroke of black ink. From one location not far from the fleet of ships, gray smoke billowed in a twisting column into the blue sky. Frail Lemi stared at it while cracking his knuckles. "What are they doing, Emre?"

Nothing good, Emre thought. "I don't know, Lem, but we're about to find out." He turned to the pilot, "Make for the smoke."

They did, and the sheer vastness of the fleet became clear. Goezhen's sweet kiss, there must be four hundred ships. Thousands of soldiers combed the sand, many preparing engines of war—catapults, ballistae, and mobile barriers. They were being placed on rafts with skimwood skis that could be hauled into whatever position the Malasani commanders wanted—either defensively, should their fleet be attacked, or as a steadily advancing bulwark that would protect their lines as they headed toward and into the city harbors. Though Sharakhai itself wasn't visible yet, Tauriyat could be seen, a misshapen lump hanging above the horizon. Emre thought he could just make out the blocky shape of Eventide.

Calamity's Reign began pulling ahead. Emre let it. As angry as Haddad had been with Emre, she'd still agreed to make introductions to her king. "Whatever happens then," she'd spat, "is up to you."

Within the hour both ships had anchored and Haddad was marching toward the camp with an escort of several dozen Malasani soldiers. Emre and the others waited on the *Amaranth.* Over an hour later a herald in bright clothing came.

"King Emir of Malasan will see you," he said.

He led Emre, Hamid, and Frail Lemi between the ships and toward the place where the smoke was lifting from the blooming fields. Hundreds of Malasani soldiers were there in a line, each bearing spears and shields, and facing the groves of adichara trees as though they expected a battalion of Silver Spears to come streaming out. Near them was a platform on skis. A dais, Emre thought at first. When he was led onto it, however, he realized its true purpose. The Malasani king, a man of only thirty summers, was clean shaven with dark hair cut straight across his brow. He was handsome enough, though he had a pert mouth that practically begged to be punched. Worse was his garb. Over a tan and orange tunic, his inlaid lap armor was nicked and dented in places. They looked inherited, those battle marks, evidence of another man's glory. Combined with the battleworn scimitar hanging from his belt, it smacked of a little boy prancing about in his father's clothes.

Also on the platform were some two dozen noblemen wearing shining, unscathed armor. They chatted and mingled as if this were some prelude to a dinner party. Haddad stood among them, silent and uncomfortable, a doe in a herd of grunting boar. She glanced Emre's way, but then returned her attention to to the nearest of the blooming fields, which was afire.

No Sharakhani thought of, much less looked upon, the adichara in a neutral way. Some revered them and, just as they regarded the asirim as holy warriors, considered the blooming fields to be hallowed ground. For many, however, even some who lived in Goldenhill or Hanging Gardens, the adichara were symbols of fear and oppression. So it was strange for Emre to see the fields like this, black smoke issuing from one of the groves, the rest laid bare beneath the light of the summer sun. They seemed strangely harmless, as if everyone in Sharakhai had been afraid over nothing for four hundred years.

As Emre and Hamid were relieved of their swords and knives, and Frail Lemi of his great spear, Umber, the herald whispered into King Emir's ear. It was then that Emre noticed a strange man standing near Haddad at the corner of the platform. He was crooked and bent and thin as a rail. He wore a golden mask with androgynous features: high cheekbones, a strong chin, full lips, and wide, elegant eyes. Along the forehead was a starburst pattern that struck a chord of memory. It was so sudden and so strong it swept Emre back to his days of living with Çeda in Roseridge. One of the illuminated books Çeda had kept in their home was a scholar's work on the gods and holy relics of Malasan. Emre could hardly read at the time, but he'd been fascinated by the masterful drawings. He and Çeda had stayed up late one night, and she'd told him about each of their gods. This mask had been the sign of one of them, but he couldn't remember which. Ranrika maybe, or Shonokh.

The king's herald finished speaking, at which point the king turned and regarded the newcomers. When Frail Lemi's sheer height and brawn registered, there was a brief widening of his eyes—the most common reaction to seeing the big man up close for the first time. Emre, Hamid, and Frail Lemi bowed, and King Emir waved for them to rise.

"You are welcome," he said in near perfect Sharakhan, spreading his arms wide as if to encompass not merely the fleet behind him, but the whole of the desert.

It was a grating gesture, perhaps meant to provoke. Haddad studied Emre with an unreadable expression. There was no doubt she was still angry with him, but there was worry in the way she kept glancing toward the blooming fields. Her attention was drawn away as the frail man in the golden mask tugged at her sleeve and began whispering to her.

Emre smiled at the king as pleasantly as he could manage. "I could say the same to you."

The king replied with a smile that could only be read as insincere.

"I've come at the behest of Macide Ishaq'ava," Emre went on, "shaikh of the thirteenth tribe. I would speak with your Excellence of our plans, and of yours, to see where our people might find common ground."

"An interesting term, common ground," King Emir said.

"Oh? How so?"

King Emir's smile was smug. He knew he had the power here and wanted Emre to know it. "It presumes you will have any ground left to call your own."

"You think we won't?"

Instead of answering, King Emir turned toward the tree line and waved. "These trees fascinate me. Do you know much about them?"

More than I'd ever share with you, Emre thought. "The blooming fields were planted by the gods after Beht Ihman to protect Sharakhai."

"They seem to be doing a rather poor job of it."

Surely he meant the asirim. And indeed, where were they? Had the Kings used them against the Malasani fleet? Had they sent them elsewhere?

As if in answer, a bone-rattling howl came from the trees. A dark figure came barreling out of the shadows. How thin it looked, how emaciated. Its skin looked dark and gangrenous. It wore no clothes, but ran naked like one of the hairless mongrel dogs that scavenged the west end for food. A second asir came a moment later, slower than the first. Limping.

Emre had been learning Malasani from Haddad and her crew over the months they'd been together, and so was able to piece together some of the questions the noblemen were asking. *Where are the rest of the asirim? Where is the vaunted Sharakhani fleet?* He cobbled together the answers as well. Mirea, they were saying. The Mirean fleet was shrieking down on Sharakhai and the royal navy had been sent to stop them, likely with the bulk of the asirim.

The two asirim charged the line of Malasani soldiers, who stood with shields at the ready. Noticeable among the soldiers was a group of about twenty. They were large of frame with big potbellies. Now that they were out in the open it was easy to recognize them for what they were: golems. Their clay bodies shimmered with bronze filings. Clothes and armor, even jewelry and sandals, were rendered into the clay and each was shaped, more or less, like the same portly man. Their faces were identical, or nearly so. Some appeared to be older than Ibrahim the storyteller, others younger than Emre, but their chins, hook noses, and arched brows were all the same. The strangest thing about them, however, were their expressions. Each was unique and, without exception, intense. They appeared fearful, angry, hateful, or filled with crazed happiness. Their eyes and mouths moved eerily, causing their expressions to shift wildly like the fickle winds of spring, but soon enough they would revert to their previous state. It was as if each was trapped in time, some brief moment of a man's life playing out over and over on their artificial features.

They plodded forward, five of them converging on the path of the first asir. The asir tried to leap over their staggered line, but one of the golems carried a net and threw it into the air with perfect timing. The asir went down in a tangle of limbs, tearing viciously at the netting with claws and teeth, managing to rip it in several places. But then two of the golems, bearing massive war clubs, battered the poor creature's shriveled form.

Nearby, the priest in the golden mask had left Haddad's side. From the edge of the platform he watched the scene play out, hands bunched beneath his chin and shivering with pleasure as the golems worked their weapons. It made him seem the sort who'd inflicted casual cruelty on others when he was young and now pined for those days of power.

The asir took blow after blow but still fought and howled and clawed, then managed to break free and tear at the nearest golem's legs. A normal man could withstand no more than a blow or two from those clubs, but the asir took a score or more before it finally fell. Still the golems pounded its lifeless frame.

As the second asir, much slower than the first, suffered the same fate, one thought kept running through Emre's mind: *These are my tribe; these are my people.* Çeda had spoken those words many times about the asirim, and while Emre had recognized the truth in them, he'd never really felt it, not until seeing them like this. It touched something deep inside him. The asirim weren't merely *his* people. They were *people.*

Some of the rage he'd felt when his brother had been murdered by Saadet ibn Sim, the Malasani bravo, returned. So did the feelings of helplessness.

"Call them off," Emre said.

But the conversation was so loud, no one paid attention.

"Make it stop!" Emre shouted in Malasani.

King Emir turned toward Emre and raised one hand. All conversation ceased. "What did you say?" he asked in Malasani.

Emre replied in Sharakhan. "I said, make the golems stop beating the asirim."

In the background came the rhythmic *thump, thump, thump* of the golems' clubs. The tips of the blunt weapons were smeared with black blood. It flew in arcs with each lift, each mighty swing down.

King Emir stepped closer until he and Emre were within striking distance of one another. "Beg for it."

"What?"

"You heard me." He waited, staring at Emre, perhaps expecting him to say something rash.

The words were right on Emre's lips. *Please stop beating them.* What did it matter if he asked? Except the idea of giving in to this man made him want to retch. This would only be the beginning.

Emre took a half step forward. The king's guardsmen drew short swords from their belts, but halted when King Emir raised a hand.

"Call the golems off. And remind your priest that respect for the dead does not include clapping like a little boy at murder."

Indeed, the priest had start clapping softly. The eyes behind the golden mask were wild with pleasure. At a touch from Haddad he froze, and his gaze swung toward Emre, who felt himself go cold. Emre had seen plenty of crazed, unpredictable men and women in the Shallows, the sort even enforcers steered clear of. That was the kind of look the man was giving Emre now, as if he were devising special tortures, things a normal man wouldn't dream of.

King Emir had the air of self-satisfaction about him, as if he'd been given the excuse he needed to do as he pleased with Emre. But he noted the priest's strange reaction as well. He turned toward him and had just opened his mouth to speak when his eyes snapped toward the adichara trees.

Emre turned and saw another asir loping out from beneath the shade. This one didn't howl as the others had. It simply ran, and with much more speed than Emre would have guessed it could muster. Strangely, it bore a sword, a great, two-handed shamshir made of nicked steel that shone dully in the daylight. The golems moved to block its path but before they could, a cough of sand lifted up from the desert and swirled around them. It swept over the platform like a gale, forcing everyone to shield their eyes.

When the sand and dust dispersed, several of the noblemen were pointing. One of them gasped. The golems were gone, nowhere to be found. A moment later Emre caught movement, a roiling over the surface of the sand. The golems had been sucked into the desert, he realized, clearing a path to the soldiers.

Arrows were fired. The Malasani soldiers locked shields and raised their swords, and still the asir tore into their line like a scythe through wheat. Man after man fell, screaming, clutching at wounds from the asir's blurring sword, clawed hand, or ravenous mouth. Some were thrown aside by gusts of wind that lifted the sand in plumes. A dozen were cut down as several golems regained the surface and squirmed, trying ineffectually to free themselves from the grasping sand. Only one was able to wade slowly forward, but it looked as though it were fighting the flow of a raging river.

With the Malasani soldiers scattered or dead, the asir turned toward the platform and howled so loudly that Emre's skin prickled from it. He found himself stepping backward even before the asir began running toward them.

The noblemen on the platform were beginning to realize what was coming for them. The asir seemed fixated on one in particular, however: the man in the golden mask. Emre heard a surprised shout behind him. A big body bulled past him, leapt onto the short rail at the edge, and bound into the air.

It was Frail Lemi with his greatspear, Umber, somehow gripped in both hands as he flew to meet the asir.

The asir lifted its sword to block Lemi's blow, but the spear, its cutting edge honed by the gods themselves, sheared clean through the pitted steel blade. Only when Lemi's massive leg kicked the asir backward did Emre realize that the asir's arm had been cleaved. Blood spurted from the stump, coating the sand in glistening black, and still the asir fought on, managing to grasp Frail Lemi's breastplate with one arm, pull itself close, and bite through the chainmail hauberk and into his shoulder.

The old man in the mask clapped and danced. Frail Lemi, meanwhile, released a surprised, reflexive sort of bellow that echoed the terror in his eyes. He was deathly afraid of the asirim, which made Emre wonder why he'd attacked one.

Lemi pushed the asir away, clubbed it with the spear's weighted end, then raised Umber high. The asir scrabbled away, but not nearly fast enough. Frail Lemi brought Umber down hard, skewering the asir, pinning it to the sand. The asir grasped the wooden haft, tried to pull itself along it to reach Frail Lemi. But its strength soon gave out. Black blood oozed from its chest, the stump of its arm, and a dozen other wounds. A dusting of sand fell across its stilling form until it lay its head back and stared sightlessly at the bitter blue sky.

The clapping and dancing of the old man subsided. His gripped hands shivered as if he were caught in the throes of ecstasy. The nobles, meanwhile, recovered themselves, though it was clear from their stiff movements and furtive glances toward the blooming fields that they were shaken. They'd badly underestimated the strength of the asirim.

King Emir, meanwhile, looked from the dead asir, to Frail Lemi, and finally to Emre. His demeanor was no longer one of a lord standing before three beggars, but of begrudging gratitude. "I'll send my herald on the morrow. We can discuss our *common ground* then."

The last thing Emre wanted to do was thank him. Still, he was about to do so—the words were right there on his lips—when King Emir took Haddad's hand and led her from the platform. To remain silent was an insult, but the king didn't so much as glance Emre's way as he left. It was peculiar, his sudden familiarity with Haddad, and at odds with the sort of air he seemed to want to project: one of self-reliance and emotional detachment. He'd been scared by the asir, Emre realized, but more than this, he'd gone to *Haddad* for comfort.

Emre watched as King Emir led Haddad up the gangplank to his capital ship. As he reached the deck, he suddenly turned and pulled Haddad toward him. She followed the motion willingly, as a lover might, as a wife might: with a smile on her face and her body leaning into his. They kissed, an ardent thing, the sort Emre had felt on his own lips many times as they lay in her bed on *Calamity's Reign*.

The two of them broke and strode away, but not before Haddad sent a brief look down toward Emre. Was it regret he saw in her eyes? Defiance? Embarrassment? He couldn't say, and then she was gone, lost to the angle of the ship's high deck.

Chapter 30

ÇEDA WAS SITTING IN THE CAPTAIN'S cabin when Melis knocked on the door.

"Come," she said.

Melis entered, her veil down, a sullen expression on her face.

Çeda took in her dress, which was caked with sand. "Brush yourself off, Maiden."

Melis looked like she'd been struck by a hammer. She stepped back outside and shook the sand off, a thing any Maiden would have done without thinking before being called to visit with the captain of a navy ship.

"Does this meet with your approval?" she asked as she stepped back inside.

It didn't, but Çeda let it go. "Take a seat," she said, motioning to the chair across the desk from her. Only after Melis had taken it and settled herself did Çeda go on. "We're set to return to Sharakhai."

"You think I'm unaware?"

"That's just it. I think you're focusing on it too much."

Melis didn't disagree.

"Sümeya and I have been talking. When we return, we'd like to try to recruit one more to our cause. To understand the lay of the land in Shara-khai. To help us find and free Sehid-Alaz."

"You want Kameyl," Melis said, practically spitting the name out, "and you want me to help you."

"Yes—"

"She'd *never* join you."

"Join *us* you mean."

Again Melis was silent.

"This is what we need to speak about. I know the asirim have surprised you. I know much has changed for you, in some ways more for you than for Sümeya. But your attitude, your insubordination, cannot go on. You are either committed to our cause or you are not."

"I'll not become a member of your *tribe*, so you can get that idea out of your head right now."

"This isn't about the tribe. This is about your doubts. Your fears for your family and Sharakhai. I see them eating away at you. One day they'll make you flinch, or doubt once too often. I see how the Shieldwives distance themselves from you."

"I was a Blade Maiden. How else would you expect them to act?"

"If it were simply that, they would treat Sümeya the same way. And they don't."

She waited for Melis to say something, anything, to defend herself. When she didn't, Çeda went on. "You can leave, Melis. You don't have to come with us to the city. You never did. You can take the skiff and go wherever you will."

For the first time, Melis showed a bit of the despondence that Çeda knew had been hiding beneath her anger. "I have nothing to return *to*."

"I know Sharakhai will be difficult for you."

But Melis was shaking her head. "I'm not talking about a place. There's nothing left to me. Nothing except—"

"What?"

"When you and I first met, we spoke of a meeting I had with King Yusam. Do you remember?"

A chill swept through Çeda's entire body. They'd been scrubbing part of the House of Maidens free of soot after an attack by the Moonless Host. Melis had confided three of Yusam's predictions about her—and that two of them had already come true. The third, Çeda realized, the one that hadn't yet come true, was the root of all Melis's troubles.

"He said you would stand beside a queen," Çeda said.

"And that I would protect her above all things," Melis added.

They'd puzzled over that word, queen, wondering if it had somehow meant Queen Alansal of Mirea. Now things had changed in Qaimir, perhaps the vision had referred to Queen Meryam. But the way Melis was looking at Çeda made it clear she thought—or feared—there was a third possibility.

"It cannot be you," she said flatly.

She thought that Çeda had somehow fulfilled the third vision. And that had broken everything she thought she knew.

"I'm no queen," Çeda said.

"I thought perhaps a King would die, that his daughter would take his place. That I would serve her faithfully until I was ready to give up my blade."

"I'm no queen."

"You know his visions can't be taken literally," Melis said.

Çeda knew firsthand how Yusam's visions often needed deeper reflection to truly understand. And it made her think about all she'd been through, what she'd done with the help of others, and all she still *meant* to do. She felt a surge of naked ambition coming from Night's Kiss, which was propped in the corner behind her. She thought it was the sword's own desires, but realized a moment later it was merely acting as a mirror, feeding off her own emotions.

Part of her, the young woman who'd hidden herself in Sharakhai and worked from the shadows to bring down the Kings, recoiled at the notion of leading a movement—*I'm no leader*—but another part of her had already accepted the truth. *I'm ambitious. What of it? The situation demands it.* And with the Shieldwives and the asirim following her, what was she if *not* a leader?

Queen or not, one of the unfortunate truths about being a leader was that it gave you no special insights. Such was the case with Melis. Çeda still had no idea how to lure her back into the fold.

"The Kings have earned their fall," she finally said. She felt like an ox trampling over a flower bed.

"The Kings may have, but you know the histories. The tribes would have killed everyone in the House of Kings whether they were innocent or not. Those in Goldenhill and the Hanging Gardens would be next."

"I'm not convinced of that," Çeda said, "but even if you're right, that's all the more reason to reach out to the people now. To tell them the true story of the thirteenth tribe."

Melis threw her hands up in the air. "That would only open old wounds! And even if we somehow convinced the tribes to forgive the Kings of all their transgressions, the people of the west end will not. They're close to rioting already. If they see a house ready to fall, they'll storm the gates of Tauriyat and do the work of Malasan and Mirea for them. Everything I've come to love will be destroyed."

"But that's just it, Melis. It was all built on lies."

"I know that!" Melis stood, her face red with rage, and drew her shamshir so quickly the ebon steel blurred, a brief shadow in the air between them.

Çeda shivered in surprise, ready to reach for Night's Kiss, but Melis wasn't aiming for her. She brought the blade down against the desk, striking with enough force to cut through the top, the drawer beneath, and halfway into the next.

The cabin door flew open, and Sümeya stood in the doorway, her sword drawn. Çeda raised her hand and shook her head as Melis unleashed the last of her pent-up rage with a second, screaming, two-handed chop. She stood there, breathing hard, refusing to look at either Çeda or Sümeya, her former commander. Then she threw down her sword, as if with that one act she could leave it all behind, and stalked from the room.

Sümeya seemed uncharacteristically unsure of herself, of what to do. She'd been battling her own demons. "Do you want me to talk to her?"

Çeda shook her head. "I will." She picked up Melis's sword and went in search of her, finally finding her in the bilge, sitting in the darkness on the ballast stones, cross-legged, facing away from Çeda. Çeda left the hatch open, allowing some small amount of light to filter in from above.

"Change was always coming to the desert, Melis."

"I know."

"We can help heal it once and for all."

"I know that too."

"So lay the past aside. Lay your former hopes for Sharakhai aside with it and look to the future. By the strength of your blade, by your wits, by your courage, we can forge it anew. Let that be the light that guides you, not the darkness of your disappointment."

Melis was silent for a time. She shifted on the stones, turning to face Çeda as the ship rocked beneath them. Her eyes were lost to the darkness, but Çeda could tell she was looking at her sword. When Çeda held it out to her, Melis accepted it. She held it in both hands, pinching it with her thumbs at the balance point, then lifted it to her forehead as if she were making a promise to the god of war. What sort of promise it might have been, Çeda had no idea. With accustomed ease Melis drove the sword home into her scabbard.

"Rezzan," she said.

"Rezzan?"

"Rezzan is Kameyl's nephew. His crossing day comes in eight days and Kameyl wouldn't miss it for the world."

Çeda sat there, stunned. Melis was offering them a way to reach Kameyl away from the House of Kings. With it came a realization.

"You didn't tell us about it because you've been afraid she'd join us." If any woman exemplified what it meant to be a Blade Maiden, it was Kameyl, and if *she* was convinced by Çeda's story, it would destroy what little hope Melis had of her life returning to normal.

"I know her brother's estate passably well," Melis said, "but we'll want to watch it for a day or two before the celebration."

Çeda leaned forward and kissed the crown of Melis's head, and the two of them left the bilge together.

Late that night they anchored and licked their wounds after the sudden battle with the Malasani ships. Miraculously, no Shieldwives had been killed. Only one of the asirim had died, Natise, who'd taken a fatal blow to the head. The rest had escaped with wounds that would heal, including one who had been engulfed in fire pot flames but had miraculously survived.

Çeda lay in her bed in the captain's cabin, a room she shared with both Imadra and Jenise. The two of them were in the galley with the others, probably drinking araq and singing songs that would be considered bawdy in even the rowdiest shisha dens in Sharakhai. It was the sort of thing women shared only with one another, and Çeda loved them for it.

Part of her wanted to join them—she would put her catalog of such songs to the test against any of the other women—but something about her talk with Melis had put her in a solitary mood. She enjoyed listening, though. Her Shieldwives were becoming a tight-knit group, and it made her proud.

Some time later the cabin door opened. Çeda thought it was Jenise, who often ended her night before the rest, but it wasn't. It was Sümeya.

"Yes?" Çeda asked.

The silence yawned between them, reminding Çeda of another meeting between the two of them alone while distant songs were sung.

"Come in," Çeda said. Sümeya did, closing the door behind her, and the roaring claps and laughter were muffled.

The space across from Çeda had two bunks. Sümeya sat on the lower, her hands in her lap.

The last time Çeda had been alone with Sümeya like this, she'd feared for her life. Sümeya had confessed feelings for her. They'd shared their bodies with one another in the desert. Çeda had felt something for Sümeya too, but she'd also used Sümeya to uncover secrets of the Kings. She felt bad about it, but she knew she would do the same all over again. The truth had been too important. It still was.

Moonlight shone through the nearby porthole, bathing Sümeya in spun silver. Her knees were only a short distance from Çeda's left hand.

Çeda didn't know whether Sümeya was here to to confess something in anger, put a spark to their unkindled love, or for some other purpose. She wasn't sure which she preferred, either, so instead of opening her fool mouth and ruining it, she remained silent, waiting for Sümeya to speak.

"Thank you for talking to Melis." Sümeya's voice was husky, but not, Çeda thought, from wine or araq. "She needed it."

"We both did," replied Çeda. "I'd been avoiding it for too long."

"Yes." Sümeya paused. "There are probably a few things we've been avoiding as well."

Çeda swallowed. "Yes."

"In the desert, on the way to Ishmantep—"

"Sümeya, I'm sorry." Her voice kept catching like a skirt being snagged by thorns. "I didn't want to learn of the Kings that way."

Sümeya laughed. "You didn't?"

Çeda, glad for the darkness, felt her cheeks go red. "I didn't want to use you like that."

Sümeya shrugged. "I would have done the same in your place."

Feeling her heart leap, Çeda reached out and touched Sümeya's knee. "No. I didn't want to use *you*. You understand?"

Sümeya's hand reached out, trailed softly over the back of her hand. The sensation traveled all the way up her arm and settled at the nape of her neck. "I understand."

"Sümeya, I don't know—" She tried to pull her hand away, but Sümeya took it and refused to let go.

"Sümeya—"

"Çeda, Leorah was right. You need to know when to shut your mouth." She shifted to Çeda's bunk and leaned in, stopping only when the two of them were breath to breath. Çeda felt the warmth rolling off her, smelled the scent of her unbound hair.

The distance closed. Sümeya's lips pressed warmly against hers.

Just as it had in the desert, Çeda's heart lifted to be with Sümeya, to have their skin touch, but there were things that needed saying, things she couldn't let go. "It's just, things are changing so quickly."

Sümeya placed kisses along her neck, the pleasure of each adding to the next until Çeda's eyes fluttered closed of their own accord and she was raking her fingers through Sümeya's hair. Çeda felt Sümeya's hot breath against her ear as she spoke. "And what does that have to do with this?"

Çeda breathed, holding herself back, forcing herself to think clearly lest she or Sümeya get hurt. "Melis was so angry. Part of her wants the world back the way it was."

"And you think I do too. Is that it?"

"Don't you? Don't you still love Nayyan?"

"The sands shift, Çeda." When Sümeya stood and slipped out of her dress, the moonlight revealed dozens of scars along her shoulders and chest, her arms and legs. "Shall we ignore it when it does?" She stood there naked, proud, vulnerable, and *wanting*. "Should we be swept beneath the dunes?"

In answer, Çeda pulled her light blanket aside and, when Sümeya slipped beneath it, swept it over both of them. The ship was still warm from the day, but the light sheen of sweat on Sümeya's skin was cool. They lay side by side. Sümeya's hand slipped along Çeda's hip, ran down her thigh. Unlike when they'd lain on the sand, Sümeya was taking her time, yet it made the flame of her passion seem all the brighter. She knew where this was headed and was in no rush to get there.

The sheer confidence in the way she leaned in, the way she withheld her touch, sent a host of butterflies fluttering in Çeda's chest. In those moments, Çeda's doubts were dispelled; replaced with a desire for Sümeya's touch that ran the full length of Çeda's body. When Çeda moved toward her, however, she found Sümeya pulling back, and when Çeda tried again, Sümeya retreated farther, this time with a smile. When Çeda grabbed the back of her neck and pulled her in for a deep kiss, however, Sümeya returned it with the same passion.

Suddenly Sümeya's lips went tight. A smile broke across her face. She laughed, a sound so pure Çeda nearly laughed with her. She would have, had the desire in her not been so strong.

When their lips met once more, Sümeya's lips were soft. Their tongues played as Sümeya pulled the blanket down, exposing Çeda's breasts, her belly. Sümeya's touch became more insistent. Her lips closed on Çeda's hardening nipple. Her hand slipped down along Çeda's thigh then between her legs, never breaking contact. When she touched Çeda, when her fingers toyed with her, a wave of pleasure ran through Çeda that was so great, so welcome, she moaned without meaning to.

The conversation outside the cabin dropped. There might have been a few laughs.

Çeda didn't care. As the conversation resumed, Çeda grabbed the hair at the back of Sümeya's head and pulled, exposing Sümeya's neck. She placed kisses against her soft skin, feeling Sümeya's pulse beneath her lips, while her other hand roamed Sümeya's well-muscled back. And when she found that same place between *Sümeya's* thighs, she heard a long, satisfied groan.

For a time they were playful as a clear mountain stream. Çeda enveloped Sümeya, and they drifted, rushing toward the rapids in ceaseless, unknowable currents until the two of them crashed, loud and vibrant and joyful in the sun.

Chapter 31

As Davud, Esmeray, and Fezek were being led toward the safe house by Cicio, the curly-haired Qaimiri, Davud wondered why Sukru had come for Anila instead of him. It was clear he'd waited until the two of them were separated. The Blade Maidens had been sent after Davud, but Sukru himself had chosen to go after Anila, which meant he either considered her more dangerous, or more important to his plans.

Fezek lumbered at the rear of the group, wearing the new hooded robe they'd found for him. He hated wearing it. Said he wanted to feel the light of the sun on his skin.

"Can you even feel it?" Davud had asked once.

Fezek had shrugged. "Not as such. But I like to imagine I could."

As they turned a corner onto a nearly deserted street, Fezek looked past Davud and Esmeray to Cicio. "Is it much farther?"

Cicio called over his shoulder, "You ask that question one more time, ah? I put you back in the ground."

"I was only wondering if we were close," Fezek grumbled under his breath. "Always so touchy!"

Davud didn't bother replying. Say a word and Fezek was likely to bend the conversation back toward his poetry, which was about as interesting as a braying mule. As Fezek remained blessedly silent, Davud's thoughts returned to Anila and the reasons Sukru had allowed her to learn the ways of necromancy in the first place. He'd asked her several times about it. She'd confessed how Sukru had come to her in his palace and given her some books that detailed the rather brief lives of necromancers.

One was the chronicle of a famous man who'd lived centuries ago, a man who lost all ten of his children to a brutal encounter with a drug lord and had nearly suffered the same fate as his children. They'd been tossed into the pit of bone crushers the drug lord kept as pets. The father had stood before the pile of bodies, his eyes afire with white light, a cold fog rolling off his frame, and had called his children back from the dead. Despite their hunks of missing flesh, despite tendons cut, throats ripped out, they'd risen and killed the bone crushers, then raided the drug lord's compound in a night of terror that had come to be known as Black Malahndi.

As dawn arrived, the man's children fell lifeless to the ground, one by one. The man himself lasted another two days. The Silvers Spears found him staring numbly at his dead children, a smile on his face and tears in his eyes. He'd been swiftly delivered to King Sukru for questioning, whereupon Sukru had recorded his account. It, and several more like it, had been enough to put Anila on her way to becoming a necromancer.

"But surely Sukru gave some hint as to his purpose?" Davud had asked her.

"Never," Anila had replied. "It felt like he was curious more than anything else."

When Davud shared his thoughts with Esmeray, she'd only shrugged. "You're searching too hard. Why does Sukru need a reason other than to gather more power?"

"I suppose he doesn't, but when he came for me, he *did* have a purpose, which I doubt he's abandoned, despite King Kiral ordering him to do so."

Esmeray had given him a side-eyed stare, then a smile of understanding broke over her face. She poked him in the chest. "You're *jealous*. You're wondering why *you*, with all the power the gods saw fit to grant you, weren't taken first."

"I'm not *jealous*. I'm worried for Anila."

"By the Great Mother's teats, Davud"—she laughed until his cheeks burned, in a way that was somehow equal parts endearing and infuriating—"you're aware you can be both, right?"

He felt he should be angry at the implication he would ever put himself above Anila's safety, but part of him knew she was right. He exhaled noisily, and it became an awkward laugh. In that moment he spotted movement along a side street. Ten doors down, a large cat was hugging the walls of the three-story homes. The serval from the banks of the river had found them again.

"Is it much—" Fezek began.

"Be quiet," Davud whispered, and rushed Fezek, Esmeray, and Cicio farther up the street. From the mouth of an alley the four of them watched the cat prowl toward them. When it crossed their path it slowed, its tail went stiff, and the hair on its back stood up, as though it had heard a mouse in the walls.

Davud was already weaving a spell to steal the breath from the serval. Esmeray, watching, snatched both of his hands. "No," she breathed, and cast a spell of her own. Her hands moved in quick, precise strokes. She was much better than Davud had given her credit for. And that was before he realized she was casting two spells simultaneously, one with each hand.

As the serval slunk nearer, Davud felt the hair on the back of his neck stand on end. He expected clay pots to start flying from the tops of the buildings at any moment, but they didn't, and soon the large, spotted cat had come to a stop only a few paces from Esmeray. It looked suddenly unnatural, however. It stood stock-still and hardly reacted when Esmeray leaned down and picked it up. She was careful, Davud noticed, never to allow its eye contact with the road ahead to be broken.

The index finger of her right hand had blood on it, taken from a small wound on her palm, courtesy of her blooding ring. She used it to draw a pattern on the cat's chest. The sigil for *forget*—no, *deny*—and something else Davud couldn't make out.

"Add yours to it, Davud. A drop in the center."

She'd left a place in the sigil for it. He complied, and dabbed a drop where she'd indicated.

When she set the cat down, it paced away with the same sort of ease it had shown before catching their scent.

"What happen now, ah?" Cicio asked.

Esmeray glanced his way, but then fixed her eyes on Davud once more. Why did she always seem so amused with him? "It turns someone else into its quarry and follows them instead."

"Whom?" Davud asked.

"*Whom* . . ." Esmeray exaggerated the word back at Davud, then laughed. "Whomever it finds most interesting, collegia boy."

Fezek and Cicio were both smiling while staring at Davud. Davud, meanwhile, felt his face redden worse than it had in some time. "And if there are others on our tail?" he asked in a rush.

"Then we'll take care of them, too."

It was intricate spellwork, what Esmeray had just done. He motioned to the retreating cat. "Will you teach me?"

Esmeray seemed affronted by the very question, but then the look faded. "If you're nice."

He didn't have a chance to ask her what constituted nice before she left him to join Cicio. She spent more time talking with him than Davud would have liked.

They resumed their walk toward Ramahd's safe house, which turned out to be a tiny room over a locksmith's shop, accessible from the small yard behind his home. Seeing them safely inside, Cicio headed for the door.

"Where are you going?" Esmeray asked.

"My lord say bring you here safely. He no say nothing about watching over you like some fucking wet nurse." And with that he closed the door, leaving them in the tiny space.

In one corner, where the low, sloping ceiling met the floor, were several small crates containing various parts for locks. Four pallets lay spaced about the rest of the floor, with blankets wrapped around each. Esmeray flopped onto one of them, the skirt of her dress billowing as she did so. She looked like a hopeless gutter wren sitting at the edge of the street.

Davud sat on the pallet across from her. "Sukru will send more than cats after me. He has enough blood to chase me for months. Years."

Esmeray was looking at him wistfully.

"What?"

"The Enclave knows of a way to deal with such things. It isn't permanent, but it may not need to be. There's a good chance Sukru will assume you're dead when his attempts to find you produce no results."

"What—" He swallowed and felt his face flush. Esmeray was a good deal prettier than he'd realized when they'd first met. "What do we do?"

She smiled. She looked fierce when she smiled, and he liked that. "The Enclave knows of a way to taint our blood so that our signature, the trace we leave behind, is altered. It makes mundane tracking spells fail, and many of the more complex ones as well."

"Mundane?" Now it was Davud's turn to laugh. He was immediately glad he did for it rekindled Esmeray's smile. "I think you've been in the Enclave too long."

She shrugged. "Perhaps. It involves an exchange of blood. Once done, the protection that applies to us will be passed to you. And then no one, not Sukru, nor Queen Meryam, nor even the Enclave, will be able to track you by use of your blood, even had they a ewer-full. I warn you, though. The first time it's done, you'll feel sick. Hot. You'll fall into a fever dream not unlike when the change first overcame you."

"As bad as that?"

"No," she said, "not so bad as that."

"How long does it last?"

"It's different for everyone. For most, one night. For those stronger in the red ways, as I suspect you are, it could take days."

Days . . . Days lost in trying to save Anila. But what else could he do? He couldn't very well rescue Anila without it.

"Very well," he said.

"Very well," she echoed.

She slipped off the pallet and crawled the short distance between them until she was close enough for Davud to feel the heat coming off her. Bakhi's bright hammer, her scent . . . She smelled of lemongrass and ambergris and a strong, womanly musk that made her seem all the more exotic. It felt vaguely threatening to have her so close, but Davud's body was tingling so much he said nothing. When she took his chin in her hand, however, and leaned toward him, tilting her head, he reeled back.

"Is there no other way to exchange our blood?"

"There is," she replied, "but this is how it was done for me. And it is how I will do it for you." Her eyes stared into his. "Unless you wish me to stop."

He swallowed, wondering what Anila would think of this. *She wouldn't care,* he told himself. *She's never thought about you that way.* Even so, it felt like a betrayal when he shook his head no.

"Good," she said, and pressed her lips to his.

It was warm, like a kiss, though he doubted Esmeray thought of it as such. She sucked his lower lip in and bit him, hard enough to draw blood. He'd grown accustomed to this sort of pain, but still he winced. The mixture of the slickness of her lips and the closeness of her body was making him more aware of himself than he'd been in a long while. He felt clumsy and foolish, a boy still growing into his body, but he also felt more *need* than he ever had before, even more than the days he'd spent in the desert with Anila.

"Now you," Esmeray said, her voice husky.

He did as she asked. He sucked her lip into his mouth and bit it. She inhaled sharply. And then the two of them were kissing softly, exchanging blood, his mouth filling with copper as they shared a moment that lit Davud from the inside.

He slipped a hand around her neck. She did the same to him, lay him down on the pallet, and pressed her body against his. His hands slipped to the small of her back. Hers gripped the side of his head and held him still as she straddled his hips and began to writhe.

When he slipped one hand up to her breast, she stiffened and grabbed his wrist. He stopped immediately, knowing he'd taken it too far.

"I'm sorry," he whispered.

He saw no fright in her eyes, no anger, but still she pulled away. Their lips made a smacking sound as they parted. "That's enough," she said. He wasn't sure if she meant his advances or their exchanged blood.

Davud's mouth was warm. It was filling with spit, some strange reaction to Esmeray. He swallowed hard. "Could—could you do this for Ra-mahd too?"

The look of surprise on her face made it clear that was a misstep. "I've offered Amansir help, but no, he doesn't get this." She pushed him hard onto the pallet. "Now close your eyes. It will come on quickly."

"Where are you going?" he asked as she slipped toward the door.

"You'll need water. Lots of it." She wiped her lips with the back of one hand. "And the Enclave will be searching for us. Best I cover our tracks."

Davud was feeling bold, and he tried to hide his smile but was perfectly sure he'd failed.

"What?" she asked.

"You said the effect was temporary."

Unlike Davud, Esmeray didn't try to hide her smile at all. "So?"

"That implies we might need to do this again."

"Well that depends on whether you live long enough for it to be necessary, doesn't it?"

Davud swallowed the growing lump in his throat and hoped his reddened cheeks weren't as obvious as they felt. "How long?"

She returned to the bedside and leaned over him until they were face to face again. "Wouldn't you like to know?" With one quick, powerful kiss, she was gone.

Davud stared at the door a long while. He soon found, however, that Esmeray had been right. A heat was starting to consume him, and he wondered if the wonderful, queasy feeling in his chest was due to that or to Esmeray.

Don't be stupid, Davud.

As he lay down and stared at the ceiling, he breathed deeply, savoring the scent of lemongrass and ambergris and a strong, womanly musk.

Chapter 32

Count Mateo Abrantes of Qaimir stepped out of the araba, taking care that his trick knee didn't buckle, then tugged down his uniform jacket. Mighty Alu but the desert was hot. And the worst thing about it was he couldn't build up a proper sweat. Nor did water seem to help. The desert air was a thief, stealing all comfort from him.

He climbed the steps to the Temple of Alu. He'd arrived the previous night and had just been driven in from the Qaimiri embassy house. It was a time-honored tradition to visit the temple, and he'd not risk angering Alu now, not when so much depended on it. It was a way of welcoming Alu from the seas, of inviting his protection. *A thing I'll have great need of in the days to come*, Mateo thought.

Inside the temple, the priest sprinkled Mateo's hands with salt water from the Austral Sea, then left him in peace to pray. A short while later, a man entered. "Welcome, friend," Mateo said, as any good follower of Alu would, but then he looked at the man properly and realized who he was.

Ramahd Amansir stood beneath a scalloped archway holding a bag over his left shoulder, leaving his right arm free. When Ramahd noticed Mateo's eyes drifting to his sword, he said, "I only wish to talk."

Mateo had thought Duke Hektor mad to take this meeting. They'd all heard the rumors of how Amansir had betrayed their queen. But Hektor had always been bothered by the manner of King Aldouan's death. There was no denying that the way Meryam, Hamzakiir, and Ramahd had swept into the capital, then taken Aldouan with them when they left, was strange. Hektor *wanted* there to be something wrong with Meryam's tale. He wanted the real story behind his brother's death, not some fanciful tale of an ehrekh somehow finding them by chance in the desert. But that was precisely what worried Mateo. If a man wants to believe in something desperately enough, he'd do so, truth and reason be damned.

"Speak your piece, Lord Amansir."

What followed was exactly the sort of story Mateo had expected. A tale of Hamzakiir being ensorcelled by Meryam. Of Meryam pulling his strings and leading her father to the desert. Of Meryam summoning Guhldrathen that her father might be killed, clearing her way to the throne of Qaimir. "Now that I look back on it," Amansir said, "I think she was manipulating me as well. Grief stricken as she was, she ensured that *I* was the one to bargain with Guhldrathen to save the two of us."

He finished with the tale of Kiral the King of Kings and how Meryam had set him up to die at the hands of Guhldrathen and put Hamzakiir in his place. From the bag he withdrew a severed head, which he proceeded to set onto the floor so that its sightless eyes were staring up at Mateo.

For long moments Mateo stared back at it. There was no doubt it had many of King Kiral's features, and yet . . . "This is a wild tale, and the very fate of our country rides upon the truth of it. I've always thought you a forthright man, Lord Amansir"—he waved to the head—"but I couldn't rightly say whether this is Kiral or not. I only met him once, many years ago."

"It's him," Amansir said. "Many others will corroborate it."

"Perhaps, but even if they do, who's to say *you* didn't kill him? Who's to say you're not trying to aid one of Meryam's rivals? There are many who might do so. Many who might be pulling strings to discredit our queen and sow discord."

He glanced over one shoulder. "I'm not asking you to believe me outright. Ask the queen for her version of events, but be prepared to look beyond her lies."

Mateo stared at the head, increasingly skeptical that the stony face was Kiral's at all. "And if I'm still not convinced?"

"Let's set aside Meryam's crimes for the moment. I'm going to tell you precisely what will happen when you go to her." Amansir rolled the head back into the bag. "She will reacquaint herself with you, ask careful questions about your recent past, and your family's past, especially as it relates to her father, the throne he vacated when he died, and any inclinations your or anyone in your house might have had to place another on the throne."

Mateo suddenly felt awkward in his own skin. How much did Amansir know? How much did the queen know? Mateo had made no moves himself, but he'd been involved in a dozen conversations with both sides of the family. Even Hektor, the late king's brother, had come to listen to their appeals, and while he mightn't have seemed ready to overstep his niece to seize the throne, neither had he seemed wholly opposed to the notion. Hektor was a careful man, but they all knew that with a bit more convincing, he would come around to their way of thinking.

And then the crate had arrived, sent all the way from Sharakhai with orders to be opened only before a meeting of Qaimir's grand council. Inside lay the body of a man. Gasps of horror and recognition swept across the council. It was Gautiste Remigio, a young noble who several years earlier had been sent to Sharakhai to serve the embassy. The corpse's skin was white and taut, and the gaping wound in his gut made it look like he'd been gored by a bull. The servant who'd accompanied the crate from Sharakhai poured a stream of blood from a phial—first upon the eyes, then the lips, then into the slightly parted mouth. Along the corpse's chest and throat and mouth, the skin took on an unnatural shade of pink, but its extremities turned blue. Its veins stood out in rhythmic, pulsing black.

The naked body moved, standing on limbs that cracked and popped. Its eyes spread wide, an unnerving stare set among wild streaks of crimson. When it turned its head to take in those who'd come for council, all in that room knew it was not Gautiste who looked upon them, but Queen Meryam herself. In the end, Gautiste's gaze came to a rest on Duke Hektor, and a ragged voice began to speak.

"I have come to assure you that your queen is safe, that the *crown* is safe, and that I have begun to unfold plans that will enrich all of Qaimir, particularly those in this room. Fear not over what happens in the desert. Worry not that the throne in Almadan remains unfilled for the time being. It will not remain so for long. And know that when all is said and done, Qaimir's allies will be richly rewarded, while her enemies, wherever they may lie, will be punished as they deserve."

With those last words, the gaze lingered on several: a duke, a duchess, and a count, those who'd been most vocal about overthrowing Meryam. Gautiste's corpse had then collapsed, and the council had devolved into a rush of anxious conversation. Mateo had learned later that Gautiste had not been killed by Meryam, as some had initially feared, but had died fighting for the queen on the Night of Endless Swords. That knowledge did little to blunt the message itself, which had been anything but subtle. It showed the type of reign Queen Meryam was preparing and the fate that awaited those who opposed her.

"Meryam knows the conversations that took place in her absence," Amansir said.

"I only listened," Mateo said. "I made no moves against her."

"Which is why you're still alive. But make no mistake, she will never trust you. She'll listen to your story. She'll take your counsel for the looming war and the part Qaimir should play in it. And then she will ask for your blood."

Mateo's head jerked back in surprise. "She wouldn't."

There had always been an uneasy balance between the nobles of Qaimir and the blood magi. Wars had been fought, and in the end, a compact was made: The blood of nobles would never be requested by any blood mage, not even one of royal lineage. It might be given willingly in a time of need, but it was too precious and dangerous a resource to otherwise be surrendered.

Amansir's look had turned sympathetic, like a father for a son who knew too little of the world. "I know Meryam better than anyone," he said. "She's drunk with power and thirsty for more. But mark my words well. That same thirst has given birth to a paranoia that was intense *before* the Battle of Blackspear. It's only grown worse since."

"And what would you have me do? Go to the embassy house and clap the queen in irons?"

"Ideally, yes."

"And failing that?"

"I expect you to behave as Hektor bid you, to observe and act as Meryam's loyal servant until he arrives." Amansir hoisted the bag over his shoulder and backed away toward the rear entrance of the temple.

Mateo waved to the temple around them. "Why meet at all, then?"

"Because it had to start somewhere. Never fear, Mateo. There's more to come."

"Such as?"

Amansir shook his head. "We'll speak again when the situation has become clear to you." He lost himself down the hallway, but his voice echoed back. "When you'll be rather more amenable to what I have to say."

Mateo left the temple in contemplative silence. He returned to his coach and was driven back inside the walls of the House of Kings to the Qaimiri embassy. Shortly after, he was summoned by the queen, who had apparently arrived for one of her increasingly rare days away from Eventide, the palace of Kiral King of Kings. She wore the golden raiment of a queen but was so thin she looked like a dying pauper. It was a wonder she remained seated in her chair.

They discussed a great many things by the hearth in her apartments. The numbers of ships in the fleet. The soldiers, the war effort. The names of the blood magi who had accompanied the fleet. He thought Meryam would be pleased, but she was in a dark mood, her gaze often wandering to stare beyond the nearby walls, toward the palaces, perhaps, along the slopes of Tauriyat.

"Is there anything more I can help the queen with?" Mateo said near the end of their discussion.

"Hmm?" She was staring northward again. "Oh, yes, there's one last thing. I'll be leaving, Vice Admiral Mateo."

"What? When? Why?"

"I'm leaving Sharakhai tonight to stop the advance of the Mirean fleet."

"*You?* But why?"

She snorted as if she'd been asking herself the same question. "To prove my worth to my fellow rulers."

"Have you not already summoned your fleet to help them in their war? Were you not instrumental in the defeat of the Black Spear?"

Queen Meryam waved her hand dismissively. "I'm going, Mateo. I'll return as soon as I'm able. Until then, I hope you'll work diligently with the Silver Spears to prepare for the fleet's arrival."

"Of—Of course, my queen." He bowed his head, lower than he should have, really. He was just so relieved. Amansir had been wrong. Which called into question everything he'd said. *That bloody head could have been anyone's.*

"Is there anything else, Count Abrantes?"

"No, my queen." He left her apartments only to discover a woman sitting behind a desk in the adjoining antechamber. She was stunningly beautiful, with curly hair that fell past her shoulders. It took him a moment to connect the woman to the name.

"You're Amaryllis," he said in practically a stutter. "Welcome."

Amaryllis smiled. "It's kind of the count to welcome me to Sharakhai."

Mateo tried hard to hide his embarrassment but was sure his momentary cringe had given him away. "I meant to say: it's good to finally meet."

A bowed head. A practiced smile. "Rest assured I feel the same."

"Well." Mateo put one hand behind his back and tipped his head to her. "I hope to see you again."

"There *is* one last thing, Count Abrantes."

"Yes?"

Amaryllis pulled open a drawer in the desk and retrieved a glass vial with a flared mouth and a cork stopper. It had a bit of clear, green-tinted liquid within, an anticoagulant. Mateo hadn't noticed it before, but Amaryllis was wearing a blooding ring on her right thumb. Its thorn jutted out past her first joint, ready to pierce skin.

"I beg your pardon?" Mateo said, though Amaryllis had yet to actually request his blood.

Her smile might have been meant as calming. It was certainly alluring, but somehow that made it all the worse. "With the queen leaving for the warfront"—she waggled the vial at him—"she'll need a way to contact you."

Mateo felt pinpricks of fear traveling up his scalp until it felt like a thousand spiders were dancing there. A moment ago Amaryllis had seemed an ally, but now everything he knew about her rushed in like a gale off an angry sea. Stories of how gifted she was at subterfuge and disguise. How adept she was at gaining the rooms of those she'd been sent to kill, no matter how well protected. Amaryllis was one of Qaimir's master assassins, and she was hold-ing a vial meant to house Mateo's blood.

"This is quite extraordinary."

"A fact our queen acknowledges. But we live in extraordinary times, Count Abrantes. There really is no other way."

The way she'd said those last words. They'd not been uttered as appease-ment, but as a warning. For a moment, instead of Amaryllis's beautiful face staring at him, it was Gautiste's, his blood-streaked eyes glistening while Meryam spoke through his mouth. *Her enemies, wherever they may lie, will be punished as they deserve.*

Bits of Lord Amansir's story returned to him. The blood mage, Hamzakiir, taking Amansir and Meryam to the desert. Meryam ordering Amansir's death. The unearthing of a desert grave after the Battle of Blackspear, when Hamzakiir's long face had given way to Kiral's.

Mateo blinked the visions away. He had known Meryam since she was a child. She'd been an ambitious girl who'd grown into an ambitious woman. But to do all of that? To kill her own father, to kill a King of Sharakhai as well, because she coveted the desert's Amber Jewel? In that moment it seemed preposterous.

So he held out his hand, and felt the sting as Amaryllis pierced his wrist and collected his blood in the vial.

Mateo left the antechamber, but lingered in the hallway outside. He heard the door to Queen Meryam's apartments opening, heard Amaryllis's voice carry. "My queen, King Alaşan has arrived. He's waiting—"

And then the voices faded as the inner apartment doors were closed.

"You've business to attend to I'm sure, my lord." One of the two guards-men outside the door was motioning to the curving stairs leading down to the main floor.

"What?"

The man gestured again, insistent, as if Mateo were a lesser lord. He felt he ought to be angry, but just then a change overcame him. His worries over Queen Meryam began to fade, replaced by a warmth he hadn't felt in a long while toward anyone but his wife.

A moment ago he'd been worried over his future. A moment ago he'd been curious what the queen wanted of King Alaşan, one of Sharakhai's *lesser*

Kings. With each step he took down the curving stairwell, however, his worries faded further.

He left the embassy house content in the knowledge that he'd made the right decision. As for Amansir, well, the man was simply too dangerous to trust. When he presented himself again—*if* he presented himself—Mateo would clap *him* in irons and hand him over to the queen.

Chapter 33

WHEN ANILA WOKE, it was like she'd never left Sukru's palace. She lay in the same bed, staring at the same ceiling in the same room she'd occupied after recovering from the terrible, frigid burns she'd sustained in the caravanserai of Ishmantep. The door she'd made rot in order to escape had been replaced with one made of iron. The two tall windows now had iron bars on them. In all other respects the room was the same, including the table near the hearth where she'd spent long hours studying the texts Sukru had brought for her.

With the sun shining brightly through the windows, everything was telling her to rise, that it would do her good, but she felt so very lethargic. The farther fields were calling again, and it was all she could do to resist.

I could let go, she mused. *It would be so easy.* The passageway was just there, close enough to touch, and like a lover's embrace, it made powerful promises. *Here will you find love,* it said. *Here will you find care and understanding. Here will you find all that has been missing since the day the colfdire consumed you.*

"Not true," she whispered softly. "Davud loves me. Davud cares."

But Davud didn't *understand*. He didn't know what it was like to live beneath that constant lure, nor with the pain that plagued her. She missed the friends she'd spent so many long nights with. Those she'd laughed and cried with. Those who'd been consumed by Hamzakiir and his foul plans. She missed Collum's wit. She missed Meiwei's sweetness. She missed them all.

She lay back. Closed her eyes.

Just let go, she told herself. *Let go, and find peace. Let go, and deny Sukru the satisfaction of his torture, or whatever it is he has planned.*

Anila shook her head a moment later. *What a weak and bitter broth you brew.* Using Sukru to mask her own cowardice brought no sense of calm. It only stirred up memories of his crashing through the cellar door with his whip, of his lashing Fezek practically in half, of that infernal whip somehow wrapping itself around her wrists and neck before she'd had a chance to do more than push herself off the bed. The whip had tightened like a noose, cutting off her air supply. She'd been in pain and afraid and also, she recalled now, elated that it was all, finally, coming to an end.

The next thing she knew she'd woken in her room in Sukru's palace. She squinted at the sun's brightness, tried to rise from the bed, only then realizing her arms and legs were chained to it. The despair that followed was nearly enough to make her give in. As sad as it was to admit, she missed the anger that had kept her alive, the will to have her revenge against Hamzakiir.

But fear is a motivator too. Fear can keep you alive, at least for a little bit longer.

She'd wanted to see Hamzakiir dead, but she'd also wanted to see Davud safe. She'd wanted to see him *live*. He'd left the cellar room with Esmeray to meet with Lord Amansir. Had he ever come back, or had Sukru found him too? Was he still alive?

In the weeks since Ishmantep, the call of the other side had never left her. Her rage had allowed her to create a state of near-perfect balance: close enough to call upon the power of the farther fields, far enough to avoid its lure. But everything had changed the day Davud shared the rumors with her: Hamzakiir had been found in the desert, slain by an ehrekh. Since then, it had been a slow and steady slide, a losing battle that saw her anger fade more by the day. The only thing that kept her from giving in was the careful curation of reasons to reignite her anger.

Today that reason was Davud. But she was exhausted, so she did the one thing she'd become quite good at. She forced herself to sleep.

When she woke again, it was to a jostling of her bed. Her eyes were so heavy she was barely able to open them. But open them she did, to find herself strapped to a stretcher and being carried by a pair of Silver Spears. Where she was going she had no idea, nor did she have the strength to ask, and soon she'd fallen into slumber once more. She was consumed by dreams of fire and ice, the two alternating constantly while people screamed.

A peculiar odor lifted her from her dreams. It was a stale smell, a sort of decay that nearly but did not quite mask the more delicate scents of jasmine and sandalwood. It was cold, and the dead air was laced with a crisp, mineral sort of smell.

Upon cracking her eyes open, she found herself in a subterranean vault with pillars spaced around an expansive room. Iron sconces gripped flickering torches, but the light they threw wasn't nearly enough to fight the oppressive darkness.

She was on a platform of some sort. A sarcophagus, she realized. In a mausoleum. She could see the telltale signs of individual tombs along the distant walls now that she knew what she was looking for. There were several other sarcophagi like the one she was lying on, but only a bare handful.

She felt a pale ghost of her anger return as King Sukru, wearing a rich khalat of brown and gold, scraped his way up the few steps to the side of her sarcophagus. He grunted as he moved, making it clear how much his joints pained him. His bald pate was reddened, his face splotchy, though the color began to fade as he stared at her with his small, ratlike eyes.

"You led us quite the merry chase."

Whatever anger she'd mustered was already seeping away. She knew she ought to care about her fate, but the simple truth was that, other than faint relief that Davud wasn't here with her, she didn't.

"You left many wrongs in your murderous wake. Raising young Bela for your foul purposes. Slaughtering my personal guardsman, Zahndr, who, despite what you might think, petitioned for leniency for both you and Davud. The butchering of my blood, my kin."

"Your brother was going to kill Davud."

"A right he'd earned."

Her dull, muted anger flared to life anew. "You would claim that a game in which you determined the rules, a game that cost countless men and women, and surely children as well, their lives was a *right*?"

"The Kings were granted the desert by the gods themselves"—Sukru leaned forward, as if daring Anila to strike him, a telling posture given that she was bound and at his mercy—"and that means everything in it."

Anila wanted to spit in his face, but she didn't have it in her. She was so very, very tired.

She woke at a slap from Sukru. "Stay with me, girl. This shan't take too much longer."

She hadn't even realized she'd fallen asleep.

Sukru nodded to the Silver Spears, who unstrapped Anila and forced her to stand. Sukru stepped down. His clothes ruffled along the floor as he swept toward another sarcophagus. There, four more Silver Spears stood to attention, one at each corner of the sarcophagus. When Sukru snapped his fingers, they lifted the lid and carried it away, exposing the interior.

Sukru moved to the far side. It was then, as Sukru stared down with something like reverence, that Anila understood what he meant her to do, and more importantly *who* he meant her to do it to. It came as no surprise, then, when the Spears had half led, half dragged her to the sarcophagus, that she was met with the pale body of a man who looked very much like the ancient King standing opposite her.

It was the Sparrow, King Sukru's twin brother, a blood mage who'd been hidden from the public eye in the centuries since Beht Ihman. His sarcophagus was filled nearly to the top with ice. Anila felt its deeper chill. The Sparrow's body was cradled in what looked to be oiled canvas, surely to protect the skin from exposure. The skin of his face and neck was pale, tinged blue in places. He'd been cleaned carefully but there were still signs of his final struggle: a circular, purple-black contusion along the crown of his head and a deep neck wound that had been stitched back together with silk thread, clearly by an expert hand. Zahndr had delivered the head wound, but the other, the one that had killed him in the end, had been delivered by the animated corpse of young Bela, courtesy of a long splinter of wood she'd driven into his neck with all the dispassion of a headsman.

"You want me to raise him," Anila said. She could feel the gossamer thread that connected his body to the farther fields.

"No," Sukru countered. "I want you to bring him back to *life*."

She lifted her eyes and tried in vain to blink away her sleep. Her eyelids felt heavy as hundredweights. But there was fire in her voice when she said, "I would *never* do that."

The look he gave her was both disdainful and self-assured, the sort a priest might give to a child who's refused to perform his prayers. "We'll see about that."

He stared into the darkness and snapped his fingers. Soon after, the sound of footsteps came. They were accompanied by a soft hiss, as of something being slid across the floor. A woman was being dragged by a pair of Silver Spears, her head low and lolling.

"No," Anila whispered.

The woman hadn't lifted her head, but Anila recognized her figure, the cut of her hair. She recognized the sound of her voice even though she was only burbling softly like a drunk. So it was that when the guardsmen came to a stop and one of them gripped the woman's hair and lifted her head, Anila saw the face of Meral, her mother, staring back at her.

"In the time since you've left, I've gone to great lengths to learn more about those who practice dark magic. Necromancers. Black magi, some call them. Those who tread the paths of the dead are consumed with a desire for revenge. Was it not so for you? Did your burning hatred for Hamzakiir not fuel your will to live?"

Anila couldn't take her eyes from her mother, who stared back with pleading eyes. "Please let her go." Anila said. "I'll do as you wish."

Sukru's lip curled as he looked her up and down. "Well I'm afraid I'll need more assurances than *that*. A moment ago you said *never*." He returned his attention to Anila's mother. "Beyond the matter of will, however, is the way. I'm guessing you raised that ghul shortly after you escaped my brother's tower. I'd also guess that right now you couldn't raise another, even if you wanted to. Such things take power, and for you, standing on the threshold of the farther fields as you are, the power it would take would likely kill you before you managed it. The few records I've found have repeated the pattern over and over again: the anger that sustains necromancers keeps them alive only so long as their revenge is gained or their will runs out. But history records one who lived beyond the days normally granted to people such as you."

At a snap of Sukru's fingers, the Silver Spears who'd led Anila to the sarcophagus swept back in, took her arms, and forced her toward her mother. They stopped several paces away. Sukru, meanwhile, moved to Meral's side and held out one hand. The Silver Spear nearest him reached behind his back and retrieved a long sliver of wood. Anila paled as she realized it was the very one Bela had driven into the Sparrow's neck to kill him.

"Dear gods, no," Anila said, as it dawned on her what Sukru meant to do. "You don't have to do this."

"I beg to differ. Given what I want from you, I'd say I have no choice in the matter."

Anila tried to rip her arms free, but the Spears were ready. They held her tight as Sukru took a fistful of Meral's hair and held her steady.

"Please, Anila," her mother said, "He has your father and your sister too. Just give him what he wants."

"Oh, have no fear of that." Sukru lifted the wood and held its point to Meral's neck. "She will."

"Let her be!" Anila pleaded. "I'll bring the Sparrow back to life! I will!"

Sukru turned back to her with a greasy smile. "Indeed, you will," he said, and with a jerk of his body drove the wood into Meral's neck.

"*No!*" Anila screamed. She fought with all her might, but she was too weak, the guards too strong.

With all the calm of a man going for his morning constitutional, Sukru stepped away and nodded to the Spears who held her. The Spears let Meral go, and she fell to the floor with a sickening slap. Blood pooled beneath her, mirrorlike. As she clawed at the rough stone, Sukru stared on, sometimes at Meral, sometimes at Anila, but always with a look as if he were enjoying every dram of pain.

"Memma, I'm sorry," Anila cried.

But her mother appeared not to hear. Her movements slowed, and then she went still.

Sukru was patient. He waited until Anila lifted her gaze from her mother to stare at him. "It will take time," he said, "before your disbelief turns to anger. But it will, and I trust it will be enough to give you fresh vitality, especially as you remember your mother's words. Do as I wish, and I'll release your father and sister before I send you to the farther fields. Do not, and they'll die before your eyes as your mother did."

Anila's ears were ringing so badly she hardly heard his words. Tears streamed down her face as the sight of her mother lying dead on the floor and Sukru standing so calmly beside her was etched into her mind. She prayed her mother would wake. Prayed she would move again.

But of course she knew it couldn't be so. She'd *felt* her mother's soul leave her body. She called to it now. She hadn't the use of her hands, so the effort was imperfect, like calling for a friend in the midst of a sandstorm, but her mother heard. Anila was sure she'd heard.

Sukru stepped forward and slapped her hard across the face. "No, no, no, Anila. You'll save it all for my brother." He waved to the stretcher. "Take her back to her room. She needs time to steep in her hatred."

"Yes, your Excellence."

The guards carried her back to the stretcher and strapped her in. Anila tried calling to her mother again, tried calling into that same strong wind, but her mind was drowning in sorrow, and her words were met only by the sounds of the storm.

Chapter 34

ALONG THE SLOPES OF AN ESTATE known as Stormhaven, Kameyl strolled between two chest-high rows of grapevines. In her left hand she held her ebon blade, Brushing Wing, still in its wooden scabbard. Grapes hung from the vines like clutches of pearls half hidden by lazy, fluttering leaves. In a rare concession to the demands of fashion, Kameyl wore a fetching dress of bronze and blue. She quite liked how it matched her skin tone. And besides, it wasn't every day her favorite cousin crossed the threshold into manhood.

Hearing footsteps approach, she glanced back to see Rezzan sprinting to catch up after having a last word with his weeping mother. A tall boy, he'd inherited the family frame. His sea green silk kaftan was embroidered with thread of crimson and burnt umber along the cuffs and neck. His trousers were stuffed into tall, elkskin boots with matching threading. The golden circlet on his brow kept his long hair back from his face. The style of his raiment was common enough among the houses of Goldenhill, but the royal bearing in him would be plain even if he'd worn sirwal trousers and a vest. His father had fostered it in him since before Rezzan was old enough to sprint along the vineyard's endless rows of vines.

Rezzan finally caught up and fell into step alongside her. As the hubbub of the massive gathering behind them dwindled, so did the tightness in his frame. He wasn't normally the nervous sort, but it was an important day.

Kameyl was nervous too. She wanted him to do well. War stood on the horizon, and Sharakhai had need of all the good auspices it could get. There would be many brave deeds done in the days to come, many heroes made; who could tell besides Thaash himself whether Rezzan would be one of them?

"Don't concentrate on the cut," Kameyl told him as they trudged along a sharper incline.

"I know," Rezzan replied. "I'm to concentrate on the fig falling."

She glanced sidelong at him as they walked. "Have you decided who you'll give them to?"

Rezzan shrugged. "Almost. I'll know once they're cut."

It was a decision Rezzan had been putting off for days, but Kameyl let it be. Cloud his mind now and he'd likely bungle the whole affair. Soon they'd reached the top of the low hill where an ancient fig tree stood. After considering the branches carefully, Kameyl drew Brushing Wing and sliced one free, a branch with three plump figs on it. She caught it neatly in one hand.

As she slipped her shamshir back into its scabbard, Rezzan waited expectantly, but Kameyl held on to the branch. "There's something we need to discuss." She jutted her chin toward the desert, and Rezzan followed her gaze. Beyond the cluster of Stormhaven's amber stone buildings, beyond the patchwork of Goldenhill's rich estates, beyond a swath of rocky land and a sweep of amber sea, a dark line dominated the horizon. The line was made up of warships. Hundreds of them. The Malasani were on Sharakhai's doorstep. With the royal navy sent to slow down the Mireans—the more deadly of the two invaders—there were no warships left to blunt the arrival of the Malasani fleet.

It felt strange to be holding this ceremony today when the war might begin that very night, but Rezzan's father, Kameyl's brother, was an important man in Sharakhai. And the old ways must be honored, even in times of war. Perhaps *especially* in times of war.

"Do you think they'll go home soon?" Rezzan asked.

There were those in Sharakhai, Rezzan's father among them, who believed Malasan had not come to attack, but rather to use the situation to exact as many concessions as they could—fewer tariffs on their caravans, freer trade agreements, favored status at the auction blocks—and that once accomplished their fleet would return home beyond the mountains.

"No," she replied, "I don't think they'll go home soon."

"You think they'll attack." His voice was doubtful, almost dismissive.

"They *will* attack. And soon."

Rezzan looked doubtful. "I don't know, Kameyl. Everyone's been saying—"

"There's something I want you to do, Rezzan, when they come."

"Father says it will only be a matter of weeks before—"

"Listen to me!" Kameyl said sharply. "When the battle begins, it will be quick. The walls may hold for a time"—she pointed to the horizon—"but have no doubt the Malasani are hiding surprises in those ships. If they break through, they will make for Goldenhill, perhaps even *before* they make for Tauriyat. They know the sorts of riches that can be found here. They know that those most likely to be ransomed for handsome prizes will be found here as well. So expect it."

"We know, Kameyl, but—"

"Rezzan, sometimes you're altogether too much like your father. Close that fool mouth of yours and open your ears. The Malasani are not here to barter. They have not come to win trading rights for their caravans. And they have not come this far to fall short of their prize: the Amber Jewel itself, Sharakhai, a thing they've coveted for centuries. They will come with a thirst for blood. So when you get word that the walls have fallen, you will take your mother and as many others as you can convince and go to the tunnels. Take them to the caves and flee in the yachts."

Generations ago, secret tunnels had been built below the estates of Goldenhill. They led to a series of natural caves along the southeastern edges of Sharakhai. Most of the highborn knew about the tunnels—others would as well, including some of the Malasani—but few knew the caves had been prepared with dozens of small racing yachts that could be used to flee the city. The Malasani would spot them sailing away, of course, but by then their commanders would be focused on the invasion, not on a handful of yachts. And even if the Malasani gave chase, they'd not catch them; those yachts were some of the fleetest in the desert.

"Kameyl, truly—"

"Promise me, Rezzan."

He looked as if he were about to deny her, or make light of it and say she needn't worry, as if he knew the first bloody thing about the situation; but he must have seen something in her face. He'd always been that way with her, knowing when she was deadly serious and when she wasn't. "Very well," he said at last.

"Say the words, Rezzan."

Rezzan sucked on the inside of his cheek. "I promise, I'll see them to safety."

"Good." She offered him a rare smile. "Now come, you've figs to cut. A warning to you, nephew. If the ritual ends and your mother isn't holding one of those figs"—with a hard shove she sent him stumbling forward—"I'll be using that sword to cut the tiny sausage you call a cock from between your legs." She caught up to him and put him in a headlock. "Are we understood?"

Rezzan pulled away, annoyed. "I was always going to give her one."

"There's a good boy." Kameyl laid an arm across his shoulders and hugged him close.

"Stop treating me like a child," he mumbled.

"When you cut these figs cleanly, you'll have earned a bit of my respect and the manners that come with it. Until then"—tightening her arm around his neck until his head was just next to hers, she kissed his cheek loudly, a thing she knew he hated—"I'll treat you how I please."

He pulled himself away with a scowl and a glance toward the celebration. "They're *watching*," he said, wiping his cheek.

But Kameyl only laughed and held Brushing Wing out for him to take. Rezzan, his red-faced indignation evaporating like rain, accepted the sword with a smile and, Kameyl was pleased to see, no small amount of reverence.

Together, they returned to the celebration. At the center of Stormhaven's grounds a pavilion stood between the stables, the servant's houses, and the long, low building where the grapes were pressed. When the hundreds gathered there saw the two of them coming, a great roar lifted up. Soon the ceremony had begun and Rezzan was swinging Kameyl's shamshir to cut the figs. The first cut was brilliant. He nearly dropped the fig as it fell, the crowd gasping around him, but then he was smiling and handing it to his mother. It had all been an act, Kameyl realized. Soon the second was cut, and the third as well, to roaring applause, high ululations, and a beaming Rezzan.

Soon the feast was upon them and the crowd began to filter into the pavilion. As Kameyl was making to follow the others in, Rezzan caught up to her at a jog. Holding Brushing Wing for her to take, he sent a nervous look back the way he'd come. "Yndris is here from the House of Maidens."

Accepting the sword, Kameyl looked and spotted a shadowed figure standing in an archway that led inside the estate proper. A Blade Maiden stood in the shadows, her veil across her face, but it was clearly Yndris. Kameyl would recognize her impudent stance anywhere. Not far from where she stood, two tall akhalas, one copper, one bronze, were tied to a paddock gate. *One for Yndris,* Kameyl thought, *the other for me?*

"She has news," Rezzan said, then leaned closer. "She said it was about King Husamettín."

"He's been found?"

Rezzan nodded. "Apparently."

Kameyl hadn't realized how tense she was, but at this news her body relaxed. Few knew it outside the House of Kings, but four Kings had traveled to the desert in search of Çeda, and only three had returned. Husamettín had been thought killed or captured when he'd attacked one of Çeda's yachts.

"Where is he?"

Rezzan shrugged. "She didn't say."

The sound in the pavilion lifted up as someone shouted and half the tent laughed. "I'm sorry, Rezzan." She gripped his arm. "I've been looking forward to this day for a long time, but duty calls."

"Of course," he said, though he was clearly disappointed. "Will you be back?"

"I don't know. Save me some cake, won't you?"

He nodded and headed inside, a smile lighting his face as a group of his friends called in unison, "Rezzan!"

Kameyl jogged toward Yndris, and the sounds of revelry faded behind her. Yndris, always impatient, turned and stepped through the nearby archway, surely so they could speak where they wouldn't be overheard. Annoyed, Kameyl followed. Who Yndris thought might eavesdrop on their conversation Kameyl wasn't sure. And if she was so worried about it, why not speak on horseback on their way back to the House of Kings?

When she reached the archway and entered the short tunnel beyond, Yndris was just entering a courtyard that contained a well-tended flower garden.

"Well do you want to talk or not?" Kameyl called to her, but Yndris kept walking, not even bothering to look back.

Soon Kameyl reached the garden, which had red gravel paths and flower beds whose blooms were all some varying shade of blue. Four massive topiaries stood in the center of the beds, each trimmed to resemble a mystical animal. Yndris waited at the center of the garden beneath a large, square arbor choked with green ivy. The ivy wrapping around one of the stout wooden posts obscured her face.

Almost as if she doesn't want to be seen, Kameyl thought.

Her heart beat faster as she stepped carefully along the border path. As she moved, the woman—Kameyl was now certain it wasn't Yndris—moved with her, so that her face remained hidden.

Kameyl drew Brushing Wing. "Whoever you are, you'll come to regret the steps that led you here."

"I already regret them," the woman said, "but not for the reasons you think."

She recognized the voice. How could she not? She'd obeyed orders from the woman who owned it for years. And so it came as no surprise as Kameyl reached the path leading to the arbor that she found her former commander, Sümeya, standing before her. Her Maiden's Black had been altered so that the cut of her skirt and the set of her turban made her look more like Yndris's, at least from a distance. She'd also mimicked Yndris's churlish body language. It had been enough to fool Kameyl, but she refused to be fooled again.

Never taking her eyes fully from Sümeya, she scanned the roof line and the windows overlooking the courtyard. She listened carefully, and reached out with her senses, feeling for heartbeats. Her senses felt dulled without the use of the adichara petals, and she'd never been one of the more gifted at it to begin with, but she was relatively certain she and Sümeya were alone.

The gravel crunched beneath Kameyl's boots as she took measured steps forward. She stopped several paces away from arbor's entrance, just out of sword's reach. "What possessed you to come, Sümeya?"

"To convince you to join us."

Kameyl laughed. "Join *you*?" Her fingers flexed against the well-worn hilt of her shamshir. "I suppose next you're going to start spouting nonsense about the thirteenth tribe."

"It isn't nonsense. Much of what they're saying is true."

Kameyl stabbed Brushing Wing at Sümeya's chest. "And how would you know?" Kameyl took a half step forward. "Were you alive when it happened? Are you somehow privy to more knowledge than the Kings?"

Sümeya backed away but hadn't yet dropped into a fighting stance. "All I'm asking is for you to listen."

"In all my time in the Blade Maidens, I came to respect only a few. Melis was one of them." As she advanced another half step, Sümeya retreated into the sunlight, maintaining their distance. "You were too," Kameyl went on, "but that's all been shattered. I don't trust you. I don't trust Melis. And I *certainly* don't trust Çeda. So if that's why you've come, to spout her traitorous nonsense, then I'm afraid you've made a grave miscalculation."

When she took one long stride forward, Sümeya sidestepped into one of the flower beds, putting an arbor post between them. "The asirim were enslaved on the night of Beht Ihman."

As Kameyl moved faster, circling the post, Sümeya shifted in a rush of lithe, balanced steps to the next path over. So Kameyl ducked under the arbor, ready to charge. Sümeya, sensing blows were near, finally drew her sword, but seemed reluctant to do so. She drew the scabbard as well, holding it like a second sword.

"They've been slaves for four hundred years," Sümeya went on. "That is the truth you must come to see. And you will if you but listen with your heart and your mind."

"Save it," Kameyl said. "You can tell it all to King Cahil."

And with that she sprinted forward. Sümeya retreated, her sword and scabbard at the ready. Kameyl was so eager she nearly missed the sound of the nearby heartbeat, nearly missed the telltale signs of the thin rope that lay along the ground.

She leapt as the rope was pulled taut. Even so, the rope snapped tight higher than Kameyl thought it would. It caught her right ankle, and she stumbled hard but managed to keep her feet.

Sümeya was on the move from the moment the rope tripped her. She blocked one awkward swipe of Kameyl's sword with her wooden scabbard, then dropped and snapped one leg out, catching Kameyl across both legs just as she was starting to recover her balance. Kameyl fell but rolled away quickly and came up at the ready.

On her left, a woman in green camouflage lunged from behind the nearest topiary. It was Melis, holding two fighting sticks. She unleashed a flurry of tight blows, but Kameyl blocked them all, then sent a devastating back kick into Melis's chest. Melis grunted, off balance, and fell hard when she tripped over a line of small, flowering bushes.

Sümeya reengaged, her skill with a blade and her economical movements on full display. It was difficult for Kameyl to find any openings, but she was so full of rage she pressed her former commander steadily backward. Sümeya blocked only with her scabbard, surely so that the fight wouldn't be heard as far as the pavilion.

"Please, Kameyl," Sümeya said as she retreated beneath the arbor. "I'm only asking you to listen."

But Kameyl wouldn't. She'd rather die than swallow the lies of traitors. Behind her, Melis was regaining her feet, so Kameyl pushed Sümeya hard. It was then that she heard movement on the arbor's roof. Leaves rustled. Wood splintered.

It happened so fast she didn't even have the time to look up before a heavy weight crashed down and bore Kameyl to the ground. Brushing Wing flew from her hand. Kameyl struggled mightily to free herself, but an arm had already wrapped around her neck. When she drew her knife, ready to stab at her attacker, a hand was suddenly there, gripping her wrist.

The tattoos on her attacker's hand confirmed Kameyl's fears, that her third assailant was Çeda. She struggled to break free, but Çeda's grip felt inhuman, like stone.

A petal, Kameyl thought. *She must have taken a petal.*

The knowledge did her no good, however. She was starting to black out.

"Kameyl, please," Çeda said. "We need your help."

"Never," she grunted and drew a ragged breath. "You speak only in lies."

Sümeya crouched before her and stared with regret. "Then we'll take you to someone you *will* believe."

Kameyl refused to wonder who. She only struggled harder. But Çeda replied in kind, tightening her grip on Kameyl's neck until the sunlit world of the courtyard went dark.

Chapter 35

BRAMA WAS BELOWDECKS in one of the Mirean dunebreakers' larger cabins. The room, meticulously clean, was grim. Indelible stains marked the floorboards and the surface of the lone table. The strong scent of the solution used to clean the room could not quite cover up the morbid scents beneath. It was the room used by their field surgeons, for amputation mostly, or for other operations involving the body's viscera.

A plain-looking man of thirty summers lay on the operating table, a foot soldier. He was naked, with a folded white sheet laid across his legs and pelvis. A damp cloth covered his mouth and nose, somewhat muting his soft snoring. The air was laced with a sharp, piney scent, traces of the anesthetic that had put the man to sleep. His symptoms were strong but not severe. He had traces of the scourge around his eyes and inside his lips. More around his fingernails. Brama had wanted to try to heal someone deeper in the throes of the disease, but the queen had insisted on prudence.

"Heal one," she'd said, "and you may certainly heal more."

Near the head of the table stood Mae, whom Behlosh had cured the previous night. She seemed diminished without her armor, but her high leather boots, simple silk trousers, and belted tunic let Brama see the woman she'd been before being saved by her qirin, Angfua. Already the dark color around her mouth and eyes had faded, leaving her skin a dusty gray instead of purplish black. The inflammation had decreased considerably, and her coughing had all but ceased. More promising was the fact that she showed almost none of the shakes that afflicted other scourge survivors. It was as complete a recovery as anyone could have hoped for, and was likely to get better with time.

Her gaze wandered to the reliquary hanging from the chain around Brama's neck. Like the one he'd given to Behlosh, it was an amulet with a lid and compartment. Resting inside the compartment, visible through the amulet's weave of golden strands, was a black bone the size of a grape. The amulet itself was heavy, the bone even more so.

And why not? Brama thought. *The weight of the entire fleet rests on it.*

The door opened and Juvaan stepped inside, followed by Queen Alansal, who looked to be in a dark mood. Brama could see it in Juvaan's face as well. Word had come only an hour before that Alansal's nephew, a general in her fleet who'd been suffering the worst of the scourge's effects, had passed. Alansal had surely taken time to look upon his body, even if from a distance, before it was ferried to an open grave with the others who'd died over the course of the day.

Alansal's black silk dress swept behind her as she sat across the operating table from Brama. When Juvaan had taken his place beside her, she said, "Alu-Waled is dead."

Brama felt his mouth go dry. Alu-Waled was the Sharakhani alchemyst who'd had the biggest hand in the creation of the scourge. Brama wanted to console the queen—after all, with Alu-Waled's death went all hope of finding a cure in time to save her fleet—but what could he say? "What happened?" he said numbly.

Queen Alansal seemed unwilling to explain further, so Juvaan did. "He managed to form a rope by braiding strips of cloth torn from his khalat. He tied them to a ceiling beam and hung himself."

The implication was clear. Though Alu-Waled had already confessed that there was no hope in finding a cure to the scourge, Queen Alansal and everyone around her had still been holding out hope that he could. With that possibility gone, and Rümayesh still adamantly standing behind her claim that it lay beyond her power to heal the scourge, even with the bone of Raamajit, their last, thin hope lay in Brama.

The sheer weight of responsibility squeezed Brama, made it difficult for him to breathe. More than two thousand had already succumbed to the scourge. Another three thousand were sick with it. Even if Brama healed the man lying before him, how could he possibly stem this tide?

He echoed Alansal's words. *Heal one,* he told himself. *Heal one.*

Queen Alansal waved to the man on the table. She was so distracted she spoke in Mirean, but Brama understood well enough. *You may begin.*

Brama nodded to Mae, who took up a scalpel and made two precise cuts in the man's chest in the same places she'd been pierced the night before by Behlosh. A small moan escaped the man, and he stirred, but as Mae pressed two clean bandages to the wounds, he fell silent once more. When the flow of blood had stemmed, Brama unscrewed the top of the reliquary and rolled Raamajit's bone onto his waiting palm. A rush of power swept through him. It was so strong, so swift, his knees went weak from it, forcing him to grip the edge of the table until the dizziness passed.

Before he could think overmuch about it, he popped the bone into his mouth. It felt gritty on his tongue. It tasted of minerals and copper and something sour, like turned milk. The dizziness became more pronounced as his perceptions swelled. He felt the man's body. Felt his soul. He felt Mae's as well. And Juvaan's. And Alansal's. He felt the hundreds upon hundreds of others in the hospital ships to the west. He even felt the bright press of soldiers in the main encampment before he managed to steel himself and draw his awareness back to the small room inside the dunebreaker.

Queen Alansal was a distraction. She glowed brighter than anyone else, and the steel pins that held her black hair in place glittered, trailing light like shooting stars whenever she moved.

By taking deep breaths, Brama was able to stem the tide of power, and once that happened, it began to settle and he was able to focus on the man on the table once more. As Behlosh had done with Mae, Brama draped his fingers over the man's shoulders and pressed his thumbs to the wounds. He'd been able to sense the man to some degree a moment ago, but in touching his flesh the veil was lifted. Brama sensed the compression of his heart, the drawing of his breath. He felt his troubled dreams, filled with images of a chase through a dark forest and the sound of howling wolves. More than anything, he felt the scourge spreading through his body like a growing stain, reaching ever deeper into healthy flesh.

Again came that revolting combination of curiosity and pleasure, but Brama refused to linger on it. Do that and he would surely fail. He did as Behlosh had done. He needed to separate the scourge from the man's body, but found he was only able to tear it away. It came like cobwebs, and however much he tore free, the scourge returned, rushing in like floodwaters wherever he managed to clear some of it from the man's flesh.

He tried not to rush. But the man's reactions—the quickening of his breath, the tripping of his heart, the splotchy reddening of his skin—urged Brama to make haste. He gave in to the urge, finding that only by moving faster and more violently could he make headway against the disease. He tore at the scourge and was able to stay ahead of its ability to return to the places he'd cleared, but the man's condition was worsening.

"Brama?"

A soft voice. Mae's.

Brama spared a look for her. She was worried. The man's eyes were wide open. His whole body was rigid, his teeth clamped, the muscles along his neck taut as sail lines. But gods, so much of the scourge still remained. Brama could stop, but if he did, what would all of this have been for?

"Brama."

He ignored Mae and worked faster. His tearing at the dark taint of the scourge was both frantic and desperate. Slowly but surely, however, he managed to strip much of it away.

"Brama!"

Not yet. He was so close! His own breath came in great heaves as he ripped the last remnants of the disease from the man. He was free of it at last.

Then Mae was pushing him away. His hands lifted defensively, he blinked and saw the man's state clearly for the first time since he'd started. He wasn't breathing. His heart was weak. Faltering.

Brama pushed Mae away and returned to him. He placed his hands on the man's chest, but had no idea what to do. It was like trying to repair a crumbling statue. His slightest touch only made it worse.

"Bakhi," he breathed, "please don't take him. He doesn't deserve it. Take me instead."

His plea fell on deaf ears. Nothing he did seemed to slow the dimming of the man's soul. The brightness within him faded. The frail beating of his heart stopped altogether. And then all was still.

Brama lifted his hands. Stared through his tears at the blood covering them. He tried to swallow the twisting knot inside his throat, to no avail. He looked up and saw Queen Alansal staring fixedly at the man with an expression of numb shock. She'd believed Brama. She'd given up one of the most powerful artifacts in all the world so that he might find a way to help her people, and he'd failed her.

"We must try again," Juvaan said, leaving unsaid that each failed attempt would cost a life.

His words snapped Alansal from her reverie. She stood from her chair in a rush, stared down at the table, at the dead man upon it, then swept toward the door. "Take him from our camp and ensure that he leaves."

"My queen—" Juvaan began.

But the queen cut across him. "Inform the generals. Finalize our preparations to set sail for Sharakhai." She stopped at the threshold, looking back with a grim expression. "If the Sharakhani Kings wish to visit death upon our people, then we shall return the favor."

And then she was gone.

Worse than the disappointment in Queen Alansal's face, worse than his own disappointment, was the fact that Brama had felt something terrible in himself as the man's soul had departed. A rush of pleasure, stronger than anything he'd felt before, had swept through him. It was Rümayesh's taint, but it had been happening so often it didn't feel like Rümayesh anymore. It felt like *him*, as if this were now a natural part of him.

Dear gods, what's happening to me?

He could almost hear Rümayesh laughing.

The bone was taken from Brama, of course. And then, as the queen had ordered, Juvaan led him on horseback to the edge of camp. He offered him Kweilo, but Brama refused.

"She'll only be in danger if she remains with me." He slipped down from the saddle and handed the reins to Juvaan.

"Where will you go?"

Brama shrugged. "I don't know."

An uncomfortable silence passed between them. "I know you tried," Juvaan said. "That's more than many would have done."

Brama nodded, and then Juvaan was off, riding back toward the Mirean camp in the distance. Brama felt exhausted. The experience of trying to heal the soldier had weakened him greatly. The bone of Raamajit held incalculable power, but Brama had spent so much energy simply trying to harness it.

Brama walked away, eventually losing sight of the caravanserai and the great fleet. Near midday, dust rose along the horizon and more than a dozen Mirean scout ships came into view, sailing south toward the Kings' fleet. Brama watched them for a time and then, without really meaning to, began walking back toward the Mirean camp. He kept wondering how many of those sailing for war would return. A fleet of fifty thousand had left their homeland. Would a fifth of them return? A tenth? And when they met the Sharakhani fleet in battle, would the Kings' forces become infected? Would the scourge breach the walls of Sharakhai?

When pressed, Alu-Waled had said it wouldn't affect the populous of Sharakhai. He had twisted the disease to have devastating effects on those of Mirean stock, leaving those of Sharakhani blood practically untouched. But even if the disease's peculiar tastes held true, there were still tens of thousands of Mirean descent living in the city. And there were those of Kundhunese and Malasani and Qaimiri blood to consider as well. The disease might primarily affect Mireans, but who could say what might happen to those from other nations?

The Kings had taken a terrible risk in the release of the scourge, and only the fates knew what would become of it. *I'll place my bets on the cruelest option*, Brama thought. The fates were nothing if not cold-blooded bastards.

Soon Brama saw the edges of the caravanserai, the encampment, and far from them, the seven hospital ships. He headed for the mass grave, where most of the thousands who'd already died were buried. There was a line of flatbed sleighs leading up to it, each one piled high with the dead. Another hundred bodies waited to be lifted and laid next to their brothers and sisters in the long, deep trench. Dozens already lay there, their arms crossed over their chests, knives held in their hands, or the occasional sword. Some few, those who'd lost loved ones recently, had sapphire orchids clutched in both hands. Rock buzzards circled above. More had landed nearby, waiting for their chance at the corpses, which those tending to the dead were careful never to give them.

"Brama?" He turned to find Mae wearing the lacquered armor of the Damned once more. She rode toward him on her qirin, which released a noisy trumpet of a call and a sputtering gout of fire as it came to a halt. "Why are you here?"

What could he say? He wasn't even sure why he'd come, other than to wallow in his own failure. He motioned to the trench. "I only wished to pay my respects."

"Pay . . . respects?" Mae had trouble with the words.

"To wish them good journey."

Her qirin clawed at the sand as Mae considered his words. "I never thank you, for helping us. For healing me."

"You don't have to—" But he stopped when Mae raised her hand.

"I was angry. What happen to Shu-fen." She pointed to the place where not so long ago the Mirean fleet had anchored. "What happen to us all. I thought it your—how you say it?—your fault. You and Rümayesh. But it not your fault, Brama."

Brama didn't know what to say, so he remained silent.

"The other ehrekh," she went on. "Behlosh. I wear the armor of the Damned proudly. But I think I could not take you to him to be healed. I don't think I'm brave enough."

"You're plenty brave," Brama said, grateful he'd managed this much, to save Mae.

She looked to the trench and the line of sleighs. "Do as you say. Pay your respects. But then you must leave." She put her hand on the hilt of her dao. "I have no choice. You understand?"

"I understand," Brama said. "Thank you."

She nodded, kicked her qirin into motion, and began helping the others with the bodies. Brama watched them, pulling the dead bodies from the sleighs, dragging each carefully, respectfully, into the trenches and giving them a weapon or some other memento to carry with them into the afterlife.

The sun fell, but there were so many bodies to deal with they set up torches and lanterns and continued into the night. The stench of it was horrendous.

Brama heard a buzzing, felt a presence coalesce along the sand behind him.

Brama didn't need to turn to know who it was. "Come to admire your handiwork?"

"This isn't my handiwork," Rümayesh replied, "but that of the Kings."

"It was in your power to stop. It still is."

Rümayesh's heavy footfalls approached. She crouched beside him, arms over her knees, the discordant look of a beggar girl about her once more. Her tails swished across the sand. As had been the case for the past several days, he could feel none of her emotions, but he knew her manners well; she was caught in one of her rare spells of introspection. It was in these times that he might speak to her, truly speak to her, free from the fits of rage or cruelty that often overtook her.

Brama took out the glass vial, the one filled with powder from the bone of Raamajit. Tulathan, the barest sliver in the sky, was rising in the east. Brama stared at it, wondering if the goddess, waking from her slumber, could hear them.

"I was going to use this to sever our bond," he said.

He thought Rümayesh would be angry. Rail against him. But she didn't. She remained calm as a desert sunrise. "Why didn't you?"

Brama shook the vial, setting its contents to glittering in the dim moonlight. "Who is Behlosh to you?"

She swiveled her great horned head and looked at him, and Brama expected her to refuse to speak of it, but to his surprise she nodded once, as if she knew the moment had come.

Brama, afraid of saying anything that might break the spell, merely waited.

"I'll share with you something few mortals have ever known." She turned her attention back to the mass grave. "When my lord Goezhen was still young, he toyed with the stuff of creation, a knack he'd stolen from Iri, his maker. He made many creatures. Some beautiful but simple, others you'd most likely consider foul. Many had a thirst he wasn't aware he was granting them. They roamed the desert in numbers in those days. They plagued the sands. But Goezhen grew bored with them and allowed many to wither and die when the old gods began granting the people of the desert miracles to put them down. What Goezhen truly wanted was to create something like man. He worked for many long years, mimicking what he thought Iri and the other gods had done. But the bitterness in his heart prevented him from creating in the same way his maker had done."

"He has no love in his heart?"

"He does, but mostly for Iri, and some of the other elder gods. And love is a strange thing in any case. Bitterness and hatred are its closest kins. So it was with Goezhen. He began to make the ehrekh in pairs. We each had *another half*, as the people of Qaimir are so fond of saying, except of the ehrekh it was quite literally true."

"Behlosh is your other half," Brama said with certainty.

"He is. Was. It is not the same thing as being lovers, nor brother and sister, nor dear friends, though all of these are close. We share the same soul."

"But why would he craft you in such a fashion?" Brama asked.

"Goezhen?" She shrugged. "He thought we would create new life with one another. Something he'd been hoping to achieve since long before stealing Iri's power. It was the greatest of the elder gods' gift to this world—life begetting life—and Goezhen wanted that power as well. In this he failed. None of his creations had it. It was a power Iri, surely sensing Goezhen's purpose, had kept well hidden. But what it did give us was an undying sense of one another. A simple urge to be with one another."

Brama couldn't help but think of the urge Rümayesh had placed in him while she was trapped in the sapphire. When Ramahd, the Qaimiri lordling, had stolen it—thereby stealing Rümayesh—a great relief had washed over Brama. It hadn't lasted, though. His relief had faded and been replaced with a compulsion to find her. It led him to set her free of imprisonment, to take her hand and wander the desert with her.

"You found a way to free yourself," Brama realized. "Behlosh is no longer your other half."

Rümayesh's laugh was a low rumble that attracted the notice of the grave workers. Brama saw them by their lanterns, peering into the darkness. Unable to locate the source of the laughter, they went about their business, noticeably faster than before.

"I did," Rümayesh admitted. "As was true of many of us, Behlosh and I grew weary of one another. Then we began to hate each other. Yet every time we parted, our desire to be with the other rose, and it only grew stronger the longer we remained apart. But what if there was a way to change it? To break the bond Goezhen forged within us?"

"That's why you bond with mortals," Brama said.

"Yes. It's how I found my first love. It's how I came to live in Sharakhai while the sigils on the walls kept others away. It's how I was able to shatter my bond with Behlosh at last. He was driven mad by it. He came for me. He even tried to break down the walls of Sharakhai before the Kings came and stopped him. Many years later, I made the mistake of allowing my love, Lirael, to leave the city. It had been many years since Behlosh was driven from the city. But he'd remained patient, waiting, and he found her." Rümayesh fell silent and then said, "He was not kind."

"All the more reason to oppose him now."

"I wouldn't be opposing Behlosh but my lord Goezhen."

"Why would he care what happens here?"

"I cannot say. But he was adamant. He told me to leave the fleet be, or suffer his wrath."

"And yet you traveled to the Kings' fleet. You found Alu-Waled and placed him at the feet of Queen Alansal."

Rümayesh looked displeased. "What of it?"

"You wouldn't have done that if you thought there was no possibility he would find a cure for the scourge. You *wanted* him to find a cure. You did it because Goezhen forbade *you* from interfering on their behalf but said nothing about delivering them someone who could."

"I'm forbidden from disobeying my lord."

"Are you? You said it yourself! You found a way to break the bonds of your making, to release yourself from Behlosh. If that isn't disobeying your lord, I don't know what is." Brama stood and moved in front of her. Like this, him standing, Rümayesh crouched, they were nearly eye to eye. "Do you know what Behlosh said to me after he healed Mae? He said that his mind still lingers over Lirael's taste. He healed Mae and took the bone of Raamajit, knowing I wouldn't be able to heal them all. The bitterness of my failure pleased him greatly. But you could deny him that pleasure."

"This is a weak gambit, Brama." She feigned amusement, but there was doubt in her eyes.

"And yet you're tempted. I know you are. That's why you've closed yourself off to me, because you fear I'll reach your wicked heart." He waved to the dead in the trench. "How many Liraels have died already? How many are now threatened? Imagine what it would be like to save them. Relief and love such as you've never experienced would flow. And it will all be because of *you*."

For a moment while he spoke, a little of their shared bond returned, and he felt her uncertainty.

"I beg you," he went on. "Help them for Lirael. Help them for the others you've joined hands with, for whatever it is you've come to love about us." He stood and tossed the glass vial of powder to the sand. "Help them for me." He lifted his sandaled foot and stomped his heel onto the vial. It broke with a crunch, and the air filled with the scent of power. "I'll remain with you. I won't try to escape."

Near the trench came a raucous squawking sound. An old man was chasing away buzzards that had managed to get close enough to peck at the corpses. As he chased one away, waving his shovel, several more swept in. The other workers came quickly, shouting, bearing shovels of their own.

As the spectacle unfolded, Rümayesh seemed unfazed. As emotionless as those buzzards. And yet, after the birds had been chased away, her eyes met Brama's, and she said, "Very well."

Chapter 36

EMRE RAN LOW AND QUICK through the moonless night. To his left was Hamid. On his right, Frail Lemi. Ahead, lit only by starlight, was the dark shape of *Calamity's Reign*, Haddad's dhow. They crept toward the rear of the ship, then crouched, waiting for the guard Haddad always kept on deck.

A short while later they saw him. Haddad's first mate; Emre could tell by the way he leaned toward his left side when he walked, favoring the side that had taken the most acid damage from the wyrm. They waited for him to head to the foredeck, then ran hard for the ship's stern, where Frail Lemi stood on the skimwood rudder and hoisted Emre up until he could grab the sill of the shutters to Haddad's cabin. She always latched them, but one of the latches was faulty. Shift the window toward the old hinges just enough and he could slip it free.

He did, and it released with a soft tick, swung outward, and he was inside the empty cabin. Hamid slipped in behind him with an oiled ease. Frail Lemi remained outside, lying low on the rudder so that, with his dark clothes, he looked like part of it.

Wary of any sound, Emre and Hamid made their way along the ship's central passageway toward the hold. It was several hours before dawn and the ship was quiet, but it wasn't uncommon for someone to be up, making night soil or pissing over the side of the ship or sneaking into the galley to steal a bite while the cook was asleep.

They heard snoring, and a cough from a crewman in a cabin, but reached the hold without incident. Hamid lit a lantern and shone its golden light over the crates, ropes, and dark hull boards. Several hammocks were still hanging from the thick beams, reminders of the days before the battle with the wyrm and the Blackspear soldiers, when *Calamity's Reign* operated with more than a skeleton crew.

After taking a pry bar from a hook affixed to the hull, Emre used it with care to open the same crates Haddad had shown him. Unlike the last time, he wasn't satisfied with seeing the topmost layers. He dug beneath the straw and the clay pots and found it to be shallow, hardly deeper than his fingers were long. The rest of the crate was filled with burlap. The same was true of the others they opened. The crates of fine wooden bows had been similarly faked, one layer at the top with nothing beneath.

Haddad had been worried about discovery of the deal she'd made with Tribes Kenan and Halarijan. She'd paid Shaikhs Dayan and Neylana and asked them to give her some of their goods so that if any came asking, she could point to them and say it was for trade, when really their agreement had been about something else entirely.

"You see now?" Hamid whispered.

It burned Emre to admit it, but Hamid had been right all along. Even after seeing Haddad with King Emir, he still hadn't wanted to believe it, but he could no longer hide from the truth: Haddad had been playing him for a long time, perhaps from the beginning.

Without answering, Emre began putting the lids back on the crates. Soon the two of them were working their way back through the ship, up the ladder, and into Haddad's cabin.

"You go on," Emre whispered when they came to the window.

"No," Hamid said. "This time we're *both* talking to her."

"I have more to talk to her about than just this."

"You mean you want to fuck her one last time."

"Keep your voice down," Emre rasped, "unless you want to see our bones fed to the Great Mother."

Hamid said no more, but neither did he make a move toward the window.

"We still have the treaties to consider," Emre finally said. It wasn't the whole of his reason for staying, but Hamid didn't need to know that.

"And you think *she's* going to help you get them?"

"We have to protect the tribe first."

"Exactly. Which is why the tribe should send a message: slit her throat so all know not to take us lightly."

"This isn't Sharakhai, Hamid."

"And we're no longer children, Emre. Time for you to grow up and act like a man."

"I'm speaking to Haddad alone."

Hamid shook his head in frustration but finally relented and began climbing through the window. "This is the last time I look the other way for you."

Emre said nothing as Hamid slipped down and into the night. As the soft sounds of his and Frail Lemi's passage faded, Emre closed the window, sat in the captain's chair, and waited.

He was still there at dawn when Haddad walked into the cabin. Golden light angled in harshly through the shutters, slicing Emre into alternating layers of light and shadow.

"Hello, Haddad."

Her first mate, coming up behind Haddad, glared at Emre. "Told you I saw them sneaking away from the ship."

He drew his knife and tried to step past Haddad, but Haddad grabbed his wrist and tilted her head back toward the passageway. "Give me some time."

Her mate pointed the tip of his knife at Emre. "He's a snake, this one. He and all his friends from the lost tribe."

"I said give me some time."

The mate fumed, but in the end drove his knife back into its sheath and stalked away.

Haddad quickly closed the door. "What are you *doing* here?"

"We need to talk."

"Emre, if you're here about King Emir, I . . . I didn't expect things to happen so quickly. I was angry and—"

"This isn't about Emir."

She looked genuinely confused, but there had been a flash of worry as well. "Then what?"

"Sit," he said, and kicked out the stool by the desk.

She chose to sit on her bed instead.

"I opened the crates," he said, watching her reaction carefully. "A handful of ointments from Tribe Kenan. A few bows from Halarijan. The payment you gave—what did you call it? Good Malasani gold?—wasn't for trade, nor to grease the skids for future treaties, as you claimed. You paid them to stay out of the alliance. Your king fears a united desert."

Haddad stared at him with a flat expression. She couldn't deny it. Not any longer.

It was why she was so upset when Shaikh Dayan left, not because Emre had spoiled her agreements with Tribe Kenan, but because she feared her work to thwart the alliance was unraveling. That's why King Emir sent her to meet with the eastern tribes in the first place. It's why she remained after the battle with Onur and the wyrm, and later, the Battle of Blackspear.

"Emre, I don't know why you've come here, but whatever it is—"

"I've come for the asirim."

She stopped. Whatever she'd thought he would say, it hadn't been this. "The asirim?"

"You saw what's happening to them. They're innocent in this."

"How can you call them innocent? One of them killed a dozen men in a blink. It nearly killed Emir!"

"The asirim were defending themselves. Defending their home, which your king was burning."

"If you think they should be left alone as the army moves into Sharakhai—"

"That's *exactly* what I think. The asirim are at the beck and call of the Kings, but some have weakened over time or become dormant after taking tributes in the city—"

"Drinking the blood of the innocent, you mean."

"Because they're *forced* to, Haddad. They're compelled."

"Aren't they holy warriors? Who gave their lives to protect Sharakhai?"

The chair creaked as Emre leaned forward. "You were there when the wights were summoned from Mesut's bracelet. You saw how they fought the Kings. You saw Kerim as well. Those were my people, and so are those who lie trapped beneath the adichara."

Haddad sneered. "You don't know who your people are. You told me yourself."

He pointed beyond the ship, toward the blooming fields. "Haddad, you may justify it however you like, but those are *people* out there, and they've suffered enough. Most of the asirim have already been summoned by the Kings. Do you know who's left? Those weakened by time, or grief, or by the wounds they've sustained in slavery to the Kings."

"You call what happened yesterday *weakened*?"

"Or those addled by time. Or too lost in their grief. My point is that you're killing innocents."

"It's war, Emre."

Now it was Emre's turn to sneer. "You would hide behind that as an excuse for murder?"

She paused, lost in thought or worry or both. When she spoke, it was with a softness that was so rare Emre knew she was convinced. "He won't stop simply because I ask him to."

"Then don't simply ask. Make him see that burning the adichara isn't worth it. Make him see that they'll remain there if they're left alone."

"They're dangerous, Emre. The Kings could still use them against us."

"If that were true, the Kings would already have done so, or would have sent them against the Mirean fleet." Haddad was unsure of herself, so before she could say anything more, Emre went on. "Leaving the asirim alone would mean much to Macide in our coming talks."

It wasn't much of a bargaining chip—by now King Emir knew how weak the thirteenth tribe was—but he also knew that Macide, its shaikh, held sway in the desert. Dayan had been convinced to join them. At least five tribes had banded together, and that number was only likely to grow. The alliance might soon account all thirteen tribes among its members, or a good many of them in any case, and Macide would be chief among them for hav-ing begun the process. Making friends with him now could pay dividends for generations.

Haddad stood and opened the door. "I'll try, Emre."

He stood and was about to head for the passageway but paused when it seemed Haddad was about to speak. She opened her mouth several times, but then seemed to settle her internal debate with a sharp nod. "He'll listen to reason."

He was almost certain that wasn't what she was originally going to say, but let it pass without comment. Her sudden change of mood reminded him of another thing that had been bothering him. "Who is the priest to you?"

"The priest?"

"The one in the golden mask. Shonokh?"

She blinked several times. Her cheeks flushed, a girl caught with her hand in the candy jar. "He's the high priest of Tamtamiin."

Of course, Emre thought. He remembered at last the passages Çeda had read to him about the god from her illuminated book. Tamtamiin was both male and female, the god of a thousand hearts, a protector who'd given birth to the bounty in the fields and forests of Malasan; and mercurial, a goddess tame as a summer glade, angry as a wounded wolf, fickle as the autumn winds.

"He seemed smitten with you," Emre said, recalling how he'd tugged at her sleeve and whispered to her on Emir's wooden platform.

She shrugged. "He always has been, since I was a child."

"Perhaps he could help you to convince your king. Are the ways of Tam-tamiin not the ways of peace, after all?"

At this, some of the fire in Haddad's eyes returned. "I hardly need you to teach me the tenets of my faith, Emre."

"No, I don't suppose you do," he said, and left *Calamity's Reign* under the sour gaze of her first mate.

Chapter 37

THE EARLY EVENING AIR was warm as Çeda climbed onto deck from the *Red Bride*'s hold. Nearby, Jenise and another Shieldwife had bows at the ready, arrows nocked. "Is all ready?"

Jenise nodded, at which point Çeda whistled the signal for *advance* and walked down the gangplank to the sand. Night's Kiss hung from her belt rather than River's Daughter. The sword seemed eager for the scene it knew was about to play out, which was about as perfect a response as Çeda could have hoped for.

The sky was a vast well of azure blue that gave way to a host of purples and pinks in the west. Tulathan, suspended above the eastern horizon like a watchful eye, was nearly full. *Not the best of omens*, Çeda thought, but she and Mavra had agreed that dusk would be best. It was when the asirim's minds were most active.

Fanned out in a circle ahead of Çeda were the other five Shieldwives, each wearing their sand-colored dresses, each with shamshirs and bucklers at the ready. Çeda nodded to them, then turned to find Husamettín emerging from the hold, his hands tied behind his back. The same rope was looped around his neck, the slipknot ready to cinch should he begin to struggle.

Melis followed closely behind the King, one hand gripping the rope around his neck, the other her drawn shamshir. She pushed Husamettín down along the gangplank, then brought him to a halt before Çeda with a sharp tug on the rope.

Husamettín took in the women around him, his face a wreckage of cuts and bruises, then stared at Çeda, waiting with the sort of calm that came with centuries of walking the earth. "Is my other daughter afraid to face me?"

"By the time we're done," Çeda said, ignoring his comment, "I will have two things from you: first, how best to approach Sehid-Alaz's cell through your palace, and second, whether Sehid-Alaz's condition is truly irreversible. I would rather you gave us this information of your own free will. I meant what I said. It isn't too late for you to help save Sharakhai. Give me this, Husamettín, and erase some of the stain on your honor."

Husamettín's dark eyes peered into hers. "If that's truly what you wish"— his words were slurred, evidence of the broken jaw, courtesy of Çeda's boot—"then you're wasting your time."

"'It is the smallest of men who clings to lies in hope that they might save him.' Isn't that what the Al'Ambra says? All you've stood for has been a lie, Husamettín. Correct it. Correct it before you pass beyond these shores, and give life to those you've wronged."

Çeda thought she'd miscalculated his willingness to speak. She felt certain he'd decided against it, choosing instead to let them torture him. But she *needed* him to speak. Everything depended on it. She was ready to threaten him when his nostrils flared and he regarded her with a new intensity.

"They *have* life." The shadows of dusk played strangely against the muscles along his neck. His eyes were reddened and watering, a small glimpse into the pain his broken jaw was giving him. "They have purpose. Given to them by the gods themselves."

"You can't believe that."

"You wish to quote verses?" His eyes were fiery, his expression intense. It was the most emotion she'd ever seen from him. "'Let not your heart blind you to what you know is right. Let not a thousand die when one brave soul might take their place.'"

He would have her believe that the asirim had acted as heroes, saving Sharakhai when the tribes had banded against it. Despite herself, despite knowing the stakes of this conversation, Çeda felt her emotions ready to boil over. *Draw me*, came a voice. *Let me taste his blood.* She quelled the sword's urges immediately. She'd come to know its moods, and that to give in to her emotions made it all the more difficult to think clearly. With a deep inhalation, she calmed herself. "You would stand before me and say the asirim acted *bravely*?"

"Our cause was just!" Husamettín swallowed hard, an act that took long moments to recover from. "If the gods came to me today and promised they would save Sharakhai from her aggressors, I would do it all again."

"You would give up your brothers and sisters again?"

"The city was ready to perish! You claim compassion drives you, yet you ignore the fact that everyone in Sharakhai would have died. Suad, the Scourge of Sharakhai, master of all twelve tribes—"

"Thirteen," Çeda said.

Husamettín's eyes burned at her. "You claim to know so much. But you don't know what it was like. Suad killed everyone—everyone!—in every caravanserai on his way to Sharakhai. None were left to flee. Mothers, daughters, sons. The old, the sick, the infirm. They were all put to the sword, their bodies defiled in mass burnings. I saw them with my own eyes. He would have taken the city and killed everyone, including your precious tribe!"

"You admit it, then, that against their will you gave the thirteenth tribe to the gods?"

"They became heroes!"

"No!" Çeda stabbed one finger at him as she spoke. "They were lambs, sacrificed on an altar of your making!"

"They saved *countless* others!" Husamettín was shouting now, but he halted when he heard a hollow wooden thump behind him. He turned and saw, beneath the ship, the lower hatch swinging free. Through the opening dropped an impressive woman in a dress of blue and bronze.

It was Kameyl.

As she strode forward, dumbstruck, Sümeya dropped from the ship just behind her. Kameyl stepped over the starboard ski, her eyes fixed on Husamettín. The Shieldwives parted for her with a reverence that surprised Çeda. Kameyl bore no weapon. She was in the same dress she'd worn on her brother's estate. And yet she looked more powerful than any woman here.

After Kameyl had woken, it had taken a full day for her to agree to this one meeting with Husamettín where she would conceal herself from him and listen, and make her judgments from there. Husamettín turned halfway toward her, taking her in with no small amount of confusion. He looked to Çeda, then back to Kameyl, and understanding dawned on him: Kameyl had been listening the entire time, and now one of his most ardent supporters knew the truth.

His face turned angry and red. Kameyl, meanwhile, met Husamettín's eyes and spoke two words—they were simple, but felt like a punch to the throat.

"You lied."

Husamettín had that look of righteousness about him, as if he thought himself a brother to the desert gods, an equal.

"All of you lied," Kameyl went on, "about *all* of it."

"We didn't lie, Kameyl Beşir'ava. The asirim *are* our holy avengers."

Kameyl shook her head and chose her own quote from the Al'Ambra. "Thou shalt not suffer your neighbor to keep a man against his will."

Husamettín's brow creased. "And who do you think the wise women were quoting when they first penned the Al'Ambra! It was the desert gods themselves, the very same gods who laid the burden upon the asirim!"

Kameyl, nearly of a height with Husamettín, looked over his shoulder to Sümeya. Holding out her hand, she said, "Give me your knife." Sümeya looked to Çeda, but the moment she did, Kameyl shouted at the top of her lungs, "Give it to me!"

When Çeda nodded, Sümeya took her kenshar from its sheath, flipped it in one easy motion and handed it to Kameyl.

Kameyl snatched it and grabbed Husamettín's pepper gray hair with her free hand. She wrenched his neck back, then lifted the knife and brought it toward his forehead. When Husamettín resisted, she slipped her arm around his neck and flipped him over her hip and down to the sand so violently that a whoosh of breath escaped his lungs. She followed his movements effortlessly, straddling him while retaining her grip on his hair.

He strained mightily at his bonds, but the rope around his neck was already tight and his own movements were only making it worse. Kameyl ignored his struggles, his reddening face and the bulging veins in his neck. Using the tip of the kenshar, she began to carve lines into the oily skin of his forehead. An arc. A line. Three bloody points.

Husamettín's face was a study in pain and anger and rage-filled impotence. But Kameyl would not be denied. She continued to carve his skin until she had completed the symbol. The ancient sign for *deceiver*. It was a shameful sign in the desert. Only the sins of rape and murder ranked higher.

By the time she was done, blood was pouring down Husamettín's face. She rolled off him and pulled him up by his hair, allowing all to see what she'd done. After wiping the bloody tip of the knife on his surcoat, she handed it back to Sümeya, then turned to face Çeda.

"Call them," she said. "I know where to find Sehid-Alaz, but you'll need your own answers when it comes to lifting the curse the King has placed on him."

Çeda looked beyond the circle of Shieldwives. "Come, Mavra. It's time."

A dozen paces distant, the sand churned. Shapes lifted. Ungainly Mavra came first, then tall Sedef and limber Amile and all the rest. The Shieldwives backed away as the asirim approached Husamettín. Most stopped a few paces away, surrounding the King in a rough circle as Kameyl, Çeda, Sümeya, and Melis gave them room. Mavra, however, continued until she stood just before him.

For the first time, Husamettín seemed afraid. Truly afraid. An unseen battle was being waging between him and the asirim. He was trying to command them to attack Çeda and the others, and they were resisting.

"Halt." The blood running down his face made him look like a speaker for the dead, a mouth for those who'd already reached the farther fields. "Halt!"

The skin of his face, stained crimson, began to quiver as he struggled to reassert his power over them. But he couldn't. Their bonds had been reforged. The old ones still existed, but the ritual they'd completed with the Shieldwives eclipsed them. Helping them was the fact that the women they'd bonded with stood just behind them, lending them support, which prevented Husamettín from inveigling his way into their minds as he'd done with so many asirim.

Mavra stood before Husamettín. She reached up and took his head in both hands. He tried to resist, but Mavra's grip was undeniable. She called upon her centuries of anger, her sorrow, and drew Husamettín's head inexorably toward her. Then she licked the wound Kameyl had lain upon his brow.

Husamettín's head arched back, as did Mavra's, her movements a twin to his. A rush of anger and regret and blood thirst swept over Çeda and the Shieldwives like a malediction. The asirim wailed, and Çeda had the urge to moan along with them, but this ritual was for them alone, so she and the Shieldwives remained silent. The asirim craned their necks, their bodies contorted—movements brought on by their bottomless sorrow and the bitter exultation that accompanied the very notion of taking, after all these years, something, anything, from the Kings.

The closest thing in Çeda's experience was the last time she'd held her mother's hands in Dardzada's apothecary. It had been in those moments before Ahya pulled free and slapped Çeda for disobeying her. The memory was a mix of misery and fear and pain and a desperate sort of love, and yet Çeda cherished it for the simple fact that it was the last time they'd touched.

Husamettín bared his bloody teeth. His breath rushed harshly through the gaps, sending red spittle spraying over the blackened skin of Mavra's face. His struggles had weakened, but Mavra still held him tight. Çeda could feel her digging deep, heedless of the pain she caused, heedless of the state she might leave him in. She wanted only one thing, an answer to the riddle Çeda had set for her: How could they free Sehid-Alaz once they found him?

The moments stretched. The sun set. Tulathan, indifferent to the pain of the King she'd sworn to protect, trekked across the sky.

Please, Çeda prayed, *let her find a way.*

When Mavra finally released Husamettín, he collapsed to the sand and lay there, unmoving. Each noisy breath lifted small clouds of dust and sand before his lips. He sounded like an old man weeping in bed, trying to hide his shame from his wife.

Mavra limped toward Çeda, looking as though she bore the weight of the desert upon her broad shoulders, and spoke in a reedy whisper. *"It's time for you to go to Sharakhai, daughter of Ahyanesh."*

Çeda hardly dared to speak. "You've found a way?"

"I've found a way. Free Sehid-Alaz, and together we will lift his curse."

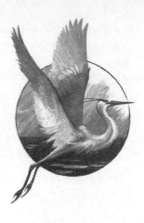

Chapter 38

ON A PLAIN OF DARKEST GLASS lies Ramahd Amansir. Silver Tulathan and golden Rhia are coins affixed to a velvet sky. Scree blows across the brittle ground with a sound like a fine Mirean wind chime. There comes a distant sound, rhythmic, pounding. It drums up memories of a terrible beast with jaundiced eyes, but when Ramahd stands and draws his sword he sees but a frail feminine form striding toward him.

"You cannot hide forever, Ramahd."

"I don't need to, Meryam."

"Oh?" She stops some ten paces distant and unfurls a whip with two barbed tips. "And why is that?"

"Do you suppose the news of your betrayal will remain hidden from the Kings forever?"

"Forever?" Her smile widens, grim beneath the light of the twin moons. "No, Ramahd. Not forever."

With that her arm snaps forward. Ramahd is ready, however, and cuts the whip. Its two severed ends fly through the air like snakes, but the whip mends itself. The braided leather regrows, this time with three heads. She uses it to strike again. Ramahd slices the whip over and over, and each time it divides and regrows its length.

Ramahd is weary beyond words, which perhaps explains why he doesn't remember his purpose until he and Meryam are fully joined in battle. He *wanted* Meryam to find him—it's necessary if his plan is to succeed—but she hasn't come for him in some time. And she's distant. Very distant. Are the two related in some way?

He isn't sure, but he's glad she's being forced to spend more of her power to try to find him. It will help to weaken her, a woman who always pushes herself to the edge. Indeed, he already feels it. She's ready to give up. It's in that moment that he presses her. He steps toward her, cutting the whip with greater ease. Soon the weapon no longer divides and regenerates.

He sees it then, a grand web fanning out around her, thin tendrils connecting Meryam to many others. Hamzakiir is there, as are Mateo, various servants in Eventide, and more servants in the Qaimiri embassy house. She maintains dominion over dozens. Some of the links are bright. Others are weak and fading, perhaps those she used days or even weeks ago.

He's captivated by it, so much so that his attack pauses and Meryam, angry that he'd got the better of her even momentarily, is back on the offensive. His sense of the web vanishes as she lashes out with the whip again and again, each strike bringing her a little closer.

"Wake up!" Cicio was shaking him so hard his pallet shifted against the attic floor. "Alu damn you, Ramahd, she's *coming*!"

Ramahd was still in the throes of lethargy, but when Cicio's words registered, he levered himself up and began the process of locating Meryam's grasping tendrils and cutting them off before they came near.

"Well?" Cicio said when he began to breathe easier.

Ramahd nodded. "We're safe. She hasn't found us."

"You're sure?"

"I'm sure."

Cicio considered this while his eyes glanced nervously toward the door. "And the web?"

He nodded. "I found it."

"Do you know how to use it?"

"No," Ramahd admitted, "but I'll find a way." He'd known the web would be there, but he'd had too little time with it to find a way to free Mateo without Meryam learning of it.

Cicio's expression made it clear he wasn't nearly as confident as Ramahd, but in the end he nodded. In silent concert, the two of them traded places, Cicio lying in the bed, leaving the blankets crumpled to one side in the heat of the night, Ramahd taking the stool near the bedside. Davud and Esmeray lay on their own pallet nearby. Davud was still in the throes of his fever, and Esmeray was cradling him against her chest. As angry as that woman always was, she'd certainly warmed to Davud. It did Ramahd's heart good to see them so, legs tangled, their worries briefly forgotten after falling asleep in one another's arms.

Cicio was looking at them too, but didn't seem consoled in the least. "We lost Vrago," he said.

"Yes."

"We lost Tiron."

"I know."

"It's time we get Mateo or go after Meryam herself."

"Mateo hasn't been seen outside the House of Kings since he arrived in the city." Cicio started to argue, but fell silent when Ramahd held up a hand. "It may not matter much anyway. Mateo can do nothing until Hektor arrives. It's better if we wait for the fleet."

"That may be too late. And they *are* near. They must be by now."

Ramahd couldn't argue. Mateo had told him the fleet would be no more than two weeks out when they'd spoken in Alu's temple. That time was fast approaching, and Cicio was right—Mateo might not leave the House of Kings before then. And when the fleet *did* arrive, there was no telling what the Malasani fleet would do. The war would consume Mateo's days, possibly even take him away from the city. The time was now. Free Mateo from Meryam's spell of domination and they would have him. And if they got *him* on their side, Duke Hektor was sure to follow, and the tide would truly turn against Meryam.

"We'll find a way," he told Cicio.

"I'm sick of this fucking city, Ramahd. I'm sick of the heat. I'm sick of the dust. I'm sick of the incessant press of people. It makes me feel like a fish in a net that keeps tightening. I want to go home to my wife. I want to see my son. Mighty Alu, I want to feel rain on my face again. Instead we sit here like does in a glade, waiting for the huntsman's arrow."

"I want to go home too." The first thing he would do is visit the graves of his wife and child, then swim in the Austral Sea, immerse himself in the cold swells to his heart's content. He squeezed Cicio's shoulder. "Sleep."

Cicio closed his eyes and eventually slept. Meryam's presence, meanwhile, faded until it was lost entirely. She knew Ramahd had awoken and that she'd have no chance to catch him now. Needing some fresh air after his close call, Ramahd went outside to the small yard behind the locksmith's home. Fezek was there, staring up at the stars, as he often did at night. "Beautiful, is it not?"

There was no denying it, but the scene was strange. As in his dream, the moons were full. Beht Zha'ir, the night of the asirim, had returned to Shara-khai.

"I never thought I'd see the day," Fezek said in that wistful, wheezy voice of his. Ramahd knew precisely what he meant. The city was silent. No howls of the asirim. No cries of fright or pain. "Too bad it never happened while I was alive. It mightn't have felt so eerie."

"No," Ramahd said, "it's eerie when you're alive too."

The city still observed the dictates of the holy night: perfect silence, no lights lit. Ramahd wasn't certain what had happened to the asirim, but surely it had something to do with the looming war, the Kings summoning them for some other purpose.

Fezek pulled his clouded gaze away from the night sky to look at Ra-mahd. His eyes had unsettled Ramahd in their early days, but now he merely found them sad.

"Have you saved us once again from the attentions of the terrible queen?" Fezek asked.

"A bit dramatic, don't you think?"

Fezek shrugged. "It's what the people want." When Ramahd paused, confused, he went on. "I've started composing an epic."

Despite his lethargy, Ramahd laughed. "Planning your visits to the tea houses already?"

Fezek stared down at himself. "I rather think the shisha dens would be more appropriate, don't you?"

"Perhaps. Do you know how it ends?"

"No," Fezek admitted, "but I'll be able tell you soon enough." He returned his gaze to the sky. "Was it the field of glass again?"

"Yes."

"Hard times." Fezek liked to think he could interpret Ramahd's dreams to find some hidden truth about Meryam they could exploit.

"I finally found what I was looking for." Ramahd knew it would lead to wild speculation on Fezek's part, but he didn't care. He needed to get it out.

"Oh?" Fezek said.

"Meryam was weak, and a grand web appeared around her."

"A web. Conspiracies."

"In a way. The threads in the web are the bonds she's created to others through use of their blood."

"Mmmm . . ."

"Hamzakiir's was the strongest among them."

"Yes, I see. She's taken quite a shining to him, which he hasn't returned. It's difficult to love a queen."

"It doesn't mean that at all, Fezek. She's dominating his mind."

"Yes, but you said yourself one still has will."

"And you think underneath it all, Hamzakiir actually loves Meryam?"

"Love is a complicated thing," Fezek replied easily. "Take you, for example."

"What about me?"

"You say you hate Meryam, but you love her as well."

The silence of the city pressed in on Ramahd. He supposed he might have admitted it to himself but he had no idea anyone else had picked up on it, much less *Fezek*.

"Well," Ramahd finally managed, "Hamzakiir has no love for Meryam, I can tell you that."

"You said you're looking for a way to free this Madano."

"Mateo."

"Yes, well." Fezek took a rasping breath, as if he were building up to something grand. "My mother used to weave baskets."

Ramahd lowered his head into one hand and began rubbing his temples. "Fezek . . ."

"She was good, but she was creative as well. Sometimes too creative. She'd weave patterns of ribbon into the reeds in the shape of animals, fish, birds, flowers. One time she made one of Tauriyat, complete with the palaces."

"Fezek, I'm tired."

"But she would often change her mind. She'd spend all that time creating a beautiful image, but then she'd become dissatisfied, and she'd undo it and start all over again."

Fezek paused, waiting for Ramahd to see his meaning, but for the life of him Ramahd couldn't understand it. "So?"

Fezek sighed, the same one he used when no one appreciated his latest bits of verse. "She'd use the same ribbon, the same reeds. The old image was lost, replaced by the new, and no one, including my mother, would know by looking at it that the old one had ever existed."

Ramahd stared at Fezek, who finally looked satisfied.

"Fezek, I could kiss you."

Fezek's head jerked. His cloudy eyes widened. "Oh, very well."

Ramahd left him there, ran up to the room, and woke Cicio. "I've got it," he said.

Cicio rubbed the sleep from his eyes. "Got what?"

"A way to bring Mateo to us."

Chapter 39

IT WAS NIGHT WHEN ANILA WAS GAGGED, taken in chains to a prisoner's wagon, and driven down King's Road. Through a small window, Anila could see that the driver had no light to speak of—no moons in the sky, nor lighted lanterns hung from hooks at the front of the carriage. It was so bloody dark she feared they would tip off the edge of the road and fall to their deaths. But they didn't, and soon they reached the Sun Palace, where she was led inside by a pair of Silver Spears and taken deep below the palace.

She'd walked this path before, but as a free woman with Davud. Four of the Kings had accompanied them as King Sukru led them all to the large cavern where the roots of the adichara met, where the strange crystal stood glowing, where Yerinde herself had demanded the Kings lay Nalamae's head at her feet. So it came as no surprise when the Silver Spears brought her to that very same cavern, nor was she shocked to find King Sukru already standing near the crystal.

Still, her breath quickened at the sight of him. She immediately worried that he had her father or sister, Banu, waiting nearby to convince her to do what he wanted, but thankfully she saw no sign of them.

Three days had passed since her meeting with Sukru in the crypt. She'd been fed her daily meals. Her chamber pot had been emptied. Beyond that, not one of the guards had spoken a word to her, and she'd had no indication of whether her father and sister were well, or for that matter still alive. That first night she had resolved, over and over, never to do Sukru's bidding, but by morning those feelings had been eclipsed by fear for her family. And she worried that Sukru might still betray her and kill her father and Banu even after she'd done as he asked.

The day after her mother's death had passed in a haze. She'd hoped it was a dream. She'd told herself it was a trick, that her mother was still alive, somewhere. By the following morning, however, she'd accepted the truth, and the lethargy brought on by news of Hamzakiir's death all but vanished. Her ability to call on magic returned, along with her sense of death in others, no matter how faint. Her endless thoughts of revenge against Hamzakiir, nearly extinguished, had been rekindled and replaced with a desire to see Sukru dead.

As the Spears led her across the cavern, it burned her that Sukru had been right about all of it, a feeling that only intensified the closer she came to him. How she longed to drain the life from him. Even from this distance she could sense it: the decay that was peculiar to the Kings of Sharakhai. They'd staved off death for so long that their bodies seemed eager to embrace it. Like a boulder on the edge of a precipice, she need but tip the balance; the rock's weight alone would do the rest.

Or it would if it weren't for the other notes she smelled, the more delicate scents of jasmine and sandalwood and rose. These were the work of the healing elixirs they drank, one of the many gifts the desert gods had granted them. It was some distillation of the adichara that had kept them alive for so long and, despite her desires, might keep her from unleashing the pent-up decay that had been building for centuries within him.

"Unchain her," Sukru said.

The Spears did, then retreated to the cavern's entrance. Beside Sukru was a massive bird cage hanging from an ornamental stand. It might have been one of those from the Sparrow's tower. She couldn't be sure. When she came closer, she noted a variety of species within. A handful of firefinches shared space with a tailrunner, two thornbills, and a small host of saddlebacks. They chirped and chirruped, the sounds fairly swallowed by the immensity of the cavern and its soft, spongy floor and walls.

The birds were bathed in violet light, thrown off by the nearby crystal, which was twice as tall as Anila and shaped like a wedge. The lowest reaches of it were lost to layer upon layer of thin, tendril-like vines, while the top of the crystal was situated just below a thin root that hung down from center of the cavern's roof. For a moment, Anila's hatred of Sukru was forgotten. This was a wonder of the desert. If only its secrets could be unlocked.

"Where is the Sparrow?" Anila asked.

"You will begin with the birds." Sukru opened the cage and crooked a finger near an ivory-breasted thornbill. He nudged it until it hopped on, at which point he pulled the bird out and closed the cage door. "When you have mastered them, you will move on to animals of increasingly large mass. And only when you have mastered *those* will you be allowed to begin the ritual on my brother."

"I've told you," Anila said, staring at the bird as Sukru stroked its back, "I haven't the ability to grant it real life."

"We shall see." With the sort of assured movements that made it clear he'd done this before, Sukru wrapped his hand around the bird's head and began to suffocate it. "Before today, necromancers have only managed to summon ghuls. The result has always been men, women, even children, who have at best been poor reflections of their former selves. You are one of the few people who know why. Their souls are but tattered remnants. They're torn, part of them in the farther fields, another here in our world. I have no doubt, were we able to walk with their other halves in the world beyond, we'd find them every bit as incomplete as the one that resides here. This, however . . ." He regarded the monolith with naked reverence, all but ignoring the dying bird in his hands. "This gift from the gods will change that."

"What do you mean?"

"I suspect," he went on, "you will find it not only easier to summon the dead when near the crystal, but that the soul will be delivered whole, or near enough that it makes no difference."

Anila had felt many souls since learning about her power. She'd witnessed deaths, and had watched in wonder as their souls had left for the world beyond. She'd seen others who were already dead, and felt the threads that ran from their bodies to the farther fields. She'd tugged on some of those souls, forcing them to inhabit their bodies once more, but it was as Sukru had said: the results had been incomplete at best.

As the thornbill in Sukru's hand went still, his purpose and the way the crystal figured into it came clear, and yet it was still strange to feel the bird's soul move so sweetly through the crystal.

When Anila had first begun testing the limits of her burgeoning power, she'd done so on a firefinch, the very one Sukru's brother, the Sparrow, had been using to communicate with Davud in secret. Davud had walked in on her during one of those first experiments and found the finch lying at the bottom of the cage, apparently lifeless. He had assumed that she'd killed it and brought it back to life. She hadn't, though. The finch's soul had merely been suspended over the threshold to the farther fields.

That was how *this* bird, the thornbill, felt. It was child's play, laughably simple, to draw its soul back. The bird fluttered. It stood on quivering limbs and shook its head as it might under a fresh downpour of rain. In a burst of movement, it fluttered up, wings thrumming, and was lost to the deeper darkness of the cavern.

"But," Anila said, already seeing several problems, "it won't be so easy with one who's been dead as long as your brother has."

Sukru's stare was merciless. "Then you'll simply have to work that much harder, won't you?"

The scent of his decay was so strong she wondered how long it would take her to send *him* to the farther fields. She quickly buried the thought. Her father's and sister's lives depended on her compliance. As did her mother's, if her plan was to work.

"There are also his wounds to contend with," Anila said, "and the state of his decay."

"Let me worry about that," Sukru said sharply.

Anila's fingers were shaking so badly she gripped them tight and straightened her back. What she was about to say was dangerous, but there was no other way. "You don't have to hide it from me," she said. "I know what you plan to do."

Sukru often looked angry when he was surprised, as if he couldn't stomach even the smallest amount of embarrassment. Now he seemed calm, which felt infinitely more dangerous. "Pray tell."

"You plan to use the elixirs that keep you alive to heal his wounds and restore his body once his soul has been returned."

He looked her up and down, reassessing.

She pressed on. "But you won't want to make him the first subject."

"Won't I?"

"No. You'll want to try it on someone else first. Someone with a similar wound. Perhaps someone who's died more recently so that I might prove that it works before you risk your brother's life."

Sukru's eyes went flat. "You're suggesting I allow you to resurrect your mother."

"It's only prudent." Anila's heart was beating so madly she heard the rush in her ears. "She's the perfect way to prove it will work. If I can resurrect her, you can heal her and watch her for a time to be sure she's stable. Then you'll be certain it will work for your brother."

"When I'm offered a bargain," Sukru said, "I like the terms to be plain."

"Very well. Allow me to save my mother, and I'll do as you wish."

"You'd do what I wish anyway."

"This is your own brother we're talking about. Wouldn't you rather I do this willingly, even gratefully? I would be working not only with the confidence of having done it before, but with the knowledge that my family has been safely released from the palace. I would be resurrecting him wholly committed, knowing that you could return them to the palace if you so wished."

Sukru sneered. "And now you're asking that they are released from the palace!"

Anila kept her voice as calm as she could. "They know nothing about what we're doing here."

Sukru paused, considering. "You're a perceptive girl," he finally said.

"Yes," Anila said, knowing exactly where Sukru was headed with this.

"And you're smart."

"Yes."

"Were I to reveal the second, necessary step to resurrecting them, the part that comes after your work, you know that I couldn't allow you to leave the palace."

He would kill her. "I know, and I would still do it gladly, knowing my family was safe."

His face pinched in annoyance. "I would hardly call living in a city surrounded by invaders *safe*."

And with that she knew he'd agreed. She was well aware that he might change his mind, but this was her best hope for saving her family.

"Not safe, true, but alive and with a chance for more life."

He glanced at the bottom of the cage where, to her surprise, a blue-breasted saddleback lay on the wood shavings and bird droppings. It was unmoving, dead. She'd been so fixated earlier on the fluttering of the others she hadn't noticed it.

"Very well," he said, taking up the dead bird. "Perform your miracle again. Work with zeal, for it won't be easy as your subjects grow in size. Then you can summon your mother back from the dead. Return her to this world whole, do the same for my brother, and I shall consider our bargain complete."

"You'll free my family? All of them?"

"Yes, I'll *free* them," he spat, and held out the saddleback's stiffened corpse for her to take. "Now get started."

Anila accepted it and repeated the ritual. Sukru had been right. It was much more difficult, not in finding the thread that led to its soul—the bird hadn't been dead for that long—but to return its soul intact. By the time she was done an hour later, she was sweating and short of breath, but the bird . . . Gods, she'd done it. Its soul had been drawn through the crystal successfully and its body had begun to twitch.

Sukru took it immediately and used a glass pipette to deliver three drops of a clear, bright blue liquid into the bird's open beak. As they watched, a second miracle occurred: the bird's dull feathers regained the color they'd been lacking; its movements—frenetic, even spastic, moments ago—became more natural. It peeped twice, then sang a longer song.

With more care than Anila would have expected, Sukru placed the bird back inside the cage. It gripped one of the many branches, still for a time, then it flapped its wings and moved about, more alert than moments ago.

Sukru's normally sour face looked pleased, even satisfied, though he was clearly trying to hide it. "That's enough for today," he said. "You're shivering from exhaustion."

"Very well." He was right, she was shaking, but not from exhaustion. "Very well," she said again, then turned and walked toward the Silver Spears, who would return her to Sukru's palace. She worried he would call her back, worried he might sense her pleasure. But thankfully he didn't, which left her to contemplate what she'd sensed while using that strange crystal.

Just as it had enabled her to ferry a soul back from the land of the dead, she was certain she could do the reverse. *And when I do it to you, King Sukru, not even your bloody elixir will be able to save you.*

Chapter 40

SMERAY WAS RIGHT. Davud was felled by a terrible fever over the days following their bloody kiss. He could hardly keep his eyes open for more than a few minutes at a time.

When wakeful, he relieved himself in the chamber pot. He ate soup filled with root vegetables and pork laden with so much lemon and herbs it was almost overwhelming, but Esmeray insisted. He stretched and ran in place several times a day so that he wouldn't lose more days regaining his strength after the fever finally passed. But when he did he grew dizzy, and he ached so terribly that he often lay back down after only a short while on his feet.

Thankfully she was right about it not being as bad as the change he'd undergone in Ishmantep, his passage to becoming a blood mage. Those had been dark days. The experience had swept over him like a storm, nearly killing him. This time it was no worse than a bout of influenza.

On the morning of the fourth day after Esmeray's kiss, the fever finally broke. Davud woke to find Fezek sitting crosslegged beside his pallet, staring at him with those cloudy eyes.

Davud pushed himself up, his night shirt damp with sweat. "Gods, Fezek, how long have you been there?"

"Since dawn yesterday. We thought you were going to die."

"We did?"

"Very well, *I* did."

"Hoped you mean."

Fezek shrugged. "I wouldn't mind having someone to talk to."

"Fezek, talking is *all* you do."

"About what it's like, I mean. You can't really understand what I'm going through until you've experienced it yourself."

Davud stood on trembling legs, if only to shake off the feeling of being weakened prey beneath the stare of a vulture. "And this would improve your situation how?"

Fezek shrugged. "You know what they say about the miserable."

"Yes, that they drown those around them in misery too."

"No, that only through misery can we truly know happiness."

"Let me guess: you wrote that."

Fezek sniffed. "I rather like it." He might have been affronted. It was difficult to tell on his decomposed face.

Davud felt exhausted and weakened from lack of food, but the aches in his muscles and joints were all but gone. "I need a night out," he told Esmeray later. "Take me to an oud parlor."

She looked as though she didn't consider it the best idea, but then she shrugged. "I know a place."

As they walked through the old city, bells began to ring. It took only moments for the sound to spread throughout the city. When they arrived at the oud parlor, a small cellar room with painted blue walls and golden lamps, they heard why. The Malasani, who for over a week had seemed content with burning the blooming fields and slaying any asirim scared up from the roots, had suddenly abandoned the practice.

"The asirim put the fear in them," one man said. "Saw the face of Thaash, they did. They know now, mark my words, the gods are coming to save the city."

"No," the proprietress shot back. "The gods have abandoned the city. That's why the asirim left. They've returned to Goezhen who made them."

Whatever the reasons, all agreed on one point: that the Malasani king had repositioned his fleet closer to the mouth of the southern harbor.

Dozens, hundreds of war machines were being moved into position and with no threat of a counterattack from the royal navy, an assault on the city was imminent.

A musician played his rebab in one corner while his wife sang. The sound mixed with both the hum of conversation and the warmth of the araq. One might almost forget that the city was under siege, and that Anila was trapped in a palace with the cruelest of the Kings. He felt instantly guilty.

"You can't help her if you're not ready," Esmeray said. She poured him another helping of araq from the small green bottle she'd ordered.

"I know," he said, and downed a healthy swallow.

"Hey. Hey!" Esmeray's perpetual frown was back, and she was staring in wide-eyed horror at his glass, which was now half empty. "I'm fairly sure you've heard the word *savor*, yes?" She lifted her glass and took in a long inhalation. Her eyes fluttered closed and she smiled like a lotus addict taking a deep breath off a shisha, then allowed herself a small sip. "*Savor* it."

Hiding a smile, he copied her and noted the smoke and cinnamon and caramel. He was no connoisseur, but it was impossible not to appreciate the finish and its strong, almost citrusy burn. "Well, well," he said, lifting the glass to the lamp flame between them and taking another look at the pale golden liquor.

Esmeray was clearly pleased but was trying to hide it. *She's an odd one,* Davud thought, *difficult to predict.* But he liked that about her. It brought him back to his days at the collegia and the pleasure he found not merely in the solving of a difficult theorem, but in working at it, uncovering its mysteries bit by bit.

"I spoke to Ramahd this morning," he told her. "He wants to free the admiral, Mateo, tomorrow night. As soon as that's done, we'll go to free Anila."

She stared into his eyes. The lamp lit her from below, and made him realize how full her lips were. "I'm no scholar like you, but don't you think it wiser to rest for a few days?"

"I feel fine," he said. "Or I will. And Anila's been there for too long already."

Esmeray considered him, but not in a critical way. She seemed surprised, as if she hadn't expected it of him. "Very well."

"You don't have to come."

"I'll come."

"I'm not going there to find Sukru. In fact, I hope we *don't* come across him. I'm only going to save Anila."

"I'll join you."

"It's just . . ." How could he tell her? "I want you to stay."

Her head jerked back, then she looked at him anew, her eyes narrowing, as if she'd just realized something. "You're trying to protect me." Before he could say a word, she was laughing, her head thrown back. All eyes turned to them, though as her laughter faded, those watching thankfully returned to their own conversations.

Disregarding her own advice, Esmeray downed what remained of her drink in one go and poured herself another. "Let me tell you something, Davud Mahzun'ava. I don't need protection. Not from my father. Not from the Enclave. Certainly not from *you*." She looked like she was going to down another full glass, but she stopped herself. As her araq swirled, amber in the lamplight, she pointed at Davud. "You think because we *kissed* you can prevent me from doing as I wish? I don't know how things were in your posh home in Goldenhill, but that isn't how things work in the west end."

"I was born in Roseridge. I've lived my entire life in and around the bazaar."

"Then you should know!"

"Know what?"

She looked as though she was going to laugh again, but she took it no further than an amused smile. "Give me your hands."

Davud swallowed, and did as she asked. He felt the suppleness of her skin, the cleverness of her fingers as she repositioned his hands. "Did you feel what my brother and sister were doing before Ramahd unwound their spell?"

"Not exactly. It happened so quickly."

"Think back."

He did, recalling how intricate the spell had seemed, how tight the weave. "It felt like they were weaving it together."

"Yes," Esmeray said. She lifted her forefinger, on the tip of which was a fresh drop of blood, shining in the dim light of the room. She reached out and touched it to his lips.

Davud, his eyes glancing nervously about to see if anyone was watching, opened his mouth and took her finger in. He tasted the blood, felt the small rush of power that accompanied it. Esmeray kept her finger there just long enough to make a circling motion inside his mouth, which he made no move to stop.

When she withdrew it, she said, "Now concentrate on the flame."

"And do what?"

"Wait. Watch. Feel."

Davud did. He didn't know what she meant to do, but for the moment he was simply glad to be with her. He felt warm inside. Tingly. The very air seemed to cradle them.

The flame flickered. It fluttered, altering from its typical lilac-leaf shape. The tip thinned and lengthened, a thread that circled the flame as if it were nothing more than a skein of sun-bright wool. Up it wound, then curled in on itself like a knot viper until it had made a new shape, something like a gilded cage.

It returned to its normal shape with a barely audible *whuff.*

"You felt my touch?" Esmeray asked.

"I did."

"Good. Now join me."

When the flame lengthened, he watched her workings more carefully. It was like stepping behind her as she worked a piece of blown glass.

"No," she said, and the flame snapped back. "Like that you'll only feel what I do. You cannot simply observe. You must *join* me."

Taking a deep breath, he nodded and tried again. As the spell formed between them, he let himself be drawn like smoke into a column of heat. He became a part of the spell, guiding it with Esmeray. Instead of a single thread curving back on itself to form the tiny cage, many threads did, creating something so intricate he would need to bend closer to appreciate it all.

Like this, the flame altering, creating new shapes as they watched, Davud felt Esmeray more intimately than he'd ever felt anyone. They were not one, but neither were they separate. They were *together,* acting in concert in a way that was so intimate it brought tears of joy and wonder.

He blinked them away, and the flame snapped back. The song finished and another began, eliciting raised glasses and smiles all around. A woman near the door released a high warbling call taken up by several in the crowd.

Esmeray never took her eyes from Davud's. She watched him carefully in the wavering lamp light, reached out and wiped away his tears.

"I didn't know such a thing was possible," Davud finally said.

"Because you've learned under two men who would never work with another mage like this." Her eyes glanced down at the flame. "But now you see what it can be like. I can help you, Davud. So can Ramahd. Together we can do this. Together we can do more. Isn't that what the philosophers at the collegia teach you about consciousness? That we can be more than the sum of our parts?"

"It is," he said, surprised.

"So it is with magic. So it is with people."

Davud felt like he was going to burst. He leaned in and kissed Esmeray. She returned it, and though Davud felt the amused gazes watching them, he kept kissing her until Esmeray released his hands and sat up straight. She brought her glass beneath her nose and drew in a long breath, eyes closed. "Together?"

Davud smiled and took a sip of his drink, feeling more relieved than he'd felt in a long, long while. "Together."

Chapter 41

BRAMA ENTERED A CIRCULAR tent that had been hastily erected in the small hours of the morning. Dawn was breaking. The eastern wall of the tent was lit in a burst of molten brass. The tent had gone up for the express purpose of having Rümayesh prove her ability to heal. After Brama's failure, it had taken some time to convince Queen Alansal, but she realized that this was the only chance she had to save her people. This time she'd insisted that they start with one of the sickest, to prove that there was hope for all.

So it was that at the center of the tent, Rümayesh loomed over a bedridden soldier, a man deep in the throes of the scourge. His face was almost entirely black and ashy. As were his fingernails, toenails, armpits, and much of his shoulders and hairless chest.

Brama considered Alansal's choice imprudent, but when it became clear she wouldn't bend, he had used it to insist that Rümayesh be given the bone of Raamajit, a thing both he and Rümayesh thought would be necessary to halt the spread of the disease. Alansal had reluctantly agreed but had yet to hand it over. She still held the reliquary, as she might a baby bird, while staring at the diseased soldier, perhaps wondering if she was making a terrible mistake. Her thin eyebrows pinched, and she twisted the cap and spilled the bone into the waiting hands of Juvaan, who brought it to Rümayesh.

"You may begin," Alansal said.

Rümayesh's eyes were alight as she took in the fabled artifact. As all those in the tent stared with awe, she pinched it between two fingers and pressed it to her forehead. Where it touched, her ebony skin parted, wrapped around it, subsuming it until the bone was lost beneath her skin and all that remained was a misshapen lump on her forehead.

She glanced at Brama with an expression he could only describe as ravenous, but it was gone almost as soon as it came, and she was turning toward the soldier and placing her right hand on his chest. Her hand was so large it wrapped around his ribs. The man's nostrils flared. His breathing, already rapid, sounded shrill over the tent's flapping walls and ceiling. His brow furrowed. His mouth made a circle. His eyes were wide and white and horror-stricken. It was such a stark contrast to the euphoric expression on Rümayesh's features, it made Brama's gut twist. He could only imagine what was running through her mind as she experienced the soldier's steadily increasing panic.

He chose not to think about it. He didn't care about her motivations so long as she finished what she'd started.

As Rümayesh pressed down on the soldier's chest, Queen Alansal stared rapt. She swallowed hard, a childlike fear on her timeless face, as a white mist lifted from the soldier's mouth and nostrils. It was thin and diaphanous, and dissipated like morning fog. As had happened with Brama's attempt at lifting the scourge, the soldier's body went rigid as stone, but he seemed in no danger of losing the battle against the scourge. In fact, unlike Mae's healing at the hands of Behlosh, much of the black, diseased tissue seemed to be healing as well. Only light halos of gray now marked the edges of his mouth and nose.

Soon Rümayesh lifted her hand, stood as high as the tent's ceiling allowed, and regarded the man. He'd fallen asleep, Brama realized. His light snores now filled the tent.

"The scourge was deep within him," Rümayesh said. "He'll likely sleep for a day or more."

Queen Alansal looked between Rümayesh and Brama, then flicked her hand to the waiting servants. The soldier was taken away and another took his place, a stocky woman with an angry purple birthmark on her right cheek who was in just as poor a state as the soldier had been. Alansal watched as the second victim was healed, and a third and a fourth, each time the strange fog rising from their open mouths. Rümayesh was not tired yet, but Brama could see how taxing each healing was for her, even with the power of the bone.

As the fifth victim was brought into the tent, Brama beckoned Juvaan closer. When he came near, Brama whispered to him. "I must speak with your queen."

Juvaan shook his head. "Let this play out."

"The longer we wait, the worse it will be. Better for her to understand and make her decision now."

Juvaan stared at the thin rail of a man now lying on the cot. "Very well."

Juvaan spoke to Alansal, who at first shook her head. When Juvaan pressed, however, Alansal looked at Brama and a heated if hushed conversation began. When Rümayesh had finished healing the sixth man, Alansal nodded crisply to Juvaan and left the tent with her escort.

"Be politic," Juvaan said as he reached Brama's side.

They retired to the main pavilion, where Queen Alansal was already seated on her dais. She said to Brama, "I have had no chance to thank you for all you've done." She tipped her head to him, her steel hairpins and the tower of her elaborately styled hair tilting with her. "We are all in your debt."

Brama shook his head. "I did little."

"You're being modest. Rümayesh would not have returned without your efforts."

Perhaps, Brama thought, *but Rümayesh is the one taking the risk.* Over the course of the entire morning, he'd worried that Behlosh or Goezhen himself would come storming over the dunes to take their revenge against Rümayesh for her disobedience. "I didn't wish to see so many die. Not like this. But your Excellence, there's something we must discuss."

"Go on."

"There should be no illusions about how quickly Rümayesh can heal the afflicted. It takes time. And the worse they are, the harder it will be."

"Come to your point."

"I advise you to have her treat those least affected by the disease, not those who are deepest in its throes."

Alansal took in his words with a nod. "And in doing so leave those on the hospital ships to die."

"Yes," he replied. "There's no way around it."

"No," Alansal said flatly. "We cannot abandon them."

"We won't if we can get ahead of the spread. Rümayesh has promised to work as quickly as she can, but even so, she must focus on those newly affected first so the spread of the disease stops here in the camp. Only then can we aid those in the hospital ships."

For the first time in Brama's presence, Alansal seemed truly disheartened. "There are over three thousand aboard those ships."

"And more are being sent to them every day. The head must be cut from this snake."

There was still a danger that Rümayesh couldn't keep up with the spread of the disease, but Brama was confident they would be able to turn the tide. The Mirean fleet was nothing if not disciplined. With everyone on the lookout for symptoms, the afflicted were quickly being separated from the healthy. The rate of infection had already been slowing. With more specific instructions being sent throughout the fleet, that would continue and allow Rümayesh to treat those who'd only just been infected.

Queen Alansal sat straight as a ship's mast. "It will be as you say. We'll delay our advance against the Kings until enough are ready. Another week, perhaps, and then our assault will begin in earnest." She paused then, a polite but strained smile on her lips. It was about as emotive as she ever got, which made it clear how important her next words were. "Rümayesh is already doing enough to earn Raamajit's bone. But I would still ask her to fight for us. Our strength has been sorely wounded. Nearly one in ten have already died, with more to follow."

Brama wiped the sweat from his brow. "You could always return to Mirea."

The queen's smile became drawn and thin. "You can say such a thing, knowing what they've done to us? The Kings must pay."

Brama tipped his head to her. "As you say, but you seem to think I have a greater influence over Rümayesh than I actually do."

The wind was storming, causing the pavilion's roof to roll and snap. "There is no one with any greater," Alansal said.

In truth this entire experience had soured Brama to the prospect of war. He'd seen it as inevitable, something he could do nothing about, and had hoped that somehow he might use it to free himself from Rümayesh, but the scourge had changed him. *Rümayesh* had changed him. The very idea of witnessing two fleets clashing and standing by as Rümayesh reveled in their pain and sorrow, made his stomach turn. Worse, he knew that *he* would revel in their pain as well, even as he was revulsed by it. He'd rather he and Rümayesh go into the desert and do as she'd promised: live like gods for a time, see the wonders of the desert. If they did that, it would leave Queen Alansal with few choices. With her fleet in jeopardy, perhaps it would convince Alansal to return home. The Kings were cruel masters and deserved to be deposed, but war could lead to the sacking of Sharakhai and a conflict that would last years, perhaps decades.

He was about to deny Queen Alansal her request when he heard a shout. More voices closer to the pavilion cried out. And then footsteps neared. They shushed across the sand, coming closer to the pavilion wall along Brama's left.

A shadow appeared on the canvas. And then the fabric was split, rent by the slice of a sword. Through the hole flew a woman wearing a red dress and turban that were caked in sand. Brama had never seen one before, but he knew what she was at once. One of the Unseen, the Bloody Nine, one of Husamettín's Kestrels. Behind her came a second woman, also in red.

Several of the Damned were already on the move, ebon blades drawn. One was felled almost immediately as the two Kestrels worked in concert, one blocking as the other sliced across his midsection. The second went down in a similar manner with a slice across the backs of his legs. Another pair of the Damned approached with a good deal more caution. They waited as others, who'd drawn their bows, loosed arrows at the Kestrels.

The Kestrels, however, wasted no time. The first snatched an incoming arrow in mid-air and used it to stab one of the queen's warriors in the neck. The other, farther back, dodged three arrows neatly, each of which punched through the tent wall behind her. The fourth she sliced in a blurring cut, then engaged the Damned standing before her. A torrent of ringing steel followed. The Kestrels took blows to their armored dresses, but none were enough to stop them, and soon one was breaking away, flying headlong toward Queen Alansal.

Arrows streaked the air. Shouts filled the pavilion, most calling for the queen to retreat, but the queen would not shrink away. She drew the steel pins from her hair and faced the oncoming Kestrel while her hair flowed down around her shoulders. The Kestrel leapt up to the dais, smooth as a bounding lioness, sword raised high in a two-handed grip.

As the Kestrel's blade swung down, the queen's arm blurred in an upward arc, cutting across the shamshir's path.

A metallic shearing sound sound rose above the shouts and sounds of battle. A high-pitched ringing followed as pieces of black, glinting metal flew everywhere, some of it striking Brama. The Kestrel hardly paused. She wielded the remaining hunk of blade as she would a long fighting knife, but the queen was ready. As the Kestrel sliced once, twice, the queen retreated, maintaining proper balance, proper distance. On the Kestrel's third swing, the queen held her ground, blocked a swift kick with her shin, and drove both hairpins into the Kestrel's chest.

The Kestrel's eyes went wide. She tried to bring what was left of her sword across the queen's neck, but her swing was slow and desperate. Alansal ducked beneath it and used that momentary opening to drive a pin through the Kestrel's defenseless neck.

"My queen!" Juvaan called in Mirean.

The other Kestrel, the shorter of the two, had a bowstring drawn to her ear, the arrow aimed for the queen. As she released the string, Queen Alansal, in a sinuous movement that made the fabric of her skirt flap, snaked around the other Kestrel so that, instead of taking the queen, the arrow took the Kestrel's sister in the chest.

No sooner had the arrow struck than Queen Alansal's right arm whipped forward. Her hairpin spun, flashing in the muted sunlight as it flew through the air before burying itself deep the second Kestrel's forehead. Her whole body quivered for a moment, her bow slipped from her hand, and she fell face-first onto the carpets.

For a moment, all was silence in the pavilion. Then drums were pounding, the sound coming from one of the ships, an urgent rhythm that was picked up by more drums on other ships.

"Make ready!" someone bellowed in Mirean. "To arms!" More orders were called, nearly all of which were lost on Brama. Over and over, those two phrases repeated: *Make ready, To arms.* The only other words Brama could pick out were the Mirean words for *south* and *fleet.*

The queen went to the fallen Kestrel and wrenched the steel pin from her forehead. After wiping away the blood on the Kestrel's dress, she twisted her hair, replaced both pins, and headed through the tear in the wall. Juvaan followed her, as did many others, including Brama.

They all stared toward the southern horizon, where a cloud of dust was rising. Ships could be seen at the forefront, like the vanguard of a storm.

The Kings' fleet, at long last, had arrived.

Chapter 42

RAMAHD STANDS ALONE beneath a bright desert sun. Off the strange, glasslike surface of the plain that surrounds him, an oppressive heat lifts. He's been waiting a long while, wary for the telltale signs—the pounding of the earth, the smell of burnt myrrh, a wavering shape in the distance— but so far there's been nothing.

Where are you, Meryam?

He resists the urge to call to her. *Do that, and she'll suspect.* So instead he waits, hoping he hasn't wasted another night.

A shift in the very fabric of the world alerts him. When he turns he sees her: Meryam, walking across the plain in a black dress with full sleeves. She bears a long, curving bow. A quiver filled with arrows hangs from her belt.

Knowing he cannot give himself away, Ramahd retreats while Meryam, quick as a striking snake, draws an arrow and lets fly. With a wave of his arm, Ramahd shatters the arrow, but there's already another on the way. He breaks this as well, amazed she has such reserves of strength.

"How long do you think you can keep this up?" he asks her.

"As long as I need to."

Another arrow loosed. Another shattered.

"And meanwhile," Ramahd says, "Qaimir is brought closer to the edge of ruin."

"Closer to the edge of glory."

"No, Meryam. If you'd take the time to look, you'd see that holding the desert is a dream."

"Dreams can come true, Ramahd." Meryam stops ten paces away, a wide grin on her face. "You might have realized it yourself if you didn't always dream so small."

A flurry of arrows fly from her bow, and Ramahd shatters each one. He'd come with the purpose of luring her, but he hadn't expected her to be so revitalized. Even worse, he feels the sudden presence of another. He glances behind and sees Hamzakiir walking toward him. He bears a bow as well.

Mighty Alu protect me.

That Meryam hasn't called upon Hamzakiir before is a sign of her stubbornness and pride. By the same token, his presence here now is a sign of her desperation, and Meryam is always at her most dangerous when she's desperate.

Ramahd retreats across the broken plain, trying to keep both of them in view. Their attack is relentless, however. One arrow punctures the linen of his trousers. Another grazes his shoulder.

Before coming here, he debated whether he should *allow* Meryam's spells to strike him—it might give him the precious moments he needed to locate his prize—but now the choice has all but been taken from him. He can't fight both of them forever, and he refuses to wake himself and let this opportunity pass him by. Only the fates knew when the chance might come again. So he fights them off for as long as he can.

And then an arrow strikes him dead in the chest.

Near Bent Man Bridge, in the center of the Haddah's dry riverbed, Cicio waited in a skiff. The sail was up and gathering wind but the anchor was down and hooked into the earth by Cicio himself so that they wouldn't risk moving before they were ready.

Ramahd lay in the bottom of the skiff beside an effigy made of hay wrapped in rough burlap. Esmeray sat at the prow, Davud on the skiff's centermost thwart, while Cicio manned the tiller. The three of them each had effigies of their own, resting beside them like oversized rag dolls. The ghul, Fezek, had been left behind in the workshop. He was always yammering at the wrong time, wavering between how impossible life was for the poet in modern Sharakhai and how great he might have been had a large and rather stubborn peach pit not become lodged in his throat.

In the days leading up to this night, Cicio had warned Ramahd that the two young blood magi would foul things up—the two of them were clearly, almost disgustingly, in love—but Ramahd had insisted, and Cicio was pleased to find he'd been wrong to doubt their abilities. When the time had come, they'd got right down to business, working together to cast spells, one to camouflage the skiff, another to alert them should anyone come blundering by.

They'd been quiet since, but Davud was becoming restless. "I feel like a fish trapped after springflow," he said.

"How long do we give him?" Esmeray asked.

Cicio pressed his fingers to Ramahd's neck. His pulse was steady, and his body had shown no signs of the spasms that came when Meryam was near. "As long as he need."

Along Bent Man Bridge, a squad of Silver Spears walked south along the Trough, talking jovially, loudly, about the drinks they'd earned after some scare with a squad of Malasani soldiers. Just then a tremor ran through Ramahd, and a moan like the opening of an old door escaped him. Cicio expected the Spears to turn, for one of them to call out, but they didn't. They kept walking, and their conversation faded, melding into the hum of night life along the Trough.

Ramahd's body went stiff. Tremors ran through him and then he lurched violently. Cicio was tempted to wake him, but Ramahd had made it clear he must be left to wake on his own.

"Be ready," Cicio whispered as he watched the banks of the Haddah for any sign that Queen Meryam's agents had found them.

Cicio scratched at the center of his chest where his skin was tickling, the spot where he felt certain a Blade Maiden's arrow was aimed. He wasn't afraid of much, but there was something about those bloody women.

Davud pointed to the northern bank, where several dark shapes were coming into view. Soldiers on horses. Cicio snapped his fingers twice and pointed to the opposite bank, where there were more riders exiting an alley. From the second group came a gut-wrenching howl, the call of an asir. It was followed by a second and a third.

"Fucking shit." Cicio cut the rope to the anchor and the ship glided into motion. "Fucking shit!"

They'd known Queen Meryam would send Maidens, but the asirim? Everyone had thought them gone from Sharakhai; not a single one had howled on Beht Zha'ir. *Clearly they managed to keep a few,* Cicio thought. As the skiff gained speed, he raised his crossbow and sighted along it, waiting for the asirim to come. *Hurry, my lord.* An asir howled again, this one so high, so shrill, it sent a shiver of fear running through him. It went on for so long he grit his teeth against it lest he start wailing too.

"Gods of the desert, no," Davud breathed.

"What?" Cicio hissed.

A man on a bright silver akhala rode out along the Trough. The rider, tall and impressive, had drawn a two-handed shamshir that fairly glowed in the night.

"It's Hamzakiir," Davud said. "Hamzakiir is coming."

"So what are you going to do?" Esmeray spat, and began weaving a spell. "Curl up like a little boy?"

The three asirim charged toward them over the rocky ground. Cicio lifted the double crossbow to his shoulder, aimed at the closest of them, and let a bolt fly. The crossbow thrummed. He heard a sharp whine, saw the asir stumble, but it was up again a moment later. The crossbow kicked as he squeezed the second trigger. The asir whined again, its speed flagging, while the other two galloped past it.

Along the bottom of the skiff, Ramahd's body was beginning to thrash. *Mighty Alu,* Cicio thought as he drew his shamshir, *hurry, Ramahd, or we won't live to see the sunrise.*

Ramahd feels the shaft sticking out of his chest.

He touches it with one hand, and through it feels Meryam's will, feels the focus of her attention, which is on a skiff easing into motion along the

Haddah. He feels those to whom she is bonded. Hamzakiir is the strongest of them, but from Meryam's state of deep concentration he feels two Maidens as well, the wardens of their respective hands.

Meryam feels what they feel, hears what they hear. She passes orders to them and they obey. She is near the point of exhaustion, but is intent on finally capturing Ramahd, so much so that she can focus on little but that one place in Sharakhai, that one mission. In doing so she's let her guard down. Ramahd feels the ship's cabin in which she lay, staring at the beams running across the ceiling as she orchestrates things from some distant part of the Shangazi.

Ramahd feels for the threads. Mighty Alu, there are so many, and each is a silhouette in the night, making it nearly impossible to tell them apart. The more time he wastes, the more likely the Maidens and Hamzakiir will have them, but he can't afford be clumsy either. If Meryam gets even a hint of what he's doing, she'll know everything.

He grips the arrow shaft tighter, pulls it deeper into his chest. The pain becomes bright as a newborn star and nearly throws him from the dream, but he remains and more importantly is given what he needs. The pain is like a flash of lightning in the night. In that bright, momentary image, the bonded souls of Meryam's grand web are revealed, and Ramahd pinpoints the one he's searching for: Mateo Abrantes, his countryman, a vice admiral in the fleet whom he must free from Meryam's influence in order for the next part of his plan to work.

It isn't enough to expose Meryam to the Kings of Sharakhai. Do that and she will likely retain Qaimir's throne despite her crimes. No, he needs allies in Qaimir too, and the way to them is through Mateo and Duke Hektor.

For Ramahd, dispelling magic is simple enough. It is akin to the slice of a knife. The swing of a sword. But the *altering* of a spell is something altogether different. With Mateo, he's dealing with a spell Meryam already forged between them. It allowed her to know his whereabouts, to communicate with him, to dominate his mind and body if need be. For Mateo to regain free will without Meryam's suspecting, he cannot mindlessly cut the spell in two. He needs to unweave it, leaving the threads of the spell intact, then make it anew.

As he begins the delicate process, Mateo's silhouette dims, and Ramahd is forced to pull on the shaft of the black arrow once more. The pain makes him careless. For several, heart-pounding moments, he's drawn to the Haddah. He sees the skiff through his own eyes and is certain he's ruined it all.

But then his gaze shifts. He sees the skiff flying along the Haddah through *Hamzakiir's* eyes. Sees the asirim giving chase. One nears and leaps high into the air, ready to fall upon Davud, but before it can it strikes a magical shield that flares to life in a burst of azure light. As Hamzakiir urges his horse into a gallop and casts his own spell to shatter the magical shield, Ramahd regains himself and the scene fades.

As quickly as he dares, Ramahd continues, tugging at the threads of the spell until they're free. Then, just as Fezek's mother did with the ribbons and reeds of her baskets, he begins the process of remaking the design.

When the vision fades, Ramahd pulls the arrow deeper into his chest, this time with both hands. Searing pain runs through him, and with it the bright flash of lightning. He sees the Maidens on their horses as they near the skiff. Sees Cicio, one hand on the tiller, firing more bolts from his crossbow at the galloping asirim.

As the brightness fades, Ramahd sees Mateo. This is the last time he'll be able to do it; Meryam's curiosity is rising and she'll surely investigate if he tries it again.

So on he weaves, reworking the threads of Meryam's bond, pulling them just so until the weave is tight. The design is still intact, but it's different now, the spell rendered almost useless. From a distance it will be indistinguishable from the previous spell, or so Ramahd hopes. Assuming that's true, Mateo will awaken from the compulsion Meryam has over him. And when he does, he'll return to Alu's temple in Sharakhai, and Meryam will be none the wiser.

Done at last, Ramahd rips the arrow from his chest.

Cicio guided the skiff around a bend in the river. They were well into the Shallows and taking a bend, one of several that cut snakelike through the city's poor western quarter. The skiff, powered by a gale Davud had summoned, was moving faster than a prized akhala. It bucked and twisted and shifted in the wind, and it was all Cicio could do to keep it on course.

He had no idea how they'd made it this far. Davud had summoned a great wind to propel the craft at breakneck speeds, and two of the asir had still caught up to them, but over and over they'd been rebuffed by the wild, bright spells cast by the two magi.

The Blade Maidens had quickly joined the asir on their black horses. Each bore a bow, which they used with frightening speed to send a steady rain of arrows against the skiff. The shield had been proof against the first volleys, but then one of the Maidens had given a sharp whistle. An order, though what it might mean he had no idea—not until a split-second later, when the next arrow came speeding in. A great shattering pattern appeared as if the domed shield were made not of arcane energy, but cerulean glass.

Esmeray let out a yelp, not from being struck by the arrow, Cicio realized, but from the shield breaking. The only thing that had saved her from the arrow was that in piercing the shield its path had been altered, forcing it to bite harmlessly into the wooden hull.

More arrows followed. Each produced another bright flash and a rent in the shield. Each made Esmeray grunt as she gritted her teeth and concentrated harder to keep the spell alive. They were hypnotic, those blue, spitfire flashes, and nearly made Cicio lose control of the skiff when the starboard ski thudded over a massive rock he hadn't been able to see. When one of the arrows struck the gunwales, he pulled it out and saw that it was tipped with black. Ebon steel, he realized, able to pierce Esmeray's magic where mundane steel could not.

Arrow after arrow came homing in on Esmeray as the Maidens' deadly aim adjusted to the effects of the magical shield. But Esmeray was smart. She adjusted the shield, altering the angle. Eventually, however, there were simply too many. One sunk into the meat of her thigh; another grazed her shoulder.

Just then Davud adjusted the wind. They were already outdistancing the horses, so he could afford time to force the wind toward their enemies. It scoured the riverbed, and struck with such force that the asirim were picked up and blown toward the bank and several of the horses toppled. The other horses were spooked. They slowed and shook their heads or reared as the wind tore at exposed skin and eyes and nostrils.

A mountain of dust had already been lifted, but Davud shifted the wind again, drawing it toward them to cover their passage. Cicio continued to guide the skiff, but peered beyond the cloud for the greatest danger: Hamzakiir on his silver akhala. Unlike the Blade Maidens, he hadn't taken the path down to the riverbed. He'd ridden along the riverside instead.

Cicio saw no sign of Hamzakiir, however, and the sounds of pursuit faded. They'd been fortunate thus far, all things considered, but Cicio knew it couldn't last. Davud was tired. Esmeray was bleeding. And Ramahd had yet to wake. They were nearing the point where they had to pull off their final trick or lose themselves to the Blade Maidens. Cicio lifted his loose, straw-filled effigy into place beside him. Davud did the same with his, tying it in place with the twine they'd prepared earlier so that it looked like someone was slumped over the side of the gunwales. He leaned Esmeray's into the crook at the ship's prow before helping her with the arrow in her thigh.

The fourth simulacrum they left lying beside Ramahd. But Ramahd himself . . . Mighty Alu, he said it wouldn't take long. Every moment since Ramahd had spasmed had given Cicio hope he was waking. But Ramahd had only continued to moan, to curl his shoulders as if he'd been struck in the chest—his hands even moved there as if grasping an arrow shaft—but he still wasn't awake.

Davud pulled the arrow out of Esmeray's thigh and cauterized the wound with one glowing finger. Esmeray sucked air through her teeth each time he touched her skin, but to her credit didn't cry out from the pain. The skiff neared the final bend before heading east toward the city's ancient inner walls. Their plan depended on their abandoning the skiff.

"No time left," Davud said, echoing Cicio's thoughts.

Cicio looked back to the great cloud of dust. He could just hear the sound of galloping horses over the wind. An asir howled, making Cicio's skin crawl. After one last look at Ramahd, he nodded. "Very well," he said, and tied the tiller into position.

With Davud's help, Cicio lifted Ramahd and held him tight along the port gunwales. Other than a few light twitches, Ramahd was a dead weight. Cicio levered his legs over and did his best to take the drop gently and to cushion Ramahd's fall, but the craft was still moving at great speed and they fell hard. Despite the two thick shirts he wore, the skin along his back and shoulders felt like a grater was being taken to them. The pain flared a moment later. The thick cloth of his trousers were torn and his hip took a nasty cut along the stones. But it could have been worse, and Ramahd hadn't sustained much more than deep scrapes along his cheek and forehead.

Davud followed and was similarly awkward in his landing. Esmeray, meanwhile, had remained in the skiff. She moved about the craft, touching each of the effigies. Something inside their chests glowed red, flaring like a windblown ember before fading to nothing. As she touched the one at the rear, Cicio felt his heart trip, felt a sympathetic heartbeat pick up inside the crude form at the tiller.

The last one complete, Esmeray leapt from the skiff. She crouched as she landed, arms spread wide to balance herself, and somehow managed to keep her feet as she came to a skidding halt.

Then the four of them were off, Cicio and Esmeray carrying Ramahd between them while Davud used the wind to shift the angle of the skiff so that it continued along the riverbed toward the dark, looming line of the old city walls. He caught up to them just as they were maneuvering Ramahd up the bank and behind an old, overturned apple cart. Moments later, the Blade Maidens and their horses burst from the cloud of dust like death's servants.

Onward they galloped, hunting the skiff, the asirim bounding and baying in their wake. All knew the Blade Maidens could follow one's heart, likely the asirim could as well, which was precisely why Esmeray had cast her spell over the effigies, one that mimicked their heartbeats while masking their true hearts.

As the dark silhouettes of the Maidens and asirim dwindled, Ramahd finally stirred. He groaned and his head lolled. He opened his eyes and took in his surroundings, clearly confused. He stared down at his chest, at the spot his hands had been clutching, then took in Cicio with a weak smile.

"It's done," he croaked.

"Remain quiet, my lord," Cicio replied in Qaimiran. "We're nearly safe."

Indeed, as they headed into the cramped streets of the Shallows, Cicio was amazed that they'd somehow succeeded. But that was when he heard it, a soft patter against the ground behind them.

He turned just in time to see one of the asir, the smallest of them, barreling into his chest. He was thrown backward onto the dry ground and took a bite to one shoulder, a rake of claws to his chest and neck. The ravenous face of an emaciated child was inches from his own, its lips pulled back to reveal yellowed teeth glistening in the darkness, slick with his own blood.

Its strength was incredible. He couldn't fight it.

But then, Alu be praised, it was being lifted off him. Not by Davud, nor Esmeray, but by Fezek the ghul. The asirim hissed and cut at him, tore his bluish skin, but Fezek seemed not to care. With his own inhuman strength he slammed the asir down onto the dusty street then stomped on its head with a crunch. It twitched once, then went still.

They were just turning up a street when they heard hooves, saw a tall silver akhala enter the street ahead. Hamzakiir, in his guise as King Kiral, sat high in the saddle, the silver sword, Sunshearer, held easily in one hand.

"Perhaps I should have remained at home," Fezek said in his reedy voice. Then he picked up a massive wooden beam from the pile of a partially collapsed structure and loped toward the King.

Bright orange flame whipped from Hamzakiir's hand and struck Fezek in the leg. His leg shattered and he fell.

"Oh, *great*!" Fezek shouted, not in pain or surprise, but heartfelt annoyance.

A black serpent of potent magic flew from Esmeray's hands toward Hamzakiir. He cut it in two with Sunshearer. He did the same with next, and the next. By then Esmeray had fallen to one knee, her magic spent. Cicio stared, unsure what to do. Ramahd, recovered at last, broke away from Cicio, but halted when he saw what was happening.

Hamzakiir was staring intently at Davud. And Davud, in turn, was staring back. Either could have cast a spell and launched it at the other, but neither did. Some unspoken agreement seemed to pass between them. What it might be, and what might have caused it, Cicio had no idea.

Davud, never taking his eyes from Hamzakiir, waved for them to continue down the street without him. "Go."

Cicio wasn't about to question it. He went to pick up Fezek, and Ramahd helped. Together with Esmeray, they did as Davud had instructed. They moved slowly, warily down the street, gazes alternating between Hamzakiir on his tall horse and Davud, who looked like a hero from ages past, Bahri Al'sir orchestrating another of his famous escapes.

Hamzakiir glanced at them only once. He looked confused, a man lost. When they turned the next corner and Davud rejoined them, the clopping of the silver akhala's hooves resumed, fading until they were swallowed by the night.

Chapter 43

IHSAN SAT IN A SIMPLE WOODEN chair in a cell beneath Eventide. Nearby, in his usual position in the corner, was Zeheb, their fallen King of Whispers. Blankets covered the walls, three layers of carpets were lain across the floor—protections meant to save Zeheb from himself when he slipped into one of his fits.

King Beşir, leaning against the wall near the door, sniffed loudly. Arms crossed over his chest, an air of impatience on his drawn face, he looked like a particularly well dressed shisha den tough. "Can't we hurry this along?"

Ihsan glanced up, allowing a bit of his annoyance to show through. "I don't know if you recall, but sifting through the whispers took him plenty of time even when he was sane." Still, they *had* been at it a while. He snapped his fingers before Zeheb's eyes. "Are you searching for him, Zeheb? Have you found King Emir?"

Zeheb, wearing only night clothes, sat with his legs pulled up to his chest, rocking back and forth like a child who'd become lost and had given up on ever being found. His cheeks were sunken, his eyes lifeless. With fully half his former bulk gone, his skin hung in drapes, which made Ihsan wonder whether Zeheb's dispassion for food and drink would eventually do Ihsan's work for him.

Over the past several weeks, another King, usually Beşir but sometimes Cahil or Sukru, had joined Ihsan to oversee his interrogations. It was tacit admission of Kiral's distrust of Ihsan. The most surprising thing about it wasn't that Kiral had taken this measure, but that he'd started doing it only after Meryam had become his wife.

"Come, Zeheb." Ihsan allowed a trickle of power to leak into his words. "We need to find where King Emir is before the attack begins."

It was a tricky balance, these interrogations. He could easily have used more power, but he couldn't have this burbling brook of a man speaking too openly. To be sure, he needed Zeheb to say *something*—he didn't want the other Kings to suspect he wasn't trying, after all—but there was real danger in it. Zeheb knew too many of Ihsan's secrets, which was of course the reason Ihsan had pushed him over the edge into madness in the first place. The more power Ihsan used, the more lucid Zeheb became, and the more lucid he became, the more likely he was to say something Ihsan would come to regret. So he kept his power to a minimum, if he used it at all, when others were here to witness it.

"Zeheb, tell me where King Emir can be found."

Zeheb mumbled, his head rocking against the thick padding affixed to the wall, his eyes distant, his lips quavering. Something about stone and sand and darkness. And noise. "*Hissing. Kissing. A thousand hearts missing.*"

Beşir frowned. "Why, after decades of threats from his father, would Emir choose to attack now?" Despite the man's skill at dealing death, Beşir was not often given to violence, but just then he looked like he was ready to push himself off the wall and beat the answers from Zeheb.

King Emir was the son of Surrahdi, the Mad King of Malasan. Surrahdi had died, apparently of natural causes, just a few months ago. For years the Mad King had professed a desire to snatch the Amber Jewel from the Kings of Sharakhai—never to Ihsan's face, of course, never to *any* of the Kings, but the rumors in Samaril, their capital, were rife. There had been several times over the past decades when Ihsan had been sure an attack was imminent. Their spies and informants had confirmed as much. But the invasions had never materialized.

None would admit it, but the Kings of Sharakhai had all breathed a sigh of relief upon learning of Surrahdi's death. After the news had arrived, they'd thought their eastern border safe, at least for a time. King Emir wasn't shy about wielding the power of the throne, but he'd inherited only a portion of his dead father's truculence. Which made Beşir's question a good one. Why now, only *after* the Mad King's death, had they found the nerve to invade?

"It may be as simple as Mirea choosing to invade as well," Ihsan reasoned. "They didn't want to see the city taken by another power. Or we might look no further than blood. Emir might have believed invasion was the only way to uphold his father's legacy."

Beşir's long face grew longer. "Perhaps, but their own borders are not secure. They're in the midst of a five-year drought. From all you've said, Emir seems a reasonable young man—a pragmatist, I think you said of him once. Why would he risk so much on this gamble?"

"We may be giving them too much credit," Ihsan replied. "They may be interested in sacking the city before the stronger force from Mirea arrives."

"A move that might help see them through the next year or two, but which would harm their prospects of trade for decades to come."

"No doubt you're right," Ihsan said. "Who can say what the mind of the young king might hold?"

Beşir's eyes grew flinty. "I daresay our chief diplomat might."

Ihsan knew he needed to take care lest Beşir fly into another of his rages, a thing he'd become famous for since killing his own daughter in front of Yerinde and all of Sharakhai. "Alas, I've shared all I can on the matter." He jutted his chin toward Zeheb. "Perhaps if I'm allowed to work alone with our friend here, we might get the answers we seek."

Beşir flung a hand at Zeheb. "Can't you *make* him make sense?"

"Were his mind whole, yes." Ihsan put on a look of regret while staring into Zeheb's ceaselessly moving eyes. "But like this, we're lucky to get as much as we are . . ."

"Then let's give him to Cahil again."

"Are you forgetting how badly it went when we tried?" It had been a huge relief to Ihsan when Cahil had got nothing. Zeheb's ravings had only become worse and more unintelligible.

"Well, we have to do something!"

"We are."

With a terrible grimace, Beşir pushed himself off the wall and thrust one long, dextrous finger at Zeheb. "I lost Kara over this!" His face, already flush, had turned a deep shade of red.

Beşir hadn't, in fact, lost Kara over their inability to get straight answers from Zeheb, nor their attempts at learning more about King Emir, but Ihsan kept those thoughts to himself. "Yes," he said calmly, "so let's honor her memory and do this right."

Beşir rolled one shoulder, working it slowly. He'd taken the healing elixirs—more than was prudent given how few of them remained—yet the wound he'd taken from Çedamihn's sword was still not fully healed. No one was certain why. Although, Çeda's heritage being what it was, Ihsan had a few guesses.

Beşir stared at Zeheb a long while, then spun and opened the cell door. "Just hurry up about it, will you?" He left, slamming the door behind him.

As his footsteps faded, Ihsan returned his attention to Zeheb, who was whispering more loudly than before. "Now," Ihsan said, putting more of himself into his words, "what have you found, my old friend?"

His words felt blunt as an old plowshare. It happened. He'd learned as much centuries ago while exploring the limits of his newfound ability. At first, those under his power had simply done what he'd said, but the more he used it, the more effort he'd needed to put into the commands. Eventually it became a battle his mind and body waged in concert. He would shiver and sweat as though suffering a fever. And then it simply stopped working, forcing him to end his experiments in a rather ruthless, though not altogether unexpected, manner.

It was the second reason Ihsan used his power sparingly on Zeheb. The slow and steady accretion of resistance was real. For years, Ihsan had been funneling resources, information, and money to the Moonless Host, all with an eye toward weakening the other Kings. Zeheb didn't know all of it, but he knew more than enough to send Ihsan to the gibbet. The day Ihsan could no longer control him was the day the chances of Zeheb revealing something damning increased exponentially. Soon, Ihsan knew, he would need to end this, but that time had not yet come. Zeheb might still prove useful.

Zeheb mumbled, his eyes flitting to and fro as if he were caught in a fever dream. At first Ihsan couldn't tell what he was saying. And then he realized Zeheb wasn't speaking Sharakhan. He was speaking Malasani. *"Flawless, modest, goddess."*

"Which goddess?" Ihsan asked. "Nalamae?" None of the other desert goddesses could be described as modest. He hoped Zeheb might have stumbled on a clue to Yerinde's plans. But it mightn't be a desert god at all. It might be one of Malasan's gods. "Is it Ranrika? Or Tamtamiin?"

At this Zeheb's eyes lit up. He turned toward Ihsan with a look of perfect clarity. "Her tenets are being kept."

"Whose?"

"They are not befouled."

"Whose, Zeheb? Tamtamiin's?" She was an androgynous god who shifted between man and woman at whim. She was the goddess of love and compassion and empathy. "Has someone broken her faith?" Ihsan asked.

"They are *not* broken!"

"No," Ihsan said, not understanding what was happening, nor who Zeheb was speaking to, but unwilling to let the opportunity pass him by. "But some are saying it."

"Who? Who? Tell me who they are and they'll lose their heads." Zeheb's eyes went glassy and his voice went soft. *"Tell me, spell me, fell me."*

Ihsan tried to ask more, but Zeheb only continued to whisper, and Ihsan was soon forced to give up. It was odd, this episode. Not only had Zeheb echoed someone's thoughts clearly, Ihsan had conversed with them *through* Zeheb. To Ihsan's knowledge it had never happened before.

Interesting, the phrase he'd used. *Lose their heads.* There were plenty who might say that in jest, but Zeheb had seemed deadly serious about it. Only a few might use it in such a manner. And given that Ihsan had told him to search for King Emir, and that Zeheb had spoken in Malasani, had Zeheb been speaking for the Malasani king?

Ihsan left and returned to the halls of Eventide, climbing its interminable stairs until he reached a veranda that overlooked the eastern and southern reaches of Sharakhai. He squinted at the brightness of the vivid blue sky, which was stippled with clouds that seemed to glow from within. Kings Sukru, Cahil, Beşir, and Nayyan, wearing her disguise as Azad, were speaking with one another. King Kiral, standing with his hands on the stone railing, stared out over the southern reaches of the desert, where the Mala-sani fleet was arrayed.

In the courtyard below, wagons were arriving with supplies for the feast that would take place that night. It felt strange to be celebrating Beht Re-vahl, the night the Kings defeated the last of the wandering tribes, but it would be even stranger not to. The desert's observances must be maintained after all, perhaps now more than ever. Abandoning them would be akin to spitting in the face of the gods, a thing none of the Kings, even Ihsan, would dare to do.

He joined the other Kings and their vizirs and viziras, and confessed his inability to learn much of anything from Zeheb. They'd hoped to find King Emir and notify the commander of the Silver Spears before their attack began, but it wouldn't happen today. Kiral looked disappointed, Sukru groused and Cahil sneered, but they let it pass. The Blade Maidens and Silver Spears stood ready in any case. They'd made their plans for any number of points of attack from the Malasani fleet, though right now they felt Husamettín's loss most keenly. The man was inflexible as granite, but Ihsan knew of no better strategist.

By and large, they were now waiting for King Emir to tip his hand. The city could withstand an attack for weeks, perhaps even months, but they counted on reinforcements from Qaimir well before then, and more from Kundhun. If Meryam and the royal navy could stave off Queen Alansal and her fleet to the north, then things would be looking up for Sharakhai once more.

Ihsan noted how strangely Nayyan was acting. In her natural form, the one she always wore in the privacy of Ihsan's palace, she showed signs of carrying their child. Those signs might be masked now—hidden by the magic of the necklace that transformed her into the likeness of Azad—but the child was still there. Nayyan could feel her, she'd told him more than once, and she was still affected by the mood swings that came with bearing a child. The explanation might be as simple as that, Ihsan thought, but he suspected not.

Before he could get her alone to ask about it, everyone's attention was drawn eastward.

"They're moving," Cahil said.

From this vantage Ihsan could see them, the Malasani fleet closing in. It looked like the desert had come alive.

"You look like you've stumbled upon your own grave," Nayyan was saying.

Ihsan's fingers had begun to tingle. The vision of the moving desert . . . The fleet sailing closer . . . "King Kiral," he spoke numbly, lost in the words of the journal that had inspired this vision. He could see King Yusam's journal, could see Yusam's script clearly. He just couldn't recall which journal it was.

Kiral turned to him.

"I need to review Yusam's journals." When Kiral stared at him dumbly, he said, "The Blue Journals."

Yusam recorded many of his visions in journals, placing those he thought most crucial to the success of the Kings into journals with blue covers. Ihsan had once had free access to them, until Kiral had ordered them taken to Eventide.

Except Kiral looked as if he had no idea what Ihsan was talking about.

Beşir swept into the silence. "Why do you need them?" His long face was dour and displeased, as if he'd been left out of some important secret.

When Ihsan paused, Kiral seemed to recover himself. "One of the passages you read," he said carefully, "it relates to this day?"

"It does." The importance of the moment was crawling over Ihsan's skin like a host of insects. "It mentioned ships sailing toward Sharakhai"—he waved toward the Malasani fleet—"exactly as we see before us."

Kiral seemed lost, perhaps waging the same sort of internal battle that so often plagued him of late. Finally he waved toward the palace. "Go. Tell us what you learn."

Ihsan wasted no time—he sprinted into the palace, making for Kiral's library. Each passing moment made it feel like their fate was being sealed. Something big was about to happen. Something crucial to the future of Sharakhai and, more importantly, to the Kings' place in it.

After gaining access to the room with the Blue Journals, he pulled out a dozen he thought likely to contain the passage in question, and found it after a short search. Yusam's description of a fleet sailing slowly toward Sharakhai.

This was an important vision in and of itself, one that might advise them on the course of the coming battle, but it was also a precursor to another event. Yusam had said as much in the marginalia. He had written often about how the strongest of his visions were not major turning points in the fate of Sharakhai, but rather, *precursors* to other major events, and it was up to him to find the related possibilities and decide what might be done to either prevent it or ensure that it happened, depending on the favorability of the outcome.

Running his finger quickly down the margins, Ihsan found the mention of the other journal. As he'd suspected, it was one of those he'd had copied only to have that copy, and three others, turn up missing. A thorough search of the palace had ensued—Ihsan had even used his power to ensure he had the truth from those likeliest to know what had happened—to no avail. No one had been able to tell him where the journals had gone. A theft in his own palace, though why anyone else would be interested in a handful of Yusam's journals, he couldn't say.

He retrieved the referenced journal and flipped through its pages. His fingers couldn't turn them fast enough. He read through the account of a vision of Eventide, which mentioned passages deep underground. It spoke of a fallen King. Of the drawing of dark blades. Of a chase and a bird of prey preparing to attack. In the margins, Yusam had written: *A kestrel?*

The fallen King was clearly Sehid-Alaz, who, after Husamettín's capture, had been moved to Eventide. Near the end of the passage, Yusam mentioned a woman in a blue dress running along a stone wall. She was described as being young and pretty with piercing eyes, and a dark halo surrounded her: the shadow of the kestrel. Several other women, also dressed in blue, ran alongside her, but Yusam was careful to note that the kestrel's shadow always followed the first woman, whose dress shifted to white the longer she ran. *She had a conniving look about her,* Yusam had written, *not unlike a desert fox.*

A fox, Ihsan thought, *or a maned wolf.*

Curiously, the account mentioned the kestrel opening its mouth, as if to release a cry, but nothing came out. Ihsan had read enough of these accounts to know that the effect said something about the kestrel, a limitation of some sort, most likely. Her voice was silenced. *Does she die?* Ihsan wondered.

Then came a mention of a silent observer, a woman cloaked in shadow and holding a pair of knives. *At the base of a hill, she stands in darkness,* the passage read, *though a corona surrounds her belly.*

"Oh, gods, no," Ihsan whispered, immediately knowing to whom that line referred.

Then Ihsan came to the last line. He read it twice, and felt his face go pale.

After slapping the journals closed, he replaced them on the shelves and sprinted for the dungeons.

Chapter 44

ALONG THE HALLS OF EVENTIDE, Çeda pushed a cart stacked with crates of lemons, herbs, and dates. Ahead of her, Sümeya pushed a similar cart piled high with bags of rice. They were two of a dozen servants heading toward the kitchens. The carts' wooden wheels clattered along, adding to the general din as hundreds of cooks, servants, and entertainers prepared for the coming feast. Somewhere, a choir of children practiced, their sweet voices echoing through palace.

Like all the women in the train of carts, Çeda and Sümeya wore plain woolen dresses dyed robin's egg blue. The white hats covering their hair, foreheads, and chins completed a look that was, to put it mildly, unattractive. Which was perfect, of course. The more plain their garb, the more they blended in. Çeda's only regret was that the hats had no veils. Few had ever seen her or Sümeya's face, but that did little to quell Çeda's fears. It felt as though someone would point to the two of them at any moment and cry, "Traitors! Traitors in our midst!"

Çeda's buckler was strapped around her waist, River's Daughter along her back, its hilt resting snugly between her shoulder blades. Like Sümeya, the shamshir's length was hidden not only by the folds of her oversized dress and the thickness of the fabric itself, but by the long tail hanging from her cumbersome hat.

As they neared the kitchens, Çeda scanned the hall for Kameyl, who'd snuck away to find Sehid-Alaz nearly an hour ago. The palace chef, a stick of a man with a frayed mop of black hair on his head, was just exiting the kitchens with a group of six Blade Maidens in tow. They walked confidently by his side, especially their warden, a woman Çeda would never fail to recognize. It was Yndris, the daughter of King Cahil, a woman Çeda had nearly killed, and would have had she not been saved by her father's store of healing elixirs.

A hand of Maidens was typically five, but here was a sixth wearing a rust-colored dress and turban that were of slightly different design from the Blade Maidens'. Çeda had never seen one before, but she'd heard of them. She was one of the bloody nine, King Zeheb's Kestrels, his highly trained assassins.

Çeda breathed a sigh of relief as they headed toward the feasting hall en masse, the chef relaying the food he was serving, which servants would be attending the Kings, and so on. Çeda and Sümeya followed the others into the kitchen and unloaded their carts, but instead of filing out with the others, Çeda pulled Sümeya aside.

Around them swirled a mad press of cooks, assistants, worktables with piled ingredients, hanging pots and pans, and serving dishes of every imaginable size. The sound of chopping, of clanging and pounding, of orders being called, filled the hot air, which was laced heavily with the scents of garlic, mint, thyme, and lemon. On the far wall was a wide hearth with several coal fires glowing fitfully within. Hanging from hooks or set onto iron grates were a dozen iron pots of varying sizes. One was a massive stock pot, big as a wine barrel. A rotund woman in a stained apron was standing beside it, sliding diced carrots from a cutting board into the roiling broth.

"We can't give Kameyl more time," Çeda said. "The wagons are nearly empty." There was no telling were the chef might assign them next.

Sümeya stared beyond the hearth to the corner, where an archway led to the servant's quarters. Kameyl had gone through it on her winding way toward the dungeons.

After considering briefly, Sümeya nodded. "Let's go."

They were just heading across the kitchen together when Kameyl strode through the very same archway, pushing the food cart she'd left with ahead of her. The shelf's top cart was empty save for a layer of burlap, which hung over the sides, completely obscuring the lower shelf. Seeing them standing there, Kameyl nodded once, then stopped the cart near a chopping block where two young cooks worked feverishly with cleavers, reducing a mountain of red onions to dice. The cooks gave Kameyl no more than a glance as she swept the pile of peelings onto the cart, then headed grim-faced along the kitchen's central aisle toward Çeda and Sümeya.

Çeda turned, ready to head for the kitchen's exit, only to be met by the mop-haired chef, who bulled his way past Çeda and Sümeya, heading straight for Kameyl. Placing himself in Kameyl's path, forcing her to stop the cart, he put his hands on his hips and spread his legs wide. "And just where have *you* been? I do your lord a *favor* by taking you on, and this is how I'm repaid?" He leaned forward and sniffed the air while peering into Kameyl's eyes. "Are you on the reek?" He stabbed a finger toward the archway she'd just come from. "Is that where you were? Having a smoke before coming back to work? Well I won't have it, I tell you. I won't have it!"

"Finding a place to relieve oneself isn't a crime," Sümeya said as she rushed in front of him, "nor is getting lost in a palace as big as this."

The chef's attention, however, had been taken by something else. With the hubbub of the kitchen playing out around him—everyone assiduously avoiding his gaze—he stared hard at the pile of onion leavings, then at the burlap curtains hiding the contents of the lower shelf. He made a move to grab the cloth, but Sümeya snatched his wrist and stopped him, at which point the chef, in a surprisingly energetic move, rolled his arm around hers and ripped his hand free. "Un*hand* me!"

Sümeya held her hands up in a placating gesture. "There's no need to become hysterical, my lord."

"Hysterical?" He grabbed the cart and yanked on it, but he may as well have been trying to take Bakhi's hammer from his bronze statue in the great hall. Kameyl was too strong for him, and kept the cart in place. "This is the most important night of my *life* and you're telling me not to become *hysterical?*"

They were all standing there, no one sure what to say next, when the burlap cloth bulged and two blackened, shriveled hands, bound at the wrist, fell out and slapped against the tiled floor. Several emaciated fingers twitched while the chef stared open-mouthed.

His cry of alarm was cut short when Sümeya shot a hand into his throat. As he ducked forward and began to emit wet choking sounds, Sümeya put her one arm around him. "My lord!" she cried, and began leading him away. "My lord, are you all right?"

While all eyes followed the chef, Çeda crouched and slipped Sehid-Alaz's bound hands back beneath the curtain. To this point, she'd felt nothing from him—a byproduct of the soporific Kameyl had given him to quell his madness—but now she felt a glimpse of emotion, a chaotic flash of light in the darkness.

By the gods, he was waking. *Please, my Lord King. Stay calm.*

But it was not to be. As Kameyl pushed the cart toward the kitchen's entrance, a long, low moan came from the bottom of the cart. A childish whine followed, a sound no one in Sharakhai would confuse with anything other than what it was: the call of an asir.

"Bakhi preserve us." The large woman in the apron was staring at the cart, backing slowly away. All around, looks of confusion were turning to fear.

The chef, meanwhile, had managed to stop coughing long enough to point at Çeda and Kameyl and rasp, "Take them!"

Çeda thought he was talking to the cadre of cooks and servants, but when they all rushed toward the edges of the room, it left a clear path along the kitchen's central aisle, revealing a woman clothed in black, her face veiled, her eyes wide and angry.

It was Yndris.

To me! she whistled sharply, summoning her fellow Blade Maidens.

"Go!" Çeda said, and shoved Kameyl back toward Sümeya.

As two more Maidens appeared in the doorway behind Yndris, Çeda ran to the massive stock pot, grabbed a meathook from a hanging rack, and used it to pull on the pot's lip. With a great heave, she hauled the pot off its iron grate.

All turned to madness as it tipped it onto the floor with a bang, disgorging its contents across the room. The cooks and assistants all scrambled away, hoping to avoid being scalded by the boiling soup. They crowded Yndris and the other Blade Maidens, preventing them from advancing.

Kameyl, meanwhile, turned the cart around and rushed it through the archway tunnel. Sümeya and Çeda followed, but Sümeya came to a halt as soon as they were out of sight. She drew her shamshir, then ripped her dress along the side and pulled out her buckler as well. "Go on," she said. "The hallway cuts around and exits close to the feasting hall. Make your way from there to the wagons."

It took every ounce of will Çeda had to obey the order, but she did. She caught up to Kameyl, and the two of them rushed the cart along the hallway. No sooner had they turned the corner than the sound of steel rang loudly behind them.

By the time they reached the central hall, the palace had devolved into a hornet's nest. Servants fled the sound of battle. Silver Spears rushed toward the kitchens in the wake of the Blade Maidens. Beside Çeda, Kameyl put on a good show, glancing over her shoulder in dismay. Çeda didn't have to act to look worried. She was deathly afraid Sümeya would be overwhelmed, but they'd all agreed that getting Sehid-Alaz out was the most important thing.

Passing through the palace's grand entrance, they reached the courtyard. Their path to Melis and the wagon she guarded was blessedly clear. Çeda and Kameyl were dragging the cart as quickly as they could across the gravel when another long moan came from beneath the cart.

"Please, my Lord King," Çeda whispered to him, "cry no more."

But it did no good. He wailed louder, and it was no longer pitiable, but filled with bile and anger and spite.

"We're taking you to safety," she added. "We're taking you to our people."

But her pleas had no effect. His mind was a swirling maelstrom of fear and anger and an overriding desire to obey the will of the Kings. He struggled even more, straining against his bonds. His wail grew until it made Çeda want to curl up like a sick child. She tried to strengthen their bond that she might calm him, but it had precisely the opposite effect. The onslaught of his raw hunger made her nostrils flare, made her lips pull back in a terrible grimace. He wasn't fully awake yet, she realized. He was still dreaming, and the only thing Çeda could think of to help was to draw him back down toward darkness.

Ahead, Melis had climbed onto the back of a wagon. Clothed similarly in a blue servant's dress, she made it look as though she were backing away from the moaning asir in a bid for safety. The driver, buying it completely, leapt onto the bed, drawing his knife as if to protect her, which was precisely when Melis leaned into him and gave him a mighty shove off the wagon.

"Hey!" he cried as he tumbled to the ground.

Melis took up the reins while Çeda lifted Sehid-Alaz and bore his awkward, loose-limbed weight onto the wagon bed. Çeda crawled beside her King and whispered "Shhhh," into his ear. A long groan escaped him. She could feel his madness fighting her, but when she imagined sand blowing through an adichara grove, and summoned up the rattle-leaf sound of the wind through the branches, he quieted and went still.

Kameyl had drawn her shamshir and buckler from inside her dress. And just in time. She lifted her buckler, blocking an arrow with a sharp *ting* as it came streaking toward Çeda. She sidestepped another and ducked a third as a squad of Silver Spears came rushing across the courtyard toward the wagon. The Kestrel, running with a spear hoisted up over one shoulder, ran alongside them, a blood-drenched raven among a flock of doves.

Just as the wagon was pulling away, the Kestrel threw her spear, which flew through the rear wheel's spokes, splashed the gravel, and struck deep into the ground. With the spear's haft caught between the spokes and the rear axle, it stalled the wagon's movement. Kameyl wasted no time. She lifted her sword with both hands and with an almighty roar brought it down against the haft, shearing it in two.

The wagon lurched into motion and began building speed. As the clopping of the horses' hooves filled the courtyard, Sümeya, still clad in her blue servant's dress, burst from a tower and sprinted along the wall walk. Giving chase were three Blade Maidens and a squad of Silver Spears. Çeda watched in awe as Sümeya, in a fearless move, leapt between the battlements and launched herself beyond the wall.

Melis whipped the horses harder and sent them careening around the curve that would lead them to the barbican. Arrows came streaking in from the Silver Spears stationed atop the wall. One clanged loudly off Kameyl's shield. Others whipped over Çeda's head. Then she saw an archer aiming for Sehid-Alaz. Çeda tried to block it, but the arrow was too swift and punched deep into Sehid-Alaz's chest.

Sehid-Alaz's jaundiced eyes went wide. His mouth became a perfect circle, revealing his red mouth, his boneyard of teeth. A wail of surprise and pain escaped him. It grew in intensity, so loud it rattled her bones. Fear and madness coursed through her—a small window into Sehid-Alaz's mind, though the knowledge did her little good. She curled onto the bed, her hands clamped over her ears as she devolved into primal, childlike terror.

The horses, thank the gods, galloped on, but as they passed beneath the barbican, the echoed sound became so intense Çeda found herself screaming along with Sehid-Alaz. The barbican shook. Cracks formed through the stones. Entire sections crumbled and fell. Pieces crashed onto the wagon bed. One as large as a mastiff came thundering down against the rear corner. The wood gave. Shards exploded outward, several piercing Çeda's left cheek and neck. A long sliver sunk into Kameyl's right forearm as she twisted away from the impact.

The entire wagon bucked and bounced, but luckily the wheels and axels held. On they flew, crossing the drawbridge and following the gentle curve that would lead them to the first of the switchbacks along King's Road.

Behind them, although the barbican continued to crumble, the rumbling was lessening now that Sehid-Alaz's long moan was finally coming to an end. A great cloud of dust billowed up and around it, obscuring the courtyard. Unfortunately, the way hadn't been completely blocked. As Melis was slowing down for the switchback, a dozen Silver Spears on horses emerged from the cloud of ivory dust.

Çeda's ears rang, a high-pitched remnant of Sehid-Alaz's scream, but above it she heard a bell tolling in Eventide, a warning to the other palaces and to the House of Maidens that enemies had been spotted. They weren't getting out, Çeda realized, not the way they'd planned. They'd hoped to pose as servants being sent to fetch more food for the feast, but that was impossible now, and the prospects of bulling their way through or climbing the walls had just become infinitely more difficult.

"Yah!" Melis called, whipping the horses as they pulled onto the long section of road ahead.

Behind them, the Silver Spears had just reached the switchback, but instead of following, they turned off the road and began riding down at a steep, dangerous angle, surely so they could cut off the wagon's escape from the road below. Soon they were among the scrub brush, and then lost from view entirely as the wagon followed a curve in the road.

Kameyl swung her sword up and pointed along the slope of the mountain to their left. "There she is!"

Dust rose along the slope in two places. One was from Sümeya as she careened down the mountain. Behind her, the Kestrel and three Blade Maidens gave chase, and it was clear they were catching up to her.

As they approached the switchback, Melis pulled hard on the reins. The horse's hooves skidded along the gravel. Sümeya burst through the brush along their left, her arms windmilling. Sümeya was bleeding heavily along her right side, and the Kestrel was right behind her. As the wagon careened past, Sümeya continued to run full tilt, then launched herself in a mighty leap up to the bed. Çeda caught her in a crash of bodies, halting her movement.

The Kestrel followed with long, powerful strides, then launched herself as Sümeya had. Kameyl moved to meet her, blocking the Kestrel's initial swing, but the Kestrel had planted one foot on the rear wagon wheel. Its spin and the Kestrel's speed launched her high into the air.

"Melis!" Çeda called, already on the move toward the front of the wagon.

But the Kestrel's target wasn't Melis. She soared beyond the driver's bench to land on the yoke between the rumps of the galloping horses. She pulled hard on the reins. Çeda whistled *danger, disengage* as both horses veered sharply right, enough that the wagon wheels were turned at an awkward angle.

Steel rims scraped against the road and the wagon skidded sideways, its momentum dragging the horses with it. The Kestrel jumped free moments before the front left wheel collapsed and the wagon tilted sharply.

Çeda tried to jump, but too late. She flew through the air while the horses screamed. Wood crashed thunderously against stone and gravel. The wagon tumbled along King's Road.

Çeda came down hard near the left side of the road, the rear of the twisting wagon narrowly missing her. She saw bodies flying, saw the horses being dragged by the wagon's momentum. She rolled and struck her head hard with a sound like breaking stone, then came to a skidding stop near the steep drop-off along the side of the road.

She sat up shakily, saw the Kestrel limping toward her over the dirt. The

Kestrel's armor had been torn badly along one leg and she walked with a pronounced limp, but otherwise seemed none the worse for the wear.

The earth is shaking, Çeda realized. *It's the horses. The cohort of Silver Spears.*

The Kestrel glanced their way: a wall of proud akhalas and soldiers in white. Çeda thought the Kestrel might wait for the Spears to arrive, to take Çeda and the others back up to Eventide for questioning, but instead she fixed her gaze on Çeda, her murderous intent plain.

Çeda reached for River's Daughter but found that it had been flung away during her fall. She reached for her knife instead, but was so dazed she didn't realize she was still wearing the blue servant's dress until her hand found only a simple belt of white silk at her waist.

"The Kings will suffer your traitorous presence no longer," the Kestrel said.

Just then an arrow struck her in the chest. She stared in confusion at the approaching Silver Spears as another arrow flew in, catching her through the left calf. Then the Kestrel was on the run, fleeing down the mountainside as more arrows chased her, and was soon lost in the wiry foliage.

Çeda turned, utterly confused as to why the Spears would have attacked their own. She had her answer a moment later. The front ranks of the Silver Spears spread wide, revealing a familiar-looking man dressed in the helm, armor, and livery of a Silver Spear. Çeda couldn't quite pin why, but he looked like he didn't belong in a uniform like that. He looked bloody awkward wearing it. It was only as he spurred his horse toward her that Çeda recognized him. Breath of the desert, it was King Ihsan, the Honey-tongued King.

Chapter 45

"HALT!" IHSAN CALLED, allowing power to leach into his voice.

Everyone around him—the Silver Spears on their horses, the three Maidens near the wagon, Çeda and her traitorous allies—froze. Even Sehid-Alaz, who had been twitching on the ground along the roadside, stilled. But not the Kestrel. She kept sprinting down the hillside as if she hadn't heard.

Because she hadn't, Ihsan knew. She was the same Kestrel who'd attacked him in the carpeted hall of Zeheb's palace. The one Zeheb had ordered deafened. Knowing the zealotry of those women, the Kestrel had probably done it to herself.

She kept running, hardly hampered by her wounds, and was quickly lost to the scrub brush. Hopefully she'd die on the mountainside, but Ihsan could spare her no more mind. The billowing dust from the destroyed barbican had hidden this exchange from nearly everyone in Eventide, but there was still much to do to see Çeda to safety and arrange a believable excuse for his absence.

He waved to the women who'd been thrown to the ground as the wagon tumbled. He saw who they were now. Sümeya, Melis, and Kameyl. "Lift

Sehid-Alaz," he said, and pointed to the rear of a nearby horse. "He'll ride with the captain. Mount the horses."

He had them wrap Sehid-Alaz with a blanket salvaged from the wagon and debated leaving Yndris and the other two Blade Maidens behind. He considered killing them as well. But it might be he could use them, so he decided they would all accompany him down the mountain.

Soon enough they were mounted and ready to ride. Ihsan was about to order their advance when he noticed Çeda staring south with a confused look on her face. Several of the Silver Spears were as well. He turned and saw something he couldn't quite understand at first. From this vantage, Sharakhai's southern harbor was laid bare. Many ships had already fled the city. Some remained, looking like forgotten husks in an ancient ruin. In the center of the harbor, near the tower and the complex of inner docks surrounding it, a cloud of dirty amber dust was rising.

A strange welling of fear bubbled up inside him. He wasn't even sure of the nature of it until he saw figures emerging from the cloud. Dark shapes, stark against the sun-bright sand. They flowed in a stream toward the outer docks and the city's streets. The wind shifted, revealing dozens, hundreds, emerging from what appeared to be a giant hole in the sand. *A tunnel. They'd somehow dug a tunnel all the way to the center of the bloody harbor.*

Zeheb's words returned to him. Sand and stone and darkness. *Hissing. Kissing. A thousand hearts missing.*

He'd been talking about the golems. From this distance, the harbor looked like a disturbed anthill, but these were no insects rushing to protect their home. This was an advance force meant to attack the city's inner defenses before they were ready.

Çeda, mounted with Sümeya behind her, stared intently at the conflict. "Golems," she said.

Ihsan knew it was true, but he knew how rare they were. They were considered sacred, a part of the one who'd granted them life through their hidden rituals. They had always been considered protectors, not aggressors, a belief Ihsan had once thought would never be forgotten or misused. Yet here were hundreds of them, attacking a foreign city. Already they were pressing along the quays, heading toward the Trough and the gates of the outer walls.

"Come," Ihsan said.

They pushed hard to reach the bottom of the mountain, thankfully seeing no sign of the Kestrel as they reached level ground and rode hard for the House of Maidens, which was busy but had few enough Maidens left inside its walls. They were met by a pair of Blade Maidens at the inner gates, but Yndris rode at their head and gave the story Ihsan had given her: that they'd been ordered down the mountain by King Kiral, that the Silver Spears were being sent to the battlefront, and the four servants accompanying them had been caught in an unfortunate accident and were being sent back to their lord in Goldenhill.

The two Maidens looked over the squad of Silver Spears. Their eyes passed over Ihsan without recognizing him, but they recognized Sümeya and Kameyl and Melis and Çeda. As their eyes widened, Ihsan said simply, "You will let us pass."

Their eyes glazed over and their postures relaxed. "Go on," one of them said to Yndris.

As they headed through the gates, Ihsan tarried and said to the two Maidens, "You'll remember the story you were told by Yndris and nothing more."

"Of course," they said.

Soon they were in the streets, where the complexion of the city had already changed. There were crowds near the House of Kings—it was Beht Revahl, after all—but they were starting to disperse. The most important thing now was to get Çeda and the others beyond the walls. Only then would he consider Yusam's vision safely circumvented. With the Malasani army arriving, no avenue to the south of the city was safe, and the western harbor would take them near to the Shallows, which Ihsan wasn't willing to risk. So when they reached the Wheel, he led them north.

The traffic in the street made way for them. Fear was plain on the faces of those they passed, but many looked to Ihsan and the rest with some small amount of hope. For the first time in a long while, Ihsan saw himself stripped of his power, wandering the city like a commoner, living a life as they lived it. He knew he had little conception of what their lives were truly like, but in that moment as he rode along the Trough, he felt the people's fear. Sharakhai was *his* city, and he'd always been confident that he could defend it. For the first time in many, many years, he was no longer sure.

One way or another, Sharakhai was about to change. Would Malasan take the city out from underneath him? Would they weaken the city's defenses while hardly lifting a finger? Or would the terrible visions King Yusam had seen in his mere, where Sharakhai and the land all around it had been laid to waste, come to pass?

They rode through the gates of the inner wall, which had been prepared for an attack but still stood open. As they neared the city's outer wall, its twin portcullises were just being lowered into place. *It keeps getting worse,* Ihsan thought. His decades, his centuries, of planning felt like they were unraveling in the course of an afternoon. *But what is there left to do but forge ahead?*

"Those on the capstan!" he called. "Halt!" And left his order at that.

The gate shuddered to a stop halfway down, and they rode through. They were committed to his ill-conceived plan now: get Çeda to the outskirts of Sharakhai. Get her and the others on a skiff. Or give them leave to ride their horses into the desert to the ship that surely awaited them. Then he could set about cleaning up his own mess.

Soon they reached the long curving quay that hugged the harbor's inner edge. In the distance, across the harbor's mouth, barricades and other fortifications had been set up and were being manned by dozens of Silver Spears. It was a way to blunt any attack while still allowing some few supply ships into the city before the war began in earnest. The barricades were just being pulled back to let a small caravan to leave. Three junks and a fat, three-masted uru led the way. At the rear, however, was a sleek ketch, which looked to be the swiftest among them.

"There." Ihsan looked to Yndris and pointed to the ketch. "Tell them you're commandeering the ship and give it to Çeda and the others."

"Of course, my lord."

They headed down a nearby ramp to the sand while Ihsan watched impatiently. He had to return to the House of Kings immediately. He'd started to formulate his rationale for being gone for so long, but it was imperfect and would need a lot of consideration before Kiral or, gods curse her, Meryam would believe him.

On the sand, Yndris reached the rear of the ketch and began speaking with the captain, who stood at the gunwales. The captain looked displeased, but nodded once when Yndris put her hand on her sword. But then there came a deep rumbling and a sound like the rattle of leaves over stone.

Ihsan stared at the sand. "Gods, no. Not here." He pulled at the reins and spun his akhala toward the ramp. "Not now."

He spurred his horse into a full gallop and saw what he had feared: clay heads lifting from the sand near the center of the harbor. They occupied a space that was little larger than a fighting pit, but more heads appeared as he watched. Shoulders and torsos rose. Arms swam as the golems' powerful legs brought them nearer to the surface.

Beyond the golems, Yndris and the rest had turned. Their horses skittered away, but their riders kept them under control. They weren't going to flee. Ihsan had given them an order, and they would continue until it had been obeyed, golems be damned.

Ihsan had to warn them away from the danger. He had to break the command he'd given them, at least until he could think of a new one.

He charged onward. "Get away!" he shouted. "Back away from the golems!"

But the sound! Bakhi's bright hammer, he'd never heard the like. The rumbling continued, but it was the strange hissing sound that made his ears itch, made his skin crawl, made him cringe. It was the sand, he knew. The sand and golems' ability to power their way through it.

A hundred golems had already reached the surface. The majority headed toward the city itself, where they would presumably try to batter down the gates. They had clay-colored skin with a metallic sheen. And their faces. It took him a moment, but Ihsan realized he knew that face. They wore the face of Surrahdi the Mad King of Malasan, but they were all of different ages. Some young. Some old. Some ancient, as Surrahdi had been when he died.

They weren't moving with any great speed, so Ihsan was able to skirt them easily while a new, desperate plan replaced the previous. He shouted and waved with one hand toward Yndris and the cohort of Silver Spears. "Attack them! Attack the golems!"

At the very least, they would slow down the golems enough for Çeda and the others to escape. If he was lucky, every last one of them would die, apparently sacrificing themselves for the good of Sharakhai, allowing Ihsan to cover his tracks that much better.

At last, they heard him. The Silver Spears turned and met the approaching line of golems. The three Blade Maidens joined them, swinging their shamshirs. Swords struck, sinking deep, but the golems' flesh was clay and a deep wound meant little to them. They grabbed several horses' reins, tore them down to the sand. They bashed their great fists against the helms of the Silver Spears, caving them in. The Maidens were more careful than the Spears, and fought with speed and ferocity.

Past the line of spears, Sümeya, Melis, and Çeda watched Ihsan's approach from the backs of their horses, sitting still as statues. "Go!" he cried, "Go!" But he had no idea if they heard him. The rumbling was so loud he could hardly hear himself.

Behind him, the sand frothed like the shores of the Austral Sea. More heads lifted. The hooves and fetlocks of his horse sunk into the sand and it stamped and tossed its head, eyes rolling, then screamed as it tried to escape.

Beyond the growing madness, Sehid-Alaz had fallen to the sand. The blanket fell from him as he lifted himself up, his jaundiced, sunken eyes crazed. He stood before the approaching golems, arms spread wide, and gave a cry that seemed to shake the foundations of the city. Ihsan reeled from it. His horse, which had managed to stay above the slipsand, reared and tipped. It squealed as it fell, and Ihsan fell with it.

The last glimpse he saw of Çeda and the others was as the golems nearest Sehid-Alaz shook, then shattered like pottery. A golem suddenly blocked his view. It stared at him with wide, crazed eyes, then bent over him and gripped the front of his hauberk.

It pressed him down, into the soft sand beneath him.

Ihsan called upon his power. "Release me!" But the golem ignored him. "Release me!" he called once more, putting all the power he had left into those words.

To no avail. Deeper and deeper he went.

The last thing he remembered, as the sand swallowed him whole, were the wild eyes of that grinning golem, intent upon his death.

Chapter 46

DAYS PASSED IN THE MALASANI CAMP. Despite King Emir's promise, he did not call upon Emre to attend him. Emre hated being so close to their bloody great army, an army that was about to invade his home, but he had no choice but to wait.

He saw no sign of Haddad during that time, but whatever she'd said to the king seemed to have worked. The attacks on the blooming fields ceased, and their soldiers steered clear of the groves. Occasionally one of the golems would range into the trees, but after a few days those forays stopped as well.

The golems were still a surprise. Weeks ago Emre had asked Haddad about this very thing. "Why not steal souls to do it?" he'd asked her one night while lying in bed. "They could create an army."

"The soul must be given willingly," Haddad had replied firmly, "and we would never do that, not for war. Golems are holy, blessed by water from the spring where Tamtamiin, god of a thousand hearts, died. They are made to protect and preserve, not to destroy."

Had she been lying? It was certainly possible, but in this he suspected she'd been sincere. Her own brother had given a piece of his soul to breathe life into her bodyguard, Zakkar, which made the subject seem not merely holy but sacrosanct. It was far more likely that the ways of Tamtamiin had been twisted, usurped by their priests, or perhaps by King Emir after his father had died.

Then one night around the fire, Old Nur, their cook and surgeon, said, "It's Surrahdi, the Mad King." He'd been talking with Darius and Frail Lemi, who'd been recounting his fight with the asir.

"What is Surrahdi?" Emre asked.

"Hmm?" Old Nur said.

"You said it's Surrahdi. What is?"

"The faces on those fecking golems."

"Lower your voice!" Hamid said, looking beyond the light of the fire toward the Malasani encampment. "You're worse than the bloody asirim."

Frail Lemi laughed, his teeth glistening in the firelight. "He's saying you howl like a jackal, Nur."

Old Nur glanced sidelong at Lemi, then spat into the flames and returned his gaze to Emre. "I saw him in Ashdankaat when the Mad King gathered all his soldiers and marched on the caravanserai. Saw him clear as day, as close to me as you are now."

It had nearly sparked a war. Haddad herself had sailed there and talked her king down before the Kings of Sharakhai had become involved.

"You're sure it's him?" Emre asked.

"Sure as your mother hangs a red lamp outside her door! Didn't you notice how similar the face is to his son—to King Emir? You mark my words. Those golems were made after his death, and to look like Surrahdi. A way for the Mad King to take part in the conquest he wanted so badly."

It could be, Emre mused. Everyone had heard the stories of the Mad King of Malasan's desire to invade the Shangazi and take Sharakhai for his own. But the might of the Twelve Kings had always been too fearsome. Even the Mad King had known his chances of wresting the desert from them were slim—it was no easy thing, even now that the city's defense was weakened by being forced to meet enemies on two fronts. And the royal navy might have sailed north, leaving the city vulnerable, but they could return at any moment.

"I don't like it," Hamid said, "sitting here. I feel like a desert hare, waiting for the wolf's jaws to close around me." He was sitting by Darius, who gently stroked Hamid's back with his good arm. "Ask to speak to him again."

Emre had done so three times already, but he did so again the next morning, and received the same infuriating answer from King Emir's herald. "Your request will be brought before the king." A day passed. Then two. And still they sat. Still they waited.

Then one day the golems disappeared.

Emre had seen them walking about since he'd arrived, eerie as ghosts. They seemed to have minds of their own at times. They seemed *curious*, even with the odd expressions they wore on their faces. There were moments when they seemed to be living a strange half-existence, as if a man had been swallowed by clay and still lived somewhere within. At other times they were like clockwork beasts, moving around with no purpose, no human emotion despite their human masks.

To have them all vanish put Emre on edge. Where had they gone? And to do what?

Three days after their strange disappearance, it became clear that the Malasani were readying their assault on the city. Emre watched from the vulture's nest as their ships were outfitted with soldiers and sailed toward the city. They stopped just short of the entrance to the southern harbor and set the ships up in a defensive line. Sledges loaded with barricades and catapults. Other machines of war were readied. Behind them, battalions of soldiers ordered themselves in tidy formations.

It was a strange sight indeed—Emre's home on the cusp of invasion, everything he'd known about to change, and the knowledge that there was nothing he could to do stop it.

Near midday, Emre, Hamid, and Frail Lemi were summoned to attend King Emir. He stood on one of three ships positioned directly behind the lines. Emre was brought up to the foredeck, where a dozen of his personal guard stood watch, many surveying the sand beyond the ship, some few watching Emre with cold eyes. Shortly after their arrival a thickset woman helped the man with the golden mask onto the foredeck. The eyes behind the mask took Emre in, they took in Hamid and Frail Lemi as well, but in the end paid them little mind. He seemed fixated on the city. The woman helped him to the gunwales, where he stared in wonder at all that was happening beyond the ship. He looked like a boy on his day of passage, eager to receive his gifts.

Emre stared at the starburst pattern on the mask, wondering at his presence. One would assume a high priest would have been brought to advise his king, and yet Emre had never seen the king consult him, nor the priest offer up a single piece of advice.

Ahead, two blocky towers guarded the open channel leading to the southern harbor. The channel itself was choked with large boulders and chains and iron barricades, preventing the Malasani ships from entering the city. Thousands of Silver Spears stood in ranks, ready to meet the advance of the Malasani army.

Emre was starting to wonder why he'd been summoned when King Emir waved to the way ahead. "So it begins."

Beyond the channel's rocky arms a cloud of amber dust lifted in a plume over the harbor. As it drifted east, occluding the richer sections of the city, Emre heard a rumbling sound. Faint cries followed. Shouting, calls of fear, orders being passed on a grand scale, filtering to them on the other side of the rocks as if this were all merely a dream. But it wasn't. It was the beginning of the Malasani invasion.

The golems, Emre realized. The golems were inside the harbor and were being unleashed on the city. And so it came as no surprise when a dozen clay shapes, then fifty, then a hundred, rounded the channel in the distance and came lumbering toward the Silver Spears. The ranks of Spears reacted with discipline, but even a small distraction would give the Malasani forces a huge advantage, and what were they to do, in any case, against opponents who could not be felled by normal means?

As their rear forces converged on the golems, a horn sounded, and the Malasani army charged. A great roar lifted from them as they ran. Sand kicked up in their wake, which painted the entire, burgeoning battle in amber, making them look beatific, a host blessed by the gods themselves.

By Emre's side, Frail Lemi watched the battle unfold with widened eyes. So often the big man reveled in combat, in inflicting pain, but there were times, like today, when he reacted as a child would. He stared in wonder, his brow furrowing as if he couldn't quite understand what he was seeing. Emre took one of Frail Lemi's massive hands in his and squeezed it, and Lemi seemed to calm.

"Why did you ask me here?" Emre asked the Malasani king.

King Emir turned as if he were surprised by the question. "This is what the Moonless Host wanted all along, wasn't it? The destruction of the Kings?"

We wanted the Kings of Sharakhai to fall. We didn't want to lose the city to some usurper. Emre had known this day was coming. He knew the might of Malasan would be enough to take the city. But to see it . . . To see the ranks of soldiers pouring into the harbor. To see the golems in the far distance storming the city. He felt as though a pit had opened up beneath him, and that all he ever knew—the Shallows, Roseridge, the western harbor, the pits, the bazaar, the sights and sounds and smells of the spice market—was being drawn down with him, to be lost forever.

This was why King Emir had summoned him. He wanted Emre, the emissary from the thirteenth tribe and the alliance, to see it. He wanted stories of it to be taken back to Macide and the other shaikhs that they might know fear before talk of any *terms* began. It would no longer be treaties and trade agreements the King of Malasan would want to discuss, but the terms of their surrender.

"The Moonless Host is no more," Emre said. It was a galling thing to admit, but it was true. "The thirteenth tribe, *all* the tribes, want peace in the desert."

King Emir turned and seemed to take Emre in for the first time. "Peace?" He pursed his lips and played at considering the notion. "Tell me, were you to gain your alliance, if all the desert tribes banded together, would you sue for peace?"

"The desert tribes have long been divided, pitted against one another by the Kings. It's only natural that we come together once more. To trade, to share. And yes, to work toward peace."

"And yet the last time the tribes banded together, four hundred years ago, it was to make war on Sharakhai. It was to raze the city to the ground."

"That is no longer our wish."

King Emir laughed. "Is it not? Let's be honest, you and I. You, the one Macide sent to treat with the enemy, would rather gut a Malasani than shake forearms with him."

"Not true."

The king's eyes were wide and incredulous. "Isn't that the very promise you made to your brother?"

Emre felt his ears turn red. Haddad had told him. She'd told him about Rafa, told him how he'd vowed to kill the man who'd murdered his brother, and his shame when he found he couldn't because Çeda had done it for him. She'd told the king how it had burned within him until he joined the Moonless Host, a group that reveled in the sort of violence he wanted to inflict.

"Where is Haddad?" Emre asked.

The king turned back toward the growing sound of battle. "Exactly where she deserves to be."

"What is that supposed to mean?"

They were interrupted by the sudden wild movements of the man in the golden mask. His hands gripped the gunwales until his knuckles turned white. He shook and hooted like a bird performing a mating ritual. "A King!" he shouted. "A King! A King! A King!"

His caretaker spoke soothing words into his ear, but the man would not be consoled. His shaking became worse until Emre thought he'd tip himself over the edge of the ship. "To me, children! To me! To me!"

Only when King Emir moved to his side and whispered into the madman's ear did his wildness ease. He whispered back to Emir, while the battle raged. The overwhelming ranks of Malasani soldiers, along with the chaos created by the golems, had allowed them to push the Silver Spears back and gain the mouth of the channel. The golems in the harbor were now moving into the city. They drove through the streets like an implacable surge of mud and sand. The entire scene was surreal. It made Emre feel homeless and adrift watching the sacking of his city.

He wasn't sure how much time had passed before he saw a group of golems walking from the eastern part of the city toward them. They crossed the dried banks of the Haddah and trudged steadily closer, until Emre could see that they were dragging something with them. Or some*one*. A soldier. A Silver Spear in a commander's uniform.

The golems threw him onto the sand before the ship, where he lay unmoving. The man in the golden mask stabbed a finger toward him. He went on tiptoes, a child returned home to find a new pet waiting for him. "He of the forked tongue!" he cried. "He of the hated dozen!"

A King, he'd said earlier, and now the mention of a forked tongue. Emre stared closer. Could it be King Ihsan? Emre had never seen him up close.

In a blur of movement, the man in the uniform of a Silver Spear spun and pulled a strange, triple-bladed knife from his belt. As dense as Emre knew the flesh of the golems to be, it severed the leg of the one nearest him and hacked through the neck of another. When a third swiped clumsily for him, it cut neatly through the golem's grasping wrist.

Four of King Emir's guards had bows at the ready, arrows nocked and sighted, waiting for their king's command. But before Emir could say a word, the man on the sand trumpeted a single word.

"Halt!"

It cut through the sounds of battle. Emre felt himself still, suddenly unable, unwilling to move. A part of him knew he should disobey, but he quickly disregarded the thought as foolish, a fleeting whim. Beside and around him, Emre saw everyone go still. King Emir. Hamid and Frail Lemi. The woman and the masked man and the guardsmen.

The battle before the prow of the ship was short and sweet. Ihsan drove his knife into the chests of the last two golems, moving faster than Emre would have given him credit for, and the golems stilled. *You're a fool, Emre. Ihsan might not be known for battle, but he was blessed, as were all the Kings, with speed and reflexes beyond that of mortal man.* When it was done, Ihsan shaded his eyes with one hand and squinted up at the men and women frozen on deck. He had a wry look on his face. He didn't look pleased, exactly, but curious, as if he wondered at the fates' purpose in delivering him here.

He walked alongside the ship, momentarily lost from view. Soon there came the sound of his footsteps thumping hollowly over the deck, ominous against the distant din of battle. King Ihsan came into view, discordantly clothed in the uniform of a Silver Spear. He looked at Emre, glanced over Hamid, gave Frail Lemi a good long look, clearly impressed. The King's face was coated in amber dust and he had a cut along one temple that had bled, coating the right side of his face with dust-ridden blood. He surveyed the deck, particularly King Emir's personal guard.

Again Emre had the urge to break free from the prison his body had become, and again he tossed the thought aside as daft and dim-witted, something Frail Lemi might have come up with.

"Guardsmen," King Ihsan called, "draw your knives and slit your throats."

As simple as that, a dozen men drew kenshars and ran them across their own necks. One by one they thumped to the forecastle deck. Blood pooled beneath them, turning dusty planks into mirror-smooth reflections of a cloud-strewn sky.

Ihsan turned his back to them and stood before King Emir. "Well, well," he said, "our would-be conquerer."

Emre couldn't see King Emir's face clearly, but he saw his throat constrict over and over. Ihsan was smug, but the way he gritted his teeth gave the impression he was struggling to maintain his power.

With his triple-bladed knife he waved to the encampment beyond Emir's capital ship. "Is this all of it, then? Your ships? Your men?"

"It is," King Emir replied.

"It was a solid gambit," Ihsan mused. "The golems. Racing ahead of Mirea. But it wasn't enough, was it?"

"It . . ." King Emir swallowed. "It appears not."

Ihsan smiled a handsome smile. "It appears not." His gaze slid to the man in the golden mask, who stood among the expanding pools of blood. Ihsan peered more closely, then tilted his head like a dune fox listening for voles. "By the gods who breathe, could it be?"

The crooked man shivered. The little finger on his right hand twitched. Ihsan noticed, then peered into his eyes as if by doing so he could see the face hidden behind the mask of Tamtamiin. He placed the tip of his knife to the chin of the mask and lifted it until it slipped from the old man's head and thudded against the deck in one of the pools of blood. It came to a rest upright, smiling, half its golden face smeared in crimson.

The old man was revealed. His face was familiar to anyone who'd been in the Malasani camp. They'd seen it a hundred times in the faces of the golems. It was Surrahdi, Emir's father, the Mad King of Malasan.

Ihsan laughed long and hard. The sound of it filled Emre with genuine mirth. He wished he could laugh as well, but the King's command still compelled him.

"I will admit you had me fooled. But now I wonder." He lifted his knife. "What will happened to the golems when you die?"

With his free hand he reached for Surrahdi's wispy hair.

Surrahdi burst into movement with a cackle of laughter. Ihsan, taken by surprise, swiped with his knife and Surrahdi took a deep cut along one forearm but continued his frenzied charge and snatched up both of Ihsan's wrists. Surrahdi was not a large man, and he was frail, but Ihsan was not large either. Ihsan tried to retreat, but tripped over one of the guardsmen.

Down both men went, Surrahdi crashing his head against Ihsan's. Ihsan, dazed, lost his grip on his knife. Again and again Surrahdi brought his head down, laughing maniacally all the while. "The Honey-tongued King! The Honey-tongued King!"

He took up Ihsan's knife with both hands and brought the pommel crashing down against his skull.

Ihsan's eyelids fluttered. "Stop," he said in a long slur. "Stop." But Surrahdi continued, somehow immune to Ihsan's words of command.

Only when Ihsan fell unconscious did Surrahdi still his wild movements. Then he reached the fingers of one hand inside Ihsan's mouth. "Let's see if it tastes like honey!"

He drew Ihsan's tongue from his mouth as far as it would go, then plunged Ihsan's own knife into his mouth, deep between his teeth, cutting one side of his mouth in the process. Back and forth Surrahdi sawed. Ihsan woke again, thrashing. He tried to throw Surrahdi off him, but Surrahdi was bent close, impossible to dislodge.

In a burst of movement Ihsan arched his back and clubbed him. Surrahdi fell away, but not without an arc of blood stemming from Ihsan's mouth. Surrahdi was laughing higher than ever.

Suddenly Emre was free. He could move again. So could the others, who staggered before pulling themselves upright.

Surrahdi regained his feet. His robes were filthy with blood, and in his hand he held a hunk of flesh. Ihsan's tongue. He stared at it, eyes crazed. Then popped it into his mouth and scampered away, arms and legs flailing like a frog gone upright. Left on the deck, King Ihsan writhed, holding his mouth and moaning terribly.

Chapter 47

INSIDE THEIR ROOM ABOVE THE WORKSHOP, Davud and Ramahd helped Fezek onto a stool. Fezek was missing the lower part of his right leg. It was an indicator of just how tense it had been that he'd remained silent on their harrowing way back from the Shallows. He hadn't mentioned anything about the leg itself or the way Hamzakiir had blasted it off. As soon as the door closed, however, he motioned to it with a look of deep sorrow. "It was my favorite."

"Fezek"—Davud wanted to be sympathetic, but—"how could you have had a favorite leg?"

Fezek shrugged and waved to it again, as ineffectual as a bull at a milking contest. "I just did, and it was that one."

While Esmeray began sewing the wound, Ramahd's man Cicio spun Davud around and pointed a finger in his face. "What happen with you and this King, ah?"

Davud knew the question was coming, but what could he say? *Hamzakiir awakened me to the red ways? A bond formed between us when he did, and to-night that same bond stirred something within him?* It was the truth, but it would be the height of foolishness to admit it. He needed them to help with Anila, and he couldn't have them doubting his heart or his purpose.

"I don't know," Davud said.

"No?" Cicio stared between Davud and Ramahd. When Ramahd merely shrugged, Cicio went on. "Then why he stare at you so long? What he say to you?"

"He didn't say *anything*."

Ramahd stood behind Cicio, both literally and figuratively. "Then how do you explain him letting us go?"

"I'm almost certain Hamzakiir knows he's trapped," Davud finally said. "Tonight, Meryam's concentration surely slipped. It must have allowed him some free will."

Cicio stared at Ramahd, perhaps hoping he would contradict Davud's explanation, but Ramahd shrugged again. "It could be. Meryam was tired. More than she's been in a long while."

Cicio's frustration seemed to drain all at once. "Mateo is free, then? He'll come to us?"

"I think so."

"When?" Cicio asked. "When he come?"

"Soon, I think. Meryam expects the Qaimiri fleet to arrive within a few days. Mateo, assuming he now understands the danger we're all in, will want to make arrangements before that happens."

"Then we'd better go tomorrow," Davud stepped in.

Ramahd stared, noncommittal, even a bit confused.

"To help Anila," Davud added.

Ramahd and Cicio shared a look.

"Mateo might come tomorrow," Cicio said.

Ramahd looked as though he was considering a delay, but Davud wasn't about to let that happen. "We're leaving in the morning to get Anila out."

"We leave when Ramahd say we leave, ah?"

"You owe me," Davud replied evenly. "War is about to spill over the walls, and I've left Anila alone for too long already."

Cicio stepped up to Davud so that they were chest to chest. "What I tell you, you fucking shit?"

"Please." Fezek got up on one leg and was hopping toward them with both hands raised. But Cicio shoved him back and he flew, arms windmilling, back onto the pallet. "Hey!"

Suddenly Cicio had his knife beneath Davud's chin. Davud felt Esmeray working a spell, which died a moment later, courtesy of Ramahd. Davud refused to summon one himself. He was exhausted and it would only make things worse anyway.

Instead he looked straight into Cicio's angry eyes and said, "There's no time left. We're leaving in the morning to get Anila."

Cicio's nostrils flared. He looked as though he were about to do something rash—teach Davud a lesson, or worse—but then Ramahd touched his shoulder. He pulled him back until Cicio drew his knife away from Davud's chin.

"You've got everything ready?" Ramahd asked.

When Davud nodded, Ramahd nodded back.

"Very well, then. We leave in the morning."

The sun had yet to rise as Davud stood with Esmeray in their small room above the workshop. Ramahd and Cicio stood nearby, dressed in light armor. They had swords, knives and small fighting shields at their belts. Cicio also held a small crossbow, cocked and ready. Fezek, meanwhile, whose right leg below the knee had been fitted with a peg leg, seemed positively giddy with excitement.

"An entirely new chapter to add to my epic," he said.

Davud had half a mind to leave him here, but he was simply too valuable, giddiness or not. "Just remember why we're going," Davud said, and from around his neck retrieved a leather necklace, to which was attached a golden triangle. Using one corner of the triangle, he pierced the skin of his index finger. On one palm he drew the sigil for *passage*, and on the opposite, *doorway*. He repeated the ritual on the palms of Ramahd and Cicio.

"If you have need, press your palms together"—he mimicked the motion but didn't complete it—"and a portal to wherever the golden triangle is will be opened." He showed them the triangle. "I'll send the bird ahead to gain us a way in. As soon as we're through and into the palace, I'll send it back for our escape."

Esmeray seemed impressed. "It's smart, Davud. Just be careful you don't spread yourself too thin."

She was right. It took effort to maintain a spell that allowed any one of them to summon, but it was important. They needed a way out. When he offered the same to Esmeray, she raised her hand.

"It would only weigh on my mind."

When she nodded to Ramahd, he reached back and opened the door. A short while later, a spoon-tailed warbler flew through the door and landed on Esmeray's outstretched finger. The bird's bright azure wings stood out against the blacks of their clothing and the grays of the worn wooden planks.

"As we've done before," she said to Davud, "but don't attempt to guide the spell. Lay your presence over mine like a cloak, so you can learn the shape of it. Understand?"

Before Davud could respond, a sound rose up from outside. There was a rumble. Davud swore he could feel it though the soles of his feet. War drums beat. Horns blared. Shortly after came the shouts and cries of hundreds, thousands.

"Best we hurry," Ramahd said. "This may play out in our favor."

Davud nodded to him, then waved for Esmeray to begin.

He had no ability to control animals in a fine-grained way. Esmeray, on the other hand, had been able to call the serval to her, so Davud had asked her to prepare a bird of her choosing for their assault on Sukru's palace.

As she'd instructed, he felt the way she cradled the bird's mind. It fluttered its wings, fighting her momentarily, but Esmeray's intent nestled over the warbler like soft cotton. It coalesced, tightened, without the bird even realizing it. Mundane spells, those that gathered and released power in crude, elemental ways, were simple to cast, relatively speaking, and took no great amount of concentration on the part of the caster.

Living creatures, however, had blood and minds of their own and were much, much trickier to affect. It was as intricate as clockmaking and easy to foul or to do clumsily, but Esmeray placed the spell on the bird without it even realizing it, and soon both she and Davud had been granted a second sight and a form that was not their own. It felt strange to be lifted into the air, to beat limbs that were not his. But it didn't take so long as he'd thought to orient himself, and he could move his own body while still sensing the bird's.

Davud held the golden triangle out for the warbler to take. The bird pinched it in its beak and was off, flying through the door and over the city. At first Davud saw only stone and mudbrick buildings, and a bit of the white-studded sky. Then the entire neighborhood opened up to him, nestled as it was inside the old city. Not so far away lay the sprawl of the collegia grounds; the Wheel at city's center where Sharakhai's two largest streets, the Trough and the Spear, met; the patchwork estates of Goldenhill and Black-fire Gate and Hanging Gardens. To the right, the great southern harbor yawned in a swath of ships and sand. Hundreds of piers raked outward from the quays. More were clustered around the great watch tower in the harbor's center. Many of the piers were empty, their owners having fled the looming conflict.

In the center of the sand there was a great lifting of dust. It billowed up as dozens—hundreds—of clay figures crawled from the sand and began pouring toward the docks. Davud had no idea what was happening, but it was clear the Malasani assault had begun.

The fates had shone on them at last. Not even prayers could have led to a better distraction.

The bird winged toward Tauriyat and its thirteen palaces. It made its way steadily toward one in particular, roughly halfway up the mountain, and flew around it, guided by Davud. He brought it to the large open space within the palace grounds where the gardens were, the walking paths, the boneyard where Anila had first raised the young girl, Bela. The bird arced along hallways, then flew down to the dungeons. Finding only two men held there, it wended its way back up and made for Sukru's apartments. Silver Spears tried to wave it away, as did an old woman with a broom, but the apartments were otherwise empty.

The bird left and fluttered its way to the small courtyard with the fig tree where Davud had first met the Sparrow's firefinch and received the golden triangle. The windows were open, and the bird flew in to find two women in fine clothing staring intently at a half-finished game of aban on the table between them. Davud was getting nervous, and it showed in the erratic pattern the bird described in the air. As the women stood, wondering at the warbler's sudden presence, it darted back outside, then returned to the palace's cavernous hallways. He guided it along several passages before coming to a door that gave him pause.

He nearly passed it by because it looked so different. Sukru had given Anila her own room so she could live and study in peace. This was the same room, but the old wooden door had been replaced with one made of iron.

"I've found it," Davud said to those in the room back in the city. "Be ready."

He guided the bird outside, hoping to fly in through an open window, but the windows were closed and barred. He flew back and, seeing no one in the hall, forced the warbler to land and set the triangle down.

He combined the symbols for *passage* and *doorway* in his mind, and the triangle, now floating in the air above the floor, began to grow. In the attic above the workshop, a similar opening grew, triangular in shape, rotating just as the one in Sukru's palace was. Ramahd, Cicio, and Fezek climbed through it, followed by Esmeray and Davud. He immediately dispelled the sigils, and the triangle shrunk and fell into his waiting palm.

He gave the triangle back to the warbler and bade it fly with all haste back to the attic in the city. Ramahd and Cicio, tense and ready to act, watched both ends of the hallway. Fezek stared through the door as if spellbound. It was Anila, Davud knew. He did that from time to time, entranced by his maker.

Esmeray, meanwhile, knelt before the door. She placed one hand over the lock and closed her eyes. Davud felt her working a complex spell that maneuvered the internals of the lock.

Somewhere distant, a door opened. Footsteps echoed. Voices approached along the hallway adjoining this one. As Ramahd and Cicio readied to defend them, Esmeray opened the door and swept inside. The rest rushed in after her, closing the door as quietly as they could behind them.

"Davud?"

Anila was sitting in a high-backed chair, her black, snakeskin hands laid over an ancient leatherbound tome on the table before her. She wore a fine, patterned dress of ivory and gold and a black hijab that matched. She stood, staring at all of them, especially Esmeray.

Esmeray caught her stare, turned, and knelt before the door again, but not before sparing a glance for Davud. *Why didn't you tell me there was still so much between you?* her look said. But then she was bent to her task: locking the door to conceal their entrance.

"What are you doing here?" Anila asked. She didn't seem pleased at all.

"We're here to get you out," Davud said. He tried to put enthusiasm into his voice, but the way Anila was looking at him, with confusion, even disappointment, prevented him.

"Davud, I . . ."

Suddenly her situation struck Davud full on. She was under lock and key, but the room looked comfortable otherwise. There was a dying fire in the hearth and she had a steaming mug of tea beside her books.

"What's happening, Anila?"

"Davud, I can't leave."

Esmeray snorted. Ramahd watched on with confusion. Fezek looked as if he might cry.

Davud felt like he'd been punched in the stomach. "Anila, we *have* to leave."

"I can't. Sukru . . ." From somewhere outside came the boom of a door closing. "They're coming for me," Anila said in a low voice, "and there's too much to explain. But I have to stay, Davud. He has my family. He has my mother."

Seeing they had little time, Davud forced the spoon-tail to land in a small, vacant lot that backed up against a curving alley. It would have to do. "We can come back for her." He hated the pleading in his voice.

"You don't understand," she said, glancing toward the door. "I have to bring her back. The crystal in the cavern . . . I have to prove I can do it before I bring the Sparrow back."

Davud reeled. "You're going to bring him *back?*"

Anila's chin jutted. "If it will save my mother, yes."

"Anila, think about this."

"I have."

"No, you clearly haven't. You're aiding a man who will kill you, your mother, *and* your family, the moment he has what he wants. Come with us." He motioned to the slowly turning portal, which revealed a corner of the dusty yard, where mountains of broken urns were piled haphazardly. Sounds filtered through the portal—a distant roar, a battle being joined—but they were muffled, as if it were a dream.

"We can save your family on *our* terms, but only if we leave now."

"I *can't*, Davud. I don't know where they *are*. And my mother is dead. Sukru had her brought before me in the catacombs below the palace, and he used the same bloody piece of wood on her that Bela used to kill his brother. And now I'm the only one who can save my mother. I can't do that anywhere but here."

Anila's arms were across her chest, her head held high. She looked unassailable in that moment. Nothing Davud could say was going to convince her to leave.

Footsteps approached the door. Ramahd, meanwhile, was standing to one side of Anila, and slightly behind her. He glanced at her meaningfully, then to the spinning portal. He was ready to take her by force if need be and, gods forgive him, Davud considered it. It was obvious she was blinded by hope, and working with Sukru could only end tragically. If they left, they could find a way to free Anila's father and sister. And her mother . . . Well, if she was truly dead, then it was a lost cause already. The dead could not live again. Not truly.

But if he did this, there would be no going back, and Anila would never forgive him. And what right did he have to make this decision for her in any case?

As much as it pained him, he knew he couldn't do it.

The footsteps came to a stop, leather soles scraping against the stone outside the door. Davud nodded to Anila and whispered, "I'll find a way to contact you."

Anila nodded back, a grateful look on her face. She waved animatedly to the portal as a key clinked into the lock. Davud, Esmeray, Ramahd, and Cicio filed quickly through. Fezek came last, but not without a longing look toward her. Davud cut off the spell while yanking Fezek the rest of the way through. The sounds of battle became sharp and loud. The wind tugged at

Davud's clothes. As the golden triangle shrunk, Davud saw Anila step in front of the portal to hide it from view. And then she was gone, and the triangle fell to the street with a soft tinkle.

"I'm sorry." He stared at the others, at a loss for what to say. "I had no idea. I endangered your lives for nothing."

"No shit, ah?" Cicio said. "Why you no talk to her first?"

"I was worried Sukru would sense it. He has some ability in magic. I thought the element of surprise worth the risk."

"Yes, well." Ramahd looked to his right, where the clash of steel and men screaming made it clear that the conflict had somehow reached this deep into the city. It sounded as if the edges of it were only a block or two away. "We'd better get out of here before we start picking up the pieces."

Davud sent the warbler off with the triangle to fly the rest of the way to the workshop. Then he and the others headed north. And just in time. Behind them, a cadre of Silver Spears were backing into the alley. A dozen were fighting a lone Malasani soldier. A *clay* soldier. He was taking blow after blow from spears and swords both, though none seemed to slow him. The skirmish was lost as they took a bend in the alley, but they'd gone no more than ten strides before the way ahead was blocked as well. Dozens, hundreds of Silver Spears were engaged with more golems who, like the first, seemed impervious to harm.

A wall of golems were on their way, and the Silver Spears were breaking at a near panic. *So many of them,* Davud thought, while everything he'd read about the golems of Malasan spoke of how rare they were.

There was no time to worry about it now. The warbler had made it to the workshop and while the area might not be safe much longer, it would give them time to plan their next steps. He summoned the portal once more, uncaring if any of the Silver Spears spotted them. Some, in fact, after seeing Esmeray and Cicio jump through, seemed to think it a convenient escape and began running toward it.

"Gods, hurry up!"

They all made it through, and Davud closed the portal, just in time. The pleas of the soldiers were cut short, and they were back in the room above the workshop. Ramahd, Cicio, Fezek, and Esmeray seemed frozen after their harrowing escape.

No, Davud realized. Not *seemed.* They *were* frozen.

No sooner had the thought occurred to him than he realized *he* couldn't move either. Like the others, he was trapped.

Footsteps scuffed over the floorboards. A Sharakhani woman with broad lips and merciless eyes came into view. It was Prayna, the de facto leader of the Enclave. Next to her came a young Mirean woman, an old, wrinkled Kundhuni, and a Malasani man with a golden disk painted on his forehead. Meiying, Undosu, and Nebahat, the three other members of the Enclave's inner circle.

Davud could feel the weave of their spell, all four working together to trap Davud and the others in a web as intricate as it was effective.

"You were warned," Prayna said.

"Cowards," Esmeray grunted.

Prayna regarded her calmly. "The Enclave has survived dozens of challenges to our existence for hundreds of years. We will suffer neither you nor an outsider precipitating another."

Esmeray looked as though she wanted to say more, but couldn't. Davud was similarly bound. Surely the others were as well. Soon they were all being led away from the workshop. Through the streets of Sharakhai they went, war echoing in the distance, until Davud heard a scuffle behind him.

From the corner of his eye he saw Prayna stumble and fall to the street. He couldn't turn his head, but he heard footsteps sprinting away, then a sizzling sound followed by a grunt of pain. As a great boom sounded in the distance, Prayna regained her feet. "Leave him," she said while dusting off her clothes. "We've been in the open long enough."

As they walked away from the conflict, Davud breathed a sigh of relief. He didn't understand it all, but he knew enough to know Ramahd had just escaped.

Chapter 48

As Sukru had vowed, he insisted Anila take small steps with the crystal as she learned its ways. He demanded she resurrect a falcon, a bird whose neck he had snapped in front of her. She accepted the still-warm bird from him, trying and failing to ignore the fact that so many animals were suffering because of her.

"The thornbill is alive?" she asked him. "It's acting normally?"

"It seems to have no ill effects." When it came to praise, Sukru was stingy as a moneylender, but even he couldn't hide his optimism.

Anila looked about the spacious cavern, at the Silver Spears stationed near the entrance. "Are we safe here?"

Even when Sukru pulled himself up from his typical hunched position he was shorter than Anila, but he somehow made her feel small with that piercing, ratlike stare of his. "What do you mean?"

"Aren't you worried about Kiral's command to leave the crystal alone? Or that Yerinde might return?"

His look turned dark, an expression made alien by the strange purple light emanating from the nearby crystal. He motioned to the falcon. "You would do well to worry about that bird and leave the business of gods and Kings to others."

"I'm only thinking of your brother."

Sukru laughed his petty laugh. "You're only thinking of your mother. Now begin, girl. I want *progress*."

She began as she had the last time, finding the silklike thread of life, following it through the crystal, and calling to the soul beyond. She'd thought it might be easier since the falcon had only just been killed. And indeed, finding it was not difficult, but drawing it through the crystal proved to be a much greater challenge than she'd given it credit for. She had to make sure its soul was returned intact, to ensure it would be healthy once returned to its body. And that, as large as it was, was no simple matter.

She managed it, though, now glad of the previous attempts. The experience helped, though it still took her over an hour to complete. And worse, she was exhausted. Sweat tickled her scalp, rolled down her forehead, along her spine, between her breasts. When she was finally done, Sukru took the bird and administered the healing elixir. In moments the falcon had opened its eyes and was flapping its wings again. Its neck was cocked at a strange angle, but it soon straightened. Minutes later it was in a cage and one would never know it had been harmed.

Over the course of the following week, she did more. A large desert owl. A serval cat—which she failed at the first time. She knew she had failed the moment it returned to its body. It was glaze-eyed, and became violent, managing to break from Sukru's grip and scratch his neck and face. Sukru recovered, gripping it in his thick leather gloves, then strangled it before her eyes.

"I trust," he said to her after calling for another, "you'll try harder next time."

He was red-faced and angry. He blamed her for having to kill the cat, and he wasn't wrong. She'd become desperate near the end, feeling that its soul was being torn in two, and she had forced it back into the corpse quickly, which had only served to tear it further.

"I will," she promised, though not to him. She needed to master this for her mother.

She resurrected the second serval, after which they moved on to three different dogs: a small pit bull, a racing hound, then a great Kundhuni mastiff. She learned from each, her skills growing, but they were becoming progressively harder as well. She was at her wit's end with the mastiff, at the edge of her abilities to keep such a large soul intact. In the end, she'd managed it, but only after four grueling hours. She stared at the massive dog as it walked, tentatively at first, then with growing energy, about the cavern. Except for the fact that it whimpered and shied away from the crystal, it seemed hearty and hale.

After each new attempt, she and Sukru discussed it, both of them judging her ability to move on to a more complex form of life. At first she could continue with only a few hours rest, but as it progressed it took a day or more to regain her strength. She was so exhausted after the mastiff, she was dizzy from it. She *ached*—and feared she would need a week to recover.

Sukru watched her closely. "It's taking you longer each time."

"As we knew it would."

"Yes, but I wonder if you've the stamina to finish what you've begun."

"I've enough."

Sukru stared at her doubtfully.

"I've *enough*," she said again. "I've learned from each one, and I'll be ready again after a bit of rest."

He seemed unconvinced, but said nothing.

Three days later, the door to her room burst open and, breath of the desert, *Davud* swept in, along with Ramahd Amansir, Fezek, and that bitch mage, Esmeray. What in the great wide desert had happened since she'd been taken to Sukru's palace Anila had no idea, but there'd been no time to find out. She felt terrible for denying Davud. He'd risked so much in coming to the palace. But she couldn't go with him.

In the hours following his departure, she was terrified Sukru would learn of it. The moment he did, surely her chance to heal her mother would be taken from her. The days passed without incident, however, and one day he came to her in her room and said the words she was so desperate to hear. "Mortal man is next."

"Very well," she replied, wondering why he'd decided to tell her here and not in the cavern.

He snapped his fingers, at which point the Silver Spear standing in the doorway stepped aside. A moment later, Anila's sister, Banu, was led into the room. It was a strange mixture of fear, relief, worry, and anger that greeted

Anila upon seeing her. Banu was bound and gagged. Bruises discolored her face, especially along her right cheek and jaw, which was dark purple and yellow with a fantastically large bruise, at the center of which was a weeping laceration. Elsewhere were smaller cuts and scrapes, as if her face had been raked over stones. Her beautiful black hair had been shaved, a deep mark of shame for the women of the city. It was uneven, as if it had been done with a knife, and revealed pale skin and freckles and cuts with dried blood caked around them.

Banu was squinting, as if the light in the room was too much for her. Still, she held Anila's gaze, pleading. *Save me*, her eyes said. *Save me from the King and the dungeons and the punishment I'll receive should you deny him.*

"Why would you do this?" Anila asked. "I've done all you've asked."

"Your father became unruly."

"He wouldn't have. Not if he knew Banu was being held."

"You doubt the word of your King?"

"You are not my King."

Banu's eyes went wide. Anila knew she shouldn't have said it, but she was so angry they were out before she could stop herself.

Sukru regarded her with cold calculation. "You're not ready to try the ritual on your mother." He snapped his fingers. Immediately, one of the Silver Spears took out his kenshar and held its edge to Banu's neck.

"I *am* ready! You know that I am."

"It isn't your *ability* I'm concerned about. It's your will."

"I'll do it. I only need practice."

Sukru waved to Banu without looking at her, as if she meant no more to him than the thornbill they'd raised at the outset of their journey.

"I know why you're doing this," Anila said quickly, questioning herself even as she spoke. But if she didn't do *something*, Sukru would order her sister killed. "You fear I haven't enough hatred for you. But believe me, none of it is gone. I harbor as much for you as I did when you killed my mother. More, now that I see how my family has been treated."

Sukru held his hand out, and the Silver Spear handed over his knife. "One can always use more."

She raised both hands in a placating gesture. "Do this, and I'll wonder when the blade will be taken to my father. I'll question my every step, and it will undermine everything we've already worked for. The balance is already so delicate."

"You have enough hatred?" he asked her calmly. "You have enough power?"

For the first time since her mother's death, she allowed her contempt for him, a thing that burned inside her like molten rock, to show on her face. "Oh, have no doubt of that."

Sukru considered Banu. He lifted the kenshar, placed the tip against her temple, and dragged it roughly along the skin of her cheek. Anila had never seen her sister look so scared. Sukru, meanwhile, looked like a fishmonger bored of his work. "See that you are." He handed the knife back to the Spear and swept toward the door. "We start with your mother tomorrow."

The Silver Spears followed, taking Banu with them. She only had time to give Anila one look that was half relief, half terror before the iron door boomed shut.

Anila stared at her mother's still body. She'd been delivered to the cavern inside a wooden crate. As Sukru's brother, the Sparrow, had been, she was wrapped in oiled canvas, cradled by ice. Her skin was ashen. Her face slack.

"Enough of your bloody reunion," Sukru said as he approached her over the spongy surface of the cavern. "It's time to begin."

Anila ignored him. She looked up at the tall, glowing crystal, then ordered the Silver Spears to shift the crate so that her mother's feet were pointed at it. When it was done, she stood at her mother's head, ran the backs of her fingers over her mother's cold skin, touched the smile lines along her cheeks. How rarely her mother used to smile, Anila mused, how lovely she was when she did.

Come to me, Anila said to her. *Come near, for I may only have one chance at this.*

"I said *begin.*"

Anila lifted her gaze. "If you wish your brother to be whole, you'll grant me the time I need."

For the first time in all their time together, Sukru seemed taken aback—not out of concern for Anila, nor her mother, but for his brother. In that moment the trappings of the Reaping King were stripped away, leaving only the brother of a man who'd died. He became human. Mortal. And it made Anila that much more furious with him, that he would cause so much pain to get what he wanted, like the fables of the petty child king of Kahram La. In her mother, Anila saw her sister, Banu. Saw her *own* childhood: growing up in and around the halls of Goldenhill. And she saw Sukru strip it from her with the thrust of a shard of wood.

Her anger was a pile of embers waiting to be awakened. She would see her mother reborn. She would bring her back from that distant shore to live the life she was meant to live. And then she would see Sukru dead. She would never have a better chance at it than this. Sukru would be wary, but he would also want to see how her mother woke. And he would be calm in the knowledge that he had Anila's father and sister hostage. It was merely a matter of striking quickly, before he had a chance to react.

When Sukru was a ghul in service to her, she would force him to kill the Silver Spears. The same ones had been here all along; the same ones who'd beaten and tortured Banu. They would die, and then she would raise them too, and force them to bring her to Banu and her father. And if any stood in her way, she would take their lives as well. Of all of this she was certain. As certain as she'd been of anything in her life. All it took was her will. And her will, Bakhi as her witness, was as vast and deep as the Great Mother herself.

So it was that Anila began the ritual. So it was that she followed the dim thread of her mother's soul to the world beyond. So it was that she gathered it, cradled it like gossamer, and bore it toward her mother's cold, lifeless body. It was a ritual performed in slow increments. Often the currents of life and death carried her farther away, or threatened to tear her mother's soul in two, but Anila was ready for it all.

When at last the soul was near, she felt her mother's awareness expand. A world she thought she'd left behind was hers once more. There was pain. She had no desire to return, but Anila coaxed her. *Remember your daughters. Remember your husband. Remember the feel of the desert sun on your face, the feel of the wind as the Great Shangazi stirs. Remember the glow of the twin moons, their beauty as they shine over the desert's Amber Jewel.*

It was enough. Her soul returned. Filled its former vessel.

Her eyes twitched. Her lips parted, and she took a shallow, rasping breath.

Sukru rushed in and Anila stepped away so he could tip a vial of the softly glowing elixir over her mouth. He allowed only drips at first. Like parched earth that shed rain too quickly, she could only take so much at one time.

Anila watched, rapt, seeing color return to her mother's cheeks, her lips, then her forehead and hands. She heard her mother's breath change from a terrible rasp to something like normality. Saw her fingers begin to twitch. Her eyelids begin to flutter.

The elixir was nearly gone. It was nearly time.

Anila breathed deeply of the cool cavern air. The scent of decay was strong from both Sukru and her mother, but she isolated Sukru's. The scent of the adichara was strong in him, a hint of the elixir's incredible healing powers, but she sensed another part as well, the decay the elixir *had* been masking for four hundred years. *That* was what she needed to intensify. It would accelerate the rot within him, and once it began, there was nothing he could do to stop her.

She'd just begun when she sensed something else in the cavern. Something *other*.

She paused her efforts. Peered deeper into the cavern's darkness. Was there an outline there? A man hidden in shadow?

Her mouth went dry and her skin prickled, starting at her scalp and running down her back, arms, and legs.

There in the darkness was a well of power, a thing as old as the Shangazi itself. A thing that had had a hand in its making, or surely in its shaping once forged by the elder gods. It was no mortal that studied her from the darkness, no demon of Goezhen's making, but a god. Bakhi had come, though why, she had no idea. Perhaps the ritual had drawn him. Or her desire to kill Sukru. He might have come to take Sukru by the hand and lead him to the farther fields himself.

But what if he hadn't? What if he'd come to watch over Sukru instead? What if, after granting the Twelve Kings protection those centuries ago, he'd come to ensure that nothing ill befell Sukru?

All the confidence she'd had moments ago drained from her like wine from a broken ewer. Her hands shook terribly. She gripped them tight lest Sukru see. The worry that Bakhi would stop her, or that he would wreak his vengeance upon her and her family, had taken hold, and once it had she couldn't shake it. What could she do but watch as Sukru finished? What could she do but stand by as he stepped back and gave her one sharp nod, allowing her to approach her mother's side?

She did, and all the joy she should have felt at seeing her mother reborn was instead a cold pit of terror yawning inside her, because at any moment Sukru might change his mind and take her from Anila all over again.

"Anila?" her mother said with chattering teeth.

"Yes, memma. I'm here."

Anila helped her out of the cold wooden crate and wrapped her in a thick wool blanket. She held her mother tight, knowing her last, best chance to escape had just passed her by.

"I feel so cold," her mother whispered.

"I know, memma," Anila whispered back. "I'm sorry."

As she huddled within her blanket, shivering terribly, Anila led her from the cavern, refusing to look back toward that veiled corner. She felt the god's stare on her back, though, felt her own awkward movements more acutely because of it.

She might have sensed amusement. Or perhaps it was a deep-seated pleasure. She couldn't be sure. And then she was gone, down the darkened tunnel, the cavern's purple light dimming behind her.

Bakhi watched from the recesses of the cavern. He waited while the woman left with the soul she'd returned from the land of the dead. What a strange thing to behold, to feel in his bones. So near to the crystal, it had felt for a moment as if he were on the other side. How sweet the feeling. And then the soul had crossed and the way was closed to him once more.

Ancient grudges stirred within him, but he suppressed them immediately. He hadn't given up yearning for the touch of the elder gods—none of them had; none of them *could*—but he'd long since given up trying to justify the actions of the elders. They'd done what they'd done, and that was that.

When the King and his soldiers in silver left the cavern, he stepped from darkness and approached the crystal. As his footsteps faltered, then stopped altogether, he had the strangest feeling. Moths in one's chest, mortals called it. Before this wondrous thing, an artifact crafted from the blood of mortals, he felt new again. Full of hope and wonder but fear as well, just as Iri and Annam and Raamajit and all the gods of creation had prescribed.

He longed to touch it, especially after what he'd witnessed, but he'd grown accustomed to halting undeniable urges. Instead, he lifted his right hand. Cradled within was a bird. This creature, the very thornbill the necromancer had raised, had found its way to the surface, desperate for food, desperate for water.

Its desires had changed, however.

It fluttered, tiny within the cage of his hand. When he spread his fingers wide, the bird remained, resting on his palm. It blinked, turned its head this way and that. Then flew straight toward the crystal.

He heard a soft thump as it struck. The bird's dead body fell lifeless to the roots, but Bakhi hardly noticed. Like a ripple in a pond, the bird's soul had returned to the land beyond, and the waves of that event were still emanating slowly outward. He reveled in each one until he could feel them no more.

He stood staring down at the bird's body. The roots opened, drew it down, until it was gone.

He left the cavern, taking one of the many winding passages, and as he walked felt traces of the trees that rimmed the city. He wondered at all that had happened since the night he and his sisters and brothers had granted the Kings their power. Walking the knife's edge of fate was difficult for any length of time, but they'd managed it for over four hundred years, and now their careful curation of events had led them here. Things were nearly at an end, with so many elements positioned just so: the Kings themselves, Mirea and Malasan encroaching on the city, Qaimir ready to enter the fray, Kundhun stirring, the tribes riling. A thousand thousand threads, all interweaving, telling a greater story, not that of mortal man, but of the gods themselves.

He left the tunnels choked with roots and eventually came to a cavern of crystals, the very one that Macide and the Moonless Host had traveled through on their way to King Külaşan's hidden desert palace. He took the same path and reached the catacombs, a set of stairs, and finally the palace itself. Soon he stood in the spot where Çedamihn Ahyanesh'ala had killed Külaşan the Wandering King. In that grand space, beneath a dome of wondrous mosaics, stood another, a woman as tall as Bakhi with silver hair and skin of palest blue.

"Were you sensed?" she asked in the old tongue of the desert.

"I was," he answered in the same tongue, "as you foresaw."

"And still you went . . ."

"How could I not?"

"I tell you, it is unwise."

"It changed nothing."

"So you say, but even you cannot see the threads the fates themselves now weave. Do not make the same mistake as Yerinde."

"A course *you* approved." The sound of his laughter filled the space beneath the high dome. "Old enmities die a slow and painful death, do they not?" When Tulathan chose not to respond, Bakhi went on. "Come, there's no part of you that wishes Yerinde might be left behind?"

It was an ancient theory to which all the gods subscribed: the notion that to meddle directly in the lives of mortal man was to bind oneself to them, to bind oneself to this earth.

"I bear no ill will toward her, not any longer, but if she so desperately wishes to forge the fate of this world, then so be it. And I don't recall you arguing when Yerinde put forth the idea, nor when Thaash provoked her into making the effort herself." Yerinde had seemed desperate, almost blinded, when they'd talked of stopping the Kings from investigating the crystal. It was Yerinde who'd put forth the notion of its creation after all, she who'd spent centuries creating more primitive versions of it.

"Well"—Bakhi shared a wink with Tulathan—"she always has had difficulty weighing the consequences of her actions."

Tulathan's smile was somehow both pleasant and wicked. "That she has."

The two of them walked, falling in stride with one another with an ease that felt ancient as the dawn. "What now?" she asked. "Have things been set aright?"

Bakhi nodded. "I believe they have. The doorway works."

"And is it strong enough?"

"No. Not just yet."

"When?" she asked as they followed the stairs up toward the desert.

"Not long."

Chapter 49

WHEN IHSAN CRACKED his eyes open the thing that registered first wasn't the pain. The pain had become a constant, a thing akin to the heat of the desert on a late summer voyage, a thing that plagued him day and night. The pain was his enemy, but it was an enemy he knew he couldn't be rid of, and so it wasn't that, but the sound of his own moaning that entered his mind first. Moaning helped *soothe* the pain, helped him forget the ruin of his mouth.

As he pushed himself off the cell floor within the Malasani prison ship, spit gathered. It made him swallow, which made the pain soar, which made him salivate more. Then the coughing started. Each one felt like swallowing a lit torch. On and on it went. He buried his head between his knees and pulled himself tight. It did little to stop the coughing, but it kept his body from convulsing so much.

Slowly, the coughing fit subsided and the pain diminished, but it was slow as the sunset. He smelled the blood trickling down his throat. He even tasted it a bit, but only barely. His mouth felt vacant and pathetic, like the temple of a forgotten god. As if to prove to himself that it had actually happened, he rubbed the jagged remains of his tongue against the back of his throat. It burned, but like a canker he couldn't stop working it.

Two days had passed since that day on the Malasani capital ship. The image of Surrahdi crouching over him played over and over again in his mind. The Mad King's face had been crazed. Eyes wide with that terrible grin that showed each and every one of his long, yellow teeth. And the smell! Goezhen's balls, Ihsan would carry it to the farther fields. A fetid stench that accompanied the sawing motions of Surrahdi's arm as he used Ihsan's own knife—Ihsan's own knife! He nearly laughed at the irony—to take his tongue from him.

"For the love of all the gods," came a woman's voice, "close that tireless mouth of yours."

For a moment, Ihsan did. He'd forgotten he wasn't alone.

This deck of the prison had a dozen small cells along its central passageway, each set aside from the others with iron bars. In the cell across from him was a bedraggled woman. She leaned against the hull, hands hanging over her propped-up knees, staring at him as if he were the cause of all that had gone wrong in her life.

"You lost your tongue. Fine." Her Sharakhan was heavily accented by the more guttural Malasani language. "Do *I* have to suffer for it?"

He stopped moaning.

"Good. Now keep it that way."

With that she closed her eyes. Even with her cut lip and black eye and all the other contusions and cuts marring her face, even with exhaustion weighing on her, Ihsan could tell she was beautiful.

Despite his troubles, despite his pain, he was curious. What combination of events had led her here? For the first time since Surrahdi had skipped away with his tongue, Ihsan tried to speak. The pain it summoned brought tears to his eyes, and caused another coughing fit.

It was starting to subside when the woman's eyes shot open and she spoke with the tone of an oud parlor doorman. "What did I tell you?"

He realized he was moaning again, and stopped.

She tried to sleep once more, but perhaps felt Ihsan's gaze on her because she soon gave up on it. "Is it true, then?" she asked in Malasani. "You're King Ihsan?"

What point was there in denying it? He nodded, then pointed to her and tilted his head just so, a gesture in Malasan which was synonymous with asking a question.

"I'm Haddad."

Though the movement pained him, Ihsan bowed his head in greeting. She didn't return the gesture.

"It must be difficult seeing everything you love taken from you."

Part of him felt like he should be angry at this turn of events. And he supposed he was, but more for Nayyan's sake than his own. Nayyan and their unborn child. This felt like a reckoning that had always been coming. A reckoning he and the others all deserved. If anything, he was surprised it hadn't come sooner. He couldn't explain to Haddad, however, so instead he pointed to her in her cell and raised his eyebrows in an expression of irony.

She looked about at the other cells, which were empty save for the one at the end, which held a figure dressed in rags with a rat's nest for hair. "Yes, I know how it feels, but I was never a King. I didn't have so far to fall."

He crept closer to the cell bars and reached out into the passageway between them. Into the dust he drew—upside down so that Haddad could read it—the Malasani sign for *how?*

She stared at the sign, then laughed a bitter laugh. "The better question is how *you* got here." When he pointed to the dusty boards again, she shrugged. "I listened to the wrong man. You?"

He drew the sign for misfortune.

She laughed again, and this time it was a genuine, soul-pleasing sound. "Misfortune indeed."

He pointed to *how?* for the third time. He hadn't retained his throne for more than four hundred years without persistence.

"In truth," she said, "I was trying to protect Sharakhai. Or one small part of it in any case." She seemed to want to tell the tale, which Ihsan found was often the case. Get someone talking about themselves, even for a little while, and a hundred doors to their heart were revealed. Then it was simply a matter of choosing the next one to open.

She spun a tale of her mission to the east, how she'd come to spy on the desert tribes as the owner of a small trading company. After a bit of prodding, she told him how she'd met King Emir. How the two had fallen in love. "Or so I'd thought," she said, suddenly much more conscious of her cuts and bruises than she had been a moment ago.

Shortly before the assault on the city had begun, she'd brought the pleas of the thirteenth tribe, as spoken by their emissary, Emre, to her king. She asked him to stop the attack on the blooming fields, saying out loud what everyone already knew: that the attack on the blooming fields was a fruitless endeavor. King Emir let her speak her piece then asked her about her time with the Sharakhani emissary, whether she enjoyed his company, how necessary it had been to sleep with him.

"He was the one who told *me* it might come to that. He *encouraged* it so long as it would help secure Malasan's future and ensure peace with the tribes for long enough to take Sharakhai."

Ihsan wiped the dust and wrote in it anew. *And when he learned the truth?*

"He flew into a jealous rage, claiming I'd put the safety of Sharakhai above that of Malasan." She turned her head and spat on the deck boards. "Empty words. He knew as well as I did that his attack on the blooming fields was useless. He admitted as much. And then, two days after I was thrown in here, I learned that he'd ordered the attack to cease!"

The news of Emre was interesting. He was a childhood friend of Çedamihn's who'd joined the Moonless Host. Ihsan had thought him little more than a foot soldier, a lesser player in the game at best. But Haddad's story was forcing him to reconsider. Why would a man, once a scarab of the Moonless Host, try to protect the asirim? It struck him how quickly the thirteenth tribe were embracing the history that Ihsan and the other Kings had spent centuries trying to erase. Most of the Kings had believed a war of disinformation would be enough to discredit the thirteenth tribe's story and suppress the truth. But now Ihsan knew he'd been right all along. As much as he'd tried to convince himself otherwise in the years after Beht Ihman, stories like those of the lost tribe were undying flames. One might bury them for a time, but eventually they would work their way back to the surface and light the world aflame.

Now he saw why Haddad had opened up to him so quickly. She had an unspoken desire to hurt King Emir. She might not even know it herself, but it was there, and it was a thing he might trade on for something infinitely more important to him.

King Surrahdi, he wrote on the floor. *Did you know he was alive?*

To say Haddad's expression was guarded would be an understatement. He thought asking had been a mistake, but then she offered, "It wasn't common knowledge."

She'd avoided the question, which hinted at how loyal she was to the throne. Was it merely out of habit? She was speaking to a Sharakhani King, after all. There was only one way to find out: keep her talking.

Surely Emir wouldn't have hidden it from you.

She was silent for a time. "No."

Ihsan smoothed the dust and wrote, *Did you know he was creating his army?*

She shrugged. "Yes."

And no one spoke against it? He put on a look of confusion, the sort parents gave to their children when they'd done something shameful.

"No. Why would they?"

She'd spoken too quickly. She knew the shame Ihsan was hinting at—any Malasani would—but had chosen not to take the bait. In reply, he drew the ancient symbol for one of their holy trinity, Tamtamiin, god of a thousand hearts.

She stared at the symbol in the dust for a long while before answering. "What Surrahdi did was for the good of our people. That honors Shonokh and Ranrika as well as Tamtamiin."

Ihsan wrote the ancient symbols for love, compassion, and empathy, Tamtamiin's primary attributes, those to which one was to adhere when working in her name. Golems were always created from a place of love. They were used to remember and honor family. They had no place in war save to defend the life of those from whom they'd been made and their loved ones. To use them for acts of aggression was forbidden. In fact, before now, Ihsan would have thought it impossible. Were they not given life from the spring Tamtamiin herself had summoned from the earth? Were they not bound through that connection to adhere to her teachings?

So the lore of the golems went. Ihsan had read many such texts in his travels to Malasan. And yet Surrahdi had made hundreds of them and was using them for war. It was easy to point to greed as the justification behind it. Surrahdi had always coveted Sharakhai. But to do so was to underestimate the importance of the triumvirate in the lives of the Malasani, particularly those who sat the throne, who were raised to worship all three in equal measure.

The Mad King, Ihsan thought, *was named the Mad King for a reason.*

Surrahdi had inherited the throne just short of his twentieth summer. He'd seemed normal in those days, if a bit aggressive toward the desert and Sharakhai. But he'd changed over the years, becoming not only more truculent, but more unstable as well—one point short of a crown, went the joke in the halls of Tauriyat. Knowing what he knew now, he had to wonder: Had creating the golems driven him mad? Had he been creating them for decades? Creating even one was a trial on the soul that left one weakened and feeling broken—*I feel unmade,* one woman had written centuries earlier.

Decades spent at this one task, Ihsan mused. *The man might be mad but I'll give him this much: he's tenacious.*

Knowing Surrahdi's penchant for symbolism, Ihsan guessed he'd made a thousand of them. *A thousand hearts missing,* Zeheb had said, which was another moniker for Tamtamiin. It was sacrilege, to do such a thing. He would have tried to justify it in many ways; creating enough to pay homage to the goddess was surely one of them.

Still, it was a high crime. He found himself wondering why the ruling families of Malasan and the priests in their temple halls would have allowed it, but he laughed at himself a moment later. Surrahdi's boldness had brought decades of prosperity to Malasan. As so often proved true, the comforts of this world trumped those of the next.

Do you feel no shame? Ihsan wrote.

"What does my shame matter? It isn't my place to say."

Ihsan swallowed involuntarily and immediately gasped. For long moments the pain was overwhelming. When he was able to look at Haddad again, he tapped the space above his dusty words.

"It isn't my *place.*" Haddad turned and stared intently at the occupant of the far cell. "I'd mind my business if I were you."

The woman in the far cell, who wore a host of tatty rags, gave no reply except to turn and face the hull. It was in that moment that Ihsan thought he recognized her, but the remembrance was lost as a sudden coughing fit overtook him.

Haddad's words filtered through his pain as she snapped at the tatty woman, "Now keep those goggly eyes fixed anywhere but here."

Heavy footsteps approached the door at the end of the large room. Ignoring his pain as best he could, Ihsan stretched an arm between the bars and wiped the words from the decking. The door swung open a moment later and in stepped the turnkey with a tray. They were each given flatbread and water but, lo and behold, Ihsan was given something extra. A glass of araq. The turnkey stared down at Ihsan, then glared at the araq and emitted the sort of displeased grunt an ox might make when whipped by its master. Then he lumbered away.

As the turnkey left and closed the door, a conversation that had clearly begun earlier resumed. "I'm telling you, we're not going anywhere," a voice said, "not until the golems have recovered."

"They know—" the turnkey began, but the rest was lost as the door slammed shut.

Do they indeed? Ihsan mused.

He picked up the araq and sniffed it, immediately recognizing its scent. It was an extremely good glass of araq from Bhylek House, one of Sharakhai's finest makers. He wondered if it was poisoned, but what would be the point? They could poison him any time they wished. He took a sip and it burned the severed end of his tongue badly. He didn't care, though; his mouth hurt anyway. He might not be able to taste much, but he could smell plenty. When the pain passed, he took a deep, long whiff, and found it to be aged perfectly, with just enough water lily to counterbalance the sharper notes of lime peel and orange. The faint notes of pepper and oak completed one of the most satisfying scents Ihsan had ever had the pleasure of inhaling.

He held it up to the light from the portholes, admiring the shallow, sunflower depths, then reached out through the bars, offering the glass to Haddad. She stared at it, then shook her head. Ihsan shrugged and took another sip as memories of the many late nights sipping the same liquor on his palace veranda returned to him.

It was a message from King Emir. An insult. They'd taken the city, the glass of araq said, or enough of it to begin stripping Sharakhai of her riches. But it only served to reinforce Ihsan's way of thinking. The very fact that King Emir would try to rub Ihsan's nose in their conquest only proved how eager they were to overlook Surrahdi's shame. *They know*, the turnkey had said before the door closed. The golems understood Surrahdi's shame, because each retained some small piece of his humanity.

You cannot believe creating so many golems honors Tamtamiin, Ihsan wrote to Haddad when they were alone again, *nor Shonokh, nor Ranrika*.

She remained silent, perhaps hoping he'd give up, but if so, she'd severely underestimated his resolve. He wiped it away and tried again.

You're willing to jeopardize your place in the farther fields, the future of your entire nation, to protect a king who would treat you so?

He didn't have to gesture to her bruises or her cut lip for her to understand what he meant. She seemed to notice his gaze, and averted her eyes, perhaps embarrassed over them. She didn't have to say a word for him to understand the shame and worry she must feel at the way King Emir and his father had chosen to conquer the desert.

Is Sharakhai worth the burning of your faith?

"You seem to think I have some control over my king. I have none."

You need no control of your own. Emir is devout. Control will be found through faith.

"Yes Emir is devout, but so is Surrahdi."

Then use their devotion against them. Remind them of the teachings of their faith.

She pointed to her face. "I did! Why do you think he did this? I tried using his faith to get him to stop the attack on the asirim."

Then appeal to others. There must be a dozen who could convince him.

"They've tried! Why do you think he parades around in the high priest's robes? He took them for his own after murdering the woman who last held that title, because she dared speak sense to him. Why do you think the golems keep dying? Deep down he knows what he's doing is wrong. But does he recognize his crimes when it happens? No, he only makes more of them. Like plastering mud over cracks, he hopes to repair his fractured mind or at the least cover his shame. But it only drives him deeper into madness."

Ihsan's hand froze above the deck boards as the implications of her words sunk in.

The golems are dying? he wrote.

Haddad stared at the writing in the dust. She swallowed hard, then looked into Ihsan's eyes, the embarrassment clear on her face. She'd divulged one secret too many.

Just beside *dying* he wrote, *Why?* Then tapped both of them hard.

Haddad leaned back against the hull. "You're a clever man. Figure it out."

He tried to learn more, but she refused to so much as look at him. Even when he tried to speak with his ruined tongue, a sound like lowing cattle, she kept her gaze averted.

Ihsan fell into silence. He wasn't sure what he'd expected out of this conversation. He'd wanted information, perhaps the beginnings of a plan to get himself out of this camp. But somehow he'd ended up with a thread that, when pulled just so, might unravel the entire Malasani army. It was too early to start tugging on it, but the time would come.

His gaze drifted to the woman in the far cell near the door. She was curled up on the floor and staring at him, her arms wrapped around her head. He was just about to rattle his door and point at her to look away when he realized how intimate the position was. And how very familiar.

He nearly laughed. *How rich,* he thought idly. Two days ago he'd contemplated killing himself. Now he could think of nothing but the satisfaction of seeing Surrahdi's grand vision come crashing down around his ears. And yet, even with the help of the woman disguised as a shabby prisoner, it wouldn't be easy.

He'd been feeling sorry for himself these past few days and in his grief had abandoned one of his primary tenets: that one controls one's own fate, always, even when it seemed it wasn't so. But how to make it happen? He had few enough strings to pull.

He stared at Haddad. At how forlorn she looked. She might be manipulated, but not by him. Her defenses were too high. Who, then, might he use? He thought back on everything she'd told him, and landed on the one who had accompanied her here, the one she'd slept with to gain his trust, the one who'd urged her to speak to King Emir.

The young scarab, Emre.

He wouldn't take direction from a Sharakhani King easily, but he'd cared enough about the asirim to try to save them; he might care enough about Sharakhai to do as Ihsan wanted.

The woman in rags opened her mouth and mimed sounds coming out, a request to speak aloud. Ihsan shook his head no. If Haddad were to learn he had an accomplice, it could all fall apart. He made his fist fall slowly behind his arm, mimicking the sun setting behind the horizon.

The woman nodded and lay her head back down. Ihsan, meanwhile, listened to the sounds of the Malasani war camp.

Chapter 50

"THE KING WILL SEE YOU NOW," said the Malasani guard to Emre. He wore the red armor of King Emir's personal guard. He was, however, newly appointed to the role, the others having killed themselves four days ago when King Ihsan ordered them to slit their own throats. Emre thought the city would have been taken by now, but the Kings' forces had put up a stiff defense at the inner walls. And, perhaps more telling, something strange had happened with the golems. Many of them, if the rumors were true, had suddenly, all in concert, turned and walked away from the conflict. They'd returned to the southern harbor and huddled in one large mass as if waiting for something. What they might have been waiting for, Emre wasn't sure. To recover, he supposed, but from what? The golems might have a sliver of a soul within them, but that didn't mean they had feelings, did it?

Emre followed the guard into the pavilion. Hamid, by Emre's side, ducked under the flap, took one look at the king sitting on the far side, and said under his breath, "Fuck me. I'm surprised he doesn't walk on stilts."

The pavilion's floor was not carpets over sand, but a series of interlocked wooden platforms. And King Emir himself was sitting on a throne, which in turn was on a dais. Along with the movable platform the king used to watch the war, it gave the impression of a man who found the sand of the Great Mother so offensive that he refused set foot upon it.

The first thing Emre noticed when they came closer were the bloody cuts and bruises on King Emir's knuckles. The king noticed and, rather than hide them, sat straighter in his throne and gripped the carved lion's heads at the ends of the armrests, as if daring Emre to make mention of them. Emre didn't. He bowed instead, only deep enough that it wouldn't be considered an outright insult. Hamid, standing on Emre's right, did as well, though clearly it was a reluctant gesture. For once, Emre didn't care.

Near the King's side, sitting on a padded chair, was Surrahdi. He was once again wearing the mask of Tamtamiin and a robe of golden flax. The way he sat, legs crossed on the seat, exposed his ankles and sandals. His hands were in his lap, ever moving, a ceaseless flow of unconfined energy. It was a strange parody of innocence, the pose of an unruly child, not that of a man who'd helmed one of the most powerful nations in the known world.

"We meet under an auspicious star," King Emir said when they'd risen. "Isn't that what you say in the desert?"

Surrahdi giggled and spoke behind his mask. "An auspicious star indeed."

"It is," Emre replied, doing his best to ignore Surrahdi, "though the expression is used for ill portents, not fair."

"For that you use favorable winds, yes? May we meet as the sands blow calmly along the dunes?"

"Among others, yes." Emre was already annoyed with the king's smug attitude. "Does this mean you've considered our offer?"

King Emir gave a conciliatory smile and waved to the low stools below the dais. The stools were so low that Emre and Hamid would have to sit cross-legged, forcing them to look up to Emir like children being scolded. Emre made no move to comply with the request. Neither did Hamid, who stared at the king with a calm expression, eyes half-lidded. It was as emotionless an expression as Emre had ever seen on him, which showed just how angry he was.

"We would not take more of the king's time than is necessary," Emre said to him.

Surrahdi had practically been vibrating in his chair, his hands clasped beneath his chin, but at Emre's words he stilled, as if terribly disappointed.

King Emir considered Emre and Hamid, suddenly much more serious. "Your message said you wish to conclude our negotiations."

Emre nodded. "Yes. I have other business to attend to."

"As do I. I have a city to take, the blooming fields to worry about, and the extermination of your precious asirim to deal with." King Emir paused, waiting for a reaction. When Emre didn't give him the satisfaction, he said, "I wonder, did you realize when you convinced Haddad to beg for my mercy that you were only delaying the inevitable? Did you suppose I would let the asirim be once the city was mine?"

"I'm not here to speak of them," Emre said.

"And yet you sent Haddad to speak of them *for* you."

"The asirim have suffered enough."

"Then you shouldn't mind quick deaths for them all."

Emre calmed himself before speaking. The king was trying to goad him, and he refused to take the bait. "Your Most Grand Excellence, I have not come here to discuss the miserable souls who live beneath the adichara, but to lay an offer at your feet."

"Oh? And what would that be?"

"Ships, spears, swords, and shields. Plus the men and women to wield them."

King Emir glanced over Emre's shoulder to the pavilion's entrance and the golden city beyond. "You think we have need of a handful of ships from the thirteenth tribe?"

"My offer no longer comes from the thirteenth tribe alone, but from the people of the desert, the united tribes."

"United tribes, is it?"

"Yes."

Emre had debated with Hamid and Old Nur long into the night how to present this offer. It was a bargaining chip Macide had given him leave to use if he felt it would help secure the tribe. Emre hadn't wanted to use it, but it was clear that King Emir wasn't taking their offer to discuss trade in good faith. Old Nur had been against it. Hamid, surprisingly, had sided with Emre. Emre had been convinced Hamid would hate the idea of fighting alongside the Malasani, but his desire to harm the Sharakhani Kings had won out.

"The Malasani presence in the desert will be short-lived," Hamid assured them over the fire. "Let us wound the Kings, draw their blood while we can."

He'd insisted they offer to fight *alongside* the Malasani fleet, independently, not as a part of it. Emre had agreed, both with Hamid's reasoning and his demands, but Emre had a greater purpose as well. King Emir needed to know that the tribes were not to be trifled with. Even if he declined, the offer itself was a declaration of a desert united. At the least it would force the Malasani king to think twice before threatening the tribes, even the least among them, or risk uniting them all against him. And at best—should Malasan come out ahead in this war—it might lead to peace with the people of the desert, a peace found through strength, not capitulation.

"Yes, well," King Emir said, "we will see what comes of your alliance. Meanwhile, you would offer us a handful of ships?"

"Not a handful. Fifty. And two thousand spears to add to your cause."

Near King Emir, Surrahdi stood and began to dance about the dais. "Fifty!" He performed a jig behind the throne. "Ships, ten and forty, sail the desert grand! Ships ten and forty, across the amber sand!"

King Emir tried to use his father's outburst to cover his surprise, but Emre had seen how his brows raised. "Two thousand spears, you say, when I have thirty thousand at my beck and call."

"Thirty thousand, and the upper hand here in Sharakhai, but a storm gathers on the horizon. The Kings have stopped you at the inner walls, and Qaimir is on their way to relieve them. I would bet that Kundhun also sails for Sharakhai, and we both know it won't be to aid you, King Emir, but to rid the city of its invaders. And then there is Mirea. Two fleets meet in the northern desert. Whether the Kings win or the Queen of Mirea does, it means trouble for Malasan. You have no allies here to call upon. But you could have, my king."

King Emir considered a long while. The wind blew strongly for a moment, sending the pavilion's tent poles to creaking. "Fifty ships and two thousand spears."

"Just so."

"And what would you ask in return?"

"But two small requests, neither of which will cause the King of Malasan any great suffering."

At this, Hamid glanced toward Emre. Last night they'd agreed to a single demand, not two. He said nothing, however, and soon King Emir was waving a hand for Emre to continue. "Go on."

"First," Emre said, "we would like King Ihsan to be delivered to us."

All around the pavilion, Emir's courtiers began talking in low tones, until Emir himself stomped the heel of his boot onto the dais and silenced all. "You want the King of Lies?"

"He has done more harm to us than you can ever know. He must pay for his crimes."

To this King Emir replied easily, "Rest assured he shall! The Honey-tongued King has much to answer for in Malasan as well."

Emre bowed his head. "Whatever insults and injuries Malasan has suffered, those levied against the thirteenth tribe have been infinitely worse."

Surrahdi became animated once more. His gaze flitted between King Emir and Emre. "So juicy and sticky sweet! The honeyed tongue of the Honey-tongued King!"

King Emir, meanwhile, considered the demand. He'd put on a doubtful expression, but Emre had never felt more sure of a thing. King Emir might not know it yet, but he would give Emre this. King Ihsan wasn't nearly as important to him as winning the desert. So it came as no surprise when he nodded and said, "Your second request?"

"That Haddad return with us to act as your emissary to the desert people." He kept his tone neutral, and had chosen his words carefully, so as not to give King Emir the impression that he knew more than he was letting on.

Two nights ago, a figure had stolen into Emre's cabin, a feminine form wearing a black dress. A Blade Maiden wearing a necklace made from the thorns of an ehrekh. Emre could hardly believe his eyes. Çeda had crossed paths with just such a woman in the blooming fields. They'd traded blows, but Çeda had managed to escape, and the encounter had led her and a good many people, Emre included, down long and winding paths to places they could never have dreamed of a few short years ago.

Emre had nearly sounded the alarm, but the Maiden had put her finger to her lips. She'd been unarmed, and had made no threatening moves, so Emre had waited. After closing the door, she'd stepped closer and spoke in a low voice.

How strange her story seemed at first. Golems and gods and mad kings. Indeed, the longer she spoke, the more incredulous it sounded, especially when she revealed that much of it had come from the Honey-tongued King.

"How could you possibly know all this?" he asked her. "King Ihsan is in a prison ship."

"As was I, until I felt it time to leave."

Emre had stared at her, doubting, but he knew the capabilities of the Blade Maidens better than most, and he eventually nodded, a sign for her to continue.

A plan had followed. A desperate plan, to be sure, but it might just work, Emre thought.

The pavilion's canvas snapped, and a smile lit King Emir's face. "Surely, you're joking."

Emre replied easily, "I assure you I am not."

Hamid leaned toward Emre and turned his head away from the dais. "Don't do this," he muttered.

Emre ignored him. "She's the perfect choice for ambassador," he said to King Emir. "She knows us well already. She's met Macide and Aríz and several other shaikhs. She knows, as well as any Malasani, how we live in the desert."

Animated and smug a moment ago, the king was now serious as a black laugher. "Knows you well . . ." Gods, his face was turning red.

Emre pretended not to notice. "Just so," he said. "She's a tough negotiator, but in my dealings with her she's always used a firm, even hand. And her tongue, well . . . I'll admit it can be harsh at times, but also quite soft when the need arises."

King Emir stood in a rush. "That's enough."

Emre played dumb. "Your Excellence?"

"Bring her," he said to a nearby guard.

The guard nodded and left the pavilion.

What followed were several minutes in which the only person who seemed willing to move, or even make a sound was Mad King Surrahdi. He pranced around the dais, hands high in the air, twirling as if he were on a mountaintop trying to summon one of the rare efrit. He seemed, instead of insanely joyous as he was most often, genuinely concerned, to the point that he might do something rash.

Emre tried to ignore him, but found it impossible when he stood before his own son and asked in a calm, collected voice, "Will you kill her?"

"Sit down."

"I always liked her, you know."

"I said sit down."

Emir's were the words of a scolding father, and came as no surprise given Surrahdi's antics. More curious was the fact that King Emir didn't use it more often. After speaking with the Blade Maiden, however, it all made sense.

"They let Surrahdi act the fool," she'd said, "because they cannot bear to face the truth that lies beneath. They've stood by, allowed his grand plan to unfold, and now no one can acknowledge the shame lest it shame them all."

The Blade Maiden had been unsure how best to force King Emir's hand, but Emre knew his type well enough. He was a man who saw confrontations as having only one winner: himself. "I'll ask for her," Emre had told the Maiden. "King Emir will do the rest."

No sooner had Surrahdi returned to his chair than Haddad was dragged into the pavilion and thrown at King Emir's feet. What followed was not unexpected. The brutality, however, was. King Emir backhanded Haddad, and when she tried to recover, did so again.

"Stop!" Emre cried, and stepped forward.

The king's guard intercepted him. When he tried to bull past them, two held his arms while a third drove a mailed fist into his gut. He curled around the blow, and his breath whooshed from his lungs, but he was up and fighting a moment later, struggling to break from their grasp.

King Emir glanced over at him, eminently pleased, then continued to pound Haddad with his fist. Emre thought he might kill her then and there to show him who had the upper hand. But he stopped a moment later, and allowed her to collapse against the dais and curl into a ball. "Haddad is mine to do with as I please. You understand?"

"If she offends you so much," Emre said, "let her live out her days in the desert."

Haddad's sobs filled the pavilion. King Emir stepped over her cowering shape and stood at the edge of the dais so he was staring down at Emre. Then he hauled one arm back, gripped his gauntleted hand into a fist, and punched Emre in the face. Emre staggered back and fell. Blood coursed down from his nose and along his lips. It dripped from his chin in a stream as King Emir glowered.

"What's mine is mine." He stepped down from the dais and punched Emre again. "Haddad. Sharakhai. Your precious blooming fields and the vermin below. The entire bloody desert." When Emre retreated, stunned, Emir rushed forward and backhanded him. Emre's world tipped sideways. His vision filled with stars.

On the dais, Surrahdi was jumping up and down like a spider monkey. "Kill him! Gut him! See what's inside!"

Four guards dragged Hamid from the tent. Two more hauled Emre to his feet while another gripped his hair and forced him to hold King Emir's gaze.

"Two thousand spears . . ." Emir spat into Emre's face. "Take your worthless crew and your tumbledown ship and return to your master like the flea-ridden cur you are. Tell Macide that when we're finished with Sharakhai, we're coming for his tribe. Tell him we're coming for the others as well, however many join your precious alliance. The only promise the shaikhs will get from me is that I will feed their bones to the Great Mother."

Ten of the King's guard and dozens of Malasani soldiers accompanied them to the *Amaranth*. When they were aboard, they waited on the sand, and when they felt they were moving too slowly began shooting arrows into the hull and masts and rigging, making a sound like barking dogs as they did so.

As the sails were set and the *Amaranth* picked up speed, Darius brought Emre a wet rag. Emre accepted it and began wiping the blood from his face. It was only as the Malasani camp was falling below the horizon that Hamid came to Emre, fuming. "You mind telling me what that was all about?"

Emre shrugged. "I'll tell you all of it. I promise." He looked at the setting sun. "For now, we need to make preparations to circle back."

Hamid's sleepy eyes were neither amused nor surprised. "No, Emre."

"Yes. We're going back," he said to the gathered crew, "and we're going to steal King Ihsan out from under their fucking noses."

Chapter 51

ÇEDA STRODE DOWN THE GANGPLANK of the *Red Bride* and took to the open sand, heading for the sunshade Sümeya had set up that morning. Behind her came Sümeya, Melis, and Kameyl, all wearing their Maiden's black. Jenise and the other Shieldwives came next, all in tan fighting dresses and turbans that made them look like sandstone statues. None bore swords, including Çeda. What was to come was a ritual of openness and understanding. It would be a rebirth of sorts, a ritual in which swords had no place.

Walking, loping, crawling on an intercept course were the asirim—eight dark, hunched shapes that clustered around a ninth, their King, Sehid-Alaz. They'd pulled the arrow from his chest, allowing the wound to close and his body to start to heal, but his mind was every bit as fragile as Çeda had feared. He walked with a strange gait and shied at sudden movement. Even clouds occluding the sun brought on momentary seizures of fear and confusion. As had been true in Eventide, Çeda could feel the chaos within him. His mind was a roil of emotions that was difficult to be near. The only reason she could be close to him now was the calming influence of the other asirim.

Alone he was like a wolf separated from its pack and beaten mercilessly. He hardly knew himself anymore and was aggressive, lashing out at any perceived threat. Twice on their flight from Sharakhai—after their strange, almost dreamlike escape with King Ihsan—he'd tried to attack Sümeya, perhaps because he smelled on her the scent of her father, King Husamettín. Çeda had intervened both times, slowly talking Sehid-Alaz down until he'd returned to his usual position: a tight ball in the bottom of their skiff.

On their reunion with the *Red Bride*, however, Mavra and her children had been able to shelter him from the storm. The beaten wolf was reunited with his pack, allowing him to find some semblance of peace, though only while cradled by their love. He'd lost his courage in Eventide's dungeon, his will to fight. He'd lost his identity. And all knew that the moment he was left alone, the madness would return. The curse Husamettín had laid upon him was a wound that might never heal. Which was precisely why they'd all gathered together, to begin the process of lifting that curse.

When they reached the sunshade, Çeda sat cross-legged on the sand. Melis set her a bamboo needle and tap and a clay pot that contained a special ink. The ink, the same as she'd made for Jenise and Amile and all the rest, had been prepared in a ritual using the burnt branches and flowers of the adichara.

"I would have you stay," Çeda said to Melis as she began to back away. She took in Sümeya and Kameyl as well. "All of you."

"We've discussed this," Sümeya said.

"Yes, but I've reconsidered. It's true that you aren't bonded to these asirim, but Sehid-Alaz should feel your presence as well, for in you he cannot help but feel hope."

The sun shone harshly against the acid-damaged side of Kameyl's face, evidence of their fight against Hamzakiir's shamblers in the ancient temple beneath Ishmantep. "Hope?" she scoffed.

"Yes. Hope that there are those in Sharakhai who can see beyond the rule of the Kings." She motioned to the sand around her and addressed all of them. "Sit."

After a look shared among them, they complied, forming a triangle around Çeda. Her Shieldwives followed, two between each of the Blade Maidens, forming a loose circle around Çeda. They made themselves comfortable. It would be a long day.

Mavra, her footsteps heavy on the sand, led Sehid-Alaz to stand before Çeda. A sickly-sweet smell accompanied them, a scent Çeda had come to associate with all the asirim. Mavra bade him sit with gentle tugs on his arm. It was only when the asirim had closed around the sunshade in a wide circle, however, that Sehid-Alaz complied. He was shaking. Nervous, angry, confused.

Mavra left him there and stood before Çeda. *"I'm glad I didn't tell my story with the ink,"* she rasped, *"for his is the larger tale. Mine is but part of his."*

Çeda could only smile. They both knew it might not work. And they both knew the alternative if it didn't.

As Mavra stepped away, Çeda lifted the needle and tap and stared into Sehid-Alaz's jaundiced eyes. There was so much confusion, so much innocence there that Çeda nearly wept, but she held back her tears. He needed to see her strength, to take heart and do what needed to be done. "I would have you take these, Sehid-Alaz," she said to the ancient King. "I would have you tell your tale."

Mavra settled herself in the outer circle. As one, she and her children closed their eyes and tipped their heads toward the sky. As if a weight had been lifted from his shoulders, Sehid-Alaz's back straightened. His breath lengthened.

Çeda held out the needle and tap. "Tell your tale and be freed."

Sehid-Alaz took one long breath, then nodded. "My child," he whispered, then accepted the offered implements with quivering hands. Çeda slipped her arms out of her fighting dress and gathered the fabric down around her hips. She leaned forward, offering her back as a canvas. Sehid-Alaz knelt behind her. He was still conflicted—the curse still weighed on him—but with those gathered around him he was as unburdened as he was ever going to be. As the sun rose, he slowly began to tap the ink into Çeda's skin.

Her upper back was already covered in the tattoos made by Dardzada and Leorah. In this space Sehid-Alaz added to the tale, embellishing it, adding nuances Çeda could never have understood on her own. It was as if Sehid-Alaz were laying down the branches of the story, those events that had happened in recent memory. Near midday, however, he began to ink more into the middle of Çeda's back. As the sun began to set, he motioned for Çeda to lie on the sand so he could work on her lower back.

Throughout the day they paused for water. For food. To relieve themselves. They took time to stand and stretch. The asirim, however, never moved. Ever vigilant, they protected their King. And Sehid-Alaz never stepped foot outside the circle. He would often stare at the dunes longingly, or at the sand just outside the circle in fear, as if it might swallow him whole. But he seemed relieved each time they were ready to start again.

They continued until nightfall, and throughout the entire next day, during which Sehid-Alaz's spells of fear and confusion came less often. Indeed, the dark storms within his mind, held at bay by Mavra and the others, seemed less intense as well. He sat straighter, and occasionally hummed an ancient tune as he inked his tattoo across Çeda's back.

Only once during that time did they feel anything from Husamettín himself, despite his being belowdecks on the *Red Bride*. He tried to break through their circle to reach Sehid-Alaz, to command him, but their precautions had sheltered Sehid-Alaz from the influence of the Kings, at least so long as they remained vigilant. After Husamettín's intrusion, Kameyl left the circle and returned to the ship. She'd hardly gone belowdecks when they felt Husamettín's presence diminish, then vanish altogether.

Kameyl returned with bloody knuckles and spots of crimson spattered across her right cheek. "He won't bother us again," she said. And indeed, they continued unhindered.

Çeda promised herself she'd not look at the tattoo until it was completed, but her will broke on the third night and she looked in a mirror. A thrill ran through her when she saw it: a tree, a lone adichara. Its thorny branches reached up among the other tattoos, though it never obscured them, as if Sehid-Alaz was well aware that his story was the background to her tale. The tattooed blooms, each with thirteen petals, were open and wide and faced the sky. Some rested along the tops of her shoulders, others along the nape of her neck and across her shoulder blades; still more reached around her ribs. It was beautiful. Sehid-Alaz had the hand of an artist.

The texture of the bark and thorns, though. There was something strange about it. She twisted in her bed on the ship, feeling the burn from the tattoo as she did so, and drew the mirror close to her ribs so she could examine one of the branches more closely. And gasped. The pain along her skin became a tingling sensation.

The mottled bark and thorns had names written into them. They were so small they looked like a part of the bark. No, she corrected herself, not part of. The tree was made up *solely* of names.

The names of the asirim, she realized. Hundreds upon hundreds of them, with much of the tree's trunk and roots still to be filled in. And then it struck her. *He's naming all of them, every single one taken on the night of Beht Ihman.* Only the blooms were left untouched by names, as if they were set apart, something *other* than his people, which she supposed was true. There was too much of the twin gods, Tulathan and Rhia, in those bright flowers.

She wasn't sure how to feel about it. She was honored, but the sheer weight of those names was a lot to bear.

"Sometimes it's good to carve a statue from your dreams," Sümeya said after Çeda shared her thoughts that night.

It was an old saying, referring to how focusing one's efforts can make a thing come true.

"I just hadn't realized how many asirim there were. It feels like they're watching from all across the desert, from the world beyond as well."

"Isn't it what you've wanted all along? To have a part in their freedom?"

"Yes and no. I wanted to see them freed. I wanted to help where I could. But this makes it feel like it's my burden alone."

"It isn't, though. You are his voice"—she motioned to Çeda's back—"and those are his words. Let him speak."

"I'm honored to be his voice. It's just that the more I feel the weight, the more it feels like I'm going to fail them."

"I feel the same way about Sharakhai."

They continued for several more days, Sehid-Alaz taking the time to fill in more and more of the adichara tattoo. Çeda was beginning to worry, though. Sehid-Alaz seemed to have hit a plateau in terms of progress toward his freedom, while she was becoming more and more aware of Husamettín, still captive in the hold of the ship. She felt others as well—the other Kings, in all likelihood. The chains that had always bound the asirim still bound Sehid-Alaz, and Çeda became increasingly worried they were *never* going to break.

She considered going back to the valley below Mount Arasal to seek Nalamae's council, perhaps her power as well, but rejected the notion as risky and short-sighted. Do that and the Kings might be led straight to Nalamae.

Late that night Çeda returned to the ship to find Sümeya and Melis asleep in their narrow bunks. Jenise was in her lower bunk reading an old beaten copy of the Al'Ambra by lamplight. She looked up from it as Çeda removed her dress and pulled back the covers from the bunk across from Jenise's. Her green-and-gold eyes were bright, as was the unkempt mop of her sun-bleached hair. "What's troubling you?" she asked Çeda.

Çeda lay on her stomach, the only position that allowed her to sleep. The salve Sümeya applied helped, as did the bandages, but the pain still flared. She winced as she punched her pillow into shape and lay her head against it. "You should sleep," she told Jenise. "We've another long day tomorrow."

"Far be it for me to tell you what to do, Çeda, but I think *you're* the one who needs sleep."

"I'm fine," she replied.

Jenise closed her book with a frown. "My father used to say that sometimes the path to the peak of a mountain lies not in moving doggedly ahead, but in backtracking, resting, and trying another way." Her gaze drifted downward to the space beneath Çeda's bed, where River's Daughter and Night's Kiss lay side by side. "Perhaps now is one of those times."

Before anchoring here, Jenise had urged Çeda over and over again to kill Husamettín. "Why wait? There's no question of his crimes. It's time he was punished for them."

"He'll pay," Çeda had replied, "but his knowledge is valuable, and there's too much at stake to rob ourselves of it. He is our sole source of information about Sehid-Alaz's curse."

"We have Sehid-Alaz himself!"

"Sehid-Alaz is bound by chains he cannot see."

"Husamettín put the curse on him. Killing him will undo it."

"The *gods* put this curse on Sehid-Alaz. Husamettín has merely twisted it for his own gain." Before Jenise could reply, Çeda had cut her off. "We'll still have that option tomorrow, but if we kill him today, we'll never learn anything from him."

Jenise hadn't been pleased but let it go. Now, though, she seemed ready to fight. "I don't believe, as others do, that you're afraid to kill your father. But your hope that he'll suddenly repent just because he's being forced to face his crimes is naive. Husamettín has said nothing, and he never will. So we lose nothing by killing him. Quite the opposite. It may be the answer to our prayers."

"We wait until Beht Zha'ir, the night of the asirim," Çeda said. "By then the tattoo will be complete and we'll know." The holy night was three days away.

"By then it may be too late." She motioned to Çeda's back. "With the ritual complete, perhaps Husamettín's curse will be woven between the names in that tree."

Çeda turned her head to the hull and shut her eyes. "Get some rest, Jenise."

It took a moment, but Jenise blew out her lamp and settled herself in her bunk. Çeda could feel Night's Kiss calling to her, urging her to do the very thing Jenise recommended.

Thou hast only to take the blood of thy father for thy King to be freed.

Just then Çeda heard movement above her. She turned and saw the moon-kissed outline of Sümeya staring down at her from the bunk above. She knew they'd been discussing the execution of her father, knew Çeda was considering it now, but she said nothing, and neither did Çeda.

Schid-Alaz continued the tattoo over the next two days, and Çeda's worries grew. Like a root, it had gained purchase within her mind and was creeping inward, splitting over and over until her skull felt consumed by it. Would Sehid-Alaz be freed when the tattoo was complete? Would the gods be angry if he was? And it if didn't, would she kill Husamettín, her own father, perhaps losing her only link to the answers she needed?

Sehid-Alaz filled in more and more names, shading the tree until it looked deep and perfect and real. Çeda's bond with him grew, and yet he seemed little changed. He might walk straighter. He might be focused when the other asirim were around him. But after the ritual was complete and the asirim broke to return to the desert, he seemed to shrink in on himself again, a shadow of the brave soul who'd saved Çeda from King Mesut on the Night of Endless Swords.

Çeda couldn't bear to be around anyone that night, so after the evening meal, she left for a walk beneath the stars. On her return she sensed that one of the asirim had parted from the others. It was Mavra, and Çeda could tell she wished to speak privately.

"What is it, grandmother?"

Mavra knelt along the top of a broad dune, her hands held tightly in her lap. She looked simultaneously young and terribly, terribly old. When she spoke, she closed herself off to the others and used her true voice so that no one but Çeda could hear her.

"*The others were so close to being freed . . .*"

"Who," Çeda asked, "your children?"

Mavra nodded. Her sense of shame was strong and growing stronger, and there was only one thing Çeda could think of that might have caused it.

"When you looked into Husamettín's mind," Çeda said carefully, "you said you'd found a way to free our King."

Mavra's eyes were distant, star-filled. "*I'd hoped that when we had him away from Sharakhai, surrounded by his loved ones . . .*" A gust of wind scoured the dune. Sand fell along its leeward side, hissing like a horned cobra. "*I hoped we'd be able to overcome the bonds of the gods.*"

"But that wasn't what you saw, was it?"

"*No.*"

She'd hidden the truth because it was too painful. "What *did* you see, Mavra?"

"*I pressed him for a way to free our King, and he fought me, and for a long time held me, held us, at bay—*"

"Mavra, tell me!"

Tears rolled down her cheeks like constellations shifting in the heavens. "*I saw Husamettín himself taking a sword to Sehid-Alaz. I saw Sehid-Alaz fall, gripping the sword in his hands. In that moment, only as he was dying, did I see him freed.*"

A tingling sensation ran from Çeda's scalp to the nape of her neck. This was the step she'd feared all along, that after everything, after all Sehid-Alaz had done to protect her, she would be forced to kill him. It was why the Kings had saved Sehid-Alaz, why they'd never killed him themselves. They needed him to keep control of the asirim.

Çeda stared up at the moons, silver Tulathan nearly full, golden Rhia only slightly less so, and came to a decision. Tomorrow was Beht Zha'ir. She would give it the day. If Sehid-Alaz still hadn't been freed by nightfall, she would use Husamettín's solution.

Tears forming in her eyes, Çeda held her hand out to Mavra. "Come. This isn't a time to be alone."

Mavra looked to her, then shifted her bulk and stood with Çeda's help. Çeda led her back to the asirim, where they all huddled with Sehid-Alaz sheltered at their center. They all knew now, they'd felt it from Mavra, and the asirim wailed long into the night. This time, Çeda wailed with them.

Chapter 52

BRAMA STOOD ON THE FOREDECK of Queen Alansal's dunebreaker, which sailed behind the vanguard of the Mirean fleet. These tall ships were even more impressive from the deck. Were it not for the ceaseless swaying, Brama would feel as though he were standing on a tower not sailing a sandship.

"Today is the day Sharakhai falls."

Brama turned to see Mae climbing the stairs to the foredeck. She had her lacquered armor on, her great helm too, its demon mask hanging to one side, ready to be buckled in place. One gauntleted hand rested on the pommel of her tassled dao. Her opposite arm was fitted with a metal fighting shield. She was silent and grim, ready to take her measure of Sharakhani flesh to avenge her people.

On the deck behind Mae, her qirin, Angfua, fought its chains. A pair of handlers tried to calm it, to no avail. The beast stretched its neck and clawed at the deck boards as the chains that bound it clinked and shinked and clouds of steam and smoke erupted in streams from its nostrils. It knew that battle was near and, like Mae, was eager for it.

As Mae stepped beside him, Brama motioned to the Kings' galleons. "Don't be reckless. The Kings haven't ruled for centuries for no reason."

Mae was already shaking her head. "No, Brama. Their time has come. The queen's water dancers foresaw it before we even left. Their fleet will fall, and then we sail to the walls of the city and tear them down too."

Brama wasn't so sure, but what could he say? He knew enough about Mae to know her belief in Queen Alansal was unwavering, as was her devotion. "And when you have the city?" he asked. "What then?"

Mae shrugged as if it were the most asinine question she'd ever heard. "We reap the glory."

"*Glory?*" Brama caught his balance as the ship plowed over a dune. "Glory from war is a mirage. It will fade, and when it does, you'll see it was misery all along."

The tension on the ships was rising. Throughout the chain of command, soldiers were being thrust into positions of authority before they were ready. But like Mae, they were angry, fueled by a thirst for revenge.

And Alansal had decided to play a card even the Kings wouldn't be prepared for. At the center of the Mirean vanguard, directly ahead of Queen Alansal's ship, were the seven hospital ships. The queen had gone to them and asked if they would fight for her. The answer from those assembled on the decks had been a great, ceaseless roar. They were not in good health—even from this distance, Brama could see the way some of them shook as they walked—but when given the chance, they would unleash their rage. The fight, as they said in the streets of Sharakhai, was about to go from knuckles to knives.

From the quarterdeck behind him, a heavy drumbeat rolled, a call to all ships in the fleet for a change of heading. It was repeated along the line. As the ships adjusted course, a series of signals using bright red and yellow flags was passed from the vanguard ahead. A grizzled soldier watched with a spyglass and relayed the information to Queen Alansal, who stood amidships near Mae's qirin. Brama understood little, but he heard a word in Sharakhan. *Asirim.* It was enough to stoke all of Brama's childhood fears of the creatures. He knew their history now—that the asirim were members of the thirteenth tribe, cursed on the night of Beht Ihman—but what did it matter if they'd been set against the Mirean ships? They would rend his flesh, or Mae's or Queen Alansal's, just as easily.

He heard a low buzzing sound behind him and turned to find a host of black beetles swarming onto the deck. The swarm pressed tightly then solidified into Rümayesh. She thudded closer, staring out over the amber expanse of desert, the vanguard of Mirean dunebreakers, and the Sharakhani fleet beyond.

"So we come to it," she said.

Her voice was low and loud, but Brama knew her well enough to sense how weakened she was. She'd remained on one of the ships farthest back to heal some fifty more scourge victims the queen had selected personally, most of them key officers and specialists in the fleet.

The queen joined Brama, Mae, and Rümayesh, wearing a billowing ivory dress with long red ribbons along its sleeves. Her hair was held in place, as always, by her two steel pins. She looked calm and ageless, but hungry as well. "Are there Kings aboard those ships?"

Rümayesh stared ahead. The lump on her forehead where the bone of Raamajit was buried stood out in the sunlight. Her rust-colored eyes narrowed, then blinked lazily. *Gods, she's halfway to exhaustion.*

"Well?" the queen asked.

The muscles along Rümayesh's jaw worked. Her brow furrowed. "I cannot tell," she said.

She's worried, Brama realized. Tired or not, it was an unsettling thing with a creature as powerful as an ehrekh.

"Why not?" Alansal asked.

A look of cold understanding dawned on Rümayesh. "The Queen of Qaimir is protecting them."

"Queen Meryam has come . . ." For some reason this seemed to please Alansal. "I wonder if the water dancers were right. King Kiral may have left this effort to her and her alone, preferring to remain in Sharakhai himself and prepare for Malasan's approach."

Rümayesh remained silent, but looked more alert. When she'd been trapped in the sapphire, Queen Meryam had conspired with Ramahd Amansir to have the gemstone stolen away so that she could gain its power. She'd used the stone to tug at the strings of power in Sharakhai and eventually joined the Kings in their quest to see the thirteenth tribe destroyed. But then Amansir, Emre, and Brama had stormed Meryam's ship, and Brama had managed to break the sapphire, thereby freeing her. Brama was still cut off from Rümayesh's emotions, but he could see how fiercely her fury burned.

"I will take the queen, if that is your wish," she said to Queen Alansal, a request bordering on a demand.

"Very well. Find her and kill her. Do this, and our bargain is complete."

Rümayesh's quirk of a smile revealed a hint of leonine teeth. "Very well."

Brama felt how eager she was to taste of death. More sickening, he felt his *own* eagerness. People hadn't even started dying yet, but he wanted it. He wanted it badly. The discord between that need and his simultaneous disgust was what made Brama realize that Rümayesh's walls had slipped. Weeks ago she would have wanted nothing more than revenge on Queen Meryam for having stolen the sapphire away and then using her as she might some menial servant. That urge was still there, but it felt almost like a dying wish.

"No," Rümayesh said to him. And just like that, his sense of her feelings was cut off. "You don't know me so well as that."

"I know you as well as anyone has ever known you."

She gazed into his eyes with an inscrutable expression. There was a sadness about her, though why that might be he had no idea. Before he could press her about it, she exploded into a cloud of beetles and lifted from the deck. Up she flew, swarming, undulating in the blue sky like a flock of blazing blues, moments before the fire pots began to soar.

All across the ships in the vanguard ahead, the Damned mounted their qirin with short spears and shields to hand. As Mae approached, Angfua was unchained by its handlers and guided to the foredeck. Fire pots crashed over the decks of the vanguard and the return fire from the Mirean ships struck the Sharakhani galleons as well.

Closer and closer the two lines came. A sudden gout of sand flew up at one of the dunebreakers, fouling the sails, and a dozen dark shapes could be seen flying up and onto the deck. These were the asirim, howling, storming the deck as ranks of Mirean soldiers moved to respond. But the asirim were terrors, scything through the Mirean soldiers' defenses. One of them, a rangy thing missing one arm, reached the pilot's wheel by bulling forward, heedless of the wounds it sustained. It took down the pilot with a single sweep of its claws, and began to pull sharply at the wheel. The ship heeled hard to the starboard side and crashed into another of the vanguard's ships, causing havoc all along the left side of the line. Another ship far to the right drifted harmlessly away as a smaller group of asirim howled aboard.

Cat's claws struck all along the vanguard, wrapping around struts and fouling ships' skis, causing the impressive line of Mirean ships to falter. Fire pots crashed. But the Mirean ships were not crippled as much as the Sharakhani fleet might have hoped. Their decks and sails had been treated, and the fires ignited by the shattering clay pots often burned themselves out before causing much damage. Those that did take were quickly snuffed out by the crews. And the ships were so bloody large, their yards of canvas so vast, it often took three or four cat's claws to slow them down at all.

Both lines of ships allowed passing lanes as they neared. The dunebreakers at the center of the Mirean line, the hospital ships, were different. They had no fear of ramming the Kings' galleons; some even had iron caps along their prow. All seven ships crashed hard into the Sharakhani line. So great was the dunebreakers' weight that many of the Kings' galleons' hulls were crushed and driven backward across the sand. As the interlocked ships came to a sliding halt, the scourge victims on the hospital ships roared in unison, a terrible, fearsome sound, and stormed over the decks of the galleons.

"*Hoyup!*" called Mae.

Brama turned just in time to see her charge over the deck on her qirin; smoke trailed from its nostrils and flame burst from its mouth as it leaped over the gunwales toward a passing galleon. All across the second line of Mirean ships, the Damned charged and leapt like antelope over the gunwales of their ships to land on the decks of the Sharakhani galleons. Cerulean fire swept across the Kings' ships as the qirin used their fiery breath and clawed at the Silver Spears who met them. The Damned, meanwhile, stabbed mercilessly with their short spears or fired arrows expertly at Sharakhani officers.

A dark shape blurred through the air to Brama's left. An asir, its bellow forcing all who heard it to cower in fear, moved with inhuman quickness, tearing through the Mirean soldiers as it made for Queen Alansal. Another leapt onto the gunwales only a few paces from Brama. It stretched its head forward, mouth open, a ravenous expression on its shriveled, blackened face.

Brama thought it was going to howl like the others, but instead it barked at him, a deafening sound. A moment later, an invisible wall struck him full on, and he was thrown backward.

He fell onto the deck, stars in his vision while a ringing sound replaced the asirim's earth-shattering bay. The ship bucked. He saw masts above, blue sky beyond, a vision replaced suddenly by the asir's blackened face. One clawed hand pierced his chest, its fingers gripping his ribs to keep him in place while its other arm lifted, ready to deliver the killing blow.

A blur of white passed overhead. A flow of black blood arced, streaking the sapphire sky, flecking the ivory sails.

Suddenly the asir was rolling away and the queen was standing above him, her steel pins gripped in her hands. They glinted in the sunlight as she raked them across the asir's body. They tore through bone and flesh alike. The asir scrabbled away, staring at the terrible wounds in its chest with a crazed expression. It looked human in that moment, afraid and alone. It managed to come to a stand, clearly hoping to flee, but Alansal was already flying forward, her ivory dress billowing in her wake. She delivered another blurring swipe of both pins, and then the asir was gone, lost over the gunwales, its arms flailing at open air.

Queen Alansal took Brama's wrist and pulled him up while, in the distance, Rümayesh's black cloud of beetles streaked toward a galleon, one of three that had remained deep behind the battle lines. Roiling balls of flame streaked upward from the galleon, released from the hands of a woman standing alone on the foredeck. Queen Meryam.

Whether the flame did any damage or not, Brama couldn't say, but the cloud wasn't slowed. It twisted and twined ever closer to the deck. When it dropped below the height of the foremast, a cascade of fire burst into the air between it and Meryam. A sheet of flame enveloped the beetles. Some curled into smoke and lifted with the flames. Most, however, seemed trapped by the rapidly closing net.

But then a tall, dark shape dropped from the inferno. Rümayesh landed on the foredeck. One of her three tails struck Meryam, sending her spinning backward. With a long stride forward, a second tail slipped around Meryam's neck and lifted her. Queen Meryam managed one last burst of bright, emerald-green flame. Rümayesh reeled from it, arms protecting her face. But then Meryam was trapped, her forearms gripped within one of Rümayesh's massive hands.

The battle around Brama was madness. Soldiers screamed. Ships crashed. The asirim howled, interspersed by the rattle of incoming arrows and the whoosh of fire pots crashing and coughing out their flames. Among it all, Brama heard a new sound, a drone of slowly increasing intensity. With it came an indescribable and rapidly growing fear. He looked over his shoulder to find a gray cloud approaching. It flew low over the ships. Brama saw soldiers, Sharakhani and Mirean alike, cringe as it swarmed across the decks.

Locusts, Brama realized. *Behlosh has come.*

The drone became so loud it prickled Brama's skin. His fear rising to new heights, he put his arms over his head and cowered. Soon, however, the cloud was past Alansal's ship and speeding toward the galleon where Queen Meryam, still trapped, struggled against Rümayesh's grip. Rümayesh was saying something to the queen, but turned as the locusts neared.

In that moment, Meryam was able to free herself. The sleeves of her dress smoked and burned to cinders as she lifted her hands, revealing the skin along her wrists and forearms, which glowed like a forge while her hands lit like the sun. Rümayesh released her, but Meryam refused to let it go so easily and snatched Rümayesh's wrist with both hands.

Where she touched, Rümayesh's skin burned, gray smoke rising. Rümayesh released a terrible roar as Meryam gripped tighter and Rümayesh's hand, burned clean through at the wrist, dropped to the deck. Rümayesh stumbled and fell against the nearby shroud, then swung her other arm at Meryam. Shards of black flew across the deck in an arc, many catching Meryam before she'd had a chance to defend herself.

As Meryam fell and was lost behind the gunwales, Rümayesh pushed herself off the shroud and stalked forward. She'd not taken two steps, however, before the swarm of locusts swept her up and carried her away from the galleon. A moment later, Rümayesh's body shattered into a million buzzing beetles, but it hardly seemed to matter.

Again and again her darker shape could be seen trying to slip free of the net, but the locusts would simply bulge outward and sweep them up once more. In moments they were lost behind the line of ships.

Chapter 53

HAMZAKIIR KNEW THAT when Queen Meryam left for the warfront, she'd taken with her several ewers of wine laced with his blood. Meryam had been forced to leave to prove her willingness to defend Sharakhai, but she could hardly allow Hamzakiir to go untended. Do that, and she might as well give up her plans in Sharakhai. All depended on her ability to control the King of Kings, to appear, at least in the early days of her rule, every bit his equal.

Meryam had left and days had passed, each one like the last. Hamzakiir's evenings had often been spent with the queen. He would sit in a chair that overlooked the city and wait. She would come to him after having drunk the wine, the blood within it forging a link between them. They would discuss the day's events, and Meryam would prepare him for what was to come.

During the day he would tend to the duties of state, and the running of his household, ensuring that Meryam's will was done. Time passed dreamlike, even the meetings he held with King Alaşan and several of the other *lesser Kings*. What he hadn't previously appreciated was the extent to which they had Meryam's ear. What the lesser Kings might gain from the relationship was clear: more gold, more status, more recognition. He knew they were dissatisfied with what they were being given and were petitioning for more. They wanted more say in the both the inner and outer workings of Sharakhai. What *Meryam* might gain was not so clear, and try as he might, Hamzakiir could never piece it together. He felt confused almost all the time. A side-effect of Meryam's spell, perhaps.

But then the fates delivered him a name. Word came in the form of a scroll that burned itself upon reading. He told Meryam of it that night, unable to stop himself. "The Enclave has sent word," he found himself saying. "They've taken the young blood mage, Davud Mahzun'ava, along with several others, and await your instructions."

Meryam asked questions, but Hamzakiir hardly listened. The mere mention of Davud's name had sparked Hamzakiir's sense of identity in the past. What was it about the young blood mage that had caused it? It was Davud's quickening, he realized. Hamzakiir's own spells had set Davud on the path to becoming a blood mage. Such things created a bond between the two magi, and might explain why Davud had acted as a touchstone.

Meryam's words brought him back. "Send word that they're to kill him," she was saying.

"But Sukru . . ."

Sukru had demanded both Davud and the woman, Anila, when they were found.

"Make it clear," Meryam said, "that there is to be no evidence of his capture. Sukru will never know."

"Very well."

"And have them deliver Ramahd's man, Cicio, to you. Give him over to Mateo once it's done."

He could sense her displeasure that Ramahd hadn't been captured as well. "What should I tell Mateo to do with him?"

"You needn't worry about that."

She has Mateo too, then . . . She must.

"As you say," he replied.

Meryam left, and his mind became muddied once more. That night, he dreamed of a voyage on the ship with the collegia graduates. He dreamed of Davud being hauled up to the deck. He dreamed of speaking to him about his awakening.

He woke in a sweat with a desperate plan, and wondered if it was already too late.

No. The scroll on which he was to write his reply to the Enclave was still on his desk. He sat down and stared at it. He lifted the quill from the nearby inkwell. The cold sweat he'd had on awakening turned hot. Sweat trickled along his forehead as he held the quill over the paper. A spot of ink fell, splattering.

The queen wishes for Cicio to be delivered to me. The young mage, Davud . . .

He swallowed. Licked his lips and wrote on.

The young mage, Davud, should . . .

A terrible headache consumed him. *Should be killed*, is what Meryam had instructed him to write. But he couldn't. The thin parchment felt like a life-line in a storm. *That's because it is*, he told himself. *Davud is your lifeline. Fail to save him now, and you will never resurface. Not until she's done with you, and what do you think will become of you then?* He'd be given the same treatment as Kiral. Buried in the desert. Lost and forgotten. And why not? Everyone thought he was dead already.

His entire body shook as he continued to write.

The young mage, Davud, should accompany him. Bring them both to the catacombs at midnight.

There were tears in his eyes by the time he was done. He stared at the paper, hesitant to take the next step. But take it he did, lighting it aflame. Blue flames rushed across its surface, sweeping the words away. The blues were now muted and ghostlike, especially along the edges. For a long while it floated just above the veined marble desktop. Then words written in a bold script appeared in bright cerulean lettering.

It will be as you say.

The paper, which had seemed caught in time, burned brightly once more, reducing itself to dust.

Slowly his heartrate returned to normal. He'd done it. He'd done it! The trick now was to keep the information from Meryam.

As it turned out, it wasn't difficult. That night, Meryam told him that the Mirean fleet was less than a day's sail from their current position. The scourge they'd unleashed on their fleet had inflicted heavy damage, but word had come: Queen Alansal had found a way to heal it, likely with the aid of

Rümayesh or Behlosh. The Kings' Kestrels were being positioned to assassinate Queen Alansal and battle was about to be joined. Meryam kept him only a few minutes, and asked if all had been done as she'd commanded.

"Yes," he replied.

It was partly true, which was the only reason he could get the word past his teeth. Still, the act made his skin crawl, and he nearly confessed his sins at once. Meryam had seemed content, however, and had cut off their communication a moment later.

He breathed a sigh of relief. Then felt something blossom inside him, a thing he hadn't felt in a long, long while—a thirst for revenge. Since his capture in Viaroza, his time with the Moonless Host, his days as Meryam's slave, he'd felt little except confusion and fear.

But now at last the way was clear.

He'd be free of Meryam. And then he'd see her head on a platter.

Chapter 54

WHEN THE CELL DOOR CLINKED OPEN, it was as if Davud had awoken from a dream. He was lying on a bare wooden plank that made him ache just to move on it. Light filtered in through a small, barred window high above him. His hands, effectively encased in steel, were trapped in a locking device. An iron bar affixed to the locking mechanism at his wrists prevented them from coming near one another—a precaution that, whatever its origin, made an effective deterrent for a blood mage.

Bakhi's swift hammer, how his head hurt. He'd been drunk only twice in his life. Both times had made him feel like leather left too long in the sun. He'd developed wicked headaches, and his mouth felt and tasted like moist jackal fur. Those experiences, as bad as they'd been, paled in comparison to how he felt now. His entire body ached. His head throbbed so badly that when he sat up he could feel it pulsing along his temples.

For long moments he leaned over the edge of the bed, trying to piece together all that had happened, but before he could do anything more than recall his surprise at being taken by Prayna and the other high magi of the Enclave, the door to his cell was opened and in walked King Kiral.

No, Davud told himself. *This is Hamzakiir, not the King of Kings.*

Hamzakiir held the key ring in his hand. It jangled as it spun and snapped into his waiting palm. He repeated the motion several times. It was then that Davud realized something was wrong.

"My Lord King?" Davud said, feeling it important, for now, to maintain the ruse.

"Do you know where you are?" Hamzakiir asked in Kiral's baritone voice.

"I assume I'm in Eventide."

"And do you know why you're here?"

"The Enclave gave me to you," Davud answered. "You requested it."

"You've had an interesting journey since your days as a collegia student. Your focus was on languages, was it not?"

Davud was more than a little confused. Hamzakiir knew quite well he'd made a focus of studying the languages of the desert and beyond. That momentary confusion, however, paled in comparison to the bewilderment he felt when Hamzakiir, his eyes never wavering from Davud's, took hold of his manacles and slipped a key into the lock. Just as Davud was casting his gaze down, Hamzakiir reached a hand to Davud's chin and forced him to look up, to hold his gaze, or rather, to *not* look at what was happening to his wrists.

Was Hamzakiir letting him go? If so, why not just do it? Why this strange conversation? Davud had no idea, but what was there to do but wait and see?

He maintained eye contact, and Hamzakiir finished unlocking the manacles. He set them down with such care they hardly made a sound. As he shifted the conversation to Davud's time in Ishmantep—which Hamzakiir would know much about and Kiral little—he took Davud's hand and used one finger to trace a pattern on his palm.

A sigil, Davud realized. *He's drawing a sigil, and he's repeating it over and over.*

It was difficult to concentrate on the sigil while continuing their conversation—though Hamzakiir made it quite clear with squeezes to Davud's wrist when he went silent that he *should* keep talking. Over time, however, Davud was able to picture the sigil in its entirety. It hovered in his mind's eye, and he recognized it. Pieces of it, in any case. He saw the base sigil for *mind* and *self,* and also one that meant *combine* or *join.* There was more to it that was unknown to him, but what did that matter? It was clear that Kiral wanted him to use it now, on him.

Indeed, a moment later he took Davud's opposite hand and led it until the tip of his forefinger was touching Hamzakiir's own palm. A warm pool of blood was there, created while he was tracing the sigil on Davud's hand. Its meaning was clear: use the blood to draw the sigil onto his own palm.

Davud did so with confident strokes; he had a mind for sigils and skill in painting them in blood. He was less sure of its meaning, and that presented a problem. It was normally necessary to know what effect he hoped to bring about. When Hamzakiir touched his finger to his tongue, Davud did the same, using his bloody finger. In that moment, Hamzakiir looked away, as if his attention had been caught by some noise from outside the small, stone-lined cell. It was a ruse, Davud knew, so that Hamzakiir wouldn't see what Davud had done. So that he'd have no memory of it.

When viewed under the light of Meryam and her domination over Hamzakiir, the strange conversation and his actions began to make sense. It was all a ploy, meant to hide his true intentions from the queen. And so it came as no real surprise when the world melted away and Davud found himself standing before the rather more thin figure of Hamzakiir instead of Kiral. He wore a robe cut in an ancient style, made with a fine material dyed in a patchwork of rusts and rubies and reds. His beard was long and his eyes were sharp, as sharp as they'd been in Ishmantep.

"You've come a long way," Hamzakiir said. "That's no simple sigil to draw, much less master, on your first attempt."

Davud stared at the world around them. Instead of the walls of a cell, he was surrounded by a canvas of constantly changing images. Kiral walking the halls of Eventide, or sitting with Queen Meryam, the two of them alone at a candlelit table, or moving through forms with his great, two-handed shamshir in a courtyard, the sun gleaming off Sunshearer's perfect, bright steel. One even showed Kiral whipping himself, his back a curtain of blood. Without exception, the surroundings were indistinct, sharpening only when Hamzakiir turned his attention there.

Over and over they changed, as if Hamzakiir's mind was flitting from one to the next to the next in an attempt to distract himself from his underlying purpose in the moment with Davud. *This is a construct,* Davud realized, *a place of Hamzakiir's making where they could talk freely, safe from the attentions of Queen Meryam.*

"We've little time." The memory behind him changed to Kiral and Davud sitting in the dungeon cell, their words muted and distanced. "So I trust you'll forgive my bluntness. I need your help, Davud." He swung his arms to the shifting kaleidoscope around them. "I have to free myself from this prison!"

"Oh? Well, I trust you'll forgive *me* if I'm not in the mood to help you with anything."

"Yes, we'll come to that." Hamzakiir turned to look at one of the visions, which shifted from nondescript sandstone to a large, leatherbound book. "Meryam keeps a tome of her sigils, many gleaned from ancient Qaimiri texts. She used one of them to bind me to her, and I've found no way to break it. Not yet. But if I could see the sigil and read the text that supports it, I could find a way for you to free me."

"For *me* to do it?"

"Who else? It may pain me to say it, Davud, but you are my last real hope."

Davud was drawn to an image of Kiral sitting in a padded chair, staring into a roaring fire. "The Enclave has sent word," he was saying. "They've taken the young blood mage, Davud Mahzun'ava, along with several others, and await your instructions."

Meryam's voice drifted to him, ghostlike. "Send word that they're to kill him."

Davud had been able to hear the other memories, but none so clearly as this. "A threat now, alongside your *request* for help?"

"Not a threat. Merely the state of things in Sharakhai. Meryam is aware of you. And when she learns of my betrayal, she will work doubly hard to see you dead." How strange it felt for the queen to have taken note of him, even more so to have ordered his death. "You're a threat to her," Hamzakiir said, answering his unspoken question. "All blood magi are."

"Not the Enclave, though."

"Make no mistake, Davud. Meryam might consider them a *contained* threat, but they're still a threat. The day will come when she'll turn her attention to them and, believe me, it won't be to offer her hand in friend-ship."

Davud waved to the fading memory of Kiral before the fire. "You bring me here. You show me this, so I'll what? Do as you wish without another word? I'm not the same wide-eyed collegia graduate you found crawling from the hold of your ship."

"No, you've changed greatly." Hamzakiir's gaze, spoke of contentment, even pride in Davud. "Which is why I've not come empty-handed." He waved to yet another memory, which resolved from the blurry patchwork. It showed King Sukru sitting in a large room with many of the other Kings.

"I have something more urgent to bring to the council in any case," King Sukru was saying. "The matter of Davud Mahzun'ava and Anila Khabir'ava."

Beside him, Cahil asked, "Who?"

"The two magi," Sukru spat, the words loud and jarring.

Cahil's smile was patronizing, his features distorted and wild, dreamlike. "Why didn't you just say *the magi who killed my brother and escaped my palace?*"

Sukru, his anger flaring, turned to Kiral and Meryam. "I request permis-sion to speak to the Enclave and demand they be delivered to us."

Hamzakiir stood before the memory. "Dousing the fire in Ishmantep was an amazing feat. Your use of Anila's blood, your mastery of magic even as new to the red ways as you were. Sadly, it resulted in her being placed on death's doorstep."

"Get to your point."

"You want to save her. You have since you left Ishmantep."

"And?"

"Come, Davud. I can help you. I know how to heal her."

"How?"

He shook his head. "No. Not until I've been freed."

"You're asking me to *trust* you?"

"Have you not found me a man of my word in the past?"

"I've found you to be a usurper. A murderer."

Hamzakiir's smile showed teeth. "No better or worse than Meryam, then."

"What makes you think I would do *anything* for you?"

"Because you, Davud Mahzun'ava, are in terrible, terrible trouble if you don't." Memories swirled as Hamzakiir walked behind him. "Find the sigils in Meryam's book. Free me, and save yourself as you do. When it's done, I'll give you everything you need to heal Anila."

He was right—Davud *was* in trouble—but the thought of freeing Hamzakiir, of unleashing him on the city and the desert again, terrified him. No matter that he might be ridding them of Meryam at the same time.

"Where's the book?"

"We have a deal, then?"

"Where's the book?"

Hamzakiir weighed his words, debated offering the information as a show of faith. In that moment, the memories around them all changed to Meryam in varying states of fury. *He fears her*, Davud realized, and it made Davud fear her too. If a man as powerful as Hamzakiir had been taken by her and treated this way, what hope did Davud have? Meryam was like a wolf in the forest. She'd caught his scent, now he had two options: to fight or flee.

Except fleeing was no choice at all. Hamzakiir was right. Meryam would eventually learn of his disobedience, and when she did she'd kill Hamzakiir, then tear the city apart until she'd killed Davud too. So why not fight?

Hamzakiir thought himself clever in tapping into Davud's greatest weakness: his compassion. Davud freely admitted it, but it didn't mean everything had to be on Hamzakiir's terms. Davud would see this through, but he would do it *his* way. He waited, calling Hamzakiir's bluff.

The scenes shifted to more neutral memories of Kiral, often in a position of power over others. Meryam could be seen in none of them. "Her book of sigils is in the shrine to Alu, safeguarded by spells."

"Do you know the ones she used?"

"Most of them, yes, and ways that you might bypass others."

"Very well," Davud said, "but I have one condition."

Hamzakiir feigned calm, but the scenes around them blinked, showing his disquiet. "Name it."

"You will arrange for Esmeray to join me."

"Who?"

"The blood mage captured with me."

Remembrance dawned on Hamzakiir's face. "Impossible," he said flatly.

"You demanded *my* release. And the release of Ramahd's man . . ."

"Yes, but Esmeray is of the Enclave, one of their own."

"I need her, if you want this done."

Hamzakiir considered, the images shifting to letters he'd written, to a piece of paper that burst into blue flame. "Very well."

Three days after Davud's strange conversation with Hamzakiir, guards brought someone into the cell across from his. Davud reached the window in time to see the gaoler and a Silver Spear leading a woman to a cell. He recognized Esmeray's dress, her dark turban and wild braids.

Without so much as a glance toward Davud, the two men closed the door to Esmeray's cell and walked away, arguing loudly about how soon each thought the deadly Malasani golems were going to return to Sharakhai.

"Esmeray?" Davud ventured when they'd gone far enough. Hearing no response, he waited for the door down the hallway to clang shut. "Esmeray," he tried again, "it's Davud."

Again his words were met with silence.

"Why won't you speak to me?"

"Be quiet, Davud."

"You don't understand. I don't know what they told you, but I arranged for you to be brought here."

"How very kind of you."

He didn't understand her tone. Had the guards treated her unkindly? Had they beat her?

"We can escape."

It took her a long time to respond. "I can't escape. Not this."

"Esmeray, what happened?"

"Leave me alone."

"No. We've got to leave, and I need your help to do it. I haven't the sigils to work these locks nor the power to blast them apart." She went silent again, but Davud refused to let it be. He had no way of contacting Hamzakiir. And even if he did, he had no idea if he could help. "Esmeray, what happened?"

For a long time, no answer came. He thought she'd gone to sleep. But then he heard the sounds of shuffling footsteps. Her hands gripped the iron bars of her window and her face was lit from the darkness.

Davud recoiled. "Gods, Esmeray, what happened?"

Her eyes, once a deep brown, were now a bright ivory color. They made her look ghostlike, a visitor from the lands beyond.

"I've been burned," she said, as if that explained everything.

"What's that?"

She seemed to be staring *through* him. "My magic, Davud. It's been burned from me."

He didn't need to ask why. It was her punishment for siding with Davud and Ramahd against the Enclave's wishes. "Is there no way to reverse it?"

She laughed silently, as if he were a child who'd just asked if he would live forever. "No, Davud, there's no way to reverse it."

Gods, this is all my fault. The Enclave were making a point. King Kiral had demanded Esmeray, and they'd given her over, but not before exacting punishment. Showing that they were not at the beck and call of the House of Kings. *What in the wide great desert am I to do now?*

Get her out. He had to get Esmeray out.

"The spell," Davud said to Esmeray. "The one to work a lock. Show me."

She stared at him sightlessly, and made no move to comply.

"Esmeray, show me the sigil!"

As she stepped away, her hands dropped from the bars and her face was lost to shadow. "No."

Chapter 55

O N THE MORNING OF BEIIT ZHA'IR, when all the others had left the ship, Çeda remained behind and took a bundle from beneath her bed. She set it on the mattress and unwrapped it. Two shamshirs lay side by side: River's Daughter, the sword Husamettín had given her when she'd become a Blade Maiden, and Night's Kiss, Husamettín's own two-handed blade.

The call of Night's Kiss was strong. *Take the blood of thy father . . .*

Part of her wanted to obey, to use it if Sehid-Alaz, as feared, had still not been freed by the time the sun set. She realized a moment later that Night's Kiss was in her hand, already half-drawn. She drew it fully from its scabbard. The blade's undying thirst was now hers. How lovely it would feel to quench it.

His pain will last but the draw of a breath, the sword cooed to her. *Then will come a sweet release, a man made anew.*

"Çeda?" She turned to find Sümeya staring at her from the passageway. Her eyes dropped to Night's Kiss. "Is all well?"

Çeda sent the sword back into its sheath with a clack and threw it onto the bed. The thought of using that sword to slay Sehid-Alaz, an object that embodied Husamettín like no other thing, a gift from the gods themselves, made Çeda recoil in disgust. She thought again, as she had many times before, of losing the sword in the desert, but like always, no matter how wise it seemed at first, the urge melted away like wax before a fire. Taking a deep breath to clear her mind, she snatched up River's Daughter, strapped it to her belt, and left the ship before she could change her mind. She'd worn no blade in the ritual before now, but she wanted her trusted friend with her this day. It might be an implement of war, but it gave her courage. It gave her hope.

As the day wore on, however, and Sehid-Alaz came closer and closer to finishing his work, her hope vanished. The bond they were forging wasn't enough. As she lay on the sand, she gripped River's Daughter like a talisman, willing Sehid-Alaz's bonds to be broken.

But they weren't. And then it was done. The names were all written on Çeda's back, the ritual complete.

She'd slipped back into her dress and stood. Sehid-Alaz stood as well. He stared at her with his chin held high. He knew they'd failed. He knew what had to happen.

"I'm ready, Çedamihn Ahyanesh'ala," he said to her.

"I'm not," Çeda replied.

"But you must be, my child."

She felt his readiness to depart these shores. She'd never felt as close to any of the asirim as she felt to Sehid-Alaz in that moment, not even Kerim. And yet the walls around him were still impenetrable. There was so much he wished to say, but couldn't due to the curse that chained him. For a moment she caught a glimpse of the man he once was: caring, vibrant, earnest, but also proud. Perhaps too proud at times.

Night fell and the twin moons rose. Çeda ordered Husamettín to be brought from the ship. This burden was hers. She would take Sehid-Alaz's life, but Husamettín would witness it. And then she'd take his life as well.

"You're sure about this?" Sümeya asked.

"You think Husamettín deserves to live?"

Sümeya replied with a level stare, "He's a useful bargaining chip, one you'll never get back if you kill him now."

For a moment, Çeda considered it, but then shook her head. "Bring him."

Sehid-Alaz was led to a rocky patch beside the oasis. They would bury him here that others might one day visit his grave. Husamettín would lie in the desert, his grave unmarked.

All gathered round. The measured song of the crystalwings drifted from the oasis's verdant pools. The baked smell of the desert waned, replaced by a faint mineral sweetness. Sehid-Alaz knelt, ready.

Some distance away Sümeya, holding Night's Kiss, forced Husamettín to his knees. Kameyl and Melis stood nearby with ebon blades drawn. The King still wore his stained, ripped kaftan. His long pepper-gray hair was unbound, his face like stone, the sigil Kameyl had carved into his forehead plain to see. *Deceiver*, it proclaimed. Husamettín seemed conscious of it, but he held his head high. Not an ounce of regret marred his features, nor did anger, as if all had been ordained from the moment Tulathan had handed him his sword.

Just then the wind tugged at the ripped fabric of his kaftan, and the moonlight shone on the battleground of scars that covered his stomach. He glanced down, twisted his torso a bit, and the wind blew the fabric back in place.

Mavra, meanwhile, was disconsolate. Regret rolled from her in waves.

"This isn't your fault," Çeda said to her. "You merely bore witness."

Çeda faced Sehid-Alaz and drew River's Daughter. The hunger coming from Night's Kiss was strong. It was jealous. This night of all nights it demanded blood. *Soon,* Çeda thought, and a hungry silence stole over the obsessed mind buried in that blade.

"I'm sorry it's come to this," Çeda said to Sehid-Alaz.

"I know."

He quavered like a newborn lamb, and she was reminded of the time they'd first met, when he'd kissed her forehead near the banks of the Haddah. As he'd done then, she leaned in and kissed the dry skin of *his* forehead.

"Go well," she whispered, and retreated a step.

As she drew River's Daughter back, the call of Night's Kiss became deep, almost irresistible. *His pain will last but the draw of a breath!*

Çeda lowered her sword. Her fingers had begun to tingle. *A man made anew,* the sword had said earlier. She turned to look at Husamettín. Stared down at his belly, where his riddle of scars was almost but not quite concealed. For the first time he seemed discomfited. Worried.

"Mavra," Çeda said without taking her eyes from the King, "when you saw the vision of Sehid-Alaz's death, what sword was Husamettín holding?"

Mavra said nothing in reply. When Çeda reached out to her, Mavra closed herself off so quickly, so strongly, that for a moment Çeda felt dizzy. "Mavra, what did you see?"

Her fear bloomed like wildfire. She took a step back, shaking her head as if the answer was unthinkable.

Çeda sheathed River's Daughter. "You saw him using Night's Kiss, didn't you?"

"No!" Mavra shook her head violently. *"No, no, no!"*

Çeda wasn't sure if her denials were in answer to the question or a plea for Çeda to stop. It didn't matter. Çeda knew she was right. She was as certain about this as she was about Husamettín's god-given weakness. Night's Kiss was a two-sided coin, his blessing *and* his curse.

"Give me the sword," she said to Sümeya.

Mavra's fear rose to new heights. *"Please,"* she begged. *"Not that."*

"Don't you see?" Çeda drew the two-handed shamshir. "You saw the truth. His fears playing out. The sword will make Sehid-Alaz *new*. It will remove the curse!"

Her face averted from the sword in a grimace, Mavra placed her considerable bulk between Çeda and Sehid-Alaz. *"Souls taken with that sword are lost forever."*

"Mavra, get out of my way."

"No!" Mavra charged forward. *"Our King will have his peace!"* Breath of the desert, she was fast! She lifted to her full height and bore down on Çeda, grabbing her arms. But Çeda was ready. She drew on the tattoos along her right arm, on the puckered wound, the kiss of the adichara, and a strength filled her. She felt it from all her tattoos now, not just the one Zaïde had inked into her skin. It was as if Sehid-Alaz had completed something that had been only half finished beforehand, bringing all of it into sharp relief.

She shifted Mavra's bulk, then hooked her ankle and threw her to the sand. She sprinted for Sehid-Alaz, Night's Kiss drawn back, buzzing in the night, but suddenly something tall and dark was streaking toward her. Sedef.

Before she could dodge, she was tackled and borne to the rocky ground. Pain exploded along her jaw as Sedef struck her. She lost Night's Kiss, managed to roll out from underneath him, but Sedef grabbed her, preventing her from coming any closer to Sehid-Alaz.

But then Kameyl came flying in, one shoulder lowered as she crashed into Sedef. Melis was there too, sending a spinning kick across his jaw just as he was recovering.

"Go!" Melis shouted, and shoved Çeda away.

Melis and Sümeya and Kameyl were all there, intercepting the asirim. Çeda's Shieldwives joined them. All of them together didn't stand a chance against Mavra and her children, not without their swords, but they didn't need to hold them off for long.

Çeda sprinted toward Sehid-Alaz, grabbing Night's Kiss on the way. A panicked howl came from one of the asirim. Wind and sand shoved Çeda back, but when she raised her right hand, palm facing outward, and rooted herself to the desert, the wind lost all strength.

Sehid-Alaz, arms wide as if in welcome, watched as Çeda closed the distance between them. Tears streamed freely down Çeda's cheeks. She didn't want to do this—desert's sweet embrace, she didn't even know if it would work—but it was their last, best chance. And if it *didn't* work, she prayed it would give their King the peace he deserved.

Releasing a guttural cry, she swung with all her might. Night's Kiss bit deep. Sehid-Alaz's jaundiced eyes went wide. His jaw swung open, lips quivering. The storm of biting sand returned with renewed life. It scoured Çeda, made her cower. Sehid-Alaz was reduced to a silhouette. He fell to the sand, clutching his side. He clawed at the stone, a long howl coming from him at last.

For long, terrible moments, Çeda, the Blade Maidens, and the Shieldwives fought the asirim. Over the sound of the ceaseless wind came shouts of surprise and pain and rage.

An indomitable weight fell on Çeda. *"You dare?"* Mavra screamed, and clubbed Çeda hard. *"You dare?"*

Over and over again she struck, Çeda doing her best to twist from the blows or fend off her mindless attacks without retaliating.

Then suddenly the wind began to die. The sand began to settle. *"Enough,"* said a voice, cutting through the storm like a knife. *"Enough."*

A hand touched Mavra's shoulder.

Her body tightened, and she pulled away from Çeda. A figure could be seen through the dust: Sehid-Alaz, numinous in the light of the moons. He was dark-skinned and thin, but stood as tall as Çeda had ever seen him. He moved among the asirim, who stilled on hearing his voice. The Shieldwives and Blade Maidens backed away, wary and waiting, unsure of his intentions.

Like a shepherd among his flock, Sehid-Alaz strode between them, touching each in turn, lifting their pain and fear and anger. They spread their arms to the moons as if they were elated, blissful, unencumbered by the curse of the gods for the first time in four hundred years. Night's Kiss had drunk Sehid-Alaz's blood but had fulfilled its promise. It had made him anew, and in so doing lifted the curse the gods had placed on him. He was free at last and now was freeing others.

At first Çeda could hardly believe what she was seeing. Then she spread her arms as well and began to laugh. It was an unbridled expression of joy, a thing she could hardly contain. She didn't *want* to contain it. The thing she'd been searching for for so long was finally here.

"Çeda?" Sümeya called in a concerned voice.

She was peering into the darkness, into the desert. Çeda looked too, and realized Husamettín was gone. She looked everywhere. Near the ships. Toward the pools of the oasis. Across the desert dunes. But he was nowhere to be seen.

"Please, Great Mother," Çeda breathed, "don't do this to me."

But the Shangazi was indifferent to her pleas. Husamettín had slipped away during the confusion. They organized a search immediately and asked Sehid-Alaz to help. But it soon became clear Husamettín was masking his presence, and all evidence of his passage had been lost to the scouring winds.

Near daybreak, Sehid-Alaz turned sharply north, where the peaks of the Taloran Mountains could be seen, a scattering of misshapen coal. It sent a chill down Çeda's spine, for among those mountains stood Mount Arasal, the tallest, where much of the thirteenth tribe now lay hidden. It was also the place Nalamae and Leorah had gone after parting ways with the *Red Bride*. Where Sehid-Alaz watched, a bird emerged from the morning's darkness. Çeda feared a return of the deadly sickletail, but she felt none of Yerinde's influence on this bird. It was a lyrewing, a songbird with copper wings, a mantle of brass, and a broad fan of a tail. "Sail north! Sail north!" it warbled in high tones. "The tribe is attacked! The goddess bids you come!"

Sehid-Alaz had gone perfectly calm. He turned to Çeda. "The King of

Swords might still be found." His voice was deep and resonant, filled with emotion. "He's still near. He must be."

Çeda tried to sense Husamettín, but felt nothing. "I weep that he's slipped through our fingers, but we cannot risk Nalamae. The search for the King of Swords must wait for another day. Come," she called to the others. "It's time we went to the valley."

Sehid-Alaz regarded the gathered asirim, then the women, the mortals who'd risked everything to save him. Finally, he nodded to Çeda.

They set sail a short while later. As the sun broke the horizon, Sehid-Alaz stood on the foredeck and released a long whistle, a trilling note that made the hair on Çeda's arms stand on end. On and on it went, and Çeda was sure that it wouldn't stop until it had reached every corner of the desert.

"What's he doing?" Jenise asked her.

"He's calling the asirim," Çeda said. "He's calling his children home."

Chapter 56

BRAMA WATCHED AS THE ROILING cloud of insects was lost behind the line of Kings' galleons. Few would know it, but the course of the battle had just turned at Goezhen's behest. Brama still didn't understand why—who could know the will of the gods, after all?—but it was clear Goezhen was trying to alter the outcome of the battle. Indeed, trying to alter the course of the desert, perhaps to the Kings' benefit.

He was tempted to let the gods have their way, but he was beginning to hate being a pawn in the games of others. And there was no denying his deeply seated desire to save Rümayesh, even after all she'd done. He was perfectly aware that he was being manipulated, but the knowledge was bitter comfort; it was times like this, times of high emotion and confusion, that he was least able to withstand the desire to aid Rümayesh.

Something loomed on his right. He turned to find sails and masts and rigging speeding toward Queen Alansal's dunebreaker. He backed away and stumbled as the prow of the Kings' galleon crashed across their starboard bow. The deck tilted beneath him, its nose dipping, and then Brama was flying over the gunwales toward open sand. He went weightless, limbs rag-doll flailing, and struck the sand hard alongside a dozen others, Queen Alansal included.

Pain blossomed across Brama's body as he pushed himself to a stand. The sound of plodding hooves approached and mixed with the din of battle, and Brama turned to find Mae riding toward them on her qirin. *A godsend,* Brama thought. *How else could he reach Rümayesh in time?*

He rushed to the queen and helped her to stand. She was badly shaken. Her eyes vacant, she stared at the battle around her as if struggling to understand it. "Let me go with Mae," he said to her. "Let me save Rümayesh."

As the royal guard converged, Mae came to a halt and her qirin released a bellow that sounded like a war horn. Queen Alansal stared at the qirin, brow furrowed, mouth working as if she *wanted* to say something but couldn't find the words.

"Queen Alansal!" Brama shouted. Finally she turned her attention to him. "Rümayesh will die without our help. If you wish to survive this battle, let me go with Mae to save her."

Alansal took in the battle anew, then nodded to Mae. "Take him wherever he wishes to go."

Mae's face was hidden behind her grinning demon mask, but Brama could sense her hesitation. Likely she wanted to remain with the queen, but she didn't question the order. She spurred Angfua toward Brama, the two of them locked forearms, and Brama swung into the saddle behind her. With Brama holding tight to her waist, Mae snapped the reins. "Hiyah hup!" came her shout, and both of them leaned into the qirin's powerful surge.

Brama pointed to a gap between two oncoming galleons. "There. Rümayesh and Behlosh were lost behind those ships."

They flew over the battlefield, the wind whipping Brama's curly hair. The qirin's speed was breathtaking. Even with two riders, it put an unburdened akhala to shame.

Far ahead, one of the Mirean ships had come to a halt. Two great doors along the port side groaned open and crashed against the sand. A pair of massive compartments were revealed, pens for the mighty gui shan. They were as big as houses, with shells like turtles and great, steel-capped horns curving up from the center of their broad heads. Each had a wooden platform affixed to their backs, at the front of which stood a rider holding chain reins attached to a bit in the gui shan's beaklike mouth. Another soldier held a long pole, which he used to tap against the gui shan's skull.

The great beasts lumbered forward on legs the size of tree trunks, while their riders pointed them both toward a galleon that had just come to a halt. When the beasts were properly aligned, the men began to strike the back of the gui shan's skull over and over. One did so with such gusto Brama thought surely his crop would snap.

The gui shan's grunts resounded over the battlefield. Then they began rumbling forward, gaining more and more speed. Like a boulder rolling downhill, they pounded over the battlefield, an undeniable force. Two asirim swarmed up the lead gui shan's back and attacked the rider and the crop man but even when both had been killed, the gui shan continued its charge toward the galleon.

Brama stared as Mae guided her qirin, ahead of one and behind the next. The amount of pain and death all around him was dizzying. He felt it so acutely. It was perfectly lovely, like a hazy autumn sunset. A lover's caress. It made his heart soar, this grand tableau of blood and savagery. It was their passage to the farther fields that attracted him so, their deaths the most beautiful thing he'd ever seen. And he was *jealous* of them, he realized.

Breath of the desert, please make it stop. He felt torn, a man in pieces, a slave to the feelings Rümayesh had placed inside him and lit like a bonfire.

At a thundering bellow, Brama looked over his shoulder to find the gui shan ducking their heads before crashing into the hull of the galleon. Their steel-capped horns pierced the thick wooden hull and for a moment they seemed to be wedged there, stuck, but they used their massive front legs and lifted their heads, and the galleon lifted with them. With a deep, resonant call, their legs churned and the galleon tilted further and further until it reached the point of no return and tipped under its own weight. Its masts and rigging crashed with a thunderous boom across the deck of another Sharakhani galleon.

On the sand nearby, a qirin was going mad, its dead rider fallen on the sand behind it. The qirin was doomed to die, but it would wreak vengeance before it did. Indeed, an asir was engulfed in flames, then trampled by the qirin's hooves, even as the asirim slashed at the beast's underbelly.

The scene was lost as Mae guided her qirin beyond the last line of ships and thankfully the feelings of euphoria ebbed. "There," he said, pointing Mae toward the twisting cloud of insects in the distance. As Angfua flew toward it, Rümayesh regained form, plummeted, and struck the sand hard. As amber dust coughed into the air around her, the cloud of locusts floated gently down, as if Behlosh knew he had won.

The locusts coalesced, and Behlosh alighted onto the sand like a vengeful god. With two of his four arms he lifted Rümayesh's unconscious shape. Blood trickled in a black stream from the incinerated stump of her right arm, turning the amber sand beneath to bistre.

The urge to flee was strong and growing stronger. The drone of the locusts had vanished, but not the fear. Brama was certain Behlosh would turn at any moment and unleash his terrible power against them.

Mae turned in the saddle. "Take this," she said, handing him her short spear.

He accepted it, and became immediately entranced by its construction. The fear from moments ago vanished, replaced by a wonder for all that was now opening up to him. He felt some small spark of life in the spear's haft, the barest echo from the tree that had given it up. He felt the steel cap and the leaf-shaped head working together to hem it in.

Ahead, Behlosh was using one clawed hand to carve symbols over the lump where the bone of Raamajit had been subsumed beneath Rümayesh's skin. Brama could *feel* him doing it. It was numb and distant but felt as if Behlosh were scratching into *Brama's* skin.

Mae, oblivious, had taken up the bow that rested beneath her left leg and grabbed three diamond-head arrows in her right hand. Hardly pausing to look, she strung the bow, drew, and fired in as fluid a display of archery as Brama had ever seen. The arrow blurred in flight, then snapped into sharp relief as it sunk into Behlosh's thigh. Mae strung the second arrow as Behlosh roared and turned. One hand waved in a broad arc before him.

"Down!" Mae yelled, and ducked.

In a heartbeat, a wall of sand and stone swept toward them. He *felt* its approach. It was the power of the bone, he realized, the power of Raamajit. Rümayesh was somehow sharing it with him.

He swung Mae's spear in an upward arc, and the storm of sand lifted up and over them. The wind was still strong, but it did no more than blow the qirin off its path. After a momentary stumble, Angfua galloped on, and when they neared Behlosh it released a tight gout of fire.

The stream of fire caught Behlosh along his taurine legs in the same moment Mae's third arrow flew, but Behlosh was ready, and caught the arrow with a sweep of one arm. The flame of Angfua's breath was interrupted a moment later as Behlosh's tail lashed out and connected in a terrible blow across the qirin's neck.

Angfua bucked and snapped, Mae dropped her bow and held out her hand. "Give it to me!"

She meant the spear, but Brama couldn't release it. The weapon had somehow become the focus he needed to guide the power of Raamajit. Behlosh stared at Brama with a glint in his eye and swung his arms in arcane rhythms, two over his head, the other two over his heart.

Suddenly Brama felt as if he'd been caught in the swell of a river. It pressed on him. Pressed against Mae and the qirin as well. Backward they went, the invisible river carrying them downstream.

They were thrown from the saddle as Angfua began to thrash. Mae unbuckled her helm and threw it to one side. Her mouth worked soundlessly, and she grasped at her throat as if she were suffocating. Blood streamed from her eyes and nose and dripped from her ears. The qirin released a pitiful trumpeting sound as it clawed at the sand. A gout of flame sprayed from its mouth. Then blood began pouring from its flaring nostrils and its blue, saurian eyes.

Brama held the spear before him like a talisman as Behlosh took one long stride forward. Eerie sounds issued from his mouth, an arcane chanting of sorts, but it was distant and dreamlike.

Brama knew Mae's spear was possessed of no extraordinary abilities, and yet it felt like something primal, a thing the first gods had forged before the making of the world. He hoisted it over his shoulder and felt its potent weight. With a grunt he slung it toward Behlosh.

The spear flew hungrily, perfectly, and neither wind, nor pull of earth, nor arcane workings of an elder ehrekh had command over it. It struck Behlosh dead in the chest. Brama knew the skin of ehrekh was proof against weapons made of mundane steel, and yet the spear impaled Behlosh. Struck him through.

The ehrekh's eyes went wide as he was driven back. One hand gripped the haft, not even trying to remove it; just holding it, as if Behlosh couldn't quite believe what happened. His other arms windmilled while reaching back to break his fall. He crashed to the sand and writhed. With all four hands, Behlosh tried to dislodge the spear. A great groan of pain escaped him, and the muscles along his arms bunched, but the spear remained. He tried one last time, the effort weaker, and then lay still.

Brama wasn't sure how long he stood there. Mae and her qirin lay motionless, the workings of Behlosh's spell having unraveled, and Brama knew he should go to help them, but he was stopped by languid movement to his right.

Rümayesh.

She watched as Brama approached. She'd seen what he'd done. *No*, Brama thought, *she hadn't merely seen it. She'd had a hand in it.* Brama had, too, in the guiding of that raw power, but when he'd lofted the spear he'd felt more spectator than actor. In a moment of perfect clarity, he now understood why. How could he, a mere mortal, have worked the bone of Raamajit? How could he have mastered that ancient artifact, when he'd failed so miserably with the soldier in the hospital ship? The simple truth was he couldn't.

A blood mage like Meryam might, maybe a woman like Alansal, steeped in the knowledge of magic's inner workings, but not him.

He trudged past Behlosh's corpse and stopped several paces from Rümayesh. It felt strange to see such a powerful creature laid so low. Hand missing. Limbs lying at strange angles. She looked like an effigy of sticks and string waiting to be burned.

Brama waved to her. "I could heal you." He may not have mastered the stone, but he felt its power still, and he could do this much. "I could heal you. But if I do, you must let me go."

Rümayesh stared with those rusty red eyes. Her throat worked and a pitiful sound escaped her, but her eyes remained flinty, unyielding. He felt her trying to influence him, but he shut her out.

"I know what you've done," Brama went on. "I know what you're trying to do."

Rümayesh smiled a leopard's smile. Her teeth were smeared with blood so dark it was almost black. "Then you know there's no going back."

For weeks now, since before Brama had arrived at the Mirean encampment, Rümayesh had been working her way into Brama's mind and body. He could feel it, her tendrils within him, her roots growing deep. All those times she'd hidden herself from him, he'd thought it because of the secrets she was keeping about her lord Goezhen and the commands he'd given her. And perhaps that was one of her purposes, but the greater truth was she'd slowly been displacing his soul, and replacing it with her own.

It all made sense now. The feelings of twisted pleasure at the pain of the scourge victims, the feelings of hunger and jealousy as mortal souls departed for the farther fields, his growing awareness, not just of Rümayesh's mind, but her shape. During the battle with Behlosh, he'd used the bone at her behest, but his body had felt like a marionette—she'd not yet taken all the strings, but she wasn't far from it either. And for his part it almost felt as if he could . . .

He tried to lift her arm. And found, Bakhi strike him down, that he could. It felt like his own arm, his own body. He felt her trio of tails, and when one of them lashed, Rümayesh smiled, her eyes drifting toward the movement. She was forcing them to trade places, and unless he did something about it, she would soon succeed.

Rümayesh's smile widened when she saw the terror in his eyes. "You should never have thought to part from me, Brama."

"*That's* why you're doing this?"

Her smile faded. "No, but it did force me to hurry my plans."

Brama shook his head, feeling ever more hopeless. "Mortals aren't made for such things. I'm no ehrekh. I'm no child of sand and stone."

"Men would kill for the power you're about to inherit. *Have* killed for it. You can live out your days a god. You can witness the dying of the desert."

"I don't *want* to! I want to live my own life and, when the time comes, leave this world for the next."

"As do I."

Brama started. That was it, he realized. She hoped to become mortal, and by doing so, have her soul pass to the farther fields when she died.

Rümayesh sensed his thoughts. "It is something that has eluded even my lord Goezhen, though he desires it so." There was a glint in her eye, a hint of the wonder she now felt. "At last, I can rejoin my Lirael."

"No," Brama said. "I won't let you." He had enough command over the bone to do it, and she was too weakened to stop him.

One of her tails slapped the sand. "Then sever our tie and be done with it."

"You'll die when I do."

"So will you, Brama."

She was right. He could feel it. Their souls commingled, and destroying one would destroy the other. "I don't care. I don't accept the future you've written for me."

Rümayesh closed her eyes and the wind gusted. Sand tickled her ebony skin, collected in the thorns of her hair before another gust lifted it away. When she opened her eyes once more, they were resolute. "Would that I had such free will."

To be driven by a hunger such as hers. To be given a taste of relief from time to time, but never finding the satisfaction she craved. He recalled the wonder he felt at seeing the desert in the manner of the ehrekh. A new world had been opened to him. But at what cost? To feel joy but not sorrow? To feel hunger as other souls drifted toward the farther fields?

He refused to live like that.

Gripping both hands into fists, he summoned the power of the first gods. He felt the bond between them. Thin and ghostlike before, it was now bright between them, a cord made of light. Rümayesh watched with a look that seemed to welcome what he was about to do. He ignored her. He no longer cared what she wanted.

With one last look toward the horizon, he severed their link. A terrible pain ran through him. It burned like the summer sun. It cleaved Rümayesh from him, and in doing so tore his soul in two.

The last thing he recalled was spindrift lifting from a dune like the curl of a horn. Then it dissipated, and was gone.

Brama woke to someone calling his name. It was distant. Dreamlike. Even when he opened his eyes and saw Mae hovering over him, it sounded like cotton had been stuffed into his ears. As the blood smearing Mae's cheeks, mouth, and chin registered, a keen ringing rose up, smothering what little he *had* been able to hear.

He was lying next to Rümayesh. His knife was held loosely in his right hand though he couldn't remember having drawn it. The fingers of both hands were bloody and his head hurt terribly. He dropped the knife and felt along his forehead. There he found a lump. Something was under his skin. Something hard.

By the gods, Raamajit's bone.

"What did you do?" he asked.

Confusion replaced the worry in Mae's eyes.

"What did you do?"

"I did nothing, Brama. You did."

She'd found him crawling toward Rümayesh. He'd taken his knife and used the tip to gouge at the skin of her forehead, then, after liberating the bone, he'd cut his own forehead and pressed the bone to the wound.

The bone had kept his soul intact. The part that still remained within him, in any case. But it wasn't alone. Rümayesh's was there as well. He felt *unwhole*, made of two parts, a man stitched together. *The Torn Man,* Brama thought. He began to giggle. Then laugh. *The Tattered Prince, sewn together from the torn remains of two tattered souls.* His laughs soon devolved into long, wracking coughs.

He rolled over and held both hands to his head to stem the terrible pain. Time passed. How much, he wasn't sure. But the next thing he knew, Mae was helping him to stand. She tugged at his sleeve, spoke to him, but the ringing sound in his ears had returned and he heard little. He wasn't ready to leave in any case.

He gazed down at Rümayesh, who lay there, lifeless. It felt impossible. He'd been with her for so long he thought he'd never be free. *You still aren't,* he thought. *There's a part of her inside you yet.* He couldn't think about that, though. Not now. He examined Behlosh, the simple yet remarkable spear still lodged in his chest. Brama tried to lift it, but he was too weak and it wouldn't budge. When he drew some power from the bone, however, the spear lifted free, as if it had been waiting for him all this time.

"Brama, we must go!"

Mae's words sounded as if they came from the other side of the desert.

He nodded, and together they walked to her qirin and rode back toward the main cluster of fighting. Hundreds of warriors from both sides fought—over the sand, on the decks of ships, in the rigging above. Near the center of it all, Queen Alansal and Queen Meryam were locked in battle. Sharakhani and Mirean soldiers lay dead all around them, as if something had exploded near the center of their conflict.

Queen Alansal did not cut an imposing figure, but she looked like one of the first women compared to frail Queen Meryam. Somehow, though, Meryam's skeletal frame made her seem more dangerous. She looked wild, like an animal caged and underfed, ready to do anything to stay alive. She swung a whip of fire from one hand. A sound like thunder rolled across the battlefield as she wielded it against Alansal, who dodged several strikes. But then one was too quick, too precise, and she was forced to block it with one of her steel pins. The end of the whip curled around it, spraying fire while doing so, and Alansal caught much of it. Even from this distance Brama could hear her scream of pain.

Another strike came in, which Alansal also blocked imperfectly. Her dress was on fire and another two strikes came in rapid succession. The second crashed against her dead on.

"No!" Mae screamed, and urged Angfua to move faster.

Queen Meryam strode toward Alansal, who had fallen face-first onto the sand. Meryam was saying something while pointing to the Mirean ships, no doubt demanding Alansal's surrender.

Alansal pushed herself off the ground. As she regarded Meryam, only paces away now, the flames along her dress flickered and went out.

Queen Meryam drew her flaming whip back, but before she could strike, a steel pin flew from Alansal's hand, glinted in the air between them, and struck Meryam deep in the chest, just above her heart.

Meryam staggered backward, her left hand gripping the head of the long pin. Somehow managing to keep her feet, she sent her whip lashing.

By then Alansal had gouged the sand with the other pin. A bright thread of chromatic light lit where the pin touched it, as if the sand were nothing but fabric, and Alansal had just cut her way through it. She rolled into this tear in reality, slipping from view and narrowly avoiding the lightning strike of Meryam's whip. Another flaming strike came just after, but Alansal was gone, and the strange doorway was closing behind her. As it snapped shut, a great gout of sand lifted into the air and a thunderclap resounded over the battlefield.

Meryam was thrown backward. She fell to the sand and lay there, unmoving, as a dozen Blade Maidens who'd been rushing to her aid reached her and spirited her away. Queen Meryam might be wounded, but it was clear the Sharakhani forces had the upper hand. Everywhere Brama looked, the asirim were causing devastation. The Maidens and Silver Spears had taken dozens of Mirean ships. There were pockets of resistance yet—the Mireans had tens of thousands of warriors at their command—but without their queen, and without Rümayesh to aid them, it was a losing battle.

Mae was riding toward a fellow soldier, one of the Damned, assaulted by two asirim. Mae drew her sword and shouted over and over, trying to draw their attention, and Brama lifted the spear, hoping to impale one of them as he'd done to Behlosh, but he felt none of the power he'd felt earlier. The bone of Raamajit felt closed, deadened, a storehouse of power still, but one for which the keys had been inexplicably lost.

The asirim were raking their claws over the defenseless qirin warrior. But suddenly they stood and their heads swiveled east. Another asir a dozen yards beyond did so as well. All across the battlefield, the asirim were breaking away from the conflicts, be it on the deck of a ship or on the sand, and turning east.

Mae pulled up as the two asirim ahead began loping across the sand. Others followed. Soon, everywhere Brama looked the asirim were bounding across the desert, heading toward the same unknown destination. The Blade Maidens called to them, ordering their return, but the asirim bounded away like a pack of black laughers on the hunt.

It gave the Mireans heart. Led by several of Queen Alansal's generals, they launched a counterattack. And then Brama heard a sound that astounded him: horns from the Sharakhani ships calling for retreat. The Mireans charged full on, hoping to catch them, but they were overeager and disorganized, and the Sharakhani forces were not toothless. A counterattack spearheaded by the Blade Maidens inflicted terrible damage, and soon the Mirean generals had had enough. They beat their signal drums, calling for their troops to regroup.

"What just happened?" Brama asked, watching as the Kings' galleons began sailing south.

Mae unbuckled her demon mask and let it hang loose. "The goddess of luck has granted us her favor."

No, Brama thought. *This wasn't luck.* Something very strange had just happened. The prevailing desert winds, which had dominated for over four hundred years, had just shifted, perhaps for good. "Come," Brama said, pointing toward the Mirean ships with his spear. "Let's help where we can."

Mae glanced back at him, an inscrutable expression on her face.

"What?" Brama asked.

Still she remained silent.

"Mae, what is it?"

"I thought after battle, you go."

Brama paused, a bit dumbstruck. In truth, he'd had no idea what he would do after the battle. He hadn't been sure he'd make it out alive. He still wasn't quite sure what he wanted to do with his life, he wasn't sure what he *could* do, given the realities of Rümayesh and the bone in his forehead, but he was struck by how much Mae seemed to care. It was then that he realized what a good friend she'd become, and how much he didn't want that friendship to end.

"I don't want to go, Mae. Not yet."

Mae stared at him a good long while. As reserved as she always was, he couldn't tell if she was pleased or not. "Good," she finally said. Then a smile broke over her face, quickly hidden as she spurred her qirin into motion.

Chapter 57

WITH THE EASTERN HORIZON a swath of citrine and gold, and the rest of the sky a star-splashed indigo, the *Amaranth* sailed toward the southern reach of the Mirean encampment. Emre stood on the foredeck, scanning the profile of the other ships. It was obvious they weren't accustomed to fighting in the desert. Their hundreds of ships were arrayed in loose clusters, some small, some quite large. Some of the ships' anchors hadn't even been lowered.

A dozen gaps presented themselves as the ship sailed deeper into the camp, but Emre had Darius hold off on entering. He was on the lookout for the prison ship. He'd never seen it, but King Ihsan's Blade Maiden had described it well enough: an old desert sloop with poor lines and a snub-nose due to a broken bowsprit.

"There!" called Frail Lemi, raising one musclebound arm to point to a curving arc of dhows and sloops and a large Malasani barque that looked strangely out of place among the smaller ships. Near the middle of that arc was the snub-nosed sloop. "That's it right there, ain't it, Emre?"

"That's it, Lem."

Frail Lemi beamed while Darius, his weakened arm hardly a hindrance, adjusted the *Amaranth*'s course. When they came within an eighth-league of the camp's outer edge, a bell began to ring on one of the Malasani ships. The alarm was picked up on several other ships. And more beyond those.

Darius piloted the *Amaranth* brilliantly, skirting twin clusters of rocks that squatted like a pack of hyenas in the dim morning light. Frail Lemi stood on the foredeck, holding the ship's anchor. The anchor was tied to a thick hawser that Old Nur had spent the night reinforcing. The other end of the hawser was wrapped around the mainmast, circling it five times. The slack was piled in a tight coil on the deck between the foremast and the mainmast, where the end of the hawser had been secured to a heavy iron ring.

Emre, holding a thick shield, drew his shamshir and slid to the starboard gunwales. "Archers!" he called, seeing a dozen bowmen moving into position on the Malasani ships and the sand before them.

Frail Lemi moved to gunwales behind Emre and ducked low. Hamid in turn crouched just behind Frail Lemi, holding a sword and shield as Emre was. Darius brought the ship in line with the prison ship. The rest of the crew sat on the main deck and gripped the hawser with thick leather gloves. The arrows began to fly a moment later. One thudded hard into the bulwarks near Emre's head. Another punched through the foresail. A third struck the pilot's wheel, startling Darius. From then on came a steady rain of barbed shafts.

As they approached the prison ship Frail Lemi stood and began swinging the anchor above his head. Emre used his shield to protect Frail Lemi's large frame as best he could, as did Hamid behind him, but they needed to give Lemi room to spin the anchor.

That Lemi could throw it was amazing enough. The anchor was iron, with three great hooks, meant to dig into the sand and prevent a ship from drifting in stiff winds. Plenty on board could lift it, but only Frail Lemi could hurl it far enough to wrap a mast, or use the trick he'd shown them to make the hook catch.

The *Amaranth* sailed closer. Arrows flew. Several bit into Emre's shield. Hamid's as well. One grazed Frail Lemi's shoulder. He flinched from the pain, but kept the anchor spinning. Then one took him above the knee. Another sliced his forearm. The hawser slipped, but with a great roar of pain and singular focus Lemi pulled it back, regained the rhythm of his swing, and with an almighty heave launched the anchor through the air.

The hawser trailed like a snake behind the anchor. The arc of its flight carried it just to the right of the foremast, at which point Frail Lemi snapped the rope to his left and tugged sharply. The anchor's forward momentum was arrested and it slipped around the foremast, wrapping clumsily once, twice, then catching the hawser's own trailing length like a grapnel.

"It's caught!" Emre bellowed. "Be ready!" Then he leapt onto the foredeck of the passing desert sloop.

Hamid followed. The two of them rolled over one shoulder and came up at the ready, swords and shields in hand as they advanced on the approaching guards. There were five of them, but the first two were old, and no swordsmen at all. Both were felled with quick sword cuts to legs and chest.

The others were more skilled, and blunted Emre and Hamid's advance. They even began pressing them back. The key thing, though, wasn't to win the battle outright, but to prevent the guards from reaching the foremast and cutting the tow rope.

Behind Emre came a sizzling sound—the rope had pulled tight around the *Amaranth*'s foremast and its slack was letting out. Emre felt the deck of the prison ship move beneath his feet. He braced for it, as did Hamid.

"Watch out!" one of the Malasani guards called, but too late.

The ship lurched into motion, and two of the soldiers fell. The others twisted and windmilled their arms as they tried and failed to keep their feet. Emre was back up in a flash and engaging the man who'd called out the warning, who'd also regained his feet. Hamid, meanwhile, dispatched a gangly fellow with a merciless slash to his unprotected neck.

When the hawser's slack finally ran out, it thrummed low, like the string of some grand instrument. They'd all worried, even Old Nur, that the hawser might snap, but it held and the prison ship was yanked into faster motion. Nur had measured the length perfectly. The prison ship's snub bowsprit was nosing over the stern of the *Amaranth*, which allowed Emre's crew to leap aboard, swords and shields at the ready.

Two of their crew were taken down by arrow fire, but the others crowded the deck and the Malasani guards had no choice but to surrender. They dropped their swords and raised their hands, but Hamid roared and cut his man down anyway. The lone man standing watched Emre nervously.

Emre pointed over the side of the ship. "I'd leave now if I were you."

Before Emre had even finished, he was heading for the gunwales. Over the side he went, landing with a soft thud and a spray of sand.

Soon enough Emre, Frail Lemi, Hamid, and the others had dispatched the soldiers. For a moment, Emre could only stare. By the gods, the ship was theirs.

Two of the crew had remained aboard the *Amaranth* with Darius and were launching fire pots at ships they passed, largely to sow confusion and buy them time. Old Nur's laughter filled the dry desert air as the pots crashed onto the decks of several dhows. Ship after ship, fire coughed and black smoke billowed.

"And fuck your mother, too!" Nur called.

The rest of Emre's crew set about the business of readying the prison ship to sail, focusing on raising the foresail first. Emre and Hamid, meanwhile, headed belowdecks.

There was a moment when Emre was sure he'd been lied to, that this was all an elaborate joke, or a trap, and that neither Haddad nor King Ihsan would be found in the cells below. His heart crawled into his throat as he landed on the floor and peered into the darkness.

Then at last, at the far end of the hold, he saw them. The Honey-tongued King, his neck and clothes filthy with his own blood, and in the cell across from him, Haddad.

Hamid found the keys in the gaoler's cabin and threw them to Emre with a look that made it clear he refused to be the one to free them. As Emre opened Haddad's cell, a twinge of regret ran through him. She had massive purple bruises and deep cuts across her face. One along her neck glistened, still weeping after the beating she'd received from King Emir.

"Well?" she asked. "Are you just going to fucking stand there?" The expression on her face was unreadable. There was relief in her eyes, but the rest of her, especially the way her fingers kept flexing, spoke of anger, of grim determination.

But anger at whom? Emre wondered, *me or King Emir?*

King Ihsan smiled as Emre unlocked his cell, and waited with a pleasant expression on his handsome, middle-aged face. Were it not for the dried blood marking his skin and the Silver Spear uniform, one might think he was heading for cardamom tea and biscuits. The effect was so smug Emre was tempted to leave him aboard the ship, but he and King Ihsan both knew he wasn't going to do that, which made it all the more infuriating.

"What?" Emre said to him. "Nothing smart to say?"

It was a crude insult, but Emre was annoyed that he'd fallen into the Honey-tongued King's plans. His god-given power might have been taken from him but the man still knew the way to the hearts of men. When Ihsan, clearly sensing Emre's discomfort, allowed his smile to widen, Emre grabbed him by the front of his stained surcoat and shoved him into the passageway ahead of him.

"Get on, then."

With Emre following, and Haddad coming last, they filed up the ladder to the deck, then toward the *Amaranth*.

The prison ship's foresail and mainsail were set, and with the wind waxing in the growing heat, both ships were gaining good speed. The sun was cresting the horizon dead ahead while the alarm bells chorused behind them. The first few ships of what was likely to be a small armada were setting sail, preparing to give chase. Indeed, nearly two dozen, mostly swift Malasani dhows, were soon cutting lines in the sand, hounding the *Amaranth*'s wake.

As the encampment dwindled into the distance, Emre ordered every yard of canvas on the prison ship set, but it was not a fleet ship, so they did the only thing they could. Emre waited for the first cluster of Malasani ships to approach, then tied the wheel into position so it would veer into their path. As Emre sprinted across the foredeck and leapt onto the Amaranth, Lemi brought Umber down across the gunwales and cut the towing rope.

It worked better than they could have hoped. The *Amaranth*'s crew shouted in joy as the prison ship crashed sidelong into the lead dhow, forcing it wide of its chosen path and catching two more ships in the mess. But even three ships down they still had a score of others to lead the chase.

As the sun rose, the wind began to bluster. Sudden gusts lifted sand and blew it across the dunes in great swaths. Emre prayed to Goezhen for a sandstorm to hide them, but it was not to be. An amber haze was beginning to form, but it wasn't nearly enough to mask their position. Plus, as the sun continued to rise, the wind's strength peaked and began to ebb.

Slowly but surely, the Malasani dhows were closing the distance.

Frail Lemi couldn't take his eyes from them. "Not long now," he said said, gripping Umber's haft.

"No, Lem. Not long now."

Instead of watching the ships behind, Emre moved to the foredeck and studied the way ahead. Along the horizon, an angry line of black rocks separated sky from sand. Last night he'd been so sure they could make the hills before the Malasani. Now it was looking more and more grim.

Emre scooped up a bit of dust and sand from the deck and gripped it in one hand. He brought it to his lips and allowed it to sift between his fingers. "I've never asked you for anything," he whispered to Bakhi, "you know this. But if you were ever to grant me anything, grant me this. Let us reach those bloody black hills."

"There!" Darius called, waving two points off the starboard bow with his good arm. "There!"

Emre looked where he was pointing and whooped. In the sand ahead of the *Amaranth*, stretching all the way to the low hills, was a rare pattern in the sand, a light chop that was difficult to navigate if you didn't know how.

"We sail crisply!" Emre bellowed. "We need to make the defile before they do!"

"Aye!" the crew cheered, knowing they had a chance now.

"What?" Emre leapt to the gunwales and stared about, taking in every crewman. "Do I sense doubt?"

"Nay!"

He thrust a finger at the trailing ships. "Will you allow those jelly-boned curs to catch us?"

"Nay!" It was a roar this time.

"Then accept what the Great Mother gives us! Ride the dunes smartly. Embrace the wind. For you know those clumsy dogs can't sail her as *we* can!"

There came a chorus of whistles and laughs. "Dead right!" one of them yelled.

"Dead right," Frail Lemi echoed. He was staring aft with that look he got when violence was near. He looked if he wanted to leap aboard the first enemy ship to come close and cleave every man who stood before him with his ruddy great spear.

As Emre leapt down from the gunwales, King Ihsan was looking at him as if he hadn't quite expected that from him. He gave Emre a respectful nod. He actually seemed impressed, but Emre didn't care what he thought. He had a crew to lead.

Darius set to it, calling out adjustments to the set of the sails to catch the fullness of the wind, and the crew responded with the sort of ease gained only from months of sailing together. Darius was a master pilot. This Emre already knew. But now he slipped into an almost trancelike state.

"A ship is like a ewer catching rain," he'd once told Emre. "The larger the funnel the more rain you can catch. But capturing the water is only half the equation. Everything about the ship, the way you sail it, acts like cracks in the clay. The skis, how well waxed they are, how battered from the desert sea, the weight of the ship, the position of the cargo, they're all cracks, leaking water you'd hoped to save. Some of it you can do nothing about, but catch the wind right and sail her properly, and it becomes art, a beautiful one if you can master it."

Indeed, the *Amaranth* was like a yearling oryx, maneuvering the dunes with speed and grace. The dhows behind them, meanwhile, were like a pack of hyenas bounding over the desert. Time and time again they plowed mindlessly against the dunes, sending sprays of sand into the air. Often they got caught in the gutters, which slowed their speed considerably, and they slipped farther and farther behind.

But Emre could see that it would be a short reprieve. Closer to the hills the sand evened out, creating a flat stretch that would favor the dhows once again. Indeed, as they sailed closer to the defile between two long stretches of jagged, inhospitable rock, the dhows began to regain the distance they'd lost, rather too quickly for Emre's tastes.

Using the spyglass, Emre scanned the defile carefully.

"Anything?" Hamid asked, standing beside Emre at the forward gunwales.

"No." Emre shook his head. "But they'll be there."

"And if they aren't?"

"Then our blood will feed the Great Mother," Emre shot back. "Now get ready."

Behind the *Amaranth*, the Malasani ships had fanned out in a wide, undisciplined arc. A lone arrow, dark against the blue sky, lifted from the lead ship. It fell short, but it was like a silent signal between a murder of crows. More lifted up. Then more still. Soon the sky was thick with an unsteady stream of them coming in from all angles.

The *Amaranth* returned fire. The ship had few cat's claws to launch with its lone catapult, but Old Nur always seemed to know the right angle to use. Over and over the weighted ends of the claws would fly, the chain between them wriggling like a snake. With frightening accuracy it would wrap around a dhow's forward struts and gouge furrows in the sand, slowing the ship and fouling its steering.

By the time the cat's claws had run out, six dhows were falling behind the pack, with more slowed down by the suddenly hobbled ships ahead. Old Nur moved on to fire pots, but the Malasani had started launching them as well.

One crashed in the *Amaranth*'s wake. Another struck just short of the transom. A third smashed into the stern, sending a spray of burning oil across the quarterdeck, the transom, and the rudder below. As they neared the mouth of the defile, more struck to either side of the ship. By some miracle none of the Malasani cat's claws managed to wrap the *Amaranth*'s struts. But the arrows were taking their toll. Darius's bad arm was clipped. A crewman, drawing back an arrow of his own, fell to deck when one caught him deep in the abdomen.

They were just short of the defile's mouth when a fire pot struck the center of the *Amaranth*'s deck. Old Nur had been going for the final few fire pots, stored in a reinforced locker, when it landed at his feet. Flames engulfed him. He screamed, flailed and ran, trying to escape the flames, and in his blindness fell overboard.

The rest of the crew were trying to douse the flames, but they'd caught along the foot of the mainsail. Hamid, Emre, and the rest worked quickly to spread the dousing agent, a blue powder, from the buckets staged all about the ship and it worked, but they were going to lose the sail. The flames licked upward, eventually burning a hole through it, but Emre still refused to order the sail down. They needed all the wind they could get.

Finally, blessedly, they entered the steep canyon, the Malasani ships just behind them. The soldiers aboard their ships, men and women alike, stood at the gunwales and roared, stabbing their swords into the air, their thirst to take the *Amaranth* at a peak now that the end of the chase was near.

The defile was narrow but still wide enough for several ships to sail side by side. The deeper they went, though, the more the steep canyon walls closed in. The Malasani ships were forced to go two by two, then single file.

The *Amaranth*'s crew were just beginning to get the fire on the deck under control when two more fire pots crashed into the stern, engulfing the entire quarterdeck in flames and splashing Darius with burning oil. Frail Lemi smothered him with a blanket quickly, shouting with impotent rage all the while.

Ahead, the defile reached its narrowest point. It was barely wider than the *Amaranth*'s skis. But the ship was now madness. The crew were trying to put out the fresh flames with more blankets and the dousing agent, of which very little remained. Ihsan and Haddad were throwing the last of their buckets onto the fresh fire at the stern. Darius had fallen and rolled away from the pilot's wheel. Hamid had followed, as had Frail Lemi, who was trying to pat out the flames with swats of his massive hands, leaving the ship without a pilot. Emre swept in and took the wheel, careful to avoid the flaming spokes.

The narrow gap ahead worried Emre more than the fire. The *Amaranth*'s sails might be aflame, but the wind through the defile was so strong it was carrying them forward at speed.

He glanced behind, then up to the flaming, smoking canvas above him. They stood no chance of fighting the Malasani. And when they'd passed this narrow gap, the valley opened up and they would never stay ahead of the Malasani ships, not as the *Amaranth* lost more and more wind to fire. Emre stared at the narrow path ahead.

"I have to crash the ship," he said to no one in particular. "I have to crash it and block the way. We can stop their ships and make a run for it after."

His decision made, he began angling the ship so it would come to a scraping halt against the rocks on the port side. But then he caught movement higher up. There was a young man in a red turban and thawb. Emre recognized him immediately. It was Shaikh Aríz, and he was waving a shamshir high in the air. When Emre waved back, Aríz used the tip of his sword to point farther along the defile.

Relief flooded through Emre. "Hold on!" he shouted as an arrow flew past him, making him flinch. He hoped the others were listening, but he couldn't spare a moment to look. "Just a bit longer!" He steered carefully but their starboard ski still jumped over an exposed rock, causing the entire ship to shift and rattle. The rocks came so close he could reach out and touch them. Then, by the grace of the gods, they were through.

Behind them, from the rocks they'd just sailed past, a dozen men in red thawbs and turbans rushed onto the sand. They hauled massive iron barricades across the narrowest point of the defile, then scattered as the first of the dhows came flying in.

Both of the dhow's forward struts were shattered by the barricades. A great gout of amber sand splashed high into the air as the ship's prow dove nose first into the ground. A moment later, the rudder was ripped free as well. The ship veered, then tilted sharply, the sudden pitch of the deck launching crewmen and equipment over the starboard side.

The next ship came crashing in, to be crippled by the combination of the barricades and the mangle of shattered wood left by the first ship. The next, though it did its best to avoid the barricades, suffered the same fate.

The ships behind them had seen the danger and had started to slow by means of the large rakes dropped from the sterns of their ships. Even so, five more were caught in the trap, and more beyond those sustained damage as they crashed into the mortally wounded ships. The rest came to a halt, the crew working feverishly to bring their sails in.

In that moment, several hundred warriors in red rose from their hiding places along the canyon walls and began firing arrows. More heaved fire pots onto the ships. In moments, every Malasani ship was aflame, engulfed to varying degrees by roiling orange fire and black smoke. The soldiers and crew who escaped the fire were taken down by arrows and, though some few tried to set up a defense with shields and return fire, Tribe Kadri's numbers were simply too great.

In little time it was done. Only two ships managed to flee west.

Men and women rushed toward the *Amaranth*, many bearing buckets of dousing agent. They put out the ship's flames and worked like fury to make the necessary repairs to the ship. They had a joyous reunion with Aríz, but this wasn't the time or the place to celebrate. They needed to find a safe place for the tribe to rest. And there was more for Emre to do yet to see his plans through.

Soon they were off, sailing east to meet the rest of Tribe Kadri. As they exited the defile to the east, Emre looked back at the column of smoke lifting in the distance. Then he took in Haddad and King Ihsan, who stood near one another amidships. King Ihsan seemed haggard—like many of the crew, he'd sustained burns from the fire—but there was a look of satisfaction on his face, as if the complex dish he'd just cooked had, despite many troubles along the way, turned out splendidly.

Haddad, however, had an intense look about her, as if she were on the verge of some momentous decision. *And well she should,* Emre thought. *This had all been for her.*

Chapter 58

WHEN ÇEDA SPIED DOZENS of sails raking the horizon, she and everyone else aboard the *Red Bride* feared the Kings' ships, but it soon became clear they were ships of the desert tribes, not the royal navy. Midday approached, and the makeup of the small fleet began to come clear. The *Drifting Sun*, Macide's fleet cutter, sailed alongside three other Khiyanat ships, their mainmasts flying the blue pennant of the tribe with its white mountain peak. The pennants of the ships sailing behind them revealed more: the Black Veils of Tribe Salmük, the Red Wind of Masal, the Standing Stones of Tribe Ebros and the Amber Blades of Ulmahir; there was even one from the Raining Stars of Tribe Tulogal.

When they came within hailing distance, word came that Macide wanted to speak to Çeda. "You've done well," Çeda said after she'd swung over to his ship.

Macide had that look of his, the one that spoke of the task being a heavier burden than he would ever let on. "Not nearly as well as you, it seems." He motioned to Sehid-Alaz and the other asirim huddled on the deck of the *Red Bride*. Their numbers had swelled to more than a score, some few asirim who'd been near having intercepted the ship on its journey toward Mount Arasal.

Çeda shared her story, and Macide pressed her on King Ihsan, wondering what he might have been doing before being taken by the Malasani golems.

"I've no idea," she said, "but he seemed intent on saving us."

"From everything you said, I'd guess he was intent on saving *you*."

Çeda thought back on it. "He might have been." It felt so peculiar, though. Why would Ihsan have risked so much for her?

"Well," Macide said, "I suppose it's fortunate that the Malasani took care of him for us."

"Don't be so sure of that."

Macide's dark eyebrows rose. "He has a golden tongue. You think the gods gave him the ability to breathe beneath sand too?"

"I saw the golem pull him up and drag him away. The gods are nothing if not cruel, and the crueler path is for him to cross our path again in the future."

When she finished, she said, "It can't be a coincidence that we met you on the way here."

"You're right."

He told her how he'd sailed to a gathering of six tribes. Masal and Salmük were already part of the alliance with Khiyanat, the thirteenth tribe. Over the next several days, Macide and the other two shaikhs had presented an offer to the rest: join us in mutual protection against the Kings; join us that we might protect the sands from the interlopers who seek to take it for their own. Once those threats had been met, we can decide what to do with Sharakhai together. By the end of their deliberations, Ebros and Ulmahir had agreed, and Tulogal, while stopping short of joining the growing alliance, had agreed to consider it further, to provide aid and, perhaps most important of all, to deliver the same offer to their allied tribes to the west.

"We were considering going with Tulogal to hold another council when a lyrewing arrived. 'Nalamae commands you, return to the valley,' it said. 'The King of Shadows is coming.' We set sail that very day, and here we are."

"And Emre?" asked Çeda. He had been sent on a similar mission to the southern tribes.

Macide shook his head. "It's too soon, Çeda. We won't know for some time yet."

She tried to hide her disappointment, though she knew full well she wasn't doing a very good job of it. How she missed Emre. His face. His bright smile. His stupid jokes.

Macide looked like he was about to say something when a low humming sound filled the air. His gaze drifted toward the *Red Bride*, which sailed along their starboard side. Near the bowsprit, Sehid-Alaz was spinning Night's Kiss through the air in a blade form Çeda had never seen before. Something ancient, perhaps, or a thing of his own making. The sword had changed since Beht Zha'ir. It was still hungry, but now bowed to Sehid-Alaz's will, as if the act of making him anew had joined the two of them. Or perhaps its hunger had been sated. Who could tell? Whatever the case, Çeda was glad to be rid of the blade.

"It's too bad about Husamettín," Macide said.

"At least Kameyl gave him a kiss to remember us by."

"A scar on his forehead is hardly the punishment he deserves. His bones should be feeding the Great Mother."

Macide looked so much like his father, Ishaq, in that moment, all righteous indignation, that Çeda laughed.

"You think it a joke?"

"I think I have more of a right to be angry than you do. Husamettín's time will come."

He seemed no more pleased, but he nodded. "I suppose what's done is done. And the asirim"—he jutted his chin toward the *Bride*—"they're free now?"

"Yes."

"All of them?"

"All of them."

He seemed skeptical.

"It's true, Macide. They're free. Free of the Kings. Free of the gods' curse. And Sehid-Alaz has summoned them to the valley."

Something unreadable passed over Macide's face, some combination of relief and gratitude, perhaps, but it was there and gone in a moment. "I hope so," he finally said. "The question now is whether they'll arrive in time."

Çeda shrugged. "They're spread across the desert but many, we hope, will be near enough to help."

Macide stared toward the mountains. "I fear they'll be too late. We arrive tomorrow. We'll face another half-day's march toward the valley and the old fortress where the tribe is taking shelter. It might be days, weeks, before the bulk of the asirim arrive, and until then we'll have thousands of Silver Spears to contend with. Blade Maidens. King Beşir."

"Beşir . . ." Çeda repeated. "He should be dead already." She explained his attack in the desert, how Rhia had been full and yet he'd suffered no ill effects.

"Yes," Macide said, "about the bloody verses." He nodded to one of the crew. "I've a present for you."

"A present?"

Macide smiled and stroked his beard, showing off the viper tattoo on his forearm. The burly crewman returned a short while later with a man named Ulman, a fellow so thin, so ancient, Çeda thought he might crumble away into a pile of sand. He looked nervously at Çeda, then Macide, then seemed to find something terribly interesting on the deck boards between them.

"Go on, grandfather," Macide said.

The man's freckled brow furrowed, and then he recited a poem:

From golden dunes,
And ancient runes,
The King of glittering stone;
By inverted thorn,
His skin was torn,
And yet his strength did grow.

While far afield,
His love unsealed,
'Til Tulathan does loom;
Then petals' dust,
Like lovers' lust,
Will draw him toward his tomb.

Bakhi's bright hammer, it was Külaşan's bloody verse, the very one she'd used to catch Külaşan at his weakest. She'd shared it with Macide and many others from the thirteenth tribe, but how did this man, who looked like he'd spent his entire life in the desert, know it? Given that Macide had described this as a *present*, she was certain Ulman had more to share with her.

"Do you have more of the bloody verses, grandfather?"

Ulman nodded.

"But how did you find them?" she asked.

He looked distressed, as if he were trying hard to remember, but couldn't.

"His great-grandfather was a librarian at the collegia," Macide answered, "and then the personal archivist for King Onur, where he found rather more than he'd bargained for. Stumbling upon the verses, he feared for his life, for his family's life. He never shared what he'd learned outside his family, but he did share it with them, and so these three bloody verses were passed down to Ulman."

"Three verses," Çeda breathed, praying to the fates they weren't the ones she already knew. But how could they be? Macide wouldn't be acting like the cat who'd swallowed the canary if they were.

"Yes, and given our conversation a moment ago, I suspect the second is one you'll be pleased to hear." Macide nodded to Ulman, who recited it with a good deal more confidence than he had the first.

From deepened vale,
A King most hale,
Sincere entreaties lost;
Fought he alone,
On plain of stone,
Yet there his fate embossed.

Thaash did see,
In King of three,
A foe made long ago;
Said Thaash to King,
Your words shall ring,
Yet true name brings you low.

"Your words shall ring," Çeda breathed. Her fingers and toes had started to tingle like they did when she was young, when her mother would return from one of her night-long excursions to the blooming fields. "It's Ihsan's."

Of all the bloody verses, she wanted King Ihsan's the most. Memories of her mission to the top of Mount Tauriyat swam before her. Ihsan had been there, waiting, and she'd been undone by a word. The very notion of having something to counteract his power made her shiver with excitement, yet in the same breath she was crestfallen. *True name brings you low,* the verse said.

"I don't suppose your grandfather gave you Ihsan's true name?"

Ulman shook his head, deflated, and resumed his careful inspection of the deck.

"Gods," Çeda said, "to come so close."

"I was disappointed as well," Macide said. "There are a few things I'd like to discuss with the Honey-tongued King. But it's more than we had yesterday."

There was no denying it. And Çeda had to admit it was sobering. The random finding of Ulman was yet another reminder that the survival of their tribe had been accomplished through the effort and sacrifice of hundreds, thousands of brave souls over the centuries since Beht Ihman. Çeda had often thought of her mother as a lone actor, but she wasn't. She'd been a part of a grand web, one thread of knowledge supporting the next supporting the next. Those who came before had given Ahya a head start and allowed her to take things further, which in turn had helped Çeda. And here was another tale, different from hers but still part of the same web: Ulman's great-grandfather finding one small bit of information, one weapon in the struggle, and handing it down through the generations.

"Now for the most interesting part," Macide waved to Ulman a third time.

Ulman spoke a third verse, and this time his voice was commanding, a renowned actor casting retirement aside for one final performance.

Sharp of eye,
And quick of wit,
The King of Amberlark;
With wave of hand,
On cooling sand,
Slips he into the dark.

King will shift,
'Twixt light and dark,
Through doors where borders lie;
Yet he who plays,
In bright of day,
Is drawn 'neath pewter sky.

"The lines are different," Çeda said.

Macide nodded and repeated the second stanza as Çeda had recited it to him:

King will shift,
'Twixt light and dark,
The gift of onyx sky;
Shadows play,
In dark of day,
Yet not 'neath Rhia's eye.

"I'm not surprised there are two," he said. "The Kings worked hard to hide the bloody verses, but they couldn't hide everything. Naturally they tried to muddy the waters by putting out false verses."

"Which leads us to an interesting problem. How do we know Ulman's verse is the true one? Where there are two there might be three."

Macide folded his arms and shrugged. "We don't know. We can't."

Ulman looked embarrassed, as if he'd done something wrong. "Under a pewter sky, there are no shadows."

Çeda blinked. Of course he was right. And it made a sort of sense. Many of the curses the gods had lain upon the Kings bound their powers and weaknesses together. "If we were to catch Beşir beneath a cloudy sky . . ."

She looked to Macide, who nodded. "It makes as much sense as anything else."

"More than that." Çeda turned to look at Mount Arasal in the distance, which was stark under a bright sun. They were deep into summer, where cloudless blue skies dominated. "But it would take a miracle to find ourselves beneath gray skies for our battle."

Macide jutted his chin toward the mountain. "There *is* a goddess holed up in that fortress."

Çeda turned to look and realized a bird was flying toward them. The lyrewing had returned. It approached, spread its copper wings, and alighted on the bowsprit. In high, ringing tones it began to speak. "The King of Shadows arrives. The attack on the fortress begins!" It repeated this three times and then stilled.

Çeda approached it with care, worried it might fly away. "Very well," she said. "Can you take a message back to the goddess for us?"

The bird waited, calm, its black eyes blinking.

Çeda told it her plan, then repeated it, and a third time. The lyrewing listened. It fanned its wings and craned its neck toward the sky. When she'd finished it repeated, "Drawn 'neath pewter sky!" and launched itself into the air.

It flew toward the mountains until lost from sight along the shoulders of Mount Arasal.

Chapter 59

As the days in Eventide's dungeon stretched on, Davud felt certain he was right about Hamzakiir. Had he been able to, he surely would have sent some word, or arranged for Davud to escape. But he hadn't, which made Davud wonder just how much Meryam suspected. Hamzakiir had implied they were still in contact with one another even though she'd left the city. Did she suspect treachery? Had she learned about Davud and Esmeray? No, Davud reasoned. If she had, their necks would already have met the executioner's blade.

Davud tried again and again to reason with Esmeray, but she'd fallen silent, refusing to speak to him at all. He tried to open the lock as well. It wasn't easy. With the manacles still on and the bar between them forcing his hands apart, he'd resorted to biting his lip and using his tongue to spread the blood directly onto the metal plate covering the lock. Using one's own blood produced weak results. Factor in the sloppy way he'd drawn the sigil and how difficult it was to affect the metal and it added up to an effort destined to fail. He managed to rattle the lock's internal mechanisms, no more.

Then one day Davud heard words that sent a chill running through him. "Things were never *cheery* before Queen Meryam arrived," the gaoler groused to the Silver Spear who always accompanied him on his rounds, "but at least one could live without fear."

The Spear, who was young, and seemed new to Eventide, said, "The queen changed him."

"Bloody right she changed him, for the worse! Does everything have to be so dark and dreary? It's part to do with the war, but mostly it's her." There came the distant clank and creak of the dungeon door opening, and the gaoler's voice dropped. "You didn't hear me say this, but I'll be glad if the war keeps her away. Glad if it keeps her away for good."

"I hate to throw sand in your tea," the Spear said, "but it's not going to happen." The gaoler gave a noncommittal grunt, his favorite response, and the Spear went on. "A ship arrived late last night with word that the queen is returning ahead of the fleet, perhaps even today."

The rest was lost as the door clanged shut.

Davud stared through the window of his cell door. "You heard them," he called toward Esmeray's cell. "We've no time to waste. We have to leave."

A hollow silence followed.

"Is this how you plan to repay the loss of your brother's life? When you're reunited with Deniz in the farther fields, will you explain you couldn't be bothered to avenge his death?"

"Be quiet, Davud."

But he wouldn't. He couldn't. "The Kings *took* him, Esmeray. They *tortured* him. Experimented on his body, likely before *and* after his death. You would lie there in your cell and accept it?"

"I told you to be quiet."

"Does Deniz love you so much that he'll overlook your cowardice? Or will he look you in the eye and tell you the truth, that you utterly failed him?"

She came to the window, staring at him with those bone-white eyes of hers. "Keep my brother's name from your lips."

"Then make him proud! Help me!"

"I can't! I can't help anyone anymore!"

"Yes, you can! You can start by teaching me how to open this lock."

She shook her head. "It would take days, weeks, to teach you. I can see from the way you've been fumbling with it."

The words Davud was about to say died on his lips. "You can see it?"

"Yes, see but not touch. Do you know how maddening that is?"

Davud's mind drifted to an oud parlor, where the two of them had spun candlelight. "Esmeray, if you can feel it, then you can guide me."

"I told you, I can't work magic."

"No, but you could provide the structure, the framework."

"It doesn't work like that." She spoke the words, but they were soft, uncertain as a sand mouse.

"Try."

Esmeray's bright white eyes cast downward. She stared at the lock, her hands gripping the iron bars of her cell window, her expression turning to one of sorrow. "I'm scared, Davud."

"I know." The admission revealed how staggeringly deep her fear ran—Davud didn't know her well, but he knew her well enough to know it took a lot for her to admit a thing like that. "But you're not alone, Esmeray." He reached out with what little power he had from his own blood. "Guide my hand."

The power was there, raw and unformed. It was the sort that could harm *him* if he wasn't careful. But he'd grown adept at summoning and holding power before its use.

For a long while she remained perfectly still. He was sure she'd decided against helping him, that the combination of the loss of her magic and her fear of the Kings was too much to bear, but then he realized she *was* trying.

He felt it, on the very edge of perception: a skeletal framework so diaphanous, so frail, it might crumble the moment he lent power to it. It didn't, though, and he found it hungry for more. Esmeray was the trellis, he the verdant growth, each helping the other, becoming stronger over time, until finally the spell's potential reached the point where they had to use it or suffer the effects of its feedback. Davud wasn't adept enough to do so, but Esmeray was, and guided it against the lock's inner mechanisms with a deft hand. Davud felt the tumblers shift. Felt each lift to the proper height. Felt the lock itself turn, the metal creaking softly as it did. The steel tried to foil the workings of the spell, but Esmeray was a master craftsman, guiding all until it was done and the door shifted on its hinges.

Doing the same to his manacles was trickier, but they managed it together, then unlocked her cell door as well. By then Davud was standing
there, waiting. He could see the fear and doubt warring within her, which
was sobering after the joy and perfection he'd felt while weaving spells with
her. *Esmeray's reality is not yours*, he told himself. He wasn't dependent on
other magi to walk the red ways. Esmeray now was.

It struck him then how callous he'd been, how uncaring of her feelings.
He was still new to magic, yet it had already become a part of him. What
must it be like for her, a woman who'd known magic since she was a child,
whose entire family knew its touch? Magic had defined her, and it had all
been stripped away.

He squeezed her hands. "We'll make Sukru pay for what he's done."

Esmeray squeezed back. "And see Anila freed."

He wasn't sure if she was ready for it, but he was grateful that she'd be by
his side. "Yes," he said, then led her down the hall toward the dungeon entrance.

They worked together to cast a sleeping spell on the gaoler. It was morning, but the man was halfway there already, leaning back in his chair and
staring at the ceiling. After unlocking the door, Esmeray took the gaoler's
knife and used the tip to carve a shallow wound along her wrist.

When she held it out to him, Davud paused. She seemed both vulnerable
and powerful in that moment. He placed his lips to the wound, felt the rush
of power. But he wasn't thinking about spells and escapes. He was thinking
about Esmeray. Without knowing when he'd made the decision to do so, he
leaned toward her and pressed his lips to hers.

She stiffened, surprised, then backed away and held two fingers to his
lips. "We'll have time for that later," she said, offering the blood once more,
though not, Davud noticed, without a quickly hidden smile. He took more,
then healed the wound with a sizzling swipe of his finger.

After Esmeray guided him in another spell to make attention slip from
them—a more refined spell than the one Davud had used to make it through
the checkpoint at the city walls—they were up and into the palace. They
passed many in the halls of Eventide, and yet the two of them walked calmly,
hand in hand, and no one stopped them. Few even looked their way, and
those who did turned away as if they'd seen Davud and Esmeray every day
of their existence in the palace.

Soon they came to an ancient door, iron-barred and peaked at the top—the one Hamzakiir had shown Davud in his dream world. It was Meryam's shrine to Alu, where they would find her book of sigils.

"She won't have left it unattended," Esmeray said.

"No," he agreed.

This spell, at least, Davud knew well—a way to perceive the traces of extant magic—but Esmeray still helped, adding slight modifications to the sigils he drew upon his hands, which had the effect of broadening the search and intensifying the results. Davud passed his hands over the door and saw it, a dull red glow.

"The trick"—like Davud, Esmeray was staring closely at the door's surface—"is to unweave the threads of the spell without breaking them." Working together, they unraveled the spell of detection, holding the threads in place as if the spell were only half-cast, then unlocked the door and stepped inside. "Then we retie them as they were." She did exactly that, with a skill that made Davud blink in awe.

Inside, they found a room of stone walls and stark decoration. There was a marble pedestal with a basin of salt water—water from the Austral Sea, no doubt. On the walls, banners depicted the crest of Qaimir and Alu's symbol, a wave crashing against stone. There was a padded bench to kneel upon and pray before the altar, which was a simple block of granite.

Of Meryam's book, however, there was no sign. Not that either of them had expected anything else; Queen Meryam wouldn't have left it just lying about. They searched the room more closely, looking for hidden compartments in the padded bench, in the walls, in the floor, and the massive piece of granite. They even tried to look *under* the bowl of water, but the blasted thing was fixed to the pedestal beneath. They searched for spells as well, as they had on the door, but found nothing.

Exasperated, and more than a little nervous, Davud said, "Could she have woven a spell too fine for us to detect?"

Esmeray shrugged, looking behind the Qaimiri banner for the tenth time. She let it slip through her fingers to lay against the wall, looking as intense as Davud had ever seen her. "She might have."

Suddenly they heard several sets of footsteps in the hall outside. A woman's voice accompanied them. A self-assured voice. An angry voice. "A *full* council," she was saying. "The greater Kings and the lesser, or their vizirs if they're unavailable."

"Of course," came a man's voice.

"You've found King Kiral?"

"Not yet."

"Then *find* him," she was saying, "and tell him to wait for me in my apartments."

There was a pregnant pause. "I'm to tell King Kiral to come and wait for you," he said, "in your apartments?"

"Just so." And after a brief pause, "Now!"

"Yes, your Excellence."

One set of footsteps stopped, then resumed and dwindled, while the other approached the door.

Esmeray waved Davud close. He moved toward her as silently as he could. She was already casting a net outward, a new framework for a spell. With an ease that surprised him, he added his power to it, and followed her guidance, feeling the complex sigil as it burned within her mind, to cast the spell that was meant to mask their presence. Davud felt it fall about his shoulders like a cold, heavy cloak just as the door opened.

Queen Meryam, a small woman in a dress that might have been sky blue were it not so filthy with dust, swept into the room and closed the door behind her. She had tiny, half-healed wounds all over her face, as if she'd lost a fight with an exploding pane of glass. She smelled like a campfire.

She didn't move to the altar, as followers of Alu often did after travel, but to the pedestal and the basin of water atop it. Without preamble, she slid one hand into the water and reached far deeper than the depth of the water would seem to have allowed. She reached so deeply everything up to her armpit was submerged. Except the water hardly made a ripple, nor did it spill over.

When Meryam withdrew her arm, she held a book in her hand. Her arm, the cloth of her sleeve, and the leatherbound tome were all perfectly dry. She took the book to the pedestal and flipped it open to study a dozen different pages, peering at the sigils carefully, reading the notes beneath. She drew several in the air before her and they glowed until she wiped a hand through each, banishing them so that she could start anew. She remained in place for nearly an hour, with Davud and Esmeray only two paces away.

Suddenly Meryam stood. She shivered violently—a thing that made her skeletal features stand out—then cast her gaze about the room. Davud's skin prickled and Esmeray stiffened in his arms. He swore he felt something *lick* the surface of the spell that hid them. But then Meryam's suspicions seemed to pass. She closed the book with a snap, shoved it back into the water, and left the room with the sort of stormy look that didn't bode well for whomever she was about to see next.

They both breathed a sigh of relief as her footsteps diminished.

"Goezhen's sweet kiss," Esmeray whispered.

"Please don't invoke the name of the gods," he whispered back as they moved to the basin.

Even knowing there was a spell upon it, it was difficult to find, much less unravel. But they did, and eventually Davud felt confident enough to reach in and retrieve the book. It felt heavy, not merely due to its considerable weight, but its importance to the events unfolding in Sharakhai.

"Where now?" Esmeray asked.

"We can't stay here," Davud replied.

Remaining in Eventide would be dangerous. Meryam could return at any moment and when she found the book missing she'd likely scour the palace to find it. And they couldn't just go to Hamzakiir now. They needed time to study the book, to find the sigil Meryam had used on him.

"We need time to think," he said.

"Time to plan," Esmeray added.

They both looked at each other, remembering what Meryam had said. She'd called a full council, which gave them the perfect place.

They said it together.

"The Sun Palace."

Chapter 60

THE SMALL DUNGEON beneath the Qaimiri embassy house had only two cells. Cicio slept in one of them, leaning against the corner formed by the metal bars. He might have lain near the walls if it weren't for the rats. The farther he could get from their holes, the longer it took them to pluck up their courage and nip at his clothes or his skin. Even so, it only afforded him a few minutes of sleep at a time. He woke to the feel of scuttling and kicked them away with a long, frustrated shout.

"You need to be faster," a young man said in Qaimiri from the cell across from him. Cicio didn't know what he'd done to land himself in a cell, but he seemed to have been there a while. "Break their necks. Leave some lying about. They won't bother you after that."

Cicio stared at him closer, realizing the dirt had made him look older than he really was. "That's a load of shit."

The boy shrugged and lay back down. "Suit yourself," and he lapsed into silence.

Cicio gave up on finding sleep. His head against his knees, he listened to the wealth of sounds coming from the floor above: clomping footsteps, crisply barked orders, the thud of furniture being moved. Over the past few days, the servants who'd come to bring food and change the chamber pots would occasionally linger with the gaoler and talk, spilling news of Meryam or the assault on the city or other, more mundane tales. Through these small exchanges, Cicio began to glean a better picture of the state of things. The war was ready to boil over again. After a strange pause in their offensive, the Malasani were mobilizing once more. But it might not be so easy as they'd thought. Duke Hektor had arrived only the night before with the vanguard of the Qaimiri fleet. And now King Kiral had summoned a war council, surely at Meryam's behest.

It gave Cicio some small hope. The necromancer, Anila, had refused to accept their help, choosing to remain in Sukru's bloody palace when escape stood before her. The entire, stupid, risky operation had been for nothing, and ended up allowing the Enclave to surprise them when they returned to the workshop attic. Cicio laughed silently. Maybe Anila hadn't been so short-sighted after all—had she come, her leap from the pan would have landed her right in the fucking fire.

There were only two bright spots in this whole mess. First, Ramahd himself was free. He'd struck Prayna across the face, stunning her, then ran down the street. The Enclave had tried to stop him—Nebahat had even managed to strike a glancing blow with a flickering green ball of energy released with the wave of his hand—but after that, Ramahd had been too quick, too adept at cutting them off from their spells. Perhaps more importantly, *Mateo* was free as well. Surely he'd spoken to Duke Hektor by now? If not, he soon would. And once Hektor was on their side, everything would change.

Footsteps clomped heavily down the stairs, making the steps groan. Cicio turned, expecting to find the gaoler, but instead saw the silhouette of a man, portly around the middle, broad across the shoulders, and bald save for a strip of reddish-brown hair that wrapped around his head.

"Come to gloat?" Cicio asked as he stood and faced Basilio, Qaimir's primary ambassador in Sharakhai.

"After all you've done, I think a bit of gloating is in order."

When Basilio stepped closer, Cicio noticed the finery he was wearing, the sort one would use for a formal function. He had a smug look Cicio wanted to drop kick off his face. "You're back from the Enclave," Cicio said, starting to understand what Basilio's return to the embassy house might mean. "The Enclave has bowed to Meryam's will . . ." It was only a guess but he could tell from Basilio's satisfied reaction that he'd hit the mark.

"Yes," Basilio said, "and your gambit has failed."

Cicio felt cold. He'd returned to the city with Ramahd, the head of a King, and a plan, but Meryam had undone them at every turn, and now she'd secured yet another piece of the power structure here in Sharakhai. Making it all the more bitter was what Basilio was hinting at with their failed gambit. He hardly dared think it, lest it turn out to be true, but it was right there on Basilio's smug face. Something had happened to Mateo or Hektor or both.

"That's right," Basilio went on, "Duke Hektor was caught spreading your lies. He, Mateo, and a dozen co-conspirators were found to be traitors to the crown and hung last night."

Shit, Cicio thought. *Fucking shit.* There had been a flurry of activity last night. Horses arriving. Muffled conversations in the courtyard. There might have been a struggle. The boy in the cell was giving Cicio a look like he understood. But he couldn't understand. They'd come so close, only to fall short in the end.

"Mighty Alu," Cicio breathed, "you were King Aldouan's man once."

There might have been shame in Basilio's eyes, but before he could reply a voice called out, "Yes, and now he's my man."

Footsteps took the stairs down, sounding crisp and light, hardly making the old boards creak. Meryam, dressed in a fine, hay-colored gown cut in the flaring Qaimiri style, reached the grimy dungeon floor and strode toward Cicio's cell. Her hair was pulled into a tight bun with stylish wisps hanging just beside her temples. Tiny white pearls accented the dress, echoing those strung on the bracelets and earrings she wore. Clashing with the refined look was a simple, red-beaded necklace, some childhood memento given to her by Meryam's sister, Yasmine, who'd died at the hands of Macide Ishaq'ava and the Moonless Host.

Basilio, his mouth working soundlessly, seemed as surprised as Cicio at her sudden presence.

"Leave us," Meryam said.

The look on Basilio's face, deflated as a child caught stealing, was enough to make Cicio smile. His smugness was short-lived, however. As Basilio bowed and took the stairs up, Meryam's state of health registered. There'd been rumors, even down here in the dungeon, of how badly she'd been wounded in her battle against Queen Alansal, yet here she was, thin as a beggar girl, perhaps, but otherwise looking perfectly healthy.

"You're using the elixirs." She had dozens of the fabled draughts at her disposal, perhaps hundreds. There was the cache Hamzakiir had stolen from King Zeheb's palace, plus any King Kiral had managed to secret away. It was how she'd been able to push herself so hard these past many months.

"To the victor the spoils," Meryam said as she paced before his cell. As the light struck her at different angles, he noted the tiny, faded scars all over her face. "Did Ramahd tell you about the man King Sukru had in his employ, the one who could unravel spells, who could cut them off before they even began?"

Ramahd had never mentioned him, but Davud had. "Some fellow named Zahndo."

"Zahndr," Meryam countered, "and he had some utility."

Some utility? Cicio thought. And then understanding dawned. "You want Ramahd by your side. And you want me to help you get him."

She held up her thumb and forefinger and peered at him over the gap. "We're this close to taking the Amber Jewel, Cicio. Sharakhai is nearly ours! What use is there in fighting me anymore?"

She might be doing this only to get to Ramahd, to capture him and have him killed, but he suspected there was more to it. She was trying to hide it, but there was a tightness to the way she was talking, like this was more important to her than she wanted to let on. In the end, it was a matter of looking at the greatest threats to her obtaining what she wanted. With the Kings in hand, who was left, and who was Ramahd best positioned to help her defeat? "It's the Enclave. You want him to protect you against the Enclave. You don't trust them."

She stared at him as if he were a fool. "I don't trust *anyone*, Cicio."

Cicio couldn't help it. He laughed a bitter laugh that filled the cramped subterranean space. "Have you ever said a truer thing in all your life?"

In a rare show of the Meryam of old, she smiled a genuine smile. "Probably not." The smile faded, and her pacing resumed. "Despite everything that's happened, despite all that you and Ramahd have tried to do to me, I could use him by my side. Help me to convince Ramahd, and I'll send you home. It's what you want most, isn't it?"

"You'd put him under a spell like Hamzakiir. You'd dominate his mind. Mine too."

He wondered why she wouldn't just dominate his mind now, but of course Ramahd was the one man she couldn't fool by such means. He would sense and dismantle her spell the moment Cicio neared. She needed him to accept willingly.

"It isn't all bad, Cicio. You'd still have *some* freedoms." She glanced back at the boy. "Many in this city have it worse." Then she shrugged. "But take it as you please. Basilio is seeing to the final arrangements for the gibbet."

Cicio would be lying if he said he hadn't considered this: a return to a simpler time when he hadn't been worried about the betrayal of his King by his own daughter. He wished this had all been a dream, for Meryam to have worked in service to King Aldouan. But she hadn't—she'd murdered him, and Cicio could never trust her not to do the same to him or to Ramahd if she grew worried over their loyalty.

"I'll go to the next world with my head held high, thank you."

She stared at him for a while, perfectly calm. "So be it," she said, as if she'd expected no less but had thought it worth the effort all the same.

She left without giving him another glance. Not long after, there came the sound of wagons departing the compound. And then there came a new sound, a roar: the sound of approaching battle. It was loud and growing louder. Soon his gaoler and a guard, both of them looking nervous, came and took Cicio in chains to the yard outside. The embassy house had been built against the larger stone wall of the House of Kings. On the top of that wall stood thousands upon thousands of soldiers. Many wore the white surcoats and conical helms of the Silver Spears, others more mundane leather armor; some wore no armor at all, but were outfitted with spears or swords and shields to help stem the oncoming tide.

Near the stables stood a gibbet with a pair of nooses and stools beneath. The entire manor staff had come out to watch, surely on Meryam's orders. She would want everyone to see what happened to traitors. The guard followed behind Cicio. Basilio stood with his sword at the ready, though with

Cicio chained, Basilio looked like a pompous ass. Cicio doubted the man had *ever* drawn a sword with the intention of using it.

As Cicio was made to stand atop a stool and the noose fitted around his neck, the battle suddenly roared louder. He could feel it, the sound percussive. Arrows flew through the air above the wall, and those who'd come to witness the hanging stared up with nervous eyes.

"Hurry up," Basilio said, waving his sword.

It was a strange scene. War raged behind the wall less than a dozen paces away. Wagons stood at the ready. The embassy's front gates, leading to the wider landscape of Tauriyat and the House of Kings, had been left open, as if Meryam had made provision for those in the compound to flee, but only after they'd witnessed the hanging of a traitor. As the slack in the rope was taken up, there came the sound of pounding hooves. The Qaimiri guardsmen standing at the open gate stared through it, bows to hand. None so much as lifted their weapons, however.

"My lord!" one of them called to Basilio, his eyes widening. "My lord!" And they all backed away.

Through the gates rode a small host of knights in gleaming plate and bright helms. At their head were two men. The first was a barrel-chested man in a plumed helm holding high the banner of Qaimir—he was supposed to be dead but, fucking hells, it was Count Mateo. And the second . . . Cicio wasn't a righteous man, but just then he wanted to drop to his knees and praise Mighty Alu. Ramahd had come. Ramahd had come to save him.

He wondered what might have happened for Mateo to still be alive and for Ramahd to be with him, but he had no time to consider it, for just then Basilio groaned, "Bloody gods," stepped forward, and kicked Cicio's stool out from underneath him.

The manacles on Cicio's wrists clanked as his hands shot to his throat. He tried to slip his fingers beneath the noose, but it had cinched like a vise. He kicked his legs, trying to lift himself enough to create a gap, but it wasn't enough. The world turned before him as his body swung. He found himself staring uselessly at the onlookers, his countrymen, who stared uselessly back. A keen ringing sound smothered all else, his eyes felt like they were ready to pop out, and there was so much pressure in his head his *teeth* ached. And his breath . . . Despite sucking in a lungful, it had all rushed from his lungs already. He couldn't draw another. Gods, how the fear in him spiked with the realization that he'd taken his last.

Suddenly Ramahd was galloping by on his horse. His sword flashed. The pressure on Cicio's neck released, and he collapsed to the ground. For along moments all he could do was clutch at the noose and try to breathe. He lost track of the battle, but not his fear that at any moment one of Meryam's guards would chop off his head.

Indeed, when he managed to roll over, he saw one of them stalking toward him.

"Drop your weapons!" Mateo roared, an order the wide-eyed guard immediately complied with.

The others did as well, and soon it became clear that, given the status and might of Mateo's host, all were ceding authority to him, at least until they saw how it played out with Basilio.

And that was decided soon enough. Basilio was severely outmatched by Ramahd. And what would he do if he won, in any case? He'd still have Mateo to deal with. Seeing this, he threw his sword to the ground and held his hands high.

Ramahd dropped from his horse, took up Basilio's sword, then backed away and gripped Cicio's arm, helping him to his feet.

"Cutting it a bit close, don't you think?" Cicio said in a raspy voice.

Ramahd winked. "You know how much I like drama."

Nearby, Mateo reined his horse to a jingling stop. In his hands, he held the reins of a spare horse in barding.

"I was—" Cicio coughed and cleared his throat several times. "I was led to believe you and Hektor were dead."

Mateo shared a look with Ramahd. "Well, you're half right. Hektor is dead, ambushed by a squadron of Blade Maidens."

Cicio coughed again while waving to the mounted soldiers. "And this?"

"Is a story for another day," Ramahd replied.

The roar of battle had grown louder. Some of the Silver Spears atop the wall were looking down at them, clearly wondering what was going on, but then a half-dozen ladders appeared on the opposite side of the wall. Mateo regarded it with something like worry, then leveled a grim stare at Ramahd.

"Best we get to it." He gestured with the tip of his sword to the wall. "Diversions like these don't present themselves every day."

"No." Ramahd looked to Cicio, who was breathing easier now. "We've a task ahead of us."

At first Cicio thought they might be fleeing the House of Kings, but then he noticed the sack—that bloody, fucking sack—hanging from the back of Ramahd's saddle. "We're going after Meryam, aren't we?"

"We are," Ramahd said with a sharp nod. "Assuming you're ready, that is."

Cicio hadn't seen this much energy from Ramahd in months. Hiding a smile, he snatched the reins of the spare horse from Mateo, swung up into the saddle, and stared down with a sneer. "When am I ever not ready?"

Ramahd swung up to his own horse and looked at Mateo. "Didn't I tell you?"

Mateo smiled at Cicio. "Good man."

As Mateo spurred his horse into motion and began organizing his knights, Ramahd urged his horse forward. He stopped near Basilio, who had watched Ramahd's approach with no small amount of fear in his eyes. Ramahd was still holding Basilio's sword, but now gave it a flip and held it out, hilt first, for Basilio to take.

Basilio accepted it warily. "What's this?"

"Get everyone to high ground before this boils over. Hide them on the far side of Tauriyat, and if the city's taken, make for the northern harbor and gather the ships you need, by force if necessary."

Basilio slipped the sword into its sheath, a sluggish movement that made it clear how unsure of all this he was. "This isn't over, Amansir."

Ramahd reined his horse over, then spurred it into motion. "Just see our people safe."

Then Cicio, Ramahd, Mateo, and his knights were out past the gates of the embassy house and riding hard toward the Sun Palace.

Chapter 61

ON THE *AMARANTH*, Emre led Haddad into the captain's cabin. As he closed the door behind her, Haddad went to the liquor drawer and poured two glasses of dark Malasani rum. She downed one, poured herself another, then lifted both glasses, handing one to Emre.

He accepted it, but didn't bring it to his lips.

"Drink," she said, and swallowed half of hers.

"Haddad . . ."

"I need a skiff, Emre," she said in a rush, "and a day's worth of water and food."

Emre's fingers began to tingle. "Why?"

"Because I'm going back to the Malasani camp." She finished her drink and set it down with a clack. "I need to speak with Mad King Surrahdi about his faith."

The words were bizarre and upsetting to hear, made worse by the part Emre had played. He'd spoken Haddad's name when asking for an emissary, knowing full well it would enrage the King of Malasan. Precisely as King Ihsan had predicted, King Emir had beaten Haddad right there in the pavilion in front of Emre and Hamid and all his generals and courtiers.

Ihsan had been locked away with Haddad in the prison ship for days. From the start he'd manipulated her, fanning the flames of her guilt over all Surrahdi had done in the name of their faith, at all King Emir had done as well. He'd sensed the love Haddad still had in her heart for King Emir, though, and that was something that couldn't stand.

"Love blinds," the Blade Maiden had said the night she'd come to Emre in this very cabin. "The ties between her and King Emir must be severed completely. Only then will her part in this be assured."

Emre had done the rest, goading King Emir into his perverse display of power. It had felt necessary—Sharakhai would fall without it—yet shame still filled him.

"I'm sorry," he said to her.

The expression on her bruised and bloodied face was one of disbelief. "Why ever would you be *sorry*, Emre? I'm going to save your city."

The way she'd said it made it clear she knew the part Emre had played. The realization struck him like cold water, and suddenly he saw this entire enterprise for what it was: a play filled with actors—Emre, the Blade Maiden, King Emir, and Haddad, each of them playing the role Ihsan had written for them.

"And still you'll go?" he asked.

"This isn't about you, or Sharakhai." A bit of her old fire had returned. Emre found he'd actually missed it. "It's about our standing in the eyes of our gods, our place in the farther fields, which is threatened by Surrahdi's actions."

For a long moment the two of them stared at one another, neither wanting to take the next step.

"You'll give me the skiff?"

It was a strange thing to note at a time like this, but he was suddenly aware of how far her Sharakhani had come. Her accent was still strong, but she had a command of the language she hadn't had months ago. It made him feel connected to her, and that in turn made him want to reach out and take her into his arms. But to do so now would be an insult.

"You'll have the skiff."

She nodded once and stepped toward the cabin door, but paused by his side. She stared into his eyes, and for one brief moment looked vulnerable, as if she wanted to be saved from what she was about to do. Then the yawning silence between them become unbearable, and she opened the door and left.

In the center of his tent, Surrahdi the Mad King sat in lotus position. Dawn had broken over the desert. It would be a grand day. A grand day indeed. He would have what he'd wanted for so long. The desert's Amber Jewel.

At last it would be his, his, his . . .

The very thought sent a cascade of joy throughout his many splinters of existence: the thousand pieces of his soul that lay scattered like broken glass across the landscape of Sharakhai. A beatific light glinted over their countless surfaces—not the light of the sun, but of the triform gods themselves. Shonokh smiled through them. Ranrika stared with piercing eyes. And Tamtamiin danced in a thousand different ways, each of them as beautiful as the next.

He saw in that light the pieces of himself he'd cut away in honor of the triumvirate. They stood now as testaments to his will, expressions of his faith. He would stop at nothing to see their love and their truth embraced by others. The Sharakhani first. Then Qaimir, who had much to atone for. Mirea and Kundhun would take more time, but they would come to heel. They would see the shining light of the Malasani gods.

When the sun had risen fully, his son came to him. Emir. He whispered words of conquest. The final push. The palaces would be laid bare at last. Then they would be taken, their flames snuffed, wiped from the pages of history. From their ashes a new flame would rise. A single flame, not a dozen or nine or however the Kings might number themselves these days. This had always been his promise, his gift to his son and all of Malasan. His gift to the gods themselves.

Through the fractured eyes of a fractured beast, Surrahdi saw the ancient, innermost walls of the city. Saw his engines of war pitted against them. Saw his spears and shields arrayed.

He began to laugh and clap, and his memories were kindled in the minds of his myriad children. He saw the days of his youth, felt the joy of dancing on feasting days. He tasted perfect morsels of perfect food, heard matchless verses that filled grand halls, felt his first touch of a woman, his first touch of a man.

His son, knowing his father was filled with Shonokh's ambition, and with Ranrika's careful thought, and with Tamtamiin's compassion, left the tent.

"You need not fear," Surrahdi said to him, though his son was already gone, "all is well in hand."

He smiled, and those many fragments of himself smiled in reply. Their enemy stood no chance. Not against the army he'd created in the name of the triform gods.

Soon the walls were breached. Soon they'd pushed beyond. It wouldn't be long now.

The tent flap opened once more. A soldier with wide eyes and a bloody, beaten face stepped inside and knelt before him. He recognized her. The woman who'd once had a cat named Calamity. Haddad the beauty. Haddad of the fiery heart.

But why had she come? His son, the king, was angry with her. He'd beaten her. Surrahdi thought perhaps he should be angry with her too, but he wasn't. She had always been his favorite.

She knelt by his side and took his hand in hers. "I've come to speak to you, my king," she said while stroking his skin softly.

"What about, child? What about?"

"Do you remember our time in the palace? When you walked with me in the royal gardens?"

Visions flooded his mind. Young Haddad, eager and inquisitive. He the voice of his faith, teaching her, among many other things, of how the gods had come to shine on Malasan. "I remember, child." His smile broadened, while in the distance, his many children paused. "I remember."

"That's why I've come. The things you taught me." The bruises around her face faded. As did the cuts. In his eyes, he saw the Haddad of old. The Haddad who was brightest, both inside and out. "You once spoke to me of balance."

Not once, he remembered, but many times.

She was crying now. "I would honor them, Surrahdi. I would honor them. And I think deep inside, you would too. I think you still want it." She blinked, and more tears flowed. "Will you listen?"

For a moment he could only stare at her tears. The light reflected in them was the light of the Malasani gods. Something was swelling deep inside him, a thing he'd buried so deeply, he hardly knew what it was any longer. He remembered how well Haddad had learned his teachings. How she would echo them back to him, sometimes even chastise him when he strayed from their path. If Haddad had something important to say, he would hear it, no matter how painful.

He stilled his shaking hands and patted hers. "I'll listen, child."

Haddad smiled. Her relief warmed the many pieces of his broken heart. She leaned close and whispered words into his ear, much as his son Emir had done only a short while ago, but Haddad spoke not of conquest, nor of greater glory. She spoke of the seasons of our lives, and of the land beyond. She spoke of true purpose and balance and obeisance to the teachings of the gods. And then she spoke of subversion, of the twisting of their ways. As she did, some few of his many splinters turned and regarded him from afar. The light that had glinted from them moments ago brightened, often the first sign of their curiosity.

He thought he should tell them to look away, to force them if need be, but he was captivated by the words of this woman, and so were his children.

Curiosity became wonder became shock became shame. It was a thing that happened from time to time with one or two of his children. When it did, he quickly convinced them that he was right, lest the infectious thoughts spread. The only path to salvation, he told them, was to spread the word of the gods, the *Malasani* gods. The only gods who mattered. He would tell them these things, and they would calm and their light would dim to quieter hues.

Not so today. With Haddad's whispers, more and more bent an ear. More and more shone their light on him. He thought he should be angry with Haddad—perhaps he should beat her as his son had—but how could he be angry when her words rang so true? Had the same thoughts not occurred to him?

It spread like wildfire. He heard his children whisper along with Haddad, then join her in a rising chorus. *You've taken their teachings, twisted their ways, and used them for your* own *glory, not theirs.*

Their stares became one. Their shame became his.

Laid bare was he beneath the eyes of the gods. He beat his ears so he would no longer have to listen to the words drifting in the air. *Shame. Shame. For shame.* He scratched at his eyes until they bled, that he would no longer have to look upon his children. He pled to Tamtamiin for forgiveness.

His son rushed in, fully armored, scimitar in hand. He stood there regarding Surrahdi, then Haddad, while a righteous anger built within him.

Through his guilt and his sorrow Surrahdi saw what his son was about to do. "Leave her!" he screamed. "She brought only truth and light!"

But Emir didn't care. He pulled his sword back. Haddad, meanwhile, was calm itself. She had made her peace with what came next.

With a roar that Surrahdi felt in his bones, Emir swung his sword. Haddad's body crumpled into a pile. Her head thumped and rolled against the dais, where Surrahdi held it to his face and wept.

Chapter 62

UNDER A SKY OF COBALT BLUE, Çeda marched along an arid mountain path. The sounds of distant battle had been growing over the last hour, urging them to push harder toward their destination: a hidden valley along the eastern slopes of Mount Arasal.

Beside Çeda marched Sümeya. Melis and Kameyl came next, and behind them, Çeda's Shieldwives, all of whom looked tired but determined. Everyone, including Çeda, had taken a petal. Çeda didn't need them, but she'd wanted this moment of solidarity between the Blade Maidens and the Shieldwives. The petals lent them strength, and sharpened their reflexes and senses, but also gave them a sense of sisterhood, which was every bit as important.

Behind the Shieldwives came the asirim, tireless as ever. From her position at the head of their line, Çeda could see Mavra, Sedef, and Amile walking in their crooked ways. The rest, over two dozen in all, were lost behind a bend in the path, obscured by the thick, low-hanging branches of the ironwood trees that dominated the slope. She hardly needed to see them, though. They were bright, burning brands within her mind, ready to launch themselves at Beşir and his forces so that their people might be saved.

As they took another curve in the path and assaulted a new slope, the sounds of battle came stronger. It made them move faster, but with more caution as well. Her lungs burning as badly as her legs, Çeda guided them to a tight clutch of ironwood trees. Once hidden inside, she crouched low and parted the branches. To her right, Beşir's camp rested in a clearing beside a milky green lake. The valley beyond was dominated by tall grasses, flowering bushes, and patchy swaths of ironwood, spruce, and fir.

Higher up the rocky slopes of Mount Arasal, an old fortress crouched at the edge of an escarpment. It was there that the battle raged. The roar of it was muted, almost dreamlike from this distance, but Çeda was under no illusions. She knew they were about to enter a battle that would decide the fate of the thirteenth tribe, and the outcome was anything but certain.

The most intense fighting was at the fortress's main gate, where hundreds of Silver Spears led the attack with ropes and ladders and interlocked shields. Behind them, snaking up the old, switchbacked road, were hundreds more. Just turning the final switchback was a battering ram with a wooden roof. Four warhorses and two score soldiers were pushing it higher and higher. As soon as it came into range, the resistance along the ramparts shot flaming arrows and lobbed fire pots, hoping to light the ram aflame before it came anywhere near the gates. One fire pot struck dead on, splashing burning oil everywhere. The people of Çeda's tribe whooped, their hands in the air, but their joy was short-lived. The roof of the battering ram had been treated, and the fire soon flickered out.

The fortress itself was old and crumbling, even porous. The crenelations looked like a titan had eaten parts of it away. And there were holes in the curtain wall, one so large a horse and cart could fit through it. Some had been hastily repaired. Others were barricaded, but each afforded Beşir's forces another possible point of entry. The only saving grace was that the largest openings were situated near the central part of the wall, which had little more than a strip of land before a steep plummet beyond. It gave the Silver Spears little room to maneuver. Every time they made a roaring advance into those gaps, the defenders countered with long poles and spears, or sometimes simple benches held by four or five at a time, sending white-uniformed soldiers plummeting over the edge of the cliff.

Ahead of Çeda lay the only other approach to the fortress. It led to a small, flat patch of land and a postern door. The path leading to it, the very path Çeda, the asirim, and her women-at-arms were following, was narrow and could accommodate only a few walking side by side. Beşir had soldiers covering that end of the fortress as well—it wouldn't do to make a push through the main gates only to have the enemy sneak out the back—but with so little land on which to maneuver, it was necessarily the smaller of the two forces.

Beside Çeda, Kameyl strung her bow and nocked an arrow with a long red ribbon tied near the fletching. Çeda, meanwhile, used her spyglass to scan the white-uniformed soldiers. It didn't take long to spot Beşir. He was leading the attack against the postern door with several hundred Silver Spears and two hands of Blade Maidens. He wore a mix of plate and chain, and a helm with tall orange plumes, as if he wanted to draw attention to himself.

As she'd predicted, he appeared to be completely healed from the wound she'd inflicted on him. With oiled efficiency, he loosed arrow after arrow against the fort's defenders. Adjustments were made to counter his movements, but each time they focused their attack on him, he would disappear and his arrows' deadly strikes would begin anew from a different location. The lyrewing had told them that Nalamae's magic prevented him from reaching the fortress's interior, but he was still using his ability to devastating effect. It wouldn't be long before his soldiers gained the walls or breached the postern door.

"Now," Çeda said.

Kameyl drew the bowstring to her cheek, aimed skyward, and let the arrow fly. The ribbon fluttered in its wake, bright in the sunlight, a bloodless wound across the deep blue sky. It reached its zenith, then dove like a falcon until it was lost beyond a stand of trees. The battle, however, continued to rage. Had their signal gone unnoticed? Or worse, had Nalamae become so weakened in her defense of the fortress that she couldn't begin the next phase of their plan?

"Ready the second," Çeda said.

"Wait," Sümeya said, pointing to the sky. "There."

Above the fortress, a patch of sky had turned white. It churned and roiled, expanding quickly into a thin haze. It was gossamer thin at first, occasionally breaking in places and showing a bit of blue sky before filling in like paint being knifed over canvas. The haze thickened. Long tufts of wool reached down toward the mountain slopes and spread like desert fog, reaching beyond the valley toward neighboring peaks, until the entire sky was covered by it. What had been bright white turned dusty silver, then a steely gray. The bright colors of the valley dimmed before Çeda's very eyes.

The battle had not died, but its intensity waned and many were pointing to the sky. Commanders called orders for their soldiers to regroup. On the far side of the valley, a roar lifted up. Beşir's rear guard had turned to meet a new threat: Macide and his four hundred soldiers, many of them veterans of the Moonless Host, and more warriors from the other tribes of the alliance. Beşir's forces were beset, but didn't break, and shifted with military precision to face the attack along their flank.

Through her spyglass, Çeda watched Beşir closely. Everything hinged on these next few moments.

Beşir would want to help meet this counterattack, and yet he remained near the walls. And even though the defenders had spotted him and were sending a hail of arrows on his position, he hadn't disappeared.

Çeda turned to her Shieldwives, to the asirim gathered behind them. "If we're right," she said while readying her buckler and drawing River's Daughter, "what Nalamae has just done will trigger Beşir's god-given weakness. It will sap his strength, but the odds are still grim, so ready yourselves."

They all nodded.

"Silent now, Shieldwives. Silent, lest they hear the lord of all things coming for them."

They readied their shields, drew their shamshirs. She didn't need to ask if they were ready. Their grim smiles told Çeda all she needed to know.

"Time to kill a King."

Çeda ran low and steady. The others fell in beside her, behind her. Sehid-Alaz had drawn Night's Kiss, which hummed as he sprinted through the trees. Mavra, Sedef, and the rest ran in a pack behind him, and oh, how eager they were. No longer were they powerless. The thought of taking one of the Kings made their hearts sing, so much so that several of the younger ones bounded ahead before being called back by the elders. Amile heeded no such calls, however. He sprinted ahead, weaving among the trees like a hound after the hare.

Not yet, called his bond-sister, Jenise. *Not yet! Give them warning and Beşir might escape, but fall upon them together and the King will be ours.*

Çeda thought he would ignore her too, but then he stopped, hunchbacked and hungry, chest heaving as one clawed hand tore deep into the trunk of an ironwood. Then the pack caught up to him and he retook his place among them. On they ran, silent as wolves.

Together they broke through the tree line and rushed toward the enemy. Shouts of alarm were raised. There was fear in the eyes of the soldiers ahead, but these were Beşir's elite. With their captains calling sharp orders, they turned and set spears in organized ranks. The asirim spread apart. They leapt high, clearing the wall of spears, ready to unleash havoc behind the lines.

More orders were called. Where the asirim landed, soldiers cleared space quickly, shields at the ready, swords rising and falling to devastating effect. Other asirim were met with nets launched with near perfect timing to meet them. Those asirim at the rear of the bounding pack saw this and checked their speed at the last moment, only to be stabbed.

In a blink, half of the asirim were wounded or trapped. But they were still inhumanly strong, inhumanly fast. They tore through the nets. Lashed at the legs of nearby soldiers with swipes of their clawed hands or feet. Some released bellows that knocked down entire swaths of soldiers. Standing on the fortress battlements were two more slight shapes: Huuri and Imwe, the twins who'd bonded with Sirendra. By the gods, Sirendra was there too. When Huuri and Imwe leapt into the fray, so did Sirendra. A dozen more warriors of the thirteenth tribe, incited by their bravery, raised their spears high and followed.

Huuri and Imwe might be small, but they were wild and fearful quick, even for asirim. They tore through the ranks of the Silver Spears, the pair converging on a Blade Maiden, who hadn't seen them. She turned just in time, managed a deep cut to Huuri's shoulder, but then Imwe had one arm around her neck. A sharp rip. An arc of blood. And the Maiden was lost beneath the battle.

Çeda fought alongside Sümeya, Melis, and Kameyl, using the discipline they'd grown used to. Shields and swords to hand, their hearts interlinked, the four of them became like a weave of fabric, one supporting the other, connected as they cut through their enemy's lines. They'd wanted—needed—to help with the initial push, but they had another objective. Beşir was most important; there was no telling how long the cloud cover Nalamae had provided them might last, after all.

In the chaos, however, Çeda had lost him. *Enemy commander?* she whistled.

Fled south, Melis whistled back.

Disengage, Çeda replied. *Follow.*

As the Shieldwives and the asirim fought, and more came from the fortress to help, the enemy began to break. Çeda, Sümeya, Melis, and Kameyl cut through them, careful not to get caught in a melee from which they couldn't easily disengage. The Silver Spears were giving them wide berth, however, and the Maidens who fought for Beşir were closing in on Sehid-Alaz, who wielded Night's Kiss with a terrible fury.

They gained a nearby ridge and ran down the far slope under the cover of the ironwood trees. The forest floor was soft here. It was strangely quiet with the needles above and the bed below and the bulk of the battle still raging beyond the ridge. Çeda switched to hand signs. *Spread out,* she ordered. *Search.* It carried an implied command to remain within sight of one another so that more orders might be passed. Like this, spread out in a broad line, they moved quickly through the forest.

For a moment she lost sight of Melis behind a large boulder. Shouts came from their left as a volley of arrows came flying in; Sümeya and Kameyl slipped behind the trunks of trees and returned fire on the company of Silver Spears that had spotted them.

Çeda was preparing to join them when she heard a whistle behind her. *Enemy. Southwest.*

Gods. Melis had spotted Beşir.

Join us, soonest, Çeda whistled and sprinted past the large boulder.

Melis was already thirty paces distant, following a gully at breakneck speed. Far ahead, through thicker growth of bushes and smaller trees, Çeda caught sight of orange plumes.

Halt! Çeda whistled.

Melis either hadn't heard or chose not to obey. Either way, she was soon lost to view behind a thicket.

Halt! Çeda whistled again, but Melis only kept running.

Çeda flew over the forest floor, desperate for signs of Beşir. She reached out, searching for his heart, but found only Melis's. *By Nalamae's grace, please be wary, Melis.*

The gully wound like a snake. The thicker vegetation along the banks robbed her of the perspective she'd had on higher ground but suddenly a clearing opened up before her. Surrounding it was a circle of birch trees, each spaced so perfectly it must once have been a ritual ground. Melis stood on the far side of the clearing, crouched low, her attention caught by something on the ground. An orange plume.

Just then Çeda caught movement high in the branches of one of the trees. "Melis!"

An arrow streaked through the air just as Melis was turning. It caught her in the chest and powered her backward. She fell with a soft thump while Çeda spun and searched desperately for Beşir.

She saw no sign of him, but became attuned to his heart mere moments before she felt a release of tension from the King. She sensed the path of his aim and sidestepped, felt the wind of an arrow's passage against her cheek, heard the sizzle of the fletching. She released her breath as another arrow blurred. River's Daughter was already on the move, spinning, her body twisting, until she felt the arrow *ting* against the flat of her blade. The sound went on and on, giving the clearing an eerie aura as Çeda stared up through the branches.

Beşir smiled down at her, drawing another arrow and setting it against the string of his god-given bow. She was just ready to launch herself toward the tree when the King disappeared.

Breath of the desert, no!

Nalamae had summoned the clouds. She'd turned the sky gray, robbing the landscape of nearly all shadows, and yet Beşir hadn't been affected. They'd chosen the wrong bloody verse. Or they were both wrong. Çeda had no idea. She only knew that she and Melis were in grave danger.

She spun, searching everywhere for Beşir's heartbeat. And found it just in time: Beşir's intent, his aim. She ducked as an arrow fluttered above her.

"I don't know why you're so important to Yerinde," came Beşir's gravelly voice. Another arrow grazed her thigh, catching only the leather, and his voice came from a different angle entirely. "But I lost my daughter's life to her cruelty, so I'll take yours in recompense, then I'll see those of your blood wiped from the face of the desert."

Another shift and Beşir was practically on top of her. She barely managed to lift her buckler and block the next arrow. She found him high above, straddling the branches of a tree that overhung the clearing. "You've proven to be quite the thorn in our side. But at least now I understand why."

He strung an arrow, drew it back, and in a blink was gone.

Çeda sensed him to her left. She felt as if she were moving in honey, too slow. The arrow caught her along the hip, a grazing shot that burned like a brand.

"Why?" she asked him, partially to slow him, partially because she was genuinely curious.

Beşir, another arrow already knocked, lowered his bow, his face incredulous. Using the weapon, he motioned up the slope, toward the fortress. "Because her *sister* stands beside you. But today, that changes too."

He shifted and loosed, shifted and loosed. Çeda was getting better at sensing his intent, not only when he was going to shift, but where to. But Beşir was compensating as well, releasing his arrows more randomly.

She tried to press on his heart, to cause him to stumble or delay, perhaps give her a chance to charge him or run to Melis, but he seemed to sense this as well. Every time she seemed close, he shifted and she lost all hold of him.

It was a strain, however. She could feel it in the way his heart was beating. Rapid, almost tripping. Each shift seemed to cause him more and more stress.

Then he moved too fast, disappearing twice in rapid succession so that she was turned in the completely wrong direction by the time he loosed his next arrow.

Çeda was caught completely off her guard, for the arrow was headed straight between Çeda's shoulder blades, but someone was there to intercept it. Melis. Instead of striking Çeda, the arrow punched into her shoulder. In the blink of an eye, another had sunk deep into her chest.

Melis raised her shield like a talisman against the night, but it was ineffectual. She could no longer fend off Beşir's attacks. Çeda tried to block the next arrow with her shield, but Melis stumbled into her and she missed. The arrow sunk into Melis's belly with a sickening thump.

"He's coming, Çeda," Melis said as Çeda lowered her down to the ground. The black bodice of her dress glistened with blood. "Quickly now. Something's happening in the fortress."

Çeda stood, her sword and shield at the ready. Beşir strode toward her, sword in hand, his quiver empty, and spoke with an ease that enraged her. "You may have freed the asirim for a short time, but with your goddess gone, they'll be returned to us, and all this will have been for naught."

But Çeda hardly heard his words. She was pure red rage.

A war cry erupted from her throat as she ran to meet him. Beşir met her every swing, and returned them with the same liquid ease with which he wielded his bow. He was strong, as all the Kings were, but so was Çeda. They fought beneath the boughs of the trees, and Beşir tried several times more to disappear, to catch her off her guard, but she'd become so attuned to him that she met every blow with sword or shield.

On the next shift she managed to cut his leg. She followed with a slice to his shoulder that would have taken his arm clean off had he not disappeared again.

Beşir was breathing heavily now, his confidence faded. He abandoned the use of his power, retreating, finding it more and more difficult to fend off Çeda's blows.

Then the landscape around them suddenly brightened. The clouds were breaking. A look of unadulterated fear overcame Beşir. She had no idea why, but she wasn't about to examine a gifted sword for nicked edges. After another ringing blow that he barely managed to block, she felt his intent once more, and this time it was directed up the slope. He meant to return to the fortress.

Determined he would not escape her again, she dropped her shield and lunged, managing to grasp his arm.

The shift came, and the world dissolved around her.

Chapter 63

ANILA'S MOTHER'S HEALTH IMPROVED. The terrible wound to her neck scarred over and soon looked as if it were years old, little more than a painful memory. Her eyes, so haunted at first, brightened. Her skin regained its hue. And she began to go about her day in Sukru's palace with something approaching normalcy.

The nights were the worst. Anila was there to shush her, to hold her close, but she had terrible dreams, and would wake from them in a cold sweat. She'd ask her mother what she saw, but Meral could never answer.

Although the look on her face defied her words, she would say, "I can't recall," and eventually fall back into a fitful sleep.

King Sukru came often to inspect Meral, and to question her. He asked her to work at her embroidery, a favorite pastime, and would assess her progress each time he came. Despite Anila's fears that her mother would turn out to be incomplete and broken, she was creating a beautiful piece, an amber-lark on a twisting branch. Every few days, Sukru's physic came to weigh the balance of her humors. All signs pointed to a woman who'd been through a harrowing experience but was nevertheless recovering.

"When will we be allowed to go home?" Meral asked Anila one day.

"Soon, I hope."

"Has he said why he wants us here?"

She remembered being brought to the palace, but not being forced down to the crypts, nor did she recall her own death. She assumed Sukru had brought her to keep Anila company, which would in turn help Anila as she served Sukru. Anila chose not to disabuse her of the notion.

"I'm sure it's for our own protection," Anila told her. "With the war on and all."

"Yes," Meral said. Her eyes drifted beyond Anila, beyond the walls of her room. She had a pensive look, her eyes moving wildly as if she were on the cusp of remembering it all. But then the look faded and she went back to her needlepoint.

A moment later, she pricked her finger with the needle. "Now see what I've done!" She stared at it while pinching the skin around the tiny wound. A small drop of blood grew and she began to cry, softly at first, but it quickly devolved into wracking sobs.

Anila embraced her as her mother had done for her as a child. "There, there." She rocked her back and forth, held her mother's head against her breast. "What's the matter?"

"I don't know," Meral said.

The depth of sadness in those words tore a hole in Anila's heart. She wanted to tell her. She *should* tell her. *You were dead. Sukru killed you.* But she didn't have the heart.

"I feel as though something terrible is about to happen," her mother said into Anila's shoulder. She broke away and looked at Anila with freshly troubled eyes. "I feel as though it's about to happen to you."

"No, memma, everything's fine." It was a monstrous lie, and Anila felt like a monster for telling it. "The war will come to a close, the Kings will push the Malasani horde back, and then we'll return home."

Meral brightened at this. She wiped away her tears, took Anila's hand and stroked her black, scintillant skin. "You'll come home then? You'll live with us?"

"Yes."

Another lie, which for some reason felt worse than all the rest. Anila knew very well she could never live a normal life again. She would see this done, one way another. She would see her family safe. And then she would take her vengeance upon Sukru.

The next day Meral and Anila were summoned to Sukru. Anila thought the Silver Spears might be taking them to his throne room, but the King met them on the way and led them to the palace's entrance, where many were gathering. The entire place was abuzz and Anila had no idea why until a burly keg of a man Anila had never seen before came and spoke low to Sukru. "All is ready at the ship, your Excellence."

"Very good," Sukru groused and waved the man toward what was proving to be an ever-growing line of people.

They were scared, Anila realized. There were a number of Silver Spears in their train, but also workmen, two maids, even a cook. Why in the wide great desert they would be joining Sukru was beyond Anila. Until they reached the courtyard.

Even this high up the mountain the sound of battle drifted over the ramparts. When Anila made way for her mother to enter the covered araba, one of seven ready and waiting, Sukru called, "No. She'll come with me."

Anila was ready to utter the first of several prepared objections when a tall akhala galloped into the courtyard and came to an abrupt halt near the coaches. The rider was a royal messenger wearing King Cahil's orange-and-gold livery. "My Lord King, your presence is requested at the Sun Palace. A council has been called."

"Yes, I've heard. I'll be there as soon as I'm able."

The messenger, a young, clean-shaven man with expressive eyebrows, looked supremely uncomfortable. "I was told to accompany you there, your Excellence."

"By whom?"

His horse pranced. "By my Lord King Cahil himself. He desires your counsel and the weight your throne will lend to the proceedings."

"He fears being overrun by the other Kings, more like."

"I wouldn't know, your Excellence. The fear is that the Malasani will breach the walls today."

"Do tell," Sukru said, as if only a fool would fail to see it. "Tell Cahil I'll be along shortly."

"I'm afraid I'm not allowed to leave without you."

Sukru reached to his belt and unfurled his whip. With a snap of his arm, the whip went cracking toward the messenger. The rider snatched his hand to his chest while the horse threw its head back and reared. Something went flying end over end, landing on the gravel shortly after the horse's hooves crunched down.

A finger. The man had lost his finger, and he seemed every bit as surprised as everyone else gathered around the coaches.

"Another word will cost you your head. Now go and give your King my answer."

The messenger, pale-faced, nodded. He covered his injury with his right hand and tried to guide his akhala away even as blood coursed down his left trouser leg and onto the gravel below.

He galloped away, and those in attendance entered their coaches, silent as gravestones. It was then, as Anila's mother was entering the King's coach ahead of Sukru, that she noticed the two others waiting inside: her father and sister. There were looks of relief as they embraced one another, but also looks of deep concern as they stared through the window at Anila.

It tore at Anila to have them remain with Sukru, but there was nothing for it. If she argued now, Sukru might kill one of them as a warning and keep the others for added insurance.

Down the slopes of Tauriyat they went, seven coaches, dozens of people either within, riding on the benches, or hanging off the back on the footman's platform. They hurtled along, wheels skidding as they took the sharp turns along King's Road, while far below, Anila saw something she never thought she'd see: enemy forces within the House of Kings. The western and southern walls, both of which were visible during their journey, were thick with soldiers bearing spears and swords. Ladders were set. Ropes were thrown over the walls. Siege towers rolled forward in a dozen places, disgorging men when they came near enough, most but not all of which were immediately riddled with arrows. And when the Malasani soldiers gained a foothold on the walls, more followed.

It was madness.

And then there came a breach along the southern expanse, not so far from Anila's familial estate. An entire section of wall came tumbling down in a cloud of dust. It was not large, but it didn't need to be. Malasani soldiers came marching through, first in a phalanx, shields interlocked, then as a mounting stream of soldiers that were already overcoming the unprepared resistance of the Silver Spears. A storm of Blade Maidens in their black dresses fell upon the enemy and it looked as though they were going to stem the tide.

The skirmish was lost from view as the coach took another turn, finally reached ground level, and flew toward the Sun Palace. Anila looked back, trying to see inside Sukru's araba for her family. They were too far back, however, and she was forced to watch the way ahead instead, where her worst fears were unfolding before her very eyes. To the left of the road, a wall of Silver Spears began to break. The Malasani forces burst through, many trying to surround the main line of Silver Spears. There were so many that some started to rush the wagons.

Anila knew enough Malasani to hear the words being shouted, "A royal wagon!" they shouted. "A royal wagon!"

Anila spotted the commander a moment later, a burly man with bright steel armor and a helm topped with a headdress of white plumes. He was pointing toward the train and men rallied to him, moving to intercept the arabas. The first wagon made it through their line. The second tried to skirt the road and hit a deep rut. It overturned a moment later, dust and dirt billowing as the four men on the bench were thrown free.

The third araba, just ahead of Anila's, was forced to slow as the Malasani set their spears against the wagon's four charging horses. Anila's wagon slowed as a wall of Malasani soldiers surged toward them, roaring.

Gods, we're all going to die, Anila thought, *every last one of us.*

She saw soldiers falling. Dozens of Silver Spears. As many or more Malasani soldiers. A group of Blade Maidens were surrounded, and though they cut down man after man, they couldn't stop them all. One by one, they began to fall. Nearby, a soldier who seemed made of red clay was taking blow after blow from the Silver Spears surrounding him. Farther along King's Road, a roaring wave of mounted Blade Maidens and ranks of Silver Spear infantry were rushing to protect the wagons, but Anila could already tell they would be too late.

She felt the death on the air. She tasted it on her tongue, bitter as week-old limes. As the araba came to a halt and the soldiers atop it moved to defend against the Malasani horde, Anila opened the door on the opposite side and began drawing sigils on the surface of the dry, dusty road. She felt the chill of it, saw ice crystals forming beneath her touch. She felt the dead, lying in a swath ahead of her.

She was fearful—for herself, for her family—but it was her hatred of Sukru that drove her. He'd brought her here, endangered her family. He'd killed her mother, only to have her reborn and now face death once more, all because of him.

The veil parted for her. She felt soul after soul heeding her call. Only a dozen paces beyond the wagon, a Silver Spear, whose blood coated his neck and his breastplate, opened his eyes. He pushed himself off the ground and took up his sword. A Malasani soldier cut him across his exposed shield arm, severing it, but the Silver Spear hardly seemed to notice. He slashed across his enemy's neck, then moved quickly on to the next, cutting him down from behind.

More of the fallen stood. Then more still. It was easy, freshly dead as they were, and Anila didn't need them anything close to whole. They were nothing like her mother, or even Fezek, whose resurrection she'd poured hours into to give him some semblance of his former self. No, for this she needed only their most animal instincts.

The Malasani began to notice. They turned to fight the growing number of dead. But the dead would not be stopped with a single cut, nor by two or three. They might lose a leg but still slash in passing at their enemy. They might take a spear through their gut but still hack and claw and bite. The spell was indiscriminate. Blade Maidens and Malasani soldiers alike stood and moved to protect the wagons.

The effect of Anila's spell spread like wildfire. She was shaking, nearing the limits of her power. Knowing she couldn't raise many more, she focused on the rest of the fallen Blade Maidens, forcing one after another to return to their bodies. Even so soon after their death, they yearned for the farther fields, but Anila had no mercy. The moment they were returned to their bodies, their minds filled with a zealot's lust to deal death against their enemy.

Something snapped around Anila's throat. She flinched, grabbed for it, and found a leather cord wrapped there. She was yanked back sharply and fell stumbling to the ground. "That's *enough!*" Sukru spat, standing over her. "Now get back in that bloody wagon!"

He released her with a flick of his whip. She thought of setting the dead on him. She could do it. Send dozens storming down on him. But he was ready with that whip of his. He'd cut her down before she had the chance, and then he'd kill her family for the spite of it.

She climbed back into the wagon. With the dead sowing so much chaos, the Malasani had pulled back and the Sharakhani reinforcements had arrived. The mounted Maidens were pushing deep into the Malasani ranks, breaking their lines, while the Silver Spears began hemming them in and pushing them back toward the gap in the wall. There were scores upon scores of bedraggled men and women who looked as though they'd just escaped from a dungeon. They were the prisoners, Anila realized, from the prison camps built to house the Moonless Host and their sympathizers. In a grand irony, they'd now been released in Sharakhai's defense.

The wagons rolled on and reached the grounds of the Sun Palace at last, where the gates were opened and then immediately closed behind them. They filed into the palace and down to the tunnels below. Many peeled away at a certain point, going, Anila assumed, to the ship that had been mentioned. Sukru was going to flee, she understood now. He was going to raise his brother and then flee with some few loyal followers into the desert, most likely to wait until the war was decided one way or another.

Meanwhile, Sukru, Anila and her family, and a small cadre of Silver Spears, four of whom carried the Sparrow's coffin, pushed hard to reach the cavern with the crystal. Upon arriving, Anila's family was taken to one side of the cavern. Anila's sister, Banu, eyed both Sukru and Anila with naked fear. Her father, holding Banu and Meral to him protectively, looked more helpless than Anila had ever seen him. Meral, however, was transfixed by the crystal. Her eyes were wide, her mouth parted in a look of pure wonder. She looked as if she were about to say something to Anila, but just then Sukru snapped his fingers and called Anila near.

He was standing over the ice-filled coffin. The Sparrow was exposed, the heavy, oiled canvas pulled back to reveal his chest and face. Lying there, unmoving, he looked like a simulacrum of Sukru himself, made from the whitest of clays.

"Begin," Sukru said with no preamble.

Everything was happening so quickly that Anila had no time to read Sukru properly. She had no idea whether he was ready to kill her and her family when this was all done or if he'd be content to have his brother alive once more and would leave them to whatever fate the war—and what seemed ever more likely to be a Malasani occupation—had in store for them. God, her mother's eyes. She was staring, haunted, into the violet light of the crystal.

"Quickly, girl!" Sukru's eyes were wide with rage.

She nodded and faced the crystal. What was there to do but hope? She couldn't risk her family's lives by attacking Sukru now.

She opened herself to that gateway, felt for the Sparrow's soul and found it with little difficulty. As she had done with her mother, she called the Sparrow near, gathered his soul, and cradled him to the world he'd left behind. It felt like hours were passing, but it was certainly far less. Sukru would not have remained silent for so long.

In the end she completed the ritual, though the Sparrow's soul was not without some small amount of tearing and damage as it crossed over. The man had been dead for weeks, after all.

Sukru waved to one of the nearby Spears, the captain of this small detail, and Anila was led away while Sukru bent over his brother, his back to everyone. Administering one of the elixirs made from the adichara, Anila knew. It was then that she realized. If Sukru had his way, none of them were getting out of this cavern alive. This may have been a rushed meeting, and Sukru's thoughts might be a bit disordered, but he would not fail to recognize that he was revealing one of the Kings' greatest secrets: knowledge that the elixirs like the one he was feeding to the Sparrow existed.

What a fool you've been, Anila.

In a rush, all of her anger over everything Sukru had done returned. She was just about to draw upon her power and call it down upon Sukru when she caught movement to her left. Her mother had broken away from her father and was walking numbly toward the crystal. One of the Silver Spears assigned to watch over her grabbed her arm. When Meral ripped it away and kept walking, he took a fistful of her hair and yanked her backward.

That was when her father charged forward, slipped an arm around his neck, and wrenched him away with a violent move that surprised Anila. "Unhand my wife!"

They wrestled and fell to the spongy cavern floor. The other Spears swept in, tackling her father, but in doing so left Meral alone, perhaps thinking her harmless.

Her eyes filled with wonder as she walked toward the crystal.

Anila tried to go to her, but the captain by her side grabbed her and shoved her hard toward one of his gangly soldiers, who caught her and held her tight. "Memma, no!" Anila cried, but her mother kept going.

"Halt," the captain said, and drew his sword. "Halt!"

Gods, he was going to cut her down from behind.

Desperation driving her, Anila wrenched one arm free and drew a symbol in the air. She heard a soft hissing as she did, a crackling sound, and felt how deep the well of coldness went. It traveled the entire length of her arm and slipped into her chest. She'd never felt so powerful as she did now.

She'd felt this man's age. Felt the way his heart would skip beats. Every time it did it would return heavier, like the beat of a kettledrum. She tugged upon it. Made it falter. Made it skip another beat when it tried to recover.

The captain paused, clutching his chest. He turned toward her, his face a mask of confusion, but understanding dawned as he stared at her right hand, which was even then drawing more symbols in the air. He pointed to her hand and choked out, "Stop her!" a split second before falling to his knees and dropping his sword.

The Silver Spear holding Anila stared in shock, then bent forward, staring at her hand. Anila used the moment to spin toward him and drive the heel of her palm into his nose. Backwards he flew, shouting in pain, both hands grasping at his face.

Meral was only two paces away from the crystal now.

"Memma, stop!" Anila called.

But she didn't listen. She didn't so much as turn toward Anila. Her attention was fixed on the bright crystal before her. She reached toward its surface almost sensually, as if she were taking the hand of a lover.

"Memma!" Anila was sprinting for her.

But too late. Meral's finger touched the stone, and her eyes went wide. A sound escaped her throat as her head was thrown back. It sounded like "Oh!"

The sound one might make on seeing a wasp land on your shoulder. Then Anila saw it: her soul shifting, crossing to the other side. Her mother fell soundlessly to the layer of roots, as if everything that had happened since her reawakening at Anila's hands had been a dream.

Everyone had frozen. All stared, shocked, even the Silver Spears. The Sparrow was standing too, holding his own throat while staring into the light. He was disoriented, and was likely trying to piece together what had happened since Anila had arrived in his tower and Bela had driven the wood through his neck.

"Come," Sukru was saying to him, taking his cold, wet sleeve. "Come, brother."

But the Sparrow wouldn't budge.

The wounded Silver Spear, blood still pouring from his nose, recovered and took Anila by the arm. She let herself be led away. She couldn't stand against these men physically. But all the rage she'd felt was now rushing back, eclipsing her sorrow. She desperately wanted to smother the life from Sukru, but she felt the power of the elixirs within him. He'd taken one, perhaps in anticipation of his flight from the city.

The Sparrow, too, was filled with the verve granted by the elixirs. But Meral's transfixion with the crystal and her sudden return to the farther fields had made him wonder.

"Can you not hear it?" Anila shouted to him. "It calls to you!"

The Sparrow glanced her way, then bent his focus back on the tall, glowing stone before him.

"Silence her!" Sukru ordered, then placed himself before his brother, blocking his way to the crystal.

As the bloodied Spear slipped his hand around Anila's neck, Sukru spoke softly to his brother. But the thought was now in the Sparrow's mind, and Anila was drawing on her power to strengthen the wisp of a thread that still bound him to the land beyond. He ignored his brother. Plodded forward even as Sukru put both hands on his chest to prevent him.

"Stop, Jasur!"

But the Sparrow wouldn't, and he threw Sukru aside.

Sukru tumbled to the ground but, refusing to give in, unfurled his whip and cast it about his brother's neck. He hadn't been trying to cause harm, merely to forestall his brother's march, but the tip caught the Sparrow across his mouth and chin.

The Sparrow turned, enraged, which Anila fanned by adding her rage to his. He seized the corded whip near his neck and a searing sound filled the cavern. Smoke rose from the leather braid. And then it was severed and both Sukru and the Sparrow stumbled in opposite directions.

The Sparrow turned back to the crystal, and was nearly upon it. His hand was preparing to touch its surface, when Sukru grabbed his arm.

The Sparrow spun again. His fist clubbed Sukru across the face, a blow strengthened by the Sparrow's magic, and Sukru fell like an overturned cart of mudbrick. The Sparrow stared down, as if he couldn't quite understand what had happened, then turned back to the crystal once more. In an act that echoed Meral's final, enthralled moments, he reached out, touched the crystal's glowing surface, and fell beside his brother with a sound like ruffling cloth.

Sukru's body twitched. Anila could feel his soul departing as well, joining his brother's. She let it drift as it would, then ripped it in twain, keeping some of it here in the mortal realm for her own purposes.

The cavern was stunned, unsure what had just happened, which Anila used to her advantage. On unsteady limbs, Sukru pushed himself off the cavern floor. Anila controlled him like a marionette, forcing him to look at his brother, to pick up the broken length of his whip, and regard everyone as they stared on with mouths agape.

"Go," Sukru told the Spears. Anila's order, not his. "Prepare the ship."

"My Lord King—"

"Go!" he shouted, and cracked his whip in the air.

They did, uncertainly at first, but then with a speed that spoke of relief. Anila padded over the roots toward him.

"Anila!" her father called, but she calmed him with a glance and a wave of her hand.

When she came to a halt before Sukru, she allowed him to crumple in a heap, then kicked him over so he was staring up at her. After stepping over him, one leg on either side of his unmoving arms, she sat on his chest and leaned in so close their noses almost touched. There was a look of understanding in his eyes—he knew what was happening but was powerless to stop it.

"You did well, my Lord King. You stoked my anger and we raised your brother. But now you know the siren call of the other side."

Sweat gathered on his greasy brow. His nostrils flared with each ragged breath.

"I've taken everything from you. Your power. Your blessed crown. Your brother. And now I've taken your free will, as you took mine. As you took my family's. As you took countless others'."

His eyes darted to the crystal. She felt his yearning, his need to return, however brief his stay had been. He wished to be whole. He wished to be reunited with his brother. The fact that he couldn't was tearing him up inside.

A single word issued from his throat. "Please."

"No, no, no, my good King," Anila said softly. "It won't be that easy." She smiled, showing her teeth, a thing that felt pure as winter's dawning. "It was never going to be that easy."

He didn't respond, only stared into the light, tears building in his eyes. She took his chin in one hand and squeezed until he turned his eyes to her once more.

"I only wish I could be here to enjoy your last moments of suffering, but I'm afraid I've more important things to attend to, so I leave you in the good hands of the fates." She stood and stared down at him. "I trust they'll be every bit as cruel to you as they have been to me. I've earned that much, I think."

Leaving him there, she moved to her mother and kissed the crown of her head. "Go well, memma. I'll see you soon, and we'll walk the fields together."

As the symphony of Sukru's sobs filled the cavernous space, Anila walked to where her sister and father stood staring, then took their hands and guided them up toward the Sun Palace.

Chapter 64

DAVUD, now washed and dressed in servant's clothes, carried a ewer of lemon-laced water across a bright emerald floor. Esmeray, dressed similarly, was already moving along the war council's table refilling the thick glass mugs of the Kings, their vizirs and viziras, and other members of the council who'd come to discuss the war. Given the sheer number of participants, the council had been moved from its normal chambers higher in the palace to the grand room beneath the large central dome, the one set aside for state receptions, for the welcoming ceremonies for new Blade Maidens, and the like. It was so large, however, that even though a hundred were in attendance for the war council, and the conversation was already high-spirited, the whole of it was swallowed by the cavernous immensity of the room.

It was strange for another reason as well. The complexion of the royal attendees had shifted sharply. Weeks ago it would have been dominated by the original Kings of Sharakhai. Now only Cahil the Confessor King, Kiral King of Kings, and Azad King of Thorns presided over the proceedings, and Kiral and Azad weren't even real Kings. They were Hamzakiir and Nayyan in disguise. The rest of the elder Kings, as they'd come to be known, were either dead, in which case the next in line of succession had come, or missing, in which case their vizirs or viziras were in attendance to represent their interests.

Even in his short time serving food and water to the council, Davud had learned much. Ihsan the Honey-tongued King had been captured by the Malasani. Zeheb the King of Whispers, the man Davud had helped frame as a traitor, had gone mad and was being held in Eventide—*for his own safety*, one woman said with a dubious look and a glance at Kiral. And word had just arrived, from a herald missing a finger, no less, that Sukru the Reaping King had refused King Cahil's summons. Perhaps most surprising of all was that Husamettín, the legendary swordsman, had been captured by the thirteenth tribe and that Beşir the King of Coin was still off chasing them with a portion of the Sharakhani fleet.

Queen Meryam was conspicuously absent and King Kiral seemed preoccupied at best. He was constantly staring through the table before him or beyond the walls, but whenever he was asked, most often by Cahil, if the council should begin, he refused, saying they needed to wait for Meryam.

"For what?" Cahil barked. "Are we no longer able to hold council without the Queen of Qaimir?"

"She has news from her fleet," was all Hamzakiir would say.

Davud was sure he was delaying at Queen Meryam's bidding, and was doubly sure that his looks of longing were reflections of what Hamzakiir was experiencing within his prison. The trick now was to reach him, give him the sigil that he and Esmeray had stolen along with Meryam's book, and see him freed. Davud wished he could do it now, without Hamzakiir's help, but after examining the sigil, both he and Esmeray had agreed: Hamzakiir would need to do much of the work himself from within the prison that held him.

The trouble was it was difficult to get near him. Kiral's vizira was a doddering old woman who shooed Davud away every time he came near. Seeing that she'd just left the hall, however, Davud headed toward him, only to be stopped by King Alaşan, the most influential of the lesser Kings. He was imperious, especially with the falcon-wing crown made of red gold, his father's most famous symbol, sitting atop his head.

"If we're going to be waiting here all day, order the kitchens to bring us food."

"Of course," Davud said, "straight away."

He tried to continue on toward Hamzakiir, but was yanked backward by the imposing form of King Melkani, the recently crowned son of King Mesut. "Tell him now," the young King snarled, and sent Davud flying headlong toward the passageway at the corner of the room that led to the kitchens.

The others around Alaşan—King Ohannes, Onur's son, King Umay, Yusam's son, and Temel, a King-in-waiting as his mad father Zeheb raved in the dungeons below Eventide—all watched him retreat before returning to their hushed conversation.

When they did, Davud paused. Esmeray, her eyes bright with worry, had seen the exchange but made no move to assist him. They'd agreed that both of them would try to get the sigil in front of Hamzakiir in any way they could. She was just heading toward Hamzakiir's central position at the table when Davud noticed someone watching him. Nayyan, who sat alone in her guise as King Azad, was watching everything with an intense gaze, as if she expected war to spill into the hall at any moment.

Davud rushed away, hoping Azad would take his pause as mere confusion. Davud wanted to be done with this. He wanted to free Hamzakiir so he could get the cure for Anila. But he had to be careful. He couldn't *force* Hamzakiir's awakening. They simply had to present the sigil and hope it would be enough. And he was loath to use magic to do it. He didn't know what sort of safeguards Meryam or the Kings might have in this place.

When Davud returned from the kitchen, he bore a tray of freshly baked flatbreads with herbed goat cheese, pickled red onions, and marinated olives. As he came out he saw Esmeray leaning over the table near Kiral, arranging the glasses and small plates at Queen Meryam's place setting. While doing so, she shielded the view of her other hand, which placed a piece of papyrus in front of Hamzakiir.

That small piece of paper held a copy of the sigil from Meryam's book, the one she'd marked as a combination of *shackle* and *mind* and *yield*. The paper contained the notes as well. Hamzakiir, still lost in thought, hadn't noticed it, but when Esmeray tapped the edge of the plate with one finger, he looked down. Esmeray couldn't linger, however. She moved on lest she be caught, trusting she or Davud would be able to return if necessary. The gods had shone on them in this, though. As strangely as Hamzakiir was acting, no one was trying to speak to him.

Davud made his way around the large, curving table, serving the food on his tray and doing his best to play the part of an obedient servant. He wasn't doing a very good job of it, though. He kept looking toward Hamzakiir, who was still staring dumbly at the piece of papyrus.

There was a ruckus from the entrance on the far side of the room. Gods, it was Queen Meryam, dressed as if she were heading to a royal fete. She filed in with a beautiful woman named Amaryllis and a dozen Qaimiri courtiers, some in armor, others in stylish clothes, all of Qaimiri make and coloring. She gave no apologies or excuses for her tardiness. She simply said, "Let's begin," and walked toward the head of the table.

Even so, there were many in her path, and they all seemed eager to speak to her one-to-one before the council began in earnest. She allowed herself to be detained momentarily, but it was clear she was in no mood for idle chatter. Davud made himself busy closer to Hamzakiir, who was now craning his neck downward and staring at the paper as if it were the most important thing he'd ever read. Yet still he did nothing.

There was no time left. Meryam was rounding the table and, gods, the paper was still on Hamzakiir's plate, plain for anyone to see. She would spot it the moment she reached his side.

Acting as though he were trying to ready everything before the queen's arrival, Davud reached over the table and spilled a healthy amount of water. It splashed against the tablecloth, Hamzakiir's left arm, and, most importantly, his plate. Looking embarrassed wasn't difficult. Davud bowed low. "My sincerest apologies," he said to Hamzakiir while taking his plate, and when Meryam reached their side, he bowed to her, set the base of the ewer on the papyrus, and made himself as small as he possibly could.

"Well get on then," Meryam snapped at Davud when he didn't move.

"Of course, your Excellence."

As the Kings, Queen Meryam, and all the rest were seated, the servants were led away. Allowing himself one bit of the arcane, Davud wove a spell to make the ox of a woman carrying the large tray at the head of the line trip to her knees. The tray clattered, spilling plates full of half-eaten food. As the chamberlain rushed forward and others moved to help, both Davud and Esmeray took the stairs to the gallery that overlooked the immense space beneath the dome.

They crouched in the shadows and watched as the crowd below suddenly turned toward the entrance. The low murmur of conversation rose quickly, a few shouting in alarm and pointing as a host of Qaimiri knights wearing full armor entered the room. Cicio was among them, as was Ramahd, who held in one hand a dirty, stained sack, surely the very one he'd told Davud about in the boatyard by the Haddah. As they filed in from the main entrance and spread in an arc at the foot of the table, the crowd backed away.

King Cahil rose in alarm and faced Ramahd. "Explain yourself!"

But it was Queen Meryam who raised a hand and said calmly, "Fear not. All will be explained."

Ramahd had a righteous look about him as he stepped up to the edge of the table. He took in everyone about the room, everyone but Meryam. "You've been duped, my Kings." He reached into the sack and retrieved a preserved, desiccated head whose face looked very much like King Kiral's. With little fanfare, he crashed the head down on a plate. "King Kiral is dead."

The room stared, then burst into conversation. Most stared at the disembodied head with some mix of confusion and revulsion. A few stepped away, hands to their mouths. Some shouted. It was in that moment, as all eyes were on Kiral's head, that Davud caught a flicker from a shadowed corner of the room. Ramahd jerked and felt at his neck. He stared at his fingers, expecting blood, perhaps. The knights behind him stood in a strangely stiff manner, and Ramahd himself seemed suddenly woozy, as if he'd downed half a bottle of araq before coming here and it was finally hitting him.

"What in the great wide desert is happening?" Davud whispered.

Esmeray peered at the knights with her ivory eyes. "Look closely, Davud."

He saw it then, the faint traces of a spell that wrapped the knights, holding them in place. From the shadows stepped the queen's woman, Amaryllis. She walked calmly past the Qaimiri knights to stand by Ramahd's side, where she took Ramahd's hand. Ramahd, meanwhile, swiveled his head and stared at her with a calm, almost vacant expression. By all appearances, Meryam made it seem as if everything that had just happened had been expected, a plan of hers long in the making.

"She's biding time," Davud said. "Ramahd caught her off guard, but she's looking for a way out."

In the relative quiet, the sound of marching suffused the room. From the same entrance where the knights had come in filed more soldiers: dozens of Silver Spears. More came from the servant's entrance behind Meryam, including Layth, the Spears' old, burly Lord Commander. Some held swords while others held crossbows, cocked and ready. They formed a circle, hemmed everyone in, including the Qaimiri knights.

Unlike Ramahd's entrance, some looked not the least bit surprised at this new turn of events. In fact, they seem relieved, particularly King Alaşan and his cohort of lesser Kings. There was a smugness in Alaşan's eyes as he watched Cahil gawk. The moment Cahil drew his war hammer from his belt, a dozen Silver Spears raised their crossbows and trained them on his chest. He made no threatening move toward Meryam, but neither did he return the weapon to its holster.

"You'd better start explaining yourself," Cahil said to Meryam.

Meryam smiled at him in a patronizing way, then turned her attention to the crowd, a famous playwright setting the stage for a rapt audience. "Weeks ago it came to my attention," she said patiently, "that I had been deceived. That we had all been deceived."

Beside her, the man they all thought was Kiral was turning red. He was grasping at his throat as if he couldn't breathe. The veins along his forehead and neck bulged. The strange choking sounds coming from his mouth managed to fill the grand space. Meryam, however, seemed unconcerned.

"Some months ago," she went on, "King Kiral entered into an arrangement with the blood mage, Hamzakiir. Some time before the Battle of Blackspear, it isn't clear when, Hamzakiir managed to infiltrate our fleet, perhaps under the pretense of speaking further with the King of Kings."

Davud's scalp began to prickle. This was a disaster. A terrible, unmitigated disaster. Meryam was orchestrating a story that would provide cover for her with the Kings of Sharakhai and her own countrymen. She was using Ramahd and the Qaimiri knights to lend weight to her tale, but Davud had no doubt she'd see to it that every single one of them would die when this was over.

Cahil pointed to Hamzakiir with the point of his hammer. "Why are you talking about him as if he isn't here?"

"For the very simple reason," Meryam replied, "that Kiral *isn't* here. He has been usurped, his body stolen, by Hamzakiir himself." She waved toward the opposite end of the table, toward the head. "I sent Ramahd into the desert to find the proof I needed, that we all needed, and at last he's returned. Isn't it so, Ramahd?"

Ramahd nodded and said, "Yes," but it seemed more like the answer a man deep in the throes of dementia might give, the answer he thought Meryam most wanted to hear.

A woman gasped and pointed at Hamzakiir. His face, quivering and purple, was beginning to change. His short hair lengthened into long strands that clumped together. Kiral's distinctive skin lost its pockmarks as a beard grew and turned from black to brown then streaked with gray. His well-muscled physique wasted away until what was left was a man with gaunt, harrowed features. He was nothing like the man Davud had seen in the place inside Hamzakiir's mind—that was how Hamzakiir *wanted* to see himself. The man squirming on the chair beside Meryam was the reality, a man who'd clearly been starved in the months since Davud had seen him in Ishmantep. *To weaken him?* Davud wondered. *For the sheer pleasure of torturing him?*

Hamzakiir clutched at his throat. He was being allowed to breathe, but only enough to keep him from falling unconscious. It wouldn't last forever, though. Once Meryam had finished flaunting his helplessness, a simple but terribly effective display of her power, she would kill him.

"We have to help him," Davud said. "He can't escape on his own."

"We don't know how," Esmeray whispered back.

"I have an idea. Help me."

With that he began reaching out. After a moment's pause, he felt Esmeray reaching with him, the two of them concentrating on the combined sigil they'd shown Hamzakiir.

"Kiral is dead," Queen Meryam continued, "taken by Hamzakiir and tossed aside like offal so he could take his place among the elder Kings."

There were many exchanged looks at the use of the term elder Kings— not, Davud suspected, because those in attendance hadn't heard it before, but because it struck too close to its brother-term, the *lesser* Kings, of whom there were many in the room.

"You were taken as well," Cahil said.

"I was for a time, but I found my way out. And I've fought for this day ever since. A day when I and others could be assured that Sharakhai would be threatened neither by Hamzakiir nor the mismanagement of the elder Kings."

Again the term, though this time Cahil laughed at it and said, "Mismanagement?"

"Just so," Meryam shot back. "If Kiral hadn't been so excited by Hamzakiir's offer to rid the city of the Moonless Host, a thing you were well aware of, King Cahil, this never would have happened. Nor would the city's resources have been squandered in flying to the desert to battle one of its own Kings. And neither Malasan nor Mirea would have been drawn toward Sharakhai like vultures to a weak, stumbling oryx."

For a moment it looked as though Cahil were ready to argue with her. But then his face hardened. "The Kings do as they will."

"So we've seen." Meryam pointed to the southern wall, a movement made weighty by the sounds of battle coming through the windows in the dome above. "And see what's come of it."

"That's nothing to do with you." Cahil thrust his hammer toward Hamzakiir. "As you've already acknowledged, you didn't marry Kiral King of Kings. You married a traitor to Sharakhai."

"So I did," Meryam replied easily, "but Sharakhai's safety is Qaimir's safety. And I have come to love this city as if it were my own."

Cahil gave a biting laugh that drowned out the rising sound of battle. "This city will never be yours."

"You're looking at it all wrong, Cahil. The truth is it has been *yours* for far too long. It's time new hands took the reins."

At this, King Alaşan stepped forward. He was tall and proud, and looked much like his father, King Külaşan. King Melkani, his gaze sharp and piercing, stepped beside him. Then King Ohannes and King Umay and Temel who, but for his father's mad ravings, was a King as well. They stood side by side, staring defiantly at King Cahil. These lesser Kings, the small Kings, some called them, were not so small anymore. From the servant's entrance, a newcomer to the proceedings joined them. Trailing behind the shuffling form of Kiral's gray-haired vizira was Yavuz, King Kiral's son and the next in line to his throne. Unlike Temel, he was a King-in-waiting no longer. King Yavuz stood beside the others as an equal.

Yavuz had been prepared for this, Davud realized—they all had, surely by Meryam herself—and Davud knew enough about the queen to know that she would leave none of this to chance. Even so, he was still shocked when King Azad began walking around the table toward the others. As he went, he removed a bright carnelian amulet from around his neck. Like Hamzakiir only moments ago, Azad began to change. His body took on a more feminine leaning, so that by the time he'd reached the others, a beautiful woman of some forty summers with striking features and a defiant stare had taken his place. Queen Nayyan had been revealed at last.

Six Kings and one Queen had now joined Meryam—seven in all, a majority of the power in Sharakhai to add to the power Queen Meryam herself brought to the table.

While it had unfolded, Davud and Esmeray formed the very sigil Meryam had used to bind Hamzakiir. The spell couldn't be undone by reforming it, but Davud hoped that by creating it again he could understand what she'd done and through that learn enough to unmake it. Indeed, he felt the boundaries of the spell itself. He expected something like chains around Hamzakiir, but it wasn't so. It was more like he'd been placed inside a bottle. He need only find its hidden entrance, which Meryam surely used from time to time to control him. But the prison felt perfect and seamless.

"Follow me," Esmeray whispered.

She formed a new framework, and Davud filled it with arcane power. Her sigil was perfect—it combined *search* with *substance* and *flaw*—yet try as they might, the spell wasn't working. They could find no flaw, and they were running out of time.

"It isn't too late to join us," Meryam said. The words might have been reasonable, but her tone was not. She was goading Cahil.

Cahil took in Nayyan and the six Kings staring defiantly at him. "You would put in your lot with *her*, a foreigner?"

"We're putting our lot in with one another," Nayyan replied. "We're no longer asking for our rightful seats at the table, Cahil. We're taking them." She took in the vizirs standing in for their Kings. "But fear not. There's still room for you and the others. Unlike you, we're not proposing to take what's yours."

"They were given what they deserved, and you should be grateful. You were given the mantle of a King."

Nayyan sneered as she took a loaded crossbow from the hands of a nearby soldier. "I am *taking* the mantle of a Queen"—she lifted the crossbow to her shoulder—"and I will have the rights my throne demands."

Beside Meryam, Hamzakiir shook so badly he fell onto the floor.

"This is your last and only chance to join us," Meryam said to Cahil.

Cahil's face was red. His nostrils flared as he took in the room. Then he gave everyone his answer: a blurring hurl of his hammer, directly toward Meryam. It spun, end over end, and crashed through Meryam's magical shield in a shower of bright yellow sparks. It struck a glancing blow to her head that sent her reeling backward. She tripped over Hamzakiir's body and fell unceremoniously to the bright, polished floor.

Nayyan squeezed the trigger of her crossbow. The bolt streaked the air and sank deep into Cahil's chest. All but ignoring it, Cahil leapt onto the table and flew toward Meryam. A dozen more bolts flew, some missing, others piercing Cahil's body as he ran, so that by the time he reached Meryam, a half dozen riddled his body.

By then Meryam had regained her feet. As she sidestepped Cahil's charge, one hand flew across her body and Cahil's neck twisted sharply to one side. A great crack rent the air, and Cahil fell to the floor like a rag doll. He skidded to a squeaking stop, and silence fell over the proceedings.

A skirmish erupted. Swords and daggers were drawn as those from Cahil's house and the allies he had remaining—those from Sukru's, Husamettín's, Beşir's, and Ihsan's houses—fought against the Silver Spears and those from the houses of the lesser Kings. The Qaimiri knights stood stock-still, as if with everything else that was happening, Meryam hadn't the presence of mind to command them to do anything.

Davud and Esmeray continued to weave their spell, but it was no good. The prison Meryam had formed was too perfect. But then Davud noticed something shining from within. The prison walls were translucent, which he hadn't realized since there'd been no light coming from inside the darkened walls. Now, though, he saw a new sigil, one he wasn't familiar with. It was Hamzakiir. He was trying to help them.

"Echo it," Davud said, "quickly."

Esmeray formed a framework, a perfect match to Hamzakiir's, and

Davud rushed to fill it with power. It seemed to do nothing, however. The walls were still in place, perfect.

"There," Esmeray said above the shouts and sounds of the battle below.

He didn't know what she was talking about at first, but then he saw it. A hairline crack, as if the prison were made of so much glass. He tried harder, focusing solely on pouring as much power as he could into the sigil while allowing Esmeray to guide it into her waiting framework.

The crack lengthened. More cracks formed. And then the prison shattered. It felt like a ton-weight being cut from its hauling rope, all that tension released in the blink of an eye.

Below them, the battle had devolved into a slaughter. Two dozen lay on the floor, bleeding, dying, or already dead. Davud was more concerned about Meryam and Hamzakiir, though. He watched breathlessly as Hamzakiir blinked and stared about as if he'd just woken from a long, drunken sleep. Meryam had rounded on him, her hand lifted, a ball of blue fire already forming.

Davud threw up a shield just in time. It barely held off Meryam's arcane flame. The woman was every bit as strong as Hamzakiir had been at his peak, perhaps stronger.

Meryam spun and locked eyes with Davud. As she lifted her hand toward him, a great crack sounded, and the floor of the gallery upon which he and Esmeray were hiding shifted. Great fissures appeared in the marble—Davud felt each of them like punches to his chest—then the floor beneath him suddenly gave way with a sound like rolling thunder. He and Esmeray plummeted to the main floor below and landed hard amidst the rubble.

Something clubbed Davud on the back of his head and a keen ringing sounded in his ears.

He felt Esmeray shaking him. He turned to see her mouth moving. She was saying something, but for the life of him he couldn't understand what. Suddenly Esmeray's eyes went wide. She stared beyond him. Davud turned to look too, and saw those who'd fallen during the fight—men and women he'd been certain were dead—begin to rise. They had terrible wounds, yet they regained their feet with the same sort of emotionless look Fezek had when they'd first woken him. As one they fell upon the Silver Spears and the followers of the lesser Kings and a battle that had been all but won was re-kindled. More fell on both sides and those who perished rose too, and the remaining Kings' forces were quickly evening the scales.

It was Anila, Davud realized. It must be. But he couldn't see her any-where.

Esmeray was still yelling at him, and finally he heard her words. "We have to free Ramahd."

She'd spun a framework around him, and Davud recognized it immedi-ately. It combined *corpus* with *awareness* and *shift*. It tied the two of them, Ramahd and Esmeray, together. She meant to shift whatever strange effect the poison dart had inflicted on Ramahd to her.

"I could kiss you," Davud said.

"Not now," she replied.

Davud, exhausted and lightheaded, shook his head and concentrated, then filled the framework with the last of his power. He felt the link between Ramahd and Esmeray form, then felt the spell lift the fog from Ramahd's mind. It wasn't dissipated, but instead transferred to Esmeray herself. As Ramahd yawned his mouth wide, blinking hard, Esmeray's eyes went glassy and her face turned vacant, almost pleasant—a mirror image of how Ra-mahd had looked only moments ago.

As the effect worked more fully on Esmeray's mind, the framework she'd created dissipated. Davud helped her to a stand. Woozy, his vision swim-ming, he held her tight to him and skirted the edge of the room, hoping only to get both him and Esmeray to safety.

He could see Meryam clearly now throwing azure fire at Hamzakiir, who was retreating steadily toward the edge of the great room. Each of the tight balls of flame thrown at him, however, shrank and dissipated in a flash of green as if they'd fallen into water. Meryam yelled something to the Lord Commander of the Silver Spears, who immediately lifted his crossbow to his shoulder, aimed across the room, and pulled the trigger.

As if in slow motion, Davud saw the bolt fly across the open space toward Ramahd. Cicio was suddenly there with a shield in his hands. Instead of taking Ramahd in the chest, the bolt punched through the shield. As Cicio turned to meet a charging Silver Spear with a broad sweep of his sword, the rest of the Qaimiri knights swept in to defend Ramahd.

That was when Davud saw her, Anila, standing beneath a peaked arch-way, one arm lifted as she commanded the dead. In that moment, as Davud guided Esmeray with more speed toward her, Hamzakiir dissolved into a cloud of roiling smoke that lifted up, up toward the windows in the dome. In moments Hamzakiir was gone, escaped. As Davud reached Anila's side, she was staring at that same window.

She turned and her eyes slowly focused on him. "Davud, how could you?"

Davud felt his ears burn red. She meant Hamzakiir. Since being ab-ducted, her life had been dedicated to seeing him dead, and she'd just wit-nessed Davud helping him to escape.

"No time now," Ramahd said, and pushed Davud and Esmeray into motion. "We have to get out of here."

Together they fled. The Qaimiri knights and the courtiers of the elder Kings had formed an unspoken alliance. They, along with the dead, beat a steady retreat while Ramahd protected them against Meryam's spells. Through a courtyard, they saw smoke billowing from another wing of the palace. From the direction of the smoke, a skirmish between Malasani sol-diers and palace guardsmen spilled into the hallway ahead of them, but they managed to skirt it and soon reached the Sun Palace's grand entrance, where the full scale of the battle with Malasan was finally revealed.

Everywhere there were disorganized pockets of Malasani soldiers, Silver Spears, and Sharakhani people. Among them were the black uniforms of the Blade Maidens, who caused havoc wherever they went, but they were too few to stand against so many, especially given the golems, which moved stead-fastly forward, clubbing any who were near. And though the Silver Spears and Maidens would occasionally bring one down, each small victory cost dozens of lives.

As they rushed down the stairs toward the cluster of waiting horses, Davud said, "The city is lost."

But then something strange happened. The golems stopped. Stood stock-still. One lifted a hand and pointed south. So did another. The effect spread, until all of them were doing it. Just standing there, pointing an accusatory finger like a father toward an unrepentant son. And then they went simply, utterly mad.

They began pounding over the ground haphazardly, their strange faces blooming into wild expressions of pain or agony or rage or simple, unalloyed surprise. With the verve of a zealot they tore into their own ranks, or the Silver Spears if they happened to be in the way. They seemed to be searching for something.

Other golems, Davud realized.

When they happened upon another golem, it was as if both had seen the one who'd murdered their mother, and they became bent on their destruction. The battles between them were terrible, and all, Malasani and Sharakhani alike, gave them wide berth.

"Time to go," Cicio said, who was mounted on a war horse and was holding his hand out for Davud to take.

Davud realized he'd been staring. With Cicio's help, he swung onto the saddle behind him, then off they rode. The House of Maidens had been breached, its stout gates sundered, but the forces of Malasan now trembled. With their greatest weapon taken from them, the Silver Spears and Maidens pushed the invaders back out through the gates and into the city.

Ramahd's host followed, broke through the lines, and were soon into the city proper. The sounds of battle faded, and the events of the Sun Palace felt more and more like a fever dream.

Chapter 65

W ITHIN THE WALLS of the ancient fortress, Leorah listened to the fading sounds of battle. The terrible memories of standing in the courtyard while the Kings' soldiers came ever closer to breaking through were still bright within her mind.

She knelt on a folded blanket beside the goddess Nalamae, who lay on a bed of rushes. Nalamae had never fully recovered from Beşir's arrow—it had struck too near to her heart. With Leorah's help, Nalamae had managed to stave off death, but it was a battle waged daily, and a losing one at that.

Nalamae's sightless eyes stared toward the leaden sky. The lyrewing had told them Macide and Çeda were on their way. It had given everyone in the fortress hope, but it hardly seemed to matter once the battle had been joined. Things had seemed grim until a woman along the wall had spotted Çeda's signal.

"Now," Leorah had told Nalamae, who had nodded and closed her eyes.

The sky turned gray, and the battle turned. Beşir's forces were routed and the tribe's soldiers within the walls had cheered and shouted ululations and were soon sallying forth to help with the rout, pressing the advantage while they could.

As the sounds of battle faded, the lines of combat drifting away from the fortress, Nalamae's brow furrowed. "Çeda," she said weakly. "Çeda's in trouble."

"What is it?" Leorah asked, scooting closer.

"It hasn't worked. Beşir still has his power."

They'd struggled long into the night with the two poems, Beşir's bloody verses. One seemed to indicate that pewter skies would undo Beşir. Another told of Rhia's face doing the same. But Çeda had fought Beşir beneath Rhia's light and he hadn't been affected then, just as he wasn't affected now. They'd either misinterpreted them both or they were simply the wrong verses.

"Rhia's eye," Leorah murmured. A memory had been tickling in her mind, but gods help her, she hadn't been able to remember it. "Not 'neath Rhia's eye."

She'd read a thousand stories of the gods and the Kings in hope of learning the secrets that would one day undo them. She'd used some to arm Ahya, Çeda's mother. She'd used others to help the tribe in the days since. There was one story that mentioned Rhia's eye, but Leorah's mind wasn't what it used to be, and it slipped through her fingers like sand.

Nalamae groaned. Her breathing came faster. "No," she said in alarm.

Before Leorah could ask her what she meant, movement attracted her attention. The front gate was still open from the soldiers pouring forth. Those who remained were the infirm, the wounded, the young. They were clustered around the open gate, bows or spears in hand, and their faces had transformed from a cautious sort of hope to confusion and fear. Some were backing away, hands batting the air in front of them. Leorah had no idea why at first. But then she saw them: blue moths, dozens of them, hundreds, thousands, swarming through the open gate as her people backed farther away.

The moths were bright blue, but as they started to swirl around the men and women, the girls and boys, they turned black. An old man with only one hand fell to his knees, then dropped face-first onto the stones of the courtyard. His wife followed. Then their grandchild, a girl of eight with a bright smile and dimpled cheeks. Each was harried by the midnight moths.

They spread like fog. Whoever they came near stilled their movements and fell to the ground, until the only safe place was the very center of the courtyard where Leorah rested with Nalamae. All others had fallen—asleep or dead, Leorah wasn't sure.

The moths fluttered around Nalamae but were prevented from coming near. In a column they swarmed, beating madly against Nalamae's final defense. Leorah stood with the help of Nalamae's tall staff. After steadying herself, she whipped it back and forth, trying to crush the moths, to scare them away, but they were elusive and persistent. Slowly but steadily, the area around Nalamae shrank.

Leorah shivered at movement near the gate. Through the arched entrance strode a woman, tall and fair, her hair unbound and flowing in the breeze. She wore an ancient battle dress made of ivory leather and cloth and fine chainmail and bore a long spear made of silver and light. Most striking were her violet eyes, which were cast upon Nalamae where she lay unmoving, all but defenseless. Leorah was not wholly surprised to see Yerinde here. Nalamae had feared her return, and seemed to accept it as inevitable.

"*Leave her!*" came a reedy voice.

Standing at the opposite end of the courtyard was Sehid-Alaz, bearing a long black shamshir that drew the very light from the air. Lifting the sword high with both hands, he ran toward her with a strange gait, black blood pouring from a wound in his calf. The moths swarmed him, yet he ran through them as if they were naught but autumn leaves. Yerinde turned, held one hand toward him, fingers splayed, and Sehid-Alaz slowed. Came to a stop. Stared hopelessly into her violet eyes.

Thy duties have yet to be fulfilled, King of Thirteenth Tribe, Yerinde said. *So sleep. Sleep with your children while you may.*

With this she leaned forward and kissed his forehead.

Sehid-Alaz crumpled to the ground. Night's Kiss fell to the stones with a clang, a momentary hum. With his fall, a memory was jarred within Leorah. An ancient tale of Yerinde's capture of Tulathan, how Rhia searched the desert wide for her, how her anger had come to rival the terrible fuming mountains in the southwest. She became certain that mortals had somehow managed to steal her sister and hide her away. She searched often, but was angriest when the sun was high. It became a fearful time, and some began to call the hours when the sun was brightest *Rhia's eye*, for it was when she most often descended on the wandering tribes and tortured them for information about Tulathan.

"The sun!" Leorah breathed to Nalamae. "We need the sun!"

Nalamae blinked. Her blind eyes moved rapidly, as if struggling to solve the same mystery. "Of course," she said in a rapturous voice. "Of course. I see it now."

Above, the clouds began to break and the sun shone through.

Yerinde laughed, a sound that was not loud but for a moment drowned out all else. *The solving of a riddle will not save you, sister.*

As Yerinde stepped closer to Nalamae, the moths closed in. One touched Leorah's cheek. Another her arm. And she remembered no more.

Çeda rejoined the world. It filled her senses like water from a well—the fortress wall; the dry, open ground beneath it; a fractured sky revealing more and more of the hot, glaring sun.

She'd left herself open to attack when she grabbed Beşir. He struck her with the pommel of his sword, then crashed his fist into her face, managing to release his arm in the process. It stunned her for a moment. She fell to her knees and barely managed to avoid his kick. It caught River's Daughter near the hilt, however, and she lost her grip. It went flying down the slope to her right.

She rolled away from a downward chop, blocked another kick, and regained her feet. Knife in hand, she approached Beşir. With the bright sun casting deep shadows across his face, his fear was plain to see. More than this, however, he seemed frail. His breath came in long rasps. His face was haggard and his lower jaw quivered from the effort.

He retreated, taking long, sloppy steps to move deeper into the shade of the ironwood trees. He stopped when he saw dark forms hiding in the shade.

The first to step out from beneath them was Mavra. Next came Sedef. Then Amile and Huuri and Imwe. They spread out, cutting off Beşir's escape. Apparently resolved to it, he turned resignedly toward Çeda. "You won't win," he said. "The gods themselves are on our side."

"Oh? Where are your gods now?"

With that he rushed her. He swung once, twice, and each time Çeda dodged easily. His face was a terrible grimace, as if the mere swing of a sword caused him pain. It was the sun, Çeda understood. The naked sun was causing him pain.

It was only a matter of time for her to find her opening, which she did after Beşir committed a terrible overreach in trying to slice her neck. She swept in, gripped his sword hand, and drove her kenshar, her mother's kenshar, deep into his gut.

Beşir's eyes went wide. His sword clanged to the ground. His whole body quavered as he staggered backward while fumbling at a pouch on his belt. From the pouch he retrieved a glass vial filled with a blue liquid so bright it almost glowed. Before Çeda could stop him, he'd pulled the stopper and lifted it to his lips, but his hands were shaking so badly he got no more than a drop before it slipped from his grasp and fell to the stones with a crystalline chime.

As the elixir was drawn into the thirsty ground, Beşir glanced over one shoulder, then the other, staring at the encroaching asirim. He coughed as the asirim stopped a few paces away, hungry, waiting. They were filled with such need Çeda felt it in her bones, and none was greater than Mavra's. Yet still they waited, ceding to Çeda the right to kill him.

"No, grandmother," Çeda said, "he's yours. Take him."

Beşir stared into Çeda's eyes as though he wanted to say something, but just then Mavra took him down from behind. Amile came next. Then Sedef and the twins. His screams filled the valley until his body finally lay bloody and broken and torn, his eyes staring sightlessly at the blinding sun.

When it was done, Çeda spit on his lifeless corpse, then peered down along the slope behind her, searching for River's Daughter. She'd just spotted it in a bush far below when a scream rang out from the fortress. *Nalamae*, Çeda knew instantly. The asirim cowered in fear. Çeda felt a presence within their minds that prevented them from approaching the fortress. They couldn't so much as look at it. They whined and cast their gazes down and crawled away into the trees.

Seeing the postern door still open, Çeda flew toward it, unprepared for the surreal scene that met her. Within the courtyard, men, women, children, the young and the old, along the ramparts, on the ground or within the doorways leading to the keep, all lay unconscious. Fluttering over them, so thick in some places they occluded what lay below, were swarms of black moths with iridescent wings. Nowhere were they thicker than on the far side of the courtyard, close to the main gate. They were so thick Çeda could see little within, only the hint of a feminine shape standing tall over another who lay on the ground.

For a moment it was all Çeda could do to think.

It's Yerinde. Yerinde has come.

She was speaking to Nalamae, though her words were distorted and garbled by the moths, and Çeda heard little clearly. Certain that Yerinde would send the moths for her as well, Çeda walked silently, making her way catlike over bodies, over fallen weapons, always with an eye on the thick cloud of moths.

Just outside the swarm, unmoving, was Sehid-Alaz. Night's Kiss lay on the stones beside him, the blade dark in the bright of day. Çeda crouched and picked it up, felt the blade vibrate and hum as she did so. The fluttering of the moths was all around her, strong like a sandstorm. Still, she worried the buzzing of the sword would give her away.

She was still paces away from the center of the cloud, and had no idea how she would make it inside. She might try to run through them but surely if she did the same fate that had befallen everyone else in the courtyard would befall her too. Seeing no other way, she was ready to try it anyway when she noticed a change. The moths were beginning to part, forming a corridor of sorts.

It was Nalamae, Çeda knew. Nalamae was creating a path for her to follow.

The goddess lay on a bed of rushes. The tip of a bright silver spear was stuck through her chest just above the arrow wound delivered by Beşir's bow, and a woman with long, unbound hair still held the spear. She was every bit as tall as Nalamae, but possessed of finer features and violet eyes that made her seem wicked, malevolent.

"Every touch," Nalamae was saying, her words now clear, "is another thread that binds you to them. Binds you to this world."

So I've known, Yerinde replied. *So we've all known. But it won't matter in the end.*

"Will it not?" Nalamae said.

In answer, Yerinde yanked the spear free, drawing a fresh scream from Nalamae.

Çeda, meanwhile, stepped carefully forward. She held Night's Kiss steady, willing it to silence with each step she took. The sword, its incessant buzz nearly drowned in the leaflike rattle of moth wings, bowed to her will and for once held its peace, perhaps knowing that to draw attention now would give them both away.

But the hunger in it. It had fed upon many lives during the battle. It should have been enough to satisfy its dark cravings, and yet there, before a god of the desert, it felt empty, ravenous, nearly crazed in its desires, so much so that it was difficult for Çeda to control it, to keep her steps steady.

Nalamae spoke, "There's one thing you've failed to consider."

Oh? And what is that?

"That I've had time to reflect on my binding to this world, while you have not. I've come to embrace it, while you fear it above all else. You took great care, forcing the Kings to do your bidding, preventing you from being bound to this place, but now you stand before *me*. I know the inner workings of this world like no other, and when I die, I will return to it. You, however, will simply cease to be. You will be neither here nor in the world beyond. You will become but a memory, fading through time until nothing remains, not even your name."

Yerinde looked like she'd been struck. She stared at the stones beneath her feet. She spread the fingers of one hand wide, turning it over and over as if she were coming to some staggering realization. *It cannot be*, Yerinde said as her gaze slipped back to Nalamae. *It cannot be!*

Nalamae smiled sadly. "Your quest ends here, sister."

Yerinde's face screwed up in anger. With a guttural yell she lifted her spear high and brought it down hard into the center of Nalamae's chest.

"No!" Çeda screamed and ran forward, holding Night's Kiss high overhead.

The sword became an alloy forged of potent will, of rage and hunger and patience lost. Yerinde turned with widened eyes. She tried to lift the spear, but Nalamae, her bloody teeth bared, had grabbed the haft. A long groan escaped her, and the muscles along her forearms stood out as she used both hands to hold Yerinde's weapon firmly in place.

Yerinde abandoned the spear and turned to Çeda, raising her hands and casting symbols in the air. But in that moment Çeda *pressed* on her as she had in the desert with the sickletail. The goddess paused, only for a moment, but it was enough for Çeda to close the distance and bring Night's Kiss down with all her might. The buzzing rose to impossible heights, drowning out all other sounds save Yerinde's high scream. The vibration rattled Çeda's arms, numbed them, and the blade cut down through Yerinde's shoulder and deep into her chest.

She'd lost her grip on the spear and now held Night's Kiss along the blade. Her violet eyes stared toward the horizon. One arm hung limp and useless. The other moved instinctively, heedless of the slicing of her fingers. She dropped to her knees. Fell to the flagstones.

Çeda yanked Night's Kiss free and it gave a long, satisfied purr. Yerinde stared at Nalamae, blinking rapidly, her breath coming in bursts. Blood the wrong shade of red foamed at her mouth.

And then she went still and fell to the stones, and Çeda let Night's Kiss fall with her, disgusted by the sword's deep satisfaction. The moths went mad, filling the courtyard's every inch, then they dissolved, lifting like embers on the wind. No longer obstructed by clouds of black wings, the brightness of the sun shone down, lighting the grim scene inside the courtyard in stark relief.

Çeda knelt by Nalamae's side. Both of her hands still gripped the spear, but she released one now and used it to take Çeda's hand in hers. Tears fell from Çeda's eyes, mirroring Nalamae's. In that moment, standing on the edge of death, it looked as though the goddess had some sudden realization. She gained a peaceful look, a look of brief contentment, then her eyes too went dim.

For long moments, all Çeda could do was hold her hand. Then, realizing the spear was still embedded in her chest, she wrenched it free and threw it aside.

Unable to hold it back any longer, Çeda fell across Nalamae's chest, and wept.

Chapter 66

EMRE TREKKED BACK from the city to the desert. The Malasani had pushed deep into Sharakhai. They'd broken through the walls. It seemed as though the mighty Kings of Sharakhai were ready to fall at last. But when all seemed lost, the golems had gone insane. Just as Ihsan had predicted.

When he reached the blooming fields he took his rest beneath the trees. Somewhere in the distance came the buzz of a rattlewing, then another, as if in answer to the first. The groves were unmoving, calm. There was a serenity about them, not the calming sort one might find beside a flowing river, but rather the sort one might find in the ruins of an ancient temple. *Tread carefully*, spoke the silence. *Honor the dead.*

After eating, he continued past the groves. When the adichara had dwindled in the distance he saw the skiff he'd sailed in on that morning. Sitting with his back against it, one ankle chained to an eye hook along the skiff's gunwales, was King Ihsan, who was using a wooden staff to draw designs into the sand. His black beard was longer. He wore a striped blue thawb and a white turban—simple enough garb but in them Ihsan still looked regal. It was infuriating beyond measure.

"It was as you said," Emre told him when he neared.

After unchaining Ihsan's ankle, Emre made preparations to sail. Ihsan held his staff and watched, making no move to help. Emre didn't care. He didn't want the help of a King.

He offered Ihsan a skin of water and a loaf of lemon-and-peppercorn bread he'd bought from a bakery that had somehow, improbably, been open near the northern harbor. Ihsan accepted both in silence. It was hard to believe the man's tongue had been cut out, his greatest power taken from him.

Then again, Emre thought, *perhaps it isn't his greatest power after all.* He'd managed to stop the entire Malasani army without uttering a word. He'd used guile instead, playing on the needs and desires of those around him to get what he wanted, and had done so while trapped inside a Malasani prison ship.

"Where will you go?" Emre asked him.

Ihsan drew into the sand. *I'll find my way.*

Which was no answer at all, but Emre didn't care. He'd promised Ihsan that if he saved Sharakhai, he would give him his freedom. And so he did.

Without another word, Emre set the skiff's sail, ran alongside it to give it a good shove, and leapt inside. Like the adichara, Ihsan was soon lost behind him.

A day's sail returned Emre to the swath of black rocks, a low range that had dozens of hiding places for ships, three of which were large enough for Tribe Kadri's entire fleet. Emre went to the nearest. Knowing they might have been forced to move, he was unsurprised to find it empty. The second was as well. Near nightfall at the end of his second day of sailing, he saw a man waving at the top of a hill. When he came closer, he saw it was Hamid, waving Emre toward a small, steep-walled basin. The sky was dark and overcast, which robbed the stone and sand of much of their color.

By the time the skiff had slid to a stop, Hamid had climbed down from on high along a set of ancient stairs cut into the rock.

"Where is everyone?" Emre asked as he climbed out.

Hamid jutted his chin toward the stairs. "Not far by foot but a long sail by sand. A dozen Malasani dhows were spotted along the horizon this morning. Aríz thought it best we not chance your skiff being seen."

Together they pulled the skiff away from the entrance so it wouldn't be seen from the desert, nor from the tops of the hills above—such was the steepness of the walls. As Emre dropped the anchor stone and began gathering his things from the skiff, Hamid asked, "You're done releasing our prize then?"

"Done completing the bargain I made."

"A fool's bargain."

"You'd rather the Malasani walked the halls of Tauriyat? You'd rather thousands of our own died as they imposed their rule over Sharakhai?"

Hamid spat on the sand. "I'd rather the Malasani were destroyed while the King of Lies roasts on a spit."

"That wasn't the bargain."

"Fuck your bargain."

Emre shrugged. "Better the demon you know, as my aunt used to say."

"Your auntie was a drunk."

Hamid was fixing for another fight. They'd had a terrible row in front of everyone just before Emre had left; it had nearly come to blows. Emre used to be afraid of Hamid's fits of anger, but men like Hamid fed on fear. He was like a black laugher, snorting and grunting to see just how cowardly his enemies were. If they looked like they would run, it only emboldened him, but face him squarely, prepared for a fight, and he would eventually slink away.

After strapping on his sword belt on, Emre slung his sack of food and water over his shoulder and headed for the stairs. "Ihsan has no tongue. He's lost his power. What do you suppose the other Kings will do to him when they learn of it? They'll not let him sit his throne, and even if they do he's no danger to us."

"No *danger*?" Hamid said. "He's spilt our blood for hundreds of years."

"And he'll pay for it," Emre said as he took the stairs and began climbing toward higher ground. "Just not today."

Hamid went silent as they climbed.

"Thousands were likely saved because the Malasani threat has been blunted. The Kings will be weakened, while *we* build an accord in the desert to topple any who remain."

"Yes, and you'll just love that, won't you? Macide's rising star . . ."

These little jealousies had been spilling out more often of late. Emre was just about to shoot back a reply when he realized someone else was ahead. It was Darius. He wore a black thawb and had a turban loose about his shoulders. He stood near the top of the stairs, looking at Emre with a sad expression.

"You shouldn't have let him go, Emre."

It was then that Emre realized Darius was carrying a shovel.

His heart already pounding, Emre turned, dropped the sack, and drew his sword just in time to meet Hamid's first blow. They traded several more before Emre felt the world around him shatter.

Then he was falling.

Weightless he plummeted and struck the sand hard. Darius, he realized belatedly. Darius had struck him with the shovel. *That's the other thing about black laughers,* Emre mused. *Alone they're easily cowed, but give them a pack and their leader becomes doubly dangerous.*

Emre woke to the sharp, rhythmic sound of a shovel piercing sand. His hands were bound. His ankles, too. After each crunch of sand came a soft hiss. It went on for a while before he was rolled into the hole that had just been dug for him. His grave.

He opened his eyes. Sand and grit made him close them, but he tried again a moment later and found Hamid working at the piled sand with the shovel.

"Don't," he managed.

Hamid paused a moment. "I should've done this a long time ago, Emre." Then he was back at it.

Darius looked worried, the wind swirling his unwrapped turban and his light brown hair.

"Please," Emre said.

"You shouldn't have let him go."

More and more sand piled on top of him. Emre tried to move, tried to keep on top of the growing weight, but he was bound and his limbs were leaden. There was nothing he could do. Soon it covered his chest. His shoulders. He felt the coolness of the sand against his neck. Felt it press against his cheeks. And then a layer of it was thrown over his face, stealing away the grayness of the sky, the sorrow on Darius's face. Emre managed to turn his head so he wasn't breathing it in, but more and more was piling on, the weight of it pressing ever harder. It was becoming difficult to breathe.

"Hamid!" called a voice.

Gods, it was Frail Lemi. Emre tried to shout back but the only thing that came was a muffled sound.

"Quickly," Emre heard Hamid say, "we can't let that oaf see."

There was a loud thump against the sand, then the muffled sound of footsteps, which faded and was gone.

"Where've you been?" Emre heard Frail Lemi say, a bit louder now. "I've been calling."

"Doing as we were bid," Hamid snapped. "Watching for Emre, as you were supposed to, over there."

"I was," Frail Lemi said, his voice more distant, "but I didn't see him. And then I didn't see you."

"If you can't even follow simple orders," Hamid replied, "you should have stayed at camp."

"I can follow orders," Frail Lemi replied.

What followed was a detailed list of all the times Frail Lemi had properly followed orders, with occasional interjections from Hamid, often proving that Frail Lemi hadn't, in fact, followed the orders he'd been given at all. They faded, grew softer and more distant, and all the while Emre struggled and prayed that Frail Lemi would turn back, that he'd look down into the basin and see Emre's skiff and wonder where he was. He'd see the freshly dug sand. He'd come back.

But he didn't, and the voices continued to fade until they were lost and all Emre could hear was the rattle of sand and the rush of blood in his ears. He tried to move, tried to lift his arm, but the weight of the sand only seemed to press harder.

Emre's breath was robbed from him. Stars filled his vision. And then his world went dark.

Chapter 67

DAVUD SAT ON A CARPET IN THE DESERT, close enough to a cook fire to feel its warmth. The fire cracked and snapped, casting an uneven glow over the Qaimiri soldiers gathered around it—the men and women who'd thrown in their lot with Ramahd in hope of seeing Meryam brought to justice. The sun had just set. The desert was calm. In the distance came the attenuated whine of a cicada.

Their three ships were anchored in a rough circle in a place known as the Bay of Elders. Anila had urged Ramahd to sail for it, had fought hard for it, in fact, insisting it would be safe. It was as safe a place as any, Davud supposed—leaning pillars of stone surrounded them, offering some small protection from the distant spyglasses that would surely be searching for them—though why Anila had campaigned for it, he wasn't sure.

Next to Davud, Esmeray lay on her side, staring into the fire with her ivory eyes. "You're doing it again," she said to him.

"Is a man not allowed to care for someone he loves? Besides, I could say the same of you."

Her brows pinched in annoyance. "Is a woman not allowed to mourn the loss of her closest friend?"

She wasn't referring to a person, but her magic. She'd been burned by the Enclave, robbed of her ability to use the crimson paths, but not of her ability to see them. *A more cruel curse you'll never find,* she'd said to him on their first day out of Sharakhai, *to see what you can never touch.* That she could still cast magic with Davud's help was apparently no balm.

"Perhaps it will return in time," Davud said.

"It won't. It never does."

He hesitated, wondering whether he should say any more. Sometimes Esmeray responded best to silence. But he couldn't stand to see her like this. He wanted to help. "At least there's us," he finally ventured.

To his surprise, she didn't laugh in his face, but stared deeper into the fire. "Us," she said softly. Her gaze met his, sobering in its sudden vulnerability. "And what happens when there's no longer an *us*?"

He liked Esmeray, but he wasn't so foolish as to think they were destined for one another. That was the stuff of tales told in the bazaars and oud parlors. "If not me, then perhaps another."

"Sometimes I forget how little you know." Her pale eyes returned to the fire. "There are some who could do what you've done with me, but I could count them on one hand, and there are none I trust enough to work with them so."

Davud looked to the dunes, where Anila had gone. As soon as they'd landed, she'd left in a fury, insisting on being alone, refusing to speak with him. He knew why she was angry, of course—he'd helped free Hamzakiir, the very last man in the desert he should have been helping, and hadn't even received his reward for it. He'd tried to explain it to her, but time and time again she'd refused to listen.

"Go," Esmeray said, "find her if you wish to speak."

"After she cools down," Davud said.

To which Esmeray laughed, a biting sound that turned Davud's ears red. "All that knowledge like grains of rice crammed into your skull and you can't figure it out."

Davud pinched his nose, avoiding the amused looks from around the fire. After a moment, the other conversations resumed and Davud spoke softly, "Esmeray, I'm tired. Can we skip the needling and go straight to the part where you tell me what I'm doing wrong?"

She pushed herself up, pulled him close, and kissed his cheek. "Davud, sometimes people *want* to be chased."

She was right. As Esmeray lay back down, Davud left the campfire and headed toward the gap in the rocks Anila had passed through earlier. The light of the campfire was dim behind him, the camp lost behind a great monolith of stone, when he noticed someone sitting on the rocks. He thought it was one of Ramahd's men, but then he saw the long thawb, the turban on the man's head, his long beard. Davud stopped in his tracks, uncertain whether he should be alarmed or joyous.

"I will admit," said Hamzakiir, "I worried you'd decided to abandon me to my fate."

"Yes, well"—Davud glanced along the rocks, wary of being seen—"don't think I didn't consider it."

Hamzakiir stood to his full height, nearly half a head taller than Davud. "Perhaps you did, but if so, it was little more than a fleeting thought."

"You just said you were worried I'd abandoned you."

A low laugh in the darkness. "Those were my emotions speaking, Davud. When I remembered that you're a man of honor, my fears vanished like fog over the dunes."

"I'm so pleased," Davud said, "though whether *I'm* a man of my word is no longer the question, is it?"

"No, the question is whether *I* am."

"Precisely."

Hamzakiir stepped closer over the sand. He reached into his thawb and pulled out a folded piece of paper. "There are five, and they're complex, Davud. Perform them in sequence. Take your time. Use only *her* blood, no one else's."

Davud accepted it. He swallowed hard as he stared into Hamzakiir's starlit eyes. The urge to thank him was there, but he choked back the words. This piece of paper had cost him much, and was likely to cost him more before all was said and done.

"I hope you find it," Hamzakiir said to him.

"What?"

"Whatever it is you're looking for, young scholar."

With that he walked away and was lost behind the nearby stones.

Davud stared at those stones for a long while, then, feeling eyes upon him, turned and shivered. Ten paces away stood the ghul, Fezek, still as a statue.

"I don't know that Anila will be pleased about this."

Davud was glad the darkness hid his burning cheeks. "Well perhaps you could let me tell her."

Fezek's gaze slid to Davud's left. "I'm afraid it's too late for that."

Davud followed his gaze and saw Anila standing there.

"Anila . . ." Davud stammered. "I—I was just coming to see you."

"I was just coming to say goodbye."

They stood in silence while Fezek watched. "Go to the ship, Fezek."

Fezek nodded, and walked in the completely wrong direction, his peg leg making his awkward gait even more awkward. For once, Davud didn't care about his strange ways. He held the paper up for Anila to see.

"Anila, I've got it," he said.

"Got what?"

"I told you: the reason I helped Hamzakiir. It was for this, a way to heal you."

Anila was silent for a moment. "You really think I want to be healed?"

"Well . . . Yes." He held the paper higher and shook it, as if that would explain everything. "This will make you *whole*. Things can go back to how they were."

Around them, the wind blew. Sand rattled and the squeak of pulleys being winched echoed. It sounded like it had come from the direction Fezek had walked, but that made no sense. The ships were all behind Davud. *A trick of the wind,* he told himself.

Anila stepped toward him. She was close enough to take the paper, but made no move to do so. "When I was with Sukru, he killed my mother before my eyes. He promised me a way to bring her back, if only I'd help him. I did, Davud. Together, we brought his brother back from the land of the dead. We brought my mother back, too. But things can *never* go back to how they were. Never. So it was with them." She gestured to the paper. "So it is with me."

"What happened to you is a *curse*, Anila. Let me lift it from you."

"Davud, I don't want it lifted. I would lose my power, and I won't give that up. Hamzakiir will pay for what he's done."

"A life steeped in rage isn't worth living."

"That's where you're wrong." Stepping close, she put her hand on his neck, then drew him in and gave him a long kiss with brittle lips. She whispered to him, "Killing Sukru was like a pull off the elixir of creation. It was the sweetest thing I've ever tasted, and there's one swig left."

"Anila . . ."

"Goodbye, Davud." She kissed him once more and walked away, following in Fezek's footsteps.

"Anila! Where are you going?"

He went after her, but stopped short when he came to a gap in the rocks. There, a hundred paces distant, was a ship. A bloody great ship, with a crew dressed in the ragged uniforms of the Silver Spears. They were going about the business of readying the ship to sail with the sort of movements Davud had become accustomed to during his time with Fezek. They were slow and fitful at times. But those pulling at the winches did so with powerful movements, tasks that normally demanded two or three crewman working together.

They were ghuls. All of them ghuls.

Davud remembered how he knew this place. Several years ago there'd been a massacre in the Bay of Elders. The Moonless Host had taken a Kings' ship and slaughtered everyone aboard. The ship had eventually been found but then abandoned, lost to slipsand. Somehow Anila had raised it from the depths, raised the crew as well.

"Anila, please!"

But she didn't listen. She boarded the ship, and moments later it set sail, a ship of the dead with Anila their captain. Davud watched it sail away until it was lost to the night. With the night sky and the desert below seeming more empty than it had in a long while, he took Meryam's book from the cloth pouch at his belt. The one that contained the sigils she'd collected. He placed Hamzakiir's page between two others, then closed it and placed it carefully back into its pouch.

After one last look toward the desert, Davud turned and headed toward the camp, toward the fire sheltered within it.

Toward Esmeray.

Chapter 68

THE PEOPLE OF THE THIRTEENTH TRIBE gathered around a grave, one of many that had been dug that morning. Many more needed to be dug, but they would take their time and pay their respects to the dead. Sümeya spoke words in honor of Melis. They were touching, and true, but Çeda listened with only half an ear. The battle had ended only yesterday, and the vision of Melis being struck through with arrows was still fresh.

When it was done, there were those who came to whisper a few words. Some grabbed a fistful of dirt and whispered prayers though they'd hardly known Melis. Many put a hand on Çeda's shoulder, or gave her a quick kiss on the cheek or the forehead. They offered melancholy smiles. Melis and many others had been lost, but their sacrifice had not been in vain. The tribe had been saved. Beşir had been killed and his forces had been routed from the valley and fled into the desert.

Had the story ended there, Çeda might have been glad as well, proud of the brave sacrifices her people had made, but there were the goddesses to consider. Nalamae was dead. So was Yerinde, who had meddled in the affairs of the desert for the first time since Beht Ihman.

Why? Çeda wondered. Why had Yerinde demanded Nalamae's head? What had she feared?

As it had so many times before, Çeda's thoughts returned to the only answer that seemed reasonable: Nalamae's foresight. Yerinde feared that Nalamae knew something or that she soon would. But what? And how did it threaten Yerinde? When Çeda had first learned of Yerinde's involvement, she thought the gods were meddling simply to maintain the status quo they'd established four hundred years earlier. But Nalamae had told Yerinde, *your quest ends here.* What quest? And if it *was* a quest, where were Goezhen and Thaash and Bakhi and the twin goddesses, Tulathan and Rhia? Why hadn't they stood by their sister's side?

Soon only Sümeya, Kameyl, and Çeda were left. All three took up their own handfuls of dirt and whispered prayers. "Go well," Çeda said, "and I pray that the worst is forgotten. Let the pain and fear of this world go. Live your new life with those who've come to welcome you, and be prepared to welcome those who follow. This I hope, for one day I wish to embrace you once more."

Sümeya took a while longer. Kameyl the longest of all.

When they were done, Çeda took Sümeya into an embrace. Then Kameyl. She could find no words that could speak to this moment. She had fought beside these women. They'd formed a sisterhood that transcended the Kings, their upbringing, their families, and their tribes. And one of their number had just passed.

Sümeya and Kameyl were looking at one another strangely.

"What?" Çeda asked.

"Do you want to tell her?" Sümeya asked.

Kameyl was already shaking her head. "Not a chance."

"What?" Çeda repeated.

Sümeya waved toward the grave. "When we found Melis, she was still drawing breath. She gave me a message for you."

"Stop being so dramatic. What is it?"

Sümeya looked at her soberly. "She said that in the end, the last of King Yusam's visions had come true."

Çeda stared dumbly. She knew what those words meant. When the two of them had first met in the House of Maidens, she'd told Çeda about the visions she'd received from King Yusam, and that all of them had come true save one: that one day Melis would stand beside a queen, and that she would protect her above all things.

Kameyl sneered. "I told you not to tell her. Her head is big enough as it is."

Sümeya, keeping her eyes on Çeda, ignored Kameyl's gibe. A moment later, however, a small smile crept over her and she tipped her head toward Kameyl's towering form. "She isn't entirely wrong, but that wasn't what Melis meant by it." She glanced toward the lake, where Macide was speaking with Leorah. "Your tribe has been reborn, and for that I'm glad. But Macide now gathers power, a power the likes of which we haven't seen in the desert for four hundred years. I don't doubt that all the tribes will side with him. With you. The question is, what comes next?"

"We expose the Kings," Çeda said. "We ensure that we remain."

"You must look further, Çeda, and I know you have thought on it. Will you allow Macide to continue the work of the Moonless Host?"

"He doesn't wish to destroy Sharakhai."

"No? He's told you this?"

"Not in so many words."

"You stand in a unique position, Çedamihn Ahyanesh'ala. You are of the city, and you are of the desert. Melis wanted you to hold *both* in your heart. That is what a true, benevolent queen would do."

"I'm not a queen."

Sümeya gave Kameyl a look, and she took the hint—Sümeya wanted to speak alone—but she remained a moment anyway, staring at Çeda with a humorless gaze. "Queen of the Desert . . ." She shoved Çeda hard and laughed as she walked toward a cluster of men and women who were digging several fresh graves.

Sümeya's expression became stern. She had that look of hers, the one she used when one of her Maidens was being too mud-brained for her own good. "Stop taking it all so literally," she said in a low voice. "You cannot let Macide go unchecked. *You* must have a say in how the coming alliance is forged and what will happen when it is." She leaned in and kissed Çeda on the lips, then left her there alone to help with the other graves.

Çeda watched her go, the feel of that kiss lingering, then headed toward Macide and Leorah by the lakeshore. Sümeya wasn't wrong but, breath of the desert, Macide had so much history with the tribe. Everyone looked up to him, including, in a way, Çeda. He was undeniably charismatic. How could she, an outsider half his age, ever hope to lead the thirteenth tribe much less a desert united?

Leorah and Macide both greeted her when she arrived. Leorah held Nalamae's staff in one hand. In the other she held a small silver vial, which she passed to Çeda with a half-hearted smile. "A difficult day"—she motioned to the vial—"but a hopeful one as well."

Çeda unscrewed the cap and tipped the contents, a small brown seed, onto her waiting palm. Leorah stared at the ground for a moment, then brought Nalamae's staff down against it with a thump. With Macide and Çeda both lending their weight, and the ground, soft here by the lake, giving way, a shallow hole was formed. Çeda placed the acacia seed, then the three of them pressed the dark earth back over it.

Çeda had debated long and hard over where to plant the seed. Nalamae would be reborn, of this much she was certain. And when she was, the tree would help her, as it had in her prior lives, to regain her memories. In the past, many, perhaps all, had been planted in the desert. But this valley was a place of shelter. It was a place they had won back from the Kings. It was a place of nurturing, a thing Nalamae would surely have need of once they found her.

Which was precisely why she worried over Sümeya's counsel. She couldn't remain here. She couldn't help rebuild. She couldn't even return to Sharakhai. Not yet. The growing acacia might one day call to Nalamae. Likely it would. But they couldn't wait for that; their need was too great. So Çeda's first order of business would be to find Nalamae, wherever she might be, and bring her back to the valley so that she could remember. Remember herself. Remember her power. Remember her history and that of the desert. They *had* to solve the riddle the gods had placed before them. She felt it in her bones. And she wouldn't rest until it was done.

So she would go. She would comb the desert, and find the goddess.

"You're certain you wish to leave so soon?" Macide asked.

In the distance, the asirim wailed. There were fifty of them now, with more arriving by the hour. They were free, but they didn't like the mountains. They wanted the heat of the desert, the grit of the sand. None of them had said so, nor would they, but Çeda knew they missed their homes beneath the adichara.

Çeda planned to go that very day. She would miss everyone here. She'd miss the asirim as well. It would be a beautiful day when all of them reached the valley. But there was no time to waste.

"With the asirim gathering," she said, "the tribe is safe." She hid her worries about Macide's plans behind a smile and a squeeze of his arm. "And you have the rest well in hand."

Macide smiled back, handsome with his hair long hair unbound. "You said it yourself, though. The goddess may be drawn here."

"Then she'll have many to guide her."

"We'll begin making the chimes as soon as we're able," Leorah said. They would hang from the branches by thread-of-gold.

"We just planted the seed," Çeda said lightheartedly. "I rather think you have a bit of time."

"Oh, I don't know about that." Leorah stared down.

For a moment, Çeda's breath escaped her. There, in the ground, a leaf was poking through. A thin thread of brown was lifting up.

A tree was growing in the valley, and soon would spread its branches wide.

Chapter 69

WHEN IHSAN HEARD the sound of plodding hoofbeats, he stood from his hiding place in the blooming fields and peered through the branches. In the distance a rider approached with two akhalas—one a bright copper with iron fetlocks, the other pure gold. The rider, a woman wearing a fine riding dress of cream and rust, rode unerringly toward him and dropped down to the sand when she came near. On the back of the spare horse, to Ihsan's great relief, were two large leather bags.

As the sun scoured the desert, they sat beneath the shade of the adicharas and ate some of the food Nayyan had brought. She fed him one of the elixirs, one of the few remaining created by Azad before his death at the hands of Çeda's mother, Ahya. It warmed his limbs, chased away his aches, but did not, as Ihsan had dearly hoped, do anything to heal his severed tongue. He tried the same with one of Nayyan's elixirs. She'd brought a number of both to aid him on his coming journey. The elixir felt more raw to him, more potent somehow, but in the end the results were the same. *I suppose*, he mused while staring at the two empty vials, *it had been too much to hope for*.

They shared a good amount of araq from one of four bottles of Tulogal Nayyan had packed. While they ate and drank, she told him of the war. The forces of Sharakhai had been on the brink of complete collapse when the golems had been driven mad. It had given the Blade Maidens and Silver Spears several hours to regroup. Even without the golems, though, the Malasani army was great and had reformed by the evening. They'd just begun a new offensive when five battalions of Silver Spears, joined by two regiments of Qaimiri heavy cavalry, nearly ten thousand soldiers in all, had driven into the rear of the Malasani forces. The vanguard of the royal navy had returned just in time, and while no one was under the illusion that the threat from Mirea had been stopped, the aid was a welcome relief.

Much of the Sun Palace had been lost to a terrible fire, the inner walls had been breached in several locations, the future of Sharakhai was still very much in doubt, but it could have gone much, much worse.

Ihsan in turn shared his story, writing words on the sand to give her the last of the events since they'd spoken on the Malasani prison ship.

He finished with the strange memory of the asir crawling up from the depths of the blooming fields. There weren't many left. Most had been drawn away for the war against Mirea. Those who remained were the oldest, the youngest, the weakest from wounds or disease or those still drunk on the blood of the tributes they'd taken during the last holy night.

It had been many long years since Ihsan had had call to bond with the asirim, to speak with them in any way, but his ability to feel the chains that bound them to all the Kings had never waned. Not so now. The asir had walked away from the blooming fields freed of the curse of the desert gods. It was Çeda, he knew. She'd somehow, improbably, freed Sehid-Alaz, and he in turn had freed the rest. Or perhaps the goddess Nalamae had done it. Might that have been what Yerinde feared? Might that be why she'd ordered Nalamae's death?

After the food was consumed and half a bottle of Tulogal drank, he and Nayyan made love on a soft blanket beneath the shade of the trees. He could feel the bump on her stomach. Their baby was growing. It wouldn't be long now before it was born.

Where will the desert be then? he wrote in the sand to Nayyan. It was only a few months away, but it seemed an eternity in these fickle times.

The two of them lay naked on the blanket, her back to his chest, allowing her to see his words in the sand.

"Still in our grasp," she replied. "The old Kings are all dead or mad or missing."

Missing, Ihsan mused, *is an interesting choice of words.*

Beşir was away fighting the thirteenth tribe. Husamettín was captured. Cahil, after being shot through with crossbow bolts, his neck likely broken, had disappeared, and no one knew whether his body had been spirited away or if he'd miraculously survived.

Zeheb was still mad.

And Sukru . . . Sukru had been found deep beneath the Sun Palace in the unnerving cavern with the glowing crystal. He'd been in a strange, catatonic state, with the body of his dead brother by his side. Days had passed and Sukru had held on to life, but every moment seemed a terrible misery for him. He moaned and cried, occasionally begging for release, but no one had dared give it to him. In the end, the Reaping King had suffered the same fate as those he'd committed to the farther fields. He'd passed only last night, his body laid to rest in the crypt beneath his palace.

His daughter, Selina, now Queen, had immediately joined the compact of the *lesser* Kings in their nearly complete usurpation of Sharakhai. Like a pride of lions, the young had pushed aside the old. It was their turn in the sun. Or so they thought. The battle was not yet won. There was still Beşir. There was Husamettín. And there was Ihsan himself. Not to mention Nayyan who, while she might have gone along with Meryam's plans once she'd managed to uncover them, was still Ihsan's.

Ihsan wrote in the sand, *Did I not tell you that nothing good will come of Kiral's union to Meryam?*

"It isn't all bad, Ihsan."

You should have told me about it.

Nayyan knew what he meant: her decision to ally herself with Meryam. She sniffed. "You were busy with your own plans. Always busy, and rarely a word for me about them."

I wasn't too busy for that, and you know it.

She sat up and faced him. "It was time," she said flatly.

Ihsan sat up too, and after a moment's reflection conceded the point. Wasn't this what he'd wanted anyway? Nearly all of the old Kings were gone. And the lesser Kings were indeed the lesser foes. He could deal with them in time, he was sure. The subject of Meryam, however, was a completely different matter. She had risen to power so quickly he'd developed a crick in his neck trying to watch her.

All in due time, he mused silently. *Mirea and Malasan will keep Meryam busy for the time being. And there are other things for me to worry about first.*

Ihsan wiped his words away and wrote: *I know you were the one who told Davud to kill Çeda.*

Nayyan had always been good at masking her emotions, but for once he'd caught her off her guard. Her nostrils flared and color rushed to her cheeks. After he'd had time to think about it, there really was no one else it *could* be. She was the only one alive besides himself who knew how susceptible people were after receiving commands from him. And there was the baby, who seemed to be granting her some small amount of Ihsan's power. *And lo how the desert will quake when that child becomes a woman grown.*

Nayyan had used that knowledge and her power to give Davud a command: to kill Çeda after he'd implicated Zeheb for betraying the Kings.

I know as well you set the kestrel on Çeda's scent. He paused, waiting for the information to sink home. *You read it in my copies of the Blue Journals. It's why you stole them. You saw that she'd be coming to Eventide. And likely no one would ever have been the wiser had I not remembered a passage in those same journals.*

He waited for her to confess, but he may as well have waited for one of the asir to climb up from the roots of the adichara and dance a jig.

I don't blame you, he wrote. *I can see why you'd be threatened by her.*

"Threatened?" Nayyan said with a laugh. "Why would I be *threatened* by her?"

I may, I will admit, have spent a bit too much time focusing on her.

Nayyan's chin jutted and she refused to look at him, proof he'd hit the mark.

It ends now, though. He motioned to the two large saddlebags that lay in the shade near the horses. *I've much more to worry about, and so do you.*

She began pulling her clothes back on. "Yes, well, perhaps it's time you got to that."

He grabbed her wrist. Forced her to stop. Thankfully, she didn't make a point of trying to dissuade him from this course of action. He still remembered the beating he'd received at her hands the last time his temper had gotten the better of him.

He pointed to the sand and wrote, *I beg you, leave Çeda alone. And see that Meryam and the other Kings do as well.*

"Why?"

Because I still don't know how she fits into all this. Until we do, we need to tread carefully. When she didn't reply, he wrote, *Promise me. This isn't for her. It's for Sharakhai. We both know the gods are up to something. It's time we found out what.*

Nayyan yanked her arm away and began to dress. "Very well. I'll leave your precious White Wolf alone until I've heard what you've found."

Ihsan dressed as well, then took Nayyan into his arms. *"Ma khee,"* he whispered into her ear, the closest he could come to *my queen.* He kissed her one last time, then touched his hand to her belly.

She left, taking the copper akhala. Ihsan took the golden horse over to the saddlebags, hoisted them up, and lifted himself up to the saddle. Gods it felt good to be riding again. He rode for three days and three nights, and came to an oasis far to the northwest of Sharakhai, one of several he'd plotted toward his destination, a range of low hills where he planned to remain in until he'd solved some of the riddles set before him.

That night, after lighting a small fire, he opened up one of the two large saddlebags. Within were journals bound in blue leather. Yusam's original Blue Journals, those that contained the most important visions he'd collected in his time walking the desert. He rummaged though them and found the one he'd been looking for, and by the light of the fire paged through it until he found the correct passage.

A King walks among the sands of the harbor. North or south. The vision was unclear. There is he taken by men made of stone. In the margins next to this was written: *Perhaps clay?*

He is brought before a king in disguise, a king who wears a mantle too large for him. He blusters, strutting like a cock before hens. But the true king stands just behind him. The king of a thousand hearts. The Sharakhani King speaks, but the foreign king, the interloper, does not listen. In the margins: *Perhaps he cannot hear.*

The true king, shriveled, a ghost of his former self, laughs and cackles and steals from the Sharakhani King his tongue. It's clear that Ihsan's power is feared. It is done to protect his son and his people. And yet afterward the clay men turn toward the king, accusatory. They lift their fingers and point to him in shame. The shriveled king falls to the ground from the onslaught, turns into a snake, and there withers and dies.

Ihsan had read this passage months ago but with all that had happened had forgotten it. He saw now that he'd ignore these journals at his peril. He wouldn't do so again. Too much depended on it.

The entry had half a dozen references to other, related visions. Some referenced the more mundane journals that filled the shelves in Yusam's archives.

He wished he had access to them all. But he didn't. *These will have to do,* Ihsan thought. If he'd come to trust anything, it was that Yusam had indeed had a strong intuition when it came to the most potent of his visions, those related to the larger danger he'd begun to sense, those that he or the other Kings would have some control over.

He briefly considered looking at the other references now—he was curious just how much of his own fate Yusam had recorded—but reckoned there'd be time enough in the coming weeks. He was sick of getting distracted. There was one and only one mystery that needed solving: why had the gods made their pact with the Kings? What did they hope to accomplish? And, now that their plan was bearing fruit, what, if anything, could be done to stop it?

From the saddlebag, Ihsan retrieved the very first of the Blue Journals. Then, settling himself in beside the fire, he began to read.

Glossary

aba: a loose, sleeveless outer garment woven of camel's or goat's hair

aban: a board game

abaya: long-sleeved robe worn by women, often with a headscarf or veil

açal: rattlewings, poisonous beetles

adichara: thorned trees that only spread their flowers in moonlight; their petals grant heightened awareness and strength

Adzin: a soothsayer, a "mouse of a man"

agal: circlet of black cord used to keep a ghutrah in place

Ahya (full name: Ahyanesh Ishaq'ava or Ahyanesh Allad'ava): Çeda's mother

akhala: rare breed of very large horse, "widely considered the finest in the desert"; "giants of the desert"

Al'afwa Khadar: a/k/a the Moonless Host; men and women from Sharakhai or the desert wastes, sworn to fight the Kings

Al'Ambra: old set of laws the desert tribes had used for thousands of years; precedes the Kannan

Alansal: Queen of Mirea

alchemyst: one who works in the ways of chemicals, agents, and reagents to produce magical elixirs

Aldouan shan Kalamir: king of Qaimir, Ramahd's father-in-law

Almadan: capital city of Qaimir

Amalos: a master of the collegium

the Amber City, Amber Jewel: where Çeda lives, a/k/a Sharakhai

amberlark: a pretty bird with a lonesome call

Annam's Traverse: legendary horse race, held once every three years

araba: a horse-drawn carriage

araq: an intoxicating beverage with a strong smoky flavor

Aríz: shaikh of Tribe Kadri, son of Mihir

Armesh: husband of Şelal Ymine'ala al Rafik; "the man who'd done the most to shelter Leorah and Devorah after their parents had been killed"

ashwagandha: a healing herb

Ashwandi: beautiful, dark-skinned woman, sister of Kesaea

asir: individual asirim

the asirim: the cursed, undying warriors of the Kings of Sharakhai, members of the thirteenth tribe

Austral Sea: a large sea to the south of Qaimir

Bakhi: god of harvest and death

Bahri Al'sir: a legendary adventurer, musician, and poet; a common figure in mythic tales of the desert

ballista/ballistae: a large crossbow for firing a spear

Behlosh: a male ehrekh, one of the first made by Goezhen

Beht Ihman: the night the Kings saved Sharakhai from the gathered tribes

Beht Revahl: the night the Kings defeated the last of the wandering tribes

Beht Tahlell: the holy day to commemorate when Nalamae created the River Haddah

Beht Zha'ir: the night of the asirim, a holy night that comes every six weeks. "The night the twin moons, Tulathan and her sister, Rhia, rose together and lit the desert floor."

Bent Man Bridge: the oldest and bulkiest of Sharakhai's bridges; crosses the dry remains of the River Haddah

Biting Shields: a nickname for the people of Tribe Rafik

Black Lion of Kundhun: Djaga Akoyo

black lotus: an addictive & debilitating narcotic

the Black Veils: of Tribe Salmük

the Black Wings: of Tribe Okan

Blackfire Gate: one of the largest gates into the old city, also the name of one of the wealthiest neighborhoods in the city

Blackthorn: Lord Blackthorn: pseudonym for Rümayesh as an opponent of Çeda's in the pit

Blade Maidens: the Kings' personal bodyguards

blazing blues: migratory birds that travel in great flocks, considered good luck

Bloody Manes: a nickname for the people of Tribe Narazid

Bloody Passage: a massacre in the desert in which Ramahd Amansir's wife and child were killed

bone crushers: the large, rangy hyenas of the desert

Brama Junayd'ava: a thief, Osman's "second story man"

breathstone: one of the three types of diaphanous stones; it needs blood. When forced down the throat of the dead, they are brought back to life for a short time.

Brushing Wing: name of Kameyl's sword

the Burning Hands: a nickname for the people of Tribe Kadri

burnoose: a hooded mantle or cloak

burqa: loose garment covering the entire body, with a veiled opening for the eyes

caravanserai: a small village or trading post built on caravan routes; provides food, water, and rest for ships and their crews

caravel: sailing ship

Çeda (full name: Çedamihn Ahyanesh'ala): daughter of Ahyanesh, a fighter in the pits of Sharakhai, a member of the thirteenth tribe

cressetwing: beautiful moth; also known as irindai (See also, gallows moth)

Dana'il: first mate of Ramahd's Blue Heron

Dardzada: Çeda's foster father, an apothecary

Darius: one of the Moonless Host

Davud Mahzun'ava: one of Tehla's (the baker's) brothers

Dayan: shaikh of Tribe Halarijan

Derya Redknife: female rider for Tribe Rafik; "thrice Devorah's age but also thrice the rider"

Devahndi: the fourth day of the week in the desert calendar

Devorah: Leorah's sister

dhow: sailing vessel, generally lateen-rigged on two or three masts

dirt dog: someone who fights in the pits

Djaga Akoyo: Çeda's mentor in the pits; known as the Lion of Kundhun

doudouk: musical instrument

Duyal: the shaikh of Tribe Okan

Ebros: one of the tribes; a/k/a the Standing Stones

Ehmel: was to have competed in Annam's Traverse but broke his leg

ehrekh: bestial creations of the god Goezhen

Emir: the king of Malasan, son of Surrahdi the Mad King

Emre Aykan'ava: Çeda's roommate, her closest friend since childhood

Enasia: see: Lady Enasia

falchion: short medieval sword

fekkas: a hard biscuit, can be sweet or savory

fetters: a length of tough, braided leather wrapped tightly around one of each fighter's wrists, keeping them in close proximity

Five Kingdoms: a name used to indicate Sharakhai and the four kingdoms that surround the desert

The Flame of Iri: a/k/a the Sunset Stone; a giant amethyst

the Four Arrows: one of the oldest and most famous inns along the Trough

Frail Lemi: a giant of a man; suffered a bad head injury when he was young; is sometimes aggressive, sometimes childlike

Galadan: stone mason Emre sometimes works for

gallows moth: beautiful moth; sign of imminent death but also, to those who know it as cressetwing or irindai, it is considered a sign of luck

Ganahil: capital city of Kundhun

Gelasira: Savior of Ishmantep; former wearer of Çeda's sword

Ghiza: elderly neighbor of Çeda & Emre

ghutrah: a veil-like headpiece worn by men; an agal keeps it in place

Goezhen the Wicked: god of chaos and vengeance, creator of the ehrekh and other dark creatures of the desert

golden chalice of Bahri Al'sir: from Tribe Narazid to the winner of Annam's Traverse

Goldenhill: an affluent district of Sharakhai

Gravemaker: the name of King Külaşan's morning star

Guhldrathen: name of the ehrekh Meryam consults

Haddad: a caravan owner from Malasan

Haddah: the river that runs through Sharakhai, dry for most of the year

Hajesh: Melis's oldest sister

hajib: term of respect (not to be confused with hijab)

Halarijan: the tribe of Sim and Verda; a/k/a the White Trees

Halim: Lord of the Burning Hands (of Tribe Kadri); the tribe's shaikh

Hall of Swords: where the Blade Maidens learn and train

Hallowsgate: one of the twelve towers spaced along the city's outer wall; is "due west of Tauriyat and the House of Kings, at the terminus of the street known as the Spear"

Haluk Emet'ava: a captain of the Silver Spears, "a tower of a man" a/k/a "the Oak of the Guard"

Hamid Malahin'ava: one of Macide's men and a childhood friend of Çeda & Emre

Hamzakiir: son of Külaşan, the Wandering King

a hand: a unit of five Blade Maidens

hangman's vine: a distillation that can make one lose one's memories

Hasenn: a Blade Maiden

Hathahn: Djaga's final opponent in the fighting pits before she retired

hauberk: chainmail tunic

Havasham: handsome son of Athel the carpetmonger

Hazghad Road: See: The Wheel

Hidi: one twin fathered by the trickster god, Onondu; brother is Makuo. Hidi is "the angry one"

hijab: Islamic headscarf (not to be confused with hajib)

the Hill: where the Kings live; a/k/a Tauriyat

House of Kings: a collective name for the House of Maidens and the thirteen palaces on Tauriyat, the home of the Kings of Sharakhai

Hundi: the fifth day of the week in the desert calendar

Ibrahim: old storyteller

Ib'Saim: a stall owner from the bazaar

ifin: an eyeless, bat-like creature with two sets of wings, a creation of Goezhen

Irem: a spy for Hamid

Irhüd's Finger: a desert landmark; a tall standing stone

Iri: an elder god, called three times before the sun awoke in the heavens

Iri's Four Sacred Stones: a/k/a the Tears of Tulathan (Result of the breaking of the Sunset Stone)

irindai: beautiful moth; a/k/a a cressetwing, considered a sign of luck (see also: gallows moth)

Ishaq Kirhan'ava: Macide's father and Çeda's grandfather, one-time leader of the Moonless Host, Shaikh of the newly formed thirteenth tribe

Ishmantep: a large caravanserai on the eastern route from Sharakhai to Malasan

The Jackal's Tail: smoke house known as a seedy place

jalabiya: a loose-fitting hooded gown or robe

Jalize: a Blade Maiden and one of Sümeya's hand

Jewel of the Desert: Sharakhai

Juvaan Xin-Lei: albino from Mirea and Mirea's ambassador to Sharakhai

Kadir: works for "a powerful woman," i.e., Rümayesh

kaftan: alternate spelling

kahve: a bean, a stimulant when ground and brewed to make a hot drink

Kameyl: a Blade Maiden and one of Sümeya's hand

Kannan: laws written by the Kings based on the much older Al'Ambra, laws of the desert tribes

keffiyeh: a cotton headdress

kefir: a milk drink

kenshar: a curved knife

ketch: small sailing ship

khalat: a long-sleeved outer robe

khet: a coin

Khyrn: see "Old Khyrn"

kiai: a percussive sound used when striking an opponent

King Azad: King of Thorns; makes mysterious draughts, never sleeps

King Beşir: King of Shadows, can move between shadows

King Cahil: the Confessor King, the King of Truth; known to be cruel

King Husamettín: the King of Swords and Lord of the Blade Maidens

King Ihsan: the Honey-tongued King, serves as Sharakhai's chief ambassador, known to be plotting and conniving

King Kiral: supreme among the Twelve Kings; "with burning eyes and pock-marked skin"

King Külaşan: the Wandering King, the The Lost King

King Mesut: the Jackal King, Lord of the Asirim

King Onur: once known as the King of Spears, more often referred to as the Feasting King or the King of Sloth

King Sukru: the Reaping King, controls the asirim through use of a magical whip

King Yusam: the Jade-Eyed King; sees visions in a magical mere granted by the gods

King Zeheb: the King of Whispers, rumored he can hear speech from far away, particularly
   when it relates to the Kings' business
King's Harbor: where Sharakhai's war ships dock
Kirhan: Macide's grandfather
the Knot: a district in Sharakhai; a "veritable maze of mudbrick"
kufi: a hat
Kundhun: a kingdom west of Sharakhai and the Shangazi Desert, a vast grassland
Kundhunese: a people, a language
Kundhuni: adjectival form
Lady Enasia: Matron Zohra's companion
Lady Kialiss of Almadan: a dirt dog, one of Djaga's opponents
Lasdi: the sixth day of the week in the desert calendar
lassi: a yogurt drink
lateen: a rig with a triangular sail (lateen sail) bent to a yard hoisted to the head of a low
   mast
Leorah Mikel'ava al Rafik: Devorah's sister, Ihsaq's mother, Çeda's great-grandmother
Lord Veşdi: King Külaşan's eldest living son; Master of Coin
Macide Ishaq'ava: leader of the Moonless Host
Makuo: one twin fathered by the trickster god, Onondu; brother is Hidi
Malahndi: the second day of the week in the desert calendar
Malasan: a kingdom east of Sharakhai and the Shangazi Desert
Master Nezahum: a woman on the faculty of the collegium
Matrons: healers and trainers from the House of Maidens
Matron Zohra: an aging woman, owner of an estate in Sharakhai
Melis: a Blade Maiden and one of Sümeya's hand, daughter of King Yusam
Meliz: former dirt dog, Djaga's mentor
Meryam: Queen of Qaimir; sister of the murdered Yasmine, aunt of the murdered
   Rehann; a powerful blood mage
merlon: on a battlement, the solid part between two crenels
Mihir Halim'ava al Kadri: son of the desert shaikh of the Kadri, Halim
mind's flight: one of the 3 types of diaphanous stones; is said to bestow the gift of
   mind-reading when swallowed, though the imbiber dies rather quickly
Mirea: a kingdom north of Sharakhai and the Shangazi Desert
the Moonless Host: a/k/a Al'afwa Khadar; men and women of the twelve tribes that once
   ruled the entirety of the Shangazi Desert; sworn to fight the Kings
nahcolite: a carbonate mineral, naturally occurring sodium bicarbonate
Nalamae: the goddess who created the River Haddah in the Great Shangazi desert, the
   youngest of the desert gods
Navakahm: captain of the Silver Spears, Lord of the Guard
Nayyan: First Warden before Sümeya, daughter of King Azad, Sümeya's one-time lover
Neylana: shaikh of Tribe Kenan
nigella seeds: a spice used in desert cuisine
Night Lily: a sleeping draught
Night's Kiss: the blade the dark god, Goezhen, had granted to Husamettín on Beht
   Ihman
Nijin: a desert harbor
niqab: veil made of lightweight opaque fabric and leaves only the eyes uncovered
Nirendra: a slumlord lady, rents space in rooms
Old Khyrn Rellana'ala: judge from Tribe Rafik

Old Nur: a shipmate of Emre's

Onondu: the trickster god, "God of the Endless Hills," god of vengeance in Kundhun; father of the godling twins Hidi & Makuo

Ophir's: the oldest standing brewery in Sharakhai

oryx: large antelope

Osman: owner of the pits, a retired pit fighter and a one-time lover of Çeda's

oud: a kind of lute

Pelam: the master of games, the announcer for the gladiatorial bouts held in the pits

pennon: flag, pennant

physic: a medical doctor

prat: an incompetent or ineffectual person

Qaimir: a kingdom south of Sharakhai and the Shangazi Desert

qanun: musical instrument, a large zither

Quanlang: a province in Mirea

Queen Alansal: of Mirea

Quezada: one of Ramahd's men

Rafa: Emre's brother

Rafiro: one of Ramahd's men

rahl: a unit of currency, gold coins stamped with the mark of the Kings

ral shahnad: "summer's fire," the distilled essence of a rare flower found only in the furthest reaches of Kundhun

Ramahd shan Amansir: of House Amansir; one of only 4 survivors of the Bloody Passage

Rasel: Scourge of the Black Veils; former wearer of River's Daughter

rattlewings: see "açal"

The Reaping King: a/k/a King Sukru, one of the twelve; commands the asirim using a magical whip

rebab: musical instrument, a type of bowed string instrument

Red Crescent: a neighborhood near the quays of the western harbor

Rehann: Ramahd's murdered daughter, Meryam's niece

Rengin: footman on Matron Zohra's estate

Rhia: goddess of dreams and ambition, the sister moon of the goddess Tulathan

River Haddah: created by the goddess Nalamae in the Great Shangazi desert

River's Daughter: the name of Çeda's sword

Roseridge: Çeda's neighborhood

Ruan: half-Sharakhani man who works for Juvaan Xin-Lei

Rümayesh: a female ehrekh, one of the first made by Goezhen

Saadet ibn Sim: killer of Emre's brother, Rafa; a Malasani bravo

Salahndi: the first day of the week in the desert calendar

Saliah Riverborn: a witch of the desert, the goddess Nalamae in disguise

Salmük: one of the tribes; a/k/a the Black Veils

saltstone: one of the 3 types of diaphanous stones; can be swallowed, but is more often sewn beneath the skin of the forehead. It slowly dissolves, bleeding away memories until none are left.

Samael: an alchemyst

Samaril: capital city of Malasan

Savadi: the seventh day of the week in the desert calendar, the busiest along the Trough

Sayabim: an old crone, a Matron at the House of the Blade Maidens, a sword trainer

scarab: a name for a member of the Moonless Host

schisandra: a woody vine harvested for its berries

the scriptorium: a kind of library

Sehid-Alaz: a King of Sharakhai sacrificed on Beht Ihman, cursed to become an asir

Şelal Ymine'ala al Rafik: shaikh of Tribe Rafik

selhesh: a term for dirt dog

Serpentine: a winding street in Sharakhai

Seyhan: a spice seller in the Roseridge spice market

a shade: a mission to ferry goods or messages from place to place in Sharakhai

shaikh: the leader of a desert tribe

the Shallows: slums

shamshir: curved sabre having one edge on the convex side

the Shangazi: the desert, a/k/a Great Shangazi, Great Desert, Great Mother

Sharakhai: a large desert metropolis, a/k/a the Amber Jewel

Sharakhan: the language spoken in Sharakhai and much of the desert

shinai: a slatted bamboo practice sword

Shining Spears: a nickname for the people of Tribe Masal

shisha: hookah

Sidehill: a neighborhood in Sharakhai, a nickname for Goldenhill

Silver Spears: the Kings' guard, the city police

Sirina Jalih'ala al Kenan: Mala's mother, a lover of King Mesut

sirwal trousers: loose trousers that hang to just below the knee

siyaf: term of respect for a master swordsman

song of blades: tahl selheshal; a/k/a sword dance

the Spear: a large street running from the western harbor to the gates of the House of Kings, "one of the busiest streets in Sharakhai"

Sümeya: First Warden, commander of the Blade Maidens, daughter of King Husamettín

Sun Palace: the lowest of the thirteen palaces on Tauriyat, once belonged to Sehid-Alaz

The Sunset Stone: a/k/a The Flame of Iri; a giant amethyst

Sunshearer: King Kiral's sword

Surrahdi: the dead king of Malasan; a/k/a the Mad King of Malasan

Sweet Anna: a fragrant plant

Sword of the Willow: from Tribe Okan to the winner of Annam's Traverse

sylval: unit of currency

tabbaq: a cured leaf, commonly smoked in a shisha

tahl selheshal: song of blades a/k/a sword dance

tamarisk: a tree

tanbur: a stringed instrument

Tariq Esad'ava: one of Osman's street toughs, grew up with Çeda & Emre

Tauriyat: Mount Tauriyat, home to the House of Kings, Sharakhai's thirteen palaces, and the House of Maidens

Tavahndi: the third day of the week in the desert calendar

the Tears of Tulathan: a/k/a Iri's Four Sacred Stones (result of the breaking of the Sunset Stone)

Tehla: a baker, friend of Çeda; Davud's sister

tessera, tesserae: tiles of a mosaic

Thaash: god of war

thawb: a common outer garment in the desert, consisting of a length of cloth that is sewn into a long loose skirt or draped around the body and fastened over one shoulder.

the Thousand Territories of Kundhun: another name for Kundhun, one of the four kingdoms surrounding Sharakhai

Tiller's Row: a street in the Shallows, "one of the few with any businesses to speak of"

thwart: a seat in a rowboat

Tolovan: vizir of King Ihsan

Tribe Ebros: one of the twelve desert tribes; a/k/a the Standing Stones

Tribe Halarijan: one of the twelve desert tribes; a/k/a the White Trees

Tribe Kadri: one of the twelve desert tribes; a/k/a the Burning Hands

Tribe Kenan: one of the twelve desert tribes; a/k/a the Rushing Waters

Tribe Khiyanat: the name the thirteenth tribe chooses when they form anew; khiyanat means "betrayed" in the old tongue of the desert

Tribe Malakhed: the ancient name for the thirteenth tribe, abandoned when the tribe is reborn

Tribe Masal: one of the twelve desert tribes; a/k/a the Red Wind

Tribe Narazid: one of the twelve desert tribes; a/k/a the Bloody Manes

Tribe Okan: one of the twelve desert tribes; a/k/a the Black Wings

Tribe Rafik: one of the twelve desert tribes; a/k/a the Biting Shields

Tribe Salmük: one of the twelve desert tribes; a/k/a the Black Veils

Tribe Sema: one of the twelve desert tribes; a/k/a the Children of the Crescent Moons

Tribe Tulogal: Devorah and Leorah's childhood tribe; a/k/a the Raining Stars

Tribe Ulmahir: one of the twelve desert tribes; a/k/a the Amber Blades

the Trough: the central and largest thoroughfare in Sharakhai, runs from the northern harbor, through the center of the city, and terminating at the southern harbor

Tsitsian: capital city of Mirea

Tsitsian Village: an immigrant neighborhood in Sharakhai

Tulathan: goddess of law and order, sister moon of the goddess Rhia

Vadram: Osman's predecessor in the shading business

Vandraama Mountains: a mountain range bordering the desert

vetiver: the root of a grass that yields fragrant oil used in perfumery and as a medicinal

Lord Veşdi: Külaşan's eldest living son; Master of Coin

vizir/vizira: a high official, minister of state

Wadi: Devorah's borrowed stallion

Way of Jewels: location in the city

the Well: a neighborhood near the Shallows; Osman's pits are there

western harbor: the smallest and seediest of the city's four sandy harbors

the Wheel: the massive circle where four thoroughfares meet: the Spear, the Trough, Coffer Street, and Hazghad Road

White Wolf: Çeda's moniker in the fighting pits of Sharakhai

Yael: mother of Devorah and Leorah

Yanca: Çeda and Emre's neighbor in Roseridge

Yasmine: Meryam's murdered sister, Ramahd's wife and mother of Rehann

Yerinde: goddess of love and ambition; once stole Tulathan away "for love"

Yerinde's Kiss: a honey collected from the rare stone bees' nests; used as an aphrodisiac

Yerinde's Snare: the convergence of a twisting web of streets; the most populous district in Sharakhai

Yosan Mahzun'ava: one of Tehla's brothers

Zaïde: a Matron in service to the Kings; heals and takes Çeda into the House of Maidens

zilij: a board Çeda fashioned from skimwood, used as a conveyance to glide easily over sand

Acknowledgments

This book marks the beginning of the end, the start of the second half of this grand tale. Once again there are many people to thank. Extra helpings go out to Paul Genesse for knowing the right places to push, making sure I'm staying true to the story, and for all the brainstorming sessions we had to iron out the kinks in this book. To Renée Ann Torres and Femke Giesolf, thank you once again for reading the manuscript and sharing your thoughts. It's especially valuable to have beta readers who know the story so well.

My publishers, DAW and Gollancz, and their teams deserve a hearty round of applause. To Betsy Wollheim, thank you for your guidance and your belief in the series. To Gillian Redfearn, thank you for your dreaded red pen and for forcing me to trim the story to its essence. To Marylou Capes-Platt, thank you once again for your keen eye. The copy editing stage can be brutal, but I'd much rather have that than release a book that's not the best it can be. Only two tomes left until this grand tale is done! Thank you to everyone in the DAW and Gollancz production, marketing, sales, and back office support teams for seeing this book through to publication and beyond.

I am indebted to my agent, Russ Galen, not only for this book, but for helping to ensure that the full series will see the light of day. Many thanks to Danny Baror and Heather Baror-Shapiro as well for your tireless efforts in bringing this series to readers all over the world.

To the Shattered Sands fans out there, thank you for all the encouragement, the emails sharing your enthusiasm, and all the crowing about the books. I see it and I appreciate it. The series would be nowhere without you.